FALLING BOX SET

(BOOKS 1-4)

DL GALLIE

Copyright © DL Gallie 2021

Falling Box Set (books 1-4) published 3 September 2021

Falling for Dr. Kelly 1st published 3rd March 2020

Falling for Dr. Knight 1st published 3rd June 2020

Falling for Agent Cox 1st published 3rd October 2020

Falling for Agent Cruz 1st published 3rd February 2021

Email: dlgallieauthor@outlook.com

eBook ISBN - 978-0-6489657-7-0

Paperback ISBN - 978-0-6489657-8-7

This is a work of fiction. Names, characters, places and incidents are the produce of the author's imagination or used factitiously. Any resemblance to the actual events, locales, or persons, living or dead, is entirely coincidental.

Edited by Karen Hrdlicka, Barren Acres Editing

Cover by Amanda Walker PA & Design Services

Interior formatting & design by DL Gallie

falling for
DR. KELLY

When opposites attract, it's explosive

A FALLING NOVEL

DL GALLIE

Every force has an equal and opposite attraction.
Love being the most volatile of them all.

AVERY

My life is anything but boring.
So what if I'm an introvert and prefer to focus on my career?
I was fine.
Until I met him—Flynn Kelly.
The doctor with the sexy Irish accent.
I thought we were unbreakable, until someone close hurts me in an unimaginable way.
Can two opposites fight the laws of attraction or will it end up tearing us apart?

FLYNN

I work hard, and play even harder.
When it came to women, I could have anyone I want.
Until I met her—Avery Evans.
She's quiet, shy, and everything I'm not.
But we're drawn together like magnets, sparking each other to life.
When the unthinkable happens, our differences really show.
Is our attraction about to sizzle and flame out? Only time will tell.

To Halle,
Dr. Kelly is all yours

"You know you're in love when you can't fall asleep because reality is finally better than your dreams."

~ Dr Seuss

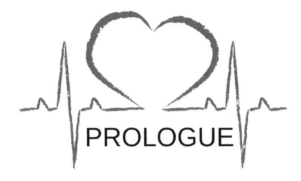

PROLOGUE

BAYLOR AND I ARE LYING UNDER HER BED GIGGLING LIKE SCHOOLGIRLS. *"THAT was awesome, BayBay. They had no idea it was me."*

"I know, Avie, I know." Bay says with a smile that lights up her face. *"We should do this again. It's so much fun playing each other."*

"It sure is." I look to my twin sister and smile, happy that of all the people in the world I ended up with her as my twin. She's my BayBay.

"I love that you're my sister, Avie."

"And I love that you're mine too, BayBay. We are gonna be twinsies forever."

"What's a twinsie?" she asks.

"It's your twin, who is also your best friend," I explain to my older twin, by seven minutes.

"Twinsies forever," she whispers back. *"Let's do it again and this time let's do it for a whole day."*

"Yes, let's do it tomorrow."

As the memory fades and reality kicks back in, a sadness washes over me. Baylor and I were close and we swore we'd be twinsies forever, and up until recently, we were. She was one of my best friends, albeit selfish at times, but at the end of the day, she always had my back and I had hers. We were there for one another when we needed a shoulder to cry on or a hug just because. But she's changing before my eyes and turning into a horrible, despicable person. My BayBay, my twinsie, is wilting away and there's nothing I can do about it. This new Baylor is harsh and not a nice person to be around. She's always been the headstrong, outgoing, and brash twin, the complete opposite to me. I'm shy, quiet, and reserved. Some would say I'm a pushover but differences aside, we always had each other's back.

I want that Baylor back.

My BayBay.

I don't like this new one.

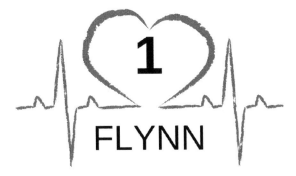

FLYNN

TODAY IS MY LAST DAY AT OASIS, WHAT I THOUGHT WAS GOING TO BE A SEX-filled getaway didn't quite turn out how I expected. The first few days I hooked up each night but they were nothing to write home about, and then I met Paige Walsh. Paige is a smoking hot red-haired vixen and, rather than getting down and dirty between the sheets with her, we became friends. Platonic, no hanky-panky, non-kissing friends…and then she got back together with her fiancé and I really was relegated to the friend zone. If I'm honest, I'm glad Paige got her happily ever after, she deserves more than a weekend fuckfest with me. My dick, on the other hand, he isn't too happy with me right now. The term blue balls is an accurate description of my nether regions at this moment in time.

I just bumped into Paige and Cam, her douche fiancé—he broke her heart and then game grovelling back, hence douche fiancé reference—but Paige is beaming right now. From the chats we had, he is the rum to her

Coke and when he followed her here, it cemented her feelings for him. *Lucky bastard*. After walking away from them, I head down to the beach for one last swim before my flight home. Kicking off my flip-flops, I pull my shirt over my head, and drop my sunglasses on top of my shirt. Looking around, I see I'm the only one here, so I pull down my boardshorts and I run toward the ocean, naked as the day I was born. When the water is to my knees, I dive in, the water is cold and a shock to the system, but it's just what I need.

Breaking the surface, I shake my head from side to side, flicking water droplets around like a dog. Floating on my back, I stare up at the sky, it's the bluest of blue and there's not a cloud in sight. I'll be sad to leave this place, but after losing Paige—not that I had her in the first place—I think getting back to Chicago is what the doctor—me—ordered.

I really needed this getaway, the last few weeks at the hospital have been crazy busy. So busy I haven't even had a chance to hook up in the on-call room. It used to be great when Kristin Payne worked there. She and I had a mutual arrangement that worked for both of us. The sex was mind-blowing, there were no feelings or awkwardness; it worked great between us. Until she foolishly went and fell in love with her childhood best friend. But in saying that, I've never seen her happier. It was no surprise when she ended our arrangement. Was I sad? Sure, but I was happy she was happy. A few weeks later, he took a job in Australia and she left with him. Leaving me and my blue balls behind.

I've had enough with the moping, so I stand up and dive back under the water. When I break the surface, I swim until my arms hurt. I'm a fair way out from shore and if I'm honest, I'm impressed with how far I swam. Looking at my watch, I see I have to get back; otherwise I'll miss my flight. Swimming back to shore, I slip my shorts back on, grab the rest of my stuff, and head to my room where I shower and change for the flight home. While I'm in the shower, like I have the last few days, I pleasure myself to thoughts of Paige, wishing ever so hard it really were her. Closing my eyes, I imagine it's her hand gripping my cock and pumping. Squeezing the tip before sliding her palm down my shaft. My balls tighten and I come over the shower wall, murmuring her name as I empty my load.

Opening my eyes, I step under the showerhead, letting the droplets cascade over my shoulders, washing away the remnants of my self-love. Soaping up, I clean myself, climb out, dry off, and finish packing.

After checking out, I jump on the shuttle bus and it takes me to the airport, where I board my flight and head back to reality.

Preston Knight, my best friend and the best pediatric doctor at Western General, picks me up. "How was paradise?"

"Paradise," I forlornly reply.

"Why so glum?" I sigh, not sure what to say to him. "Dude, like seriously, what's up?"

"I have blue balls."

Preston laughs, a deep belly laugh which echoes through the car. I'm glad we are stopped at a red light; otherwise, I'm sure he would have crashed the car. "Are you telling me, Dr. 'I have an accent, drop your panties now' has blue balls?"

Nodding my head, I sigh dejectedly, "Yep."

"How? You just got back from a fuckin' adults-only haven."

"The first few days were banging—pun intended—and then I met this chick but she was…"

"Was what?" he questions, as he pulls onto the freeway.

"She was there after a breakup—"

"Rebound sex," he interrupts, raising his eyebrows suggestively.

"I wish. The ex-fiancé arrived. He followed her to Oasis and won her back." *Lucky bastard.*

"Well shit, so why not hook up with someone else?"

"I don't know. I just wasn't feeling it. After getting cockblocked by her, I just, I don't know. If I'm honest, this weirdness goes further back. Ever since Kristin fell in love and moved to kangaroo land, I've just been out of sorts."

"Sounds like you need to get laid and you need to get laid good."

"Tell me about it. The boys are turning blue and I'm getting callouses on my hands from all the jacking off. I feel like a teenager again."

"If you like, we can go out tonight."

Shaking my head, I resist, "Nah, I need to get home, unpack, and get my head back into the game. Plus, I've got an early shift tomorrow."

"No worries, some other time then."

The rest of the trip to my place is silent. We pull up to my building and I climb out. Preston hops out and opens the trunk. Leaning in, I grab my bag. "Thanks for picking me up, man…and the talk."

"Anytime, you know that."

"Appreciate it. I'll see you tomorrow." Turning around, I head inside. The doorman, *he's new*, I think to myself, opens the door and nods at me. Nodding at the desk clerk, I push the button for the penthouse. The elevator arrives, I step in and the car whisks me up to my floor.

Stepping into my penthouse, I look around. It really is a bachelor pad, but it's *MY* bachelor pad. Everything is dark brown. My couch, the rug, the artwork. Hell, even the kitchen has chocolate brown granite and dark wooden cabinets. At least the walls are light, brightening the place up. As I head into my bedroom, I think maybe it's time to overhaul this place. If I lighten the furnishings up, it might lighten my mood as well.

Dropping my suitcase off in the walk-in closet, I head back to the kitchen and pour myself a glass of red. I'm thankful I called my house-keeper and asked her to stock up today. Not wanting a heavy meal, I prepare a cheese platter and head out to the patio. I enjoy my wine and watch the sun go down. The sensor lights flick on and I realize I've been sitting out here for hours.

Picking up the empty plate and my wine, I head inside. Placing the plate and glass in the sink, I head to bed, hoping a goodnight's sleep will reset my mood, and I'll be ready to head back to work in the morning. I drift off to sleep and for the first night since meeting Paige, I don't dream of her. I take it as a good sign and that things will return to normal.

2
AVERY

"FOR FUCK'S SAKE, BAY," I GROWL, AS I WALK INTO THE KITCHEN. IT'S already been a long day since I had parent-teacher conferences today, and then after I left school, I had to stop in at Jewel-Osco to get a few things. Placing the grocery bags on the floor in the kitchen, I look around at the mess Baylor left and shake my head. What has gotten into my sister lately? It looks like she cooked up a greasy breakfast, using every dish we own, and then left everything where it was. She even left the butter and milk on the counter. Grabbing them, I place them away in the refrigerator and grab the two bottles of wine—hey, it was two-for-one—and the other cold grocery items while I'm at it.

Grabbing my phone, I connect it to the Bose system and I groove out to The Killers, singing along to "Mr. Brightside" as I put the other food in the pantry. Turning from the pantry, I look to the sink. "Fuck me," I groan, the sink is full of dirty dishes, actually it's overflowing with greasy, grimy dishes. I shudder at the sight before me. Bay has always been the messy twin, but this is absolutely disgusting. The counter next to the sink is also covered with dirty dishes and cups. I'm embarrassed to be related to the slob who created this mess. Opening the dishwasher, I get a reprieve when I see it's empty. I get to work loading the dishwasher with as many of the dishes as possible. And surprisingly, I get most of them in, which was more than I anticipated. Once it's full, I pop in a tablet and turn it on.

Then I tackle what's left.

Filling the sink with hot water, I wash and scrub for what feels like hours. Once they are all sparkly and clean, I pop them in the drying rack, no way am I drying them up too. Then I turn my attention to the pots and pans that were left on the stove. Emptying the sink, for the third time, I clean the pots and pans and then put them on the stovetop to dry, since the rack is full but first, I need to remove the grease and food splatters from the stove. With the dishes and stove taken care of, I start on the counter-tops and cupboards because something is splattered on them. Note to self, when I move again, do not get a kitchen with white cabinets. This job takes me just as long as it did to wash the pots. The grease had started to set but with a little elbow grease—pun intended—the kitchen is finally spotless.

With a sigh, I throw the cloth into the trash, no saving that one. Leaning against the cabinets, I look around and smile. I really love our place, Bay and I made it into a real home. It suits both our personalities. The kitchen is small, with white upper and lower cabinets. The counter-tops are a speckled gray with a coffee maker and toaster sitting out for easy access. The kitchen is off the dining nook, which has a round table with four chairs. Off there is the living room, which consists of our sofa, coffee table, entertainment unit with flat-screen TV, stereo, and DVD player. It opens to a reasonably sized balcony, which overlooks the park across the road. The balcony is large enough for two chairs, a lounger, and small table. At the back of the living room is the front door and hallway, which leads to the two bedrooms and a half bath. There are faux wooden floorboards throughout and plush carpets in the bedroom. The bonus of this place, each room has its own en suite so I don't need to share with Bay. She never used to be this much of a slob but lately, her habits have been slipping.

Opening the fridge, I pull out my bottle of wine and pour myself a glass, a well-deserved glass after playing Suzy Homemaker since I got home. Taking a sip, I close my eyes and savor the taste as the pinot grigio slides down my throat. Not in the mood to cook, I put together a mini plat-ter, consisting of smoked cheese, salami, olives, and crackers. With my platter and wine in hand, I walk into the living room and my heart sinks. This room is just as messy. Not wanting to deal with it right now, I step out onto the balcony, which is surprisingly tidy.

Climbing onto the lounger, I place the platter next to me and lie back. Finally I'm able to relax. For the rest of the evening, I enjoy my wine and food. Bay doesn't come home and she doesn't call either, her behavior is concerning at the moment. However, as Cress keeps telling me, Bay is old enough to look after herself, but I worry about my twin. There's a niggling feeling deep inside my stomach, telling me she's in trouble, and I don't like feeling like this. I really hope I'm just being a worrywart right now.

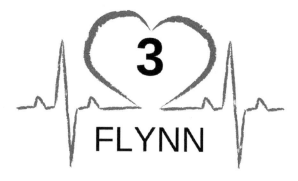

3

FLYNN

"TIME OF DEATH: FIVE FIFTY-TWO," I DECLARE, SHAKING MY HEAD IN DEFEAT. Someone pats my back in sympathy, and I let out a deep sigh. It's tough losing a patient. It doesn't matter if they are ninety or nine, a life is a life. Now the sucky part, I have to face the family and let them know that we, I, was unable to save their dad/brother/husband/son. This is the part that hurts the most. Sure, losing a patient stinks, but seeing those left behind fall apart, that's heartbreaking and it never gets easier. Thankfully, it doesn't happen all the time, but when it does, it messes with me and I doubt everything I did as the doctor on the case. Was there something I could have done to prevent the death? Did I fuck up? Doubt is a bitch, especially in my line of work.

Running my hands though my hair, I take a deep breath to prepare myself; not that you can really prepare for this. Exiting the room, I wash my hands and make my way out to the waiting room. As soon as I step into the waiting room, a lady stands up. She looks at me and without me even uttering a word, she knows. Her face pales. She begins to shake her head from side to side and lifts her hand to cover her mouth. The first tear falls as I begin walking toward her. "Mrs. Hunter" She nods but doesn't utter a word, "I'm Dr. Kelly. I was working on your husband, Paul. Unfortunately, due to the injuries he sustained in the crash, I was unable to save him." *To the point. Direct, without being harsh.* They are the words my mentor told me the first time I lost a patient and to this day, I still repeat them to myself when I deliver news like this.

"No. No. No!" she wails. She falls forward and crashes into me. She rests her palms and forehead on my chest, shaking her head from side to side repeating "No" over and over.

It isn't until a little voice says, "Mommy," that I realize he was a father. Mrs. Hunter really loses it when she looks down at her daughter. She drops down to her knees and envelops the little girl in her arms and cries harder. Seeing this causes a lump to form in the back of my throat when it really hits me: I didn't save this little girl's dad. *Fuck, fuck, fuck.*

Lifting my hand, I squeeze the back of my neck and look down at this woman and her daughter. My heart breaks for them both, it aches in a way I've never felt before. Reaching out, I rub Mrs. Hunter's back as she continues to cry, holding her little girl tightly to her chest. She's sobbing uncontrollably but at the same time, whispering to her daughter.

The little girl pulls away from her mom and looks up at me; her eyes red and filled with tears. "Why didn't you save my daddy?"

Wow, this little girl just gutted it me further with her words. I didn't think I could feel any shittier than I already do but this lil' one just knocked me on my ass once again. Dropping to my knees, I look her in the eyes. "I'm sorry sweetheart, I did everything I could to save your daddy."

She looks over to her mother, her bottom lip quivering and the tears in her eyes spilling down her little cheeks. "Daddy's not coming home," she tearfully cries.

"No, honey, he's not," Mrs. Hunter replies softly.

Reaching out, I take her hand and squeeze. "I know it'll be hard to never see or hug your daddy again, but he's in heaven now. You've now got your very own angel. He will look over you, protect you, and love you forever and ever."

The little girl looks to her mom. "Is that true, Mommy? Is Daddy an angel now?"

"Yes, honey, he is." She swallows a sob, "And what do angels do?"

"Angels ALWAYS smile down on those they care about."

"That's right."

"But if he loves us, why did he leave us?" *Wow, can this child gut me anymore?*

Her mother gasps and begins to sob. She drops to her knees and envelops her daughter in her arms, and together they cry and grieve. I give them a few moments and then reach out and squeeze her shoulder. "Sorry, Mrs. Hunter, but I need to talk to you about organ dona—"

"Yes." Her head pops up and she looks directly into my eyes. "Yes, P-p-p-p...Paul wanted to. The least we can do is make his death worthwhile."

This woman is amazing. She has just lost her husband, the father of her child, and she's turning his death into something wonderful. People continue to surprise me, and for once, it's in a great way. Nodding my head, I squeeze her shoulder tighter. "I'll contact the team and someone will be over to see you shortly to sign some forms." She nods at me as the tears continue to streak down her cheeks. With a sad smile, I once again say, "I'm so sorry for your loss, Mrs. Hunter."

She continues to nod and cry as I walk away. Just as I reach the security doors, I hear a little scream echo through the room. Looking back, I see the little girl in her mother's arms, sobbing her little heart out. Now that's heartbreaking. Leaving the little girl and her mother to grieve, I push through the doors and make a beeline for the drug room. Slipping inside, I close the door and lean my head against the wall. Closing my eyes, I breathe deeply and sigh. Quietly I whisper, "Six words have never cut me so deeply before. That little girl's life will forever be changed because I couldn't save her father."

Turning around, I slide down the wall and rest my head back. Closing my eyes again, I breathe deeply and take a few moments to compose myself. The life of a doctor is shit some days, and today it is epically shit.

Once I feel like me again, well as much as you can after an incident like this, I stand up, shake it off, and head back to work. Pushing open the door, I swallow down the lump in my throat and get back to work.

Along the way, I pass a nurse and she looks seductively at me. Licking her lips and grinning. My eyes drop to her mouth and I remember those lips wrapped about my cock a few weeks ago in the on-call room. Then I look into her eyes and I recall the days after. If it hadn't have been for Kristin saving my ass, I would have had a stage five clinger on my hands. I think she's the reason for not hooking up with anyone after Kristin left. Nodding at her, I put my head down and keep walking. *Not today, nurse, not today...or ever again.*

Once everything is finalized, and I've handed things over to the transplant team, I pop the paperwork in the correct tray for filing and head toward the doctors' lounge, thankful today is finally over. Pushing the door open, I step in and see Miranda and Grant, sitting very close together; seems there's a hot new couple at Western General. I'm happy for them, but coupledom isn't for me. I'm made for giving pleasure, not settling. We nod our heads hello as I pass by. Sitting in front of my locker, I sigh when I hear the door open and close again.

"Dude," Preston says, I look up and see him walking over to me. Standing up, we do the manly slap on the back, one-armed man hug, and then I sit back down. "Sorry about your patient," he offers, as he opens his locker and begins to change; the dude has no shame whatsoever.

"Thanks, man. How he held on as long as he did is beyond me. There was literally nothing I could've done."

"That's tough."

Nodding, I pull my scrub top over my head, leaving me in a white T-shirt; I throw my top at the laundry cart and lean into my locker for my button-down. Holding the shirt in my hands, I rub my forehead, and turn to Preston. "Drinks?"

"Hell yes. It's been a tough week."

"It sure has. Doesn't even feel like I had a vacation, but I'm glad to have the weekend off, especially after today." As I say this, I think back to my holiday and the babes I hooked up with, and in particular the lass who got away, Paige Walsh. Just thinking about her has my cock twitching. Even now, a week later, I'm still thinking about the chick I didn't fuck. She's all I can think about. A night with a random lass is exactly what I need to get her out of my head, and I need someone who doesn't work here. That's a complication I don't need right now.

Thirty minutes later, Preston and I walk into the Fat Fox Tavern. We decided to skip the bar closest to Western General. After today, I didn't want to be around other doctors where the topic of conversation always turns to work. After what transpired with the death of Mr. Hunter, I do not want to think about being a doctor. Tonight I want to fuck and forget.

Glancing around the bar, my eyes land on the most beautiful woman I have ever seen. Chocolate brown hair cascades down her back. Slim waist, from what I can tell. Legs that go on and on, *I'd like to see those sexy as hell legs wrapped around my waist…or face.* She's sitting at the bar with a girl-friend, drinking beer and doing shots. *She's doesn't look like a prissy stuck-up lass,* I think to myself, as I watch her throw back a shot. She makes a face, which on anyone else would look silly, but on her, it's sexy as fuck. She downs another shot straight after garnering a laugh from her friend. This time she shakes her head at the hit of alcohol, and it causes her tits to wobble. From where I'm standing near the door, they look like gorgeous breasts. *I wanna bury my face in them, maybe even slide my dick between them.* At that thought, my dick twitches in my pants.

Discreetly adjusting myself, Preston and I walk farther into the Tavern. We end up at the opposite end of the bar, which luckily for me, gives me a clear view of this sexy as hell vixen. We order two Guinnesses and head to a table in the back where again, I have a clear line of sight to the gorgeous brown-haired goddess who I cannot take my eyes off.

As I drink my beer, I hope and pray that later this evening, she will be riding my cock into the wee hours of the morning.

4

AVERY

My best friend Cressida (Cress) Bayliss and I have just arrived at The Fat Fox Tavern. Taking a seat at the bar, we order a round of beers and some shots. While we wait, Cress looks around the bar, no doubt scouting for tonight's hookup since she's child-free for the evening. Cress is a single mom to Lexi, and her daughter is a mini version of her mother. She's an exact carbon copy, looks and personality-wise. Good luck to Cress when Lexi is a teenager.

Our drinks are placed in front of us. We pick up our beers and tap them together and chant, "Cheers" before taking a sip. The yeasty goodness instantly relaxes me and I smile. Closing my eyes, I let the anguish of Baylor and the busy week I've had float away and vanish.

We sink our shots and I shake my head as the alcohol both burns and warms my body from the inside out. Picking up my beer, I take another drink when the sound of Cress's voice brings me back into the present.

"Ave, there's a hottie Mc-fuckin'-Hotterson behind you and he is currently eye fucking the hell out of you from across the bar," Cress says, as she lifts her beer to her lips. Moving my shoulder, I go to turn and look but she grabs my arm roughly and whisper-shouts, "No! Don't look."

My eyes bug open. "Why? If he's so hot, I wanna see," I complain. I can tell from the look in her eyes that he is a twenty out of ten.

Her eyes bug wide open and then she starts to grin, leaving me antsy— a grinning Cress can be dangerous at times. Her eyes are steadfastly locked behind me. He really must be hot if she can't stop staring. And then it hits me, he's staring at her and not me, and she clearly wants him too. *Ohh well,* I think to myself as I pick up my beer and take another sip.

When her mouth drops open, I become confused. She's stunned silent. With her eyes bulged wide open and her mouth wide open. And then I feel it, a warmth at my back.

My skin prickles.

My heart rate accelerates.

My mouth goes dry.

The air around me crackles.

I've never had a reaction like this before...and I haven't even laid eyes on this guy. Closing my eyes, I inhale deeply and spin my chair, trying to look sexy as I do, but instead, I overexert and the stool flies around faster than I anticipated and I lose my balance. Reaching my hand out to brace myself on the edge of the bar I miss, and instead, my hand lands on a body, with a thump, in the most inappropriate of spots. A grunt emanates from above me and he doubles over. "Fuck me," he groans in pain.

"Holy shitballs, I'm so so sorry. Are you okay?"

"I will be...eventually," he groans through clenched teeth, "but would you mind removing you hand from my junk?"

I'm frozen.

I'm shocked.

I'm in awe of his voice.

His looks.

His accent.

And I'm red with embarrassment.

My eyes bore into the Adonis before me. Finally my brain kicks into gear and I realize my hand is still resting on his junk. "Oh my God. Shit. Sorry," I stammer, as I remove my hand from his impressive package. I quickly pull it back and my eyes wander over his body. Oh My Fucking God, this man is gorgeous. Drop-fucking-dead-gorgeous. Brown cropped hair. Blue eyes I could stare at for hours and lose myself in. Chiselled chin, covered in the right amount of scruff. And a dimple, a fucking dimple. "I'm so sorry. Are you okay?"

"Yeah, nothing an ice pack and a beer won't fix."

"Well, I can help you with the beer," I offer.

He stares at me and nods. "Aye, I'd like that." *Holy shit, his accent is hot, so fucking hot.*

His electric blue eyes stare intently at me. My skin heats from the intensity of his gaze. I'm sure my chest is bright red and blotching with my nervous rash, or just red with embarrassment, or a little of both. My hazel eyes stare back at him and I feel a connection with him, which is weird considering I just met him.

The moment is broken when the bartender says, "What can I get for you?"

My eyes snap toward him. "Beer," I say, as I turn back to the man beside me. "A..."

"Guinness," he orders, his Irish accent again sending shivers through my body.

He offers me his hand. "Flynn, Flynn Kelly."

"Avery Evans," I reply. "Nice to meet you, Mr. Kelly."

"Doctor," he huskily replies.

"My mistake." I swallow and add, "It's nice to meet you, Dr. Flynn Kelly." Placing my hand in his, an electrical current zaps between us. It's just like those romantic moments I read about in my romance books.

"Tis a pleasure to meet you too, Avery Evans." My name sounds so sexy come from his lips, my eyes drop to his mouth, and I watch as his tongue darts out, sliding across his bottom lip.

We each hold each other's hand longer than appropriate and once again the barman interrupts us, delivering Flynn his beer. *Fucking cockblocker,* I think to myself, as I hand over a ten dollar bill to cover his drink.

"Thanks for the beer, Avery Evans." The way he says my name sets my body alight. Combine that with the intensity of his gaze and my body is a burning inferno. I love hearing his accented, deep husky voice wrap around each vowel and consonant within my name; hell, he could read the phone book to me and I'd be mesmerized. He takes a sip of beer, and my eyes watch as he swallows, it's sexy as all fuck. Yes, him drinking a beer is sexy. He places the beer on the bar top, his gaze once again boring into me. My body temperate is nearing catastrophic heat levels.

"My pleasure," I quietly offer in reply, brushing my hair over my shoulder as I stare at the gorgeous Irishman before me.

"It can be," he seductively says; as he continues to unabashedly fuck me with his eyes...again. My panties dampen. My tongue darts out and I lick my bottom lip. His eyes trace my tongue before I can register what's happening. He threads his fingers into my hair, pulls me toward him, and slams his lips against mine. My mouth opens in shock and he takes the opportunity to slide his tongue inside. My eyes close and I lose myself to the kiss. Our tongues seductively slide against one another. Our lips press together tightly. This kiss is not suitable for public, but I can't stop kissing him. My lips and tongue are moving on their own, I have no control. Sliding my hands into his hair, I pull him closer to me, deepening the kiss and our connection.

He pulls away, breaking the contact between us much sooner than I would have liked, but considering we're in a bar; it's probably for the best. He starts to lean forward and I think he's going to kiss me again. He leans in farther, his warm breath ghosting over my ear, my body buzzing from the brief contact. "Thanks for the beer," he whispers before placing a gentle kiss on that sweet spot just below my earlobe, my skin tingling where his lips caressed my heated skin. He pulls back, winks at me, picks up the pint glass, turns around, and walks away. Leaving me a panting, breathless, wet, turned on mess.

"Holy fucking hotness, Batman," Cress says from beside to me, I totally forgot she was here. "I think I need a cold shower after that."

"You and me both," I stammer, as I watch him walk away. And I can say, his ass is just as fine as the rest of him.

"You going to go after that hot piece of ass?"

I shake my head. "Nope, if he wants me, he can chase me."

"That's my girl!" Cress shouts. "Dude, two shots of whiskey...please," she hollers to the bartender. Throwing her arm around my shoulder, she leans in and whispers, "Let's loosen you up for Mr. Outlander over there."

Shaking my head, I laugh. "Jamie is Scottish. Flynn is Irish."

"Whatever!" she says in a Cher from *Clueless* tone. "They both end in 'ish, now let's liquor you up so you grow a pair of lady balls and go home with that Hottie McHotterson, and get you past third base AAAND maybe I can go home with his Channing Tatum look-alike friend?" She raises her eyebrows suggestively at me as she nods toward the pair. Turning around, I see they are both extraordinarily hot and both of them are looking our way.

Shaking my head, a laugh escapes me. I can't believe: A. That just kiss just happened and B. That Cress just said that to me, but at the same time I can because, well, it's Cress. Crass Cress was her nickname at school, and it's stuck ever since. All these years later, she still lives up to the nickname.

While she orders another round of beers and shots for us, my mind drifts to a dirty place with Dr. Flynn Kelly. Pressing my thighs together to ease the throb, I take a sip of my drink. Glancing over my shoulder, I find he's still staring at me. My heart rate increases when I see him grin at me.

Turning back to face the bar, I purse my lips and wonder if I can do it.

Can I go home with a complete stranger?

Can I have a one-night stand?

This is new territory for me, but if I'm being honest with myself, I think I want to.

Looking back over my shoulder, Flynn winks at me. With that one action, it cements my decision; I'm going home with a hot Irishman tonight.

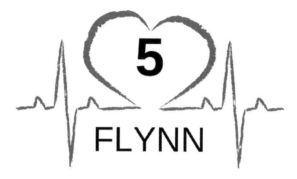

5

FLYNN

My eyes have been locked on Avery since we walked in. Even when she smacked me in the nuts, it didn't deter my want, my need, my hunger for this woman. From my seat, I watch as she sashays across the bar, her hips seductively swaying from side to side with each step she takes. My eyes rake over her body, and fuck me; this woman is stunning. What adds to her allure is she doesn't realize how goddamn sexy she is. She turns down the corridor toward the restrooms and out of sight. Waiting a few moments so I don't look like a creeper, I retrace her steps, but rather than heading down the corridor to the restrooms, I hide in an alcove off to the side, waiting for her to return. Ready to pounce and take what's mine.

Leaning against the wall, I feel her presence before I see her. Looking up, I smile as I watch her walk toward me. Before she steps out into the main bar, I grab her wrist and pull her toward me. Spinning her around, she gasps in shock as I cocoon her between the brick wall and my body.

Caging her in, I place my hands either side of her head and we stare at one another. The light is dim but as I gaze into her hazel eyes, I see them fill with desire when she realizes it's me. She opens her mouth to speak but I cover her lips with mine, devouring her mouth in a searing X-rated kiss. She slides her hands over my shoulders and runs her fingers up into the hair at the nape of my neck, just like she did earlier. The sensation causes my cock to twitch and harden between us, poking her in the belly. My heart is rapidly racing within my chest, it feels like it's going to break through my body. I've never had a reaction like this before from a kiss, I can only imagine what it will be like when I fuck her.

Her kisses become hurried, she wraps her leg around my thigh, shamelessly rubbing herself on me as we continue to devour each other's mouth. Our hands roam and explore each other's bodies over our clothes. The temperature in the alcove rising by the second, she moans into our kiss when I slide my hand down her arm and across her chest. Cupping her breast with my palm, I gently squeeze her soft plump mound. Sliding my hand inside the V of her dress and under the material of her bra, I massage and knead her breast. Her body heats under my touch with the skin on skin contact. With my other hand, I graze it ever so slowly down her body, her sexy as fucking sin body; a body I cannot wait to see sprawled naked in my bed. Gripping the hem of her dress, I slide my hand up her leg that's not wrapped around me. Skimming my finger over the top of her barely-there panties, I slide my fingers between her thighs and cup her mound.

"Please," she murmurs into my mouth, as she opens she legs wider for me. "Finger fuck me," she breathlessly growls, circling her hips onto my thigh and hand. This is an unexpected turn of events, but I'm more than happy to oblige. If I'm honest, I thought she would be quiet and meek, I like this sexy vixen side of her.

Teasing her, I run my finger in circles over her soaked panties. "Please," she cries again. The pleading in her voice does all kinds of things to me. With a forceful tug, I tear her panties off of her, the material disintegrating under the force. I thrust two fingers inside of her. They enter with ease due to her wetness. She gasps at the sudden intrusion and when I slide a third digit in with the others, she begins to ride my hand. Grinding herself against my digits. Moaning at the friction, I continue to slide my fingers in and out of her hot wet channel. My tongue mimics the motion of my hand within her mouth.

"Fuck my fingers, lass," I whisper against her lips, resting my forehead against hers, as I continue to thrust my fingers in and out of her. Her hips circling and thrusting in sync with my movements.

"Yes," she mewls.

Pulling back, I watch her face as euphoria radiates through her body. Her eyes are closed, she's lost in her pleasure. Her body tenses and she begins to scream. Slamming my lip against hers, I kiss her deeply and swallow her orgasmic cries. Her body violently shuddering as she rides out her orgasm.

She lowers her leg and stares up at me. Her cheeks are a sexy shade of 'I just came' pink. She's breathing heavily. Her chest heaving as she catches her breath.

With my eyes locked on hers, I lift my fingers to my mouth and slide them in. Licking and sucking them clean. A moan breaks free when the taste of her sweet sweet nectar hits my tongue. Her eyes widen at my motion. "You have the sweetest tasting pussy, Avery. A man could become addicted, and after just one taste, I'm addicted. I want and need more." Her cheeks darken at my words. With my eyes locked on hers, I slip my fingers back into my mouth and suck up the last remnants of her orgasm.

Leaning into her, I whisper, "Avery, I'm going to take you home now and I'm going to eat you, suck you, and fuck you repeatedly. All.Night.-Long." Emphasizing the last three words.

Nibbling on her earlobe, I pull my head back and stare at her. "Nod if you agree." She blinks rapidly before slightly nodding her head.

Without saying a word, I grab her hand and pull her out into the main bar area. Walking over to her friend, I tell her Avery is coming with me. I don't give either of them a chance to speak. Picking up her purse, I drag her out of the bar after stopping to tell Preston to make sure her friend gets home safely. He nods his head with a sly grin, and I leave the Tavern with Avery for a night I'm not going to forget anytime soon.

AVERY

HOLY SHIT, I'M LEAVING THE TAVERN WITH A SEXY AS SIN DOCTOR.

A doctor who I just let finger fuck me in said tavern.

A doctor who I *asked* to finger fuck me said tavern.

What is this man doing to me? And why do I like it so much?

This isn't me. I'm shy, reserved, and quiet. I don't leave bars with men I just met, or let them do things like *that* to me in public. From the limited conversation I've had with him, I can tell we are polar opposites but I'm drawn to him like a moth to a flame, and for once in my life, I don't care if I get burned. In fact, bring it on.

As I slip into his car, I lean back into the soft leather seat and a laugh escapes me.

"What's so funny?" he asks, as he hungrily stares down at me.

Gazing up at him, I shake my head. "It's nothing." If he knew what I was thinking, he'd pull me out of his car so fast my head would spin. He'd leave me standing in the parking lot alone and screech out of here as if he was driving in the Indianapolis 500. I keep my mouth shut because I don't want that. I want him to do exactly as he said. I want Flynn Kelly to fuck me, suck me and devour me all night long.

My mind drifts to all the sexy and dirty things I want him to do me. My body trembles at what I hope is ahead for me tonight. While I am lost in thought, he closes my door and climbs into the driver's seat. He starts the car and turns to look at me. His gaze is hungry and the desire I have for him skyrockets. I've never felt like this before. Brushing my hair behind my ear, I give him a shy smile. In return, he gives me a panty-melting grin and then I remember I'm no longer wearing any, he ripped mine off me back at the bar. Leaning across the center console, he threads his fingers into my hair, pulls me toward him, and presses his lips against mine. The kiss starts out gentle but quickly becomes heated, and he's now tongue fucking my mouth; I think this is my new favorite pastime.

Breaking the kiss, he huskily says, "I can't wait to have your sexy ass lips wrapped around my cock."

Between my thighs throbs at the thought and a slight moan slips free. He grins, and turns his attention back to job at hand, getting us back to his place as quickly as possible. He puts the car into reverse and we leave The Fat Fox for his place...and a night I'm sure to remember for the rest of my life.

Ten minutes later, he pulls into the underground parking garage for his building. Coming to a stop in his parking spot, he puts the car in park and turns off the ignition. Nerves start to kick in but the desire and need coursing through my body pushes them away. Turning to look over at him, I notice him swallow deeply. He must sense me staring at him because he turns to face me and from the look on his face, any thoughts and all fears dissipate.

Our eyes lock.

The air around us thickens..

My heart races, faster than ever before.

A force beyond my control over takes my body and I climb across the console and into his lap. Gripping his cheeks in my palms, I press my lips to his. I gyrate my hips on his hardening cock and I kiss the life out of him.

Just like he did to me, I fuck his mouth with my tongue and rub myself on his growing cock.

I've never been this brazen before, but this man brings out a side of me I never knew existed. A side I kind of like. Sexy vixen Avery is fun. He slides his hands up the back of my thighs and grips my ass, squeezing tightly as we continue to devour each other. A sound from nearby pulls us apart. Both of us breathing heavily. Panting.

"Let's take this upstairs," he growls.

Words elude me in this moment, so I nod my head in agreement when fear begins to creep in. *What in the hell am I doing?* Climbing out of the driver's side door, since I was in his lap, I wait for him to step out. He hands me my purse and after closing the car door, he links his fingers with mine and a calmness washes over me. That one simple touch instantly put me at ease. Silently we walk toward the elevators. My eyes keep sneaking peeks at him. I cannot believe this is happening. As we wait for the elevator to arrive, I dig my nails into my palm to see if this is real. To see if I'm dreaming. I feel the pressure of my nail against my skin so I know this is real. I'm not dreaming. I really did leave a bar with someone I just met and I'm about to have my first one-night stand.

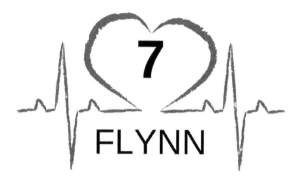

FLYNN

What is this woman doing to me?

I nearly fucked her in the underground parking garage, thank God that noise spooked us. I don't want anyone seeing her naked. I know that's rich, considering not thirty minutes ago I was finger fucking her at the bar, but it was dark and we were in a secluded alcove. Here? Anyone could have walked past and seen. I'm not an exhibitionist per se but I'm one hundred and ten percent sure Avery isn't. Sure, I've fucked in the on-call room and in my car up at the bluff when I was in med school, but never so brazenly out in public like this.

We exit my car and as I step toward Avery, I take a deep calming breath. Lacing my fingers with hers, a euphoric feeling washes over me and I pull her toward the elevator, eager to get her upstairs and naked beneath me. Pressing the call button, I stare at her out of the corner of my eye and as we wait, I notice her fidgeting. She's nervous and by the tinge of pink in her cheeks, aroused. Her nerves add to her sexiness, and I cannot wait for what's about to happen when we get upstairs. The doors open, I drop my hand to her lower back and usher her into the waiting elevator. Reaching over, I push the button for the penthouse and look back at her. Her mouth drops and her eyes pop wide open at this revelation. Placing my finger under her chin, I lift her gaze up to meet mine. We stare intently at one another as the elevator begins its journey to the top floor.

Our eyes are locked on one another and just like each time I look at her, something passes between us, it's an unspoken word of desire. The air in the car around us thickens and once again, my heart is racing profusely. At the same time, we step toward one another and our lips meet in a searing hot kiss. Our hands roam and caress. Our hearts beat erratically against each other. Blood and lust race through our veins. We both moan as our wanton sexual tension envelops us.

Sliding my hands down and around to her backside, I squeeze her ass and tap. She jumps up and wraps her legs around my waist. The feeling of her wrapped around me is far better than how I imagined it. She unabashedly grinds herself on me. My cock presses painfully against my zipper at the friction. Wrapping her arms around my neck, her breasts press into my chest, her taut pointy nipples poking me through our clothes. *I can't wait to suckle them*, I think to myself as the elevator doors open. Stepping out into the penthouse foyer, I walk us toward my front door. Pressing her into the mahogany, I dig in my pocket for my keys. If I was thinking clearly, I would have already had them out, but with her sexy body pressing against me, my thoughts were preoccupied.

With the keys finally in my hand, I take a step back, slip the metal into the lock, and unlock the door. Our lips remain sealed and my grip on her tightens as I maneuver the door open without dropping her. Multitasking with a goddess like Avery in my arms is harder than you'd think. My brain is fried, all the blood in my body is currently throbbing between my thighs, my cock harder than it's ever been before.

Stepping over the threshold, I stride into my living room and lower her to the sofa. She lies back on the chocolate brown leather and her glossy brown locks fan out behind her, creating a chocolate halo beneath her. She's fucking gorgeous. My eyes rake over her body from head to toe as I memorize each and every inch of her. "Avery, you are so fucking stunning."

Resting my knee on the sofa between her spread thighs, I slide up between her legs, gently pressing into her sex. At the same time, I skim my fingertip up her leg, her skin prickling with goose pimples under my touch. My hand keeps going and I trace the silky material up her side, across her stomach, before circling my finger around her breast. Her nipple hardens under my touch, pressing against the material of her dress.

Leaning down, I cocoon her beneath me and nuzzle into the side of her neck and massage her breast, pulling the taut peak of her nipple between my thumb and forefinger. Wishing there was no material between us. She moans as I nibble along her jaw. Throwing her head back into the cushion, she gives me full access to her neck. She threads her fingers in my hair, gently scraping her nails along my scalp. My cock twitches with each scratch.

Gazing down at her, I smirk before I lower my head and cover her mouth with mine. We kiss and lose ourselves in each other. Without warning, she flips us over—wow, she's a lot stronger than I thought—and straddles me. She grins down at me and winks. Gripping the hem of her dress, she lifts it over her head and drops it to the rug below. Leaving her in only her sexy as fuck, lace strapless bra that is doing nothing to hide her nipples. She's bare, as her panties are shredded and on the floor in the alcove back at the Tavern.

Lifting my hands, I gently caress her breasts as she rotates her hips on my cock. Pulling the lace cup down, I pinch her nipple between my thumb and forefinger, finally skin on skin contact. Her skin is silky soft, I cannot wait to burrow my face between her tits, licking, sucking, and marking her delicate skin. Her head drops back as I continue to fondle her breasts. They felt great in my hands through her dress but with nothing between us now, they are even better. Lifting myself up into a sitting position, I press my face into the valley of her breasts. Breathing her in, I groan, she even smells amazing. Licking up the side of her breast, I take one of her stiff pink peaks into my mouth. Sucking deeply, my tongue swirls around the tip before I suck again, gently biting down.

"Flynn," she huskily moans, as she presses my head farther into her bosom. Scrapping her nails across the back of my scalp, I moan against her flesh. Pulling my head from her breast, she grips my cheeks in her palms. Lifting my gaze from her breasts, I stare into her eyes. "Fuck me, Flynn," she pants as she tears at my shirt, buttons fly everywhere as she tugs the material down my arms. Throwing it to the floor, she shuffles back and begins to work on my pants. Without knocking her off me, I manage to free my cock and slip on a condom. She discards her bra and hungrily stares down at me. She bites and licks her bottom lip, and it's the sexiest thing I've ever seen. The only barrier between us now, nothing. She's gloriously naked on my lap and I cannot wait to slide my dick inside of her.

Gripping her sides, I lift her up and shuffle back onto the couch. She's kneeling across my lap. I can smell her pussy, I lick my lips. Her mouth drops open in shock as I slide my finger down her slit. She's soaked, spreading her wetness around, she lifts up on her knees and slowly shimmies forward and lowers herself onto me. We both moan as my cock slides into her wet folds. Her pussy hugs my cock tightly as she seats herself fully on me. With her eyes locked on mine, she slides herself up and down my rigid shaft. Gripping my shoulders tightly, her nails dig into my skin as she rides me like a stallion.

My left hand kneads her ass; squeezing and massaging her cheek. My other hand slides around her tiny waist and up to her breasts. Massaging gently, I tug on her nipple and pinch. Alternating back and forth between the two. "Flynnnnnnn," she moans, as I continue to fondle her breasts; they fit my hands perfectly. I can't wait to press my face into them again and that's exactly what I do. Leaning forward, I press her gorgeous tits together and lower my face between her plump mounds. I lick and suck her breasts. Gently biting her nipple, she moans and throws her head back. She runs her hands up into her hair, turning her head into her arms as she slides up and down my dick. We thrust our hips back and forth and I continue to devour her breasts. While I suck one nipple, I massage and squeeze the other. Repeating the motion over and over. She moans and groans as pleasure envelops us both. She makes the most amazing sound as her climax builds, a mixture between a wail and scream. The sound reverberates deep within me, pushing me to the edge.

"Avery, fuck," I groan, I'm teetering on the edge but I can't come. Not until she does. *She has to come before me*, I chant to myself over and over. She clenches me tighter and tighter with each thrust.

"I'm close," she cries.

Our eyes find one another and we stare deep into each other's souls as we thrust back and forth.

In and out.

Up and down.

Our bodies moving in sync. My balls tighten and I will myself not to come. *Not yet. Not yet*, I continue to chant. She slides her hand between us and flicks her clit, this sensation causes her to tense and shudder around me. Her body violently shakes and she screams, "Yes! Yes! Yes!" as her climax detonates. This sets me off and together we explode, screaming in ecstasy as we ride out our orgasm.

Our bodies quivering as the pleasure endorphins sore throughout us, she collapses forward, pressing her tits into my chest. Her hair shrouding me as we both breathe heavily and come down from our orgasmic high. She lifts her head and stares at me, her lips lift in a shy smile. "That was..."

"Yep," I say, as I tuck her hair behind her ear, cupping her face in my palm. Something passes between us, she leans forward and kisses me. This kiss is different, it's not as frenzied as our earlier ones but it's just as poignant. With her still straddling me, I remove the condom, tie it off and drop it to the carpet. Gripping her hips, I flip her on to her back. I settle between her legs and we make out like horny teenagers on a Saturday night.

She reaches around and grabs one of the condoms I dropped earlier. "Please," she murmurs into the kiss. Breaking the connection, I see what's in her fingers. Taking the rubber from her, I sheath my cock and stare down at her. She spreads her legs wide and that's all the invitation I need. With a flick of my hips, I slide inside her again. Even though I just came harder than ever before, I'm ready and raring to go once again. We fall into a rhythm, thrusting our hips back and forth. Our bodies and lips moving in sync. Our tongues caress one another and quicker than I would have liked, we both tumble over the orgasmic cliff once again.

Wrapping my arms under her, I lift her up and she wraps her limbs tightly around me. Walking us into my bedroom, I pull back the duvet and place her down on the bed. Sliding in next to her, we face one another and chat. I tell her about growing up in Ireland. She tells me about, Baylor, her twin sister. I get the feeling something is up there but I don't push it. I want to keep tonight light and fun. We continue to swap stories into the wee hours of the morning. She makes me laugh, and boy do we laugh. We share information with one another like I do with Preston; never have I done that before after a hookup, but Avery Evans is more than just a hookup. I want more with this woman. Tomorrow morning over breakfast, I'll broach that subject, because right now, her eyes are drooping and she's ready for sleep.

Pulling her into my side, she rests her head on my chest and throws her leg over mine. We blissfully drift off to sleep, wrapped in each other's arms. This is an amazing end to what was a horrendous day and I cannot wait for tomorrow.

8

AVERY

Opening my eyes, I'm disorientated for a moment. Blinking a few times, the room comes into view, but when I glance around I don't recognize anything. The walls are a dark gray, the furniture is dark, and the ever so soft bed is huge and isn't mine.

Then I remember.

Memories of last night come rushing back to me. My clit throbs as they play back in slow motion through my mind, my body tingling as I recall each and every deliciously sexy moment from last night.

A noise from beside me snaps me back to the present, and my gaze drifts to the side. I'm met with a muscular back and the hint of a butt cheek—a gorgeously firm butt cheek, if my recollections from when said cheeks were firmly pressed in my palms is correct. My eyes move north and I get a sudden urge to lean over and lick down his spine and bite his butt cheek.

What the hell? That's not me. I don't think dirty thoughts like this. Hell, I don't usually do ANY of the things I have done with this man. This man makes me do things I never in a million years would ever consider doing, but with how my body feels right now, I'm so glad he pulled me out of my comfort zone.

Rolling to my back, I stare up at the ceiling and then it happens. Panic starts to build within and a sudden urge to flee overtakes me—there's the shy, conservative, rule abiding Avery that I know. Like seriously, I'm an elementary school teacher, I don't pick up sexy as sin doctors in a bar...or go home with them. Nor do I let sexy as sin demigod's finger fuck me in public or make out and dry hump them in their car. Or have hours and hours of mind-blowing, out of the world, amazing sex. Or have naked deep and meaningful conversations at stupid a.m. with a complete stranger.

Fuck, fuck, fuck, I have to get out of here.

Movement from next to me pauses my racing thoughts. It seems during my mini mental breakdown freak-out, Flynn woke up and rolled over to face me. He's staring at me and even with a sleepy look on his face, he is the most gorgeous man I have ever laid my eyes upon. His gaze bores into me, my skin heating from the intense desire in his eyes. His gaze calms me and pushes my freak-out to the side, especially when his hand slips below the sheet and slides between my thighs. Like the whore I've turned into, I spread my legs for him, inviting him to do anything he wants to me. He rubs up and down my lips. Instantly I'm wet—whore—and his finger slides with ease into my sex. I moan at the friction and press myself into his hand. My eyes droop closed and my head rolls back on the pillow. I need more. I want more. I want Flynn like I need my next breath. *What is with this man and his magical fingers?*

My legs spread wider and I turn my head to face him, we stare one another as he continues to finger me. Pleasure builds deep in my belly. He thrusts two fingers inside, I moan in delight and close my eyes. My back arches and I whimper in ecstasy. He leans over and presses his lips to mine. His tongue licks along my lips, before sliding in and out of my mouth, in sync with his fingers between my legs. Before long, I explode around his fingers. Screaming as pleasure rumbles throughout my body.

Flynn removes his fingers, and he traces his fingertip along my bottom lip before bringing them to his lips. He slips them into his mouth and sucks. My mouth waters at seeing this. Licking my bottom lip, I taste myself for the first time. It's tart and tangy, not what I expected. He grins at me as he tugs the sheet off my body. He grabs my hand and places it on his cock, his rock-hard cock. Gripping his dick in my palm, I squeeze and flick my wrist up and down. The pad of my finger slides over the tip, spreading the leaking precum around. Our eyes are locked on one another as I jerk him off. He grips my hand and halts my movements. "I'm going to come if you keep that up."

Lifting to my knees, I shimmy down the bed, and with my eyes on him, I take him into my mouth, the tip hitting the back of my throat. Hollowing my cheeks, I suck and pump his cock. Repeating the motion over and over. His breathing becomes labored. His body stiffens and then I feel the first burst of hot salty cum hit the back of my throat. I suck and lick every last drop. I've never been into head before, but this man seems to bring me out of my comfort zone in many different sexual ways.

Pulling back, his cock pops out of my mouth. He beckons me forward with his finger in a come-hither motion. Straddling his legs, ever so slowly I crawl up his body. Kissing, licking, and nipping every ripple along his perfect body as I go. Licking up his neck, I straddle his waist and sit up. I stare down at him and smile. "You beckoned me?" I huskily say, not recognizing my sexed-up voice or this sex vixen version of me.

Flynn sits up, wraps his arms around my lower back and presses his face into my breasts. He attacks them with vigor. Each nip and suck sending shock waves straight between my thighs. My head drops back and I lose myself to the pleasure ricocheting throughout my body. My hips begin rocking back and forth; his cock hardens between us. Sliding my hand down, I grip his dick and begin to stroke. When he's hard as steel, I lift myself onto my knees and I slam myself down on him. "Fuuuuck!" I shout, as I impale myself fully on him, he's deeper than any cock has been before. He lifts his head from between my breasts. "Condom," he growls.

"I'm on the pill," I say, my eyes locked on his. There's a hint of indecision in his eyes. "I'm clean. I promise."

"I'm clean too." He smiles at me and nods his head.

Nodding in return, I begin to ride him. I've never not used protection before, I can feel every ridge on his cock, without the latex barrier it's much more intense. I grunt and groan as pressure builds within. My hips piston back and forth. Flynn thrusts up from below. He's so deep it hurts but at the same time, it's the most exquisite feeling ever. His cock is deep inside, it feels like he hits my cervix each time; it's ohh so delicious.

"Flynn," I croon, as I grip his shoulders for leverage and increase my thrusts. We thrash back and forth. The only sounds in the room are our heavy breathing and skin slapping on skin. Out of nowhere my orgasm detonates. I scream as my climax peaks, euphoria pulsates through my muscles from head to toe. My body tingling, never have I had such an intense orgasm like this before.

Flynn's body tenses against mine. His arms tighten around me and I feel him release inside me. He grunts and squeezes me as he climaxes. Collapsing back onto the bed, I fall with him. He gingerly traces his fingertip along my spine. I'm completely sated and well fucked, I drift off to sleep lying across his chest.

My full bladder wakes me, I don't want to move but if I don't it won't be pretty. Slipping slip out of bed, I walk into his en suite bathroom. It's clean and masculine, like the rest of his place. Gray tiles, white vanity. Even his towels are a charcoal gray. After using the toilet, I step to the sink and wash my hands. Glancing in the mirror, I don't recognize the person staring back at me. My cheeks are flushed, I feel relaxed and invigorated. Then I think about last night, and this morning, and with those thoughts in the forefront of my mind, I begin to freak out, again. *Shit, shit, shit. What have I done?* Conservative Avery is here, this is the Avery I'm used to and the one I know. No longer is the sexy confident vixen from last night present. Shy awkward me has returned, and she needs to get out of here and she needs to leave now.

Poking my head into the bedroom, I thank the heavens when I see Flynn is still sleeping soundly. Quietly tiptoeing out, I quickly exit his room. My heart is racing and it feels loud, like a herd of elephants trampling through the safari park. Stepping into the living room, I find my dress by the sofa. Picking it up, I slip it over my head. Then the clean freak in me appears. Picking up his discarded clothes, I fold them neatly in a pile and place them on the coffee table. Bending down, I pick up my bra, grab my shoes and clutch, and exit his place.

As I wait for the elevator, I sigh in relief that I escaped without being caught. My mind is a jumbled mess right now, and I'm ever so thankful I don't need to do the awkward morning/afternoon-after chitchat I've heard about. *How do people do this all the time?*

The elevator doors open and I press the button for the lobby. Shoving my bra into my bag, I slip on my shoes, and cringe when I realize I have no panties. I've just slipped my shoes on when the doors open to the lobby. Exiting, I race across marble floor, my heels clicking on the tiles loudly, basically announcing my walk of shame to the empty lobby, except for the concierge and doorman. Lowering my head down in mortification, I quickly race through the lobby and push the door open before the doorman can do it. Stepping out to the street, my heart is racing in my chest. I've never done the walk of shame before, and I don't ever wish to feel like this again. Looking to the street, I smile when I see someone getting out of a taxi.

Smiling at them, I carefully climb in—don't want a Britany vag flash—and give the driver my address. Sitting back in my seat, I rest my head against the headrest and let out the breath I hadn't realized I was holding. Grabbing my phone, I call Cress. She picks up on the second ring. "Afternoon, hussy."

"Morning," I reply, as I glance at my watch and realize it's almost one in the afternoon.

"Sooo…" she prompts, "how was your night?"

"Good," I say, as memories of last night play in vivid sexy high definition color in my mind, and my traitorous body zings with delight.

"Good, that's all I get good?"

"Yep. I'm in a taxi on my way home right now." Pausing, I purse my lips. I sigh and whine, "Cress—"

"I'll be there when you get home." I love that she knows what I need right now.

"Thank you," I whisper, but she's already hung up. I'm ever so grateful to have a friend like her because I really, really need her right now. I need her to help me compartmentalize everything that has eventuated in the last twelve hours.

Leaning back in the taxi, I close my eyes and then I lift my head and shoot upright. *Holy shit, I had an out of this world one-night stand and then I snuck out. I'm such a whore.* "Fucking hell," I mumble, as I lean my head against the side window and close my eyes. I feel so dirty, so skanky right now, but at the same time so alive and liberated.

Doubt starts to creep in, maybe I shouldn't have snuck out like I did but really, what other choice did I have? It's not like I'll ever see the sexy as sin doctor again.

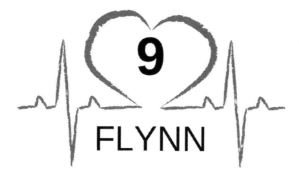

FLYNN

WITH A SMILE ON MY FACE, I OPEN MY EYES AND REACH OUT TO THE SIDE. I need to hold her against me as I wake up, but I'm met with nothing. My hand feels a cold sheet beneath it, turning my head to the side, I frown when I see the bed empty. *She must be in the bathroom,* I think to myself when I see the door closed. Lying back down, I stare at the ceiling and find myself grinning from ear to ear. Last night was beyond my wildest dreams amazing. I've slept with a lot of women but Avery Evans, fuck me, she strides to the top of the list.

It's been a while now, and she hasn't returned. "Avery?" I call out as I sit up in bed. Walking naked to the bathroom door, I knock. "Ave lass, are you okay?" Again I'm met with silence, pushing the door open I find it empty. Turning around, I walk into the living room and find it empty. Stepping around the sofa, I see her dress is gone, and my clothes are folded neatly on the coffee table. And then it hits me, she snuck out.

"Motherfucker," I groan, running my hands through my hair. Dropping down to the sofa, I rest my elbows on my knees and dejectedly sigh. She didn't seem like the person who would fuck and chuck, then again, I know dick all about her. Sure we chatted before falling asleep in the wee hours of the morning, but the topics we discussed were nothing serious.

Leaning back into the sofa, I smile as a vision of Avery riding me in this exact spot last night flashes before me. I can still smell her pussy, her sweet sweet pussy. My cock hardens thinking about her taste. My mouth waters and I imagine the sounds she made when she came. "Fuuuuck!" I growl as I grip my cock and begin to stroke. The sound of her purring like the sex kitten she is plays over and over on a loop in my mind. My grip on my cock tightens, my tugs hurried, and soon I'm spraying cum all over my stomach.

Collapsing back onto the couch, I lie here breathing heavily and think about the dark-haired angel who got away. Heading back into my bedroom, I climb into the shower and wash the remnants of my self-love away. Climbing out, I dry off and decide to head back to the Tavern, maybe she'll be back there for a quiet beverage to end the weekend.

Calling Preston, he agrees to meet me there in an hour.

An hour later, I walk in and my eyes dart around the bar, but my raven-haired beauty isn't here. Preston is and he's got a grin on his face. "Hey," he says, as I sit across from him. Picking up his drink, I slam it back. "Rough night?" he cheekily questions.

"Amazing night. Rough afternoon." I reply, flagging down the waitress, I order myself a beer and another scotch for Preston.

"That's two extremes."

"That's how the last eighteen hours have gone."

"Huh?"

"Last night and this morning were amazing with Avery. We clicked, and not just between the sheets." I take sip of beer the waitress just delivered. "Well, I thought we clicked. When I woke up just after lunch, she was gone. No note. Nothing. The only reason I knew she was there was because she folded my clothes and left them on the coffee table."

"Huh?"

"Before she left, she folded my clothes that were left in the living room last night."

"At least she's neat," he teases, as he takes a sip of his drink.

"Not what I'm focusing on at the moment." Then it hits me, he was with her friend last night, "How did you go last night?" He shrugs his shoulders. "What does that mean?"

"It means I looked after the friend like you requested."

"Aaaaand?" I probe.

"And nothing. We had a drink after you guys left and then I dropped her home."

"Really? You didn't fuck her?"

"Nope, my dick stayed in my pants. By the sound of things, you had enough sex for the both of us last night and this morning."

Shrugging, my mind once again drifts to last night, especially when my eyes gravitate toward the hallway to the restrooms. Vividly, what went down between us in the alcove flashes before my eyes.

"So what are you going to do?" His question stumps me.

"No clue. Did you get the friends details at all?"

He shakes his head but from the look on his face, he's full of shit. Something happened last night, I'd bet my left nut on it. But I know Preston Knight; he will keep this secret to himself until he's ready to share. That's one of the things I love most about the guy, he is loyal to a T.

Not wanting to bring him down with my foul mood, I say goodbye and head home to bed. Lying in my bed, I think about Avery, the one who got away. She helped me get over my blue balls, but now, it's my mind that's all messed up.

AVERY

CRESS IS THE BESTEST FRIEND EVER. TWENTY MINUTES AFTER I ARRIVE HOME, she turns up with wine, ice cream, and a gorgeous little girl. "Lexi, how you doing?"

"I'm good, Aunty A. I got to sleep at Nana's last night and then this morning, Mommy took me to the park and I got an ice cream."

"So I can see. What flavor did you get?"

"Mint chocolate chip."

"Yummo, my fav." Her face is all sticky and there's a chocolate splotch down the front of her *My Little Pony* shirt. At the moment, Lexi is obsessed with everything associated with that show. "You wanna watch some Pony while Mom and I chat in the kitchen?"

"Yessssss," she squeals in delight. She races into the living room and pulls out her beanbag and settles in while I switch it on. The theme song starts and I walk into the kitchen to find that my uber awesome best friend has a glass of wine waiting for me.

"Okay, spill," she says, as she hands me a glass of wine.

Taking the wine from her, I take a huge gulp, followed by another. "Okay, Chuggy McChuggerson, slow down there," she teases, as she takes the glass from me and tops it up—see, bestest friend ever.

Looking to her, my freak-out erupts with vigor. Tears well in my eyes. My chest becomes tight. Breathing is difficult. "Cress, I'm a big fat whore," I cry as Cress envelops me in a hug and lets me cry into her shoulder. "I slept with him so many times and it was ducking amazing." We don't swear when Lex is around. "It was the best ducking sex of my life. I'm surprised I'm not waddling today. When he was asleep, I snuck out, and now I feel guilty for leaving him like that. I can't even apologize for being such a ducking whore. At least I folded his clothes before I left."

She pulls away, holding me at arm's length and pulls a confused face. "You folded his clothes?"

Nodding my head up and down, I confirm, "Yeah, when I slipped my dress back on, I picked his clothes up, folded them, and placed them neatly on the coffee table."

Cress laughs at me. "Only you would have a one-night stand and then clean before leaving."

"Cress," I whine, "I'm a big fat whore."

"NO!," she shouts, wiping under my eyes with her thumb. "You are a sexy single gal, who had a fantabulous night ducking a hot guy."

"But—"

"NO! NO! NO! NO! NO!" she scolds. "Avery Evans, look at me." I lift my gaze to hers. "One night of amazing sex does not make you a whore. Did he pay you?"

"No."

"Then by definition you are not a whore, maybe a skank but definitely not a whore."

"Takes a skank to know a skank."

And just like that, all my whore fears are erased, but now I feel guilty for leaving. "Stop with the guilts for sneaking out," Cress says, giving me the mom eye she has down pat.

"How did you know?"

"I know all your tics," she nonchalantly says, she hands me my wine and this time, I take a small sip and savor the crispness of the white. "Now, listen to me, I will only say this once. You will not call yourself a whore for having fantabulous sex. You will not feel guilty for sneaking out like the harlot who I'm finally able to call my best friend. I'm proud, wee skankhopper. We, well you, are going to put last night with the sexy Scottish—"

"Irish."

"You are going to put last night with that sexy Irish doctor into the flick bank and move on."

"I knew you were my best friend for a reason. In half—"

"Three quarters," she teases.

"Fine, in three-quarters of a glass of wine, you've eased my fears and I feel like me again."

"Happy to be of service. Now, I want all the sexy filthy details."

Shaking my head, I take a sip. "Nope, last night is firmly locked away in my, what did you call it?"

"Flick bank," she offers.

"Yes, flick bank. Last night is safely locked away there. Now, I'm going to have a shower 'cause I smell like sex. You can order dinner and then we can watch *My Little Pony* with Lexi."

"Can't we watch something else?" she cries.

"Do you want to enrage your daughter?"

"Fair point."

With my wine glass in hand, I step out of the kitchen to go have a shower. Turning around, I pop my head back in, and say, "Cress, thanks for being you and calming me down."

"You are most welcome, babe. It's not often I get to rescue you, so it's nice to repay the favor for once…even if you won't spill the sexy schmexy details with your BFF."

"Love you," I call out, as I walk down the hallway to my room.

Cress really is the best friend I could ask for. Baylor used to share that spot with Cress, but in the last few weeks she's changed. I don't like the person she's turning into, not that I've really seen her. She's been MIA more times than not. I really hope she's okay, but my gut and twin instinct tell me she's spiraling out of control and she's about to crash and burn.

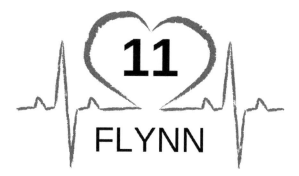

11
FLYNN

…three weeks later

I've taken an extra shift in the ER and I'm seriously regretting it. It's insanely busy today, and not just because we are short-staffed. It must be a full moon or something has been slipped into the water supply, because the cases today are batshit crazy and the patients all seem to be angry assholes with asshole family members or friends with them. With another chart in hand, I pull back the curtain, step in, look to the bed, and pause midstep. My eyes pop wide open when I see whom my next patient is… looks like picking up this extra shift wasn't such a bad idea after all. With a grin on my face, I casually say, "Hi." Stopping at the end of her bed. My eyes rake up and down her body. My eyes land on hers, but something is amiss.

"Well, hello there, handsome," she replies, her eyes lighting up but they aren't as vibrant as I remember and her hair seems lighter, but the lighting in here sucks and it has been three weeks since I last saw her. "Who knew hurting myself could be a good thing," she says, her voice deeper than I recall.

"How are you?" I ask, not the question I should be asking right now, but this woman has constantly been on my mind for the last three weeks, hell, I've even dreamed about her.

My eyes are locked on hers and my mind drifts to our night of unbridled passion together.

The moaning.

The groaning.

The thrusting.

The taste of her pussy.

The out of this world fucking.

The sound of our skin slapping together.

And then I remember she skipped out on me the next day.

Normally I don't care, but there's something about Avery that makes me want more. I felt a connection with her, and I know she did too. We meshed together in every way possible, and not just between the sheets. In amongst our marathon fuckfest, we had a deep and meaningful conversation that left me wanting more. I've never felt that before, and then she gave me my first taste of being fucked and chucked.

Shaking my head, I realize she's been talking but I have no clue about what she just said. Nodding my head, so I don't look like a complete idiot, I step to the side of the bed and place my hand on her calf, lifting up the ice pack. The spark that was there the other weekend when we touched is gone. I deflate a little on the inside, I really thought there was something between us, I guess there isn't anything there after all. Before I get a chance to ask a question, the curtain is pulled back. "Seriously, Bay, you are such a klutz at times."

That voice. My skins prickles at the sound of that melodic voice. My head snaps up and I spin around. For the second time in as many minutes, my mouth drops open in disbelief.

"Flynn."

"Avery."

We both say at the same time.

"Wwww...what are you doing here?" she stammers, her cheeks flushing as she stares at me.

"I work here." My eyes rake over her body. It seems my memory deceived me, Avery is more fucking gorgeous than I remember.

We continue to stare at one another. The intensity in her gaze causes my mind to flit back to our fucktastic night together.

Her head thrown back in ecstasy.

Her skin glistening with sweat.

Her gorgeous legs wrapped around my waist.

Her beautiful tits that fit perfectly in my hands.

The sexy sound she makes as she crashes over the orgasmic cliff.

My cock twitches at the memory.

The sound of her doppelgängers voice snaps me back to the present. "You two know each other?"

"No."

"Yes."

We each say.

We continue to stare at one another. I can't believe it's her. I'm being highly unprofessional right at this moment by ignoring my patient, but Avery is here. My Avery is standing in cubicle three. She's in front of me, in the flesh, but she's also lying on the bed beside me.

What the fuck?

My eyes dart back and forth between the two of them as I try and process this. A shrill voice breaks the silence, "Oh My God, you two totally fucked," comes from the Avery look-alike on the bed.

"Baylor, keep it down, we're in a hospital," Avery snarls. The girl in the bed sticks her tongue out at Avery. "Grow up, Sis, and have some class for God's sake. People don't need to hear you spouting this crap."

"Says the one who fucked Dr. Hottie McHotterson over here." She flicks her head in my direction. Her eyes wander over me and check me out from head to toe. It gives me the shivers and not in the good way. Her sister on the other hand, her sister causes my body to come alive just from her proximity. The woman in the bed, Baylor, her sister, licks her lips, but movement in my peripheral vision snaps my attention back over to Avery, beautiful shy Avery. She's my polar opposite in every way but I'm drawn to her like a magnet, by a force I cannot explain.

"Please ignore my sister," Avery says, as she steps closer to the end of the bed...and me. "She must have bumped her head as well as rolled her ankle." She lifts her hand and presses down on the ice pack covering her sister's ankle.

"Ouch, you bitch," Baylor whines, her face wincing in pain.

Glancing at the chart in my hands to calm myself, I look to my patient. "Baylor—"

"Bay," she interrupts and bats her eyelashes at me, clearly showing no respect for her sister. She totally knows something went on between us, yet she still flirts with me.

Ignoring her, I go on, "Baylor, I'm Dr. Kelly. Can you tell me what happened?"

She begins to speak but my eyes are locked on Avery. She's fucking gorgeous, I don't think I have ever met someone as stunning as her. Her shyness has returned and she's fidgeting by the end of the bed. Suddenly, I hear Baylor and I realize, once again, I didn't hear a word of what she just said. "Let's take a look," I interrupt her.

Placing the chart on the bed, I lift the ice pack and stare at her ankle. Her very swollen, bruised, and possibly broken ankle. Reaching out, I lightly touch her foot. She flinches and groans but the doctor in me knows she's exaggerating. "We'll get an X-ray and once we know what we're dealing with, we can go from there."

Exiting the cubicle, I walk over to the nurses' station and request an X-ray. I've just signed the X-ray request form when my skin prickles. I feel her approaching, turning around, I watch and stare as Avery hesitantly walks toward me. "Flynn, I'm—"

Shaking my head, I interrupt, "Not here and it's fine," I snap, harsher than I intended. She immediately shrinks into herself and I feel like a major dick. "Look, Avery. It's fine. If you'd prefer another doctor for your sister, I'm happy to do so. I don't want to make you uncomfortable." Where the fuck did that come from? I don't normally give a shit if someone is uncomfortable, but I really care about this woman and her feelings. She has me acting like a lovesick fool. Once again, I realize I tuned out and missed what she said. "Sorry, can you repeat that?"

She stares blankly at me. "There's no need to swap. It will just piss Bay off and a pissed-off Bay is never a good thing."

"Your sister, seems...nice," I say.

She knows I'm lying. "Mmmhmpf. That's not how I'd describe her but then again, I know my twin better than anyone." We continue to stare at one another. Everyone and everything around us fades into the background. My eyes are focused on the angel before me. The air around us zinging with electricity, just like it did three weeks ago. "Flynn, can we get a coffee sometime? It's the least I can do aft..."

"After you left me high and dry after our fucking amazing night together?" I say, arching my eyebrows.

She laughs, "Yeah, something like that." She steps toward me, rests her arm on my forearm, and lowers her voice. "I'm sorry I left how I did. I'm not normally that rude, but I've never done what we did before. In the reality of the daylight, I kinda freaked out."

"I was upset to find you gone when I woke up." Her face deflates. "Sorry, I didn't mean to upset you."

"How are you comforting me, when I'm the one..." She doesn't finish her sentence, she leaves it hanging. We stare at one another. All I see is Avery; shy gorgeous Avery. It's just the two of us, even though we are standing in the middle of the ER. That connection, that chemistry from the tavern and that night is still present. My eyes are locked on hers, my gaze bores deep into her soul. This woman who is the complete opposite to me has me wrapped around her finger. I'd do anything for more time with her. The saying opposites attract comes to mind and I'm one-hundred-percent attracted to her and definitely her opposite. I'm confident she's attracted to me too, but she's scared and I'm going to have to take control of the situation at hand.

Without thinking, I blurt, "Can I take you to dinner?"

12

AVERY

Holy shit, he wants to take me to dinner.

What kind of guy does that? I sneak out like a thief in the night and he still wants to see me, is he crazy? I offered for us to get coffee, ease our way into something, and then he counters with dinner. *What the what?* Have I been sucked into an alternate universe? An alternate freaking universe where a sexy as hell Irish god, who also happens to be a doctor, wants me. Me? Avery Evans, plain-Jane teacher. He does remember that we had a one-night stand—a freaking amazing out of this world, porn worthy one-night stand—and then I snuck out. What are the freakin' odds that he turns out to be the doctor who treats my sister? And after ALL that, he still offers to take me out to dinner. *What the what? Is this guy nuts? Oh My God, don't think of his nuts 'cause that's near his thingy, his amazing thingy that gave me the most amazing pleasure E-V-E-R!*

I'm not sure what to do.

I've never been in this situation before.

What do I do?

What's the protocol when a one-night stand asks you out when you bump into one another?

Shy me wants to run and hide and forget I ever met Dr. Flynn Kelly.

Sex-bomb vixen me, who went home with him, really wants to go to dinner with him...and then have him for dessert. *Where the hell did that kinky thought come from? I don't think or say things like that.* Crap, what is this guy doing to me? Shit, he's staring at me, waiting for my reply.

Before I can stop myself I blurt out, "Sure, I'd love that." *What the hell, Evans?*

He smirks at me as he grabs a card off the counter and scribbles on the back of it. He hands it to me and just like before, when his fingers brush against mine, an electric current zaps between us. The air around us sizzles with desire and lust. He leans in and ever so softly kisses my cheek, my cheek tingles when his lips press against my skin.

"My cell's on the back. Call me to arrange dinner," he gruffly says, his voice sending shock waves through my body and igniting my soul. Before I can say anything, he steps away. Leaving me standing here like a lovesick fool with a grin on my face bigger than the Cheshire cat.

Grinning from ear to ear, I turn on my heel and walk back into the cubicle where Bay was, but it's empty. I'm guessing she's off for her X-ray so I take a seat and wait.

I'm thankful for the few moments of peace. My mind plays everything over and over.

Our night together.

The chats we had.

The morning together before I snuck out.

Our chat just now.

The peck on my cheek a moment ago.

Lifting my hand, I rest it where his lips were. A shudder runs though me. *I'm so scared when it comes to this man but at the same time, I'm intrigued and excited.* For the first time in my life, I want to be reckless and carefree. I'm going to go for it, what's the worst that could happen?

Sitting down on the chair on the corner, I wait for Bay to return. A short while later, the curtain pulls back and she returns. She plays the princess card and flirts excessively with the orderly. The fool goes out of his way to help her back onto the bed. Sitting in the corner, I shake my head and hold back a laugh.

Stretching my arms over my head, I stretch out my muscles and then lean back and continue watch the spectacle in front of me. How freakin' long does it take to get someone back into a bed? Finally, she's settled and the orderly leaves, pulling the curtain closed behind him. "You good?" I ask, when she looks over at me.

"What do you think?" she snaps at me, "My ankle is swollen. It looks like a melon is growing out the side of it, and I won't be able to head to Vegas with the girls this weekend. But at least there's a totally fuckable doctor on my case."

My blood boils when she says this. She knows something happened between Flynn and me, but in recent, typical Bay style, she's going to walk all over me. She's going to take what's mine; just like she did with my Princess Barbie when we were eight years old. Before I can tell her to back off, the curtain opens and Flynn steps in.

He looks to me and winks, my cheeks darken and my heart begins to race faster within my chest. I'm sure if I were connected to a heart monitor, my heart rate waves would have little love hearts flashing across the screen between each beat.

"Hey, Doc," Baylor flirts.

"Ms. Evans, I—"

"Please call me Bay." She flirts and again my blood simmers.

"Ms. Evans," he ignores her–score one Flynn. "As I was about to say, your X-ray shows no sign of a break, but the ligaments have been torn. You'll be in an orthopedic boot for a few weeks to aid in recovery of the ligaments, and you will need to follow up with a physical therapist to exercise and restrengthen the ligaments."

Baylor leans forward and thrusts for tits toward Flynn. "Can't you see me through my recovery?" she purrs like a desperado.

"No," he sternly says. "I'm an ER doctor, not a physical therapist. I'll have you fitted with a walking boot and then you'll be discharged." He turns to leave and looks at me. "Ave, don't forget to call me." With that statement he exits the cubicle, and I sit watching the curtain flap with a goofy grin on my face.

"What the fuck?" Bay scoffs. "He's choosing you over me?"

My grin evaporates at Bay's harsh words and I stare at her. "What?" I ask confused.

"Dr. Hottie totally ignored me and focused on you. Why?"

Shrugging my shoulders, I try to school my face because if Bay gets wind of my feelings—not that I have any—for Flynn then she'll swoop in and steal him like she did with Mike Ciz in eleventh grade. However, this time it will be much worse because I've already slept with Flynn, and there's something building inside me when it comes to the hot Irish doctor.

"Why?" she snarls again.

"Why not?" I bitchily say in reply.

"Because I'm me and you're you. You're a boring, quiet, shy school teacher. And I'm this…" She flicks her hand up and down her body. "Who wouldn't want this?"

Maybe it's your holier than thou attitude, I think to myself. "Bay, we look exactly the same except your hair is a little lighter, so on looks alone there's no comparison. Personality-wise…" I don't finish that because I don't want to get into an argument with her.

She rolls her eyes at me. "Whatever." She crosses her arms in a huff.

Thankfully a nurse walks in before it can get any more heated between the two of us. She gives Bay the details she needs for her physical therapist, fits her boot, and then hands her her discharge papers.

With the usual Bay overexaggeration, she climbs into the wheelchair and we leave the hospital. Just as we are exiting the ER, I feel Flynn staring at me from behind. Looking over my shoulder, I notice him watching me. He winks when our gaze meets and a smile breaks free. I brazenly wink back, something I wouldn't normally do, but around Flynn Kelly I seem to do a lot of things I normally wouldn't.

We arrive back at our apartment and Bay heads to her room, slamming the door behind her. Shaking my head, I walk into the kitchen and pour myself a glass of wine. With my wine in hand, I walk into the living room and as I take a seat on the sofa, I pull my phone out of my pocket. Tucking my legs under my butt, I lean back into the sofa and grab the card Flynn gave me earlier. My nerves begin to jitter as I stare at the rectangular card in my hands. Pursing my lips, I umm and ahh as to whether I want to text him. I want to text him, really I do. But at the same time I don't. I totally don't know what to do right now. So instead of deciding, I chug back the wine in my glass. Hopping up, I refill it, and bring the bottle back with me.

Placing the bottle on the coffee table, I sit back down and take another sip. As the delicious crisp flavor of the pinot grigio hits my tongue, I decide to throw caution to the wind–a common trend when it comes to this man—and reach out to him. Adding his number to my phone, I stare at it before I whisper, "What the hell." And then I text him.

AVERY - *Hi, Flynn. It's Avery. If the offer still stands, I'd love to have dinner with you.*

That leaves the ball in his court and if he decides to ghost me, then I won't be too upset. Who am I kidding? I'll be gutted if he doesn't reply, but to my delight my phone beeps with a text a few minutes later. As I reach forward to pick it up, my heart rate accelerates with nerves. When I see his name on the screen, I grin like the Cheshire cat. Taking another sip of wine, I settle into the couch, unlock my phone, and read his reply.

FLYNN: *Hey, gorgeous. To be honest, I didn't think I'd hear from you. I thought I was going to have to resort to talking to your sister to get your number. Thanks for saving me from that. How about Friday night? I'll pick you up at 8.*

I smile at his reply.

AVERY: *Friday sounds great. I'll meet you there.*
FLYNN: *It's the gentlemanly thing to pick up his date.*
AVERY: *This isn't the olden days. I'll meet you there, just tell me where.*
FLYNN: *Let's meet at my place and we can go from there.*
FLYNN: *You remember where that is, don't you?*

Smart-ass, I think to myself as I type my reply.

AVERY: *Yes. See you Friday at 8.*

Placing my phone on the couch next to me, I shuffle back into the cushion and find myself smiling and then I sit up straight when it hits me. Holy shit, I'm going on a date with Dr. Kelly.

13

FLYNN

I'VE JUST FINISHED MY CRAZY, HECTIC, SUPER-SURPRISING EXTRA SHIFT AND I'M exhausted. Grabbing my phone, I check for a message but there's no new messages. I'm not surprised, really. As I watched Avery leave the hospital earlier, it felt like it would be the last time I ever saw her. Honestly, I'm not holding out any hope of her texting me. After changing out of my scrubs, I grab my things and head to my car. As I'm climbing in, a text comes through, and much to my surprise and delight, it's from Avery. She DID text me, seems I was wrong in regards to her. Sitting in my car, I open her message with a goofy grin on my face and read. Normally I'd leave it and check/reply once I got home but knowing it's from her, I can't help myself.

Inwardly I do a little jig as I read her reply—yep, I'm acting like teenage girl who has scored a date with the quarterback to the home-coming dance. Quickly I text back my dinner offer, and much to my delight, she replies immediately. She's either playing coy, or safe, not giving me her address but from what I know about her, she'll be playing it safe. She accepts my offer to meet at my place and with our date locked in for Friday, I throw my phone in the center console and head home.

I'm stopped at a red light and my mind drifts back to our night together. Her panting and screaming my name. The glazed-over look in her eyes when she comes. Man, I really hope we recreate and add to those memories on Friday. The honking of a car horn behind me snaps me back to the present. Looking up, I see the light is still green and I press my foot down on the accelerator and continue my drive home.

On the drive, my mind runs a million miles an hour with what we can do on Friday...and what I hope happens AFTER our dinner date. Whatever happens, I'm not going to let her slip through my fingers this time. I know I sound like a sap, but for the first time ever; I'm intrigued by a woman. I want to get to know Avery Evans. I want her in my life. I need to woo her and the wooing will start this coming Friday.

The week dragged by ever so slowly but finally, it's Friday. And just like the rest of the week, my shift passes by at a slow snail's pace. It's the slowest of slow days in the ER, and normally I'm all for a quiet shift but not today. I wanted today to fly by so I could get to tonight AND then I want for evening to go slow. *What the fuck is happening to me?* I'm A. Going on a date and B. I'm fucking excited for said date. Never in my thirty-three years have I ever been excited for a date; actually, I don't think I've ever been on a date date. Meeting in a bar to fuck isn't a date, it's a booty call with class. This is new territory for me. Do I get her flowers? Chocolates? A teddy bear? I don't know what to do and suddenly I'm nervous as all hell. What is this woman doing to me?

My shift is finally over and I hightail it out of the hospital. I brush off Preston when he asks about heading out for a drink. He eyes my suspiciously and I know that the next time I see him, he's going to grill me...but all going well, I'll have details to spill about a girlfriend. *What the fuck?* Where did that thought come from. Settle down, cowboy. Let's have our date before I start picking out china patterns. Thinking of that, my mind drifts to Avery in a white dress, standing before me on a beach. Her hair blowing in the wind. Shaking my head, I snap those crazy thoughts from my mind, pushing them deep down, and I head for home.

Stepping into my penthouse, I look around, and for the first time since moving in, it feels amiss. This place really needs a woman's touch and I think Avery is the woman to do that. Maybe after ravishing her all night long, I can ask her opinion in the morning…as long as she doesn't duck out on me again. That thought frightens the fuck out of me.

Avery Evans is invading my thoughts and changing my outlook on life. She's an enigma and I cannot wait for our date tonight to get to know her more.

AVERY

It's time to leave, I'm too nervous to drive so I order myself an Uber and it arrives quickly. The car pulls up in front of Flynn's building but I don't move. I sit here, staring at the back of the seat in front of me. Taking a deep breath, I step out and walk toward the entrance. The doorman opens the door for me and nods hello, but doesn't say anything. Smiling at the concierge, I walk toward the elevators, my heart excitedly racing with each step I take. Pressing the call button, the doors open and as I step in, my nerves kick in. I become a nervous ball of energy. My eyes watch the numbers as I travel up to the top floor. Nervously, I rub my hands up and down my dress a million times on the ride up. Biting my bottom lip, I let out a huge breath just as the elevator doors open. With a nervous sigh, I take a calming deep breath and step out into the penthouse foyer.

Holding my head up high, I walk toward his door. Raising my hand, I knock. Suddenly butterflies appear in my stomach and they begin to flap their wings rapidly. The door swings opens and when I see Flynn smiling back at me, all those nerves instantly disappear. "Hey," I greet. *Hey, really, Avery?*

"Hey," he says in reply. His eyes rake over me ever so slowly. His gaze setting my body on fire. "You look stunning, Avery." The deep timbre of his accented voice prickles my skin. Looking down at myself, I grin, *Yeah, this dress is smoking hot, thanks Cress for making me buy it.* And from the look on Flynn's face, I've knocked it out of the park tonight.

My eyes roam over him, and I too like what I see. I'm lost in everything that is Dr. Flynn ohh-so-sexy Kelly, and I can't believe I'm going out with him tonight. I feel like I've stepped into an alternate universe, hot guys don't fall me for. Bay? Yes. She's confident and outgoing. Me? I'm shy and reserved. My nerves ramp up again and doubt begins creeps in. I can't do this. I shouldn't be here. It isn't until Flynn touches my arm and smiles at me that everything settles down. The connection of his palm on me, instantly calms me. All those nerves evaporate and I feel like I can breathe again. We stare at one another. The air around us crackling with lust, desire, and everything in between.

"Evening, Dr. Kelly," I shyly offer, then I internally scold myself because I've already said hey. *Off to a swimming start here, Evans.*

"Evening, Ms. Evans," he says with a smile and wink.

My panties are now soaked. We continue to stare at one another and I'm ready to say screw dinner. I want to throw myself at the man before me and ravage him. Before my craziness comes to fruition, he steps into the hall and closes the door behind him. Stepping to me, he places a gentle kiss on my cheek and when he pulls back, my skin is tingling from the ever so brief kiss. Lifting my hand, I caress the spot where his lips just were and my smile widens. "Shall we?" he asks, offering me his elbow.

"We shall," I murmur, as I link my arm with his.

We spin around and make our way toward the elevator. We step into the car I just exited and as the doors close, the air around us electrifies once again. Standing next to one another, we not so subtly check the other out on the ride down. Flynn is rocking a pair of black slacks and a silver-gray button-down that accentuates his blue eyes, making them pop. His hair is styled in that sexy, messy man way and there's a slight five o'clock shadow gracing his chin.

The elevator arrives on the ground floor and we step out. He places his hand at my lower back and ushers me toward the exit. My heels click on the marble floor as we cross the lobby. The concierge nods toward us, and smiles. Flynn nods his head in return. "Evening, Max."

"Evening, Dr. Kelly." He pauses and looks to me. "Ms. Evans." Lifting my hand, I offer a shy wave and smile.

The doorman opens the door for us and when we step outside, I quiz Flynn, "How does he know my name?"

"I added you to the access list. That's how you got up without any concern earlier."

"Really? Why?"

"Because after tonight, I hope that you'll be visiting me often." *Whaaaat?*

He places a kiss on my temple and ushers me into a waiting car. I've been so wrapped up in this man that I didn't even notice the car idling at the curb. "Ohh, fancy. Do you always use a car service?"

"Not often, but I wanted to make tonight special."

Entering the car, I scoot across the seat and watch as Flynn climbs in beside me. I cannot help but ogle the sexy as sin man climbing in. How in the hell am I on a date with this man?

"Like what you see?" he cockily says, lifting his eyebrows teasingly.

"Meh." I shrug. "I've seen better," I playfully reply. *Wow, Avery, where is this sass coming from?*

"Really?" he counters.

"My lips are sealed." Mimicking locking my lips, I grin at him and wink. He smirks at me and a small laugh escapes me.

"I'm sure I can unseal them," he cockily replies.

He stares at me intently and then his gaze drops to my lips. My tongue darts out and I gently bite down. "I guess time will tell."

"Well then, looks like I need to up my game because, Avery, since I saw you at my door, I've really wanted to taste you again."

Swallowing deeply, I look to him seductively and whisper, "Why don't you then?"

"Because, if I kiss you now, I won't be able to stop, and I want to spoil you before I fuck you, plus, I wasn't referring to kissing the lips on your face."

My eyes bug open at the crassness of his statement but at the same time, my insides sizzle at the thought of what will come later. Sitting back in my seat, I stare out my window and grin. I really want him to kiss and ravish me. I want him to do everything to me.

Sneaking glances at the man beside me, my desire and want builds with each mile the car travels along the freeway. "You know I can see you staring at me, right?"

My heads snaps to his. "How?"

"Because I'm staring at you, lass. I'm watching your every move. You, Avery Evans, are the sexiest woman alive, and I'm lucky as hell to be on a date with you this evening." He pauses and reaches over to take my hand in his. Lacing our fingers together, he rests our joined hands on his thigh. "When I saw you standing at my door, I was tempted to say screw the restaurant. I wanted to drag you inside where I'd feast on *you* for dinner, but then the sensible side of me kicked in and reluctantly but also happily, here we are."

Holy shit, he did not just say that to me.

Holy shit, we were thinking the same thing.

My mouth opens and closes a few times, words escape me and then my brain fires and words appear. "And I thank you for that, I'm starving."

"I am too…for you."

My eyes widen at his words and my panties dampen. Pursing my lips, I lower my gaze to my lap. My heart is racing right now, my insides are a buzz and my lady bits are throbbing. Biting my lower lip, I turn my head slightly and look directly into his eyes. "And for the record, Dr. Kelly, I would have totally been down with the ravishing of option one."

He shakes his head and laughs, a deep belly laugh that's music to my ears. "You continue to surprise me, Avery Evans."

"I continue to surprise myself too when I'm around you." Shuffling around, I face him. "Flynn, we are total opposites but there's something about you I'm drawn to. I couldn't stay away, even if I wanted to."

"Avery, I feel exactly the same way."

The rest of the car trip is silent but I do shuffle closer to him. Only a hair's width separating us, my hand traces circles on his knee, brazenly going higher and higher each time. Before I do something stupid, like straddle his lap and ravage him, we pull up to the restaurant. Flynn climbs out first, and offers me his hand.

As I step out, he says, "I hope you like steak." Looking up, I smile when I see we are at Rococo's Steakhouse, the finest steakhouse this side of Texas. We head toward the entrance, before he opens the door, I tug on his hand, stopping him. He turns to look to me. I smirk at him, leaning into him I whisper into his ear, "I love a big juicy piece of meat." Stepping back, I wink before I step past him and open the door to the restaurant.

He shakes his head at me and enters the restaurant behind me. We make our over to the maître d's station. "Good evening, welcome to Rococo's Steakhouse."

"Good evening. Reservation for Kelly."

"Welcome, Mr. Kelly. Your table is ready, if you'd like to follow me."

Flynn laces his fingers with mine and we follow the maître d' into the restaurant. I've never been here before and this place is gorgeous. When you enter there's rich wooden flooring that leads into the restaurant, where it changes to a deep plush burgundy carpet. The tables are dark in color, the chairs are a chocolate brown with studded accents and burgundy cushioning. Each table has a candle for ambience. The overhead lighting is dim but enough that you can still see. The kitchen it open and you can see inside. It's a hive of activity right now, pots clanging, steaks sizzling. The chef barking orders to the staff. Next to the kitchen is the bar which runs the length of the building. The front of the restaurant is floor-to-ceiling glass and the view of the city is spectacular.

Arriving at our table, Flynn pulls out my chair for me. "Thank you kind, sir."

He lowers down and whispers, "Don't thank me, I totally did that so I could see down your dress."

Playfully I smack his arm. "You fiend."

"Only for you," he replies, before he makes his way over to his chair. My eyes watch him. Even though he's tall and massive, he moves with the grace of a ballerina. He winks at me and I realize I'm in way over my head. Flynn Kelly is going to be the death of me...and I cannot wait.

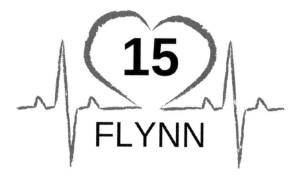

15
FLYNN

SITTING ACROSS FROM AVERY IS HARD...MUCH LIKE MY DICK RIGHT NOW. THIS woman is unbelievably sexy, and what makes her even more so, is the fact she is oblivious to how gorgeous she is. Right now, I want to be sitting next to her so I can caress and touch her. She smiles and it lights her face up, her eyes sparkle. It's in this moment I decide that sitting across from her isn't so bad after all. I can bask in her beauty and continue to check her out. Glancing around the restaurant, I look at everyone else, and no woman here compares to Avery. I just hope my cock decides to behave himself before I have to stand up.

"Flynn?" she yells, my eyes snap to hers. Her face is etched with concern.

Shaking my head to clear it, I question, "Sorry, what?"

"I asked, what do you recommend?"

With a grin, I saucily reply, "You...from memory."

Her cheeks tinge a sexy shade of pink. She bites her bottom lip. "I meant on the menu."

"Are you on the menu?" I tease.

She stares at me before leaning forward, giving me a stunning view down her dress. Her tits press together and I want the bury my face between them. They are looking mighty fine encased in satin, which so happens to match her dress, *I can't wait to see that bra on my floor.* She licks her lips before seductively whispering, "Maybe I can be your dessert later."

Cock.

Painfully.

Hard.

Again.

"You are a sexy little minx, Avery Evans. I'm totally holding you to that AND yes, for dessert I'm going to feast on you like I would a double chocolate fudge sundae. Every inch of you will be licked with my tongue and inspected with my fingers. When I've had my fill, I'll fuck you with my cock into the wee hours of the morning." He pauses. "I suggest you order the surf and turf…you are going to need your energy."

Her eyes pop open at my brashness and her cheeks darken my favorite shade of 'aroused pink.' She audibly gasps and swallows deeply. Her eyes become molten and I know she's thinking about what's coming after dinner. She goes to open her mouth in reply but the arrival of our waiter halts that conversation. She's flustered as she places her order, watching her squirm is quite entertaining. This woman continues to intrigue me.

As I watch her with the waiter, I grin to myself at how lucky I am to be here with this woman. I'm glad her sister hurt herself, as bad as that sounds, I mean it in the nicest possible way because it led me back to Avery and this time, I'm not letting her get away.

Dinner passes by quickly and smoothly, and thankfully, my cock has returned to normal. We laughed, lots, and the conversation flowed, as did the wine. There were no awkward silences. Avery and I get along surprisingly well, considering our vast differences. There is no more sexy talk but quite a few sexual innuendos are shared.

Every now and again, I'd feel her foot sliding up my calf; little minx that she is. The evening is easy and relaxed. It's utterly perfect. We finish the bottle of wine and the waiter appears. "Can I entice either of you with dessert?"

Avery's cheeks darken at the mention of dessert. I'm about to ask for the sticky toffee pudding when she beats me to the punch. "I think we're fine on the dessert front," she moves her gaze to me and adds, "you don't have what I would like on the menu." Again, she bites her lip and my cock begins to harden once again.

"Tea or coffee then?" the waiter asks, oblivious to the flirting and innu- endoes floating around.

"Just the check, thanks," I answer.

"Certainly, sir." The waiter leaves and it's just the two of us again. The air is crackling right now. Avery lifts her hand and runs her fingers across her chest, up her neck before biting on her fingertip.

"Avery," I warn. "If you keep doing that, I'm going to throw you over this table and have my dessert right here."

"I'm down with that," she playfully replies.

"Minx," I say, as I pull my phone out and message the car service to pick us up. Once the message is sent, I look over to her. "Let's go." We stand up and make our way to the maître d'. Being a gentleman, I let her go before me. My eyes rake over her backside. "Fuck, that ass," I apprecia- tively whisper. It's obviously louder than I intended because she glances at me over her shoulder, winks, and then turns around, adding an extra sway to her hips. I settle the bill, to which she offers to go halves on. "No, I asked you out, therefore it's on me."

She nods but I can tell she's uncomfortable with that. She's the first woman to ever offer to pay after we've eaten, that gesture adds to her amazingness. She cups my cheek in her palm, her thumb gently caressing my jaw. "Thank you for dinner," she says, before kissing me on the cheek and turning to exit the restaurant.

The driver pulls up just as we exit. Holding the door open for her, we climb in and the driver pulls away from the curb. If I thought the air in the car on the trip here was thick and crackling, sitting in the back of the car now, it's stifling and getting hotter by the minute. I want nothing more than to pull her into my lap and take her now, but Avery deserves more than a backseat quickie and therefore I will be a gentleman and wait. But as soon as we get inside my penthouse, then it's all fair in orgasms and more orgasms.

Not liking the space between us, I reach over and rest my palm on her knee. Gently brushing my thumb back and forth. She squirms in her seat as my hand traces higher and higher. Just as we turn onto my street, I gently brush across her mound, a small illicit moan slips from her lips and it shoots straight to my cock. *Dammit, that backfired on me.* I cannot wait to hear her moan like that when she's naked and riding me. The driver pulls into the underground garage, it started to rain halfway home so I asked him to drop us off here so we don't get wet.

The driver stops by the elevators, I climb out and quickly walk around to open her door. Offering her my hand, she places her palm in mine and I help her out of the car. As we walk toward the elevators, she pulls on my hand. I immediately think she wants to go home. Turning to face her, I'm ready to plead my case as to why she should stay, but she shocks me by gripping my cheeks and pressing her lips to mine. Her tongue pushes inside my mouth and I willingly open. My hands slide into her hair and we devour each other's mouth. I've never much been a fan of kissing before but with Avery, I could quite happily kiss her for the rest of my life. "God, I missed your mouth. It's just as I remembered," I mumble, before I press my lips against hers again, fucking her mouth with my tongue. Reluctantly, I break the connection and rest my forehead on hers. We are both panting. "Shall we take this upstairs?"

She nods her head and grins. She places a quick kiss on my lips and reaches down to cup and squeeze my cock, my achingly hard cock, which is currently painfully pressing against my zipper. It's going to have teeth indents etched into the skin. She pulls away from me and steps over to the elevators and presses the call button. Standing in shock, I shake my head. This woman continually surprises me and if I'm not careful, Avery Evans will be the death of me...but what a fucking way to go.

Joining Avery by the elevator doors, we silently wait. She reaches out to press the call button again and when she does, the doors immediately open. We climb in and I hit the 'P' for the penthouse. As soon as the doors close, the temperature instantly rises. Turning to face her, a force overtakes my body and I step to her. Walking her backward, I cage her against the sidewall with my body and grind my groin into her stomach. She moans and her sounds head straight to my balls.

Gripping her cheeks, much like she did to mine in the garage only moments ago, I slam my lips against hers. She drapes her arms around my shoulders and presses her body to mine. My arms lower and wrap around her waist as we continue to devour each other's mouth. "Ave lass, from this point forward, I want you to save all your kisses for me."

"Only if you save all your kisses for me."

"Deal."

Pressing my lips to hers again, I get back to kissing her. I can't wait to get her inside so I can kiss every inch of her delectable body. I will happily kiss no other person for the rest of my life, as long as I can continue to kiss Avery Evans. This woman has captivated me; heart, body, and soul.

The elevator doors open and with our lips fused together, I blindly step out and walk us toward my door. Without breaking the connection, I manage to open the door and step inside. She kicks it closed with her foot and as soon as the lock clicks, she removes herself from my arms. My face scrunches, as I don't like her not being in my embrace, but she shocks me —again— when she drops to her knees. She beckons me forward and I step to her. She reaches up, pops my fly open, lowers the zipper, and tugs my pants off my hips. Her eyes widen when she realizes I'm commando. Finally, I've shocked her but her surprise quickly morphs into hunger and desire.

Licking her lips, she smiles up at me. Her tongue darts out and she swirls it around the tip of my throbbing cock, precum coating her tongue. She massages my balls before taking me deep into her mouth. Puckering her cheeks, she gently sucks. My eyes drop closed and I lose myself to the sensation of my cock sliding in and out of her wet mouth. "Avery," I moan, as she continues to slide my cock in and out. Looking down at her, my cock hardens further at the sight of my cock sliding in between her delectable lips. She winks up at me and my balls begin to tingle. A sure sign I'm close. Reaching down, I pull her off me. "As much as I'm enjoying that, I do believe that YOU owe ME dessert." Seductively I raise my eyebrows but the little minx shocks me with her reply.

16

AVERY

"Maybe I want my dessert first," I counter, before I lower my mouth back to his cock and resume sucking. Lifting my hand, I begin to stroke his cock in time with my sucking. He grips my head and guides it back and forth on his cock. His body becomes rigid and the first spray of hot salty cum hits the back of my throat. I continue to suck until he's finished.

Pulling back, I stare up at him. "MMMMM, my new fav dessert."

He shakes his head. "You, Avery Evans, are a constant surprise and a little minx. What am I going to do with you?"

Shrugging my shoulders, I stand up, and as I rise, I grab the hem of my dress and lift it over my head. *Where has this bombshell version of me come from?* Dropping my dress to the floor, I'm standing before Flynn in nothing but my bra, panties, and heels. Taking a step back, I stare intently at him. My heart racing like never before. "I've always wanted to fuck wearing these heels." I lift my foot to the side to indicate my shoes. His gaze drops to them and then back up to me. My body heats at the intensity of his gaze. "And I want to be wearing these heels only," I pause for emphasis, "and I think tonight is the perfect time to make that wish come true." Reaching behind my back, I unsnap my bra and remove it. Letting it dangle from my fingertip, I drop it to the floor. It lands on top of my dress. I stare at Flynn, his eyes are full of hunger. Lust. Want. Desire. All of the above, and it's all for me. His breathing is ragged, much like mine. Even though he's just come, his dick is once again rock-hard and standing to attention. He steps out of this pants and stops just in front of me. Bending down, he throws me over his shoulder, I squeal in shock. With a slap to my ass, he turns around and heads toward his bedroom. Lowering me to my feet at the end of the bed, we stare at one another. He slides his fingers into the edge of my barely-there panties and tugs, the material snaps and disintegrates in his hands.

"Hey, I liked those," I complain, as he drops the material to the carpet.

"I'll buy you more," he growls, as he lowers to his knees in front of me. Pulling me to him, he presses his head to my mound and inhales. He places a kiss to my cleft and gently sucks. My head drops back on a moan when he flattens his tongue and slides it up and down my lips. "MMM-MM," I moan. He squeezes my ass, bringing me closer to him. I grip the sides of his head and press him farther into me.

After a soul-crushing orgasm, just from his tongue, he gently pushes me back onto the bed. Lifting to rest on my elbows, I watch as he once again devours my pussy, just like he said he would at dinner tonight. Dropping to the mattress, I lose myself as my second orgasm of the night begins to build. This man is a freakin' god with his tongue. He builds me up and just when I think I'm going to crash over the edge, he pulls back and nuzzles my thigh, teasing me. Taunting me before diving back in again.

I can't take it anymore.

I need to come.

Gripping his head, I pull so he looks up at me. "If you don't let me come, I—" I don't get to finish that sentence because he thrusts two fingers inside of me, twisting them to hit that pleasure spot. My head drops back to the mattress. He continues to thrust his fingers in and out while simultaneously rubbing my clit. I've never felt pleasure like this before. My body is buzzing. Thrumming with desire. He reaches up with his other hand and pinches my nipple. That action sets off a chain reaction of explosions. The most intense orgasm of my life detonates and explodes with such force that my body lifts off the mattress; I tremble from head to toe. My skin burns with desire. Falling back to the bed, I scream and moan as the pleasure continues to ripple through my body.

With one last kiss to my clit, my body comes back to Earth. I'm erratically breathing, like I've run a marathon. "Fuck me," I pant, trying to catch my breath and my body returns to normal.

"With pleasure," Flynn says as he stands up.

He removes his shirt, pulling it over his head in that sexy way guys do by grabbing the neck and lifting. He stands above me at the end of his bed, gloriously naked. His cock standing to attention and weeping. Spreading my legs, I lift my hand and with my finger I beckon him forward. He rests his knee on the end of the mattress and gazes down at me. "You look beautiful lying in my bed, but you know what will look even more stunning?"

"What's that?" I asks.

"Me fucking you on my bed."

"Well," I pause for effect. "What are you waiting for?" I boldly reply, as I slide my hand down my body and flick my clit. My body shudders at the sensation but it stops when Flynn rests his hand on mine.

"Ah uhh," he scoffs, "that's my job." He grabs a condom, sheaths his cock, and lowers himself between my legs. He lines his cock up with my entrance and with his eyes locked on mine, ever so slowly, he slides in. This intrusion is wonderful. Closing my eyes, I moan and enjoy the feeling of him filling me up. "Eyes on me, beautiful," he growls, as he begins to thrust his hips back and forth. Opening my eyes, I stare up at him. His muscles tense and flex as he thrusts in and out.

"Kiss me," I order.

He lowers himself down and kisses me. Wrapping my legs around his waist, I cross my ankles and the heels of my shoes dig into his ass. *This is better than I imagined*, I think to myself as our movements become frenzied. Our kisses hungry. Our teeth bumping as we thrust back and forth. My fingers dig into his shoulder blades, and I scream into our kiss as my orgasm appears out of nowhere and envelops me. My body quivers and as the remnants of orgasm number two, no three. Hell—I don't know—subsides, Flynn follows and he comes for the second time this evening.

Rolling off me, we stare at the ceiling. Both breathing heavily. "That was…"

I interrupt him, "Wow. Unfucking believable. Fantabulous. Out of this world amazing. Wow."

"You already said wow."

"It deserved two."

Rolling to my side, I rest my head in my palm and gaze at the man beside me. "Thank you," I murmur.

Rolling to face me, he rests his head in his palm like I am and smiles at me. "Why are you thanking me?"

"For tonight. I was hesitant to come on this date. I didn't want the amazingness of our first night to be replaced by an awkward dinner but..." I drift off, not sure if I want to voice this out loud.

"But what?" he questions.

"But I had nothing to worry about. From the moment I stepped out of the elevator, I was at ease. Being around you is easy. It's fun. You make me do things that I never do. You bring me to life in a different way. Hell, our first night together ticked off several of the 'never done before' boxes. I feel alive for the first time ever and I have you to thank for that."

"You are welcome and I agree. When I'm with you, everything seems easy. The world seems brighter. I'm so lucky to have met you, Avery Evans."

"I agree, Flynn Kelly. Thank you for bringing me to life."

"Thank you for letting me bring you to life."

We stare at one another, the air around us begins to crackle with desire once again. Leaning forward, I place my lips against his and before I know it, I'm riding him cowgirl style and another orgasm is crashing over me. After two or three more orgasms, hell I lost count after two, I blissfully fall asleep, naked and wrapped in Flynn's arms.

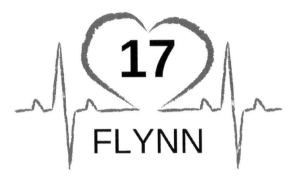

FLYNN

Opening my eyes, I look down and see her gorgeous hazel eyes locked on mine. She winks at me and proceeds to give me the best morning blow job of my life. Sooner than I would like to admit, I come with a guttural groan, spilling my seed down her throat. My cock pops out of her mouth; she wipes the corner of her lips, and seductively slips her finger into her mouth. "Morning," she whispers, as she slides in next to me. Draping her arm across my abs and tangling her legs with mine.

"Morning," I reply, brushing a tendril of hair behind her ear. "Sleep well?"

"Like the dead. You?"

"Best night sleep of my life AND the best way to wake up. On our next sleepover, I would like to book a wake-up call like that."

"Duly noted." She leans up and presses her lips to mine. The moment is broken when a loud rumble comes from Avery.

"Hungry?" I ask, just as my stomach makes its own loud grumble.

"Seems we are both hungry…for food."

"Amongst other things," I say with a wink.

Rolling her to her back, I press her into the mattress and I slam my mouth over hers. Kissing the life out of her before fucking her. After a few more orgasms, we finally crawl out of bed and make it to the shower. There we add another few orgasms to the tally before finally washing each other. Stepping out we dry off, and I hand Avery a shirt of mine. She slips it over her head and I gaze at her. "I like you wearing my shirt."

"I like wearing your shirt."

Pulling on a pair of sweats, I step to her and wrap my arms around her waist. "I especially like the no panties option." Sliding my hand under the hem of the shirt, I grip her taut ass in my palm and squeeze.

"Well, if someone hadn't shredded mine, I'd have underwear to wear."

Shrugging at her, I grab her hand and start walking out of my bedroom. "I think I need to feed you now, you're getting hangry."

Avery rolls her eyes at me and follows me into the kitchen. She takes a seat at the island counter and I whip up breakfast for us. It's a simple meal consisting of coffee and fruit. "Sorry, it's not much. I didn't really plan for the morning after."

"It's fine, Flynn. I'm not a breakfast person anyway, coffee would have been fine."

Throughout breakfast we chat and laugh.

"You guys really swapped and no one knew?"

She nods her head. "Yeah, when we were little we got away with it easily but when we got older, our differences started to show. I remember one time in high school, I pretended to be Bay and took an exam, can't remember how we were caught, but Mom and Dad were so angry at us. We kinda stopped after that."

"I bet you were a cute kid."

"Says the cute one."

"I'm not cute," I retort.

"Yeah, you are and I bet you were a heartbreaker too. Leaving broken hearts behind in Ireland and at med school."

"I can neither confirm nor deny that accusation."

"I call bullshit."

Even though Ave and I are so different, we do have many similar interests: snowshoeing, wine, socializing, we each love dumb mind-numbing games on our phones. I realize, when I'm with her, it's comfortable. It feels like we've known each other for years and not just a few weeks.

"We should totally do that one weekend in the winter." Her words warm my heart; they don't freak me out. The fact she's thinking ahead and thinking about us still being together in a few months' time makes me smile, this isn't just some fling to her and that makes me ecstatically happy, because this isn't just some fling for me either. I want more with this amazing woman. I think I could fall for her…and I hope she could fall for me too.

"Why are you grinning like the Cheshire cat?"

"You just said we should go snowshoeing together."

"And?"

"Winter is months away. You're planning in the future for us."

"And?"

"And it surprised me."

"How so?" she questions, as she grabs our breakfast dishes and places them in the dishwasher.

"Well, after sneaking out and then your hesitance to go out with me, I didn't think you were interested."

She steps around the island and in between my thighs. She wraps her arms around my neck. "Flynn, you took me by surprise that first night, and yes, it really freaked me out, but when I saw you again, something changed within me. And last night was the best night of my life. Great dinner. Amazing company. Pretty good sex—"

"Only pretty good? I think the sex was more along the lines of fucking amazing. Best ever."

"Okay, your description of the sex is better than mine and one-hundred-percent accurate. But what I'm trying to articulate is that our connection isn't just physical. It's emotional too. I haven't felt inferior or awkward once with you. You bring me to life, Flynn, I've never felt like this before."

"Me neither, Ave." Her smiles widens. "Why are *you* now grinning like the Cheshire cat?"

"You called me Ave."

"So?"

"I normally hate being called Ave, but when you do, I kinda love it."

"Well, then, Ave lass, I want to know when we can do it again."

"Do what again?"

"Last night?"

"The date or sex?"

"Both," I nonchalantly say.

"Dinner next weekend." She pauses and bites her lip, then she lifts my shirt off her body and drops it to the tiles. "As for the sex, I say now."

She walks backward and when she hits the sofa, she lies down and beckons me forward with her finger. Standing up, I pull down my sweats and walk over to her. Stopping at the end of the sofa, I stare down at her. "Shit," I mumble.

"What?"

"The condoms are in the bedroom."

"I'm still on the pill and you are still the only person I've never used protection with before."

"Are you sure?"

She nods her head. "Yes, now fuck me, Flynn."

And fuck her I do.

We spend the rest of the morning fucking like rabbits, exploring every inch of each other's body. They say opposites attract and the attraction between Avery and me, it's explosive. I just hope we can survive the fallout if it comes to that.

AVERY

FLYNN DROPS ME HOME MID-AFTERNOON. I HAVE TO SAY, LAST NIGHT WAS THE best date of my life. Flynn is so different from what I thought and he brings me to life in a way like never before. The car ride home was quiet but not awkward. He pulls up in front of my building, leans across the center console, and kisses me. The kiss is searing hot and leaves me wanting more. I'm tempted to drag him upstairs and ravage him, but my nether regions ache and need a rest.

Standing on the curb, I watch him pull away. He's off to meet his friend, Preston, for an impromptu game of basketball, with a promise to call me later this evening. When his car is out of sight, I turn around and head up to the apartment. Unlocking the front door, I step inside and instantly I'm met with an irate Baylor. "Where the hell have you been?" she bellows at me before I've even closed the door.

"I told you, I had a date."

"You left yesterday evening. It's the afternoon on the following day. I needed you," she whines.

"I'm sorry, Bay. I thought you'd be okay for one night. I'm here now, what do you need?"

"It's fine now," she snaps. "I called a friend. She came running to help when she heard I'd been in the hospital."

"Seriously, Bay. You have a sprained ankle. You were in the ER for all of five hours. You are not dying and you can totally look after yourself. I think I can have one night out for a date."

"What if I'd fallen? What if I'd have died? You wouldn't have known for hours."

Dramatic much? I think to myself as I walk inside. "Quit with the drama, Bay. You're fine. You survived the night without me."

She rolls her eyes in typical overdramatic Bay style. She was always the drama queen when we were growing up. As much as we look alike, we are polar opposites personality-wise. "Who did you go out with?"

"Flynn."

"The hot doctor?" Nodding my head, I smile as memories of last night, and this morning, come flooding back to me but her next sentence cuts me to the bone. "Why would he go out with you?" she snarls, placing emphasis on the word you.

"Why not?" I defensively ask.

"It's you. Boring Ms. Evans, grade school teacher."

"Tell me how you really feel," I joke, but in what's become Bay's new way of life, she lets loose but this time, there's vengeance and hurt behind her words.

"Okay, I will. You get everything handed to you on a friggin' silver platter. I try my hardest and I still struggle. You, are the sweet and innocent one. You always swoop in and make everything look easy and perfect. You're a new-age Mary-fucking-Poppins, and you make me sick. One of these days, you will fall off your pedestal and I will be the first person in line to laugh and laugh. Now if you don't mind, I need to rest my ankle that you don't seem to give a rat's ass about."

My mouth drops open at her response. She stands up and storms toward me, walking just fine on her ankle. She stops in front of me, breathing heavily. She sweetly smiles at me. "Don't get too comfy with your doctor."

"Why not?"

"There's no way you'll keep a stud muffin like him." She pokes me in the chest. "Dud and stud don't go together. This isn't one of those romance drivels you read. Avie, this is real life and no one gets a happily ever after." Her eyes glisten as she says this last part. "I'm going to my room to rest." She turns and walks away from me. Before she heads down the hall, she adds, "Clean up this place once you've pull your head out of your loved-up, skinny ass and remember what I said, it's not gonna last."

To say I'm shocked at what she just said to me is an understatement. I'm left standing in the living room, stunned and hurt by what just went down between the two of us. Baylor and I are different people, each to our own, but we've always been kind to one another. Just now, she was brutal and harsh; we've never been nasty like this before. She and I may be twins but apart from sharing a womb and kinda sorta looking like each other, right now, we share no other traits. She's become selfish and pushes the boundaries. Lately she expects everything to be done for her; which usually happens because she manipulates people, me included, to get her way or what she wants. She and I have become polar opposites on every level and even though she just tore me a new one, I still love her. Something is up with her at the moment but she won't let me in. She's being harsh and pushing me away to protect herself but I refuse to give up on her. She's my twinsie and I want the best for my sister. There is one thing though, I'm going to prove her wrong when it comes to Flynn. He and I will work out…I hope.

I've just climbed into bed and I'm shattered, today was tiring; emotionally and physically. My morning started out amazing, more than amazing and after ten minutes with Bay, it all went to shit. The only good thing to come from the angst filled afternoon; our apartment is now spotless. At least she can't gripe about that anymore.

From the moment I stepped through the door, nothing I did was right and she berated me at every chance. I would have preferred if she'd given me the cold shoulder, like she used to when we were little and she was in a mood. Actually, I wish she was like she was when we were little, I want my BayBay back.

My phone vibrates with a message. Picking it up, I smile when I see it's from Flynn.

FLYNN: *Nite, gorgeous. Just got to the hospital for my shift but wanted*

*to touch base before I got started. Miss you and can't wait to see
you soon*

A smile breaks free as I read his words. With one message he made all
the shit disappear.

AVERY: *That was just what I need. Hope you have a great shift Xo*
FLYNN: *Why so glum?*

My fingers hover over the keyboard, I don't know if I want to bother
him with my Bay issue, so I err on the side of caution with my reply.

AVERY: *Not glum. Just tired and missing you. Some fiend last night
kept me up for hours and hours with multiple orgasms and a marathon
sex session.*
FLYNN: *Sounds like a wonderful nite to me.*
FLYNN: *We should do it again.*
FLYNN: *Soon.*
AVERY: *That can be arranged. **wink***
FLYNN: *When and where? I'll be there. **wink wink***
AVERY: *Ummm....Let me cook you dinner Tuesday night.*
FLYNN: *What's for dessert? **wink wink wink***
AVERY: *Me **wink wink wink wink***
FLYNN: *We need to stop this. I'm sporting a major woodie right now
and I have a 12-hour ER shift ahead of me. It's not off to a good start.*
AVERY: *It will be hard **pun intended** but you'll be fine. Nite Flynn*
FLYNN: *You are going to be the death of me, Avery Evans. Nite
Ave lass*

With a smile on my face, I happily drift off to sleep and dream sexy
things about Flynn and me. Waking early, I decide to head to Western
General to surprise Flynn with breakfast. On my way to the hospital, I stop
at *Starbucks* and grab two coffees and some pastries. Parking my car, I
climb out and balance the pastries, coffees, and my handbag and head
toward the ER. Someone yells out what I think was Baylor, looking around
I can't see anyone so I keep walking, and then I hear that same voice yell,
"Fine, be a bitch then." Looking around I still can't see anyone so I turn
back around and keep walking.

Stepping inside, I look around, the waiting room is empty. As I'm
looking around, the hairs on my neck stand on end and I feel Flynn before

I see him. Looking up, he stops midstep when he sees me. His face is void of emotion and I begin to think I made a mistake in coming here, but then the biggest smile graces his gorgeous tired face. "Ave lass, what are you doing here?"

Hearing him call me Ave lass does things to me I've never felt before. I don't know whether it's his accent or just him, but whatever it is, my body comes alive being in his presence. As we walk toward each other, I find myself grinning and giddy with excitement. "Morning, Doctor," I purr, yes, I actually purr. "I thought you'd like coffee and pastries after a long HARD shift." Placing emphasis on the word hard, I smirk at him.

"I'm addicted to you, as much as you are addicted to the liquid in that cup you are holding."

"So not much then?" I playfully tease.

He shakes his head as he wraps one arm around my waist, pulling me into him. He places a kiss on my temple and my panties immediately dampen when his lips connect with my skin. A moan breaks free and when Flynn stares at me, he knows exactly what I'm feeling. "You, my little minx, are a devil." He lowers his voice and whispers, "I cannot wait to get you naked and fuck the sass out of you."

Winking, I quietly murmur, "You can try as much as you like—" The moment is interrupted when the doors to the ER slam open and a man frantically rushes in, a young boy in his arms.

"Help, I need help!" he screams.

Flynn immediately races over to the man and goes into doctor mode. I'm frozen on the spot. The once quiet ER is now swarming with the family of the child. A nurse arrives with a gurney and then Flynn and the nurse take the child from the man and place his tiny little body onto the bed and whisk him away, with his parents close on their heels.

I'm a quivering mess watching the scene before me play out. How Flynn does this on a daily basis is beyond me. Taking a seat in the ER, I decide to wait for him, since I don't have anything better to do on this Sunday morning.

FLYNN

AFTER HANDING THE LITTLE BOY AND HIS CARE OVER TO PRESTON, I LET OUT A sigh. It's always tough dealing with kids, but today is a good day, as the kid will make a full recovery after a few days in hospital. Stepping back into the ER, a grin appears on my face when I look over and see Avery is still here. She's sitting in the corner and chatting with an elderly gentleman. From my spot I watch them, she looks happy and carefree. Just seeing her so joyous warms me from the inside. The gentleman says something and it causes her to laugh, a deep belly laugh. Her giggle filters through the waiting room like music.

She looks up and when her eyes lock with mine, she smiles at me and the grin that was already on my face increases. Walking over to them, I bend down and place a kiss on her head. "Avery, you're still here." My voice is laced with surprise, because I am. I didn't expect her to wait around for me.

She nods. "Yep, I had no other plans this morning so thought I'd hang around and wait. While waiting, I met Mr. Marshall here, and he helped me pass the time." Looking to the man, I nod.

"Marvin Marshall," he says offering me his hand.

"Flynn Kelly," I reply as I shake his hand, but before we can chat more, a nurse comes barrelling over to the three of us. "Marvin Marshall," she scolds, "we have been looking everywhere for you." She stops next to me and is glaring at Marvin.

"You said I couldn't go outside the hospital. Last time I checked, the ER waiting room was *inside* the hospital." He air quotes inside. Avery and I both laugh, until we see the look on the nurse's face.

"Dr. Kelly," she sternly says in greeting.

"Hi, Helen," I reply, "How are you?"

"Better now I found this one." She hooks her finger toward Marvin. "I swear the older they get, the worse they become."

"I heard that," Marvin says.

"You were meant to," Helen spits back at him.

Marvin leans over to Avery and not so quietly quips, "I think I'm in trouble but to spend the morning with a gorgeous girl like you, it's totally worth it." He winks at her before he turns his attention to me. "Look after this one," nodding his head toward Avery, he states, "she's a keeper."

"I think you're right, Marvin," I reply, my gaze on Avery's as I say this. Her cheeks tinge that lovely shade of pink I love seeing on her.

"We need to get you back to your room, Marvin," Helen says.

Avery stands up first and offers her hand to Marvin. With a bit of a struggle, he stands up and steps toward Helen. Avery reaches out to stop him. She squeezes his arm and when he turns to face her, she leans down and places a goodbye kiss on his cheek. His face lights up like a Christmas tree and I think this morning is the highlight of his year. "Goodbye, Marvin."

"Bye, Avery." Marvin and Helen walk away. Helen walking slowly to aid a shuffling Marvin. Marvin mumbles something that garners him an evil-eyed stare from Helen. Both Avery and I laugh as we watch them exit the ER.

Stepping to Avery, I brush a tendril of hair behind her ear. "You really are something, Avery Evans."

"A good something, I hope," she shyly replies.

"A very good something." Leaning down, I place my lips against hers for a quick kiss. It turns heated and not really appropriate for the ER, but I don't care. If I want to kiss Avery, I'll kiss Avery no matter the location.

Pulling back, I rest my forehead on hers. "Give me ten to change, then I can meet you at my place?"

She nods her head. "I like that plan."

Kissing the tip of her nose, I turn and go change. Ten minutes later, I've changed and I'm racing to my car. Traffic is light this morning, surprisingly, and I make it home in good time. When I arrive, I park in my spot and rather than wait for the elevator, I take the stairs, two at a time, and make my way up to the lobby to meet Avery.

Stepping out, I smile when I see Avery waiting for me. She's leaning against the front desk, chatting with Max.

"Good morning, Dr. Kelly," Max says when he sees me.

"Morning, Max." Turning my attention to Avery, I ask, "You ready?"

"Yep." She turns to Max and says, "Have a great day, Max."

"You too, Ms. Evans."

"Please, call me Avery." He nods at her and she picks up a tray of coffees and we walk toward the elevators. Lacing my fingers with hers, we fall into step with one another as we head toward the elevators. The doors open and a delivery guy exits, we step in and I press the button for the penthouse.

"Hope you don't mind, I stopped and got coffee for me and a tea for you on the way here."

"Not at all, I'm just happy to have you here, the hot drinks are just a bonus."

"I won't stay long as I know you need to sleep."

"I'd love to sleep with you." She eyes me. "Not like that, you fiend, in the literal close your eyes sleep sense BUT if that was to happen, I wouldn't complain." I pause and then add, "I love waking up with you in my arms."

"Well, since I got a full night's sleep. How about I lie with you while you drift off and then I'll come back later this afternoon?"

"OR you can just spend the day at my place so you are here when I wake up?"

"Really?" she asks and I nod in reply, "Okay, sure, why not. Just for you, I'll spend the day lazing around in a gorgeous penthouse."

"Perfect." Leaning down, I press a kiss to her temple and breath her in.

We are quiet for the rest of the trip. Entering the penthouse, Avery heads to the living room and sits on the sofa. Taking a seat next to her, she hands me my tea. We drink them in silence. Once finished, Avery tidies up and I grab a quick shower since I didn't have one before leaving the hospital. When I step out of the en suite I smile when I see Avery is in my bed.

She's slipped into one of my shirts, and can I say, I love seeing her in my clothes. She's reading on her iPad. She looks up and the vision before me is indescribable.

Grinning down at her, I walk around the bed in nothing but my towel, when I reach my side, I drop the towel to the floor and stand there. Her gaze drops from my face and is now locked on my cock. I stand beside the bed and stare at her. She looks up at me, her cheeks once again pink, and with a wink, I pull back the covers and climb in next to her.

Draping my arm across her stomach, I snuggle into her side as she sits in bed and continues to read. She begins massaging my scalp and soon slumber overtakes me. I fall into a deep blissful sleep, snuggled into Avery.

It's mid-afternoon when I wake again. Reaching out, my hand meets a cold sheet, Avery isn't in bed and a wave of sadness washes over me. I really thought she'd stay and then I hear noise coming from the living room. Slipping on a pair of sweats, I follow the sound and stop midstep. From my spot in the hallway, I watch Avery. She's in her own little world, singing along to "Wolves" by Selena Gomez playing from her iPod, which she's connected to my speaker system.

Leaning against the wall, I cross my arms and watch as she swings her hips and wipes down the kitchen counter, oblivious to me watching her. The song changes to "Havana" by Camila Cabello and she seductively sways her hips from side to side. My cock twitches at the sight of her ass swishing from side to side. She's still wearing my shirt and I find myself grinning at the sight before me. Taking a deep breath, my smile increases when the most amazing, sweetest scent ever to come from my kitchen envelops me. That's when I notice a tray of decadent-looking iced cupcakes sitting on the counter, waiting for me eat.

She finally notices me and jumps in fright. She squeals, and brings her hand to her chest.

"Sorry, didn't mean to scare you."

"It's okay, I hope I didn't wake you, when I bake I listen to music and sing. I guess I got a little carried away." She turns to the sink and rinses the cloth.

Walking over to her, I shake my head, "No, you didn't wake me."

When I reach her, I wrap my arms around her from behind and place a kiss on her shoulder. "Morning."

"Afternoon," she says, turning her head, allowing me to place a kiss on her lips.

"You taste like frosting," I huskily murmur.

She licks her lips. "Had to taste test and make sure it had the right amount of vanilla."

"Is that so?" I ask, as she spins in my arms and drapes hers over my shoulders.

"Yep," she says. Lifting her up, I carry her and place her onto the island countertop. She spreads her legs and I step between them as we gaze into each other's eyes. Without breaking eye contact, I reach behind her and grab a cupcake. Glancing at the decadent-looking masterpiece in my hands, I inspect it as if I'm a judge on *Cake Wars*. "It looks pretty great to me, but I better taste one just to be sure."

She takes the cupcake from me and peels back the muffin paper and offers it to me. Opening my mouth, I take a bite and instantly moan. My mouth is assaulted with the delicious combination of vanilla icing and light fluffy chocolate sponge. Offering the cake to her, she leans forward and takes a bite.

"MMMMM," she moans, lifting her gaze to mine.

My eyes drop to her lips, her tongue darts out, and she gently bites her lip. *Dick, instantly hard.* Noticing a smidge of frosting at the corner of her mouth, I lean forward and lick before pressing my lips to hers for a kiss. Sliding my tongue into her mouth, I wrap my arms around her waist, pulling her into me and deepening the kiss. Our tongues slide around each other's mouth, and my hands wander up and down her back before sliding around the front to cup her boobs in my hand. Gently I squeeze her plump mounds that fit perfectly into the palm of my hand. Gently I push her back onto the counter, sliding my hand precariously slowly down her chest. Leaning over her, I lower my head and suck one of her nipples through my shirt. She moans beneath me. Her back arches. Kissing my way down her stomach, I lift her—my—shirt and circle my tongue around her belly button.

"Please," she whimpers, as she runs her fingers through my hair. Her nails scratching at my scalp.

Placing featherlight kisses along her stomach, I kiss down toward her panties. Today she's wearing plain pink cotton and I see a wet patch between her thighs. Grazing my nose up and down her material-covered slit, she moans and thrusts herself upward. Pushing on her stomach to hold her down, I suck and kiss her through the material covering her.

"Please," she whines, tugging on my hair.

Lifting my gaze, and standing up, I stare down at her. She looks utterly divine laid out on my island counter. Reaching down, I grab the sides of her panties and tug them down her legs. Dropping them to the tiled floor, I look back at my girl. She spreads her legs wide open, resting her heels on the edge of the countertop. Giving me an uninterrupted view of her pussy, her lips shining with her arousal and her clit peeking out.

"Please, Flynn," she begs and this time I don't deny her. I lower my head between her thighs and I devour her with my tongue and fingers like a starved man. If I died right now, I would die a happy man.

AVERY

FINALLY, HE GIVES ME WHAT I NEED. HIS HEAD BETWEEN MY THIGHS. HIS tongue sliding up and down my folds. His thumb pressing on my clit. A guttural moan slips from my lips when at long last, he slips a finger inside me. "Yes. Yes. Yes," I mewl. He slides two or three, I'm not sure how many, more into me. My body hums with arousal, I never want this feeling to subside. *If I died right now, I would die a happy woman,* I think to myself as I lift my hands to my breasts and massage them through Flynn's shirt. Pinching my nipples between my thumb and forefinger, I play with my breasts while Flynn plays with my pussy. Finally, my orgasm erupts and I scream. My back arches. My body clenches tight. My thighs press together, trapping Flynn between my legs. I soak Flynn's face with my juices as pleasure rockets through my body.

Loosening their vise-like grip on Flynn's head, he lifts from between my thighs, his chin and lips shiny with my arousal. He licks his lips. "Mmmm."

Sitting up, I lift his shirt over my head and scoot toward the edge of the counter. Sliding my hands into his sweats, I push them down and his cock springs free. He steps out of his pants and I reach forward and grip his erection in my hands. Giving it a few strokes before I guide it between my thighs. Lining it up at my entrance, I look up at him and whisper, "Fuck me, Flynn."

We both thrust forward and I impale myself on him. A moan slips free as our hips rock back and forth. Sliding his hand under my ass, he lifts me up and I wrap my legs around his waist. He spins around and presses my back into the wall as he continues to thrust himself in and out. His lips devour mine. He kisses his way down my neck until he's at my breasts, taking a nipple into his mouth, he sucks before gently biting the tip.

"Flynn!" I shout. "I'm close," I mumble.

Lifting his head from my breast, he stares into my eyes and continues to piston himself in and out of me. "Let go, lass."

With his words, I let go and tumble over the orgasmic edge. My walls clench around his cock. My fingers dig into his shoulders and I ride out my second release of the afternoon. My body is still buzzing when I feel him tense against me and with a gravelly grunt, he too comes. Resting my forehead against his, he empties himself inside me. Pulling away as he finishes, he stares at me, panting deeply.

He rests his forehead against mine again as we each settle our breathing. My eyes drift closed and I run my fingers absentmindedly through his hair. With my eyes still closed, I feel my body moving. I feel like I'm flying. Opening my eyes, I see Flynn is walking us into his en suite. He places me on the vanity and I watch as he spins around and leans into the shower, turning the water on. He closes the glass door and the cubicle begins to fill with steam.

Spinning back, he steps toward me and places a kiss on the tip of my nose. He reaches down and lifts me into his arms, hugging me to him. Instinctively, my legs wrap around his hips and I hold onto him like a monkey.

"You do know, I have these things called legs and I can walk?"

"Ohh I know you have killer, sexy as fuck legs, Avery, I just like having you in my arms."

SWOON, ovaries exploding, this man seriously is going to be the death of me.

"I like being in your arms too, and you also have pretty amazing legs and a sexy ass." Lifting my head from its resting place on his chest, I kiss and nibble his jaw. His scruff tickling my lips. Pressing my lips to his, I kiss him, my tongue licking along the seam before sliding into his mouth. He stops walking toward the shower and deepens our kiss.

Pulling free, we stare at one another. Our lips plump and bruised from our kiss. With a wink, he walks toward the shower and opens the door. Stepping in, the hot water hits my skin and I moan. The pressure and heat feels amazing. Dropping my head back, I close my eyes and let the water cascade down my face and body.

Flynn lowers me to my feet and spins me around. Running his hand up my side, he begins to massage my shoulders. A pleasurable moan erupts in the back of my throat. Dropping my head forward, I completely relax. The combination of the warm water and his fingers digging into my muscles is pure bliss. A contented relaxed sigh breaks free, I'm seriously in heaven right now.

"Avery, if you keep moaning like that, I will not be held accountable for what I do to you in here."

"Mmmhmpf," I reply.

Leaning forward, I rest my forehead against the tiled wall and enjoy the massage he's currently giving me. Flynn cocoons me in, the warmth from his body adds to my chilled-out state. His cock is pressing against my ass. Circling my hip, his cock hardens between us. Reaching behind me, I grip his girth in my palm and begin to stroke. He squeezes and massages my shoulders and I squeeze and massage his cock. Turning to face him, I wink before dropping to my knees. Licking my lips, I open wide and take his cock deep into my mouth. Sliding it out, I suck the tip, swirling my tongue around before sucking back down again. Repeating this over and over. Flynn moans from above and slides his hands into my hair. He guides my head up and down his shaft. Cupping his balls, I gently massage them. Flynn hisses and then I feel them tighten in my hand. With a guttural growl, he comes. I suck every last drop of salty cum down my throat. Sitting back on my heels, I gaze up at him, and I realize in this moment, I am falling for Flynn Kelly and I could quite easily fall in love with him. I get the urge to tell him, I want to tell him.

Standing up, I take his hands in mine and just as I'm about to tell him, his beeper beeps, breaking the spell on the moment.

"That'll be the hospital, I need to get that." Nodding my head, he steps out. Looking back he adds, "Be right back, don't go anywhere."

"There's nowhere else I want to be," I whisper as I watch him.

Taking the opportunity, I pump some bodywash onto my hands and begin to wash myself. I feel him before I see him, spinning around he looks sad. "What's wrong?"

"I need to go into work early. I know we were going to have dinner—"

"Don't apologize, we can do dinner another time."

"You really are amazing, Avery Evans."

"I know," I confidently reply. "I'm finished, you hop in and I'll make you a coffee to go."

"Thank you," he says, his voice saddened by having to leave. Stepping out, he grabs a fluffy white towel and opens it for me. He wraps it around my body, enveloping me in. He holds me closely to him. Resting my head on his chest, the thrum of his heartbeat relaxes me. Squeezing my arms, I look up at him. He really is sexy; looks, personality, he's the perfect complete package. He places a kiss on my nose and hops back into the shower.

Stepping into his room, I redress in my clothes from earlier and head to the kitchen. I go about making his coffee and I clean up our cupcake mess. I've just finished wiping down the counter when Flynn walks out. Our gaze locks across the room. Neither one of us says anything. I'm just about to say those three words when my phone rings, glancing down I see it's Bay. Sending the call to voicemail, I ignore her. I'll call her back after I say goodbye to Flynn. I look up and see he's slipping his coat on. I realize the moment to tell him has now passed. It's probably a good thing, it's too soon to be feeling this. We've only known each other for a short time but when I'm with him, I feel different.

Picking up his coffee, I walk toward him and pass it to him. Slipping on my coat, we exit his apartment and hop into the elevator. He gets off at the lobby and walks me out to my car. After a NSFP—not suitable for public—kiss, I climb into my car and leave Flynn standing on the sidewalk. He watches as I drive off and with a smile on my face, I head home.

21
FLYNN

WALKING AWAY FROM AVERY JUST NOW IS THE HARDEST THING I HAVE EVER done. In a few short weeks, this woman has taken up residence in my heart and for the first time ever, I think I'm falling in love. To reiterate that point, "Can't Help Falling in Love" by Elvis begins to play. If that's not a sign—not that I believe in that shit—then I don't know what is.

Walking into the hospital, a melancholic feeling washes over me, but it quickly passes when a multi-vehicle accident occurs. The ER is swarming with people and I don't have time to think. It's the wee hours of the morning when Helen comes wandering into the ER, a scowl on her face. "Hi, Helen," one of the triage nurses says.

"Hey."

"To what do we owe the pleasure, Helen?" I ask.

"Marvin in missing again."

A laugh breaks free but I quickly stop when I see the murderous look on her face. "Want some help looking for our resident Houdini?"

"Please," she says, "This shit is getting old, he's worse than the kids in the children's ward."

"Well, they do say that's life's cycle. Baby. Child. Adult. Child. Death."

"That's a pretty morbid way to think of life," she replies.

"It's true though, when you look at it."

Stepping into the ER waiting room, I look around and sure enough, Marvin is in the corner chatting/flirting with a group of young girls. "Found him," I say, nudging Helen in the arm. She shakes her head and storms over to him.

"Marvin Marshall," she scolds, and from my spot next to her even I flinch, not Marvin though. He enrages the beast that is Nurse Helen and turns to his new friends. "Ohh oh, I'm in trouble."

The girls all giggle. He says goodbye to his friends and follows a still fuming Helen back toward his ward and room. "Dr. Kelly," Helen says as they walk past.

Marvin mimics Helen, "Dr. Kelly," garnering another evil glance from Helen.

Shaking my head, I walk back into the ER and decide to tackle the paperwork I have been putting off. With my arms laden with charts, I head toward the doctors' lounge. Dropping off the paperwork, I head across to the coffee shop and grab myself a coffee—the coffee in the cafeteria here tastes like shit. With my coffee in hand, I head back and get into the paperwork.

Before I know it, the sun is shining and it's morning. My shift will be over in a few minutes and I want to see Avery. I decide that today, I will be the one to surprise her. Grabbing a quick shower, I change into denim jeans and a green Henley. Saying hi/bye to the doctors in the lounge, I race to my car and drive over to Avery's.

Traffic is a shitshow this morning and it takes me forever to get to her place. I'm agitated and antsy when I pull up out the front. Taking a few calming breaths, I cool down and climb out of my car. Looking at my watch, I hope she's awake, I don't want to wake her, but if she does happen to be sleeping, I'll just climb into bed with her. Either way it's a win/win.

Stopping at her door, I raise my hand and knock. The door opens and I'm pleasantly surprised when I see what she's wearing, then movement over her shoulder catches my eye and I realize it's Baylor at the door. She flirts but I ignore her advances, my eyes are locked on Avery's. She is unbelievably sexy this morning. Like me she is wearing denim jeans and hers hug her curves in that sexy as fuck way. She's wearing a black tank that accentuates her tiny hips and shows off the perfect amount of cleavage. "I'm here to pick up your gorgeous sister."

When I say this, Avery's face lights up. We say our goodbyes to Baylor and I escort my girlfriend to my car. On the way over, I planned a spur of the moment date. Sleep can wait, today is all about Avery Evans.

22

AVERY

HIS EYES RAKE OVER HER BODY AND MY BLOOD BOILS. I SHAKE MY HEAD AND roll my eyes and then his eyes find mine and his grin morphs into a megawatt smile that lights up his face; and mine. Ignoring Bay and her shameless flirting, he says, "I'm here to pick up your gorgeous sister."

"Awww, are you admitting I'm gorgeous?" He looks at Bay and scrunches his eyes in confusion. "You just said my sister is gorgeous. I'm her twin, therefore you think I'm gorgeous too, since we are two in the same."

She thrusts her tits toward him but his eyes are locked on me. Ignoring her he says, "You may be her twin, but I only have eyes for Avery." He steps around Bay and stalks over to me. "I only want her." Wrapping his arms around my waist, he pulls me into him, and kisses my cheek hello.

"What are you doing here?" I ask, as I stare up at him.

"We have a breakfast date," he matter-of-factly says, before he gently places his lips against mine for a sexy hello kiss that leaves me breathless. He pulls away and brushes a tendril of hair behind my ear. "Morning, beautiful."

"Morning," I manage to squeak out 'cause I'm kinda stunned right now. "I didn't realize we were doing breakfast this morning."

"Surprise!" he says, tapping the tip of my nose. "Ready to go?"

Nodding my head, I see from the corner of my eye Bay is still standing in the doorway. She's shooting daggers my way, she's pissed at being passed over by Flynn; again. "Sure. Let me grab my purse and we can go."

Grabbing my things, I link my fingers with his and we walk toward the door and Bay, who is still standing there. "Have a good day," I say to Bay as we pass. We step through the door into the hallway. Bay slams the door behind us, the frame rattling from the force, and through the wood I hear her mumbling profanities, presumably toward me. That seems to be the only way she talks to me at the moment. I can't do anything right when it comes to her right now. Something is definitely up with my twin, and normally we'd talk to one another about our worries and bounce ideas around to fix the problem. But for the last few weeks, even longer, she's been pulling away and changing before my eyes.

Flynn squeezes my hand and I can't help but smirk, for once a guy wants me and not her. I know it's petty to feel like this but I'm happy to win for once; score one for me. I play over the scene when he arrived in my head and my grin widens. Flynn ignored her advances and when he saw me, I became his sole focus. It was all about me and it felt pretty good to be the center of attention. I'm so happy right now, it's not often I get one up on her, and Flynn just helped me achieve that.

Looking over at him, I squeeze his hand back. "Thank you for that."

"Thanks for what?" he questions, his forehead scrunched in confusion.

"For ignoring her skanky, ho slutty, see-through nightie." I pause, then add, "For being you."

"Ave lass, I didn't even see what she was wearing. Well, I did, don't get me wrong." I eyeball him but he is correct, he is a man after all, and they don't always think with the right head. "I was surprised you'd wear something like that, but then you moved and my gaze gravitated over to you and from that moment, you were all I saw. Ave, when you are around, it's you and only you I see. No one else enters my mind."

My mouth drops open at his frank confession. "I feel exactly the same way when I'm around you. More often than not, I feel you before I see you." He nods in agreement. "Now, let's go eat. I'm starving."

"Well, I need to get you fuelled up because after breakfast, you are going to need lots of energy for what I have in mind."

At his words, my clit begins to throb between my thighs and suddenly I'm not hungry for food. Flynn whisks me to Maggie's, a small mom-and-pop diner just around the corner from my place. We each order pancakes, bacon, and coffee. After an amazing breakfast, we leave and I think we'll be heading back to Flynn's for some naked between the sheets fun, but he surprises me; again. Rather than heading back to his place, he heads to the The Morton Arboretum and drags me toward the Maze Garden. It's an amazing one-acre, living hedge maze, and the maze changes with each season. "Ohh my God, Flynn, this place is amazing, I haven't been here in forever The last time I was here was with Cress for Lexi's fourth birthday."

"I've never been. I've been past here many times and this morning I thought, today is the day. I'm happy to pop my maze cherry with you."

"And I'm happy to pop your cherry." Taking his hand in mine, we head toward the entrance. Flynn and I spend hours chasing each other through the maze. We get lost many times but we have an absolute blast together. We manage to find all seven of the plant rooms, something I've never done before. I cannot remember the last time I laughed this much. We finally make our way out of the maze; I was starting to think we'd be trapped in there forever. I'm sweating like a pig and I feel gross. We head into the Ginkgo Restaurant and Cafe and I take the water the he offers me. Twisting off the cap, I take a mouthful. "That was so much fun. Not what I thought would be happening today."

"What did you think I had planned for today?"

My cheeks darken and I lower my head. Flynn places his finger under my chin. "What did you think, Ave?"

"I…ummm…ahh…I thought you were going to take me back to your place and you know—"

"You know what?" From the predatory look on his face, he knows exactly what I'm referring to.

"I thought we'd be naked and doing stuff, other fun stuff."

"Why you, little minx you." He places a kiss on the tip of my nose and gazes at me. He leans down and whispers, "Let's get out of here and then we can definitely do that." He nibbles my earlobe, gently sucking.

Swallowing deeply, my body quivers when I think about what's going to happen as soon as we get back to his place. Then I remember I'm all sweaty and dirty and feel yucky. "Can I shower first? I'm all dirty and sweaty."

"Lass, you will be even dirtier and sweatier when I'm done with you, but I guess we can always start in the shower and see where we end up from there."

"I like the way you think, Dr. Kelly. Let's go," I say.

We head back to Flynn's and he makes good on his promise to get me even more sweaty and dirty. Flynn ravishes my body from head to toe, repeatedly.

All

Afternoon

Long…and well into the evening.

23

FLYNN

AFTER OUR AMAZING SEX-FILLED AFTERNOON AND EVENING, LIFE AS I KNEW IT at the hospital became hectic. It feels like I live there at the moment and I haven't seen Avery in days. I'm missing her like crazy, which surprises me. I've never missed anyone before and people can tell that something's up. I'm grouchy with the staff. I'm not myself. I know I'm being a total asshole, but I can't help it. I miss Avery. And to top it off, on Wednesday something weird happened. I was walking in for my evening shift and I bumped into Baylor. I knew it was her from the way she was dressed—short, short Daisy Dukes and a pink top, if you could call it a top, as it left nothing to the imagination. She was heading out after her a physical therapy appointment and as usual, she flirted up a storm with me. And like always, I brushed her off but she was definitely different today. She was more forceful than usual and she even tried to pass herself off as Avery at the beginning, but the walking boot clearly gave her away. Orthopedic boot aside, I'm pretty sure I know the difference between my girlfriend and her twin. She's pretty persistent, that's for sure. That girl just won't take a hint but what frustrates me the most, is that she's doing this to her own sister. *Who does that?* We are interrupted by a sketchy-looking guy; he grabs Bay by the arm and drags her away. She smiles at me as he pulls her away but it doesn't feel sincere. I'm not sure if she's going willingly but that thought changes when she catches me staring at her. Lifting her hand to her lips, she blows me a kiss, and then turns her attention back to the guy she met up with and begins flirting with him. That chick clearly has issues, how she's related to Ave is beyond me. They are polar opposites…just like us really.

Shaking off the encounter, I head into the doctors' lounge to get ready for my shift. I've just pulled on my scrubs when my phone rings, glancing down I see Avery's smiling face on the screen. Picking it up, I answer immediately, "Ave lass, how are you?"

"I'm great. I just received the most gorgeous bunch of reddish-pink roses. You wouldn't know anything about that, would you?"

"Maybe."

"Seriously, Flynn, they are gorgeous. Thank you so much."

"You're welcome, lass. I've missed seeing you this week, but I wanted you to know that I'm thinking of you."

"Flynn, it's been three days."

"That's forever in Avery time."

"Aww, are you missing me, baby?" she teases, but she's correct. I am a lovesick fool missing his girlfriend, and I'm man enough to admit it, well to myself that is.

"Hell yes, I am. Any chance you can swing by the hospital later?"

"I was there earlier visiting Marvin." *Dammit, I missed her.* I pout, yes, I pout…thankful no one is around to see me acting like a pansy.

"How is our resident escapee?"

She swallows deeply. "Not doing too good. I'm worried about him." Her voice is laced with sorrow and sadness.

"What's wrong?" I ask, as I sit in front of my locker.

"He wasn't as spirited as usual." She sniffles, "I think he's going to die, Flynn."

"Ave lass, I'm so sorry." Wishing right now I could take her into my arms and give her the comfort that she needs. "If you like, I can check on him in the morning, and send you an update before you go to work."

"You'd do that for me?"

"I'll do anything for you, Avery."

"Thank you, Flynn, I'd really appreciate that. Thank you."

"Anything for you, Avery." We both go silent but it's not awkward or uncomfortable. "Sorry to cut this short, but my shift is about to start."

"No need to apologize, it's fine, now get to work and go save some lives."

"Will do. I'll call you in the morning with an update on Marvin."

"Thank you."

"Night, Avery."

"Night, Flynn."

Hanging up, I smile when I realize I've fallen head over heels for Avery Evans. I've never felt like this about a woman before. It's new territory for me, and I'm scared to death I'm going to fuck it up, but at the same time, I'm excited for the adventure ahead.

Finally my super busy nightshift is over. I'd love to just head home and crash, but I promised Avery I'd check in on Marvin. So here I am, in the elevator on my way up to his floor. When I walk into his room, I freeze midstep when my eyes land on him in his bed. He really has deteriorated since I last saw him. He notices me standing by the door and smiles, but it doesn't reach his eyes like it usually does.

"Doc, how are ya?" he says, as he shuffles into a sitting position

"I'm good. You?" I ask, as I walk into the room.

"Fit as a fiddle." And then he coughs. It's a deep belly cough and the doctor in me winces, that's not a good cough and just as I think that, he goes into a coughing fit. He's struggling for breath, his body heaving as he tries to suck in oxygen. Racing to his side, I help him attach the breathing mask and then I take a seat and stare at him. It takes almost ten minutes for his breathing to return to normal. He pulls off the mask, "Water?" he asks, and points to the cup on his bedside table.

Picking the cup up, I hold it and the straw to his lips. He drinks and lies back down. He closes his eyes and drifts off to sleep. Not wanting to leave him alone right now, I sit back in the chair and run my fingers through my hair. Dropping my head back, I too, nod off to sleep.

I'm woken up when I feel a finger poking my cheek. Opening my eyes, I see Marvin staring at me. "Doc, you snore like a freight train."

"Do not," I defensively scoff.

"Do too," he returns like a child. "I'm surprised you didn't set any alarms off, it was that loud."

"I'm not that loud, I'm just tired. I worked a twelve hour shift last night."

"Ohh, poor baby," he teases. "When I was a spring chicken, I'd work sixteen hours a day, six days a week. Never once have I snored in my seventy-two years."

"I bet if I asked around, I'd hear that you snored." I pause and then add, "Or you'd make a cute lil' mewling sound."

"Like hell, I mewl," he scoffs. "Where's that lovely lady of yours? I prefer waking up and seeing her pretty face in that chair."

"Sorry to disappoint you, but she's at work. How about we send her a message?"

"What? Like a dick pic?"

"Marvin Marshall," a nurse scolds, as she walks in. "No respectable woman ever wants to receive one of those."

"I'm with her," I say, nodding my head toward the nurse.

"Traitor. How about a nice pic of the two of us then?" Marvin turns to the nurse. "You mind taking a pic?" he sweetly asks her.

"Not at all."

Handing my phone over to her, she takes it from me. I lean toward Marvin and wrap my arm around his shoulder. We smile for the photo. Taking my phone back from the nurse, I send it to Avery before I forget.

FLYNN: *Marvin says hi **attach photo***

"All sent."

"Good, now get out of here. I want a rest without a chugga chugga disturbing me."

Laughing, I stand up. "I'll catch ya later. Bye, Marvin."

"Later, Doc."

As I'm stepping into the elevator, my phone pings with a text.

AVERY: *My two fav men **smiling emoji***
AVERY: *Thank you for checking on him.*
FLYNN: *Happy to do it.*
FLYNN: *He seems in good spirits this morning.*

I leave out the part where I'm worried too, she doesn't need that on her plate.

FLYNN: *P.S. He wanted to send you a dick pic **shocked face emoji***
AVERY: ***Wide eye emoji***
FLYNN: *He also thinks I snore like a freight train.*
AVERY: *I plead the Fifth.*
FLYNN: *I do not snore.*
AVERY: *If you say so Thomas.*
FLYNN: *I DO NOT SNORE!*
AVERY: *Gotta get to class. Chat soon. Xo*
FLYNN: *Have a good day. Xo*

With a goofy grin on my face, I head to the doctors' lounge to grab my things. Climbing into my car, I drive home. Forgoing a shower, I strip off and collapse into bed. I think I'm asleep before my head hits the pillow. Falling into a deep sleep, I dream of Avery…and dick pics from Marvin.

AVERY

AFTER A LONELY AND LONG WEEK, FRIDAY FINALLY ROLLS AROUND. TONIGHT, Cress and I are going out for drinks, it's been weeks since we went out. Actually, the last time we did was the first night I hooked up with Flynn.

Taking my time, I run a bath and pour myself a glass of wine. Climbing into the jasmine-scented bubbles, the warm water envelops me and I sigh. Nothing beats a relaxing bath. When the water turns cold, I climb out. Wrapping a towel around me, I head into the kitchen and pour myself another glass of wine before heading to my room to get ready. Deciding on a black, knee-length halter dress, I pair it with my trusty Louboutins. Curling my hair, I slap on some lip gloss and then I'm ready to rock.

Ordering myself an Uber, I message Cress and tell her I'm on my way to pick her up. As I'm climbing into the car, a feeling of unease washes over me. Looking around, I see two guys, whom I've never seen before, loitering around the entrance to our building. They look out of place, one of them catches me staring at him, he nudges the other guy, and they both watch me intently as the car pulls away from the curb. A shiver runs down my spine, goosebumps appear on my skin, but as quickly as they appeared, the bumps and feeling vanish the farther we drive away from the apartment. Looking out the back window, I see them still standing there, watching as we turn the corner. Shaking my head, I sit back in my seat and start thinking about this evening, I cannot wait to let loose tonight with Cress.

Forty minutes later, after stopping to get Cress, we arrive at the Tavern. Walking inside, we make a beeline for the bar and excitement bubbles when I see the cocktail of the day is a mojito. Ordering two, I wait for our drinks and Cress goes to snag a table that was recently vacated by a couple. I lean against the bar and look toward the alcove where Flynn accosted me that first night. My body thrums as I remember what his magic fingers did to me...and what they do to me now on a regular basis. Grinning to myself, I grab our drinks and head over to Cress.

"Cheers," we both say in unison. We clink our glasses together and drink our cocktails. The tart, tangy liquid quenches my thirst and I take another sip. My phone rings, digging it out, I see Flynn's face smiling at me. "It's Flynn, give me a sec."

Cress nods and finishes her drink. She then mimics the drinking motion and makes her way to the bar to order more drinks.

"Hi, Dr. Kelly," I say, as I answer my phone.

"Good evening, Ms. Evans," he croons down the line. "How are you this fine evening?"

"I'm good. And you?"

"Glad to be finished for the week and looking forward to a weekend off. Today was dead quiet so it dragged and dragged. But I did see your number one fan."

"Marvin," I say with a smile, "How is he?"

"He's doing better. He escaped...again."

"Sounds like him. That definitely means he's doing better. I was so worried earlier this week. If you see him again, telling him I'll pop by after work one day next week."

"You really are a gem, Avery. It sounds loud, where are you?"

"Cress and I are at the Fat Fox."

"You mind if Preston and I join you ladies?"

"Not at all. I haven't seen you since last weekend and that was forever ago."

"Aww, did you miss me, baby?" He throws my taunt from earlier this week back at me.

"I'll never tell," I playfully reply.

He laughs and the timbre of the sound reverberates through my body, leaving me a wanton mess. "Sooo, just how badly did you miss me?"

"You'll see, and feel, just how badly I've missed you when you get here."

"You can't say shit like that to me when I'm not in the same room as you."

"Well, hurry up and get here so you can see and feel for yourself."

He groans and I laugh. "You are an evil minx, Avery Evans. Just you wait until I get there." *Dammit, this has backfired on me*, I think to myself when he says, "See you soon, gorgeous."

"Can't wait. Drive safely," I say in reply. Placing my phone down on the tabletop, I realize I'm beaming. Cress returns with two decadent looking cocktail glasses full of mojito. "I love you," I tell her, as she places our drinks on the table and takes her seat across from me.

"You only love me for my cocktails."

"Yeah, and?" I teasingly reply. Picking up my drink, I raise up in a toast. "To a fantabulous night with my fabulous girlfriend."

"Cheers to that." We both sip and let out an "ahhhh" as the refreshing drink dances on our tastebuds.

"What's got you so chipper?" Cress asks me, as she rocks to the beat of the music.

"Flynn and Preston are stopping by. I hope that's okay?"

Her eyes widen in delight. "Is it okay that two sexy as sin doctors want to stop by? One who happens to have a sexy as hell Irish accent, and the other could be Channing Tatum's twin, let me think about that…hell to the yes it's okay." She takes another drink and again moans. "I really need to get laid. Since Mom has Lexi for the night, I can do it without needing to fuck and chuck to get home to her."

"Get Cress laid is my mission tonight."

"I'll drink to that." She lifts her drink and salutes me. "I like this sassy side of you. Who knew you getting laid would also be good for me too? Prior to Flynn, you'd never suggest something like that."

"I know, right? I'm just so happy and I want you to be happy too."

"Ahh, thanks, babe, but try not get finger fucked here again, save that for the privacy of home, or at the least, the car."

Choking on my drink, I shake my head. "Why did I tell you that?"

"Because you know I need to fuck vicariously through you at the moment. This dry spell is killing me. My rabbit died from overuse, and at the rate I'm going my bullet is going to burn a hole in my clit."

"Evening, ladies," Preston sneakily says from behind Cress. He steps around her and I notice his eyes are lingering on hers. Her face goes beet red as it hits her that he heard what she just said. I burst out laughing. I'm still laughing when Flynn walks over to us with two beers and two more mojitos on a tray.

"Hey, babe," I say, hopping off my stool to greet him. I place a quick kiss on his cheek but he has other ideas: he dips me back and fucks my mouth with his tongue. This kiss is totally not appropriate for being in public, but the bliss I'm currently in makes me not give a shit. I give myself over to the kiss and lose myself in all that is Flynn Kelly. Everything around me fades away. It's just the two of us.

My bubble is burst and I'm snapped back to reality when Preston teases, "Get a fuckin room, you two."

Flynn places me back on two feet and I wink at Preston as I take my seat. "Preston, great to see you again."

"You too, Avery." He turns his attention over to Cress. "Cressida, it's nice to make your acquaintance again. Since we didn't get a chance to formally chat last time, I'm Preston Knight, pediatric doctor and this thing's best friend." He flicks his thumb toward Flynn, but I notice his eyes are locked on my best friend...and hers are locked on him too.

"Thing, really?" Flynn scoffs. Preston just shrugs his shoulders but continues to focus on my best friend. Hmmmm, interesting.

"Cressida Bayliss, but my friends call me Cress," she purrs in reply, yes my best friend purrs. "I'm a mom, grade school teacher, and this sex fiend's bestie." She nods her head at me and takes a sip of her drink, as if she didn't just insult me.

My eyes bug open at her description of me.

"And are we a sex fiend too?" Preston questions her.

She nonchalantly shrugs her shoulder and takes another sip of her drink, seductively wrapping her lips around the straw. After taking a drink, she murmurs, "You already know the answer to that..." then she adds "...and you may find out again later."

Flynn laughs. Preston's face lights up and I shake my head at Crass Cress, clearly she has been keeping secrets from me. The four of us start chatting, and I notice that Preston and Cress are ignoring Flynn and me. They only have eyes for one another. My eyes are locked on the two of them when Flynn sits next to me and affectionally squeezes my knee.

Turning my attention to him I smile. "That was quite the welcome kiss."

"Only the best for my girl."

"Your girl. I like hearing you say that."

"I like saying that."

We stare at one another. Our focus is solely on each other. It isn't until I hear Preston say, "They're eye fucking each other again."

Cress replies with, "At least he isn't finger fucking her again."

My mouth drops open in shock. "Cress," I scoff, "I'm not telling you anything anymore, and you'll have to suffice with your bullet from now on."

Preston leans into her and not so quietly whispers, "I'm more than happy to assist."

My eyes once again bug open in shock. Cress stares at him, smiles, and winks.

Flynn says, "Umm, I think I missed something."

"I wish I missed something," I say.

Cress shrugs.

Preston continues to stare at my best friend. If he was in a Bugs Bunny cartoon, hearts would be coming out of his eyes and baby Cupids would be shooting arrows into the sky.

Flynn looks lost.

And me, I just laugh. I seriously cannot remember the last time I had this much fun, and we've only been here for thirty minutes.

"Ohh, tonight is going to be a hoot."

And a hoot it was. We went from the Tavern to some new club, Tingle, which recently opened. The four of us do shots at the bar before grabbing our drinks and walking around. We find a table and settle in. My eyes gravitate to a throuple grinding together on the dance floor. She has vibrant copper hair and the two guys she's with are hot—not as hot as Flynn—but I can appreciate the opposite sex. I'm getting turned on watching them but when the music changes, they head toward the bar and out of sight.

The four of us are all well on our way to being drunk as skunks when "Acceptable in the 80's" by Calvin Harris begins playing. Flynn and Preston surprise Cress and me when they jump up and make their way to the edge of the dance floor. My mouth drops open as they both start to dance and holy-freakin-moves-Batman, the two of them are carving up the dance floor. Think Channing Tatum in *Step Up* moves—yes, I'm aware that Preston looks like him too but he also moves like him—I fucking love it.

My eyes however are locked on Flynn. His body twists and moves in sync to the beat. He's completely lost to the music, it's so good to see him relaxed. This week at the hospital has been tough for him, it's nice to see him let his hair down and chillax. This week has been tough for me too. Things with Bay have taken a turn. I'm not a fan of the new people she's hanging out with, and they keep thinking I'm her. They make me feel uncomfortable and when I confront Bay, she just laughs it off and ignores my concerns. I was ever so glad to be coming out tonight, and seeing Preston and Flynn dancing right now is making tonight amazeballs.

"Holy shit, Ave, you didn't tell me your sexy as sin doctor could dance too," Cress says.

"I had no clue. But have you seen, Preston? He's totally carving up the dance floor."

Cress and I watch as my sexy as hell boyfriend and his best friend groove away in front of us. Their moves draw in a crowd, everyone mesmerized by the two of them. The songs changes to one I don't know and both guys walk back over to us.

"Holy shit, dudes, where did you guys learn to dance like that?" Cress asks as she hands them each a beer.

"Med school," they reply in unison.

"Preston and I were the dance kings in our frat house."

"You guys were in a frat?" Cress and I ask at the same time.

"Jinx," she says, I shrug and turn my attention to Flynn.

He nods. "Yeah, Preston and I were Phi Kappa Psi at Stanford."

"I did not pick you as a frat guy."

He shrugs his shoulders. "There's still a lot you don't know about me, Avery Evans."

"So tell me then, what else don't I know about you, Flynn Kelly?"

"Weeeell, I'm crazy about this sexy as sin school teacher, and I'm pretty sure she's crazy about me too."

Shrugging my shoulders nonchalantly, I grin at him. "Go on."

"I love that when I touch her here…" He steps to me and drags his fingertip up my thigh. "…she quivers with desire and her panties dampen."

"What else?" I huskily breathe and my panties do indeed dampen as he continues to draw circles on my thigh.

He leans into my ear. "I cannot wait to get you back to my place where I'm going to strip you naked, even though this little black dress is fucking divine on you. I need you naked so I can fuck you repeatedly. All.Night.-Long. Just like our first night together."

Swallowing deeply, I look into his eyes. "I'm down with that." Reaching up, I hook my arm around his neck and bring his lips to mine and kiss him deeply. The sound of Preston slamming his beer down on the table pulls us apart. Looking over, I see him ask Cress to dance and she blushes. Yes, my best friend blushes, but she takes his outstretched hand and they head toward the dance floor. Watching them, my eyes are focused on the chemistry radiating between them.

"Wow, those two are, ummm..." Flynn says, his eyes looking at our two friends dirty—almost dry humping—dance with each other to "Pony" by Genuwine.

"Yep," I say, nodding my head. "Wanna show them how it's done?" I sexily purr.

"Hell yes. Any chance to have my hands all over your sexy body sounds perfect to me. Let's go get our groove on."

Laughing at his reply, I place my drink on the high-top table. "Don't ever say that again."

"Don't fret, don't plan on saying it again. As soon as the words left my mouth I instantly regretted them." We both laugh.

Leaning into him, I whisper with a wink, "I'll spank you later."

Gabbing his hand, I pull him onto the dance floor just as "Sexy Back" by JT starts to play. We begin to bump and grind and we take on Cress and Preston in a dance-off. Somehow it becomes Cress and me against them. Flynn and Preston totally win, they left Cress and me for dead, but watching Flynn dance is totally fucking hot.

The rest of the night flies by and it's the most fun I've had in a long time. We dance. We slam back shots like we are in college. We dance some more. We eat gross greasy food that can only to be consumed when you're drunk and then we drink some more.

At stupid o'clock in the morning, Flynn and I leave Cress and Preston at the club, they are still dancing and the two of them are getting hotter and hotter the more we drink. We stumble back to Flynn's place and once inside, we ravish each other's bodies multiple times before we pass out from exhaustion just as the sun is rising.

When I wake several hours later, I'm wrapped in Flynn's embrace. My body aches from head to toe, and I'm not sure if it's from all the dancing last night or the multiple orgasms I had once we got back here. My head is pounding and my stomach is queasy, damn shots.

Sliding out of bed, I slip on his shirt from last night and head to the kitchen to make some coffee and get some water, my mouth feels like a dirty ashtray. The only downside to a big night out is the morning after.

I've just turned the coffee machine on when my phone rings. Looking down I see that it's Bay.

"Hey, Bay."

"Where are you?" she snarls.

"Good morning to you too."

"Whatevs, where are you?"

"Not home." I don't tell her where I am because I don't want any grief from her concerning Flynn.

"Well, I need a ride. I drank too much last night and I need you to come and get me."

"No, Bay, I'm sorry, I can't."

Flynn comes up behind me and wraps his arms around me. Cupping my boobs, he squeezes them and a moan breaks free.

"Ugh, seriously, Ave? You can't wait until I'm off the phone?"

Even though I'm holding my phone to my ear, I totally forgot she was there. "Sorry, I'm busy, Bay. You'll have to Uber it."

"Some sister you are. I'd be there for you if you called me in need."

"Yeah, right," I scoff. "Grab an Uber and I'll see you when I get home." Another moan slips out when Flynn pinches my nipple.

"Is that sexy as sin doctor with you?"

"No," I snap, but it's not convincing at all.

"He'll be mine soon," she softly says, and before I can tell her off, she hangs up on me.

"Gah!" I shout, as I throw my phone on the counter. "I hate her stinkin' guts." I pause, and then playfully tack on, "You make me vomit. You're scum between my toes. Love Alfalfa." I laugh as I recite this verse and when I spin around to look at Flynn, he's looking at me like I have two heads. "It's from *Little Rascals*." He's still looking at me with a blank stare on his face, and I realize he has never seen the movie. "You've never seen it, have you?"

"Seen what?" he asks, shrugging his shoulders, utterly confused right now.

"*Little Rascals*, the movie."

He shakes his head side to side. "Nope. Never seen or heard of it."

I scoff in fake shock, "Well, then we need to rectify this. Later today, me. You. *Little Rascals*. A bottle of red and popcorn."

"Can we be naked?"

I laugh at his request. "Sure, why not."

"Perfect," he reiterates, "later we will watch *Little Rascals*, naked, while drinking red wine and eating popcorn. But first, coffee."

"I like that plan."

We sit at the island, drinking our coffee, and we chat about the movie. I pretty much tell him everything that happens since I know the movie from start to finish. Baylor and I loved the movie growing up, we must have watched it a million times over the years.

Finishing our coffee, we head back to bed and sleep for a few more hours. Seriously, I am never drinking again. I'm too old to party 'til the wee hours and then fuck 'til the sun comes up. Not that I've ever done that before, but I can unequivocally say, I'll do it again because last night was amazing and anyone who says they are never drinking again is a big fat liar, because they totally will drink excessively again.

After our nap, we order Chinese and eat our weight in Mongolian beef and watch *Little Rascals*. Like I agreed, we watch it naked while drinking red wine—see, I drank again—and eating popcorn. I recite just about every line and then we make sweet, sweet love on the sofa. I completely forget about all my concerns with my sister because I'm with Flynn.

He hops up to refill our wine and as I watch his naked ass, I realize that no longer am I falling for Dr. Kelly, I've fallen head over heels, ass over tits, in love with this sexy as sin Irish doctor, and I've never been happier.

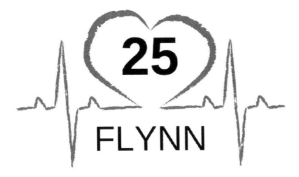

25

FLYNN

GRABBING A GLASS OF WATER, I SIGH WHEN I REALIZE IT'S BEEN THREE DAYS since I saw Avery in person. Seems three days is my limit before I turn into a total girl and start whining like a little bitch. We had a quick FaceTime chat earlier but that's not the same. She left my place Sunday at dinnertime after we spent the most of the weekend together. Apart from a few text messages and our FaceTime, I've missed seeing her...damn double shifts and life getting in the way.

Even though I'm dog-tired, I want to see her. Picking up my phone, I go to call and see if she's free for dinner, but I'm interrupted by a knock at the door. Walking over, I open the door and I'm pleasantly surprised to see Avery standing there. My mouth drops open at the sight before me. She's wearing a figure-hugging, pink dress that leaves NOTHING to the imagination, I've never seen her dress like this before. "Fuck me, you are gorgeous."

"I know," she replies.

Shaking my head at her cheeky response, my eyes once again rake over her body—shoot me—I'm male and my sexy as hell woman is here, and suddenly, I'm not so tired anymore. I've never seen her like this before. There's something different with her tonight but fuck me, I'll take it. She steps around me and walks, no, saunters in and takes a seat at the breakfast bar. She crosses her legs, ala Sharon Stone in *Basic Instinct* and I'm pretty sure she isn't wearing any panties. I'm totally digging this sexy vixen version of Avery.

"What are you doing here?" I ask, as I walk over to the wine fridge and grab a bottle of white. *It's after five and we can order* in I tell myself, as I uncork the bottle. Grabbing two glasses from the cupboard, I pour us each a glass and hand one to her. Her fingers brush mine and the zing I usually feel isn't there tonight, maybe it's because I've just finished a twenty-four hour shift and I'm shattered.

"I missed you," she says, "It's been too long since I've seen you."

"You FaceTimed me at lunch today."

Her eyes bug open and then she sexily whines, "That was forever ago."

"You are too cute."

"I know," she replies again. Something is definitely off with her tone tonight. I put it down to being super tired, I'm not even enjoying my wine and this is my favorite.

"Look, Ave lass, I'm sorry to do this, but I'm shattered after my shift. Can we do this tomorrow? After I've gotten some sleep."

She looks at me, and her face it etched with rejection. I hate that I put that look on her face, but I know if I ask her to stay, I won't be getting to sleep for a few more hours, and I just can't, as much as it pains me. I need sleep.

"Fine," she snaps, "but can you drop me home first? I got an Uber here."

"Of course," I say, confused as to why she'd Uber it here, she doesn't usually Uber it unless she's drinking. "Are you okay?" I question.

"I'm fine," she snaps again, clearly she's tired too.

We head down to the parking garage and when she climbs in, I once again get a view of her pantyless ass. I'm close to taking her back upstairs but something is stopping me from doing so.

The car ride back to her place is quiet. It's kind of awkward, but I put it down to me being a complete zombie right now, actually, I'm surprised I didn't crash on the way over here. Pulling up outside her apartment building, I walk around the hood. After helping her out, she links her arm with mine and we walk inside. We climb into the elevator and ride up to her floor. Again it's silent and awkward. The doors open and we step out. She's digging in her purse for her keys, banging on the door as she does so. Suddenly, as if she's heard something, her head snaps up and she looks at me. Her eyes take on a glint I've never seen before. She steps toward me, drapes her arms over my shoulders and gazes into my eyes. She starts leaning in when the apartment door swings opens. A smirk appears on her face and we both turn our heads. The person standing in the doorway looks shocked. Her gaze darting back and forth between us, and then her eyes well with tears, and a sinking feeling develops in my guts.

"Flynn. Bay." She steps into the hall with us. "What's going on?"

What.

The.

Fuck.

"Avery?" I question, looking between the two of them.

"Hey, Sis," Baylor says from in front of me.

Immediately, I step back and push Baylor away from me. My eyes dart between them and suddenly, everything makes sense now. The awkwardness. The unease. No spark, it's because I was with Baylor and not Avery. Had I not been dog-tired, I would have known immediately.

Turning to Avery, my hearts breaks when I see the devastation on her face. "Avery," I plead, "I'm—"

She raises her hand. "No. Don't." On a sob, she blubbers, "Just go, Flynn."

She turns on her heel and walks into the apartment. My eyes follow her as she somberly races into her bedroom. My heart shattering with each step she takes away from me.

"Well, that was perfect," Baylor smugly says from beside me. "Call me," she sweetly says as she steps toward me. She rests her palms on my chest and places a kiss on my cheek. Turning on her heel, she walks toward the elevators and steps into the car we just exited.

Shaking my head, I watch as the doors close and then I hear it, a gut-wrenching sound emits from inside the apartment. Racing in, I slam the door behind me and make my way to Avery's room, her sobs getting louder and louder.

Standing at the doorway, my heart breaks at the scene before me. Avery is lying on her bed in the fetal position, tears cascading down her cheeks. She's completely shattered and it's all because of me, and her sister. I can't take it. I step into her bedroom and plead, "Ave lass, please."

26

AVERY

"Don't, Ave lass, me!" I scream, my heart is shattering in half right now. Wiping at my eyes, I refuse to cry. He doesn't deserve my tears, I sit up and cross my legs. Taking a deep breath, I lift my gaze and glare at him. "You were..." I can't finish my sentence, the tears start again and they pour like an avalanche down my cheeks. "You were about to kiss my sister," I sniffle. Voicing that out loud shatters my heart into a million tiny fragments. "How could you?"

"I thought she was you!" he shouts in defense. Does he really think so little of me that he would try that lame excuse?

"Please," I scoff. "Don't insult me, Flynn. If you want her, go for it. I know she's vivacious and out there, and I'm—"

"Perfect," he says, as he strides over to me, eating up the distance in a few steps. Dropping to his knees in front of me, he takes my hands in his and grips them tightly, squeezing in an oddly reassuring way. "Avery

Evans, you are perfect, absolutely-fucking-perfect and...and...I love you. I fucking love you."

My mouth drops open at his declaration. I've gone from hurt and anger to shock and awe.

"Avery, I love you." He climbs up onto the bed, shuffling to his knees and with my hands still in his; he stares intently into my eyes. "From the moment I laid eyes on you, I was smitten. I had to have you. I had you and then you left, but then fate bought us back together and I was once again bewildered by you. You are the air in my lungs. The beat of my heart. You are my everything, Avery Evans." He pauses. "Ave lass, I love you."

Blinking rapidly, I process the words he just said to me. Words that resonate deep in my soul, I believe and I feel every one of those words. "I love you too, Flynn Kelly."

Wrapping my arms around his neck, I slam my lips against his and pull him toward me. Our bodies collide. We become one. This kiss is electric, it's different from the many before. The love between us radiates around my room. It envelops us and swallows us whole. Nothing else matters except for Flynn and me and our love for one for another.

Falling to the mattress with our lips fused, we let our love flow between us. I'm blissfully in love with this man and he loves me back. I love him with every fiber in my being. Nothing and no one can tear us apart.

After our declaration of love, Flynn and I lie on my bed in each other's arms. The sound of the front door opening, startles us. Baylor giggles when some guy says something and thankfully, they head to her bedroom, slamming her bedroom door with enough force to shake my room. Letting out a sigh, I look to Flynn. He knows from the look on my face that I need to get out of the apartment. Without saying a word, he lifts me out of bed. My legs wrap around him and I hang on like a monkey. He exits my apartment and carries me down to his car and away from Baylor.

The beating of his heart calms me, I'm reluctant to let him go. I want to stay in his arms forever, and as if he can read my mind, he says. "As much as I love having you in my arms, I need to let you go so I can drive us back to my place."

Nodding my head, I unwrap my legs from his waist and lower my feet to the ground. He opens the car door for me and before I hop in, I look to him. "I love you, Flynn."

"And I love you, Avery. Now get in."

Climbing in, I strap myself in and we head to Flynn's and away from my deceitful sister. My thoughts are a jumbled mess but they keep coming back to those three words, I love you. Who knew three little words, eight letters could hold so much power?

Arriving at his place, Flynn parks in his spot and we lace our fingers together and head up to his apartment. We don't say anything, the silence is peaceful. We step into his penthouse and a calmness washes over me, that is until I see the open bottle of wine and two glasses sitting on the island counter. I stop midstep and my eyes snap to his, my blood simmering and hurt courses through my veins; she was here. Any calmness I had evaporates and rage takes its place.

"Nothing happened!" he yells. "She turned up here just as I got home from the hospital. My mind isn't functioning properly. I've been awake for over twenty-six hours now. I honestly thought she was you. You two are strikingly similar but also different, and I sensed something was off but I just put it down to being overtired." He pauses. "I'm so sorry, Ave." Turning to face me, he goes to take my hand in his, but I step back. He looks to me and pleads, "I promise you, Avery, nothing happened between us. Please believe me!"

As I stare at him, I see the remorse and guilt he feels in his eyes. Stepping over to him, I cup his cheek in my palm. "I believe you." Relief floods his face at my words. "Flynn, you are mine," I emphasize the word mine, "even when you're dead tired and your mind is playing tricks on you. Your heart sensed something was up because it beats for me and only me. Just like mine beats only for you." Wrapping my arms around his shoulders, I rest my head on his chest. "You are mine, Flynn Kelly, forever and eternity," I whisper, as I close my eyes and snuggle into him.

He wraps his around me in return and kisses my head. He whispers, "I'm yours, Avery, forever and eternity." We silently hug one another. It's nice. It's perfect, and it's exactly what we need right now. I know without a doubt that he's telling the truth, but I'm so confused as to why Baylor would do this to me. To him. Something is amiss with her but that's something for another day. Lifting my head, I look up at him. "Flynn, take me to bed," I huskily whisper as I nuzzle his chin.

"With pleasure," he growls, tightening his embrace around me.

Scooping his arms under my legs, he lifts me up and carries me bridal style into his bedroom. He places me on my feet at the end of the bed. He lowers his lips to mine and gently kisses me. Pulling back, I whisper, "Be right back."

Walking over to the en suite bathroom, I close the door behind me and stare at my reflection and grin. *Flynn loves me and I love him.* Cue freak-out, but no freak-out occurs because this is meant to be. I'm happy and content with this declaration. Taking a deep breath, I pull my shirt over my head and slide my jeans down my legs; ever so thankful I wore a sexy matching set today.

Opening the door, I sexily step through and when I look to the bed, I smile. Flynn is sound asleep, snoring loudly, like he does when he's super exhausted. Walking over to the bed, I drop to my knees and remove his shoes and socks. Then I manage to get his jeans down and I begin to unbutton his shirt. He stirs. "Ave lass, I'm sorry," he sleepily says.

"Shhhh," I whisper. "Go back to sleep, baby."

He sits up and his eyes pop open when he sees what I'm wearing. "Ave, you are so fucking gorgeous," he hungrily says, his eyes immediately drooping closed before his head falls to my stomach, once again asleep.

"Sleep, baby," I say, running my fingers through his hair. Kissing his head, I whisper, "I'll be here in the morning."

Sliding his shirt down his arms, I gently push him backward and he drops back to the mattress, managing to pull me down with him. He rolls to his side and I snuggle into him, spooning. He's out cold, snoring like a freight train. Me? I'm wide awake and my mind is firing on all cylinders. Why did Bay do this? What is wrong with her? And what I can do to get my sister back?

Eventually my eyes become heavy and my last thought before I drift off to sleep is that the man I'm currently snuggling with loves me, just as much as I love him. Bay and her pettiness be damned.

27

FLYNN

WAKING UP WITH AVERY IN MY BED IS FAST BECOMING MY FAVORITE WAY TO start my day. Rolling to my side, my eyes roam over her body. Her sexy as sin body is currently encased in a black satin bra and panties combo. The sun is just rising and in the morning light, Avery looks radiant. Tracing my finger down her breastbone, ever so gently, her skin prickles under my touch and her hazel eyes flutter open, the green vibrant in the early morning light.

"Morning, beautiful."

"Morning," she huskily says, smiling at me. Even sleepy, she's gorgeous.

Leaning toward her, I place my lips against hers. Rolling her to her back, I roll on top of her, cocooning her body with mine and deepening our kiss. Sliding my hand down her side, the moment is interrupted by Avery's phone's alarm.

"I have to get to work," she sadly says. "Rain check?"

"Abso-fuckin-lutely, BUT you need to wear this again," I say, skimming my finger over the satin circling her nipple.

She closes her eyes and moans before huskily whispering, "Deal."

Lowering my head, I kiss the tip of her nose and we climb out of bed and get dressed. I drop Avery home and after a longer than necessary goodbye kiss, she climbs out of my car. I sit and watch the woman I love walk into her building. The door closes behind her and I realize how close I came to losing her yesterday…and all because of her sister. Shaking my head, I decide to head to the hospital to spend some time with Marvin before my shift starts, I'd rather be around him than on my own at the moment.

After a crazy few days, it's finally Saturday. Thankfully there have been no more doppelgänger incidents. Ave and I have FaceTimed each morning before she heads off to work, but it's not the same as a face-to-face visit; man, life getting in the way of my woman and me is a drag. I may have gone overboard with gifts this week, wanting to reaffirm to Avery that I love her and only her. To her school, I sent a huge bunch of tulips. To her home, a delivery from Agent Provocateur, that's more of a gift for me but potato/vodka. There was also a voucher sent from Allyu Spa for couple's spa day package—just need to find the time for both of us to be free—and finally, an invite to spend the night with me tonight.

Just before lunch, Ave arrives with pizza and beer; man, I love this woman. After devouring the pizza, we decide on a lazy day at home before our dinner date tonight, where I surprise Avery with new a dress and more lingerie from Agent Provocateur. I take her back to Rococo's and just like our first night here, we have an amazing time. Followed by an equally amazing sexy night in bed when we get home.

The next morning, Avery is up before me and I'm pleasantly awakened by the smell of breakfast. She cooks us pancakes and we eat naked on the couch, watching another of Avery's all time fav movies, *Empire Records*.

It's the perfect Sunday morning until Avery receives a call from Baylor. She stares at her phone for a few moments before she takes a deep breath and answers, putting it on speaker.

"Hey, Bay."

"Avery." Her tone is curt and rude.

Then it's silent, I can feel the tension building in Avery from where I'm sitting next to her. I take her hand in mine and gently squeeze, giving her the courage to go on. She takes a deep breath. "What do you want, Bay?"

"Wondering where you are? Are you with Cress commiserating over the demise your relationship with Flynn?" she says, her voice laced with such venom.

"No, I'm not." Avery defiantly replies, her voice strong. "Actually, I'm at Flynn's right now. I've spent the weekend with him."

"Even though he cheated on you?"

"He didn't cheat. He told me nothing happened between you two."

"Of course he'd say that, he's—"

"Bay, stop with the fucking lies. I've had it. Just stop."

"Enjoy it while you can, Ave. You won't get your happily ever after... mark my words."

The line goes dead. Looking over to Avery, I see that she's gutted. Wanting to distract her, I tell her to go get changed. She slips into her jeans that I love and a dark pink off-the-shoulder sweater thing.

We head to my car. "Can you tell me where we're going?" she begs, as we pull out of the underground parking garage.

"Don't you want a surprise?"

"Kinda. Sorta. Not really." She pauses. "Pleease tell me. I'll make it worth your while?" She suggestively raises her eyebrows at me.

"Lass, you'll be getting sex when we get back, so that's not really a bargaining tool at all."

"Fine," she huffs; crossing her arms across her chest she pouts like a child. It's cute but seeing her down cuts me deep.

"I hate seeing you sad like this so I'll tell you," I concede, and she instantly smiles. "We're heading to the hospital to see Marvin. I thought a visit with him would cheer you up since he always manages to make you smile."

"Ohh, Flynn, thank you," she cheerfully says.

As soon as we step into his room, both of them light up and seeing the joy on her face warms my Irish heart.

We stopped at his favorite bakery on the way and grabbed a dozen glazed donuts before stopping at Starbucks across the road from the hospital for coffees. The nurse isn't too happy to see Marvin shoveling a donut—it's actually his fourth but from the scowl on her face, I won't be bringing that up. "Marvin Marshall, you know that donuts aren't allowed on your diet." The nurse looks to me and now I'm scared. "And you, Dr. Kelly," she points a finger at me, "should know better."

Avery giggles from where she's sitting and it's nice to see her relaxed, so I take the verbal lashing with a grain of salt. If my girl is happy, it's the least that I can do. Marvin manages to win the nurse over by offering her a donut. "You were a total heartbreaker back in the day, weren't you, Marvin?" I ask, as the nurse walks out of his room, nibbling on her sweet treat.

"You betcha I was."

He looks to Avery. "If I was forty years younger, you and I would have a ball together."

"I'm sure we would," she playfully replies.

Marvin looks to me. "You look after this one, she's special. What she sees in a snoring freight train like you is beyond me."

We all laugh, at my expense. And the barbs continue throughout the afternoon. We spend the next few hours playing cards with Marvin and listening to his wild stories. He's lead an amazing life. We say our good-byes and when we climb into my car, Avery looks to me, and hesitantly asks, "Can you, ummm, drop me home?"

"Ohh," I say, deflated that she isn't staying at my place again.

"I just want to grab a few things so I don't have to rush in the morning."

Relief washes over me. "Sure can, babycakes."

"Babycakes, really?"

"Too much?"

"Just a little."

We've just pulled up to her place when my phone rings and it's the hospital. They are short staffed in the ER and need me to cover a shift. Reluctantly, I say goodbye to Avery, after getting her to agree to get her things and head to my place to wait for me. She climbs out of my car and I watch until she's safely inside. Then I head back to where we just came from, but our plan doesn't work out quite like we expected and nothing will be the same again.

28

AVERY

Flynn has just left and I'm feeling pretty great right now, actually I'm more than great. I'm on cloud a billion at this specific moment in time. The afternoon with Marvin was just what I needed, AND I've decided the Bay issue is a non-issue. I'm not going to let her ruin this for me. I've never been this happy before and nothing, I mean nothing, is going to stand in the way of my happiness, and if I know Bay, that will piss her off more than rolling over in defeat. It breaks my heart that my own sister, my twin, is trying to tear us apart but if anything, her interference has brought Flynn and I closer together. So in a way, it's a blessing in disguise.

What I'm struggling with is that she won't talk to me. Something is up. Normally, we tell each other everything but at the moment, she's a different person and I don't like this version of my sister. Yes, we've always been different, but we've always had each other's back and we'd never do anything to purposely hurt one another. I just wish she'd talk to me, I want my twinsie back.

Pouring myself a glass of wine, I think about Flynn and find myself grinning, like I do most times I think about him. We may be opposites in many ways, but I think that's what makes us, well, us. We balance each other out, like yin and yang. He brings me out of my shell and I like the version of me that has surfaced. Without him, I'd still be shy and timid, but since meeting him, I'm a lot more outgoing and I'm happy, happier than I've ever been. I'm not going to let Flynn get away, if I have my way, no one is going to stop me from keeping my man. I've said it before and I'll say it again, I'm swooning hard for Dr. Kelly and for the first time ever, I'm not going down without a fight. I will fight tooth and nail for what's mine, and Flynn is mine. I love him with all my heart and I'll do anything for the man I love.

I just hope our love for one another is strong enough to weather any storm which comes our way. "Bring it on," I say to the empty room, and I feel good saying this, even if it is only to myself.

Just as I've made this declaration, the person behind my recent anxiety and discomfort walks in, well, she saunters in as if her shit doesn't stink. I haven't seen her since we had our major blowout showdown. We've been ships passing in the night and I'm happy to have it like that. Never before have I not wanted to see Bay. Sure, we've had our differences but at the end of the day, we are sisters and love each other. We've always been able to overcome our hurdles, but I'm not sure if it's possible this time. She's never maliciously hurt me before, and I don't think I can easily forgive and forget this time.

My eyes track her movements, she seems tense and stressed. The twin instinct in me rears to life and wants to help her but I know Bay, if I push, she'll clam up and become spiteful, well, more spiteful that she has been lately. I need her to come to me on her own terms, and that means taking the brunt of her outbursts and putting on a brave smiling face. She finally notices me. "Well, well, well, look who's sulking at home, drinking wine like the loser she is." She sashays into the kitchen, dropping her Prada—fake—handbag onto the granite countertop.

"Bay," I say, lifting my wine to my lips so I don't say something I'll regret.

She stares at me, her lip lifts in a facetious way and I just know what's about to spill from her lips is going to piss me off, possibly hurt me more. "I had THE best night and morning—" she pauses and glares at me, "but I won't bore you with the sexy gritty details."

My blood begins to boil at what she's insinuating, if it had been last week, I would have fallen for her lies and deceit regarding her and Flynn, but not this week. This week I have all the information and she can no longer hurt me with her deception. I knew she could be cruel, she's always had a bit of a nasty streak but never with me. I never thought I'd be on the receiving end of her nastiness. She's always had my back. We were twinsies forever but now, she's going out of her way to hurt me.

"Sounds nice." Not giving her anything, I place my glass on the counter and half-heartedly smile at her as I step toward her. "I'm heading to my room." I dart around her but I don't get far, she grips my arm, digging her fingers in.

"You won't keep him, Ave," she snarls. Lifting my gaze to her, I see nothing reflecting back in her eyes. The final knife in my armor is when she adds, "I'll see to it."

Taking a deep breath, I ignore her and race to my bedroom. Slamming the door behind me, I slide down the wood and breathe deeply. My eyes well with tears but I hold them back, she doesn't deserve my tears. Lowering my head to my knees, I sigh deeply and take big, deep calming breaths. "Why do you hate me so much, Bay?" I whisper, wiping away a lone tear that's managed to break free. I stare into my room at nothing in particular and my phone beeps with a text. Lifting myself up, I dig it out of my pocket and smile when I see who it's from.

FLYNN: *Miss you already, sexy lady.*
AVERY: *I needed that.*
AVERY: *You know who just came home.*
FLYNN: *Do you need me to come back over?*

My face breaks out in a smile at his offer. I'd love nothing more than for him to come back, but he's at work and I don't want him and Bay under the same roof. I don't trust her one bit when it comes to Flynn.

AVERY: *Thanks, but no thanks. I'm going to crawl into bed and watch Netflix. Besides, you need to play doctor and save some lives.*
FLYNN: *We can snuggle together and watch Netflix.*
FLYNN: *I've heard I'm a good snuggler. #JustSayin*

I laugh at his reply.

AVERY: *I know you are.*

AVERY: *But I'll be fine. Other people need you more than I do right now.*
FLYNN: *Reluctantly I say fine, BUT I'm taking you out for dinner tomorrow after I sleep.*
AVERY: *Sounds wonderful. Can't wait! **blowing kiss emoji***
FLYNN: *Sleep well, beautiful. Love you. Xo*

Staring at my phone, I focus on the 'Xo' part of his text and once again I find myself grinning. Never before have those two letters, or those three beautiful words meant so much to me.

AVERY: *Nite nite. Love you too. Xo*

Standing up, I change into my pajamas and hop into bed. Closing my eyes, I drift off to sleep with a goofy grin on my face. Happy. Content and in love.

Waking the next morning, I feel refreshed and relaxed. Picking up my phone, I see I have a text from Cress.

CRESS: *Wanna do something crazy today?*

Shaking my head, I dial and she picks up on the second ring. She doesn't give me a chance to talk, she dives right into her crazy plan. Staring at the ceiling, I listen to her. Pondering her words, I sit up in bed. "I can't believe I'm saying this but sure, I'm in." She squeals in my ear and we agree to meet up in an hour's time.

Hanging up, I grab a quick shower and slip into a pair of light wash denim jeans, a black racer back tank, and my navy Chucks. Filling my to-go coffee mug, I race out to meet Cress for our crazy adventure.

Two hours later, I'm sitting across from Cress in a restaurant, after our adventure we decided to get brunch. After demolishing the most amazing three egg omelette, I sit back and stare at Cress. "I cannot believe I let you talk me into it."

"I cannot believe you agreed." We both laugh. "But seriously, Avery, I have never seen you so happy. I think a certain sexy Irish doctor was just the medicine you needed."

"And I think a certain Channing Tatum looking doctor is the prescription you need. One of these days, you are going to have to tell me what's up between you two."

She mimes zipping her lips. "My lips are sealed." She pauses and then leans forward. "But I will say—" She doesn't get to finish, because some crazy chick comes up to our table and slaps me hard across the face. "You bitch," she snarls. "It's all your fault. I wish Kye had never met you."

Before I have a chance to reply, she's storming away.

"What the fuck was that?" Cress asks, her eyes flicking between the retreating form of psycho Barbie and me. "And who the fuck is Kye?"

Shaking my head, I cup my stinging cheek. "Beats me who Kye is. " The name Kye is familiar but I cannot place it or him. "But, man, does she have a wicked left hook."

Cress looks back at me and shakes her head. We finish our brunch and then say our goodbyes. I stroll back to my car and think about the events of today. The crazy events of today, I still can't believe Cress convinced me to do it, but this is the new carefree, fun Avery and she had an absolute blast today.

Driving home with a smile on my face, I think how crazy my life is right at this moment. Meeting Flynn. Falling in love. The discontent with Baylor. Crazy Cress and our adventures together. Hanging with Marvin. My life is mostly perfect right now.

Parking my car, I decide to take the stairs as I'm excessively full from brunch. My phone pings with a text before I enter the stairwell. Digging it out of my bag, I smile when I see it's from Flynn.

FLYNN: *I need to see you.*
FLYNN: *Feel free to wear that black satin number.*
FLYNN: *Please come over. **begging emoji***
FLYNN: ***begging emoji***
FLYNN: ***sad emoji***
AVERY: *Be there soon. **wink wink***

Racing into the stairwell, I hall ass up the stairs, two at a time. I'm huffing and puffing by time I reach our floor. Running into the apartment, I quickly change into my black satin bra and panties set, as per Flynn's request, and then I slip on my purple dress from our first official date. Applying some lips gloss, I run my fingers through my hair. Blowing myself a kiss in the mirror, I can't believe how great I look.

Deciding to be brazen, before I exit my room, I pull my dress down and snap a sexy image of my shoulder with just a hint of my bra and a sexy pout. I quickly text it to Flynn and before I've left my room, I get a reply.

FLYNN: ***eyes emoji***

FLYNN: *Get your ass over here!*
FLYNN: *Now!*
AVERY: *Just leaving. Love you.*

Exiting my room, I grab my bag and car keys. Opening the front door, I come to a halt. I'm met with a burly bald-headed man and his skinny runt of sidekick and then it hits me, these are the guys from outside the building the other week.

"Can I help you?" I ask.

"Baylor."

"No, I'm not her. I'm—"

"Shut it, bitch. We want what's ours!" the bald guy bellows, spittle flying through the air. He stares me down and that prickly feeling from the other day appears. "NOW!" he growls, slamming his fist into the doorframe.

"I'm sorr—" But I don't get to finish that sentence, the skinny guy zaps me with a Taser.

Dropping to my knees, my body flinches and coils from the electrical shock. Glancing up at him, the elevator dings and in a panic the guy rears back his leg and kicks me in the ribs and in the face. The force snaps my head back and it hits the doorframe with a thud. The last thing I remember is faintly hearing my name being yelled before I'm zapped again. And then everything goes black.

29
BAYLOR

WELL FUCK, THIS ISN'T WORKING OUT HOW I PLANNED. I NEEDED AVERY TO BE sad and locked away in her room, or crying at Cress's house. But no, she's loved up with Flynn and because of me; my actions are going to catch up with her. Maybe I need to stop with the flirting and push her toward him, that way she will move in with him and I can be free to live my life without worrying about her.

Fuck, how did it come to this?

Last night, seeing her strong and not wilting, I was kinda proud of her. Normally she'd roll over but since meeting this Flynn guy, she's changed. But then so I have, the main difference is she's changed for the better. Me? I've changed for the worse and I've turned into someone I barely recognize anymore. If I'm honest, I don't like who I've turned into. I need to do something, but what? I'm in too deep now.

Picking up my coffee, I look around our apartment and realize I'm lonely and unhappy, I want to be the old me again. I wonder where Avie is right now. And that thought hurts; we always used to know where the other was. Flopping onto the sofa, my mind drifts to when things were good with us…

…Avie and I have are having a baking day. We are going to bake up a storm. Avie starts getting out the ingredients and I walk over to the sound system. Switching it on, I click into Spotify and crank up the tunes. "The Piña Colada Song" comes on and we sing along as we get our Martha Stewart on. We bake chocolate chip peanut butter cookies, triple chocolate muffins, and banana bread. While the treats are cooling, we whip up a lasagne for dinner tonight and Ave makes her famous caramel dumplings.

Looking around the kitchen I smile, Avie and I haven't had a day like this in forever. We had so much fun but right now, the kitchen looks like a winter wonderland. There's white powder all through the kitchen. We may have had a flour fight while making the béchamel sauce for the lasagne, but I'm not worried about the mess because my neat freak sister—bless her little neat cotton socks—will go all Suzy Homemaker *and have every speck cleaned up before I even start to wash the conditioner out of my hair.*

As that memory fades, I realize I need to change my life and I need to do it now. I want more baking days with her, I want the old us back. With a sigh, I come to the conclusion I need to change now. To say I'm in over my head is the understatement of the millennium. It started out innocently, but as time went on and the thrill subsided, I'd find new ways to get my thrills and now, well, now I'm screwed and not in the good, panting, sweaty naked way.

When Kye died, that was when I realized how deep in I was, but how the fuck am I going to get out of this? I tried to push Avery away to protect her, but that backfired spectacularly. Now she's hurt and lying unconscious in a hospital bed because of me, and what do I do? I pretend to be her to save my own ass.

This is spiraling out of control. I need to come up with a plan and I need to do it fast because when she wakes up, I'm screwed.

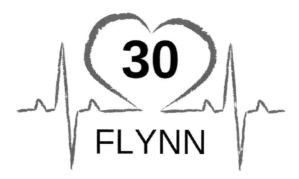

30

FLYNN

HOLY FUCKING SHIT!

The image that Avery just sent me is burnt into my retinas, and ever since I opened that message, my cock has been rock-hard. I'm pacing in front of my door, eagerly awaiting her arrival.

Thirty minutes pass and she still isn't here. I put it down to traffic.

Another thirty minutes passes and now I'm antsy. I feeling of unease settles in my stomach.

Sixty minutes have passed and now I'm worried. That unease has magnified tenfold and I'm worried as all fuck. Picking up my phone, I dial Avery but it rings out and goes to voicemail. "Ave lass, it's me, please call me back as soon as you get this message. I'm worried. I love you."

Throwing my phone on the island countertop, I stare at my front door, willing it to open. With each second that passes, the feeling of dread intensifies in my gut. Just as I'm about to call her again, my phone lights up and it's her. "Ave lass—"

"Flynn…" she blubbers, "it's…it's Bay."

"What's wrong? Where are you?" I knew something wasn't right, I should have gone to her place rather than waiting here like a lovesick fool.

"I'm at Western General." She sounds so broken, I know she's on the outs with her sister right now, but at the end of the day, Baylor is her twin.

"I'm on my way."

"Hurry."

Before she'd hung up, I was already racing toward the door.

Thirty minutes later, I race into the ER and immediately my eyes land on Avery. She's accompanied by two police officers. Taking a deep calming breath, I get myself under control as I walk toward them, eating up the distance quickly. She looks up and when her gaze lands on mine, a look washes over her before she throws herself at me. "Flynn," she cries into my chest. My arms instinctively wraps around her. She falls apart in my embrace and I kiss her head and soothingly whisper 'Shhhh' over and over.

Looking to the officers, I recognize Cooper and Devon from when an officer was shot on the job. "Hey," we all say in unison.

"Can you tell me what's going on?" I ask.

Cooper steps to me. "Before we do, Flynn, can I ask your relationship to Baylor and Avery Evans?"

"Avery here is my girlfriend."

Ave nods in agreement and he explains what happened. "It seems that Baylor was attacked at the apartment she shares with Avery, earlier this evening, by two unknown assailants. Avery here, interrupted them and probably saved her sister from getting kidnapped or worse."

"I was so scared, baby. I'm glad to be in your arms now," she says, as she tightens her arms around me, her body tight with tension.

"Avery was giving us all she can remember but she's in shock at the moment so her memories are vague."

"Ave lass, I'm so glad you weren't home when it happened." Placing a kiss on her head, I pull her back to look at me. "Do you know who they were?"

She shakes her head. "No, I don't think I've ever seen them before."

"Are they the guys from the other day?" She looks at me confused. "You mentioned two guys the other night?

"I…I don't know. Everything's all so fuzzy." She sits down and rests her elbows on her knees and sighs.

Shaking my head, I run my fingers through my hair and I sit down next to her and rub her back. "What shit has your sister gotten into?"

Her head snaps toward me and the look she's currently giving me could turn me to stone. There's such vehemence in her gaze right now. "Who says it's her fault?" she snaps.

"I didn't say that, I—" Before I can defend myself, Clay enters the ER and walks toward us.

Standing up, I step away from Avery and over to Clay. "Clay, dude, how's Baylor?" I stretch out my hand to him.

"Flynn," he says, slapping me on the back with one hand and shaking the other in that manly one-hand shake/hug. "You know I can't discuss this with you, you're not technically family."

I nod my head in understanding but Avery says, "It's fine." As she slides her arm around my waist, snuggling into my side. I breath her in but she doesn't smell as florally as she usually does.

"Avery, it seems that Baylor was shocked with a Taser. There's two red barb welts on the side of her abdomen. She has a concussion. A small cut to her left cheek that needed five stitches, but luckily no broken facial bones. She has three cracked ribs and a nasty bump on the back of her head. Her face and ribs are bruised, likely from being kicked. All things considered, she's in okay shape."

"Jesus Christ," I mutter, rubbing my forehead.

Clay adds, "She's still unconscious and we will continue to monitor her until she wakes up."

Avery is frozen beside me. Rapidly blinking as she process his words. "Will…will she be okay?" she stammers.

"Until she regains consciousness, we won't know about her mental state but physically, yes, she will recover from these injures."

Avery nods her head and then falls into a chair. Looking up to Clay she asks, "Can I see her?"

Clay nods his head. "Of course. Come with me. Flynn, technically, you cannot see her."

Nodding my head, I say, "No, I understand." I turn to Avery. "You go see your sister, and I'll see about getting her transferred to a room upstairs."

She stands up, wraps her arms around me, and kisses me. There's something different about the kiss. There's no feeling or emotion that there normally is when we kiss. I put it down the to stress of what's happened with her sister. I watch as she follows Clay but something is niggling at me. Turning to Cooper and Devon, I fill them in on the recent issues with Baylor.

Wrapping up with the officers, I head back into the ER and stop at the nurses' station and arrange a room for Baylor. Five minutes later, they tell me there's a bed on four for Baylor and she'll be moved up in a few moments. Offering to tell Avery, I make my way to the cubicle Baylor is currently in.

Stopping outside I hear her say. "Please wake up. I'm so sorry, twinsie. Please wake up for me."

Hearing her words, I smile when I realize that even though they are going through a rough patch right now, she still cares for her sister and that only makes me love her more.

AVERY

My body hurts.

My head aches.

Everything is fuzzy.

My eyes are heavy. I'm trying to open them but they refuse to move.

My body feels light, like I'm floating.

There's an incessant beeping that's grating through my brain. *Make it stop.*

Then I hear it, I hear him, Flynn, he's here but what he says confuses me.

"Ave lass, she'll be fine."

I'm not fine, I yell in my head.

Flynn, please help me. I plead, but he can't hear me. No one can hear me.

It's just me and my thoughts.

The beeping becomes louder and erratic.

There's a commotion around me, I can feel it happening but my eyes won't open for me to see. A warmth spreads over my body and I drift off into the blackness again.

I'm awake, again, and like before, everything is fuzzy.

My eyes still won't open.

My head now has a dull ache.

My body still hurts but not as much as before.

My throat is as dry as the Sahara and I need to pee really badly, then I realize I have a catheter in and reluctantly, I empty my bladder. *Eeeeew*, I think to myself as the 'Ahhhhhhhh' feeling of when you are peeing washes over me.

Laughing within my head, I try and open my eyes but like last time, my lids are heavy and weighted down. With all my might, I concentrate and my eyes flicker open. Blinking a few times, the room comes into focus. I'm in a hospital bed, huh? Confusion wraps around me.

"Avie," Bay says, leaning her head down, she grips my hand in hers and squeezes tightly. "I'm sorry you got caught up in this." I'm confused as to what she's saying. She grips my hand tighter but my lids start to droop. My body feels heavy, I can't keep them open. *No, Avery, stay awake*, I plead with myself, but the darkness wins and I doze off back into the black abyss.

I'm awake and just like the previous times, I will my eyes to open but they refuse to budge. Someone is holding my hand tightly, their grip is strong and comforting. There's a sound, I think it's a door opening. The grip on my hand disappears and I hear footsteps.

"Flynn, baby, what are you doing back here?"

What the hell?

"Just checking on my girl."

Flynn, I shout in my head. That's not me. Bay's doing it again. Flynn, I shout in my head over and over, my voice hoarse from screaming at him.

My eyes flit open and it looks like my sister and boyfriend just kissed.

My heart rate spikes. My heart is rapidly beating within my chest, it hurts seeing my sister kiss him. It's beating faster and faster. The beeping is getting louder and louder. Panic is building within me.

I try to speak but I can't. My voice won't work, I'm willing myself to speak but my body and mouth don't want to cooperate.

Flynn steps around her—me—and races to my side, he'll be in doctor mode right now, it calms me that he's on my case. My heart rate slows down. My body relaxes. I try to speak but again, nothing comes out. My eyes are on his, I'm pleading with him to look at me, but he's focused on the monitors attached to me. The monitor starts to rapidly and loudly beep and I scream inside my head for him to look at me.

Flynn! Flynn! Flynn! I scream over and over.

The door flies open and a nurse comes racing in. I beg and plead for her to look at me too but she and Flynn are chatting. Finally they turn to me but just as they do, my eyes close again. *Damn it,* neither of them saw me.

A warm feeling envelops my body from head to toe and once again I drift off into the darkness.

32
FLYNN

I'm worried about Avery. She seems on edge and not just because her sister is in the hospital. She seems different but then again, I've never been with someone when a loved one is in the hospital. The doctor in me has always been reserved and watching from the outside, but this time, I'm a part of the inner circle and I don't like it much. I definitely prefer to be on the other side of things.

Avery's eyes keep darting around everywhere. I guess she keeps expecting the persons responsible for this attack to return. When I realise that's why, I stop overreacting.

Baylor woke for a few moments just before. Avery froze but as quickly as she woke, she drifted off again. I guess her body needs time to heal. She's been through a lot. She sure is one tough cookie, but then again, she is Ave's twin, so they must be alike in that aspect. Leaving her with Baylor,

I step out and walk toward the nurses' station. Avery needs someone to lean on so I call the one person I know she'd want here, Cressida.

Dialing her number, which I got from Preston, she picks up on the second ring. "Hey, this is Cress."

"Cressida, it's Flynn."

"Hey, Doc, and I've told you to call me Cress."

"Okay. Hi, Cress, it's Flynn."

"Much better," she teases, and I find myself grinning. "To what do I owe the pleasure of this call?"

"It's Avery—"

"What's wrong?" Her voice increases an octave when she says this.

"We are at Western General. Bay is here."

"Ohh shit. I'll get Mom to watch Lexi. Be there soon."

She hangs up and I let out a sigh. Turning around, I see Preston walking toward me. "Any change?" he asks.

Shaking my head, I reply, "Not really. She woke for a bit but was agitated so they sedated her again."

"Shit."

"Yeah. I just called Cress, she's on her way." His face lights up when I mention her name. "Thanks for her number by the way."

Before I can probe him regarding Ave's best friend, his pager beeps and saves him from my interrogation...for now. He looks at it. "Gotta run. Keep me posted."

Nodding, I say, "Will do."

Aimlessly, I wander the hospital. This not being involved in the care of a patient is hard. I want to be there for Ave, but right now she's so lost in her head and worried about Baylor. Giving her time with her sister is the best for now, so I head own to the cafeteria.

Grabbing a coffee, I take a seat and mindlessly drink it. With the first sip, I scrunch my face up; I totally should have gone to the doctors' lounge and used the machine there, or better yet, to the shop across the road. My phone beeps with a text.

CRESS: *Just parked. Meet me in the ER.*
FLYNN: ***thumbs up emoji***

Grinning as I hit send because I know she hates emojis, Ave told me one day when they were texting back and forth. I thought Preston and I texting in gifs was bad, but if there was a team Olympic sport for texting, Cress and Avery would be the world champions.

Standing up, I pocket my phone, dump my coffee—if you could call it that—in the trash, and make my way back to the ER to meet Cress. She must be a speed walker because when I enter the waiting room, she's already here. She races over to me. "Flynn," she shouts. "How's our girl?"

"I don't know. She seems off. Doesn't seem herself."

"That's understandable."

"Yeah, I get that, but I don't know. I can't put my finger on it. I'm hoping you being here will put her at ease and pull her out of her funk."

"If I know Avery, she'll be putting on a brave front but on the inside, she'll be screaming and falling apart. She and Bay may not be in the best place right now but at the end of the day, Bay is her sister, and family means everything to Avery."

Nodding my head I agree with her. Avery is always there when you need her, and for her family. "Let's go then."

Cress and I head down the corridor and make our way up to Baylor's room. We step into the room and Cress immediately envelops Avery in a hug. "Ohh, Ave, I'm so sorry. Do you know why this happened?"

She shakes her head no, closes her eyes, and lets Cress comfort her but she seems stiff. Her face is ashen with worry. Stepping over to them, I wrap my arms around her from behind and kiss the side of her head. She lifts her arms and rubs her palms up my arms. Sighing deeply, she melts into me. *This is more like it,* I think to myself, *this is the Avery I know and love.* It's all starting to work out, that is until I look over at Cress, she looks concerned.

"Ummm," Cress says from where she's standing. "Flynn, can you get Ave some water, she looks parched and dehydrated."

Nodding, I whisper, "Be right back." Kissing the side of her head, I step out into the hall and stop when I see Preston hovering outside Baylor's room.

"Did I see Cress?" His eyes lighting up when he says her name. "She got here quickly."

"Yeah, she did. That woman can fly or something. She's really worried about Baylor but at the same time, she's mothering Avery, sending me to get her water."

"Well, she is a great mom. That instinct carries over in everything she does. How's Avery doing now?"

"Still the same. Still out of sorts."

"Can you blame her? Her sister was attacked outside their apartment. Any news from the police yet?"

"None yet. Until Bay regains consciousness, we won't know anything further."

From behind the door, I just exited I hear yelling. Preston and I eye each other and then we race over and open the door. Stepping into the room, I'm not prepared for what I hear.

AVERY

I'M FLOATING, WELL, IT FEELS LIKE I'M FLOATING. MY BODY IS LIGHT YET HEAVY at the same time. There are raised voices nearby. I can't quite make out who they are, this fog in my head is making everything fuzzy and confusing. Add in the ache all over my body, and I can't make much sense of anything right now.

Fluttering my eyes, they open briefly before drooping closed again, but this time they don't feel like lead. I will them open and this time success, I blink rapidly. The room is blurry but it's starting to come into focus. My throat is dry and scratchy and when I try to speak, nothing comes out.

The fog clears and now everything is bright and my hearing is back, I don't understand what they are saying, it's like they are speaking a foreign language right now. I think it's Cress and she's angry, like momma bear angry. Then her words finally register. They play on repeat over and over in my head, "You're pretending to be her."

"Am not," someone who sounds like Baylor scoffs in reply.

"Please, you lying bitch." Yep, that's Cress. "The person lying in that bed is Avery Evans. Standing before me is bitchy Baylor Evans."

She's pretending to be me? Why? I'm confused right now.

"Baylor, why?" I scream but it's my mind because my eyes droop closed and once again, I begin to drift away from reality. *No! No! No!* I plead with my body but once again, it wins.

This time rather than drifting into darkness, it's gray and hazy and I feel like I'm floating.

You're pretending to be her. Am not.

You're pretending to be her. Am not.

You're pretending to be her. Am not.

This repeats over and over in my mind. What the fuck, Baylor? I'm so confused right now, surely what I'm hearing isn't what's happening. Panic begins to fester and in my mind I shout, *She's not me* over and over.

I'm pleading, *she's not me.*

My mind is crying. Pleading. Begging.

She's not me.

She's not me.

She's not me.

I keep chanting this as I will my eyes to open.

I will myself to speak.

I will myself to move, even a fraction, but my body won't cooperate. Anything, I just want my body to do something, but all I can do is lie here and listen to them bicker and argue.

"You are not her," Cress scoffs.

"Yes, I am!" Baylor yells back.

She's not me.

She's not me.

She's not me.

She's not me.

Come on body, do something.

I shout over and over in my mind.

She's not me.

She's not me.

She's not me.

She's not me.

Please body, do something. Anything. Please.

The door opens and Flynn snarls, "Enough!"

He's here, I think to myself. The atmosphere in the room freezes when he speaks. My eyes flicker open but no one is paying attention to me. Rage is enveloping the room and I'm forgotten about.

Please Flynn, look at me, I beg. Hoping he knows, hoping he feels my presence. Hoping our love is enough for him to see through her lies and deceit.

Flynn is talking.

The girls are yelling.

The voices begin to fade away and the last memory I have before I drift into the darkness is Flynn fighting for me.

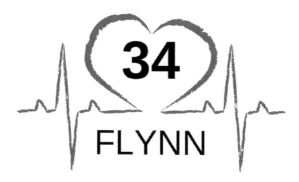

34
FLYNN

I'm looking between Cress and Avery/Baylor/whomever arguing like children. My mind is racing to process what's playing out right now. My eyes drop to the person in the bed and then flick back to the doppelgänger standing next to me. I'm so confused , I don't know what's the truth or who to believe.

"You are not her," Cress scoffs, stepping toward Avery/Baylor, poking her in the chest.

My eyes look back and forth between the two of them as they continue to throw barbs at one another.

"Yes, I am!" Baylor/Avery yells back.

"You are not Avery Evans, I bet my life on it." Cress points at Baylor/Avery and she smacks her hand viciously away.

I've had it and I explode. "Enough!" I yell, they both jump at the loudness of my voice. Even I'm surprised at the forcefulness behind it. "Just stop it," I plead. "Whoever is in this bed needs rest. You two fighting like this isn't going to help." I shake my head and stare at the body lying in the bed. "Regardless of who this is," pointing to the bed, I go on, "you both need to show some respect. She was attacked, she doesn't need this in her recovery."

"Yeah, Cressida," Avery scoffs, and with that one comment, I start believing Cress that Baylor is parading around as Avery right now.

Stepping over to Avery/Baylor, Cress, reaches out and stops to me. "Flynn, that there Baylor Evans." I stare at her, then look to Avery/Baylor. I'm so fucking confused right now. "Flynn, the person in that bed is Avery. My best friend. Your girlfriend. I know it without an ounce of doubt." She pauses. "Flynn, I swear to you on my life. On Lexi's life, the person in that bed is Avery."

"Prove it," Baylor/Avery snarls, just as the door to the room slams open, hitting the wall with a thud. Security is here, probably from the yelling and commotion echoing out in the corridor.

"With pleasure," Cress snaps. "Yesterday morning, Avery and I got tattoos." My eyes scrunch in confusion, I knew they had brunch but this I did not know. Cress grabs the hem of her shirt and lifts it up. On her left hip is what looks like Lexi's handwriting, spelling out her name within a pink and blue inkblot. "I got this yesterday. Avery, the real Avery, got one on her wrist."

The woman beside me quickly hides her arms behind her back and her face drains of all color.

"Is this true?" I hesitantly ask, my voice laced with confusion and hurt.

"Flynn, babe, she's lying," Baylor/Avery whines.

"Show me your wrist!" I demand, my voice a few confused octaves higher than usual.

"No, I don't have to prove anything. I'm Avery. I'm your girlfriend. Flynn, please…" she pleads, but I don't believe her this time.

"Uhh, yeah, you do," Cress says, stepping toward Baylor but Preston, who I've just noticed is here, wraps his arms around her and pulls her back into him. He whispers something into her ear and she instantly deflates.

Walking to the bed, I pull back the blanket and lift Baylor/Avery's arm up. Sure enough, on her left wrist is a fresh tattoo. Holding Avery's hand, I squeeze and kiss her knuckles. Then the most amazing thing happens, her eyes flicker open and this time, after blinking rapidly, they stay open and focus on me. I'd recognize those gorgeous green orbs anywhere. When she realizes it's me, she smiles and it lights up her pale bruised face. "It's okay, lass, I'm here," I say, kissing her knuckles repeatedly. Relief floods through my body that she's regained consciousness.

"What's...what's going on?" she asks, her voice raspy and dry sounding.

"What do you remember?" I ask, doctor me takes over even though I want to wrap my arms around her and hug her dearly.

"It's all hazy." She pauses and thinks. "There were two men and then," a tear escapes, "one of them zapped me and then...and then..." She's a sobbing mess now and can't talk. Sitting on the bed, I lie down next to her and pull her into my arms. Her body is shaking. She flinches at my touch.

"I'm sorry, lass." Gently I place a kiss on her temple.

She nods. "I was so scared." She burrows into my chest and blubbers.

"Shhhh, you're safe now, lass. I won't let anything else happen to you," I say, running my fingers gently though her locks. "No one will hurt you again."

Turning my head, I look to Baylor, her face is ashen with fear and shock at being caught. Avery lifts her head from my chest and looks to her sister. "Why, Bay, why?" Avery sadly asks, her voice broken.

"I'm so sorry, Avie," Baylor says, stepping to the bed she reaches across me, offering her hand to her sister. In my arms Avery tenses, she hesitates to take her sister's hand.

The room falls quiet, until Cress breaks the silence. "Are you shitting us right now, Bay. Sorry, really? That's all you've got?" Cress scoffs, her disdain for Baylor shining brightly at this moment. "You better start talking now, bitch, and don't even think about lying to us."

"Shut it, Cressida," Baylor snaps, "No one asked for your opinion. No one wants you here. Go home to your bastard child. You aren't needed here."

Cress lunges for Bay but Preston pulls her back and stops her.

"That's enough!" I roar, jumping out of the bed I step to Baylor. I'm fuming right now. She freezes at my words and stares blankly at me. "Preston, can you please ask the officers to come into Avery's room? They need to speak to Baylor here."

"Sure, no worries," he says. "Glad you're awake, Avery." He turns to Cress. "Come on, Cress."

She rolls her eyes at him but when he stares her down, she relents. "Fine." Walking to the bed, she reaches out and squeezes Ave's hands. "I'll be right outside. I'm so mad at you right now, but I'm also glad you're okay." She bends down and kisses her on the cheek. She shoots a glare at Baylor and turns to face Preston. He places his hand low on her back and guides a reluctant Cress out of the room with him. The two of them walking precariously close together.

After the door closes, I look to Baylor sitting in the corner. "Baylor, you need to start talking and you need to tell us the truth. Do not think about leaving anything out or lying." She huffs, crosses her arms over her chest, and continues to sulk like a petulant child.

Avery and I look at one another. She winks at me and flinches as she does. I wink and she grins back at me. Taking a seat next to her, I lean over and kiss on her forehead, I whisper, "I'm so glad you're okay. I love you."

"Thanks. I love you too." Her gaze drifts over to Baylor. "Flynn, can you please leave me with my sister for a moment?"

"I'm not leaving you alone with her. She pretended to be you. Hell, she's probably the one who did this and she's blaming it on two innocent guys."

"Fuck you, Flynn," Baylor angrily shouts at me. "I'd never hurt my sister like that. Never."

"Not physically you wouldn't, but you did pretend to be her on several occasions. I don't trust you, the only reason I haven't kicked you out is because I want answers."

Avery cups my cheek in her palm. "Please, Flynn? I'll be fine. Bay won't hurt me."

"I don't like this but okay." I place another kiss on her forehead. "I'll be right outside this door."

Walking away from her is harder than I expected. Stepping into the hall, Cress and Preston walk over to me, his arm around her waist. "Everything all right?" Preston asks.

"Yeah. Ave wants to speak to Baylor."

"And you left her alone with that psycho bitch? I don't trust her," Cress says through gritted teeth. "One word and I'll take her skanky ho ass down."

"You've got a live one there, dude," I say, then they step apart and pretend like nothing is going on between them.

"Flynn, are you sure it's okay to leave them alone together?" Cress asks me again

Nodding my head, "Yeah, they'll be fine. I trust that Ave can handle her sister."

Cress nods and agrees. "If anyone can handle Bay, it's Avery. Look, I'm going to head to her place and grab a few things for her, I'll be back soon."

"Thanks, Cress."

My gaze drifts to the door that I just exited, and I hope with everything I have, I didn't just make a mistake leaving Ave alone with Baylor.

35

AVERY

The door closes behind Flynn and before the door clicks shut I turn to Bay, and for the first time ever, I let loose on her. "Baylor Martine Evans, you are going to be straight with me and you are not going to lie." She tries to interrupt me, but I raise my hand and glare. She must sense that I'm more than pissed because she closes her mouth and stares at me. "For months now, you have not been yourself. You have turned into a big meanie head twatwaffle." This causes her lip to lift, mine too if I'm honest. "You have been horrible, absolutely horrible, to me and I want to know why?"

"Why what?" she snaps, crossing her arms defensively, like she always does when she knows she's in the wrong but doesn't want to admit it. She stares out the window at the darkening evening sky. I stare over at my sister and notice her shoulders are tight and high, she's hiding something. It frustrates me that she won't talk to me. Even though we're fighting right now, we've always talked to each other, and her not talking to me right now hurts more than the things she's done recently. "Why, Bay, why?" I plead again, but she continues to stare out the window. "Really, Bay, you're just going to ignore me?" Slapping my hand on the bed, I scoff in frustration when the silence becomes deafening. "What the fuck is going on, Bay?" I shout. Her head snaps to me and I just know the next thing out of her mouth will be more lies. Raising my hand, I stop her before she begins, "And don't you dare say nothing. Bay, you've been on a downward spiral for weeks now. You've become a horrible human being, I want my twinsie back. Hell, you pretended to be me—"

"We've done it before," she snaps.

"We were kids, Bay, AND if I remember correctly, Mom and Dad generally busted us." She eyes me. "Okay, they didn't always bust us, but we were kids. We did it for fun. This time, you tried to seduce my boyfriend AND when I was attacked, you pretended to be me." Pausing, I take a deep breath. I'm absolutely exhausted but I want the truth from her. "Please, Bay," I plead, "please talk to me."

She ignores me and I start to think she'll never open up and then she turns to face me; she lifts her gaze to mine and my heart breaks for my sister. Her eyes are full of despair and brimming with tears. She bites her lip worriedly. "Avie, I'm in trouble, big trouble and I don't know how to get out."

"Maybe I can help get you out. Please, Bay, just talk to me."

She shakes her head. "No, Avie, no one can. I...I've...I got mixed up with these people and I started dealing for them." My eyes pop wide open at this revelation, my sister is a drug dealer. *What the hell?*

"Are you using?"

She vehemently shakes her head. "Nope. Never, you know I'd never touch them."

"But you'll sell them."

She sadly nods her head. "The high of doing a deal is exhilarating. It's the best, most euphoric feeling in the world. I became addicted to the high of doing deals. I'd never felt power, or euphoria like this before. I knew it was wrong..." *There's the Bay I know and love,* I think to myself. "...but I just couldn't stop, and then I got in way over my head. Kye—"

"That name seems familiar."

"He was another dealer and we became close. When he tried to get out..." She drifts off but I can guess what she's alluding to.

"He was killed," I answer for her. She sadly nods her head, a lone tear falls down her cheek, which she quickly wipes away.

"Ave, all this..." She flicks her hand around at me. "This happened," she sniffles, "because of me. You're in here because they thought you were me. This is all my fault." She drops to her knees and cries. She shuffles toward the bed and rests her head on the mattress and continues to cry. I sit here and watch my sister falls apart. The grief of what happened to me and losing her friend, Kye, is crushing her right now. And seeing her like this, it's crushing me too.

She lifts her head and looks at me. "I'm sorry, Avie," she sobs, she reaches out and squeezes my hands. "I'm so so sorry." Her body shudders as she lets it all out.

"Ohh, Bay," I say. Trying to sit up so I can console her, I flinch in pain. "Arrrgh," I moan, holding my ribs.

Bays head snaps up and when she sees me holding my side, she begins to cry again, harder this time. "Ohh, Avie, I'm so so sorry. Please don't hate me. I was so scared when I came home and saw what was happening. I didn't want them to hurt me too. I didn't know what to do. I panicked and pretended to be you to save my ass, but then it kinda spiraled. I was confused. I was scared. I was emotional. Once we got to the hospital, I kept up the facade. I don't know why I did that. Please forgive me."

"Bay, come here." I beckon her to me with my fingers. She takes my hand and sits on the edge of my bed. "I get why you pretended to be me while at the apartment, but I don't get why you did it here? Or why you pretended with Flynn the other week. I don't understand that."

"I don't know why I kept it up once we got here, but it was nice to feel wanted again. I'd pushed you away and after losing Kye, I was all alone and suddenly there were people everywhere and I was hugged, and I liked that. Had you not got a tattoo, totally badass by the way, I would have eventually been found out when you woke but for those few hours, it was nice being you. You really do have a great life and boyfriend."

"You can have it too, you just need to make a few changes. What about the other week when you went to Flynn's and pretended to be me? That wasn't to save your ass, that was to hurt me."

"I was in deep at that stage. I was hoping, if I split you and your Irish hottie up, you'd hide at home and be safe. I pretended to be you to save you."

"That was a seriously dumb plan."

She shrugs. "Hey, I'd popped a few pills beforehand. I thought it was a brilliant plan. I didn't really know what I was doing."

My eyes pop open at her pill use declaration but then I remember her saying she hadn't used. "You just told me you didn't do drugs."

"Not the hard stuff. Pills are fine."

Shaking my head, I'm so disappointed in her right now. "I just...Bay, why? Why? I don't understand. You're a smart girl but this is really dumb."

"I don't know," she spits, "I was sick of living in your shadow. You're the angel twin. Great job, sweet school teacher. Me? I'm the college dropout. Always fucking up. Jumping from one shit job to the next. When this fell into my lap and it was something I was good at. I felt amazing for the first time in a long time."

"You're proud 'cause you're a drug dealer?"

"Never said I was perfect." She sighs deeply, "What am I going to do?"

"Tell the truth for starters. When the officers come back, you will tell them everything and suffer the consequences. It's time to grow up, Baylor Martine Evans."

"Wow, you used my full name again, twice in one day," she jokes and then swallows deeply. She looks at me. "I'm scared, Avie."

"And you should be, Bay." Pausing, I take a deep breath. "But I'll be here for you."

"Why?"

"You're my twin. I'd do anything for you." Reaching out I squeeze her hand and smile.

"You know if the shoe was on the other foot, I'd probably leave you at the mercy of the dealers, right?"

A laugh escapes me. "No, you wouldn't. You play tough, but underneath it all, you're just as sweet as me."

"It's a twin thing," we say in unison, and we both smirk at one another.

She squeezes my hand. "I really am sorry, Avie."

"I know."

There's a knock at the door and Flynn steps in with another doctor. "Ave lass, this is Clay, he just needs to check you over." He pauses and looks awkwardly at Baylor. "And, Baylor, the officers are outside wanting to speak to you."

She freezes next to me. "You can do this," I say, as I squeeze her hand reassuringly. She shocks me by standing up, leaning over, and hugging me.

"I love you, Avie," she sadly whispers.

"I love you too, BayBay," I say, as I hug her tightly back, using the childhood nickname I had for her. She laughs into my neck and holds me tighter; she's crushing me, and it kind of hurts but right now, she needs this. Pulling back, she looks to Flynn. "Let's do this," she says and I watch as my twin, for the first time in her life, faces up to her actions. I could not be more prouder of her, than I am at this moment.

My room is empty and the silence is nice. Lying back down, I stare at the ceiling and go over all that Bay told me. Sadness envelops me and I start to berate myself. I knew something was up, but I was so absorbed in my own life I didn't help her. I need to apologize to her next time I see her for not being there for her. Had I been, I don't think she'd be in the mess she is right now.

A few minutes later, Flynn walks back in and sits on the edge of my bed. "You okay?"

Staring up at the man I've fallen for, I nod. "As long I have you, I will be."

"I'm not going anywhere." He leans down and places his lips against mine, but our loving moment is interrupted when Marvin comes barging in. "Where is she? And whose ass do I need to kick?" He pauses and looks to me. "Ohh, baby girl. What did they do to you? And why are there two of you?"

"Marvin," I say, happy to see my friend.

He walks over and takes a seat beside me. He looks me over from head to toe again. Reaching up, he cups my cheek, "What happened, baby girl?"

"It's a long story but I promise you, I'm fine."

"Okay, I trust you. But why am I seeing two of you? Did the quacks give me too much and I'm tripping right now?"

A laugh escapes me. "No, you're not tripping. That's my twin sister, Baylor. She's in trouble but we are going to fix it."

"Really?" Flynn questions, his voice laced with shock and apprehension.

"Yep. I'll fill you in later."

"Why do I always miss out on all the good stuff?" Marvin whines, but before I can reply, a nurse steps in, pauses, and crosses her arms.

At the same time, Marvin says, "Ohh oh, I'm in trouble."

And I say, "Ohh oh, you're in trouble." He and I both laugh, garnering ourselves an angry glare from the nurse.

"Marvin Marshall, you are going to be the death of me."

"You love me," he replies.

We all laugh at his candor. And if I'm honest, seeing him just now instantly relaxes me. I hope when I get to his age, I'm still this spritely. He says goodbye to me and promises to visit again tomorrow; shocking us all, he asks the nurse if it's okay.

Placing a kiss on my cheek, he and the nurse shuffle out and I watch as he exits. No sooner does the door close, it swings open and in walks Clay; I hadn't even noticed he had left. "Okay, Kelly," he points toward Flynn, "you need to get out so I can check on my patient."

Flynn nods his head, and I watch as the man I love leaves my hospital room, and I just know that everything from here on out will be smooth sailing.

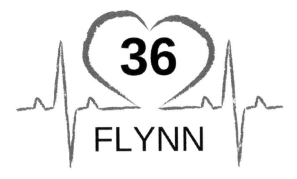

FLYNN

W<small>HILE</small> I'<small>M WAITING,</small> I <small>LEAN AGAINST THE WALL BY</small> A<small>VERY'S ROOM.</small> I'<small>M SO</small> relieved she's okay. When it hit me it was her in the bed and not Baylor, I thought I was going to die. Seeing the woman I love unconscious is not anything I want to ever go through again. Someone stops next to me and I look up to see Baylor.

"Flynn—"

"No. I don't have anything to say to you."

"That's fair."

We stand here staring at one another. "Actually, I do have one question. Why? Why would you do that to your sister? Your flesh and blood?"

She shocks me when she starts to cry. Shaking her head from side to side, she wipes at the avalanche of tears. "I'm sorry." She blubbers, "Avie knows everything and her forgiveness is all I care about, but I would like to be civil with you, for her. And in order to do that, I need to apologize to you."

"I'm listening." Crossing my arms, I lean back against the wall and wait. She doesn't speak and when I look to her, she's looking at her feet. "Baylor," she looks up at me and I see remorse written all over her face.

"Flynn, I'm so sorry I deceived you the way that I did. I didn't mean to let it go on as long as I did. When I stepped out of the elevator and saw those two guys with Avie, I panicked. Everything happened so fast and then it just snowballed from there. I wanted to come clean so many times over the last few hours but I'm scared."

"Scared of what?"

"Them coming back."

"What did the police say?"

"Not much. I hope when I go and see them to give my formal statement, that they'll have more." She steps to me and places her hand on my forearm and squeezes, for a small chick, she's mighty strong. "You need to keep her safe."

"With my life." And I mean that, I would lay my life down to save Avery, in a heartbeat.

"Thank you." She swallows deeply and removes her hand. She brushes her hair behind her ear and it reminds me so much of Ave. "You know, you really are the perfect person for Avie. You are the complete opposite to her, but they say opposites attract. You've brought out a side to my sister that I didn't know existed. I kinda like her sassy, strong side. You two are clearly attracted to one another. You can feel the love radiating from you both when you're together, and I don't think I've ever seen Avie this happy before." She pauses, and sighs. "With my recent antics, I'm glad she has you by her side."

"Even though you tried to break us up."

"Semantics but, Flynn," we stare at each other and an understanding passes between us. "You hurt her and I will fucking kill you."

With that, she turns around and walks away from me. Maybe I've misjudged Baylor, I think she's just lost. With Ave and me on her side, we'll help her get back on the right track.

Clay exits Avery's room. "All good?"

"You know I can't tell you anything." I eyeball him. "Fine, but if I get fired I'm taking you down with me."

"Fine, but she's going to be my fiancée one day so…"

"Really?"

"Yep, now, how is she?"

"She's fine, considering. No lasting damage, but she will be sore for the next few days. I'm going to keep her in for another night and she can go home tomorrow."

"Can't I take her home and watch over her? I am a doctor, you know."

"No, you can't. And don't even think about playing the doctor card."

"Fine," I relent. Offering my hand, he takes it and shakes. "Thanks, man, appreciate you taking such good care of my girl."

"Never thought I'd see the day when Flynn Kelly was smitten with a woman."

"You've met her, it's hard to not fall for her."

"I agree…just don't tell my wife that."

We both laugh. He walks down the corridor and I head back into Ave's room. Pushing the door open, the room is dark, except for the night light above her bed. Avery's eyes are closed. I take a moment to look at her. Even with a messed-up face, she really is the most beautiful woman in the world.

"Stop staring at me, you creeper," she says with her eyes still closed.

"I'm just admiring your beauty."

"I think you need your eyes tested. I feel like shit and I'm pretty sure I look like a zombie right now."

"A sexy as fuck zombie," I say, as I step toward her. "And I love you just the way you are."

"Did you just Bruno Mars me?"

"Guess I did, but it's the truth. Avery, you are the most stunning woman in the world, zombie look included, and I'm the luckiest man alive to have you as my girlfriend."

"You say the sweetest things, Flynn Kelly, now come over here so I can kiss you."

"You had me at kiss."

Bending down, I gently grip her jaw in my fingers and press my lips to hers. It's a soft and gentle kiss, but it's the most perfect kiss ever in the history of kisses. Against her lips I murmur, "I love you, Avery Evans."

"I love you too, Flynn Kelly." She pulls back, her eyes darken with desire. "Wanna quickie?"

A deep laugh breaks free, shaking my head I run my finger over her bottom lip. "Avery, I would love nothing more than to fuck you all night long, but not three hours ago you were unconscious. Your body needs rest." She pouts. "But I promise, as soon as you are one-hundred-percent, I will eat you, suck you, and fuck you repeatedly. All.Night.Long."

"You know, you said that to me in the alcove the night we met."

"I did not know this but I can unequivocally say, that was the best night of my life...it led me to you."

"I agree one-million-percent with that statement. Now get out of here, so I can sleep and heal because I can't wait to fuck you repeatedly, all night long."

"Fiend," I playfully reply.

"Takes one to know one."

After kissing her longer than necessary for a goodbye, I leave her and head home. I'm exhausted. The events of last night and today have caught up with me. Hopefully, it's all smooth sailing from here.

AVERY

"You okay? Do you need anything? Do you want me to call Flynn? What can I do?" She says all of this in one breath.

Shaking my head side to side. "No, I'm all good. What are you doing here?"

"I didn't want you to be alone so I came back. You looked so peaceful when I got here, I was going to climb in with you like we did in the past, but I wasn't sure if I'd be welcome." A tear breaks free. "Avie, I cannot express how sorry I am for what I've done recently."

Reaching out my hand, I flick my fingers at her. She jumps up and takes my hand in hers and sits next to me. "BayBay, you are my sister and I will always be here for you...even when you do stupid shit."

"You are the best sister ever."

"I know. Now you know what will make *you* the best sister?"

"What?" She wipes her nose on her shoulder sleeve and I shudder.

"That's gross, Bay."

"Whatevs. Now, what will get me into the best sister book?"

"Coffee."

"Huh?"

"Let's go to the cafeteria and get coffee."

"I'd like that."

Bay helps me slip my robe on—thank you Cress for bringing me a bag—and then she bends down to assist with my Birkenstocks. Once I'm dressed, as such, we link arms and head down to the cafeteria.

Since it's early, and we are the only ones here, we get our coffees quickly and take a seat. We each take a sip and spit it back into the cup. "Oh My God, that tastes—"

"Like shit...actually, it's worse than shit." We both laugh. "Ave, there's a Starbucks across the road, feel like a walk?"

Looking down at what I'm wearing, I hesitate but I really need coffee. "Fuck it. Sure, let's go."

Linking arms again, we head across the road and fifteen minutes later we each have a grande coffee in hand and contented looks on our faces. "Much better."

"Much."

We decide to head back to the hospital grounds, since I'm not really dressed for public viewing. I wave at Clay as we cross the road, he does a double take when he sees us. "Damn, I must be tired, I'm seeing two."

"Clay, this is my twin, Bay. Bay, this is Clay."

"We met," he growls.

"Nice to officially meet you," Bay offers. "I'm sorry about yesterday."

Before this awkward encounter can get any more awkward, Clay's pager goes off and he leaves us to race back to the hospital. I can feel Bay pulling away and retreating into herself. "Stop it, Bay."

"I'm not doing anything."

"Do I look dumb?" She goes to say something snarky and I bump her shoulder. "Don't let others' opinions or feelings affect you. Yes, you made mistakes but those who matter, as in me, are the only people's opinions you need to worry about. Now, get me back to my bed, I need to rest. This was a huge outing."

Bay nods and we continue our walk back to the hospital. A van comes screeching into the driveway. Just before we reach the doors, a man jumps out, shoves me to the ground, grabs Bay, and drags her into the vehicle, her kicking and screaming. She's fighting her assailant, but he's bigger and stronger. He throws her into the car, slams the door shut, climbs back in, and they drive off.

It all happens so quickly, I don't have a chance to call for help or do anything.

"Baylor!" I scream at the retreating van. Tears begin to well in my eyes. "Baylor!" I shout again but it's no use, the van is gone. Security rushes over to me and I look up at them. "My sister, they took my sister."

FLYNN

"FLYNN," SHE BLUBBERS

"Ave lass, what's wrong?"

"They…they took Bay," she cries, and the heartache in her voice crushes me.

"Who took Bay?"

"The guys. They finally got her. Flynn, they…they took her." She sniffs, "Flynn, I need you."

"I'm on my way."

"Thank you. Please hurry."

"I love you, Avery. And I'm sure Bay will be fine, if she's anything like you, which I suspect she might be, she'll be okay."

"I hope you're right, Flynn."

Me too. "I'll be there soon."

Hanging up, I quickly change and race to the hospital. When I arrive at

Western General, the place is swarming with police. An officer is looking over my credentials when I hear my name being yelled. Looking up I see a disheveled Avery running toward me. "Flynn," she wails as she throws herself at me. My arms wrap around her and she breaks down and cries into my neck.

"Shhhh," I whisper, "I'm here now."

She loosens her grip on me. "Flynn, they still haven't found her. They took BayBay."

"Lass, give them time. It's only been an hour."

"But—" Pressing my finger to her lips I shush her. "No buts, give them time. Now, let's get you back to your room. This won't be good for your recovery; you are still fragile yourself. You need to get strong so you're better when she gets back."

"But Bay needs me to be out looking for her."

"Ave lass, no. You can't go looking for her. Those guys have already attacked you once, I won't let them attack you again. Bay would want you to be safe."

"But I need to find her, Flynn. I need my twinsie back."

"She will be back before you know it. Now, back to bed. Let's go."

We walk inside and are immediately met with Marvin. "No need to call the popo, I was just in the nursery."

"If I thought that would work, I would call them but I'm pretty sure you'd evade them too," Helen says. "Can't wait until you are back at the home."

"You'll miss me," he teases.

"Yeah, like a hole in the head. What's going on here?" Helen questions.

"Ave's sister was taken."

"You okay, babycakes?" Marvin asks her, shoving me aside and wrapping her in a hug.

"When Bay is back I will be."

"How about I hang with you for a few hours...as long as that's okay with my keeper?"

"Do you promise to stay with Avery and not wander off?"

"Cross my heart, hope to die. Stick a needle in my eye."

"You leave her room and I might just do that. I'll come collect you just before lunch."

"Thank you, Helen," he says, his tone super cheeky. Helen shakes her head as she walks away. "Come on, let's get you into bed." He says this with a suggestive eyebrow shrug. Ave and I both laugh, but we follow him back to her room.

168 DL GALLIE

Avery does as she's told and climbs into bed. Marvin takes the chair by the window and I climb on to the bed with her.

"Young love, it's so nice to see," Marvin says. "Now, what are we gonna watch while we wait for your sister to be rescued?"

"Your choice," Ave says, her voice quiet. I can tell she's shrinking into her head again and just as I think that, her body shakes in my arms, she's crying again.

"Ohh, Avie," I say, this causes her to cry harder.

"Bay is the only one who...who calls me Avie," she blubbers; pushing her head into my shoulder, letting it all out.

"I'm so sorry, Ave."

"It's not your fault. It's those guys' fault." She lifts her head. "What if I don't get her back? I don't know how to exist without her."

"She'll be fine."

"Doc's right," Marvin agrees, "If she's half the woman you are, then those fools are in for a treat. She'll be back before lunch."

But Marvin wasn't right, it's now been three days since Baylor was taken and she's still yet to be found. It's like she disappeared off the face of the Earth. Avery is beside herself with worry right now, and I'm worried about her. If we don't find Bay soon, I don't know how Avery is going to cope.

AVERY

SHE'S BEEN GONE FOR FOUR DAYS NOW. NINETY-SIX HOURS AND THERE'S STILL no sign of my sister. I'm going out of my mind. I'm sick to death of hearing people say, "Everything will be fine" or "Bay is tough." I know she's tough, but my mind is racing right now. One minute I'm calm and think yes, she'll be home soon, and the next, I'm screaming and crying with fear that she's dead. I'm on an emotional roller coaster right now. Everyone is hovering around me like I'm going to fall apart at any second, I'm fine... ish, apart from wanting my sister back. I want some space. I just want to be left alone and with Flynn heading into work today, I might just get some peace. But noooo, I can't be trusted on my own so I agreed to go to the hospital with him. I'll hang with Marvin for the day.

I've been here for three hours and Marvin has kept me entertained, and my mind off Bay. He's just drifted off to sleep, so I take the opportunity to get some alone time. I head across the road to Starbucks since the coffee in the cafeteria here is toxic waste. With my coffee in hand, I'm walking back to the hospital when two men in suits approach me. "Avery Evans?"

Hesitantly, I really. "Yeeees. And you are?"

"I'm Agent Hall and this is my partner, Agent Oates." My eyes pop open at this, and I giggle. They both look at me in a 'yes we know our names are funny' way. They are talking but I'm not listening, I'm singing "I Can't Go for That (No Can Do)" by Hall & Oates to myself. It isn't until Hall, I think, says, "Ma'am, can you come with us, please?"

"Is this about my sister?"

"We aren't any liberty to discuss that here with you."

"Just tell me if she's okay."

A look passes between the agents. "Yes," one of them sternly answers. With that one word, I can finally breathe easily again. "Avery, if you come with us, we can tell you more."

"Can I let my boyfriend know what's happening?"

"No, not right now. Time is of the essence here, Ms. Evans."

"Fine, I'll come...but I'm texting him as soon as we leave."

"Fine."

"Actually, can you show me ID before I get in a car with you? Stranger danger and all that shit."

They both show me their identification, and much to their amazement, I quickly grab a snapshot of Hall's. Thank you, Cress, for teaching me the art of the quick sneaky pic. "For security," I say and I quickly send it to Flynn.

AVERY - *Going with Agents Hall and Oates, yes that's their names. It's about Bay. Call you soon **attach ID picture***

No sooner do I send the message and my phone starts to ring. I answer but before I can say anything, Flynn bellows down the line, "Are you fucking crazy going off with strangers?"

"They aren't strangers. They are agents, Hall and Oates, and they have information on Bay."

"You are making me fucking crazy."

"It's about Bay and I'll be fine. Besides, you have a pic of Hall's ID. If this was a setup, they would have taken me like they did Bay, rather than talk to me and ask me to come with them." Just as I say this, the police station comes into view. "Look, we've just arrived at the station, see I'm fine. I'll call you as soon as I'm done here."

"You better. Please be safe and remember I love you."

"I love you too."

Hanging up, I sigh. Suddenly I'm nervous. "Is Bay here?"

They ignore me and quietly we walk into the station. They take me into an interrogation room and when the door opens, my eyes well with tears. "BayBay," I blubber as I take her in. Her clothes are torn, her hair's a mess, and her face—her gorgeous face—is black and blue and swollen. Racing over to her, I wrap my arms around her and she returns the gesture.

Together we cry with relief at seeing one another. Pulling back, I gently grip her cheeks in mine. "Are you okay?"

She nods. "Yeah, I am."

"What happened?"

"Long story."

"Bay," I warn.

"I'll tell you, but first, I need you to sit and listen to what I have to say."

I sinking feeling develops in my stomach. I've never seen Bay like this before. "I'm not going to like this, am I?"

She shakes her head. "Probably not, but, Avery, I need to do this. I need to make amends for my actions." She swallows deeply. "I need to do this for Kye."

"Who is Kye, Bay?"

She sniffs. "He was 'the one' and because of my actions, he died. It should have been me but he protected me. I tried to walk away after that but I was in too deep. Way too deep." She licks her lips and looks at me. "Avie, this is my chance to put things right. This is my chance to make up for his death."

"I'm so proud of you, BayBay." And that's the honest truth. Last week, I was broken up and hurt over my sister but this week, I could not be prouder of her. This the Bay I know and love. She's taking charge and trying to put things right. "Okay, now, tell me the plan."

Taking a seat next to her, she tells me what's happened over the last four days. My sister is one tough chick, not many people would have survived what she went through. Then she tells me what's going to happen next; I'm a mix of unease and pride. For the next several hours, I'm brought up to speed on what's going to happen now. The more I'm told, the more I don't like it. To say I'm scared is the understatement of the century. I'm beyond frightened for my sister right now, but everyone assures me it will all work out and Bay will be safe.

I'm scared shitless with regards to what she's about to embark upon, but at the same time, I'm one extremely proud sister.

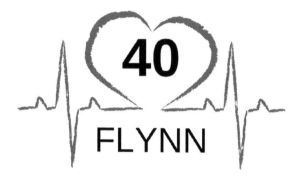

40

FLYNN

THE LAST FEW WEEKS HAVE BEEN CRAZY, MY LIFE FEELS LIKE SOMETHING FROM the movies. I've had identity swapping, mistaken identity, an attack on Avery, kidnapping, undercover work, but there's also been happiness, joy, and love. Avery and I are hopelessly in love and we are happier than ever. As much as she's putting on a brave face, I know she's worried about Bay. Bay going undercover was a shock but at the same time, it's not a surprise. She likes living on the wild side, and if I'm honest, I'm impressed with the turnabout in Avery's sister.

Life is simply perfect at the moment, and this weekend, I'm going to whisk my girl away for the dirty relaxing weekend we need and deserve. Looking up from the chart I'm finishing up, I see Helen walking toward me and smirk, clearly Marvin has gone AWOL; again. "Has our resident Houdini escaped again?"

She shakes her head and as she steps closer to me, I see devastation written all over her face. I know what she's about tell me isn't good news; so much for our perfect life right now. "No, but I wish he had." She swallows deeply. "Marvin passed about an hour ago."

Standing up, I walk over to Helen and wrap my arms around her. She hiccups a sob and breaks down in my arms. "I'm going to miss the old coot," she blubbers.

"I think we all will. The hospital just won't be the same without him here."

"I know," she sniffles and steps back, wiping the tears from under her eyes. Our moment is interrupted by a beautiful angelic voice that breaks the silence. "Hey, guys."

Helen and I both snap our heads toward Avery and without saying anything, her face drops. She knows. Her eyes well and she shakes her head from side to side as the tears break free. She drops to her knees and breaks down. "No, no, no. He can't be gone."

Helen squats down next to Ave. "Avery, honey, he's in a better place now. You know how much pain he was in these last few days."

"I know, but he's gone and I didn't get to say goodbye."

"Avery, he knew how much you cared. Since he met you, he changed. You gave him the best possible last few weeks anyone could have asked for. He loved you like a daughter."

"I know but..." She shakes her head sadly. "He wasn't just my friend, he was my family." She looks up at me and my heart breaks when I see the devastation on her face. "Flynn, Marvin's gone."

Dropping to my knees, I pull her into my chest. She lets out all her grief over the loss of her friend.

We have just returned to Avery's apartment after Marvin's funeral, today was tough, but it was also good for her, it allowed her to say her goodbyes to Marvin. As we were leaving, the funeral director gave me an envelope for Avery. I'm unsure as to when to give it to her. She's an emotional wreck right now. I'm glad that Bay and Cress are here for her. Bay can't be as much as she'd like, due to her predicament, but Ave is pushing everyone away at the moment.

Ave heads into her bedroom and I stand in the living room, unsure of what to do. Removing my suit jacket, the envelop falls out, just as Avery steps back into the room. She bends down, picks it up, and looks at it. Her eyes widen when she sees her name scrawled on the front.

"What's this?"

"The funeral director gave it to me to give to you."

"Who's it from?"

Shrugging my shoulders, I admit, "I don't know. You'll need to open it to find out."

She swallows deeply and stares at the envelope. "Will you stay with me while I do?"

"Of course I will. I'm here for you anytime you need me."

She sadly smiles before taking my hand and pulling me to the sofa. She sits down and I sit next to her. She slides her finger under the flap, tears it open, and pulls out the letter. She begins to read and tears well in her eyes.

MY DEAR AVERY,

YOU READING THIS MEANS I'M UP IN HEAVEN WITH MY HAREM OF ANGELS, RUNNING AMOK AND FINALLY LIVING PAIN FREE. YOU WERE THE LIGHT THAT KEPT ME GOING THESE LAST FEW MONTHS. YOUR FRIENDSHIP MEANT EVERYTHING TO ME. THANK YOU FOR KEEPING THIS OLD GEEZER SMILING IN MY LAST DAYS. PLEASE DON'T DWELL ON MY PASSING, LIVE FOR THE BOTH OF US. FOCUS ON FLYNN, NAME YOUR LITTLE BOY MARVIN, AFTER ME, AND KEEP THAT EVIL DOPPELGÄNGER SISTER OF YOURS IN LINE.

AVERY, YOU HAVE THE BIGGEST HEART AND I'M SO GLAD TO HAVE KNOWN YOU. IF I HAD A DAUGHTER, I HOPE SHE'D BE LIKE YOU. DON'T EVER LET ANYONE DULL YOUR SHINE, CONTINUE TO SPARKLE EACH AND EVERY DAY.

CHEERS,

MARVIN

"Ohh, Marvin," she says, wiping away her tears. She looks to me and sadly smiles. "He was the sweetest man. I'm going to miss him so much, Flynn."

Placing a kiss on her temple, I pull her into me. "He sure was. Will you be okay, lass?"

"Yeah, I will be," she says. "Can you take me to bed and snuggle with me? I just want to be held."

"Anything you need and I'll do it."

We walk into her room and strip out of our clothes. We climb under the covers and snuggle, her back to my front, just like she wanted. "Marvin wants us to name our son Marvin."

"Marvin Kelly, I like it."

"Marvin Evans has a good ring to it too."

"Dr. Evans, I like it."

She rolls over to face me. "You'd change your name for me?"

I nod my head. "Yep, whatever it takes to have you in my life is what I'll do."

"You continually amaze me, Flynn Kelly, but it will be me who changes my name, it's tradition."

"Your strength continues to astound me, and I thank the heavens every day for allowing me to meet and fall in love with you."

"And I love you too. Now make love to me, Flynn. Show me how much you really do love me."

And that's exactly what I do. For the rest of the afternoon and evening, Avery and I make love until we blissfully fall asleep wrapped in each other's arms.

41

AVERY

...six months later

AFTER THE INCIDENT OF MISTAKEN IDENTITY, ENDING UP IN HOSPITAL, BAY'S kidnapping, and the undercover sting thing, everything changed. The day Agents Hall and Oates—I still laugh at that—came to get me from the hospital, my world was turned upside down. After Baylor was rescued from B1 and B2—Bozo one and Bozo two—she was arrested for her part in the drug racket, but she offered to go undercover to help them bring down the biggest party drug operation in the state. Her offering this reduced her overall jail sentence. Had she not been arrested when she was twenty, her sentence could have wholly been suspended, but a dumb drunken night and a stolen garden gnome changed that for her. Luckily for Bay, B1 and B2 were killed when's she was rescued. They were high as kites and stood no chance against the team that was sent it. Their deaths, however, helped Bay in more ways than one. With no one to dispute her story, it played into the undercover setup and sting. Bay used them as her scapegoat with the drug leaders. They were impressed with her tenacity and she quickly worked her way into the inner ranks of the chain. Little did they know, she was gathering as much evidence as possible to bring them down.

The day it all went down, it made headline news. Bay and I hadn't spoken in a few days, so I was antsy and on edge. When it hit the news, and I knew she was safe; I could finally relax. The three months it took was nerve-wracking but with Flynn by my side, I was able to cope.

I'm so proud of my sister, but when it was all over, it was time for her to head to jail and serve out her twelve-month prison term. She's been inside for three months now and without her at the apartment, I'm lonely. I miss her like crazy, we've always been together—twin thing—so it's weird to not see her each and every day. I visit her every weekend, if Flynn isn't working, or sleeping, he comes with me since I'm generally at his place anyway. I spend most of my nights at his penthouse, basically we are unofficially living together.

Last weekend, when I went to visit Bay, Flynn had to work and it was just me. After a lengthy discussion, and a few raised voices, Bay and I decided to give up our apartment, as long as Flynn would officially let me move in.

That afternoon, I was excitedly awaiting him to get home from work. I baked to keep my mind occupied and I also cooked a lasagne big enough to feed the hospital. He stepped through the door and my excitement bubbled over. As usual, he went and had a shower to freshen up. I was a bundle of nerves while I waited so I opened a bottle of red, and I was on glass number two when he emerged, freshly showered and looking mighty sexy.

Handing him a glass, I top up mine and we head outside to watch the sunset from the patio. We are snuggling on the outdoor lounger, one of my favorite things to do. Looking up, at him, I take a deep breath and broach the moving in topic. "So, um, babe, today Baylor and I decided to give up our apartment."

His head snaps in my direction. "Okay, but where are you going to live?"

"Well, I was kinda sorta hoping you'd let me move in here…with you!"

He stares at me. Not saying a word. The silence is deafening. I start to think he doesn't like the idea of us officially living together when his lip lifts and he breaks into the biggest smile ever. "Does this mean that offi-cially you'd be waking up naked in my arms each and every morning?" Nodding my head, I open my mouth to agree, but he raises his hand and presses his finger to my lips to stop me. "So three hundred and sixty-five days of the year, you will be waking up naked in my arms?"

"Yep," I say letting the 'p' pop.

"Best.Fucking.Day.Ever," he declares.

He takes my glass from my hand and places both glasses on the deck, he then pulls me into his arms and presses his lips to mine. Then I'm flying through the air and I'm thrown over his shoulder. My head has the perfect view of his denim-clad ass as he stalks back inside. He takes me into the bedroom, strips me naked, and gently pushes me back. Falling to the mattress, I stare up at my sexy doctor boyfriend as he begins to strip off his clothes. I'm excited for what's about to transpire, but he shocks me when rather than fucking me, he climbs onto the bed next to me. He pulls me into his arms and we snuggle together naked. We drift off to sleep, wrapped in each other's embrace.

The next morning, I wake naked in his arms, just like Flynn predicted. Rolling to my side, I smile when I realize he's already awake. "Good morning," I huskily say, my voice still sleepy.

"I love waking up like this."

"Me too." Lifting my hand, I cup his cheek in my palm and run my finger along his jaw. The stubble tickling me.

"I love you, Avery Evans, and I cannot wait for this to be official official."

"Define official official?"

"Your stuff here. You redecorating this place to turn it from a drab bachelor pad penthouse to OUR love nest penthouse."

"Really? I can add a few feminine touches?"

He nods at me. "Yep, this will be your home too, Avery. I want you to be comfortable here."

"As long as I have you, that's all the matters."

He leans forward and presses a kiss to my lips and then FINALLY, I get lucky.

Sure it's crazy to be moving in together, considering I've only known Flynn for less than a year but when you know, you know. And it feels right, so we are taking the plunge and have decided to officially cohabitate together. Some say it's too soon—I'm looking at you, Cress—but we don't care what anyone else thinks. We are happy with our decision, and that's all that matters. Truth be told, from the moment my eyes landed on the sexy as sin Irish doctor at the Tavern, I started falling so this was inevitable.

…later that day

Flynn didn't waste any time and he rallied the troops and today is officially the day I move in with him. With Baylor incarcerated, it was up to me to move us out, but thankfully, with the help of Preston, Cress, Lexi, and Flynn it wasn't as daunting as I expected, packing up two people's lives. Bay and I had lived here for nearly seven years. We had accumulated a lot of crap in that time. Bay's stuff was placed in storage and my things were transferred to Flynn's, well I guess, our place.

Never in my wildest dreams did I think I'd be living in a penthouse apartment, or be hopelessly in love, but here I am doing both. I am irrevocably in love with Flynn Kelly, and today I moved in with him. Oh My God, I'm your cliché love song right now—cue sappy love song music—but I don't care. I'm the happiest I've been in a long time.

After a grueling day, Preston, Cress and Lexi have just left…together. I cannot wait to have drinks with Cress soon to grab all the gritty, sexy gossip on her and a certain pediatric doctor because there is definitely some, okay a lot, of sexual tension between the two of them. It's been going on for months now, but my best friend is playing coy. The fact he's amazing with Lexi confirms my suspicion that something is going on between them, AND Lexi is extremely friendly with him. It's like they already know one another, because it usually takes Lexi time to warm up to people, especially men due to her douche hat father, but she and Preston are buddies already.

Flynn has taken the last box down to the car and I stand in the now empty apartment. Looking around, I sadly smile. Baylor and I had some great times here over the last seven years. It was here that I got my acceptance letter to college, had my graduation party, celebrated my placement at Westside Elementary, AND it was the place where Flynn and I first confessed our love for one another.

Closing my eyes, a smile appears on my face when I feel Flynn's presence behind me. He wraps his arms around my waist and pulls me back into his chest. He nuzzles my ear and whispers, "I love you, Avery Evans, and I cannot wait to live with you."

Spinning in his arms, I drape mine over his shoulders and gaze into his sparking blue eyes. "I love you too, Dr. Kelly, now take me home and ravish me."

"Home, I like that."

"Yeah, me too...now let's go."

"With pleasure, Ms. Evans, with pleasure."

An hour later, we are standing in the kitchen by the island counter. Flynn is in a pair of denim jeans which sit low on his hips. I'm wearing my pale pink satin sleep shorts, with matching cami top, and my beige slouchy cardigan, as there is a chill in the air tonight.

Flynn opens a bottle of red and pours us each a glass. He hands one to me and when our fingers brush, a sizzling zing zaps through my body, causing me to shiver.

"You cold, Ave lass?"

Shaking my head, I smile at him. "No, I'm good."

"You are more than good, you look sexy as fuck in this." His eyes roam over me and my body temperature rises, causing me to shiver again. He takes my wine glass from me and before he places it next to his on the countertop, he takes a sip. Leaning forward, he nuzzles along my jaw. "Mmmmm, wine tastes so much better with a side of Avery."

He steps back, resting against the counter, and we stare at one another. The air around is pings with lust, desire, and everything in between. Picking up my glass, I take a sip, place it down, and pressing my lips against his for a quick kiss.

Pulling back, I stare at him and nod, "Personally, I think this wine is better with a side of Flynn."

"Agree to disagree?" he counters.

Stepping to Flynn, I cup his cheek in my palm. "Agree to disagree." I run my thumb along his chin and stare into his baby blues. His scruff is longer than usual and I wonder what it will feel like between my thighs. My cheeks heat at this dirty thought and I smirk.

"What are you smirking at?" Lifting my gaze to his, my cheeks darken further and he smiles back at me. "You little minx, you. Tell me what dirty thoughts you have?"

"Who says they are dirty?"

"You did. Your cheeks are currently dirty pink and your breathing in labored. Now, tell me?"

He rests one hand on my hips and the other on the countertop edge. Leaning back an inch, he stares intently at me. My insides quiver at the intensity of his gaze. Rubbing his cheek, I tell him what I was thinking.

"I like the way you think dirty, Avery. Now kiss me and I might make your thoughts a reality."

Closing my eyes, I lean in and press my lips ever so softly to his. Our kiss starts out soft and gentle, but it quickly turns heated. Without warning, I'm flying through the air and then I'm sitting on the edge of the countertop. Flynn quickly pulls down my sleep shorts and panties. His gaze flicks from my face to between my thighs. Spreading my legs wide, I raise my eyebrows seductively at him. His face widens in a sexy grin and he gently pushes me back so I'm lying on the countertop. He drops to his knees in front of me. With his eyes locked on mine, he kisses the inside of my leg and ever so slowly kisses up my thigh. I can feel the heat of his breath and I moan, he hasn't even kissed me where I want him and I'm already panting.

He kisses the top of my mound. "Mmmmmm, Flynn, please," I beg. I need more like I need my next breath.

"With pleasure," he growls before he licks from my taint to clit.

"Yes," I mewl, as he continues to devour me. The scruff on his face feels amazing, it heightens the pleasure coursing through me. Gripping his head in my hands, I press him farther into me. He attacks me with vigor and I'm loving every minute of it. He slips a finger inside and bends it, to hit that sweet spot that sets me off and suddenly, I'm screaming his name as I come all over his fingers and face.

He stands up to full height and gazes down at me. His face is covered in my juices, I lick my lips. Sitting up, I lean forward, grip his cheeks in my palms and press my lips to his. Since falling for Flynn, I've become a fan of kissing him after he goes down on me.

With my lips still pressed to his, I flip open his button, lower the fly, and push his jeans and briefs down his thighs. Wrapping my legs around his waist, I guide his cock toward my entrance and with a flick of his hips, he thrusts inside of me. Pistoning his hips back and forth, my body begins to tingle with orgasm number two.

"Let go," he murmurs against my lips.

It's all the prompting I need. I let the feelings envelop me and I crash over the edge for the second time tonight. Flynn soon follows, grunting through his release.

When he's finished, he rests his forehead against mine. We breathlessly stare at one another, completely sated and happy. He scoops me into his arms and walks us into the en suite bathroom, we shower and climb into bed together. Flynn lies on his back, and I snuggle into his side, throwing my leg over his. Looking up at the man who has become me world, I whisper, "I'm going to love living with you, Flynn Kelly."

"And I'm going to love living with you too, Avery Evans."

FLYNN

"All right, I'm off." She stops in front of me. "I'm so nervous."

"Why are you nervous?" Wrapping my arms around her waist, I gaze down into her sparkling green eyes.

"I'm scared I'll get there and they'll tell me it's an error and she's not coming home today."

"Bay is coming home today, tell that overactive imagination of yours to settle down."

"And you are one-hundred-perfect sure it's okay for her to stay here?"

"Of course, she's your sister. Will it suck to not be able to bend you over the island counter and fuck you when I want? Yes, but it's not forever. From what I know of your sister, she'll want her own place and independence before I get sick of her."

She smiles. "When did you get so wise?"

"I've always been wise, you're just noticing it now."

"Let me bow down to you then, ohh wise one." She steps back and bows down.

"Smart-ass." Looking at the clock, I tap her ass. "You better get going, otherwise, you'll be late."

"Okay, wish me luck."

"Good luck, not that you'll need it." *I'm the one who needs luck if I'm going to pull this off.* "Now go on, get, my other girlfriend is on her way over."

She playfully smack me in the chest. "Hardy, har-har." She kisses me on the lips and as she walks away, she looks over her shoulder. "Say hi to Ms. Palmer for me."

Shaking my head, I laugh and watch as my girlfriend, soon to be fiancée—I hope—exits the penthouse. When I hear the ding of the elevator, I race into my office and grab the fairy lights, candles, and flowers I stashed in here earlier, thankful she was in the shower when Max delivered it all. With my arms full, I head out to the patio to turn this place into a sparkly romantic wonderland.

Cress is onboard to get here around six with Lexi, who seems to be doing much better now. It was touch and go for a while after the accident, but with Preston on her case, and how he feels about Cress, it's good to see the little munchkin running around, happy and giggling again. Now, we just need Preston and Cress to pull their heads out of their asses and get their act together. Now that Lexi is healthy again, I think she will play a big part in that.

I've asked them to be here too, as I want all of Avery's 'family' here when I ask her the most important question of her, and my, life.

Time seems to be dragging by and finally my phone pings.

CRESS: *On our way up*

Cress had arranged with Avery to meet here when the sisters return, but little does Ave know that Cress was going to be here anyway. The ding of the elevator causes my heart rate to accelerate and rapidly race within in chest. The front door swings open and they all walk in.

"Hi, Bay," I say, as I wrap her in a hug.

"All set?" she whispers, and I nod my head.

A lump forms in the back of my throat and I feel like I want to throw up. I'm so fucking nervous. We stand in the foyer chatting when Avery says, "Come on in, no need to stand in the foyer all night." She looks vibrant and happy right now, and then her words register.

"No," I shout, startling everyone. "Ave lass, ummm, ahh, can I speak with you for a moment please…privately…outside."

She looks at me suspiciously but nods her head and starts walking outside. "Back in a sec." Cress and Bay both nod and grin like fools. Taking a deep breath, I follow behind her and when she steps outside, I flick the switch on the remote in my hand and the area lights up. Ave stops midstep, gasps, and covers her mouth.

Stepping around her, I take her hands in mine. She pulls her gaze to mine, her eyes sparkling and glassy with unshed tears. "Ave lass, I was falling for you from the moment I laid eyes on you at the Tavern. That first night was the best night of my life. The next morning you were gone and I was crushed, but fate had other ideas. We ran into each other again and this time, I didn't let you go. The more time I spent with you, the harder I fell. I knew you were the one for me, and I hope you feel the same way." Dropping to my knee, I pull the ring from my pocket. It's white gold with a round brilliant-cut diamond in a halo style. I place it at the tip of her ring finger. "Avery Evans, will you marry me?"

She's frozen and doesn't say anything for what feels like eternity. Then she nods her head and the biggest smile ever graces her face. "Yes. Yes. Yes. Flynn, yes, I'll marry you."

Sliding the ring on to her finger, she lifts her hand and gazes at it. Then her eyes land on mine. I have never been happier than I am in this moment. She grips my cheeks in her palms and covers my mouth with hers. Her tongue slides effortlessly into mine and our first kiss as an engaged couple is amazing.

The moment is interrupted when Cress, Preston, Lexi, and Baylor join us outside. The girls all have sparklers in their hands and smiles on their faces too.

"I'm engaged!" Ave joyously shouts.

The girls race over to her and admire her ring. Preston walks to me and we do the one-arm bro hug. "Congrats, dude."

"Thanks," I say, as I watch my fiancée with her friends. I fell hard for Avery Evans and each day I fall harder for her. I now get to spend the rest of my life with the most amazing woman in the world. I'm a lucky lucky man.

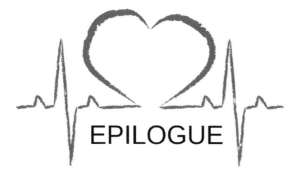

EPILOGUE

My life was plain and boring, and then one day I met Flynn Kelly and my world was turned upside and inside out. From the first moment I laid eyes on him, I started falling. We are complete opposites but as the saying goes 'opposites attract' and even though that's definitely the case with us, we go together perfectly.

I thought the day Flynn proposed was the happiest day of my life. And it was, until the day I became Mrs. Avery Kelly, but that moment has once again been trumped. Today, I gave birth to our twin boys, Marvin and Marshall. In honor of a great man who was taken too soon. His memory will live on in the form of these two little boys.

"How you doing?" Flynn asks, as he gazes down at our boys sleeping in their bassinet.

Standing up, I walk, well, shuffle, over to him and wrap my arm around his waist and look down at our munchkins. A smile graces my face. "Considering I just punched two watermelons out of my va-jay-jay, I'm pretty good. I think I'm still high though, everything is fuzzy, and I'm guessing I look like a hot mess."

"I'd say a sexy hot mess." Placing a kiss on my head, he hugs me closer to him.

"You need your eyes checked, I'm sure there's an optometrist around here somewhere."

"My eye sight is perfectly fine, Avery Kelly."

"Pffft, whatever you say." I pause. "We did good, didn't we?"

"Yep, they are perfect. Just like their momma."

"And just like their daddy. You think Marvin is up there gloating to everyone that we named them after him?"

"I have no doubt. And knowing the Houdini he is, I bet he's trying to find a way to get back down here so he can see them in the flesh."

I laugh and startle the boys. "Oops." I shrug. We each pick up a baby and like the pros we are—not—we rock them back to sleep….an hour and a half later. Who knew two, tiny, cute little beings could make so much noise? Once they are asleep again, we place them back in the bassinet and stare down at them.

Flynn pulls me into his side and kisses my head, before grabbing my hand and tugging me toward the bed. "We sleep when they sleep," he whispers, as we climb into the tiny hospital bed and snuggle.

"I love you, Flynn."

"I love you too, Ave."

He places a kiss on my forehead and I close my eyes. As I drift off to sleep in Flynn's arms, I realize I'm the luckiest girl alive. Falling for Dr. Kelly was the best decision I ever made; not that I stood a chance when it came to my sexy as sin Irish stud.

THE END!

PLAYLIST

Can't Help Falling in Love – Elvis Presley
Unchained Melody – the Righteous Brothers
Can't Take my Eyes off You – Engelbert Humphries
Sexy Back – Justin Timberlake
Bleeding Love – Leona Lewis
Love Song – Sara Bareilles
Complicated – Avril Lavigne
I Don't Wanna Be – Gavin DeGraw
Acceptable in the 80's – Calvin Harris
Pony – Genuwine
Wolves – Selena Gomez
Havana – Camila Cabello
Way Down We Go – KALEO
A Thousand Miles – Vanessa Carlton
Big Girls Don't Cry – Fergie
Hey, Soul Sister – Train
Walkin' on the Sun – Smash Mouth
Escape (The Pina Colada Song) – Rupert Holmes
American Woman – Lenny Kravitz
You've Lost That Lovin Feelin' – The Righteous Brothers
Hey There Delilah – Plain White T's
Better in Time - Leona Lewis
Halo – Beyonce
Just The Way You Are – Bruno Mars
Not N Cold – Katy Perry
How to Save a Life – The Fray
Who Knew – P!nk
Toxic – Brittney Spears
Chasing Cars – Snow Patrol
Haven't Met You Yet – Michael Buble
Just Dance – Lady Gaga
Dynamite – Taio Cruz
Crazy in Love – Beyonce & Jay-Z
Bring me to Life – Evanescence
I Can't Go for That (No can do) – Hall & Oates
Kiss on my List - Hall & Oates
Out of Touch - Hall & Oates

Private Eyes - Hall & Oates
Maneater - Hall & Oates
Mr. Brightside – The Killers
Never Tear us Apart – INXS
Lover – Taylor Swift
All of Me – John Legend

This playlist can be found on spotify.

falling for
DR. KNIGHT

They are in for the
fight of their lives

A FALLING NOVEL

DL GALLIE

**Chaos and tragedy can either bring us together, or tear us apart.
Falling in love isn't like it is in fairy tales.**

CRESSIDA

Being a single mom is hard.
But Lexi is my life, and I'll do anything for my daughter.
I just never expected tragedy to strike, or for my past to haunt us.
Or for Dr. Preston Knight to be the man who saves us.
The same man I should *never* have fallen in love with.

PRESTON

I'm the best in my field.
Being a doctor is in my *blood*.
My focus is always on my career.
Until her—Cressida Bayliss.
I've fought many battles, but never one so close to my heart.
This is the biggest fight of my life, and with my heart on the line, I can't afford to lose.

Andi, Preston is all yours.
Thank you for believing in him, and me.

"Love until it hurts. Real love is always painful and hurts: then it's real and pure"

   ~ *Mother Teresa*

PROLOGUE

WHEN I SAW MY DAUGHTER IN THE ER BED GETTING STITCHED UP AFTER THE accident at Navy Pier, I thought that was the worst possible thing to happen to me, but hearing, "Cress, Lexi has sepsis," *THAT* was the most heartbreaking thing a mother could hear. And to kick me even more when I was down, let's also add, "She has now developed pneumonia." Even with the bad news coming from the man I'm in love with, it did nothing to cushion the blow. Seeing the seriousness on his face was when I broke down. I realized in that moment just how sick my little girl was.

She was sick, really really sick; and he wouldn't promise me that she'd get better.

When Preston said those words my world imploded. After the initial shock wore off, the guilt set in. I felt like the worst mother in the entire universe, add in threats from Dickwad Dawson and the already stressful situation became even more volatile. *Fuck my life.* I should have known that life would fuck me over. Things were going smoothly and for the first time since Lexi was born, I was happy, ecstatically happy and in love. But with this kick in the guts, I didn't know if I could fix it. I wasn't a wizard, I couldn't wave my magic wand or cast a spell like Twilight Sparkle to make Lexi healthy again. My little girl, my most precious possession, was sick and it was all my fault. I should have seen the signs. I should have paid more attention. I shouldn't have been fucking around with Preston. I should have been focusing on Lexi. I should have been there for her.

I.

Should.

Have.

Known.

I'm her mom for fuck's sake! How could I have let my little girl down so badly? I should have noticed the color draining from her face. I should have seen how lethargic she'd become. I should have brought her in sooner. I should have done more. I should have been a better mom.

And now because I was following my heart, my little girl is close to death. The apple of my eye is fighting for her life and it's all my fault. Falling for Dr. Knight was the worst thing I've ever done.

1 CRESS

...five years earlier

NEVER HAVE I FELT PAIN LIKE THIS BEFORE, NOT EVEN WHEN CREED WALKED away while I was pregnant. That day was hard, but this, this is the hardest thing I have ever done. "Avery, get me drugs. Get me every fucking drug there is. It hurts so much," I scream and cry to my best friend, who has stepped up to the plate and takes the crown as THE bestest friend ever in the history of best friends.

"If you let go of my hand, I will see what I can do," she says through clenched teeth. I loosen the grip I have on her hand, and when she pulls it away, she shakes it back and forth, stretching her fingers, and then shaking again to get the blood flow back into it.

"I'm sorry," I cry and then I burst into tears. "Avery, I'm going to be a shit mom," I blubber. "I just squished your hand. What if I squish the baby? I can't do this on my own."

"Cressida Rachel Bayliss, stop talking shit—"

"But—" I try to interrupt her, but she raises her hand in a stop motion. I know she means business because not only did she middle name me, she full named me too.

"Don't make me bitch slap a pregnant woman in labor. You've got this.

You are the strongest most amazing person I know, and this baby will be lucky to have you as his or her mommy."

"Avery," I cry, tears well in my eyes and then the dam breaks. Tears pour down my face but this time instead of fearful tears, they are happy emotional tears. "You're not meant to make a pregnant lady in labor cry."

"Well, stop talking shit and I won't. Now let me go find the nurse, or Dr. Jenkins, and get you some drugs."

"I knew you were my best friend for a reason." I mean every word in that statement. Ave is my ride or die. She's my best bitch and I would be lost without her.

After my mini freak-out, Munchkin—the affectionate term I used while pregnant with her—yes, her—came quickly, like super quick. She announced her arrival into the world with a scream to rival that of Jamie Lee Curtis in *Halloween*. I'm pretty sure I was a close second with the screaming, because pushing a nine-pound baby out your hoo-ha is no easy feat. Alexis Avery Bayliss, or Lexi for short, arrived before I could get the good drugs, but as soon as they put her in my arms, everything was right with the world. The pain of the labor vanished. All my fears of being a shitty mom disappeared. I was filled with love, awe, and gratitude. My daughter is the most perfect beautiful baby in the world, I know all parents say this but in regards to Lexi, it's true.

For a brief moment, I thank Dickwad Dawson for knocking me up because if he hadn't, I wouldn't be holding my beautiful little girl in my arms right now. Guess I better let him know she has arrived, not that he'll care. My mind drifts to the day I told him I was pregnant and the events that unfolded after that...

...Sitting on the side of the tub, I look down at the four sticks sitting on the floor mat and the one in my hand. All I see are pink lines staring back up at me screaming 'You're pregnant!,' insert jazz hands. A smile breaks free. "I'm pregnant," I murmur and rest my hand on my belly. "Hey, Munchkin, I'm your mommy. I'm promise to be the bestest mommy in the world."

The sound of the front door closing startles me and I drop the stick I'm holding.

"Cress, Babydoll, where are you?" Creed shouts, as I hear his boots hit the wall by the door. I hate when he kicks his shoes off like that.

"In here," I shout, as I turn on the faucet and wash my hands to get rid of the residual pee. Creed walks in and smiles at me in the mirror. I stare at his reflection. Brown hair. Brown eyes. Square jaw. I start to wonder what our baby will look

like. Since I have dark blonde, almost brown hair, I guess she, or he, will have dark hair too. I have blue eyes so it's anyone's guess. Our skin tone is similar. But my thoughts and happiness are thwarted when I hear him growl, "What the fuck?"

Shaking my head, I turn around to see him glaring at the pile of pregnancy tests on the bathroom floor. "Surprise," I say, but when I look at his face, I don't see excitement or awe. I see anger, rage, and disgust.

"You need to get rid of it," he snarls between clenched teeth. I have never heard that tone from him before. "I'm not ready to be a father, and you certainly aren't in any shape to be a mother. You can't even boil a fucking egg without calling Mommy for assistance."

"Excuse me?" I scoff, I'm shocked at the outburst coming from him right now.

"You heard me. Me no father and you no mom." He pauses. "Hell, it's probably not even mine."

"Excuse me?" I shout again. "How dare you accuse me of cheating on you! I have been nothing but an amazing girlfriend. Sure, the timing isn't ideal but we'll make this work. I know we can. We will be a happy family."

"Yeah, we will because you're going to get rid of it."

"Ummm, no, I'm not."

"Yes. You. Are," he growls, pausing between each word for emphasis. His face turning purple from holding his breath. I can feel the anger radiating from him but I refuse to let him ruin the moment. This is a joyous time for me. For us. For our future.

"No, Creed. I'm keeping this baby. We made Munchkin together, he or she is going to be perfect and we will be amazing parents."

"Fuck this shit." He punches the mirror, the glass cracking and splintering under the force. He turns around and walks out, leaving me stunned. He turns back around. "You need to think who you want more, me? Or that thing?" He points to my belly and before I can reply, he's gone. Leaving me alone with Munchkin and my heart broken.

Dropping to my knees, I cry. My happy moment and life crushed by the one person who I thought would be by my side forever. When I have no more tears left to cry, I lean back against the tub and cradle my stomach. I look down at my flat for now abs and whisper, "I'll choose you every time, Munchkin, every time."

A few hours later, Creed returns and he drops to the floor in front of me. He takes my hands in his and lovingly stares at me. "I'm sorry, Babydoll. I was shocked, it was so out of the blue. I don't want you to get rid of it—"

"Munchkin." I say, smiling at him, "Our lil' munchkin is growing inside of me." Taking his hand, I place it on my belly and stare at him. "I love you, Creed. We are going to be fine, and this baby is going to have two amazing parents, sure we'll fumble, but together, we can do anything."

"I'll try, Babydoll, but I'm scared."

"I'm scared too, baby, but together, we can do this. We can be a family."

For the next few weeks everything was perfect, then one night he came home drunk. He wanted to fool around but I've been suffering from horrible morning sickness, so much for that disappearing in the second trimester. He got angry when I said no. "Fucking baby is cockblocking me already. Knew it was going to mess with us. I thought pregnancy made you bitches horny all the time. Knew you should have gotten rid of it."

"Not this again," I mumble, but it was obviously louder than I intended because he slapped me across the face. Cupping my cheek in shock, I stare at the man before me. He isn't the man I fell in love with all those years ago.

"Don't sass me, woman. I knew this baby was a mistake, you not putting out proves that."

He climbs off the bed and leaves, slamming the door behind him. It was three days before he returned home. He never told me where he disappeared to, and to be honest, I didn't care.

This pregnancy has been tough; I've been so sick this past week. Thankfully I have Avery and Mom to help me. Between the two of them, I've had round the clock care. The topic of Creed is never bought up, and I'm thankful for that because I don't know what to say.

When he finally came home, it all went back to normal, well for the next few weeks anyway. The day of our twenty week scan, he didn't turn up, to say I was hurt was an understatement. When I got home, that hurt intensified. I found him packing.

"What's going on?"

"I'm leaving. I can't do this. I can't be a father to that thing." He points to my bump and scowls. "I'm still not convinced that thing is mine anyway, so I'm leaving."

At his words, my heart and world shatter. Tears well in my eyes. "But—"

"There's no buts, I'm gone. You will always chose that thing over me. I'm worth more than that, if you can't see that then there's no point in me hanging around."

"Please, Creed," I beg, "Please don't leave us." Tears pour down my face as the man I love continues to pack.

He stops packing and looks at me. "Get rid of it and I'll stay."

"You know I won't do that. I can't do that."

"Then I'm gone."

"You said you love me! That you'd try. That we'd be a family."

He breaks out into a sarcastic laugh. "Love you? That's a good one, Cress. You said all the happily ever after shit, not me." He zips up his suitcase and walks *toward me. He stops and cups my face in his palm. "It's such a shame, you were such a good fuck." He taps my cheek and walks past me.*

"You said you wanted to try, remember? You said you'd be here, for us. For our child."

He turns to face me. "I said I'd try for you, not that thing. I still don't even know if it's mine." He pauses. "You had your chance, Cress, and even now, you're still choosing it over me. You chose wrong, Babydoll." He turns around and walks toward the front door. With his hand on the door handle, he looks back at me. "You did this to yourself, Cressida. In a couple of months, you'll be nothing but a fat, pregnant, ugly bitch. Because this thing you keep calling munchkin is going to steal everything from you and give you nothing in return." With those hateful words, he opens the door and walks out. Leaving me pregnant, alone, and completely heartbroken...

The door to my room opens and snaps me back to the present and away from that fateful day. A group of doctors enters for rounds, thankfully this only happens twice a day, I cannot wait to go home where it will just be Lexi and me. Looking up, I smile at Dr. Jenkins and glance around at the other doctors with her. My eyes land on a doctor hiding in the back, holy hotness, Batman, he is the most beautiful man I have ever seen. Then I realize I look like a hot mess. I haven't slept in a gazillion hours and yesterday; I punched a watermelon out my hoo-ha with no drugs. *Why, universe, why would you do this to me?*

"Cressida," the doctor says, and I internally cringe, I *hate* being called Cressida.

Shaking my head, I focus on her. "Sorry, I missed that, Dr. Jenkins?"

"Can we have a quick look at Alexis?"

Dropping my gaze, I look to a sleeping Lexi in my arms and smile. I've been doing that a lot in the last twenty-four hours. She is the apple of my eye and I don't ever want to give her up. "Umm," my voice wavers and I hesitate, "she's just drifted off."

She can see the trepidation in my eyes, but her face softens in that dreamy way it does regarding babies. "That's fine, we can come back later." And that is why I chose Dr. Stefanie Jenkins to deliver my baby: she cares and takes my feelings into account. I was not the easiest of patients, with being a first-time mom and doing it alone, but she was my savior.

Before I can say anything the group exits my room. Dr. Hottie is the last to leave, our eyes connect and the moment could not be more perfect. It's intense. It's electric. His gaze penetrates deep into my soul, my skin heats as his eyes roam over me. He winks and turns to leave. Looking over his shoulder, he says, "Congrats on the birth of your little girl, Cress."

"Thank you," I manage to utter as the door closes behind him.

He called me Cress, it's like he knew I hate being called Cressida. And his voice, ohh my God, his voice. It's deep and husky, I could listen to him talk all day long. Hell, I'd even listen to him read the phone book. Lex stirs in my arms and I realize I need to pee. I shuffle out of bed and I place her in the bassinet in my room. After using the bathroom, I climb back into bed, and drift off to sleep, dreaming about Dr. Hottie.

After that morning, I never saw Dr. Hottie again but it wouldn't have mattered anyway, a guy like him would never go for someone like me. Plus, I don't need a man in my life; I now have a baby to focus on. I'm going to be the best mom ever to my little munchkin.

2 PRESTON

....present day

Flopping down on the sofa, I kick out my legs and flick on the TV. Bringing up Disney+, I grin when I see *DuckTales* is currently playing. Lying back, I watch as Huey, Dewey, and Louie get into mischief and like usual, Scrooge McDuck is being all scroogey. Drifting off to sleep, I wake up when the alarm on my phone blares, reminding me I need to pick up Flynn from the airport. Thank God I set the reminder because I totally forgot I was to collect him today.

Hopping up, I grab a quick shower and make my way to the airport to pick Flynn up. Lucky bastard has spent the last ten days in paradise at Oasis, an adults-only resort in Castaway Grove. I'm sure on the trip back to his place, I'll hear all about his conquests...ohh how wrong I was. "Are you telling me, Dr. 'I have an accent, drop your panties now' has blue balls and callouses on his hands?"

He nods his head and sighs dejectedly, "Yep."

This is pure gold. The Irish God—according to the nurses, well anyone with a vagina, at the hospital—got cockblocked by the woman of his dreams, and he spent the last few days at the resort by himself, with Mrs. Palmer and her five daughters, watching her douche of an ex swoop in and win her back.

"Sounds like you need to get laid and you need to get laid good."

"Tell me about it. I feel like a teenager again."

"If you like, we can go out tonight," I offer.

He once again shakes his head. "Nah, I need to get home, unpack, and get my head back into the game. Plus, I've got an early shift tomorrow."

"No worries, some other time then."

The rest of the trip to his place is silent. I've never seen Flynn so down, it's concerning, and I kind of feel guilty for the teasing earlier. We pull up to his building. Turning off the car, we climb out and I help him with his bags.

"Thanks for picking me up, man...and the talk."

"Anytime, you know that." Flynn and I met in med school and we hit if off straightaway. And as they say, the rest was history. Our friendship has grown stronger over the years, he's more like a brother than a friend and colleague. I'd do anything for him, and I know he'd do the same for me too.

"Appreciate it. I'll see you tomorrow." We do the manly, one-arm, back-slap hug and I watch him walk inside. Shaking my head, I internally laugh at him and his blue balls. Climbing back into my car, I head back home. Stopping along the way, I grab some Chinese and in front of the TV, I watch old-school *Scooby Doo*—hey, I'm a pediatrician and spend all day with kids, plus I'm a big kid at heart—and I eat my sweet and sour chicken, thinking about the busy week ahead.

Friday finally rolls around, this has been the slowest week in history but it did allow me to catch up on paperwork; who knew there'd be so much paperwork being a doctor? I've just finished up a meeting with admin when I get word that Flynn lost a patient earlier this afternoon. I know my friend, he will be gutted and as his best friend it's my duty to cheer him up. Making my way to the doctors' lounge, I walk in and see Flynn sitting in front of his locker. His shoulders are down and he's ignoring everyone, but I won't let him ignore me. "Dude," I say as I walk over to him. When he sees it's me, he stands and greets me with our one-armed man hug, and then he sits back down. "Sorry to hear about your patient."

"Thanks, man." He begins to change out of his scrubs. "How he held on as long as he did is beyond me. There was literally nothing I could have done."

"That's tough," I offer in condolence, there's nothing worse than losing a patient, especially for me since I deal with kids. The death of a child always sucks ass, actually the death of anyone is rough.

Before I get to ask him about heading out for a few drinks, he beats me to it. "Drinks?"

"Hell, yes. It's been a rough week."

"That's putting it mildly."

After changing my shirt, Flynn and I hop into my car and we head to The Fat Fox Tavern. We decide on a bar away from the hospital because if we went to O'Malley's, the one closest to the hospital, the topic of conversation would turn to work and people would offer condolences to Flynn and that's the last thing he needs. Tonight he needs to get drunk and maybe hook up with a chick…giving his palm a rest and ease his blue balls.

We enter the tavern and head toward the bar; my eyes gravitate toward a gorgeous chick sitting at the bar with her friend. Her friend is hot, with blonde hair and blue eyes, but it's the other gorgeous woman I'm intrigued by. She lights up the room when she smiles and her laugh is like music to my ears. I order our drinks and notice Flynn looking in the same direction. I hope, and pray, that he wants the other chick. With our beers in hand, we walk over to a table and silently sit down. Flynn's eyes are still locked on the girls, as are mine, and I'm trying to gauge whom he's checking out.

The goddess I've been admiring looks over to us and that's when I realize Flynn is eyeing her friend. *Thank you*, I silently say to the big guy upstairs. He chugs back his beer and without saying a word, he slams the empty glass on the table, walks back to the bar but this time, he heads over to the girls. My eyes are locked on the dark-haired angel, when suddenly, the friend spins around and hits Flynn in the nuts. I clench my nuts, feeling his pain in my own balls, but I'm also laughing. It was like a scene from a black-and-white slapstick comedy. It's the funniest shit I've seen in a long time, I can't remember the last time I laughed this hard. I watch the scene unfold and shake my head when he smoothly leans in and fucks her mouth in the middle of the tavern. *The Irish fucker has done it again,* I think to myself as I watch him make out with the blonde chick, her friend watching from the sidelines grinning from ear to ear.

Picking up his beer, he walks back toward me with a smug look on his face.

"How's the nuts?" I tease as he takes a seat.

"Now they'll be purple and blue, but if I play my cards right, they won't be blue after tonight." He winks at me and takes a sip of beer.

Shaking my head, I pick up mine and drink. The woman looks to Flynn and he winks at her. I see it written on her face, she's going home with the Irish stallion tonight. Out of nowhere, Flynn slams his glass down—again—and stalks across the bar. "What's he up to?" I mumble to myself, as I watch him walk toward the restrooms, the blonde nowhere in sight.

From the corner of my eye, I see my angel sitting at the bar by herself. She looks over her shoulder and even though we are in a packed bar, our gaze connects. Time stands still. Everything around me disappears, every-thing except for her. Our eyes are locked on one another. It's intense. It's electric. It feels like déjà vu. Her gaze penetrates deep into my soul, my skin heats as her eyes roam over me. She winks and turns her attention back to the bartender. *Ohh, I'm taking this one home tonight,* I think to myself, as Flynn and her friend walk back into the bar from the restrooms together. Her cheeks are flushed and he looks like the cat who ate the canary, knowing him, he totally just did that. They stop and speak to the friend, Flynn grabs her purse and they head toward me.

"I'm taking Avery home, please make sure her friend gets home safe-ly." He tells me.

"Roger that." I salute him and wink at Avery, her cheeks darken in embarrassment. He drags her out of the tavern, leaving me alone.

Finishing off my drink, I walk over to the friend. "Seems, I've been tasked with getting you home tonight."

"Lucky me, but I don't recall ordering a handsome Uber to get me off… home," she says. *Ohh the sass on this one is on point,* I think to myself as I take the recently vacated stool next to her.

Offering out my hand, I introduce myself, "Preston Knight, handsome Uber guy."

She smirks at my smart-ass remark. "Nice to meet you." She places her hand in mine and shakes. She has a good grip. Strong. Firm, perfect to wrap around my cock. An image of her fingers wrapped around my cock, stroking from base to tip appears in my mind. Her tongue darting out, licking the head before she swallows my shaft to the hilt.

The clearing of a throat snaps my attention away from my dirty thoughts. I see her looking intently at me. "Where did you just go? You drifted off there."

"Nowhere," I say. I'm so glad she cannot see into my dirty, perverted mind right now, or my dick, which is painfully pressing against my zipper right now.

"Can I buy you a drink?"

"Really? That's what you're going with? Friendly advice, you really need to review your flirting strategies."

"How about over a drink you teach me…insert name here."

She eyes me, her gaze roaming all over my body. She brings her drink to her lips, takes a sip, and spins around to face me, leaning on the bar. "Do you think I'll go home with you, just like my friend did with your friend?"

Shrugging my shoulders, I nonchantly say, "Well, my friend's charm clearly impressed your friend…"

"What my friend and your friend do have nothing to do with me."

"So you think I'm a lesser man than Flynn?"

"I didn't say that." She pauses. "So why don't you take a seat, buy me a drink, and we will see what happens. Plus, I'm not ready to leave with my handsome Uber guy yet. You still need to complete lesson 1-0-1 in flirting." She pauses and smiles at me, it lights up her face. "And my name is Cress."

Taking a seat next to her, I signal the bartender. He nods and finishes serving the couple at the other end and walks over to us. "Two more please," I ask him, but my gaze is on Cress, sassy sexy Cress. Even her name is beautiful. "So, Cress, tell me about the woman under this sexy, sassy exterior."

"You tell me what you see," she sasses in reply.

"Well, I see a very attractive, smart woman with a sharp mind and a quick tongue."

She licks her lips seductively, my eyes drop to her tongue and my cock twitches. It wants that tongue licking him. Hell, I want that tongue licking all over me.

"You also need to add to that assessment, the mom of the most amazing daughter, substitute grade school teacher, coffee addict, and wine lover." She pauses, and then adds, "So, it seems my bestie and your bestie are going to bump uglies tonight."

"And what about you, Cress? Do you bump uglies?"

She shakes her head side to side. "Ohh, no, I don't bump uglies." I deflate at hearing this but then she adds, "I'm more of a do the horizontal tango all night long kind of girl." She takes a sip from her beer. "And what about you, Preston, who are you a knight for?"

"I'm a pediatric doctor at Western General, I guess I'm a knight to my patients. Well, I try to be anyway." I lean into her, my lips hover near her ear, she smells amazing, "I'm eager to learn how to horizontal tango...with you."

Pulling back, I gaze into her blue eyes, noting her breathing has become labored. She swallows deeply and stares intently back at me. That déjà vu feeling hits me again. Reaching up, I brush a tendril of dark blonde hair behind her ear. Running the tip of my finger along her jawline and down her neck, her skin breaks out in goosebumps, but our moment is interrupted by the ringing of her phone.

3 CRESS

HIS STARE, IT FEELS LIKE I'VE FELT IT ON ME BEFORE BUT THAT'S NOT POSSIBLE, he and I are from two very different worlds. He's a doctor, I'm a single mom and substitute school teacher, we never would have crossed paths before, trust me, I'd remember meeting a Channing Tatum look-alike like him. I'm just about to offer to teach him how to horizontal tango when my phone rings, it's Mom's ringtone. "I need to get this," I tell him. Grabbing my phone from my purse, I swipe to answer, "Hey, Mom."

"Hey, Cress. Sorry to bother you—"

"Mom, it's no bother, is Lexi okay?"

"Kinda sorta. I'm not sure."

Her answer causes my eyes to pop wide open. "What's wrong? Is she okay?" Panic sets in that I'm not there for Lexi. Instead, I'm in a bar with a sexy man. I'm a shitty mom.

"She's running a temperature and she's very lethargic, not Lexi like at all. I'm going to take her to the hospital."

I can feel Preston staring at me, he seems concerned too. "There's no need to take her to the hospital, Mom."

"No need? That's crazy, Cress. She needs to see a doctor."

"I said there's no need to get her to the hospital because I *have* the doctor. We'll be there soon. Tell her Mommy is on her way."

I don't wait for Mom to answer, I look to Preston. "We need to get to my mom's, Lex isn't well. I need you."

"You need me, do you?" he playfully teases, but when he sees the worry etched on my face, he nods his head and stands up. "Okay, let's go."

He throws some bills onto the bar for our drinks. He places his hand low on my back and if I wasn't worried about Lexi right now, my body would be thrumming from the ever so light contact with him. We exit the Fat Fox and head over to his car. It's a sleek, silver Aston Martin; it's the perfect car for the sexy doctor. He unlocks it and opens my door for me—such a gentleman—I climb in and admire the interior, and then I remember that Lexi is sick. I need to stop drooling over his car and focus on getting to Mom's and my daughter.

Pulling my belt on, my leg tics and I bite my nail. Now that I'm thinking about Lexi, I'm anxious to get home to my munchkin. Preston starts the car but he doesn't pull out immediately. He reaches over and pulls my hand away from my mouth and gently squeezes.

My eyes snap to his and he smiles. "She's going to be fine, Cress. Now, what's your mom's address?"

Nodding my head, I tell him her address, he punches it into the navigation system and I stare out the window thinking about my little munchkin and what I'm going to find when I get home. When Ave left, I should have left too. I should be a better mom, I need to be there for Lexi. I'm all she's got. Sure, Dickwad Dawson pops in every now and again, but I don't think she really realizes who he is to her, even though she calls him 'Daddy Creed,' which totally pisses him off. Even though he left me, I will never hold him back from seeing his daughter. I keep hoping that one day he will become the father he promised to be before he left, but I think I have a bigger chance of shitting glitter than that ever happening.

We are stopped at a red light and I feel Preston's hand on my thigh, I have no idea how long it's been there. I look down at his hand and then I look over to him. He's staring at me, calm and cool, the complete opposite to how I look and feel right now. "How you doin, love?"

"Worried."

"You need to stop, I know it's easier said than done but if it was super serious, I'm sure your mom would already be at the hospital with her. We will be there soon and then you can see for yourself that she's okay."

Nodding my head, I think over his words but I don't say anything because right at this moment, I don't know that everything is going to be okay. I don't know anything. Until I see Lex for myself, I'll continue to worry and fret.

We pull up at Mom's house and before Preston has even stopped the car, I'm opening the door and climbing out. Racing up the path, I swing open the front door, and step into the living room. My eyes land on Lexi and her head resting on Mom's lap. *My Little Pony* is playing on the TV. Racing over to her, I drop to my knees and press my palm to her forehead, she feels warm. "Hey, Munchkin, you not feeling well?"

She shakes her head. "Mommy, I don't feel good." She starts to cry but the mom in me knows this is a performance cry, not an Oscar winning one, but she is playing it up, that much I can tell.

"Ohh, baby," I coo, lifting her into my arms, I hug her to me. She wraps her arms around my shoulders and I rock us. Kissing her head and rubbing my hand up and down her back, she snuggles into me and I smile.

"Who are you?" I hear Lexi ask, any hint of sickness in her voice gone; the little faker.

Looking over my shoulder, I see Preston standing there. *Man that man is fine*, I think to myself and then it clicks, there's a man in my mom's house and that man isn't Dickwad Dawson.

"I'm Dr. Knight, your mom tells me you don't feel well?" I feel Lex nod her head. "Can I have a look at you?"

"You already are looking at me."

"I'm a doctor, so I can have a look at you as if you are a patient of mine?"

"But you don't have a white coat or a stesascope."

"I see you're sassy just like your mommy."

Glaring at him, I see that he's focused on Lexi. "You don't have to do that, I'm sure she's fine," I say, throwing his words from earlier back at him. My leg begins to cramp, so I stand up. Lexi gripping onto me like a monkey.

"Yes he does, Mom," Lexi says. "He's a doctor, he'll make me all better." She wriggles down and out of my arms. Walking over to Preston, she takes his hand in hers and pulls him farther into the living room. She dramatically lies down on the sofa, resting her feet on Mom's lap and stares up at Preston. *And the Oscar for fake sick daughter goes to Alexis Avery Bayliss.* I shake my head and watch Preston with Lexi.

He steps toward her. "Okay, let's have a look," Preston says, placing his medical bag down on the coffee table. He opens it up and pulls out a stethoscope. He pops it around his neck and then grabs a digital thermometer. He places it on Lexi's forehead, when it beeps I peer over this shoulder and sigh in relief when I see 99.9° reflecting back at me. "A little high but I'd say it's fine," he confirms, looking at me over his shoulder.

The look on his face is calm, cool, and collected, the complete opposite to how I'm feeling. Turning his attention back to Lex, he checks her pulse and nods.

"Can I have a quick listen to your chest?"

"How will you do that?" she asks, I'm sure more questions will follow.

"With this," he says, lifting the stethoscope from his neck.

"I thought a stesascope listens to your heart?"

Preston nods. "It does. Your heart is in your chest." He pops the earbuds in Lexi's ears and places the bell on her chest.

Her little eyes light up. "It sounds like a drum," she excitedly says.

"It sure does. Can I listen to your heart now?"

Again my compliant daughter nods her head, if she really was sick, she'd be squirming and refusing to do as she's told. "Thank you." He pops the earpiece in his ears and looks down at her. "Okay, Lexi, I'm going to pop this on your chest and when I do, I want you to take big deep breaths for me."

"Okay." She does as asked, breathing in and out deeply.

"A few more and then we're done." She keeps breathing and he moves it around her chest and when he's finished, he removes the earpiece and asks her to stick her tongue out. She sticks it out and he nods at her.

Looking up at me, he puts me at ease. "Everything sounds clear. Her temperature is a little high but not worrisome. Her throat is a little red but with rest and fluids, she'll be okay."

"Preston, are you sure?" I question. Seeing him all doctor like makes me reconsider that she wasn't faking after all. Dropping next to her, I press my hand to her forehead and check her temperature again.

He nods and smiles. "Positive. Bed rest and *My Little Pony* is what I'd prescribe."

"*My Little Pony*, really?" I say, rolling my eyes at him.

"Yep," he says, tapping Lexi on the tip of her nose in a loving way that has my ovaries clenching. My hoo-ha sings, "Touch me. Feel me."

Hearing Lexi giggle eases my worries and I watch as Preston fusses over her, seeing him with her makes me all giddy. "...and don't forget, *My Little Pony* and lots of drinks."

"Okay, Doc," Lexi coos.

"You could have prescribed *Outlander* or something."

He looks over to me. "Well, for Mommy, I'd prescribe a date...with me."

"That line ever work before?" I tease.

"Depending on your answer, I'll let you know."

"Ohh, I like him," Mom says from the sofa. "Cress, I'll take Lexi to bed, leave you two alone." Mom winks at me, stands up and holds out her hand to Lexi. Lexi hops up, gives me a kiss, and walks over to Mom.

"It was lovely to meet you, Dr. Knight," Mom says, her voice all dreamy.

"Just Preston is fine."

Lexi turns back to Preston with a quizzical look on her face. "Why are you called Dr. Knight if you is also nameded Preston?"

"My full name is Preston Knight, so people can call me Dr. Knight or Preston."

She's nods in agreement. "Mine is Alexis Avery Bayliss but people just call me Lexi, or Lex. And Mommy sometimes calls me Munchkin. I call Mommy, Mommy but Nanna and Ave called her Cress, or Cressida when she's in trouble."

"Lexi," Mom says with a laugh, "let's get you into bed so you can rest and be better for school on Monday."

"Okay, Nanna."

Lexi takes Mom's hand. "Good night, Preston," Mom says on her way out of the living room.

"Good night, Momma Cress, it was lovely to meet you."

"Momma Cress, I like that," Mom croons. I roll my eyes, this guy is smooth but it's not in a creepy over-the-top way. It's endearing and sweet. He has both Mom and Lex wrapped around his finger. Mom and Lexi walk out of the room and it's now, just Preston, me, and my thumping libido.

We stare at one another, from down the hallway we hear Lexi tell Mom, "I wish he was a real knight and not a doctor knight. A real knight would have a horse and a sword."

At the mention of sword, my eyes drop to his crotch and I imagine what his sword would look like. Breaking the silence, Preston says, "So," my eyes lift back to his, "what do you say?"

"To what?" I play coy.

"A date?"

Staring at him, I make him sweat a little. "I guess I could lower my standards and date a doctor who moonlights as an Uber driver."

He chuckles at my reply. "There is one condition to this date."

"Ohh, yeah and what's that?"

He steps toward me and whispers, "You need to teach me how to horizontal tango at some point during the evening."

"I'm sure if you play your cards right, that can be arranged." Pursing my lips, I try to hold back the smile that's threatening to break free. "When will this date slash teaching lesson happen?"

"I'm free Wednesday night?"

Not wanting to seem too eager, even though given the choice, I'd leave again right now with him. "I'll have to see if Mom ca—"

"Mom's available," Mom yells from down the hallway.

We both laugh.

"Seems we have a date on Wednesday," he says, pulling a card out of the side of his medical bag. Picking up a pen from the coffee table, he scribbles on the back of it. "Here's my card, my cell is on the back. I'll pick you up here at 7 p.m. on Wednesday." He kisses my cheek and picks up his bag. Before he walks out, he gazes at me, my body temperature rising with the intensity of his stare and that déjà vu feeling envelops me again. "Goodnight, Cress."

"Goodnight Preston."

With those parting words, he leaves.

Staring at the living room entrance, I'm all smiles. I love hearing my name pass through his lips...I can't wait to feel those lips on mine and hopefully on Wednesday, I will.

Flopping back onto the sofa, I lean back and grin, I have a date with Dr. Knight.

4 CRESS

THE NEXT MORNING, WE HAVE BREAKFAST WITH MOM AND THEN WE HEAD home. All signs of a fever and sickness gone. Once home, I put in a load of laundry and Lexi plays in her room while I continue to tidy up. As I'm putting the vacuum cleaner away, I realize I'm still smiling. Last night with Preston was pretty amazing. Nothing physical has happened between us —yet—but the connection and spark is there. I haven't felt that in a long time, not since Creed. My thoughts are interrupted when from the living room I hear the theme song to *My Little Pony*. "Fuck me," I mumble to myself.

Closing the linen cupboard door, I head out to see my munchkin. Leaning over the back of the sofa, I kiss her forehead and am happy to still feel no temperature. "Hey, Munchkin, it's a bit early for Pony isn't it?"

She shakes her head and looks up at me. "Dr. Knight said it was my medicine."

"I don't think he said that."

She nods again. "Yes, he did. He said prescribe *My Little Pony* and Nanna said prescribe means medicine when she tucked me in."

"Did she now?"

"Yep," she replies as if butter wouldn't melt in her mouth. Shaking my head, I head into the kitchen and turn on my coffee machine. I need caffeine if I'm going to deal with Twilight Sparkle and her pals...for the fifty-millionth time.

With my coffee in hand and a juice box for Lexi, I head back into the living room. Taking a seat next to Lex, I pass her her juice box and grab my phone and Preston's card.

CRESS: *Thank you for last night. Sorry to end it how we did*

Placing my phone next to me, I grab my iPad and scan Facebook and Instagram before I start playing a game. I'm just about to win this level when my phone beeps with a text, startling me and I lose. "Duck me," I mumble to myself, as I swipe into messages and smile when I see it's from Preston.

PRESTON: *Morning, love. It's fine. How's the patient this morning?*
CRESS: *She's good. Currently taking her medicine of* My Little Pony *and washing it down with an apple juice box.*
PRESTON: *That's great. How's Mommy this morning?"*

Missing you is my first thought but I can't tell him that.

CRESS: *Great, I have coffee and a healthy daughter*
CRESS: *Thank you again for checking her over last night*
CRESS: *I really appreciate it*
PRESTON: *It was my pleasure.*
PRESTON: *You can pay be back on Wednesday night **wink wink***
CRESS: *I didn't realize there was a house call fee, how will I ever repay you?*
PRESTON: *I can think of a few ways **wink wink***
CRESS: *Are you proposing sexual favors for your work?*
PRESTON: *If you're offering, I'm not going to say no...what sane man would say no to that? I was just proposing dinner...and maybe a horizontal tango lesson*
CRESS: *Maybe we can compromise*
PRESTON: *I'm open to suggestions*
CRESS: *We can discuss this Wednesday in great detail*
PRESTON: *Is it Wednesday yet?*
CRESS: *Someone's anxious*
PRESTON: *I have a hot date with a sexy as fuck woman who may, or may not, teach me how to horizontal tango...you'd be anxious too*

CRESS: *Meh, but I am looking forward to Wednesday*
PRESTON: *You and me both, love*
CRESS: *Bye, Preston :)*
PRESTON: *Later, gator*
CRESS: *Later, gator? Really?*
PRESTON: *Does later, mater work better?*
PRESTON: *Or see ya later, alligator*
PRESTON: *Or take care, teddy bear*
PRESTON: *Or bye bye, butterfly*
CRESS: *Please stop...I get it, you're a big kid at heart*
PRESTON: *That's not the only thing that's big **wink wink***

My eyes go wide at his response but at the same time, it doesn't surprise me at all. This man is an enigma and for some reason, he wants me. Well, I think he wants me, and I think I want him too.

CRESS: *No one likes a bragger*
PRESTON: *It's not bragging if it's true*
CRESS: *Who says it's true?*
PRESTON: *I do*
CRESS: *You don't count*
PRESTON: *I do too....1, 2... skip a few... 99, 100*
PRESTON: *See, I can count*
CRESS: *I'm going now.*
CRESS: *Bye, Preston :)*
PRESTON: *Goodbye, love*

God, I love it when he calls me love, I think to myself as I read back over our text messages. He really is a big kid, but he's a big kid with a heart of gold. The way be stepped up last night with Lexi was beautiful, and he was great with her.

Throwing my phone onto the coffee table, I sit back and lose myself in *My Little Pony* but my thoughts keep drifting to Preston and our upcoming date. Needing a distraction, I tell Lexi to go get dressed.

We head to the park and I push Lexi on the swings, she's always loved the swings. Out of all the equipment in the park, she always makes a beeline for the swing. We are finishing up an ice cream when my phone rings. I look at the screen and smile when I see it's Ave. "Afternoon, hussy," I tease when I answer.

"Morning," she replies, her voice rough with sleep.

"Sooo…" I prompt my tight-lipped friend, "how was your night?"

"Good," she offers in reply.

"Good, that's all I get…good?"

"Yep. I'm in a taxi on my way home right now." She sighs and then whines, "Cress—"

"I'll be there when you get home," I say without a second thought, Ave has always been there for me, now it's my turn to be there for her. Grabbing Lexi's hand, we head back to my Toyota. Once she's strapped in, we stop at Walmart and I grab the essentials: wine, ice cream, and chocolate.

Forty minutes later, Lexi and I pull up at Ave's apartment, which she shares with her twin, Baylor. I hope she's not home because at the moment, that woman is a selfish bitch and she's horrible to her sister.

Knocking on the door, I don't wait for an answer, I waltz in and notice Ave is still in last night's dress and she looks well-fucked, and on edge. She needs wine and a debrief.

"Lexi, how you doing?" she says, as she hugs my daughter.

"I'm good, Aunty A. I got to sleep at Nanna's last night and Mommy took me to the park and I got an ice cream."

"So I can see. What flavor did you get?"

"Mint chocolate chip."

"Yummo, my fav," Ave says, she licks her fingers and wipes a smudge off Lexi's face. She looks to me and smiles, but it doesn't reach her eyes. She's in Ave-freak-out mode right now. "You wanna watch some Pony while Mom and I chat in the kitchen?"

"Yessssss," Lexi squeals in delight. She races into the living room, pulls out her beanbag, and settles in while Ave switches it on. I head into the kitchen and before I do anything, I pour two glasses of wine. The theme song starts to play and then Ave walks into the kitchen, she smiles when she sees her wine waiting. It's the first genuine smile from her since I arrived.

"Okay, spill," I say, as I hand her her glass of wine.

Taking the wine from me, she takes a huge gulp, followed by another. Wow, she's in mega-freak-out mode. "Okay, Chuggy McChuggerson, slow down there," I tease, taking the glass from her and since I'm a good friend, I top it up.

Looking over to her, I see the tears in her eyes. "Cress, I'm a big fat whore," she cries. Stepping to her I envelop her in a hug. Rubbing her back, I let her cry and get it all out. "I slept with him so many times and it was ducking amazing." I smile that at a time like this, she still doesn't swear. We don't, well we try not to, swear when Lexi is around but she's so engrossed in *My Little Pony* I doubt she'd notice. "It was the best ducking sex of my life. I'm surprised I'm not waddling today. When he was asleep, I snuck out, and now I feel guilty for leaving him like that. I can't even apologize for being such a ducking whore. At least I folded his clothes before I left."

That last line stumps me, so I pull back and look quizzically at her. "You folded his clothes?"

She nods her head. "Yeah, when I slipped my dress back on, I picked his clothes up, folded them, and placed them neatly on the coffee table."

I laugh because only my friend would have a one-night stand and then clean before leaving. And that, right there, is one of the many many reasons I love her.

"Cress," she whines, "I'm a big fat whore."

"NO!," I shout. Stepping back over to her, I wipe under her eyes with my thumb and glare at her with my mom stare. "You are a sexy single gal, who had a fantabulous night ducking a hot guy."

"But—"

"NO! NO! NO! NO! NO! Avery Evans, look at me." She lifts her gaze to meet mine. "One night of amazing sex does not make you a whore. Did he pay you?"

"No."

"Then by definition you are not a whore, maybe a skank, but definitely not a whore."

"Takes a skank to know a skank."

Just like that, everything is right with the world again. "Stop with the guilt for sneaking out."

"How did you know?" she questions.

"I know all your tics, Ave." I hand her her wine back, and she takes a sip, a small one this time. "Now, listen to me, I'm only going to say this once. You will not call yourself a whore for having fantabulous sex. You will not feel guilty for sneaking out like the harlot, which I'm finally able to say my best friend is. I'm proud, wee skankhopper. We, well you, are going to put last night with the sexy Scottish—"

"Irish."

"You are going to put last night with that sexy Irish doctor into the flick bank and move on."

"I knew you were my best friend for a reason. In half—"

"Three-quarters," I tease.

"Fine, in three-quarters of a glass of wine, you've eased my fears and I feel like me again."

"Happy to be of service." I lean on the countertop and rest my chin on my palm. "Now, I want all the sexy filthy details."

She shakes her head at me. "Nope, last night is firmly locked away in my, what did you call it?"

"Flick bank."

"Yes, flick bank. Last night is safely locked away there. Now, I'm going to have a shower 'cause I smell like sex. You can order food and then we can watch *My Little Pony* with Lexi."

"Can't we watch something else?"

"Do you want to enrage your daughter?"

"Fair point."

Lifting my wine, I take a sip and watch as my best friend heads toward her room to shower. She turns around. "Cress, thanks for being you and calming me down."

"You are most welcome, babe. It's not often I get to rescue you, so it's nice to repay the favor for once…even if you won't spill the sexy schmexy details with your BFF."

"Love you," she calls out as she walks away. Grabbing my phone, I call and order Indian, then I join Lexi in the living room AND I manage to get her to watch the *Scooby Doo* movie with Buffy and her hubby. As we watch them on spooky island, my mind keeps drifting to Preston and I wonder if I will feel like Ave come Thursday morning, a dirty satisfied whore…but without the freak-out part.

5 PRESTON

CRESS AND I HAVE BEEN MESSAGING EACH OTHER NONSTOP SINCE I DROPPED her home last night. And damn, that woman can take something so sweet and innocent and turn it dirty as fuck. I thought Flynn was crass but 'Crass Cress' takes that crown. Now I'm picturing her in nothing but fuck-me heels and a crown—totally saving that for the spank bank. Hey, I'm a man.

Shaking my head, I move on from that delicious sexy thought and get back to what I was originally thinking about, a fully clothed Cress and our upcoming date. She's witty and fun and the banter over text has been amazing. And as sad as it is to admit, this sexting has been the most fun I've had in a long time. Our dirty chats aren't just sexy as fuck, they are funny, honest, and real.

Just like her.

My mind once again drifts to her and specifically her legs, her killer legs...in sexy fuck-me heels and a crown. "Fuuuuck," I groan, readjusting my hardening cock. I'm hard every time I think of her. And that's seriously messing with my mind, I've spent maybe an hour with this woman and a bit longer texting her but man, do I want that woman. Another shocker, I'm looking forward to Wednesday night. Me? Preston Knight is looking forward to a date. There's a definite spark between us. I know women have that seventh sense shit, but I'm positive she feels this pull too. I noticed the way she looked at me because it's exactly how I was looking at her and guess what, love? I'm more than ready to give you a taste of me and I'm more than ready to have a taste of her.

All of her.

She's not like anyone else I have met or been with. She's the complete package. Personality, check. Strong mind, check. Sassy, fun, and witty; check, check, and check. Gorgeous, big check. Sexy as fuck legs, check. Those legs? Fuck those killer legs are all I can think about. You may think something's wrong with me since I keep referring to her legs whereas most men love tits. Big ones, small ones, fake one. Tits ARE the first thing we notice and don't get me wrong, Cress has great boobs...there are so many sinful things I want to do to them, but it's her legs that have me drooling. I keep thinking about her tango lesson, the horizontal kind, where her legs are wrapped about me. My hands, or tongue, running up and down them...Fuck, I can't wait for my horizontal tango lesson on Wednesday. I'm looking forward to see what she's got in store. There's something about Cressida Bayliss and I cannot wait to find out more.

Flynn called and asked to meet me for drinks at The Fat Fox. I'm happy to oblige and we agree to meet in an hour. I walk in, head straight to the bar, and order myself a scotch. With my drink in hand, I find a table and wait for Flynn to arrive. My eyes flick around the bar and a smile graces my face as I think about Cress and her killer legs. My cock twitches in my pants. *Down, boy, we are in public.* My thoughts are interrupted when Flynn arrives. "Hey," he says, taking the seat across from me. He picks up my drink and slams it back. "Rough night?" I question.

"Amazing night. Rough afternoon." He flags down the waitress, and orders himself a beer and another scotch to replace mine that he just chugged back.

"That's two extremes."

"That's how the last eighteen hours have gone."

"Huh?"

He fills me in on last night—lucky bastard—and then what happened this afternoon: unlucky bastard. "The only reason I knew she was there and that I didn't dream the night up was because she folded my clothes and left them on the coffee table."

"She what?"

"Before she left, she folded my clothes that were left in the living room last night."

"At least she's neat."

"Not what I'm focusing on at the moment." His eyes suddenly

brighten. "How did you go last night?" Not wanting to share the details just yet, I nonchalantly shrug my shoulders. "What does that mean?"

"It means I looked after the friend like you requested."

"Aaaaand?" he probes.

"And nothing. We had a drink after you guys left and then I dropped her home."

"Really? You didn't fuck her?" he questions me.

"Nope, my dick stayed in my pants. By the sound of things, you had enough sex for the both of us last night and this morning." Taking a sip of my scotch, I ask, "So what are you going to do?"

"No clue. Did you get the friend's details at all?"

Without thinking I shake my head. "Nope, sorry. I was a gentleman and dropped her home like the knight that my last name is."

From the look on Flynn's face, he knows I'm full of shit but that's the best thing about our friendship, we don't push each other to open up and gossip like girls. He knows that when I'm ready to share, I will. And like always, he'll be there to listen with an open ear and a cold beer.

Flynn is pissed about being fucked and ducked and isn't in the mood to socialize, so he calls it a night. As he walks out, I think about Cress and decide to text her again.

PRESTON: *Hey, love. How's the patient now?*

CRESS: *We tried a new medicine,* Scooby Doo, *she's out cold and no further temperatures*

PRESTON: *You really shouldn't mix medicines but in this instance, I will say it was a good choice.*

CRESS: *Personally, I'd prefer* Outlander *but not sure that's appropriate for a five-year-old…what with all the sex, naked boobs and butts, and whatnot*

PRESTON: *I'd like to see your naked whatnot **wink***

CRESS: *Maybe on Wednesday I could be persuaded*

PRESTON: *Dammit, now I'm thinking about you naked in my bed*

CRESS: *Who said anything about a bed????*

PRESTON: *Dammit, woman, stop*

CRESS: *Stop what? Me being naked, caressing my breasts, water cascading down my shoulders between my thighs making me wet*

PRESTON: *Stop it or I'm driving over there right now*

CRESS: *I wouldn't be opposed to that but…*

PRESTON: *But what???*

CRESS: *But A. I'm not at Mom's. B. You don't know where I live C. I'm not at home and D. I'm not that easy*
PRESTON: *Where are you?*
CRESS: *Not at home*
CRESS: *I'm with Ave...she freaked out after last night*
PRESTON: *I was just with Flynn...he's bummed she ran out*
CRESS: *I think she is too...should we play matchmaker?*
PRESTON: *Hell no...if it's meant to be, it will be*
CRESS: *That's very philosophical of you*
PRESTON: *There's a lot you don't know about me, Cressida Bayliss*
CRESS: *It's Cress...and I can't wait for Wednesday to find out more about the elusive Dr. Preston Knight*
CRESS: *Night, Preston*
PRESTON: *See you soon, raccoon*
PRESTON: *Hang on, that one was corny...Take care, polar bear*

Laughing, I pocket my phone and head home, where I fall into bed and dream sexy things about Cress, me, her legs, and a crown...why is Wednesday so far away?

6 CRESS

WEDNESDAY FINALLY ROLLS AROUND AND TO SAY I'M NERVOUS IS AN understatement. I can't remember the last time I was like this before a date. I'd love to chat with Ave at the moment, but she's still in a funk about fucking and ducking Flynn and to add to her plate, Bitchy Baylor is at it again. It's mind-boggling that those two are twins; they are total opposites. One's a mega bitch, the other is the most beautiful human being on the planet.

I've just dropped Lexi at school and I'm folding the wash when my phone beeps with a text.

PRESTON: *Can't wait for tonight, love*

There's that love again. I get chills every time I see that in a message, I know I should reply but I'm at a loss for words. This man is doing things to me that I normally wouldn't. For instance, a date. I cannot remember the last time I went on a date. Being a single mom is hard, so apart from the occasional hookup or lapse in judgment when Creed would drop Lexi off, it's just been her and me. Am I ready to allow someone into our bubble? Am I ready to try a relationship? With Preston? The sexting has been fun, something that's totally not me but at the same time, I feel special when he reaches out to me. I'm so confused right now. My phone pings with another text and I realize I've been thinking about Preston for the last ten minutes.

PRESTON: *Cat got your tongue?*
CRESS: *No...just busy*
PRESTON: *Whatcha doing?*
CRESS: *Folding wash. What you doing?*
PRESTON: *Just pulled 3 Lego bricks out of a kid's ass*
CRESS: *No way?*
PRESTON: *Yes way, he wanted to shit bricks for show-and-tell so he shoved 3 up his ass on Tuesday last week, ready for show-and-tell this week*
CRESS: *No shit*
PRESTON: *That's why he came he...hasn't shit in a week and his ass was hurting*
CRESS: *Clearly this kid didn't prep properly, everyone knows you need to prepare for anal*
PRESTON: *Cress, he was 7*
CRESS: *Didn't think of that*
PRESTON: *Sooo, what are you open to?*
CRESS: *I'm open to most things*
CRESS: *But not bestiality...or incest...or clowns*
PRESTON: *Clowns, really? So the circus is out then*
CRESS: *NO CIRCUS OR CLOWNS*
CRESS: *EVER*
CRESS: *PERIOD*
CRESS: *I WILL END YOU IF I SEE A CLOWN OR HIGH-TOP TENT*
PRESTON: *Duly noted, no clowns*
PRESTON: *What specifically are YOU open to? **wink wink***
CRESS: *Anything...and everything else*
PRESTON: *Really?*
CRESS: *Really, really. Now I need to finish this wash and prep for a date tonight*
PRESTON: *Is this date good-looking?*
CRESS: *He's all right*
PRESTON: *Only all right?*
CRESS: *I'll let you know later tonight. Bye, Preston*
PRESTON: *Bye bye, butterfly*

Laughing, I throw my phone onto the coffee table and realize that I was pretty open and crass in our communications just now. "Crass Cress strikes again," I say to myself. Preston doesn't seem to mind, we seem to be on the same wavelengths with most things and the banter has been fun, and sexy AF. He and I get along quite well, considering he's a doctor and I'm a single mom. I can't wait for tonight to see if it was just a heat of the moment thing, or if there is something between us. He's great with Lexi and that there is the kicker. She is my everything and I will not let anyone or anything hurt her. Jinxing myself, my phone rings with *his* ringtone. Knowing that if I don't answer, he will harass me until I do, I pick it up and answer, "Hello."

"Babydoll," Creed says in a tone that grates on my nerves. How I was ever in love with this douche canoe is beyond me.

"What can I do for you?"

"So formal, is that any way to speak to your baby daddy?"

Rolling my eyes, I sigh, thankful he cannot see me right now. "Hi, Creed, how are you? To what do I owe the pleasure of this call?"

"No need to be a bitch," he snarls. "Wanna see the squirt."

"You know you are welcome to see her anytime. Just let me know when."

"Tonight."

Of fucking course he wants to see her tonight.

"We have plans tonight, can we do tomorrow?"

"What plans to do you have?"

"My plans are none of your business. You can see her after school tomorrow?"

"Fine," he huffs. "I'll see you both then, Babydoll."

Before I can reply he hangs up. Throwing my phone back to the table, I fall back onto the sofa and shake my head. Of course the universe will throw Dickwad Dawson at me when I'm about to go on a date that I'm excited about. "Fuck you, universe!" I shout to the empty room. Letting out a frustrated sigh, I stand up and begin folding the clothes again, hoping to distract myself.

I'm putting away the last of the laundry when I have an epiphany, Dawson is a moot point. He has nothing to do with my date tonight, I will deal with him tomorrow. Tonight, I'm going to go out with Preston, have a fantabulous time and teach him to tango; vertically AND maybe, horizontally too.

With a renewed excitement, I head into my bathroom and begin preparing for tonight. Stripping off, I fill the sink, grab my razor and shave —everywhere. Once I'm smooth as a baby's butt all over, I run myself a bath. A soak in the tub is just what I need to relax and mentally prepare for tonight. Drizzling in my fav soak, I climb in, moaning as I slide down. The water is a little hot but it eases my muscles and is just what I need right now. Leaning back, I close my eyes and think about Preston. My clit begins to pulse as I picture him; muscular arms, chiseled jaw, gorgeous smile, eyes that bore deep into my soul. Sliding my hand down my body, I press on my throbbing clit and moan. Lifting my leg up, I rest it over the edge of the tub and slip my finger between my folds and push it inside. With my other hand, I massage and squeeze my breast. Pinching my nipple between my thumb and forefinger. His name slips through my lips, "Preston," as my pleasure builds. Slipping a second finger in, I speed up my thrusts, squeezing my breasts harder. Closing my eyes, I shout, "Preston!" as I explode around my fingers. The fiercest self-induced orgasm I've ever had tears through my body, leaving me sated and relaxed.

Opening my eyes, I pull my leg back into the tub and slide down, submerging myself under the water. Blowing out the air in my lungs, à la Julie Roberts in *Pretty Woman*. Breaking the surface, I lean back and sigh. "Fuck me," I mumble as I close my eyes and wait for my heart rate to return to normal. Once I'm me again, I climb out, hop into the shower so I can wash my hair since I dunked myself. If I don't, I'll end up with a frizzy mop, and that's the last thing I want for tonight.

Climbing out of the shower, I dry off and slip on my robe. Plugging in my hair dryer, I dry my hair and then straighten it. I can never blow-dry my hair like the hairdresser does, it always ends up a frizzy mess—thank God for straighteners—at least I can do that. Once my hair is silky smooth, I grab some sexy lingerie and redress. Looking at the time, I see I have just enough time to grab a coffee before I head to school to pick Lexi up. Pulling on my jeans and a tank top, I grab my keys, slip into my flip-flops, and head out the door.

Twenty minutes later, I'm at school waiting for Lexi to get out. The bell rings and all hell breaks loose. There are kids and parents everywhere. Like a heat-seeking missile, my eyes land on Lexi and when she sees me she waves and races toward me. Dropping to my knees, I open my arms wide. "Hey, Munchkin."

"Hi, Mommy," she replies as I envelop her in a hug.

"You give the best hugs," I tell her, as I place a kiss on the tip of her nose.

"I know," she says with a grin. "I can't wait to sleep at Nanna's tonight."

"She can't wait for you to either."

"Will you be staying with us, like on the weekend?"

"Not tonight, sweetie, I don't want to disturb you since it's a school night."

She nods. "That's a goodly thing. You're a goodly mommy." *Damn, Baylor*, I think to myself hearing Lexi use goodly. Yes, it's a real word but it so does not fit this context. "Are we going to Nanna's now?"

"We can if you want, OR we can swing by the park?"

"Park then home then Nanna's. That's such a goodly idea, Mommy." I shake my head at the use of goodly, again.

"Okay, let's go." She places her hand in mine and we head to the car.

Twenty minutes later, we are at the park and as usual, Lexi makes a beeline for the swings. My phone beeps with a text and I smile when I pull it out.

PRESTON: *T-minus 3 hours and 12 minutes 'til my tango lesson*

A smile graces my face as I read his message. It's nice to know he's as excited as I am for tonight.

CRESS: *Remind me again what's happening in T-minus 3 hours and 11 minutes*
PRESTON: *The best night of your life will commence*
CRESS: *That's a big call to make, Dr. Knight. You better bring your 'A' game stud*
PRESTON: *Ohh, I plan to, love, AND I'm hoping to hit a home run... multiple times*
PRESTON: *See you soon you sexy, raccoon*
PRESTON: *That's totally not really sexy but you are so there's that. Laters, love*
CRESS: *Later, mater **blowing kiss emoji***

Sliding my phone back into my pocket, I watch Lexi on the swings. My mind drifts to tonight and suddenly, I'm nervous. I think I really like this guy...I can totally see myself falling for Dr. Knight.

7 PRESTON

After texting Cress about tonight, I start to wonder if I'm coming on too strong, but her replies seem to indicate I'm not, so I guess I will keep going how I am. As I climb into the shower to get ready for tonight, I shake my head. This woman is turning me into a total girl. I don't think I've ever been this excited before a date, but then again, I have never met a woman as vivacious, sexy, and intriguing as Cress Bayliss.

Stepping under the spray, the hot water hits my shoulders. Closing my eyes, I start to think about our texting/sexting over the last few days. Images of her in the shower with me run through my mind.

Water cascading down her body.

Her nipples erect, a droplet of water waiting to be licked.

The water sliding between her thighs.

Her eyes full of desire.

Her plump lips, moist and waiting to be kissed.

My cock hardens. Gripping it tightly in my fist, I picture Cress. Stopping mid-stroke, I realize I want it to be her doing this. Shocking myself, I turn the tap to cold and let go of my cock. Taking a page from Flynn, I join the blue balls club and decide to wait for tonight. Cress doing this will be so much better than my hand. Thinking of her has my cock coming to life again, so I think of saggy granny tits and it instantly deflates.

Now that my dick is under control, I soap up and wash myself, avoiding my cock because if I touch it, I will grip it and jerk it. But I want more than anything for Cress to have that pleasure later this evening. So I refrain.

Short-term pain, long-term gain.

Stepping out, I wrap my towel around my waist and walk over to the dresser. Styling my hair, I stare at my reflection. I look different, I realize my eyes are brighter than usual...I think it's to do with Cress. She's bringing me to life, prior to meeting her I was just existing. I wasn't living, she makes me want to live life...and I hope she wants to do it with me.

Stepping into my room, I get dressed. Black slacks, deep purple dress shirt with the sleeves rolled to my elbow; smart but casual. As I slip my shoes on, I start to wonder what Cress will wear tonight. Whatever she wears, I know she is going to be sexy as fuck.

Looking at the clock on my bedside table, I realize it's time to go. I'm suddenly nervous but at the same time, super excited. Grabbing my wallet and keys, I head into the garage. Pushing the button on the wall, the garage door opens. I climb into my car and start the engine, "Closer" by Nine Inch Nails begins to play. This song is sexy and dirty...*a good sign for tonight*, I think to myself as I back out of the driveway.

On the drive over to pick Cress up, I stop and grab a bunch of flowers. Not knowing what her favorite are, I grab a bouquet of sunflowers, which happens to be my mom's favorite flower. With my flowers in hand, I get back on the road and my nerves settle; that is until I open the door at her mom's. My mouth drops open at the vision before me. Cress is wearing a blood red halter dress that hugs her body in the sexiest possible way. There's a split up the side accentuating her legs, her hair is straighter than straight, and her lips are stained red to match her dress. "Fuck me, you are a vision, Cressida Bayliss."

"Cress," she murmurs, as her cheeks darken. Her eyes roam over my body and my cock appreciates the eye fucking. We silently stare at one another, the air around us thick with desire, want, and need. The moment is broken when Lexi steps beside her mom. "Hey, Dr. Preston."

"Hey, Munchkin, how you feeling now?"

"All better."

"That's great to hear."

"I took my Pony medicine, just like you said."

"Excellent," I say, offering my hand in a high five which she excitedly hits. I shake my hand, pretending it hurts. "Wow, that's a strong high five you have there."

"It's cause I eat all my veggies."

"Did you eat them all up tonight?"

"Yes…even the yucky Brussels sprouts."

I make a face. "I don't like them either." Suddenly I remember the flowers and the little something that I have for Lexi. "Give me a sec," I tell them and race to my car and grab the gifts. Walking back up the path, I hand the flowers to Cress. "These are for you," I say, pressing a kiss to her cheek.

"Thank you," she murmurs, as I drop back down and hand Lexi her gift.

She snatches the gift bag from my hand and pulls out the *My Little Pony: Friendship is Magic* DVD; her eyes light up. "My very own Pony DVD. Thank you, Dr. Preston, thank you." She throws her little arms around my neck and hugs me.

"You are most welcome, Princess."

Looking up, I see Cress holding the flowers in one hand and her other over her heart with an adorable look on her face. Winking at her, her cheeks darken. "Let me pop these in some water and then we can go."

"I can do that," her mom says from behind her.

"Evening, Momma Cress."

"Evening, Preston," she says, taking the flowers from Cress. She winks at her daughter. "You two have fun tonight."

"Mom," Cress scoffs, as she turns around to get her things. My eyes watch as she walks away and her dress from the back is just as stunning.

Momma Cress steps over to me and stares intently at me. "You hurt my baby girl and I'll hurt you. These two girls are all I have left, and I will not let anyone hurt them again. You got me?"

Nodding my head, I confirm, "Yes, ma'am—"

"Don't call me ma'am," she interrupts.

"Yes, Momma Cress. I don't plan on hurting her, or Lexi, or you. Scout's honor." I hold up three fingers and smile.

"Good." Cress walks back toward us, her shoes echoing on the floorboard. "Now you two kids have a great night," she says to Cress, kissing her on the cheek before Cress drops down and hugs Lexi goodbye.

"Be a good girl for Nanna and I will see you in the afternoon after school."

"Nite nite, Mommy." Lexi pulls away and cups her mom's cheek in her hand. Cress stands up and steps beside me. "Bye, Dr. Preston." Lexi says, offering me her fist for a fist bump.

"Bye, Lexi girl," I reply, bumping my fist with hers.

Lexi and Momma Cress head inside and close the door. Looking to Cress, I smile. "Shall we?"

"We shall," she says and links her arm with mine as we walk down the path to my car for our date, one of many…I hope.

8 CRESS

WHEN PRESTON HANDED ME THE FLOWERS, MY HEART RATE SPED UP AT THE thoughtfulness of his gift. When he handed Lexi a gift as well, my whole body thrummed with pleasure and my heart soared, especially when I saw what it was. A sob built in the back of my throat as I watched Preston with the most important person in my life, the scene before me was so beautiful. The connection he has with Lexi is strong already. I can tell that if this goes off the rails between us, she too will be heartbroken. Then Mom arrives and even she is smitten with him. Damn, we will all be gutted if this turns to shit. Maybe I need to back off and keep them apart until I know what this is between us.

Mom takes the flowers from me when I offer to pop them in water, but I'm thankful, as I don't really want to leave her alone with Preston, who knows what would occur. As I rejoin them, I bite the inside of my cheek to hold back my laugh when Mom scolds him for calling her ma'am.

We say our goodbyes, with a fist bump for Preston and Lexi—it totally melts my heart seeing that—and then he escorts me to his car. With each step we take down the path, my nerves ramp up. My eyes land on his car and I smile. "Your car is pretty sexy, Dr. Knight."

"As are you, Ms. Bayliss." He reaches around me and opens my door.

"Thank you, Sir."

"No thank you, Love. Thank you for allowing me to wine and dine you tonight."

"You just want the promised horizontal tango lesson."

"That's just an added bonus." He pauses and looks at me, his gaze heating my skin, and again that déjà vu feeling washes over me. "Cress, tonight is just the beginning of something beautiful." With those words, he closes my door. *Holy shit*, we haven't even left the house yet and I'm already swooning for this man.

He pulls into a parking garage and we climb out. My eyes rake over his car and I shake my head, this is one sexy car...for a sexy as hell man. "Shall we?" he says, offering me his elbow.

"We shall."

Linking my arm through his, we make our way to the elevator and take it down to the street level. We step out and cross the road. My eyes light up when I see we are walking toward, Las Tapas. It's a mom-and-pop run Spanish restaurant. "Ohh, I love this place."

"Me too, they make the best—"

"–paella," we say together and laugh.

Things are so easy with Preston, I can definitely see myself falling for this man and that scares me. I haven't felt like this with anyone since Creed, and we all know how that turned out.

We step inside and while we wait to be seated, we look at one another, and again that déjà vu feeling appears. "Have we met before?" I ask.

Preston shakes his head. "I don't think so, but occasionally when I gaze at you I get this feeling like we have."

Nodding my head, I smile. "It's so weird."

"Well, either way, I'm glad I get to know you now," he says, just as the hostess arrives and escorts us to our table.

Las Tapas is your typical Spanish restaurant. Gorgeous Spanish inspired artwork lines the walls, crystal chandeliers hang from the ceiling. There's custom-made bar tops with handmade Spanish tiles and natural wood. Wine racks full of wine line the walls and large windows overlook the outdoor dining area. Each table is set with candles, making it intimate and perfect for our first date, by creating the perfect romantic dining experience.

Preston pulls out my chair and pushes it in. The heat from his body sets mine ablaze, he didn't even touch me and I'm already turned on, panting and wanting more. Thankfully the waitress arrives and hands us our menus.

"Buena noches, what can I get you to drink?"

"Can I grab a glass of Tempranillo, please?"

"Make it a bottle," Preston says.

"Por supuesto," the waitress replies, turning away from us, she makes her way back to the bar, leaving Preston and me alone for the first time since we sat down.

We stare at each other across the table. I lick my bottom lip and gently bite, my go-to movement when I'm nervously excited. This man does things to me, even without laying a hand on me. I notice his eyes locked on my lips, then he looks into my eyes. His stare penetrates deep into my soul. My body thrums with desire. I swallow deeply. Neither of us has spoken but so much has been said with our eyes.

I want you.

I desire you.

I need you.

The waitress returns with the wine but we keep staring at each other. She silently opens the bottle and fills our glasses. She turns and as she walks away, I hear her silently whisper, "That was caliente."

We both laugh.

Picking up his glass, he raises it in a toast, "To the beginning of something amazing."

"I'll drink to that."

Tapping my glass against his, I take a sip and moan in delight. "Ohh wow, that's a good vintage." Looking up, I see Preston staring at me open-mouthed. "What? Do I have something on my face?"

He shakes his head, "No, that sound you just made had my mind going to a dirty sexy place...with you."

"Do tell, Dr. Knight," I playfully tease, resting my elbows on the table and my chin in my palm, blinking rapidly at him. When I stop with the blinking, I realize that probably looks like I'm having a fit rather than the sexy siren I was going for.

He leans forward, "Well..." But before he can tell me all the dirty sexy things, the waitress arrives.

"Are you ready to order?"

"The paella," we both say at the same time.

"el amor está floreciendo," the waitress says with a smile, before turning around and leaving us alone again.

"What did she just say?" I ask, my voice laced with confusion and intrigue.

"Beats me," Preston shrugs. "But she seems pretty happy right now, so I'm guessing it was something good."

"It was very good," the lady at the table next to us says.

We both turn our heads to see an elderly couple at the table.

"What did she say?" Preston asks her.

"Love is blossoming," her husband says, He takes his wife's hand in his and brings it to his lips and kisses her knuckles. She smiles adoringly at him, love radiates between the two of them. "Lucia and I had paella on our first date sixty-five years ago. Love is the food of life. Paella is life therefore paella is the food of life and love. And Lucia is my life and love. "

"That is beautiful. I wish you many more years of love and paella."

"Salud," he says, raising his wine glass toward us.

Preston and I raise ours in return and both say, "Salud." We gaze at one another, our eyes are locked on each other, as we sip the wine.

We are both quiet, processing the man's words.

Lucia and her husband stand up and leave. I watch as they walk away, he gently rests his hand on her lower back; that is unbridled true love. Looking to Preston, I smile. "Wow, can you imagine being with someone for that long?"

"I'll let you know in sixty-five years." Preston replies, the look in his eye is carnal.

Lifting my wine to my lips, I take a sip and stare at Preston over the rim of the glass. This man continues to amaze me, I keep thinking I'm going to wake up because sexy doctors don't want me. I'm a nobody; therefore this must be a dream. A fucking good dream but it must be a dream nonetheless. Preston squeezes my arm, snapping my attention back to the present and the realization that this is in fact real life.

"You drifted off there, where did you go just now?"

"Nowhere in particular. Just thinking that this must be a dream because I'm on a date with a sexy doctor in an amazing restaurant. Drinking amazing wine about to dine on a fantabulous paella. Things like this don't happen to me. Ever. Therefore this must be a dream."

"You think I'm sexy?"

"That's what you took from what I just said?"

"I took the important parts. I'm sexy and fantabulous paella."

"You are really something, Dr. Knight."

"A good something?"

"I haven't made my mind up yet," I pause for emphasis, "but if tonight keeps proceeding like this, you will definitely be getting that tango lesson before the night is over."

9 PRESTON

FUCK ME, THIS WOMAN IS SOMETHING ELSE. I HAVE NEVER BEEN AROUND A woman like her before. She's sexy as fuck. Vivacious. Flirtatious. Funny. Down-to-Earth. She is the complete package.

Our date is going smoothly. The paella is delicious, both of us moaning in delight with each mouthful. After dinner, we finish off the wine and continue to get to know one another. "...I'm pretty sure I scared Ave off of ever having kids after I nearly crushed her hand when I was in labor."

"You are amazing," I honestly tell her.

"How so?"

"You're raising your daughter alone."

"I'm not alone, I have Ave and Mom."

"No, they help occasionally. *You* are doing all the hard work yourself AND you substitute teach if needed."

"It's nothing compared to what you do."

"Don't sell yourself short, Cress. I think you're amazing and that's all there is to it. Now, would you like to dance with me?"

She looks over her shoulder and sees a few other couples dancing, that's one of the things I love about this place. People don't care, they just do what feels right, and right now, I want to dance with this woman. Her face lights up. "I'd love to."

Standing up, I step over to her and offer my hand. She places hers in mine and like each time we touch, there's a spark that jolts through me. Spinning her around, I pull her in close to me. One hand sits on her lower back, the other holds her hand between us. She rests her head on my shoulder and we sway to the music. Our bodies becoming one. Taking a deep breath, I breathe in. Her smell envelops me. "I love your scent," I whisper into her hair, breathing everything about her in again. "I could get high breathing you in."

I feel her smile against me. "I've worn this since forever," she quietly says as we continue to dance.

"What is it?"

She lifts her head and gazes into my eyes. "True Love by Elizabeth Arden."

If that isn't a sign of what's to happen between us, I don't know what is. Between her perfume name, the kind words from the waitress, and the love story between Lucia and her husband, we are surrounded by all things love tonight. I can see myself falling for Cressida Bayliss.

Cress rests her head back on my shoulder, her body molding into mine once again. She turns her head and begins to kiss and nuzzle where my neck and shoulder meet. My hand slides down her back and I cup her ass, her perfect taut ass, in my palm. She reaches down and lifts my hand from her ass, placing it back on her lower back. Making a quiet tsking sound as she lets go.

Sliding my hand back down, I squeeze her ass this time. She lifts her head and stares at me. It's the perfect moment for our first kiss. Closing my eyes, I begin to lean forward when she spins away. I realize the music has changed, to a much faster song. She holds my hand and spins in and out in sync with the music. She spins back in, this time her back to my front. She swivels her hips, which has my cock wanting to dance too. There's no hiding what she's doing to my body right now. She glances at me over her shoulder and winks. *Minx*, I think to myself as she spins out again. This time when she spins back in, she slides her hands seductively up and down my chest. She grabs my hands. "Let's dance," she huskily says. The tone of her voice heads straight to my dick and it hardens further between us. I'm frozen, I stare at the sex bomb before me. "Let's tango," she says, as she takes my hands in hers and we begin to tango.

I've always thought this was a sexy dance, but to be involved in said dance, it's even sexier than I imagined. Cress is amazing. Her body flows with the music, pressing seductively into mine and surprising me, I keep up with her. Probably because having her body pressed against mine is the most amazing feeling in the world.

As the song comes to an end, she spins back into me, wrapping my hands around her stomach. She leans her head back and stares at me over her shoulder. We are both breathing heavily. The minx, once again, swivels her hips against my cock. Not letting her win, I press it into her ass. She slides a hand between us and grips my hip, squeezing tight and rubbing her ass in circles on my cock. There's no hiding my desire for her.

"Cress," I warn, but there's no way in hell that's going to stop what she's doing. Right at this moment, I wish we were at home naked doing this.

"What?" she innocently says.

Shaking my head, I surprise her when I spin her out and pull her back in. Sliding my hands into her hair, I pull her to me, and slam my lips against hers. She slides her hands around my shoulders and pulls me closer. Deepening our kiss. As first kisses go, this one takes the cake. Our tongues bump in their own seductive dance. Breaking the kiss, she pulls back and stares at me. We are both panting, the kiss leaving each of us breathless. Ever so slowly, I trace down her spine and place my hand on her ass, gently squeezing. Her lips lift into a smile that lights up her face. She rests her head back onto my shoulder and we lose ourselves to the music, once again slow dancing.

The song ends, we pull apart, staring at one another. Cupping her cheek in my palm, I run my thumb along her jawbone before I lean in and press my lips against hers again. Pulling back, I rest my forehead against hers. "You have the lips of an angel, Cress. Where have you been?"

"Raising my little girl and waiting for you," she whispers. She takes a step back. "Now, take me home, Preston, so I can give you that naked tango lesson I promised."

10 CRESS

AS FIRST DATES GO, THIS IS THE BEST ONE EVER IN THE HISTORY OF FIRST DATES. Well, for me that's the case and I really hope it is for him too. Preston is the whole package: hot, fun, caring, charismatic, hot—yes I know I said hot twice but hello, he looks like Channing-freaking-Tatum's brother, that deserves two hots. Dancing just now was the most fun I've had in a long time. I cannot remember the last time I danced like this. Come to think about it, it would have been the night Lexi was conceived. Creed took me out to this Latin club and we danced the night away. Shaking my head, I don't want to be thinking of *him* right now. Tonight is all about Preston and me, and possibly the start of something amazing. I'm not sure I'm ready for a relationship but if anyone can sway that decision, it will be Preston Knight.

Lacing my fingers with Preston's we exit the restaurant after he settles the bill. I offered to pay half but ever the gentleman, he wouldn't hear of it. We walk toward his car in the parking garage; the only sound the echoing of my heels clicking on the cement floor. As we approach it, I whistle, "This seriously is a sexy car." I stop and appreciate the machine before me. I don't know shit about cars but I do know, this one is hot.

"I've seen sexier things."

Looking to him, my face is etched with confusion because this is the sexiest car around. "What else could possibly be sexier than this?" I ask, flicking my hand up and down his car.

He steps behind me, I can feel his breath on my skin. "You," he huskily answers, as he slides his hand around my waist, pulling me into him. My head drops back to his shoulder, elongating my throat. He darts his tongue out and licks up my neck, my skin breaks out in goosebumps, and I moan. My hips rub against his crotch, garnering a low growl from him. He cups my cheek, turns my head toward him, and kisses me. This kiss takes my breath away. If his other hand wasn't on my hip holding me up, I'd be a puddle on the floor.

Our tongues dance and caress one another, spinning to face him, I deepen the kiss. Pressing my chest to his. "Take me home, Preston," I whisper against his lips.

Without saying a word, he unlocks the car and opens my door for me. Climbing in, I watch him walk around the hood. His eyes steadfastly locked on mine. He climbs in, starts the car, and speeds toward his place.

We pull into his driveway and the door to the garage automatically opens, he parks and turns the car off. He must sense me watching him because he turns to look at me. My breathing quickens and nerves wrack through me at the intensity of his gaze.

"Cress," he whispers. Reaching over he brushes a tendril of hair behind my ear and cups my cheek in his palm.

"Pres," I whisper back, leaning into his palm.

He pulls my head toward him and he presses his lips to mine. Cupping his cheeks in my palms I hungrily kiss him back. The temperature in the car rises rapidly. Breaking the connections between us, I whisper, "Take me inside, Pres, I owe you a horizontal tango lesson and I have a feeling you will be the best student ever."

"A's all round for this boy."

"I was hoping for big O's," I playfully tease.

"I'm sure that can be arranged. Inside now, Ms. Bayliss, I'm ready for my lesson."

We climb out and head inside. Preston's place is gorgeous. Large open plan living, dining, and kitchen; which looks like it leads to an outdoor entertainment area. Chrome and black accents, it's very stylish and sophisticated. Exactly how I pictured his place. Noticing a kick-ass stereo system, I head over to it and connect up my Spotify account. I bring up a dance playlist and when I see the perfect song, I hit play. "Closer" by Nine Inch Nails begins to play. My hips move to the beat of the music. Turning around I see Preston staring intently at me, a grin etched on his face.

"This is fate, Cress."

"How so?"

"This song was playing in my car earlier this evening."

"That is the very definition of fate. Now, Dr. Knight, where would you like your lesson?"

"Come with me."

He turns around and walks down the hallway and into the master bedroom. He flicks on the lights, presses a button on the remote, which was sitting on the dresser, and the music from the living room filters into the room. Leaning against the doorframe I watch as he walks over to a chair in the corner. Untucking his shirt from his pants, he takes a seat. Leaning back, he undoes the top two buttons on his shirt, before resting his hands on the arm of the chair. He is the epitome of an alpha male right now. Sexy. Powerful. In charge. The alphaness oozing from him. Seeing him like this sets my body ablaze. I now know how Ana felt in *Fifty Shades* when Christian would watch her; I've never felt sexier than I do right now.

"The floor is yours," he says, gesturing to the space in front of him.

Pushing off the doorframe, my hips sway to the beat of the music. Running my hands up my neck and into my hair, I flick through the strands. Stretching my hands above my head. My eyes are locked on Preston as I slide my hands seductively up and down my sides. With my fingertip, I trace along my cleavage, between the valley of my breasts, down my stomach. Gripping the hem, I lift it up slightly, and shake the material side to side. His eyes are locked on my movements. Stepping over to him, I beckon him forward with my finger.

Preston slides to the edge of the chair, spreading his legs wide for me to stand in front of him. My hips continue to swing to the music. Reaching out, I undo the buttons on Preston's shirt. Tracing my finger up his chest, I circle his nipple. Stepping back, I turn round and look at him over my shoulder. Squatting down, I continue to look at him over my shoulder, standing up I bend forward at the hips, and shimmy my ass in his face. Snapping back into an upright position, I turn to face him again.

His eyes are full of desire and they watch my every movement. Stepping back, I stare down at him. "Up," I demand.

He stands before me and I slide my hands across his shoulders, dragging his dress shirt down his arms. The material drops to the floor, he's standing before me in nothing but his dress pants. Both of us panting. The song changes to "Cheap Thrills" by Sia. Pushing off his chest, I spin around in circles. Flicking my hips to the beat of the music. Preston steps behind me. He rests his palms on my hips, sliding them down to grip the hem of my dress, and begins to lift it up. "Ah uh," I say. Stepping away, I turn to face him. With my eyes locked on his, I brush my hair over my left shoulder and undo the bow at my neck, sliding my hands around my neck. Letting go of the strap, the material falls to my feet. Leaving me in my black strapless bra and matching panties.

Pushing him back, he falls into the chair. Resting my hands on the arm, I stare at him before pressing myself forward. My body hovering an inch in front of him, I can feel his breath on my chest. Standing up, I brush my chest against his face. A growl erupts from him. With a grin on my face, I step to the center of the room. Turning to face him, I call him forward with my finger. He stands up and prowls over to me. The look on his face sets my body on fire. He stops in front of me. Without saying a word, I undo his belt, pop the button, lower his fly, and push his pants down. We are now both in our underwear. Placing my hand on his lower back, I pull him into me. Taking his hand in mine, I place it on my hip. He grips my other hand and brings it between us.

With our gaze locked on one another we sway side to side. Our movements are not in sync with the music but the moment is pure perfection. He spins me out and back in again, just like we did at the restaurant. He repeats the spin and this time, I end up with my back to his front.

He hugs me to him, nuzzling my neck. "Cress, you are the sexiest woman I have ever met." I moan when he sucks my neck. Dropping my head back onto his shoulder. He finds the front clasp of my bra and flicks it open, my breasts spill free. He cups them in his palms as I swivel my hips on his groin. His cock hardening the more I press against him.

The song comes to an end, and I stay wrapped in his arms. My back to his front. Looking over my shoulder, we stare intently at one another, our chests rapidly rising with each breath we take. He lowers his head and presses his lips to mine, my eyes close and I give myself over to the kiss. He wraps his arms tighter around me, one hand cupping my boob and squeezing. The other slides down my stomach, where he cups my pussy over my panties. I moan. Breaking the kiss, I open my eyes and stare into his. My hips gently rock side to side, his cock pressing into the crack of my ass, the material of our underwear the only barrier.

We are both breathing heavily, the air around us electrified with desire, want, need, and hunger.

Preston slides his other hand down my side, gripping my hips, he tears my panties off before quickly removing his briefs. He presses me into his freed erection. The head of his cock pushing against my ass, a guttural moan breaks free. I've never been as turned on as I am right now. Sliding my hand around his neck, I run my fingers into his hair and gently tug. Our hips still circling and pressing into each other. Lowering my hand, I slide it between us and grip his cock in my palm. Squeezing.

"Cress," he groans.

Spinning around to face him, I lick my bottom lip, with my eyes locked on his, I begin to drop to my knees. He grabs me by the shoulders and pulls me back up into a standing position. He grips my ass and lifts me up, on instinct I wrap my legs around his waist and drape my arms over his shoulders. His thick shaft pressing into my stomach as our mouths crash together in a frenzied kiss. Tightening my arms around his neck, I press myself into him. You cannot tell where I end and he begins.

He sits on the end of the bed with me straddling him. Lifting myself up, I circle myself around the tip of his cock. I begin to lower myself down when he says, "Condom." Standing up, with me still in his arms, he walks around the side of the bed and sits near the head. He reaches into the side table drawer and grabs one. Shuffling back, I take the foil packet from him and tear it open with my teeth. Quickly I sheath his cock and then, once again, I lift up and circle the tip before I sink myself onto him. We both moan in delight as I fully seat myself on him. With our eyes locked on one another, I slowly begin to move my hips in circles. Pushing Preston back, he falls to the bed and I follow. He slides his hands into my hair and pulls my lips to his. Closing my eyes, I focus solely on the feel of his lips on mine, and his cock sliding in and out of me.

"Prestoooon," I mewl, as an intense orgasm detonates out of nowhere.

My walls clench around him while my body tingles from head to toe as pleasure courses throughout my body. My release sets Preston off, his body stiffens beneath me. He groans and grunts as he releases in the condom.

Falling off, I lie next to him panting. Staring at the ceiling and catching my breath. Turning my head to the side, I see Preston looking at me. "Hi," I murmur.

"Hi," he says back, leaning over to me and pressing his lips to mine. "That was the best dance lesson of my life. I think I want to sign up for more."

"I'll have to check my schedule but I'm sure I can fit you in. You are, by far, my best student."

"I better be your only student."

Nodding my head, I smile. "This is a one student only school."

"Good," he says before pressing his lips to mine again. I shudder at the intensity of this kiss; he pulls me into his side and we cuddle. Closing my eyes, I drift off to sleep completely sated and totally falling for Dr. Knight.

11 PRESTON

OPENING MY EYES, I HAVE A SMILE ON MY FACE. I HAD THE BEST DREAM LAST night, then a soft little snore from beside me garners my attention. Turning my head, I smile when I realize my dream was in fact reality from last night. Cress and I did the tango, both horizontally and vertically, and we did it both clothed and unclothed. My cock clearly remembers because he is proudly standing to attention, hoping for a replay of last night.

Reaching over, I brush a tendril of blonde hair off her forehead, gently grazing her skin as I do. This causes Cress to open her eyes. When she notices me staring at her, she smiles. It lights up her face, the blue of her eyes intensifying as she wakes up.

"Morning, Dr. Knight."

"Morning, Ms. Bayliss."

We stare at one another. She leans toward me, the sheet slipping down, exposing her tits to me. I get the sudden urge to lean forward and suck and bite them. That thought is thwarted when Cress climbs over and straddles my waist. She stares down at me and we silently gaze at one another, the temperature in the room rising by the second. She leans down and places her hands on either side of my head, her eyes boring deep into my soul. Lowering her head, she presses her lips to mine. Opening my mouth, she slides her tongue in. My hands grip her hips, when she begins grinding herself on me. Smearing her arousal on my stomach. She takes my lip between her teeth and gently bites. Letting my lip go, she kisses along my jawline to my ear. She's breathing heavily, much like I am. My heart races with each nip of her teeth on my skin. When she bites my earlobe and sucks it, I groan at the sensation. Pain and pleasure mixing together. I'm not normally into the pain/pleasure side of intimacy but with Cress, I'm willing to try anything; and everything.

Shimmying down, she stops when my rock-hard cock hits her ass. She licks and nibbles her way down my neck and across my collarbone. Sucking and biting my nipple. "Fuuuuck," I moan, increasing my grip on her hips. I want nothing more than to flip her over and fuck her but at the same time, I want to see where this will lead.

Sitting up, she stares down at me and traces the path her tongue just took with her fingertip. My skin is buzzing and burning for this woman. She circles my nipple before twisting and squeezing. I hiss at the sensation, my cock twitches against her ass. Her lips lift in a smirk as her fingertip traces over my abs. I'm not ripped but I am in shape and right now, I'm thankful for the countless hours I've spent in the gym.

She lifts to her knees and I inwardly smile at what's to come next, much to my dismay, she slides her wet pussy over my shaft and straddles my thighs. "Cress," I plead.

The little minx winks at me and leans forward. Her tongue circles my navel before she licks down toward my crotch. She purrs as she licks over the spot where she was grinding herself earlier. *I really want to taste her*, I think to myself as I lift to my elbows and watch her. We stare at one another as her tongue continues south, down to my cock. It's harder than it's ever been before, I cannot wait to see her lips around my shaft. She licks around the base, licking as if it's a melting ice cream on a hot summer's day. She licks up the side, and then back down. I growl because I want my cock in her mouth. She grips my shaft and begins to pump as she sucks one of my balls into her mouth. Humming around me, the sensation is amazing. I've never felt anything like it before.

"Cress," I pant, as I grip her head and pull her mouth off me. "If you don't suck my cock right now, I will not be held accountable for what I do to your mouth."

"Patience, Dr. Knight. Patience," she teases, as she sucks my ball into her mouth, while continuing to pump my shaft up and down with her hand. My ball pops out of her mouth and she licks around the base again, her tongue going higher and higher each time.

She lifts her head and stops. She stares at me, her tongue darts out and flicks over the head of my cock. It's throbbing. I don't know how much longer I can hold back. She winks at me and, finally, covers my cock with her mouth. It's wet. It's warm. It's fucking heaven. Hollowing her cheeks, she sucks my cock into her mouth. The head hits the back of her throat before she pulls out again. Repeating the process over and over until she opens her throat and takes all of my cock into her mouth and down her throat. This is the best blowjob in the history of blowjobs.

She cups my balls and continues to suck on my shaft. Our eyes locked on one another as she blows my mind with her blowjob skills. My balls tighten and then I come. I come like I've never come before. Cress sucks and swallows every last drop. When my cock pops out of her mouth, she wipes the corner of her lips. She leans down and ever so lightly brushes her breasts against my skin. Placing a quick kiss on my lips, she hops off the bed and walks to my en suite. I take the time to appreciate her gloriously naked ass and legs, they are perfect in every way. This ass man is very happy.

She grips the doorframe and looks at me over her shoulder, "I'll have a coffee, black, one sugar, please." She steps into the bathroom and closes the door behind her.

Shaking my head, I climb out of bed and pull on my navy lounge pants and head into the kitchen to get my girl coffee. Yes, I referred to her as my girl, I'm man enough to admit that I am falling for this woman. Grabbing out the coffee grounds, I fill the coffee maker and turn it on. When the coffee is brewed, I make two coffees—one black with one sugar and the other, with hazelnut creamer. I've just finished making them when Cress steps into the room and I pause mid-stir. She's slipped on my shirt from last night. She's rolled the sleeves up and she looks sexy as hell.

"You look much better in that shirt than I do."

"You need your eyes tested, but thank you for the compliment."

She walks over to me and jumps up on the counter. Handing her the coffee, she brings it to her lips and inhales before she takes a sip. Closing her eyes, she moans.

"Good coffee?" I tease.

Her eyes pop open and with a smile that lights up her face, she nods. "Coffee is life and this here is a ducking good coffee."

"Did you just say ducking?"

"Yeah, I'm used to saying it around Lexi so I now kinda just say it all the time."

Nodding at her, I take a sip. "She really is a great kid." I want to ask about her father, but is it too soon to pry and ask that question? I mean, we've only been on one date and really it's none of my business. Hearing her say my name, snaps my attention back to her. "Sorry, I missed what you said."

"I said, yeah she is, but Mom and Ave are a big part of that."

I decide to go for it. "What about her dad?"

She sighs, "He pops in when he feels like it."

"That's a douche thing to do."

"Well, Creed is a deadbeat so it's no surprises there, but I'd never stop him from seeing her. Just because he and I didn't work out, shouldn't mean she misses out on her father." She looks sad as she says this. "He's actually popping by this afternoon…if he shows."

"He's not reliable?"

She shakes her head, "Not really. I haven't told Lexi because I don't want her to get upset if he bails on her."

"He do that often?"

"More often than not."

"I'm sorry to hear that. Do you need to get home? Or can I offer you brunch?"

"I don't need to be home 'til later so brunch would be lovely. Can I help you cook?"

A laugh breaks free. "I can't cook to save my life, Cress. I was going to order from this little place down the street. They do the best eggs Benny."

"So you do have a flaw?"

"We can't all be perfect, sexy, and amazing like you."

Her cheeks tinge pink at my compliment. I step over to her, take her cup from her hands, and a growl slips through her lips. Gripping her cheeks in my palms, I stare into her eyes before I press my lips to hers. Pulling back, I rest my forehead against hers. "You are exquisite, Cressida Bayliss, don't let anyone tell you otherwise."

Pulling away, I grab the menu from the drawer and hand it to her. "Tell me what you want and I'll order us brunch."

She stares at me. "The Benny sounds amazing, and Preston?" She looks to me. "You're pretty spectacular too."

Wiping my mouth, I lean back in my chair and watch Cress. From the sounds she's currently making, I think she likes the Benny. "It's good, hey?"

"The absolute best. If I died right now, I'd die a happy woman."

"I wouldn't be happy if you died," I say. Pushing back from the table, I walk over to Cress, leaning one hand on the table and sliding the other into her hair, I kiss her temple. "Let's go sit by the pool, you head over and I'll get us another coffee."

She looks up at me. "You had me a coffee."

Racing inside, I make two more coffees and when I head back out, Cress is sitting on the edge of the pool, her legs dangling in the water. Placing the coffees down beside her, I go to take a seat next to her but I lose my balance and fall into the water. When I surface, Cress is laughing; the glee on her face is priceless, and even though I'm wet, that look makes it all worth it.

"Ohhhhhhh, Preston," she says through her laughter. "Are you okay?"

"I'm fine. You should join me, the water is lovely."

"I'm good thanks."

I lunge toward her but she's quicker than me and she rolls to the side, flashing me, and I'm stunned to see she's not wearing any panties. All this time she's been in my shirt and *only* my shirt. Had I known this, I would have taken her on the counter when she first entered the kitchen.

"Where are your panties?" I question, as I pull myself out of the pool. My water soaked my sweats, pulling them low. I notice Cress is staring at me.

"Inside," she nonchalantly says, as she stands up.

"Why are you not wearing them?" She shrugs. "Would you like me to slide my cock into you? Because that is the only reason I can think as to why you would be pantyless right now." I pause and stare at her. Her breathing has become labored and she bites her bottom lip. "I bet you're wet right now."

"I'm not the one who just went for a swim, therefore I'm not wet."

"Not the wetness I'm referring to. I bet you're soaked between your thighs and from the way you just clenched your legs, I bet I'm correct."

"Why don't we take a shower and you can find out?"

Walking over to her, I take her hand in mine and drag her inside. Her phone beeps with a text as we step inside.

"I need to get that, it's Mom's tone."

"I'll go start the shower." Dropping her hand, I slide my arm around her waist and pull her to me. Slamming my lips to her, I kiss her. My tongue slips into her mouth and I kiss her deeply. My hand slips between her thighs and I find her wet and ready. "I knew it," I murmur against her lips. Tapping her on the ass, I turn and walk away, leaving her to check her message.

Turning the water on, I strip off my wet clothes and climb into the shower. Closing my eyes, I step under the flow. Stretching my neck, I smile when I feel her eyes on me. Lifting my head, I can't see through the glass due to the steam. Wiping the glass, Cress comes into view and I cannot believe the sight before me. This woman is the epitome of a sex siren. She reaches behind her and "Closer" by Nine Inch Nails begins to play. Her hips swing from side to side. Her eyes are locked on mine as she lifts her hands and begins to undo the buttons on my shirt. She takes a step forward and spins on her heel. With her back to me, she pulls the shirt down her arms, the material dropping to the tiled floor. She turns back to face me and presses her body against the shower door. Her breasts flattening, she breathes against the glass, fogging it up. She winks at me, steps back, and traces her fingertip around her nipple, the tip hardening from her touch.

"Get in here now, Cress."

She licks her lip and silently opens the door. She steps into the shower stall and under the spray. Water cascades down her body. "Fuck me," I groan. "I love you all wet, Cress."

"Feel free to find out just how wet I am." She lifts her leg and rests it on the shower seat, opening herself to me. Without having to be told twice, I drop to my knees and press my face to her pussy. Flattening my tongue, I lick from taint to clit. She moans, gripping my head in her hands, pressing me farther into her.

"Preston," she mewls. "Please fuck me."

"Not until you come on my tongue."

She lifts her hands and begins to play with her breasts. I watch her hands as I thrust two fingers into her, she's soaked. Taking her clit between my teeth, I gently bite before sucking. I feel her insides clench against my fingers and with a twist, she explodes. Soaking my face with her juices, moaning my name as her orgasm erupts.

Standing up, I stare at her. Both of us heavily breathing, we leap into action together: hands exploring, lips crashing. Tapping her ass, she jumps into my arms and I press her against the wall as she sinks down onto my cock. It's hard. It's fast. It's carnal. We come together, grunting each other's names as we reach our peak.

Lowering her to her feet, we silently stare at one another as we catch our breath. "Can I wash you?" I ask, breaking the silence. She nods her head. Pumping some shower gel into my hands, I soap her up. Paying special attention to her breasts, once she's all cleaned, she returns the favor.

Once we are both clean, we step out. Handing her a towel, we silently dry off. Leaving her to fix her hair, I step into my room and change into jeans and a T-shirt. Cress steps into my room, wrapped in her towel. She drops the towel and pulls on her underwear and dress from last night.

She refastens the halter around her neck and notices me staring at her. "What?"

"Nothing, Love, just admiring your beauty." Her cheeks darken in embarrassment at my compliment. "No need to be embarrassed, Cress. I'm just stating the truth."

"No one has ever made me feel like you do, Preston. It's an odd feeling to be appreciated and wanted."

Stepping over to her, I cup her cheek in my palm. "I will always appreciate you, Cress. Now, let me get you home so you can be ready for your munchkin."

Her eyes light up at the mention of Lexi. "Thank you."

"You are welcome, Love. Now let's go before I strip you out of that dress and make you late." From the look in her eyes, I can tell she'd like that, but I know she needs to get home to her daughter and I'm okay with that. There will always be next time, and I cannot wait for a repeat of last night and this morning.

12 CRESS

Unlocking the front door, I step inside and close it behind me. With a smile on my face, I walk into my bedroom to change into something more appropriate for when Mom drops Lexi home. I don't really want my daughter to see me in last night's dress, that's not a very good example to set.

After changing into capris and a tank, I walk toward the kitchen for a much-needed caffeine boost. While I wait for my coffee, I lean against the counter and images of last night and today flash before my eyes. My body thrumming at the memory of his hands on my body, his cock sliding into me. My mouth on his cock. His tongue in my pussy. His lips on mine. A shudder wracks over my body and then I smell coffee. Looking to the machine, I see my cup of liquid gold waiting for me. Picking up the mug, I bring it to my nose and inhale. The caffeine goodness seeps into my soul. Taking a sip, I close my eyes and moan, a sound I've made many times over the last twelve hours, and sounds I hope to make again this weekend. Preston, Lexi, and I are going to have a picnic on Saturday. Normally I don't want the man I'm sleeping with around Lexi, but there's something about Preston Knight that puts me at ease and allows me to share him with her; there's also the fact she met him the same night I did.

A knock at the door halts that memory. Placing my mug on the countertop I walk to the door, swinging it open, the happiness I just felt dissipates when I see Creed standing before me. His smug face grinning at me. How I ever was in love with this man is beyond me. "Hey."

"Babydoll," he says, leaning forward to kiss my cheek. My body shuddering at his touch. "Where's the squirt?"

"She'll be home soon, you're early," I say, leaning against the door.

"I wanted to see you. Wanted to see if we could squeeze in a quick fuck before I play Daddy." He slides his arm around my waist, pulling me into me. "I know how much you love to fuck."

"Not today," I say, placing my hands on his chest and pushing myself away from him.

"What do you mean not today?" he snarls through clenching teeth.

"Exactly that, not today...or any day again."

He squeezes my shoulders and glares at me, before he viciously shoves me backward. I wasn't expecting it and I stumble, landing on the entrance table. Wincing as the corner jabs my lower left back. Lifting my hand, I rub the spot and cringe. *That's gonna bruise*, I think to myself as I stare at an angry Creed.

"Are you telling me no?" he hisses, spittle flying from his mouth.

"Yes," I defiantly say. It feels good to finally stand up to him. "Creed, we are over. You are Lexi's father and nothing more."

"Are you fucking around on me, Cressida?"

"Whom I sleep with is none of your business, Creed. We have been over for five years now, sure we've occasionally gotten together but that was just a lapse of judgement on my behalf. It won't be happening again."

"Once a slut, always a slut," he retorts, stepping into my face. His hot breath hitting my face, I smell bourbon on his breath and for the first time ever, I don't want Lexi to go with him. "Tell the squirt something came up." With that, he turns around and walks down the path to his car. He climbs in and takes off.

Closing the door, I turn around and lean against the wood, heavily breathing. The fear that built up is slowly ebbing away. The sound of a car door slamming startles me, turning around, I look through the peephole and when I see Mom and Lexi walking up the stairs, I let out the breath I was holding. Swinging the door open, I drop to my knees. "Hey, Munchkin."

"Hey, Mommy."

"How was your day at school?" I ask, my voice wavering a little. Mom notices and looks at me funny, I shake my head subtly but I know, as soon as Lexi is out of earshot, she will be questioning me. *Damn Mom knowing me so well.*

258 DL GALLIE

"It was great. Today we learnded all about trains and Trevor got a Woody–" My eyes widen at this. "–and he showed everyone."

My eyes are scrunched in confusion. "Trevor got a Woody?" I question.

She nods excitedly at me. "Yeah, Trevor got a Woody, a big one. You pull Trevor's Woody string and he says all different things. Can we watch *Toy Story* tonight, Mommy?" *Ohh, she's talking about Toy Story.* I stare at her, trying to hold back my laugh. "Can I get a big Woody too?"

"Lex, honey, why don't you go unpack your school bag?" Mom says, and I'm ever so thankful because I'm about to burst out laughing like the big immature kid I am.

"Okay, Nanna."

Lexi walks inside and as soon as she turns down the hallway, the laugh I was holding in erupts. "Oh My God, Mom. How are you not wetting yourself right now?" Mom follows me into the living room and we take a seat on the sofa.

"Because I'm worried about you. What happened? Where's Creed?"

At the mention of Creed, my laughter stops. I stare at Mom and the fear from earlier comes back. "He's an ass."

"No shit, Sherlock. What did Dickwad do now?"

"Ruined my good mood." She eyes me. "It's fine, he just showed his true colors. He won't be spending the afternoon with Lexi."

"Well, that's a bonus. The less time she spends with him the better. He's—"

"Moooom," I interrupt. "He's her father."

"Just 'cause she has his DNA, that does not make him a father. It just makes him a sperm donor and thankfully for us, there's more Bayliss DNA in her than Dawson DNA. Enough about Dickwad, tell me all about last night?"

My lips lift in a smile as I think about Preston and last night.

"Now *that's* the look I love to see on your face," Mom says. "That is the look I want to see after you spend time with a man."

"Mom." I swat at her arm.

"Sooo, how was it?"

Thankfully Lexi comes back into the room and jumps on the sofa between us, saving me from the Spanish Inquisition…for now. Mom is not just my mom, she's also my best friend. We probably tell each other more than necessary, but after Dad died and it was just the two of us, we became a team.

Lexi is still talking about Trevor's big Woody and I'm still biting my tongue holding back my laugh. Mom brings up Netflix and turns the movie on. We end up watching one and two, with a promise to watch the rest after school tomorrow. Mom leaves, without getting the answers she wants, but I know that when I get back from dropping Lexi at school tomorrow, Mom will be waiting with coffee and cake for a gossip session.

After a hot relaxing shower, I climb into bed. Wincing when I lay down, my lower back is really sore and it's already started to bruise. I'm just about asleep when my phone beeps with a text. Grabbing it off the bedside table, I smile, it's from Preston.

> **PRESTON:** *Nite nite, Love. I can smell you on my pillow, it's my new favorite scent.*
> **PRESTON:** *Is it Saturday yet?*
> **CRESS:** *It's almost Saturday.*
> **CRESS:** *My pillow smells like Tide*
> **PRESTON:** *Maybe I need to come over and rub myself all over your pillow*
> **CRESS:** *I'd rather you rub me but if pillows are your thing, who am I to stop you?*
> **PRESTON:** *Flirty minx…now I'm hard*
> **CRESS:** *Do you have a big Woody?*

I laugh to myself at my reply. I will never be able to think of *Toy Story* and Woody the same again…and I won't be able to look at little Trevor the same either. That kid has scarred me for life.

> **PRESTON:** *Whenever I think about you, I always sport a big Woody… have you forgotten already? Do we need a repeat of last night to refresh your mind?*
> **CRESS:** *My memory is just fine, but I'm down with a repeat…I do love to tango, vertically AND horizontally*
> **PRESTON:** *Dammit, Cress, I was just texting to say goodnight*
> **CRESS:** *Goodnight, Dr. Knight*
> **PRESTON:** *Goodnight, Ms. Bayliss*

With a smile on my face, I drift off to sleep dreaming about Preston's big woody and how he makes me reach for the sky.

13 PRESTON

DUE TO AN EMERGENCY AT THE HOSPITAL, I HAD TO CANCEL MY PICNIC PLANS with Cress and Lexi. Thankfully, she was understanding. Previous girl-friends would always get angry if I cancelled short notice, but not Cress. She wished me the best and said we'd catch up soon.

It's early evening when I finally get home, I'm absolutely exhausted but I want to check in with Cress. Grabbing a beer, I fall onto the sofa, put on *DuckTales,* take a sip, and message Cress.

> **PRESTON:** *Just got home, I'm shattered*
> **CRESS:** *Glad you're home safely. How was your day?*
> **PRESTON:** *Long and hard*
> **CRESS:** *I was asking about your day, not your cock **wink wink***
> **PRESTON:** *You dirty girl…I think you need a spanking*
> **CRESS:** *I'm down with that **spank spank** **wink wink***

Man, this woman continues to amaze me. She comes across as a saint but underneath she's a dirty, dirty girl…and I love it. I'm currently picturing Cress bent over my sofa; her ass in the air and it's pink with an imprint of my hand. Fuck, now my cock is hard.. Looking at the television, I see that *DuckTales* is finished and now *Scooby Doo* is on, and I have to say it's my all-time favorite cartoon. Scooby and Shaggy begin to eat a really gross sandwich, but the inner child in me kinda wants to see what it tastes like too and with that, my cock is no longer long and hard.

> **PRESTON:** *Watcha doing?*
> **CRESS:** *Eating pizza and ice cream with Lexi*
> **PRESTON:** *I like pizza and ice cream*
> **CRESS:** *Who doesn't?*
> **PRESTON:** *I'd like to eat it off of your naked body*
> **CRESS:** *Oh. I'm game for that...maybe for our next date?*
> **PRESTON:** *When and where? I'm there*
> **PRESTON:** *Plus I owe you a spanking*

She doesn't respond straightaway and I find myself disappointed. Texting with Cress is fast becoming my favorite pastime.

> **CRESS:** *Sorry, had to get Lexi to bed. Now tell me more about this ice cream eating and spanking*

I smile at her response and my cock likes it too. I would love nothing more than to drive over to her place, grab some mint chocolate chip ice cream along the way and do exactly that. "Fuuuuck," I groan as I readjust my cock.

> **PRESTON:** *Well...it would involve you naked, a tub of ice cream and my tongue...licking said ice cream off every inch of your body. Then I'd slap your ass 'til it's red. Once it's glowing, I'll let you suck ice cream off my cock, and then I'd fuck you into the wee hours of the morning.*
> **CRESS:** *Why, Dr. Knight, you are one dirty doc.*
> **PRESTON:** *You wouldn't have me any other way*
> **PRESTON:** *Care to have that picnic with me tomorrow? And maybe I can make the above a reality...my cock and I would very much like that*
> **CRESS:** *As much as I would love part two, rain check on that one. As for option one, we will pick you up at 11*
> **PRESTON:** *It's a date and a rain check*
> **CRESS:** *Good night, Dr. Knight*
> **PRESTON:** *Be sweet, parakeet*
> **CRESS:** *That's totally corny*
> **PRESTON:** *You love it*

CRESS: *Yeah, I kinda do. Nite, Preston*
PRESTON: *Nite, Love*

Finishing off my beer, I pop the empty into the recycling and crawl into bed. I'm asleep before my head hits the pillow and all too soon, my alarm is blaring. Climbing out of bed, I grab a shower and like I have all week, I remember the striptease Cress gave me last weekend. I love that she brings out her wild side with me, and her wild side meshes with mine like peas and carrots. She's the complete perfect package. She's messing with my head but hell; I'm going to do my best to hold on to her.

Stretching my arms over my head, I stretch out my tight muscles. I slept like the dead last night, and today, I feel refreshed and excited for my picnic with Cress and Lexi. Showering quickly, I pull on a pair of cargos, a Metallica T-shirt, and my Chucks. Looking at the clock, I see I still have an hour until they get here so I make myself a coffee and head out back to enjoy the morning sun. I'm totally zoned out when the doorbell rings.

Hopping up, I pop my mug on the counter and head toward the door. Swinging it open, I'm met with a smiling Cress and an anxious looking Lexi. "Good morning, ladies."

"He called me a lady," Lexi whispers to Cress.

"Then you better act like one," Cress tells her daughter.

"Good day, kind sir," Lexi says, looking to her mom with a big grin on her face. "May I do poo poo in your toilet?"

"Lexi," Cress scoffs, her cheeks darkening with embarrassment.

"It's fine, Love." I offer my hand to Lexi. "Follow me, Munchkin."

"Thank you, kind sir."

Holding back a laugh, we walk inside. Looking over my shoulder, I see Cress still standing in the doorway. "You coming?" As soon as the words are out of my mouth, I realize it sounded dirty.

Cress winks at me. "Why thank you, kind sir, I'd love to." Then she mouths 'later' back at me.

"Minx," I whisper.

"What's a minx?" Lexi asks, clearly I said it louder than I intended.

"Ummm, ahh…it's a—"

I stumble as to what to say but, thankfully, Cress walks over to us and puts her hand on Lexi's shoulder and guides her toward the bathroom. "Come on, Munchkin, let's go poo poo."

Just like that, my faux pas is forgotten…that is until I hear, "Mommy, what's a minx?"

"Less talking, more pooping," I hear Cress say to Lexi. I laugh again, you'd think after dealing with kids all day, every day, I'd be more careful, but when I'm around Cress, all rational thought evaporates and I become a bumbling teenager again. The Cress effect is strong when she's around.

"You have a pool?" Lexi screams, racing to the windows looking out to the backyard. She turns to Cress, her little face lit up like a Christmas tree. "Can we go swimming, Mommy?"

"I thought you wanted a picnic in the park?" Cress says to her, as she walks over to me.

"I want a pool picnic now. Can we, Mom? Can we?"

"I don't—"

"I'm happy to do that, if it's okay with you?"

"Are you sure?"

Nodding my head. "Not a problem at all...but do you two have suits?"

"Ohh no," Lexi dramatically says. "I don't," she dejectedly sighs.

"I have a suggestion." They both look to me. "There's a mall at the end of the street, what if we go get some swimsuits and stuff for our picnic, then we can come back here and start our pool picnic."

"That be tabolous. Can we, Mommy? Pleeeeease?"

"Yeah, Mommy, can we, Mommy? Pleeeeease?" I mimic Lexi, she looks to me and grins. Her smile melts my heart.

"Sounds like a plan to me, let's go."

An hour later, we are back at the house. Everyone has new swimwear and we have a gourmet feast to dine upon after our swim.

Lexi and Cress change in the spare room and I change in mine. I'm getting drinks together when I hear a giggle coming down the hallway. Lexi and Cress step into the room and my eyes bug open. Cress is wearing a sexy as hell, bright orange one-piece with cutouts on the sides. Lexi is wearing a pink and purple *My Little Pony*—surprise surprise—one piece.

"Can we please go swimming now, Dr. Preston?"

"As long as it's okay with Mommy?"

"Let's do this," she says, taking Lexi's hand she leads her out back.

My eyes drop to Cress's ass as they walk past. "That ass," I whisper, but again, it clearly wasn't as quiet as I'd hoped because Cress looks back at me. With a wink, she turns and keeps walking, with an added sway to her hips.

"Fuuuuck," I growl, subtly adjusting my cock.

"You coming?" Cress sasses as she opens the slider. She escorts Lexi outside, again emphasizing the swish of her hips.

"Fucking minx," I whisper to myself, shaking my head and grinning like the lovesick fool I am.

Grabbing our drinks, I head out and join them.

Cress is rubbing sunscreen on Lexi and I get excited at the prospect of rubbing sunscreen on Cress, but much to my disappointment, she leaps into the pool. Her body slicing through the water, she breaks the surface and I watch as water cascades down her body. "Your turn, Munchkin," Cress says to Lexi, who's standing on the edge.

She shakes her head. "I can't jump like you, Mommy."

Stepping beside her, I crouch down. "How about we jump together?" She shakes her head, her little body shaking with fear. It's the first time I've seen the vivacious little girl not going at it with everything she has. "What if we wade in from over there?" I point to the shallow kiddie area. I love this pool for that, I actually spend most of my time sitting in the shallow end, leaning back and enjoying a beer.

She nods her head at me and slips her hand into mine. Standing back up, we walk over to the area. I step down first so she can see how deep it is. A slight smile appears on her face as she climbs in, her face beaming when the water touches her. She immediately drops herself down, just her head hovering above the water. She stands up and walks to the edge before it drops off and looks to Cress.

"Having fun, Munchkin?"

She nods her head and the next minute, she's leaping through the air toward Cress, dive-bombing in front of her mother. Cress grins at Lexi when she resurfaces, the two of them laughing with joy. The sound is music to my ears and I find myself grinning as I watch them splash about together.

Cress looks over at me, and the smile on her face gets my heart racing. "That didn't take long," I say, nodding to Lexi who is paddling around the pool.

"She totally suckered you. This one is a water baby," Cress says, as she throws Lexi up in the air. She squeals in delight before she crashes to the water.

Shuffling to the edge, I dangle my feet over and watch the two of them swim about. I don't get out here as much as I would like and it's great to see it being used. Cress and Lexi swim toward me. Lexi climbs onto the ledge and sits next to me. Cress rests her hands on my thighs and lifts herself up. She places a quick kiss on my lips. I'm shocked that she would do that in front of Lexi.

Reaching out, I grip her hips in my hands and she hisses in pain, pulling away from me.

"Are you hurt?" I question as she jumps up and sits next to me.

She vehemently shakes her head. "I'm fine," she says, but I notice her hand resting on her lower back.

"Cress," I warn, "what's wrong?"

She looks to Lexi, when she sees that she's occupied blowing bubbles, she leans to the side and pulls one of the cutouts away from her body. My eyes pop wide open at what I see and my blood boils.

14 CRESS

"What the fuck, Cress?" he growls, anger radiating from him but it's not at me, it's for me.

"Language," I scoff, hoping to take the attention away from my back.

"What the duck, Cress? What the duck happened?"

"Nothing, it was an accident," I plead.

"Don't ducking lie to me, Cress. What happened?"

Sighing, I shake my head and close my eyes. "Not now."

"Creeesss."

I look to Lexi and he understands and nods his head. "Later you will tell me who hurt you."

"Promise."

"I'm hungry, Mommy."

"Me too," Preston says. "How about we hop out? I'll fire up the grill and then after we eat, we can watch a movie."

"Yes, yes, yes," Lexi excitedly says, splashing about in glee.

"Okay, you two, hang in the pool and I'll go cook."

Preston steps out of the pool and I stare as he climbs out. Water sluicing down his body. His muscles flexing in that delicious way. *Man, he's hot,* I think to myself as I watch him dry off. I want to be that towel. He looks over at me and notices me staring at him, he smiles but it doesn't reach his eyes like it usually does. He's angry about the bruise. To be honest, I forgot about it. It isn't sore anymore but when I bump it, or someone squeezes me, it hurts like a bitch. *Fucking Creed*, ruining things once again for me.

Not wanting to dwell on things, I focus on Lexi. Sitting on the edge of the pool, I kick my legs back and forth watching her. She's beaming right now, jumping and splashing. I wasn't joking earlier when I said she's a water baby—I'm pretty sure she was a mermaid in a past life.

Looking over my shoulder, I watch as Preston lights the grill. His face is laced with concern and I'm the cause of that. I need to talk to him and put him at ease, but I know this man, he's going to go all alpha and lose his shit when I tell him what happened. I know he cares but I can handle Creed. I don't want, or need, him getting involved in this.

With a sigh, I look back to my water baby. "Lexi, baby, time to hop out."

"Please, Mom, can I stay for a little longer?"

"If you are a good girl, I'm sure you can have another swim after lunch. Why don't you get your iPad and watch some Pony while I help Preston with lunch?"

"Okay, Mommy." She kicks her way over to me and I help her out of the water. Wrapping her in a towel, I pull out her headphones and iPad. She walks over to the outdoor lounger near the grill and reclines back. Handing her the device, she focuses on the screen and is transported to Equestria with her pony friends.

Walking over to Preston, I stand next to him. "Please don't be mad at me." I place my hand on his back, hoping to calm him with my touch.

He looks to me and shakes his head. "I'm not mad at you, I'm mad that someone did this to you."

"How do you know I didn't do it to myself?" He eyes me in a 'I'm-not-a-fool-don't-treat-me-like-a-fool' way. "Fine," I huff, crossing my arms across my chest defiantly, as I rest against the grill bench. "The other day when Creed came to see Lexi, he wanted to hook up." His eyes pop wide open and he clenches his jaw, I shake my head from side to side, "I told him no, and he didn't like it. I stepped back from him and hit the corner of the hall table."

"You stepped back? Or he pushed you?"

"A little of both."

"Cress, why are you defending him?"

"Because it's nothing. He was mad I wouldn't sleep with him."

"You were still sleeping with him?"

"Occasionally I would, yes, but I haven't slept with him in over a year. Ave would always yell at me when I would and after I always felt ashamed. When I saw him the other day, I felt nothing for him." Taking a deep breath, I continue, "For the first time ever, he didn't have a hold on me. It felt freeing and clearly I pissed him off. I don't think he meant to hurt me."

"Don't defend his actions, Cress. You never, N-E-V-E-R hit a woman."

"He didn't hit me."

"Hit, push, whatever. You never touch a woman, period."

"Well, I guess you won't be touching me ever again," I tease.

He slides his hand around my waist, pulls me into him, and whispers, "How I touch you is the *only* way a woman should be touched." He kisses my neck. "Every inch of their body should be worshipped." Kiss. "Caressed." Kiss. "Admired." Kiss. "Adored." Kiss. "Loved."

Swallowing deeply, I stare up at him. "I like how you worship, adore, caress, and love my body." Looking over his shoulder, I see that Lexi isn't looking; lifting to my toes, I press my lips to his and kiss him deeply. Wrapping my arms around his shoulders, I press myself into his body. His cock thickens between us. Pulling back, I grin, "Seems you like how I worship you too."

"You are a minx, Cress Bayliss. Just you wait 'til I get you alone."

"Ohh yeah, and what will you do to me, Preston Knight?"

"Well." He leans in, his breath heating my neck. He nibbles my earlobe and whispers, "First, I would strip you out of this sexy as fuck one-piece. Then I would lick and worship every inch of your body with my tongue. Then I'd pay extra attention to your pussy with my mouth and fingers and once you'd come on my face, I'd fuck you. I'd fuck you hard and fast and after you've come again, I'd fuck you sweetly and slowly."

My body is thrumming as I process his words. My clit throbs. "Preston, you don't play fair."

"All's fair in orgasms and war," he says. He kisses the tip of my nose and turns away to focus on the grill.

"Asshole," I mumble under my breath. "I'll go get us more drinks and the sides."

"Okay," he says, without a care in the world.

As I walk away from him, I grin as an evil thought appears. Grabbing my phone off the counter, I race into the bathroom and lock the door; I really don't want Lexi to walk in on this. Lifting my leg onto the vanity, I slide my finger under my suit, I accidentally brush my clit. I shudder and moan at the contact. "Damn you, Preston," I whisper.

Positioning my phone, I take a sexy pic of my finger under my suit and text it to Preston.

CRESS: *Payback's a bitch*
CRESS: ***attaches photo***

Washing my hands, I head into the kitchen and prepare the salad to go with the chicken breasts. I'm grabbing the plates when my phone pings with a text. Looking up, I see Preston staring at me. With a smirk, I read his reply.

PRESTON: *You are a minx…your ass is mine next time we are alone*
CRESS: *What is your obsession with my ass?*
PRESTON: *Have you seen your ass? How can I not be an ass man?*

A laugh breaks free at his reply and another evil thought once again appears. Pulling my one-piece up into my ass crack, I lean over the counter to enhance my ass, and quickly snap a pic.

CRESS: ***attaches photo***

From where I'm standing, I hear Preston moan. *Score one, Cress,* I think to myself as I carry out the salad and plates. Placing them on the table, I wink at Preston and walk over to Lexi. "Let's go wash up for lunch, Munchkin."

"Can I finish this episode first?"

"Nope, hands now, missy."

"Fine," she huffs.

Turning off her iPad, she places it on the table and I follow her inside. We are in the bathroom washing her hands, when I think about what I did in here just a few moments ago, my cheeks darken and I shudder.

Once our hands are sparkly clean, we grab some drinks and head back outside to join Preston. He's dishing up and seeing him all domesticated causes another shiver to wrack through my body.

"Mmmmm, smells great," I say, as I push Lexi's chair in.

He winks at me and takes his seat, handing me my plate. Our fingers brush and an electrical current zaps through me, my already pulsing clit now throbs. I swallow a moan but Preston notices, he smirks at me and I mouth 'asshole' at him.

After lunch, we laze in the kiddie part of the pool. The day has been amazing. Preston and Lexi get along like a house on fire, watching them together makes my heart happy. We have one final swim and then we head inside to clean up and watch a movie.

Lexi and Preston are sitting on the sofa arguing over which Pony is the best. With a smile on my face, I leave them to it and set about loading the dishwasher and tidying up. It's only fair since Preston cooked.

Closing the dishwasher, I step into the living room to join them and I stop mid-step. The scene before me is gorgeous and takes my breath away. *My Little Pony* is on the TV, Preston and Lexi are both on the sofa. He's lying on the chaise and Lexi is snuggled into his side, his arm wrapped around her and both of them are sound asleep. Someone's snoring and I think it might be my daughter. Clearly all the swimming took it out of them both.

Grabbing my phone off the counter, I snap a photo and set it as my screen lock photo. I've just set it when my phone pings with a text.

CREED: *I'm at your place, where the fuck are you?*
CRESS: *Out*
CREED: *When will you be home?*
CRESS: *Later*
CREED: *I want to see Lexi. Get your ass home now*
CRESS: *I'll be home later. How about tomorrow?*
CREED: *I want to see her now. Get the fuck back here now, bitch*
CRESS: *We will be home later.*
CREED: *You better be or I will see to it that she lives elsewhere*
CRESS: *Don't threaten me, Creed*
CREED: *Or what? Huh?*

Shaking my head, I sigh in frustration. I know not to engage him otherwise we will just go round and round in circles. Him threating to take Lexi has really pissed me off but it's also scared me, he's never threatened that before.

CRESS: *We will see you tomorrow, Creed*
CREED: *Make sure the squirt is ready when I get there*

Dropping my phone back onto the countertop, I rest my hands on the edge, lower my head, and sigh. My heart is racing right now. I know I've enraged Creed but he needs to know I'm not at his beck and call anymore...I just hope I haven't pushed him too far.

15 PRESTON

AFTER MY LITTLE CATNAP WITH LEXI, I LOOK OVER TO SEE CRESS SITTING IN the armchair. I lie here and watch her for a few moments, she's deep in thought and I don't like the look on her face. Carefully, I ease Lexi off me and I walk over to Cress. Sitting on the coffee table, I place my hand on her knee and she jumps six feet in fright.

"Shit, Preston, you scared me."

"What's wrong? You were so deep in thought you didn't even see me walk over here."

"I'm fine."

I scoff, "Cress, when a woman says she's fine, she is anything but. What's happened?"

She picks up her phone and hands it to me. Scrolling through the text thread, I read the messages from Creed, my blood boiling with each message I see. "He's threatening you?" She nods at me. "Has he done this before?" She shakes her head. "Cress, are you worried?"

She looks up at me and sadly nods, a tear cascades down her cheek. She looks so frightened right now. "Preston, he's threatening to take Lexi from me, how can I not be worried? She's my everything, Preston."

"I won't let that happen," I say.

Standing up, I lift Cress up, sit down and place her on my lap. Hugging her tightly to me, her body shuddering with fear. Kissing her temple, I run my hand soothingly up and down her leg. Resting my head against hers, I ask, "Tell me what I can do."

"This works for now." She snuggles farther into me.

"What's wrong, Mommy?" Lexi asks.

We both look up to see Lexi staring at us.

"Nothing, Munchkin, just snuggling," Cress says, any hint of her fear hidden from her daughter. She really is a remarkable mom.

"Can I snuggle too?" she asks.

"I don't think so," Cress says, while at the same time I say, "Sure, come on up, Munchkin."

Cress lifts her head and looks at me, while Lexi takes the opportunity and climbs onto my lap too. She snuggles in and the three of us sit here in silence.

"I like this," Cress murmurs.

"Me too," I confirm, placing a kiss on her head.

"And me, don't forget me," Lexi adds.

"How could we forget you, Princess?"

"You think I'm a princess?" she asks

"All good little girls are a princess, right, Cress?"

"Exactly," Cress agrees. "I was a princess when I was your age too."

"What are you now, Mommy?"

"A queen," I reply.

Cress lifts her head and stares at me, for the first time since I woke up, she smiles and it reaches her eyes.

"Well, where's my crown?" Lexi asks.

Cress and I both laugh. "Well, we better do something about that then," I say, "Next time I'm in the crown store, I'll get you one."

"And one for Mommy," Lexi says. "A queen needs a crown too."

"I will be sure to get two of their finest crowns."

"Good," Lexi says. "Can I have a lollipop, Mommy?"

"Of course, you can grab one from my bag."

She hopes off my lap and races away. I watch as she skips off, without a care in the world. Ohh to be five years old again. She returns with three lollipops and hands them to us. "Can you open this for me please, Dr. Preston?" she asks, as she climbs back onto me.

"Of course, and you know you can just call me Preston," I say, as I open the wrapper and hand it back to her.

"I know," she says matter-of-factly, "but you are my doctor friend."

"Can't argue with that," Cress adds, as she slides the candy into her mouth...my mind goes to dirty town and I remember that blowjob from the other morning. From the look in her eyes, she knows exactly what she's doing.

'Minx,' I mouth to her.

She shrugs and continues to suck the lollipop as if she was sucking my cock. My cock twitches, he feels each and every suck and lick. A low groan builds in the back of my throat.

"Mommy, I think we are crushing Dr. Preston. We should hop off him. He groaned."

My eyes widen because if Cress hops off, my cock will be standing to attention and that's the last thing I need, or want, Lexi to see.

"It's fine," I say. "I like having you two in my arms."

They both nod. The three of us quietly sit here. The moment is perfect.

"Wanna suck?" Lexi asks, offering me up her lollipop.

I shake my head side to side, "Thanks, but I prefer pink ones."

Cress scoffs and shakes her head.

"I like pink ones too but I prefer purple ones," Lexi says, popping the sucker back into her mouth.

"How about you, Cress?" I look down at her. "What do you prefer to suck?"

"I like hard purple ones," she says, her eyes locked on mine as she says this. I subtly shake my head at her.

"Me too, Mommy, can I get a hard purple one?"

Cress and I both burst out laughing, not wanting to be left out, Lexi laughs too. This makes me laugh harder. "Who knew lollipops could be so funny?"

"And dirty," Cress quietly adds.

Lexi hears the theme song to *My Little Pony* and she leaps off my lap, dives onto the sofa, and watches the TV intently. Completely forgetting about hard purple lollipops.

"Wow, she really does love that show."

"You have no idea," Cress replies.

We hop up and join Lexi on the sofa. Cress snuggles into my side and Lexi snuggles into her. Absentmindedly I play with her hair, her body relaxes into me and I smile. She was so worked up earlier due to the messages from Creed, it's nice to see her back to normal. But if I'm honest, those messages scare me. I know Cress is tough, but this Creed guy seems crazy and I fear for her and Lexi. I know she wants Lexi to see her father but if he's like this, I think she'd be better off without him. It's not my place to say anything so for now, I'll bite my tongue but if things continue,

I'll step in. I care deeply for Cress and Lexi, and I won't let anything happen to them.

They have just left, I had such a great time today and Lexi is a little fire-cracker, but then again, Cress is her mom so I wouldn't expect anything else. Popping the last of the dishes into the dishwasher, I turn it on and head into my bedroom and get ready for bed. I have a morning shift tomorrow so I need an early night.

Lying down, I stare at the ceiling, sleep eludes me right now. My phone pings with a text, picking it up I smile when I see it's from Cress.

CRESS: *Thank you for a wonderful day. Lexi and I had a great time*

PRESTON: *My pleasure. I had a ball too. Look forward to doing it again*

CRESS: *It? or me?*

PRESTON: *You are such a minx, I'm pretty sure you know what I want to do*

CRESS: *I may need a reminder*

PRESTON: *Next time we are alone, I will show you **wink wink***

PRESTON: *PS. When can I get another tango lesson?*

CRESS: *Soon, grasshopper, soon…you are my most favorite dance partner*

PRESTON: *Well, YOU are my most favorite person when it comes to persons*

CRESS: *Aww, you say the sweetest things. Nite, Preston*

PRESTON: *Nite Nite, Queen Cress*

Placing my phone down, I hop up and grab my Mac. I quickly order a present for my two royal ladies. I wish I could be there when they open them, but if I know Cress, she will send me a pic. With a smile on my face, I drift off to sleep, happy and content. My life is pretty perfect right now, nothing can bring me down.

16 CRESS

A FEW DAYS AFTER OUR AMAZING DAY AT PRESTON'S, A PACKAGE ARRIVES addressed to Princess Lexi and Queen Cress. Popping it on the dining table, I decide to wait until Lexi is home from school and we will open it together. I've finished mopping the floors when there's another knock at the door. Looking through the peephole, I sigh when I see it's Creed on the other side.

Opening the door, I put on a fake smile. "Hey, Creed."

"Dollface," he replies, the sound of his voice grating on my nerves. "Where's the squid?"

"At school."

"Ohh, thought she'd be home."

"Creed, you know she finishes at 11:45 a.m."

"I have an idea as to what we can do to pass the time." He winks suggestively at me.

"Thanks, but no thanks."

"Are you turning me down again? A slut like you always wants a piece of this." He grabs his junk and thrusts his hips toward me. "Come on, Dollface, it's been ages since I sank myself inside of your cunt."

"Creed," I warn, and just like the other week, he steps inside. He backs me into the wall, I have nowhere to go. He rests his hands either side of my head and licks along my jawbone.

"I forgot how good your skin tastes," he says, sliding this pinky down my neck.

Closing my eyes, I shudder and thankfully, a car door slamming in my driveway startles him and he pulls back. A few seconds later, Mom walks inside. Never have I been so thankful for her to pop in unannounced.

"Cress, everything okay?"

Nodding my head, I smile but I know Mom realizes it's fake. "Yeah, all good, Mom. I was just telling Creed that Lexi is still at school. I was about to offer for him to meet us at the park after I've picked her up, but you arrived before I could do that."

"Yes, it would be lovely for you to join us," Mom says, her voice void of any emotion.

"If she'll be there," he flicks his finger toward Mom, "I'll pass." He looks back at me. "Cress, you and I will fuck soon, there's no stopping it. You know it as well as I do. Just give it to me and then everyone wins."

He turns on his heel and leaves. Mom slams the door behind him and I let out the breath that I was holding.

"You okay, baby?" Mom says, stepping to me, she rests her hand on my arm; her touch instantly calms me.

Nodding, I lie, "Yeah, I'm fine."

Pulling Mom into a hug, I hold on to her. My body shaking as the fear slowly fades. Mom hugs me back and whispers, "Please talk to me, sweetheart." She pulls back and grips my cheeks in that mom way.

"It's fine, Mom. Creed is just being Creed."

She nods but she knows I'm lying, she also knows I won't talk until I'm ready, but I don't want to talk about this. Not now, not ever.

It's fine.

Everything will be fine.

But even as I tell myself this, I know it's far from the truth. Creed Dawson is a mean, narcissistic son of a bitch at the best of times, and I have just severely pissed him off. This is now the second time I've rejected him, but it's the first time I have stood my ground with him. I hope I haven't wakened the beast.

Mom helps me finish cleaning the house and then we go pick Lexi up. Lexi is excited to see Mom with me and we stop off at the park, just like I suggested to Creed earlier. I keep expecting to see him here too, but at the moment, he'll be fuming and pissed off. Lexi will be the last thing on his mind, and I'm grateful for that. Never before have I not wanted him to see her, but now I don't want him anywhere near my daughter.

The time at the park is a blur, I'm thankful Mom was with us. My mind wasn't where it should have been, focusing on my daughter. If anything had of happened to her because I was lost in my head, I would never forgive myself. Lexi is my everything and I will do everything in my power to protect her, that's my job as her mom and it's a job I take seriously.

When we walk in the door, Lexi immediately sees the box on the table. She points to it. "What's that, Mommy?"

"It's a package for us," I tell her.

She squeals in delight. "I never get presents unless it's my birthday or Christmas. What is it?"

"I don't know, how about we open it and see?"

"Yes!" she screams in excitement and races to the table, pulls out the chair, and climbs up. She drags the box to her and pretends to read the label. "What does it say, Mommy?"

"It has our address on it and it's addressed to, Princess Lexi and Queen Cress."

"That's us. Dr. Preston called us Princess and Queen on the weekend."

"It might be from him then," I tell her.

"Let's open it, let's open it," she squeals in delight, the sheer joy on her face is priceless right now.

Pulling at the tape, we open the box. Lexi pulls back the flaps and her eyes widen. "Ohh, Mommy, I'm a real princess now."

Peeking over her shoulder, I see two plastic crowns. A smile graces my face and I shake my head. "Preston," I murmur to myself.

"Can we wear them?" Lexi excitedly asks, her body buzzing with excitement.

"How about we have our shower and then we can?"

"Okay...and can we call Prince Dr. Preston to say thank you?"

"We can try but he might be at work."

"Deal." She jumps down from the table and races into the bathroom. First time ever she hasn't argued when I've told her to have a shower.

An hour later, we are both freshly showered, in our pajamas, and wearing our crowns. The lasagna is in the oven warming and we are watching, surprise, surprise, *My Little Pony*.

"Can we call Prince Dr. Preston?" Lexi asks as the cartoon comes to an end.

"Sure," I say. Leaning forward I grab my phone and bring up Preston's contact details.

"Can we Face call instead?"

"We can try."

Lexi settles on my lap and we call Preston. He answers immediately and I smile when I see he's shirtless, his chest glistening with sweat. "Thank you, Prince Dr. Preston, I love my crown," Lexi says before he can even say hello.

"You are most welcome, Princess Lexi. You look beautiful."

"What about Queen Mommy?"

"Queen Cress is also beautiful."

"Why thank you, Prince Preston," I say, bowing my head down. He winks at me and even though I'm in my nightie wearing a plastic crown, I do feel beautiful. The hungry look in Preston's eyes sets my insides ablaze.

"No, Mommy, he's Prince Dr. Preston."

"Ohh, I'm sorry, thank you, Prince Dr. Preston."

"I'll let it slide just this time since you both look stunning in your crowns."

The oven beeps and Lexi wriggles in my lap. "Dinner's ready. Bye," she says, jumping down from my lap.

"Guess that means I have to go." He nods. "Thank you again for our crowns."

"Maybe you can wear it for me sometime…only that."

"That can be arranged."

"Moooooom," Lexi sings from the kitchen.

"I'll talk to you soon."

Hanging up from Preston, I pop my phone down. I am totally falling for Dr. Knight and I'm pretty sure, he's falling for me too. Walking into the kitchen, I turn the oven timer off. Taking out the lasagna, I dish it up. Lexi and I eat at the dining table, proudly wearing our crowns and pretending to be royals.

Over the next few weeks, the taunts from Creed increase. From the horrible text messages to the verbal lashings I get each time he's here to collect Lexi, he's progressively getting worse. And to top it off, when Lexi gets home from spending time with him, her behavior and language is atrocious. She has never acted out like this before.

Hopping out of the shower, I pull on my jean shorts and a white linen long-sleeved shirt and roll the sleeves up. Looking at the clock, I see that Creed will be here soon to pick Lexi up. She's excited and beaming because today he's taking her to the circus. That's one outing I'm happy for them to do together because well, clowns. Those smiling assholes give me the heebie-jeebies, being trapped inside a tent with them is NOT my idea of fun.

There's a knock at the door and Lexi races to answer it. She opens it and Creed is standing there. Leaning against the doorframe as if his shit don't stink and I can tell from the look on his face, we are going to fight before they leave.

"Daddy Creeeeed," Lexi excitedly says.

"Dollface," he says to me, my skin tingling and not in the sexy way it does with Preston. I notice that he doesn't greet Lexi, or get angry at the 'Daddy Creed' tag.

"Her name is Mommy or Queen Mommy."

"Like fuck she's a queen," he sneers at Lexi.

"Please don't speak to her like that."

"I'll talk to MY daughter however the fuck I want. Get your things, Squid, we're gonna be late."

Lexi turns and skips to her room to get her shoes and jacket, unaware of what's about to unravel between Creed and I.

"Creed," I warn when I know that Lexi isn't in earshot, she doesn't need to see us argue. "You—"

"What? What the fuck do you have to say? Finally wanting a piece of this?" He thrusts his hips and points to his cock.

"I'll pass, thanks."

Clearly this pisses him off because he steps inside and slams me into the wall. "One of these days, slut, you are going to beg me to fuck you and I'll fuck you good. Sluts like you like it hard and fast and rough. I'm getting hard just thinking about slamming my cock into your cunt. Strangling you as I pound into you. Watching the oxygen seep out of your body as I continue to fuck you like you've never been fucked before. Sluts like you love being fucked like that."

"Mommy," Lexi says from the entry to the hallway.

Shoving Creed off me, I swallow deeply and drop down to my knees. I stare at her and smile. I want to change my mind about letting her go with him but I know that deep down, he will never hurt her. His issue is with me, not her. "You have a good time at the circus with Creed."

"Daddy," he snarls from above us. First time ever that he wants to be called Daddy, what's up with him? His behavior is very odd at the moment.

"Creed will drop you home after the circus." Placing a kiss on her head, she hugs me and leaves with Creed.

Closing the door, I lean my head against the wood and the tears begin to fall. I need Preston. On autopilot, I grab my bag and keys, jump into my car, and drive over to his place. Walking up to his front door, I ring the bell. A few moments later it opens and as soon as I see Preston, I launch myself at him. Wrapping my arms around his neck.

"Cress, Love, what's wrong?"

"Please just hold me," I say as I cry into his neck. I hold on to him for dear life, he's the lifeline I need right now. Without saying anything, he lifts me into his arms and carries me bridal style inside. He sits down on the sofa and hugs me tighter to him. Nuzzling my head into his neck, I continue to cry. I'm a sobbing mess right now and I can't stop, the flood-gates have opened and they are pouring out.

Placing his fingers under my chin, he lifts my head so I'm looking at him. "Cress, Love, you're scaring me."

Nodding my head, I sniff and stare at him. Still unable to speak.

He wipes his thumb under my eyes, wiping away my tears but as soon as the skin is dry, new tears wet it again. Lowering my head to his shoulder, I close my eyes and hold on to him. His embrace and kisses on my head calm me.

The tears finally stop, lifting my head, I stare at him. He cups my cheek in his palm, I lean into his touch. "What do you need, Love?"

"You," I whisper. "I just need you."

17 PRESTON

"You, I just need you." She wraps her arms around me tighter.

Lifting her head, she sadly smiles, leans forward, and presses her lips to mine. Gripping her cheeks in my palms, I kiss her back. Pouring everything I have into this kiss. I feel her body melting into mine.

"Make love to me, Preston," she whispers against my lips. "Please."

Pulling back, I stare at her. She looks so broken, so vulnerable right now. I'd love nothing more than to sink myself balls deep inside of her, but at the same time, I want to know what's upset her so much.

"I will, on one condition."

"Anything," she says.

"After you need to tell me why you were a blubbering mess on my doorstep just now."

She swallows deeply and then nods. Standing up, she unbuttons her shirt slowly. Then she pushes the linen off her shoulders and the material flutters to the floor. She reaches behind her back to unclasp her bra. The straps fall down her arms, baring her breasts to me. Her gorgeous plump breasts. "You have the most gorgeous breasts, Cress."

She straddles my thighs and stares intently at me. The light in her eyes is returning. Leaning forward, I suck a nipple into my mouth. "Preston," she moans, her head dropping back as I lick, suck, and bite her breasts. She runs her fingers up the back of my neck, gently tugging on my hair. My cock thickens beneath us.

Cress grips my cheeks. "Make love to me, Preston."

Who am I to deny her? I stand up with her in my arms and walk into the bedroom. Placing her on her feet, we stare at each other as we undress. Our eyes are locked on one another, the air in the room thick with desire. We are both naked and panting. Stepping to her, I slide my hands around her waist and press my lips to hers. She drapes her arms around my shoulders and kisses me back. It's soft, it's sensual, it's the definition of a perfect kiss.

Spinning her around, I lay her back on the bed. Staring down at her, I have never seen a more stunning vision. Her hair is fanned beneath her, creating a golden blonde halo. Against the darkness of my comforter it looks like it's glowing.

"You are magnificent, Cress," I say, nudging her legs open with my knee. I cover her body with mine. My cock is at her entrance, she pleads with her eyes for me to push inside of her and I do exactly that. Her walls hug my cock as I slide in and out. I stare down at her as I thrust my hips back and forth. Our eyes are locked on one another; nothing else exists right now except Cress and me. She lifts her leg, hooking it around my lower back, allowing me to thrust deeper. I can feel my balls tingling but I will myself not to come before her, she needs too and right now because I don't know how much longer I can last.

"Come with me," she moans. She reaches up and cups my cheek in her palm, that one action means everything to me. She clenches around me and screams, this causes me to explode with her.

Together we ride out our orgasm. I somehow feel closer to her in this moment. Her hand is still cupping my cheek, she runs her finger along my jawline. She stares intently up at me and murmurs, "I love you, Preston."

I look down at her and smile. "I love you too, Cress."

We gaze at one another, our love enveloping us. She slides her hand behind my head and pulls me down to kiss her. Our tongues gently caress one another, sliding in and out of our mouths. My cock hardens as we continue to kiss, I know Cress can feel it because she smiles into our kiss. She flips me onto my back and rests her hands on my chest, lifting to her knees she slides herself down my cock. Our eyes are glued together as she rides my cock. Lifting my hands, I caress her breasts. Rolling her nipples between my thumbs and forefingers. Her head drops back, and she slides her hands into her hair in that sexy way. She flicks her hair up, the strands dropping back down; never have I seen anything more sexy than a naked Cress riding my cock.

"Come for me, Cress," I say, as I press my thumb to her clit.

This sets her off and she moans my name as she comes for a second time. She clenches down on me and I too come.

She collapses onto my chest. I hug her to me, running my hand up and down her back. She lifts her gaze to mine. "I really do love you, Preston."

"And I really do love you too, Cress."

She lowers her head back to my chest and sighs deeply. She knows that we need to talk. I don't want to push her but it's killing me not knowing why she was so upset earlier. "I met Creed my last year at college." She hugs me tighter and continues, "I saw him in the local coffee shop. He looked across the room at me and our eyes met, it was lust at first sight. We fell hard and fast for each other. After graduation, we moved in together. Life was great. I had a teaching job at the same school as Ave, I had a great boyfriend, everything was prefect but it slowly started to fall apart. Creed changed, I don't know exactly when it happened, but he started to become nasty, saying horrible things to me. He'd always apologize and things would go back to normal. When I found out I was pregnant, I was over the moon...until Creed came home. He wasn't happy and told me to get rid of it. He also accused me of cheating and that it probably wasn't even his. He left but came home a few hours later all apologetic. I accepted his apology and things were good. For a little while anyway. It all went to shit when I was twenty weeks, he missed the scan and when I got home, he was packing. He said some really horrible things and walked out. I was pregnant, alone, and heartbroken." She lifts her head and sadly smiles at me.

"Cress," I say, brushing her hair off her face. "You really are remarkable. That must have been really hard to go through."

"It was. Thankfully I had Mom and Ave, those two were my everything, until I gave birth to Lexi that is. She became my whole world the moment I laid eyes on her."

"What happened after she was born with *him*?" I place emphasis on the word him.

"Much to Mom and Ave's disgust, I reached out to let him know he had a daughter. No surprises he didn't give two shits, that was until I bumped into his mom one day at the store. When I told her what happened she was so angry with her son. After that he made an effort but as time went on, he drifted away. I'll never stop him seeing his daughter, I see that too much at school. That just hurts the child. Just because I have an issue with Creed, Lexi shouldn't miss out on seeing her dad. Even if I do think he's a big dick."

"More people need to be like you in situations like this." I pause. "So what happened today?"

She sighs and closes her eyes. She hops up and starts to pace. My eyes watch her walk back and forth. She swallows deeply, stops, and stares at me. "Over the years, I've had weak moments and I'd give in to Creed and his charm. I'd sleep with him and deep down, I always hoped that he'd stay and we'd become a happy family. I realized that was never going to happen so a few months back, I decided it wasn't healthy for me to keep going back to him. I told myself that I'd stop sleeping with him. He doesn't like being told no, and for the last few weeks his anger at being told no has been building. The verbal attacks have been getting worse, and I'm pretty sure he's bad-mouthing me to Lexi too."

"Is that why he shoved you the other week?"

She nods, her eyes full of tears. "He's slowly unravelling, Preston. He's slapped me before but he's never been violent. I'm almost scared to let Lexi spend time with him, but I'm scared of what he'll do to me if I stop him from spending time with her. Deep down I know he won't hurt Lex—"

"Are you sure about that?"

She looks to me as the first tear falls. She shakes her head and wipes it away. "I really don't know." She cries, the tears are now pouring down her cheeks.

Hopping off the bed, I stand up, wrap her in my arms and let her cry. I whisper, "Shhhh," over and over to her, consoling the woman I love as she lets out all her grief concerning Creed-fucking-Dawson.

"Preston," she sniffles into my chest, "what am I going to do?" I hold her tighter to me and place a kiss on her head. She is literally shaking with fear., My heart hurts for her.

"We will get through this together, Cress. I won't let anything happen to you or Lexi." I press another kiss to her head as I say this.

Shaking her head, she lifts her head and looks up at me. "I can't ask that of you."

"You're not asking, I'm offering." We silently stare at one another, she processes what I just said. A smile graces her face.

"Thank you," she sadly says, she seems so broken right now.

I need to take her out and keep her mind off this. We can come up with a game plan later. "Okay, you need to go take a shower and then I'm taking you out for coffee and cake. Then we will pick something up for dinner and be waiting at your place for when Princess Lexi and douche dad get home—"

"His nickname is Dickwad Dawson."

"I like that." I place a kiss on her nose. "Now go shower, you stink like sex."

"I wonder why that would be?" she teases.

"Well, when a penis enters a vagina over and over again, that's called sex."

"Guarantee what we did has a much better description than that."

"I was paraphrasing," I nonchalantly say. "Now shower." I turn her around, tap her ass, and push her toward the shower.

She looks over her shoulder at me. "You can always join me."

"Cress, if I join you in the shower, there is no way I won't fuck you again and next time I do, I want to take my time and show you how much I love you."

She stares at me, processing my words. "Fine," she huffs. "I have fingers, looks like I'll just have to look after myself."

"Can I watch?"

"Why, Dr. Knight, I didn't realize you were a voyeur."

"When it comes to you, Cressida Bayliss, I will voy like no-one has ever voyed before."

"You say such the sweetest things but if you ever call me Cressida again, you'll be getting reacquainted with Mrs. Palmer and her five daughters." She blows me a kiss, turns around, and walks into the en suite and turns the shower on.

Sitting on the edge of my bed, I process her words. Creed Dawson is a real piece of work and I meant what I said earlier, I won't let anything happen to her or Lexi.

18 CRESS

It's been a week since my mini meltdown and a week of radio silence from Creed. He wasn't impressed that Preston was here when he dropped Lex home after the circus. I think he had it in his head that giving me a few hours of 'me' time would result in me wanting to jump his bones. That will never happen again. The Creed train has left the station, and Cress is happily on board the Preston Express, not that there is anything express about this man. Even a quickie with him is anything but quick. My mind drifts to the day after my meltdown…

…*Preston pops around after his shift. Lexi's eye light up when she opens the door and sees him. I think it was more to do with the bunch of lollipops for her rather than him. She lets him in and they both join me in the kitchen. He places a kiss on my cheek and winks, my body instantly buzzing from just a kiss. He must sense my reaction because he mouths 'later' to me.*

He opens a lollipop for Lexi and hands it to her. "Yuck," she says, dumping it into my coffee cup.

"Lexi," I scoff.

"It was a green one, Mommy, that's yucky."

Shaking my head, I pull it out of my cup and pop it into my mouth. Preston opens a purple one and hands it to her. "Thank you, Prince Dr. Preston."

"You are welcome, Princess Lexi. How about you go watch some Pony before I take my two ladies out for an early dinner?"

"Really?" she excitedly asks.

"Of course."

She races out of the kitchen into the living room, a few minutes later the theme song to Pony starts. Preston stalks over to me, pulls the lollipop from my mouth, grips my cheeks, and kisses me.

"Well, hello to you too," I say, taking the lollipop from him and popping it back into my mouth.

He has a carnal look in his eyes, he leans forward and whispers, "Cress, I am going to feast on your pussy and you are going to remain quiet. You make a peep and I stop. Nod if you agree."

My head nods, as if I'd say no to that.

He places his hands on my shoulders and pushes me into the corner farthest from the living room. Dropping to his knees, he pushes my dress up my legs. His touch sets my body ablaze. He kisses my clit through the material of my panties, which are completely soaked. He slides them down my legs and I step out, kicking them to the side. I lean back against the counter, pushing my pussy into his face. With his eyes locked on mine, he grips my hips in his hands and licks me from taint to clit.

A moan escapes my lips. "Cress," he warns before he thrusts his tongue back into me.

Gripping the edge of the counter, I close my eyes and give myself over to him. I'm panting as my orgasm builds. He pulls back suddenly, leaving me unsatisfied. Reaching up, he takes the lollipop from my mouth and pops it into his mouth. He sucks it before tracing the candy around my clit. My eyes widen when he slides the sucker between my lips. "Ohh God!" I pant, as he pushes it inside of me. Biting my lip, I hold back a moan as he continues to push it in and out of me.

He sucks and nibbles on my clit as he vigorously pumps the candy in and out of me. His eyes are locked on mine as the pleasure within me grows.

"Come for me, Cress," he whispers against my sensitive bud, his words set me off and I come all over his face and the lollipop.

He pops the sucker into his mouth and sucks. "Fuck, Cress. Your taste is so much sweeter mixed with this lollipop, a Cress pop is my few fav candy."

He rises up, leans his hands on the counter either side of me, cocooning me in. We stare at one another, I'm still panting from my quick and intense orgasm. Reaching out I squeeze his cock. "Maybe I should—"

"Mooommy," Lexi yells, "I need to go poo poo." He rests his forehead against mine and we both laugh. "Mooooomm," she yells again.

"You head to the toilet and I'll be in in a sec."

"Okay," she yells back, and we hear her race down the hallway.

Taking the lollipop from him, I pop it into my mouth and wink. Dropping down, I grab my panties and pull them back on before going to deal with Lexi and her ill-timed poop...

I'm snapped back to the present when Lexi yells out, "Moooooom, I need to go poo poo." A laugh escapes me, it's like time repeating itself.

"Coming," I yell.

Lexi and I are snuggling on the sofa, watching *Frozen 2*. My mind is not on the movie, I keep thinking about Preston. I don't think I have ever been happier than I am right now. Preston came into my life at the exact moment I needed him. If it weren't for him, I don't think I would have survived Creed's taunts over the last few weeks.

I love him with all my heart. Not only does he love me but he loves Lexi as if she were his own. Seeing the two of them together absolutely melts my heart. Who would have thought my best friend and I would both be blissfully in love at the same time? And with best friends too? When I think about Ave, I smile and as if she can sense me thinking about her, my phone rings and I'm met with her smiling face.

"Hey, Ave."

"Hey, yourself. It feels like forever since we've spoken."

"I know, right? But someone is all loved up and I have been trumped as your person."

"You will always be my person, Cress, but Flynn has a dick and you don't."

"Avery Evans, I have never heard you speak like that before. I wholeheartedly approve of you finally joining the Crass Cress club."

"I wouldn't go that far. Anyway, what's new with you?"

"Creed's a dick."

"That's not new. What did Dickwad do now?"

"Got mad when I wouldn't sleep with him."

"You turned down sex? Are you sick? Or is there something you're hiding?"

That's when it hits me, I haven't spoken to Ave about Preston. Actually, I haven't seen her since she hooked up with Flynn.

"How about we meet for drinks on Friday night, and we can catch up on the gossip?"

"I would love that, Ave. Message me when you're in the Uber on your way to Mom's."

"It's a date...and I want all the gossip."

"Same goes for you."

"Deal."

We say our goodbyes and then I call Mom and lock in a sleepover for Lexi. As predicted, she was happy to have her granddaughter for the night.

Life is perfect at the moment and I cannot wait to let loose with my bestie tomorrow night.

Lexi and I spend the day pampering each other. Me getting ready for my night out with Ave, and Lexi because she really believes she's a princess at the moment.

After getting dressed—me in jeans and a sparkly top, and Lexi, in the princess dress Preston bought her—we jump into my car and head over to Mom's. As we are pulling out of the driveway, I notice a gray sedan on the other side of the street. I've never seen it before, it pulls away and I shake off the weird feeling.

Just as I pull up at Mom's, my phone pings with a text. After hustling Lexi inside, I check my message.

AVERY: *In Uber now...let's get our drink on*

CRESS: *See you soon **cocktail emoji times 3***

Mom tells me I can pick Lexi up anytime and for me to have a great time. A car horn beeps. "That'll be Ave." I walk over to Lexi, "You be good for Nanna, I'll pick you up tomorrow."

"Love you, Mommy." She hugs me and sits next to Mom on the sofa.

"Have fun," Mom says, as I walk out to the Uber.

Climbing in next to Ave, I smile. "Hey hey, babycakes."

"Babycakes, really?"

"Yeah, not one of my finer greetings but the night is young, I have all night to come up with some awesome one-liners."

Forty minutes later, we pull up at the Fat Fox. Walking inside, we head to the bar and excitement bubbles in the both of us when we see the cocktail of the day is a mojito. "Winning," I say, as I order two. Ave waits for our drinks and I go grab the table recently vacated by a couple.

A few minutes later, Ave arrives with our drinks. She hands one to me and we raise our glasses. "Cheers," we say in unison. We clink our glasses together and drink. I moan as the tart, tangy liquid quenches my thirst; I take another sip when her phone begins to ring. Her face lights up and one guess who it is. "It's Flynn," she says, "give me a sec."

Nodding at her, I realize that my drink is nearly empty. Chugging back what was left, I point to the bar and mimic drinking. Ave nods at me and I make my way to the bar to order more drinks. It takes what feels like forever to get our new drinks, as I return to the table, Ave says, "I love you," and hangs up, just as I place our new drinks on the table.

"You only love me for my cocktails," I tease.

"Yeah, and?" she sasses back in reply. She picks up her new drink and raises it up for a toast. "To a fantabulous night with my fabulous girlfriend."

"Cheers to that."

We both sip and let out an, "ahh," as the refreshing drink dances on our taste buds.

"What's got you so chipper?" I ask, my body swaying to the music.

"Flynn and Preston are stopping by. I hope that's okay?"

My eyes widen in delight, as much as I was looking forward to girls' night, I've been missing Preston this week. I realize I haven't answered her and from the look in her eyes, she's about to grill me for information so I quickly say, "Is it okay that two sexy as sin doctors want to stop by? One who happens to have a sexy as hell Irish accent, and the other could be Channing Tatum's twin, let me think about that...hell to the yes it's okay." Taking another sip, I moan, *Man, this is a good mojito.*

Looking to Ave, I sigh, "I'm gonna get laid tonight."

"Get Cress laid is my mission tonight." Ave states but little does she know, I'll be going home with Preston. I'm not sure why I'm not telling her about him. I kinda like the mystery of it and I haven't felt this way about a guy since Creed. This is all new and exciting for me.

"I like this sassy side of you, Ave. Who knew you getting laid would also be good for me too? Prior to Flynn, you'd never suggest something like that."

"I know, right? I'm just so happy and I want you to be happy too." *I am happy*, I think to myself.

"Ahh, thanks, babe, but try not get finger fucked here again, save that for the privacy of home, or at the least, the car."

She chokes on her drink and shakes her head at me. "Why did I tell you that?"

"Because you know I need to fuck vicariously through you at the moment. My rabbit died from overuse, and at the rate I'm going my bullet is going to burn a hole in my clit."

"Evening, ladies," Preston says from behind me, my eyes bug wide open at what he just heard. My cheeks darken with embarrassment, while my best friend, possible ex-best friend just laughs at me.

Tonight is off to a swimming start and I cannot wait to see how the rest of the evening progresses now that Flynn and Preston are here.

19 PRESTON

As soon as Flynn and I enter The Fat Fox, I immediately spot the girls. My eyes always gravitate to Cress whenever she's in the room. Flynn leads us over to the girls and when we arrive, I hear Cress talking about a vibrator. "Evening, ladies," I say, startling Cress and causing Avery to laugh. She immediately stops laughing when she sees Flynn. The two of them make out like lovesick teenagers. I can't help but tease them, "Get a fuckin' room, you two."

Flynn places Avery back on her feet, she winks at me as I take a seat. I watch the two of them and I realize, she really is the perfect person for my best friend. Sure they are total opposites but as the saying goes, opposites attract.

"Preston, great to see you again," Ave says sweetly.

"You too, Avery." I turn my attention over to Cress, who's quiet for a change. "Cressida," I tease, "it's nice to make your acquaintance again." I play that we don't know each other because we haven't had 'that' chat yet. From the look on her face, she seems anxious to play coy so I continue, "I'm Preston Knight, pediatric doctor and this thing's best friend." Our eyes are locked on one another, she looks fucking amazing tonight and I cannot help but admire her beauty. Even in jeans and a simple top, Cress is the sexiest woman in the place.

At stupid o'clock in the morning, Flynn and Ave say their goodbyes. They can hardly keep their hands off one another. Cress and I stay at the club for a little while longer. Our dances are becoming more and more erotic, they are borderline not suitable for public. I'm glad Cress is in jeans because if she wasn't, who knows what I would have done.

"Let's get out of here," I whisper into her ear, as her body shivers against mine.

She nods her head. I order us an Uber and link my fingers with hers. When we make our way outside, the cool night air slaps us in the face. Cress shivers, I drop her hand and pull her to me, my front to her back. She rubs her ass against my cock. "Cress," I warn, "you need to stop that or I'm going to drag you into the alleyway over there, pull your jeans down and fuck you."

"I'm down with that," she sasses back.

Clearly sexual threats don't work with her but luckily for me, our Uber pulls up. We climb in and I reconfirm my address with the driver. Surprisingly, Cress behaves on the trip back to my place, but as soon as I unlock the front door, she turns into the sexual deviant I love. We don't make it past the entryway before I'm balls deep inside her. This woman will be the death of me, but death by Cress would be a wonderful way to go.

Eventually we make it to bed. We fall asleep naked and happily wrapped in each other's embrace...not knowing that in the coming weeks, things will change in a way that no one sees coming.

20 CRESS

WAKING THE NEXT MORNING, I FEEL LIKE SHIT. I'M TOO OLD TO PARTY THE night away like I did—I'm not twenty-one anymore—but man it was fun. My body hurts and I don't know if it's from all the dancing or the mind-blowing sex when we got home. I cannot remember the last time I had a night like that.

Reaching over, I'm met with a cold sheet. Opening my eyes, I notice I'm alone in bed. Sitting up, I hear splashing from outside. Climbing out of bed, I head out to the pool area. Leaning on the pool gate, I watch as Preston does lap after lap. He swims up and down, flipping around and swimming back. His body cuts through the water like a hot knife in butter; smooth and with ease. His muscles stretching and flexing with each stroke. He reaches the end, stops, and stands up; his back is to me. His muscles taut as he runs his hands through his hair, removing the excess water.

"Morning." I say, startling him, as I open the gate and step into the pool area.

He turns to face me and when he notices I'm still naked, his eyes fill with heat. "Good morning, Love." His eyes roam over my body, my skin heats even though I'm at the opposite end of the pool from him. He beckons me forward with this finger.

Shaking my head, I purse my lips and take a seat on the edge of the pool. My legs dangle in the water, it's colder than I anticipated and my body breaks out in goosebumps. With my eyes on his, I trace my finger down my neck, across the tops of my breasts. I circle my nipples before tracing down my stomach, spreading my legs open. He stalks toward me as I run the tip of my finger up and down my folds. He stops in front of me and places his hand on top of mine. He takes control. Pressing his hand to mine, as he slips our fingers between my lips. Sliding them up and down, he presses into me, only to pull back and slide them back up toward my clit.

"Please," I moan. My body is on fire. Every nerve ending alive and buzzing.

"This is *my* pussy, Cress. You need to remember that."

Before I can agree, he pushes my hand aside and thrusts two fingers into me. Spreading my legs wider, he lowers his head and sucks my clit into his mouth. If I thought I was on fire before, I'm now a fiery inferno. Every fiber within engulfed with desire and lust. He slips a finger into my ass and I explode.

"Prestoooonn," I mewl, falling backward as the most intense orgasm of my life detonates. Lifting my hands, I squeeze my breasts and clench my legs around his head as he continues to suck my clit and pump his fingers in and out of both my pussy and ass. The orgasm that never ends continues to erupt and I ride it out.

Lying on the edge of the pool, I'm breathing deeply, coming down from my orgasmic high. My body is still buzzing when I sit up and stare at Preston. He has a satisfied smirk on his face. "Don't look so smug, Dr. Knight, you haven't got off yet."

"Cress, giving you pleasure gives me pleasure. Now come here and kiss me."

Sliding into the water, I shiver when the cool water hits my heated skin. Swimming over to Preston, I place my arms around his neck and pull him toward me. Our lips press together, I lick along his seam, slipping my tongue into his mouth. He slides his hands down my body and lifts me up, I wrap my legs around his waist. His cock is harder than steel, circling my hips on his cock he groans into my mouth. He walks us back until I'm pressed up against the pool wall, pushing himself inside. My head drops back and I meet him thrust for thrust. Even though I just had an intense orgasm, my body begins to thrum once again.

Lifting my head, I stare into his green orbs and I give myself over to him. Our bodies rock back and forth. The pleasure builds and builds. "Let go, Love," Preston croons and I do exactly that, the pleasure envelops me and for the second time this morning I reach my climax. Moaning into his mouth, I ride out my orgasm. Soon after, his body stills and he too comes.

We stay wrapped in each other's embrace as our breathing returns to normal.

"I love you," I whisper, as I continue to stare at him.

"I love you too, Cress. You are everything I didn't realize I was missing. Both you and Lexi mean everything to me."

My heart melts at his words, cupping his cheek in my palm. I smile, "You mean everything to us too. We are lucky to have met you." It's crazy to be feeling like this after such a short amount of time, but when you know, you know. I'd be crazy to let a man like Preston go. I will do everything I can to keep him because I'm happier than I've ever been before.

"How about we go pick her up and take her to the park for a picnic?"

"She'd love that...and I would too."

He kisses the tip of my nose and lifts me up, placing me on the edge of the pool. He lifts himself up beside me. We sit with our legs in the pool, I rest my head on his shoulder. The moment is perfect, absolutely perfect.

We head inside to shower before we pick Lexi up and my phone pings, I deviate to my purse on the hall table. "I'll get this and meet you in there."

"Don't be long," he says, and I watch his naked ass walk away from me.

Picking up my phone, I deflate when I see the messages are from Creed. They started an hour ago and there are quite a few of them.

CREED: *Where the fuck are you?*
CREED: *Answer me, bitch*
CREED: *If you don't answer me, I will make your life a living hell*
CREED: *Where the fuck are you?*
CREED: *Cressida fucking Bayliss*
CREED: *Fucking tell me where are you!*

My heart rate speeds up as I read through the messages when my phone rings in my hand. I cringe when I see it's Creed calling. I know that if I don't answer, he'll just keep harassing me. Taking a deep breath, I answer.

"Hello," I say, my voice strong.

"Where the fuck are you?" he snarls.

"Hello to you too, Creed," I sass back.

"Don't fuck with me, bitch, where are you and Baby Girl?"

"We're out, and her name is Lexi, not Baby Girl, it's creepy when a grown man refers to a child like that."

"I can call her squid or Baby Girl, or Kid like you call her Munchkin."

"You don't have the right to use a nickname with her. Her. Name. Is. Lexi."

"Get fucked, now, where are you?"

"Out," I snap back, anger coursing through my veins right now.

"I can see that, I'm at your house."

"We won't be home 'til later, you are more than welcome to stop by then…or tomorrow." *Or never*, I silently add.

"Of course I'm welcome, I can stop by whenever the fuck I want. You need to start remembering your place, Cressida. Don't make me angry. You will regret it if you do. You wouldn't want something to happen to Baby Girl now, would you?"

"Don't you threaten my daughter, Creed." I snarl, thorough clench teeth. "You—"

"I can say, threaten, and do whatever the fuck I want."

He hangs up before I can reply, my eyes well with angry tears but I refuse to cry another single tear over this man. Shaking my head, I close my eyes and take a deep breath. I'm so lost in my head; I don't hear Preston come back into the room. "Cress, Love, what's wrong?"

Lifting my head up, I look to Preston. I open and close my mouth a few times, no words come out and then my brain finally fires. "Just Creed being Creed," I tell him but he knows I'm hiding something. I won't let Creed get to me and ruin what has been an amazing night and morning. If I do, he wins and he doesn't deserve to win. I won't allow him to win.

"How about that shower?" I say, as I walk past him and head into the en suite. Turning the shower on, I step in, close my eyes, and let the water wash away all my worries.

Opening my eyes, I see Preston staring at me through the door. His gaze calms me, I know with him on my side, I'll be fine. He will give me the strength I need to stand up to Creed…I hope.

21 CRESS

THE FOLLOWING SATURDAY IS A BEAUTIFUL CLEAR DAY SO MOM AND I TAKE
Lexi to Navy Pier. Preston is working all weekend which sucks, but I get to
spend time with my daughter and mom, so it's still a win. We pack a bag
and I make sure to pack her inhaler just in case her asthma kicks up from
running around and all the excitement. Last time we went, I didn't have it
on me and she had an attack. I won't be making that rookie mistake again.

As usual, I get more texts from Creed, and they all ask the same two
things, 'Where the fuck are you?' and 'Ready to fuck yet?' Ummm, no, hell
will freeze over before that happens again. Even if Preston wasn't in the
picture, that ship has sailed. It's left port, never to return again. Creed and
I are officially done in that respect. Unfortunately, he's Lexi's father so he
still has to be a part of our lives.

It's really busy here today, people are obviously lapping up the warmer
weather. We have just gotten off the Ferris wheel and Lexi is beaming.
She's jumping up and down all excited when she steps into the path of a
kid on a scooter. The two of them collide and it's nasty.

My poor lil' munchkin gets hit and knocked down, with the kid and his
scooter landing on top of her. She screams out and begins to cry. "Lexi!" I
scream, as I race over to her. "Why didn't you stop? Or go around her?
She's only a kid."

"I'm so sorry," the teenage boy says, as he rolls off Lexi, pushing his scooter to the side, he looks down at her. "Are you okay?"

"Of course she's not," I shout, "you just crushed her with your scooter. There's blood everywhere.

One of the friends says, "Ohhhhhhh shit, Dustin's gonna get it."

"It's okay," Mom placates, "it was an accident." Trying to calm the situation.

"Mom, she's bleeding and a kid was just on top of her. It's anything but fine," I snap at Mom.

"Where is she hurt?" the boy asks, he's worried and I don't know if it's for Lexi, or his own ass.

"Lexi, baby, look at Mommy."

Lexi is wailing and crying. Tears stain her little cheeks, she has a gash on her arm and leg. She's covered in blood. She must be in a lot of pain. The boy who hit her rips off his shirt and presses it to Lexi's arm. "Brent, gimme your shirt for her leg." The friend peels off his shirt and presses it to her leg.

"What are you doing?" I ask, watching as they both spring into action and tend to Lexi.

"We just did first aid at school, we're putting our training into action."

Dammit, I can't yell now. They are actually helping, I can feel Lexi start to calm down. She flinches each time they hold their shirts to her body but her tears are subsiding. "Well, you are both doing a great job."

"Lexi, baby, look at Mommy, don't look at the blood. Focus on me and my voice."

"Moooommmy, I bleeding," she cries.

"I know, Munchkin, I think we will have to stop by the hospital."

"I want Prince Dr. Knight."

"I will see if I can arrange that, but he might be busy."

Mom takes over looking after Lexi while I pull out my phone and call Preston. It goes straight to voicemail, I leave a message but I also text him.

CRESS: *Lexi had an accident, on our way to the ER. Please come if you can*

Putting my phone into my pocket, I bend down and pick Lexi up. "Nanna and I will take you to the hospital now." Looking to Dustin and Brent, I smile at them. "Thank you for your help. I'm sorry she jumped in front of you."

"It's okay," the boy who hit her says, "she reminds me of my little sister, Alexis."

"That's my fullded name," Lexi tells the boy.

"Well, if you are like my sister then I know you'll be fine. She's tough, it must go with the name."

"I'm tough AND a princess."

"Wow, that's a double whammy right there. I have no doubt you will be fine then, Princess Lexi."

"Mommy, he called me princess."

"Thank you again, Dustin," I say. "And sorry for yelling at you."

"It's okay, I'm sorry, too. I should have been more careful."

Turning around, with Lexi in my arms, Mom and I race to the car and head to the hospital. Mom drives and I'm in the back with Lex. My phone pings with a text and I pull it out.

PRESTON: *I'm in the ER, see you when you get here. Give my princess a kiss for me*

CRESS: *Will do. See you soon*

"That was Preston, he's waiting at the ER for you."

Lexi nods at me. Her tears have stopped, that's a relief. "How you doing, Munchkin?"

"My leg really hurts, Mommy."

"I know, baby. Preston will make you all better." Looking up, I see Mom pulling into the hospital grounds. "We're here," I say and just as I say that, the car door swings open. Preston is standing there staring down at us.

"Princess Lexi, what happened?"

"I got hurtded," she says, lifting her arm and leg to him, wincing as she moves in my arms.

"Well, let's get you inside and all cleaned up."

Shuffling across the seat toward the open door, I pop one leg on the ground but Preston bends down and takes her from my arms. She cries out in pain and it breaks my heart. Seeing your baby hurt is the worst feeling in the world, but I know Preston will look after her.

Following them inside, we head toward a cubicle where an older nurse is waiting for us. "Okay, Princess," Preston says to Lexi, his voice soft and caring, "I'm going to pop you on the bed here and have a look at you." Lexi nods her head. "And Mom," he looks to me and with that one glance, I know Lexi and I are in good hands...I may also be a little turned on seeing him all alpha doctor like, but now isn't the time for that, "how about you sit on the other side and hold this brave princess's hand." Nodding my head, I do as I'm told.

The nurse squeezes my shoulder. "She's in good hands, Dr. Knight is the best."

"He sure is," Lexi says. "He bought me a crown."

The nurse nods. "Ahh, you must be *the* Lexi we've all heard so much about." She looks to me. "And you must be Cress." The look she gives me is like that of a proud mom, beaming over her son.

"That's us," I say.

"I'm Andi, Preston's number one nurse. Your munchkin really is in good hands, and I'm not just saying that because of who you are to him, I'm saying that because he really is the best."

Nodding my head, I process her words. I'm shocked that someone from his work knows who we are but at the same time, my heart fills with joy that he's talking about us with his work colleagues. But if they know, I'm guessing Flynn will know and that means Avery will know…but if she knew, she'd call me to tell me she knew and she'd be pressing me to get all the gossip. Therefore, I don't think she knows, but now I'm wondering if she does know and she just hasn't said anything because she's waiting for me to let her know. I really need to arrange a coffee date, or cocktails so I can fill her in on all things Preston and me because I'm rambling to myself right now and I don't ramble, that's Ave's job.

Lexi cries out when Preston pours something over the cut on her leg. She has my attention now. Taking her hand in mine, I coo, "Shhhh, Munchkin, you are big and brave. You'll be okay."

"Right you are, Lexi," Preston says. "I just need to clean this and then we can pop a bandage on it." He looks to me, "No need for stitches which is good."

"Okay," she nods, "can I have a pink bandage?"

"I have something better in mind, after I dress it, how about I pop a *My Little Pony* Band-Aid on it and if we sweet talk Andi, I'm sure she will give you a couple to take home too."

"Really?" Lexi says, her voice laced with excitement.

"Only the best for my most fav patient."

Thirty minutes later, Lexi is all bandaged up—surprisingly, neither one needed stitches—and we are now on our way home.

We say goodbye to Preston and Andi, I don't get a chance to ask if he's able to come over later after his shift because he's whisked away on another case.

Traffic is terrible this afternoon and it takes us forever to get home. We stop at McDonald's and get Lex a happy meal for dinner. She eats most of it. Mom tidies up and I bathe her and get her ready for bed. Lexi is wiped out and as soon as her little head hits the pillow, she's out cold.

Sitting beside her, I stare and watch her sleep, she's my everything. I love her with all my heart. I always have, and I always will until my dying breath.

Kissing her on the forehead, I walk back into the living room and smile when I see Preston sitting with Mom on the sofa. A bottle of red is open and he's telling her about med school and being a doctor. Leaning against the wall, I watch as he and Mom chat. Creed never did this, it was always about him.

He looks over his shoulder and smiles at me. "She asleep?"

Nodding my head, I walk over to him. "Yeah, I think she was asleep before her head hit the pillow." Kissing him on the cheek, I snuggle in next to him. The next thing, I know, I'm in bed, snuggled next to Preston.

His alarm goes off at stupid o'clock; he kisses me on the forehead and leaves for work. I drift back to sleep but I toss and turn. I wake with a fright from a horrible nightmare: Creed took Lexi. I was spinning around in a crowd, screaming for her, but everyone just went about their business as if my worst fear hadn't happened.

After that, I can't sleep. Deciding to hop up, I head out to the kitchen and notice Mom asleep on the sofa. Grabbing the blanket from the back of the armchair, I cover her and step into the kitchen to make a coffee. With my cup in hand, I sit at the island and think about my dream.

"What's wrong?" Mom asks, as she grabs a mug and makes herself a coffee.

"Bad dream."

"Lexi's fine, Cress. You need to stop worrying."

"I'm her mom, it's my job to worry."

Over the next week, that dream plagues me each night; it's worrying because Creed has stopped texting and stopping by. It's radio silent from him. Preston on the other hand, has stopped by each day to check on Lexi and me. And I blissfully fall asleep in his arms…until I wake with a start from my recurring nightmare.

22 CRESS

On Sunday morning, Mom pops by early. She tells me to head out and take some me time. "I'm fine, Mom," I tell her, but she gives me *the* mom look. "Fine, I'll see if Ave is free for brunch."

"Good," Mom says, and she heads into the kitchen, no doubt making banana pancakes for Lexi.

Picking up my phone, I text Ave.

Cress: *Wanna do something crazy today?*

I've just stepped out of the shower when my phone rings and it's Ave. "Hey hey, lady."

"Hey, so what's this crazy adventure you have in mind?"

"Weeell, I wanna get a tattoo today and you are going to get one too." The line goes quiet, I pull it from my ear to see if we are still connected. "You still there, Ave?"

"Yeah," she answers.

"So, what do you say?"

"I can't believe I'm saying this but sure, I'm in."

I squeal in delight. "Great, I'll text you the address and meet you there."

"Sounds good, see you soon, Crazy Cress."

"Crazy Cress, I like that."

Two hours later, I'm sitting across from Ave, after our tattoos we, well I, decided that we'd get brunch too. I'm sipping on my coffee after eating my weight in waffles.

"I cannot believe I let you talk me into it," she says, popping a grape into her mouth.

"I cannot believe you agreed," I say, as I grab her wrist and look at her new ink under the wrapping, "but seriously, Ave, I have never seen you so happy. I think a certain sexy Irish doctor was just the medicine you needed."

"And I think a certain Channing Tatum looking doctor is the prescription you need." My eyes bug open, so she does know something. "One of these days, you are going to have to tell me what's up between you two."

I mime zipping my lips. "My lips are sealed." Then I lean forward. "But I will say—" I don't get to finish what I was going to say cause come crazy bitch slaps Ave across the face, yelling about some dude named Kye.

Before either of us have a chance to reply, she's storming away.

"What the fuck was that?" I question her. "And who the fuck is Kye?"

She shakes her head, cupping her cheek. "Beats me who Kye is. But, man, does she have a wicked left hook."

We finish our brunch but the atmosphere has changed since our encounter with Rocky Balboa and we decide to call it quits. We say our goodbyes and I head home to my munchkin and Mom. I'm looking forward to chillaxing on the sofa and preparing for the week ahead.

A couple days after my brunch date with Ave, I'm sitting at home when my phone rings, I don't recognize the number, without thinking, I swipe and answer, "Hey, this is Cress."

"Cressida, it's Flynn," he says, his Irish accent really thick and ohh so sexy.

"Hey, Doc, and I've told you to call me Cress.

"Okay. Hi, Cress, it's Flynn."

"Much better," I tease. "To what do I owe the pleasure of this call?"

"It's Avery—"

"What's wrong?" I say, sitting upright, my heart racing as I await his reply.

"We are at Western General. Bay is here."

"Ohh shit. I'll get Mom to watch Lexi. Be there soon."

Hanging up, I grab my bag, and tell Lexi she's heading to Nanna's and I need to go out for a bit. I call Mom after strapping Lexi into her car seat and tell her I'm on my way and what's happened. When I pull up at Mom's, she's waiting out front for me.

Climbing out, I unstrap Lexi, and she runs inside. Mom envelops me in a hug and tells me that everything will be fine and to keep her updated.

Racing to the hospital, I find a parking spot. Before climbing out, I grab my phone and text Flynn to let him know I've arrived.

CRESS: *Just parked. Meet me in the ER.*
FLYNN: ***thumbs-up emoji***

Growling when I see the thumbs-up emoji—emojis are fun but a thumbs-up is just plain rude. I shake my head and race into the hospital to meet Flynn. A few moments after I arrive, I see him and shout as soon as I see him, "Flynn, how's our girl?"

"I don't know. She seems off. Doesn't seem herself," he says, his voice laced with concern.

"That's understandable, her sister is in the hospital and unconscious." I say, hoping to ease his worries.

"Yeah, I get that, but I don't know. I can't put my finger on it. I'm hoping you being here will put her at ease and pull her out of her funk."

"If I know Avery, she'll be putting on a brave front but on the inside, she'll be screaming and falling apart. She and Bay may not be in the best place right now but at the end of the day, Bay is her sister, and that means everything to Avery. Family always comes first is her motto."

He nods his head in agreement but he's clearly worried. "Let's go then."

As soon as we enter Bay's room, I race over to Ave and wrap my arms around her. She's stiff, even when Flynn embraces her. My eyes roam over her and I can feel what Flynn is sensing. Something is off with my best friend right now and it's more than her sister being attacked. Then I look at her arms and it hits me, it's Baylor standing before me and Avery is in that bed. *Fucking bitch* is pretending to be her, I need to get to the bottom of this and she's more likely to talk/confess if Flynn isn't here.

"Flynn, can you get Ave some water, she looks parched and dehydrated," I ask him, I need him out of this room so I can confirm my suspicions.

He nods and kisses Bay/Ave. "Be right back." My blood boils when he kisses her, *fucking bitch-faced cunt.*

The door closes behind Flynn and I stare at Baylor. "You're pretending to be her, aren't you, Baylor?"

"Am not," she scoffs in reply and that adds to my suspicion. That's how Baylor would talk, not Ave.

"Please, you lying bitch. The person lying in that bed is Avery Evans. Standing before me is bitchy Baylor Evans." *Once a bitch, always a bitch,* I think to myself as I stare at her. "You are not her," I growl at her, anger building that she's doing this. Why she's doing this?

"Am so!" Baylor yells back, her reply once again reconfirming my suspicion that Bay is playing games again.

Before I lose my shit with this bitch, the door opens and Flynn snarls, "Enough!" Clearly our yelling garnered some attention, and I'm still no closer to proving that Ave is in that bed.

His eyes flit between Baylor and me. "You are not Ave," I say again, poking Baylor in the chest.

"Yes, I am!" Baylor yells back, but I notice her voice waivers.

Pointing at Baylor, my anger builds, "You are not Avery Evans, I bet my life on it." She smacks my hand viciously away.

Flynn yells at us both, I've never heard him angry like this. I know this commotion isn't good for Ave, but I need to get everyone to see that this is Baylor and not Avery.

"Yeah, Cressida," Baylor sasses and it's with these two words that I know I'm one-hundred-percent correct and from the look on Flynn's face, he too is starting to doubt the bitch before me.

Pointing at Baylor, I tell Flynn, "That is Baylor standing there." Then I stare down at my best friend in the bed. Lifting my gaze, I glare at Baylor before looking to Flynn. "Flynn, the person in that bed is Avery. My best friend. Your girlfriend. I know it without an ounce of doubt." I pause waiting for him to agree, but he still looks conflicted. "Flynn, I swear to you on my life. On Lexi's life, the person in that bed is Avery."

"Prove it," Baylor snarls.

"With pleasure," I say with glee. "Yesterday morning, Ave and I got tattoos." Grabbing the hem of my shirt, I show my new tattoo. As I look at my new ink, I smile. On my left hip, is a pink and blue inkblot with Lexi's name in the center in her handwriting. "I got this yesterday. Ave, the real Avery, got one on her wrist."

Baylor quickly hides her arms behind her back. *Busted, you stupid bitch,* I think to myself as her face drains of all color. Even when Flynn confronts her, she still tries to play off that she's Ave.

"I don't have to prove anything." She pleads, "I'm Avery. I'm your girlfriend. Flynn, please…"

"Uhh, yeah, you do," I say, stepping toward Baylor. The urge to hit her is strong and had Preston not wrapped his arms around me, I would have. I was so worked up that I didn't even notice he'd entered the room.

"Down, girl," he whispers into my ear, his voice instantly calms me and I melt back into him.

Closing my eyes, I take a deep breath and compose myself. Opening my eyes again, I watch as Flynn goes over to Ave and lifts the blanket covering her hand. As soon as he realizes that the person in the bed is Ave, he kisses her knuckles. Her eyes open and I think I stop breathing at seeing this. "It's okay, lass, I'm here," Flynn croons, as he continues to kiss her knuckles. Relief etched all over his face, he really does love her.

My eyes well with tears at the scene before me, that is until Bay steps toward Ave and says she's sorry. She thinks one word, five letters, will make this all okay. The more she says sorry, the more my anger builds again. "Are you shitting us right now, Bay?" I snap. "Sorry, really? That's all you've got? You better start talking now, bitch, and don't even think about lying to us."

"Shut it, Cressida," Baylor snaps at me. "No one asked for your opinion and no one wants you here now. Go home to your bastard child. You aren't needed."

I see red at her words and I lunge for her. Luckily for her, Preston holds me back because I'm ready to tear shreds off of her right now.

Once again, Flynn bellows at Baylor and me. I know he's right but I can't help it, my best friend was attacked. She's lying in a hospital bed and the bozos responsible are still out there, and to top it off, her bitch of a sister pretended to be her.

Flynn asks Preston to get the officers in here. He nods. "Sure, no worries." He looks to Ave. "Glad you're awake, Avery." He then turns to me. "Come on, Cress."

I roll my eyes at him, but from the look on his face, I know not to defy him right now. "Fine," I huff. Walking to the bed, I reach out and squeeze Ave's hand in mine. "I'll be right outside. I'm so mad at you right now, but I'm also glad you're okay." Kissing Ave on the cheek, I glare at Baylor and walk out of the room with Preston close behind me.

"Love, you need to calm down," he says as soon as the door closes.

"Do not tell me to calm down. My best friend was attacked and her whore of a sister pretended to be her. I think I'm allowed to be pissed off."

The door to Ave's room opens and Flynn steps out, in sync Preston and

I turn around as Flynn walks over to us. "Everything all right?" Preston asks.

"Yeah. Ave wants to speak to Baylor."

"And you left her alone with that psycho bitch? I don't trust her," I say through gritted teeth. "One word and I'll take her skanky ho ass down."

"You've got a live one there, dude," Flynn says to Preston. He clearly knows about us and then I feel guilty that I haven't spoken to Ave about Pres and me. I guess now isn't the time but as soon as she's out of the hospital, it's time to tell her about us.

Preston shrugs and winks at me, I roll my eyes at him and shake my head. "Flynn, are you sure it's okay to leave them alone together?"

He nods his head. "Yeah, they'll be fine. I trust that Ave can handle her sister."

I nod and smile. "Yeah, if anyone can handle Bay, it's Avery. Look, I'm going to head to her place and grab a few things for her, I'll be back soon."

"Thanks, Cress."

Turning on my heel, I leave the two of them and head to my car. As I climb into my car, I realize I didn't say goodbye to Preston, and then I start to feel like a bitch.

CRESS: *Sorry for not saying bye.*
CRESS: *I just need to process all of this*
PRESTON: *It's okay, Love. Be sure to find me when you get back. Love you*
CRESS: *Love you too*

How does that man do it? With one text message he's calmed me down. Pulling out of my parking spot, I race to Ave and Baylor's to grab some things for her.

An hour later, I've dropped Ave her things. She looks better already and says that she'll be fine. Bitchy Baylor is nowhere to be seen, thank God for that. Like he has a sixth sense for me, Preston walks down the hallway when I exit Ave's room.

"Hey," I say, as I look up and see him.

"Hey, you calm now?"

"I was always calm."

"Liar liar pants on fire. I could feel the rage simmering when you were in my arms."

"If Flynn was in that bed and his twin did that, wouldn't you be all stabby and ragey too?"

"Yeah, I guess so," he says.

"No guessing about it." I pause and look up at him. "Can I have a hug?"

"Always," he says, wrapping his arms around my waist. He pulls me into him, I rest my head on his chest and slide my arms around him. His embrace relaxes me and since I got that call from Flynn, I finally relax. Lifting my head, I look up at him and smile. "What time do you get off?"

"I can get off anytime I want," he says with a wink, "But my shift finishes in about an hour."

"Can you stay at my place tonight?"

"Of course." He leans down and presses his lips to mine. I open my mouth and kiss him back. I know we are in the middle of the hospital but right now, I don't care. I need Preston like I need my next breath. "I love you," I whisper against his lips.

"I love you too."

Resting my head back on his chest, I close my eyes. I feel happy, content, and loved.

23 PRESTON

Wow, what a day.

Attacks, identity swapping, and a kid who thought he could fly like Superman off the front balcony of his house. FYI, he couldn't and ended up with a compound fracture to his left leg, a snapped wrist, and surgery.

My crazy day is finally over and I'm on my way over to see Cress and Lexi, which is now the best way to end a hectic day. But most of all, I want to see my girls. As I approach my car, I see someone leaning against it. Their head is down and I don't know who it is. "Can I help you?" I ask. They lift their head and when I see who it is, I sigh. "Get off my car," I growl, coming to a stop in front of him.

"Stay the fuck away from them." He snarls.

"Or what?"

"Don't test me, doctor boy. I can make your life a living fucking hell."

"I think I'll let Cress decide if she wants me in her life. You better be careful or she will put you out of her life. She's already kicked you out of her bed." That was a low blow but this guy has pissed me off.

"I'll be back between her thighs soon enough, fucking her tight cunt. She's a fucking whore, one dick won't be enough for her. Just you wait."

"How can you speak about her like that? Cress is the most amazing mother and woman I know."

"Fuck off she is. She's a whore. Plain and simple. You are just the latest fucker to fall under the spell of her pussy."

"Warning noted. Now, get the fuck off my car. Don't make me tell you again."

He pushes himself off my car and stops in front of me. I can feel his breath on my face. He stares at me and I notice his eyes are dilated, blood-shot, and glassy. The trifecta when it comes to drug use, he is on some-thing pretty strong. My guess would be coke.

"Stay the fuck away or I will make life really hard for the bitch." He shoves me in the chest and staggers away.

Turning around, I watch him skulk out of the parking garage. That man really gets on my nerves. Once he's out of sight, I climb into my car and head over to see my girls.

On the drive over I contemplate telling Cress about Creed's threats to me, but she has enough going on so I decide to keep it to myself for now. I will do everything I can to protect Cress and Lexi.

Knocking on the door, I wait for it to open. When it does, I smile when I see Lexi. She looks tired. "You okay, Princess Lexi? You look flushed."

"What does that mean?"

"A bit red in the cheeks."

"I just raced to open the door. Mommy said we couldn't eat 'til you got here, so I was excited when I heard you." She grabs my hands. "Come on, we can eat now." She pulls me inside and shouts, "Mooooooomm, he's here...dinner."

A laugh escapes me as she drags me into the kitchen. Taking a seat at the table, I look at the spread before me and grin. Working long hours, I don't often get home-cooked meals, so I feel like a king and I can't wait to dive into the roast chicken, with all the veggies, and fresh dinner rolls.

"Hey, Love," I say to Cress as she walks into the kitchen.

"Hey," she says, placing a quick kiss on my lips before she sits next to me. She looks tired and drained.

"You okay?" I ask, reaching over to take her hand in mine. She looks down at our joined hands and then up at me again, something is going on because her eyes are dull right now.

"Yeah, just a lot going on."

"Do you want to talk about it?"

She looks to Lexi, then back at me. "Maybe later."

"It's a date." I smile at her and for the first time since I arrived, she smiles. That light is back in her eyes. I stare at her, she really is the most beautiful woman in the world.

"Can we eat now?" Lexi asks.

"Yes, Munchkin, we can." Cress dishes up and the three of us dig in.

After eating everything on my plate, I lean back in my chair. "Oh My God," I say, resting my hands on my stomach, "Cress, that was the best meal ever."

"You better have saved room for dessert."

Looking to her, I raise my eyebrows. *I'd love to have her for dessert.*

"It's not that," she laughs, "Lexi and I made apple crumble."

"Mommy let me sprinkle the cimmamon."

"Are you trying to fatten me up?"

Her eyes drift to my dick, she looks at me and shrugs. 'Minx,' I mouth. She blows me a kiss and stands up to grab dessert. My eyes watch her ass as she walks away. I lick my lips, she really does have the finest ass in the history of sexy asses.

After the best apple crumble I have ever eaten, I clean up the kitchen while Cress gets Lexi ready for bed. I've loaded the last dish in the dishwasher when she comes out. "Hey, can you have a look at Lexi's leg? The cut is taking forever to heal and she says it still hurts."

"Sure." I follow her into Lexi's bedroom. Sitting on the edge of her bed, I look at the cut. It's a little red around the edges and inflamed. "How long has it been like this?"

"I only noticed it tonight."

"Okay, let's wash it again and I'll pop some antiseptic onto it. Over the next few days, keep an eye on it. If it doesn't heal in a day or two, I'll prescribe some antibiotics for her."

"Should I be worried?" Cress questions.

Shaking my head. "Nah, it looks okay to me. I don't think we need to worry." That seems to ease her worry.

Cress and I tuck Lexi in and then I take her to bed. I make love to her before drifting off to sleep with the woman I love tucked into my side.

24 CRESS

The following week is crazy and I'm not just referring to the taunts from Creed. The week started out with me picking up some sub work. Mom was only too happy to watch Lexi for me and on Wednesday, when she was stuck, Preston swooped in and saved the day. He picked Lexi up and the two of them spent the afternoon together. When I got home, I found them inside a blanket fort watching, *DuckTales*—I think Lexi now has a new favorite show. I don't think it's so much the show, it's that Preston likes it and she likes Preston very much.

Kicking off my shoes, I join them in the fort and snuggle in. Completely content and sated with Lexi and Preston. I'm currently in my happy place with the two people I love the most.

There's a knock at the door but no one wants to move so we ignore it, we stay in our fort watching *DuckTales*. The knocking stops and then my phone blows up with text message after text message. I shield them from Lexi but Preston being Preston, he glances at the screen. His jaw clenches and he growls low in his throat as he reads the messages.

CREED: *Open your fucking door, bitch*
CREED: *Stop being a whore and answer me*
CREED: *Cressida fucking Bayliss, do not ignore me*
CREED: *Fuck you, bitch*

CREED: *I want to see Lexi tomorrow. Let me or else you will pay*
CRESS: *I'm working tomorrow, you can collect her from school*
CREED: *Maybe we can have some fun when I drop her home*
CRESS: *I told you, not going to happen*
CREED: *Just give in and fuck me already*
CRESS: *Good night, Creed*

After texting with Creed, I'm on edge. I excuse myself from the fort and go to the kitchen. Grabbing a bottle of white from the fridge, I pour myself a glass.

"You okay?" Preston asks, as he wraps his arms around me from behind, pulling me into his chest. His embrace instantly calms me.

Placing my glass on the countertop, I place my arms on top of his and snuggle back into him. "Yeah, I'm fine."

"Cress, I know that when a woman says fine, she is anything but fine."

Spinning around, I drape my arms over his shoulders. "Seriously, I'm fine. Creed just doesn't like being told no, if I let him spend time with Lexi, he'll back off."

"Are you sure?"

Nodding my head, I smile. "I'm sure." But even as I say those two words, I have no idea. I don't think Creed would hurt Lexi but then again, I have never seen him like this before. I really don't know what to do.

Preston and I get Lexi off to bed and then we grab the bottle of wine and head out to the back deck since it's a lovely night. Preston and I drink our wine in silence. Each of us in our own heads. When the bottle is finished, I offer for him to stay, but he declines since he needs to be at the hospital early. He kisses me goodbye and I watch as he drives away.

With a sigh, I lock the screen and front door before I climb into bed. My last thought before I drift off to sleep is that I wish I'd met him first and he was Lexi's dad.

The next afternoon when I get home from school, I decide to clean the house so that tomorrow I can spend the entire day with Lexi. I turn on Spotify and get to it. Two hours later, I'm on the last job, vacuuming. "Shake it Off" by Taylor Swift comes on and I shake my booty around the living room as I finish the floor. I can feel eyes on me and when I look over to the door, I see Preston standing there, staring at me through the screen.

Jumping in fright, I rest my hand on my chest, "Dude, you scared the absolute shit out of me. Why didn't you knock?"

"And miss out on seeing you shake your booty, hell to the no."

Walking over to the door, I open the screen. As soon as I do, he slides his hand around my waist, pulls me to him, and presses his lips to mine. My leg lifts in that way they do in romantic movies. Our moment is interrupted when, Creed growls. "Are you finished tongue fucking my wife?"

Pushing away from Preston, I look to Creed. "I'm not your wife."

"Whatever." Creed looks to Preston. "Who the fuck are you?"

"Preston Knight," he says, offering his hand to Creed. "Pleasure to formally meet you, Creed."

My eyes widen at this, *Preston has met Creed before? When? And why did he not tell me?* Creed looks at Preston's hand and refuses to shake it. "So you're the asshole, she's slutting it up with."

"Excuse me," Preston fumes. "You don't speak to me, or Cress like that."

"Pres, I've got this," I say, resting my hand on his arm. He looks to me and nods. I can see the anguish in his face, he wants to protect me but he knows this is my fight. I smile up at him. Then I hear a little voice, "Mommy."

Looking down, I see Lexi walk up the stairs behind Creed. "Hey, Munchkin," I say, dropping down to my knees and opening my arms to her. She walks over and hugs me tight; she seems sad.

"Hi, Mommy."

"Did you have fun with Daddy Creed?" He growls at that name and I can't help but smirk at my slight win. She shrugs at me and my heart breaks for my little girl right now. She's never returned from being with Creed sad like this. "Why don't you go put your things away. I'll be there in a moment."

"Okay, Mommy," she sadly says. She looks to Creed. "Bye, Daddy Creed." Then she turns around and races inside.

"What happened? Why is she sad?"

"She wouldn't stop talking about the fucker standing next to you. I told her that he'll move on soon, no one hangs around a slut like you." I can feel the anger radiating from Preston, I step between him and Creed, the last thing I need is a fight breaking out between the two of them.

"Creed," I yell, "You cannot say shit like that to her. She's a little girl for fuck's sake."

"Well, it's the truth. If we arrived a few minutes later, you would have been fucking him right here in the doorway. I'm not sure this is a suitable environment for my daughter to be in anymore."

"Fuck you, Creed," I seethe through clenched teeth. "I'm the one who has been here for her ever since I found out I was pregnant. You pop in whenever you feel like it. You taunt me when you don't get your way and now, you are referring to me as a slut to my daughter. Some father figure you are."

"She's my daughter too," he snaps back.

"She might have your DNA but you certainly are no father."

"What? And he is?" He flicks his finger toward Preston.

"He's more of a father than you ever will be."

"Don't push me, bitch." I feel Preston step forward at this, I block him but I don't know how much longer I can hold him back. "If I want to, I can make your life a living hell, Cressida. Just you remember that." His gaze roams over my body and I shudder at the lewdness in his gaze. "See you round, Dollface."

He blows me a kiss and walks away. Leaving me fuming. "Cress," Preston says from next to me, "are you okay?"

Nodding my head, I bite my thumbnail. "I need you to leave."

"What?" he shouts. "Why?" Preston reaches for me and I pull back.

"I need you to go, Preston. I need to focus on Lexi right now."

"Cress—"

"No," I shout. "Preston, I need time to think. Please?" I plead, cupping his cheek in my palm, I stare at him. "Please, I need to focus on Lexi tonight."

"I don't like this but if you insist."

"I do, I need some alone time with Lexi tonight. My little girl needs me."

"I'll give you tonight, Cress, but I'm not going anywhere. You, me, and Lexi, we belong together like Huey, Dewy, and Louie belong with Scrooge."

He kisses me on the temple and walks out. Standing in the doorway, I watch him climb into his car and drive away. Closing the door, I lock it and engage the deadlock. Turning around, I slide down the wood and rest my head on my knees. Did I just push the best thing to ever happen to us away?

My phone pings with a text, without looking, I know it's Creed. Pulling it out of my pocket, I open and read his messages, instantly regretting opening it.

CREED: *I'm better than that doctor asshole, he will not take my place in Lexi's life. You try and push me out and I will file for custody.*
CREED: *I know people and those people will ruin you.*
CREED: *Don't push me*

Tears well in my eyes as I read his texts over and over. "Mommy," Lexi says from the hall. Looking up, I see her standing there staring at me.

"What's up Munchkin?" I say, as I stand up and wipe at my eyes.

"Where's Prince Dr. Preston?"

"He had to go home."

"Ohh," she sadly says.

"How was your afternoon with Daddy Creed?"

"I didn't have fun. He was kinda mean when I talked about Prince Dr. Preston and *DuckTales*."

"Don't let that worry you. How about we build another fort, watch *DuckTales* and eat mac 'n' cheese in the fort?"

"Can we sleep in there too?"

"It's a school night tonight, but maybe we can on the weekend?"

"Really?" Her eyes widen in delight.

"Of course, Munchkin."

"Yesss," she squeals, her little face lit up with joy.

"You get the pillows. I'll get the blankets." Before I've finished saying that, she's racing away and just like that, my daughter is happy.

For the next few hours, I focus on Lexi and I forget all about Creed's threats, but guilt from pushing Preston away begins to fester.

After watching a whole season of *DuckTales* and eating our weight in mac 'n' cheese, I bathe Lexi and get her off to bed...leaving me alone with my thoughts and guilt.

Pouring myself a glass of wine, I curl up on the sofa. I grab my iPad to read but my mind keeps drifting to Preston, and specifically how I spoke to him. How I pushed him away. And how he said he's not going anywhere. I feel like a total bitch and now, I need to apologize. Looking at the clock, I realize he'll be sleeping but I text him anyway, this way he can wake up to an apology message.

CRESS: *I'm so sorry, Preston. I acted like a total whorebag bitch. I took my fears and anger out on you, and I shouldn't have done that. I'm so sorry.*
Please know that I love you with all my heart and soul. I've never felt like this about anyone before. It's been Lexi and me for so long and I

freaked out at the prospect of losing her. Until I met you, she was my
everything. Now you both hold that spot in my heart.
CRESS: *I'll see you soon…Gotta go, buffalo Xo*
CRESS: *PS. I'll leave the corny sign-offs to you…that was really bad*
CRESS: *PPS. Love you long-time*

I hit send and I really do hope I see him again soon. I really hope Creed hasn't ruined this for me.

25 PRESTON

Preston, I need time to think. Please?
    Preston, I need time to think. Please?
    Preston, I need time to think. Please?

Those seven words play on a loop in my head. The look of hurt on her face at Creed's words gutted me. Her sending me away gutted me. I've fallen hard for this woman and even though she just pushed me away, I know I've finally found 'the one.' It's fucking crazy to be talking like this after such a short period of time, and considering she sent me away tonight, but when you know, you know.

Cress is it for me.

Lexi too. I love that little girl as if she were my own.

My phone pings with a text, picking it up, I see it's from Cress. As I read her words, a smile graces my face and I know we'll be fine.

PRESTON: *No need to apologize. It was a rough afternoon. I love you too. I'll pop round after my shift tomorrow.*

She texts me back immediately.

CRESS: *I promise to make it up to you*
PRESTON: *Naked horizontal tango? **wink wink***

CRESS: *That can be arranged. I'd do anything for you, Preston, anything!*
CRESS: *I love you unconditionally.*
CRESS: *Nite nite, Preston*
PRESTON: *I'd do anything for you and Lexi too. I hope you know that.*
PRESTON: *Love you xo*
PRESTON: *Nite, Queen Cress*

Placing my phone on the side table, I lie back and finally relax. *I love you unconditionally* are the four new words now playing over in my mind as I drift off to sleep.

The next day, I'm called into Dr. Jenkins' office. She's sitting behind her desk, her shoulder-length dark hair straight as usual when I enter. She pushes up her glasses and smiles as I enter. "Preston, how are you?" she asks, as she walks around her desk and ushers me to the seating area in her office. Perks of being chief, a nice large office.

"Good, today was quiet so it was a good paperwork day."

"You better not have jinxed it by saying the 'Q' word." We both laugh. "You are probably wondering why I called you in here today." I nod my head. "I've heard that Boston," my eyes widen that she knows, "is interested in you leading their new pediatric wing. I want to know what I can do to entice you to stay."

"How did you know? They only emailed the offer a few days ago, and I haven't spoken to anyone about it yet."

"It's my job to know, Preston. I didn't get to this position because I slept my way here. I got it because I'm the best, as are you. I don't want to lose you. The hospital doesn't want to lose you. So, what will it take for you to stay?"

"I...I—" I'm stumped, I have no idea what to say right now.

"Think it over and get back to me."

Standing up, I shake her hand and walk out, thankful that my shift is over because I have a lot to think about but before I can think about work, I need, no want, to go see my girls.

Jumping into my car, I drive over to Cress's. I pull up and there's a gray sedan parked out front. Looking to the house, I see Cress talking with a guy in a suit. Climbing out of my car, I walk up to them. Cress looks pale. "Cress, Love," I ask, "is everything okay?"

She looks at me blankly and nods. Then she looks back to the man, "As I said, Agent Cox, apart from handover with my daughter, I don't know what Creed gets up to. Hell, I don't even know where he lives."

"Okay, thank you for your time." He hands her a card. "If you think of anything else, please don't hesitate to contact me."

"What have you gotten yourself into Creed?" she whispers to herself after I close the door. Escorting her to the sofa, I sit next to her.

"What was that all about?"

"He's an agent with the DEA. Seems Creed is into some bad shit, he was questioning me about him."

"Fuck, seriously?"

"Yep, just when I think it can't get worse regarding him, this happens."

"What are you going to do?"

"What can I do?"

"Maybe you need to speak to a lawyer?"

"I can't afford that."

"I'll help you if you need," I offer.

She shakes her head and takes my hand in hers. "Thanks, but I can't take your money. I'll figure this out."

Her response doesn't surprise me at all. "Well, my offer is there any time."

"Thank you," she says. She looks at me, my cock twitching at the heat in her eyes. "Now, where's my hello kiss?"

"I'm so sorry." Reaching over, I pull her onto my lap and press my lips to hers. Breaking the kiss I rest my forehead on hers. "Hi."

"Hi," she replies with a smile. "How was your day?"

"Crazy."

"DEA crazy?"

"Not that crazy but still crazy. I got a job offer—"

"That's amazing, Preston. Congrats."

"It's umm ahh, in Boston."

"Ohh," she says, no longer elated at my news. "So you're moving?"

"I don't know. My boss here offered me anything I want to stay here in Chicago."

"Wow, that's great. What are you going to do?"

I shrug. "I don't know. Leading a pediatric unit would be amazing, but my life is here…you and Lexi are here."

She shakes her head. "No, don't base your decision on us." I go to interrupt but she places her finger on my lips. "You need to do what's best for you and your career. I would never stop you from doing that, BUT in saying that, I really hope you stay cause I kinda like having you around." She grinds herself on me, my cock hardening beneath her.

"God, I love you," I say, leaning over I press my lips to hers. Before she can process what's happening, I flip her onto her back, cocooning her under me on the sofa. "What time is your mom dropping Lexi home?"

"Any minute now."

"Dammit, I'll just have to settle for this for now." Pressing my lips to hers, I fuck her mouth with my tongue. She moans into my mouth, and my cock hardens further between us, painfully pressing against my zipper. She swivels her hips, pressing against my dick harder. "Cress," I warn into the kiss. She giggles against my lips and continues to circle her hips. "You are a minx," I say, nipping her bottom lip between my teeth. I slide my hand between us and up under her skirt. I cup her pussy, pressing my thumb into her clit. This is pretty steamy but I can't stop what I'm doing. I need to be inside of her now.

"Yes," she mewls, closing her eyes. Her head drops back elongating her neck, leaning down I lick from her shoulder to under her ear. "Fuck me, Preston," she whispers, pulling her panties to the side, I'm about to push my finger inside when the front door swings open and Lexi yells, "Mooooommmy, I'm home."

Cress freaks out and shoves me off her. I land on my back on the floor with a thud. "Uggh," I groan. Looking up at her, her cheeks are flushed and she's never looked more beautiful.

"Duck, I'm so sorry," she says, her comment sets me off and I start to laugh. She laughs too.

"Mommy. Prince Dr. Knight. What's so funny?" Lexi asks, this causes us both to laugh even harder.

"Come on, sweetheart," Momma Cress says. "Let's unpack your bag and then Mommy and Doc P. will get you that snack I promised."

"Okay, Nanna."

Lexi skips off. Momma Cress looks down at us, shakes her head, and smirks. She follows after Lexi while Cress and I continue to laugh. I feel like a teenager getting busted again.

Once composed, Cress and I hop up. Pulling her into my arms, I hug her. "I love you," I whisper into her hair.

"I love you too." She kisses my cheek and heads into the kitchen to prepare Lexi her snack.

Taking a seat at the island, I watch Cress flit about the kitchen. She looks happy, and I realize I don't want to ever see her unhappy again. I don't think I'm going to accept Boston. But before I make up my mind, I need to talk to Dr. Jenkins and see if she was serious. I think I have an idea that will benefit both myself and the hospital.

"Cress," I say. "I need to go. I'll call you later."

Placing a kiss on her cheek, I squeeze her ass and walk out, passing Lexi and Momma Cress on the way. "I'll see you ladies later."

Racing down the path to my car, I look up and see Creed leaning against the hood. "Creed." I growl, anger building as he pushes off and steps toward me.

"Clearly my words the other week fell on deaf ears and that bitch, or you, haven't heeded any of my messages. Stay the fuck away."

"And if I remember correctly, I told *you* to stay away. Cress and Lexi are better off without you in their life."

"I'm her father, you can't stop me from seeing Lexi and if you try, I will make life difficult for the bitch, and you. Last chance, fucker."

"You don't scare me, Creed."

"You should be scared, Doc. I know people and with one call, I can make you disappear, or even better, I can ruin your career. Don't test me."

"Warning noted. Now, get the fuck off my car."

Not wanting to engage with him any further, I walk around to the driver's side and unlock my car. I stare at him over the roof of my car. "Maybe it's you who needs to stay the fuck away. Leave Cress and Lexi alone to live their lives."

"Fuck you, asshole." He flips me the bird and saunters down the street like his shit don't stink.

Climbing into my car, I sit and watch him slither into his piece of shit car and drive away. With a sigh, I start my car and head to the hospital. Once I've spoken with Dr. Jenkins, I'll deal with Creed and his threats. I will not let him or anyone hurt those I love.

26 CRESS

Preston has stayed at my place every night this week and each night after making love, I've fallen asleep wrapped in his arms. Thankfully, I haven't had that horrible nightmare. He has slipped into our life perfectly. It's like he's always been a part of our family. Watching him with Lexi fills my heart with so much joy.

Each morning, we make breakfast together and then go our separate ways. I'm in the middle of the grocery store on Tuesday when I get a phone call from Lexi's school, telling me she's unwell and I need to come and get her.

Abandoning my shopping cart, I race to the school to pick her up. As soon as I see her, I know something is terribly wrong. She's clammy and pale. Her breathing is labored and her heart is racing. I take her straight to Western General and call Preston on the way.

As soon as we arrive, like when she cut herself, he's waiting for us. He opens the back door and I swear I hear him mumble, "Shit." Lexi is whisked inside, I leave my car out front, I don't care if it gets towed; my daughter needs me.

It's chaotic, Preston and Andi immediately spring into action. The two of them work in sync like a well-oiled machine. I watch from the sidelines, helpless to do anything. Lexi is admitted to the children's ward immediately and when this happens, I know it's bad. They insert an IV, run tests and other things, but I'm too emotional to focus right now.

Things have settled down and now we wait for the results to come in. I sit by her bed and stare at her little body in the bed, biting my thumbnail. It's amazing how quickly she got sicker, I feel like a crap mom for not focusing on her more. I should have known something was up when I dropped her at school this morning. I should have known. Lexi is sound asleep right now. Her chest rising and falling as she breathes. Her skin is so pale and she looks sick, really really sick.

How did I miss this?

A few hours later, Preston enters Lexi's room. From the look on his face, I know it's not good. My world crumbles around me when Preston says, "Cress, Lexi has sepsis."

Collapsing to the floor, the tears break free. "Nooooo," I cry.

Preston takes me into his arms and I cry. "Cress," he quietly says, "we need to move Lexi up to ICU. Then we will need to do a spinal tap so we know exactly what infection we are working with. While we wait for the sepsis workup, we will administer a broad spectrum antibiotic and as soon as we get the results, we will change her antibiotic to treat the specific infection." I listen to him speak but nothing he says really registers, he's in full-on doctor mode right now. He's serious and to see him like this, adds to my fears for Lexi.

"Will she be okay?" I ask.

He looks at me. "I will do everything I can to make sure she is."

"Will. She. Be. Okay?" I ask again. "Preston, tell me the truth," I snap.

"I can't tell you what you want to hear right now, Cress, but know that I'm doing everything I can."

"Well, do more!" I shout. "I can't lose her, Preston. I just can't."

"Cress," he pleads.

"Preston. You need to fix her. Please." Walking away from him, I sit next to her bed until Andi returns with an orderly so they can move her up to ICU.

Once she's settled in ICU, I take a breather. I step outside and lean against the wall, sliding down I sigh. I need my mom. Grabbing my phone, I call her. "Hi, Cress," Mom says when she answers.

"Mom," I blubber.

"What's wrong?"

"It's Lex, she in ICU."

"What's happened?"

Tears pour down my cheeks. "She has sepsis, Mom. How did I not know she was so sick? I'm the worst mom ever."

"Stop that nonsense," Mom says. "I'll swing by your place and pack you both some things. I'll be there soon. And, Cress?"

"Yeah?"

"She's strong. She's a Bayliss. Give her a kiss from Nanna and tell her I'll be there soon."

"Thanks, Mom."

Hanging up, I head back into ICU and I sit next to my little girl. Taking her little hand in mine, I bring it to my lips and kiss her knuckles. Her eyes flutter but she's so exhausted she can't open them. Running my hand across her forehead, I lean down and press my lips to her temple. "I love you, Munchkin. Please get better. Please."

Closing my eyes, I rest my head on the bed next to her and holding her hand in mine, I drift off to sleep. I'm woken when someone squeezes my shoulder. Turning my head, I see Creed standing there, the look on his face is murderous.

"Thanks for fucking letting me know she was in the hospital," he snarls.

"Creed."

"What lame-ass excuse do you have, huh? I had to find out from your mom that she was here. What the fuck, Cress?"

"Excuse me, sir," Andi says, "You need to calm down and curb the language."

"Ohh fuck off," he sneers. "This bitch here didn't tell me that my daughter was in the hospital."

"This woman," Andi says, "hasn't had a chance to."

"She called her fucking mother, she had time to call me. She's just being a bitch."

"Last warning, sir, you use language like that again and I will have no choice but to call security. Now, I suggest you leave and calm down. Once you are calm, you can come back. Lexi doesn't need this right now."

"Everything okay here?" Preston asks, as he walks in.

Creed looks to Preston and his face turns red. "I want a new fucking doctor," he snarls.

"Dr. Knight is the best that we have, sir," Andi says. "I assure you, your daughter is in excellent hands."

"As is my wife when it comes to this fucker."

"Creed," I snap. "Now is not the ducking time. Lexi needs us. If you want to stay, stop being a jackass and focus on her."

"Fuck this shit," he bellows and storms out of ICU, passing Mom in the doorway.

"Cress," Mom says, and as soon as I hear her voice, the tears start again.

"Mom," I cry, standing up I race over to her. Mom wraps her arms around me in the way only a mom can. Wrapping mine around hers, I cry into her shoulder.

"Shhhh," she coos. "It's all going to be okay."

"It's not, Mom, my baby is sick, so so sick and I missed it. I'm a shit mom."

"No, you are not. I won't let you talk like that. Now, you are going to go to the bathroom and wash your face. Then you will go to the cafeteria, get a coffee, and once you are calm, you will come back and be strong for your daughter."

"I'm not leaving her."

"Yes, you are," Mom says. "I will call security myself if I have to. You need to look after you too. Now go. Coffee. Now."

"Come on," Preston says. "I could do with a coffee too." He looks to Andi. "Please page me as soon as the results are in, or if anything changes."

"Can do, Bossman." She turns to walk way and then looks over her shoulder. "And take her across the road for coffee, the stuff in the cafeteria is shit."

He nods and takes my hand, normally that calms me but not this time. I'm so highly strung. All I want right now is for Lexi to get better. Reluctantly, I let him escort me over to the coffee shop because I know my mom, she really will call security if I don't go. Deep down, I know she's right. I need to calm down so I can focus and be here for Lexi.

27 PRESTON

CRESS AND I ARE SITTING IN THE COFFEE SHOP ACROSS THE ROAD FROM THE hospital, waiting for our drinks. She's biting her thumbnail, something I've noticed she does when she's anxious, sad, or her anxiety is through the roof. They call my name and I go get our drinks. I place Cress's coffee in front of her, she looks at it but doesn't pick it up. She goes back to staring into space. Her refusing coffee proves that she's not okay.

"Cress, Love, talk to me?" She looks at me, her mouth opens and closes a few times. "Please," I beg.

"You really want to know what I'm thinking right now?" I nod my head. "My daughter is in the in ICU," she sneers, "'cause I missed the signs. I'm her mom for fuck's sake. I should have known something was up. It's my fault. I should—"

"Cress, it's no one's fault."

"I'm not finished," she snaps. "I should have paid more attention. I should have been focusing on her one-hundred-percent of the time, not spending it with you." She pauses, takes a deep breath, and from the look in her eye, she's moved from anger to rage. "And then there's you. You're a fucking doctor, and you didn't see this happening right under your nose. How? How did you not see what was happening to my baby girl?" She pauses and swallows. "Preston," she cries. "How did this happen? How did we both miss this?"

Tears are pouring down her face. Hopping up from my chair, I walk over to her lift her up, sit back down, and wrap my arms around her. "Shhhh," I whisper. "Cress, you need to keep thinking positive. Lexi is tough. I will do everything I can to get her better."

"You promise?"

"Yes, I promise to do everything I can."

"No, promise me she will be okay?"

Shaking my head, I tell her honestly, "I can't promise she will be okay but, Cress, I won't rest until she's better."

"That's not enough. She needs more. I need more." She hops off my lap, walks out of the coffee shop, crosses the road, and heads back to the hospital.

Rubbing my forehead, I sigh. I want so much to tell her it will all be okay, but I can't. I never make a promise like that because I cannot guarantee it will be okay, but I promise I will do everything humanly possible to get Lexi well again. I wish I could promise what she wants, but I can't promise that, I just can't.

A voice from behind snarls, "Ohh look, she's finally seeing that you really are a fucking piece of shit."

"Creed," I say through clenched teeth. "Fuck off, I'm not in the mood for your shit."

"And I'm not in the mood to sit around a hospital waiting for my daughter to get better 'cause you fucked up."

Standing up, I get in his face. "I didn't fuck up. This is no one's fault. Kids get sick, it's a part of life."

"You were too busy fucking that slut to see what was happening. You didn't see her getting sick right before your eyes 'cause that woman's cunt was all you could think about." The coffee shop falls silent, everyone's eyes are on Creed and me. He steps closer, his nose millimeters from mine. "You missed this, Knight, this is on you." He pokes my chest. "If my little girl dies, I will sue your ass for everything you have, *and* I'll make sure that Cress hates you with a vengeance."

Shoving him, he stumbles backward. I step toward him, my heart racing as my anger rises. I want to knock this fucker out. My blood is boiling at the words coming from his mouth. "Fuck off, you piece of shit. You don't care about Lexi or Cress." My fist clenches and I'm so close to hitting him. "Do everyone a favor and fuck off."

His eyes drop to my fist, his lip lifts in an evil smirk. "Go on, hit me. Just another thing to add to the list of things that you are going to go down for."

Raising my arm, I pull back ready to knock him out but someone covers my hand and stops me. "I don't know who you are," Flynn says, "but you need to walk away."

"Fuck you both," Creed snaps. "Enjoy your last days as a doctor, Knight." He storms out of the coffee shop. My eyes follow him as he walks down the street and away from the hospital.

Flynn stands in front of me and squeezes my shoulder. "You good?"

Looking at him, I shake my head side to side. "Not really, no."

"Wanna talk about it?"

"Not really, but I know you, you'll make me talk."

"Good, now start talking."

"I did fuck up, Flynn. I missed this. I'm a doctor for fuck's sake, how did I miss her being this sick?"

"I don't know the specifics but I do know you, you are a fucking great doctor, Preston."

"Tell that to that little girl in that hospital. To Cress, the woman I love. Lexi is in the ICU 'cause I didn't pick up on the signs. I should have looked at her cuts more. I should have done more. I should have—"

"Should have what?" Flynn snaps. He stares at me and I shrug because I really don't know what I could have done. "Exactly. Now, pull your head out of your ass and focus. There's no point in going over what-ifs right now. Right now, you need to concentrate on what you can see and do. Be the best doctor for Lexi and be there for Cress."

"She hates me right now."

"She doesn't hate you. She's just a mom who's worried about her daughter."

I stare at my best friend and process his words, I don't agree with him at all. "You're right," I say to placate him. "Lexi and Cress need me right now. They need me to be on top of my game so I can get her through this."

"That's the Preston I know."

We exit the coffee shop and head back to the hospital. I check in on Lexi, but there's been no change and until we get the work up, we won't know how to treat whatever she has effectively.

It's been two days since Lexi was admitted and I think I've slept for maybe four hours. I've set up camp in the doctors' lounge. Lexi is my only case right now, until she is out of the woods she is going to have all my attention. To make matters worse, my princess now has pneumonia too. Her little body is wilting away and it's all my fault. I should have picked up that Lexi wasn't well. This is on me and no matter what anyone says, this is my fault, but I will do everything in my power to make sure she makes a full recovery.

28 CRESS

I'VE LOST COUNT AS TO HOW MANY DAYS IT'S BEEN NOW; I THINK IT'S THREE, no four days, and there's been no improvement. Not only does my baby girl have sepsis from the cut on her arm, not her leg like I thought since that was the one she was complaining about. She now has pneumonia due to her already compromised respiratory system; damn the asthma that runs in the family.

I've just had a shower, at the insistance of Andi, Mom, and Ave. Avery and I have been texting constantly, I told her not to come. I can't handle seeing the anguish in her face too, and thankfully, she's doing as I asked. Earning her the title of 'bestest friend in the world.'

Walking back into Lexi's room, I lean against the doorframe and stare at her little body hooked up to all the machines. Emotion overcomes me at the sight of her. Racing to the side of the bed, I take a seat and stare down at her. Her cheeks have color today but she still sleeps a lot. "I'm so sorry, Munchkin," I whisper, brushing a tendril of hair off her face. "I've let you down. I will never let you down again, just please, please pull through. Please get better, please, Munchkin, please." Lowering my head to her bed, I cry. Gut-wrenching sobs break free as I let it all out.

This is all my fault.
This is all my fault.
This is all my fault.

This is all my fault.

I keep repeating this over and over as the tears continue to fall. A hand touches my back and I know whose hand it is. Lifting my head, I turn my head to see Preston staring down at me. He's got that 'I'm sorry' look and I'm sick of seeing that look on everyone's face.

"Cress—"

"No," I snap, standing up, I turn and face him, "If I hadn't have been fucking around with you," I poke him in the chest, "Lex would not be in that bed right now. This is all my fault." I pause. "Actually, it's all your fault."

"Cress, no, it's no one's fault." He tries to soothe me but deep down I know this is all my fault. I'm projecting my fear right now, but it feels good to be angry. If I focus on how mad I am, I don't dwell on the fact that I fucked up.

"I'm her mother, goddammit. I should I have seen her getting sick. I should have known." Dropping to my knees, I shake my head and cry. Looking up at Preston, I see anguish on his face, "I can't lose her, Preston. I can't. She's my everything." Another wave of sobs break free. "Please save my baby girl. Please, Preston, please."

He squats in front of me and envelops me in his arms. "Cress, I will do everything humanly possible to save her." His warmth and words are comforting and I lean into him. Closing my eyes, I cry into his chest. My sobs have eased but I still feel like the shittiest mother in the world. Taking a deep breath, I pull back and look up at Preston, like always with us, that déjà vu feeling encompasses me and something passes between us. I can feel him giving me the strength I need to go on.

Movement by the door catches my attention and I look up into the glaring eyes of Creed.

"Creed, you're back," I say. Pushing away from Preston, I stand up and walk over to him. Preston follows, standing close behind me.

"I'm checking on *my* daughter," he snarls. "She still not any better?" He pauses but continues, not giving me a chance to talk. "I really think we need a new doctor, Babydoll, the current one is clearly shit."

Preston tenses behind me. A lump forms in my throat at the harshness of his words but what surprises me most is, I wonder if he's right? Is Preston too close? Is our relationship compromising his care of Lexi?

"Do you want to sit with her for a bit?"

"Like you can fucking stop me," he snarls, stepping into the room. He walks past us and shoves his shoulder into Preston. Looking to Preston, I apologize with my eyes. It's no secret that Preston and Creed can't stand one another, actually no one can stand Creed. Not even Andi and she loves everyone.

"I'll stop in later," Preston says. "Text me if you need anything or there's any change. If it's urgent, get them to page me." He presses his lips to my temple. Closing my eyes, I draw strength from him. He exits the room and when I turn around, Creed is staring at me, I don't like the look in his eyes right now. Taking a deep breath, I walk over to the bed and sit. Creed sits and takes the chair on the opposite side.

"How is she?" he asks. I'm shocked at his question, he hasn't once asked about her. He normally just sits here and yells at everyone.

"There's been no change. The pneumonia was unexpected but her lungs will slowly get better. She's currently on several antibiotics but until they start working, it's a waiting game."

"How did this all happen?" he questions, not a hint of malice in his voice. It almost seems like he cares.

"I don't know," I dejectedly say.

"How can you not know, you're her fucking mother?" And there's the Creed I know.

"That's rich coming from her absentee father," I angrily snap back.

He stands up and holds on to the end of the bed. He stares at me and I shudder from his leering gaze. "Maybe it's time I see my lawyer about getting custody, since you seem to be doing such a stellar job."

Jumping to my feet, I race toward him. "Over my dead body will you ever get custody of Lexi."

"That can be arranged," he nonchalantly says, staring at me with a sinister smirk on his face. "Maybe it's time I become less absentee."

"Why, Creed, why? Why now, after five years, do you suddenly give a shit about her?"

"'Cause it fucks with your mind, Dollface, and fucking with you is a favorite hobby of mine and since I can no longer fuck you, I will fuck with you. I hold the power here, you should remember that." He steps toward me and grips my chin roughly. He glares at me. "Enjoy the time you have with her because when I'm done, you will have nothing. N-O-T-H-I-N-G. You will be begging for me and my cock, and guess what? I won't give you shit. You will be all alone and it's all yours and lover boy's fault because you couldn't look after my daughter." Before I can say anything, he presses his lips to mine. He grips my upper arms tightly, trying to gain access to my mouth. "Bitch," he snarls against my pursed lips before he turns on his heel, storming out of Lexi's hospital room.

"Ohh God," I cry, covering my mouth as his words sink in.

"Cress," Preston says from the doorway, "is everything okay?"

Spinning around I stare at Preston. Swallowing deeply, I storm over to him and lose it. "You are the reason Dickwad Dawson is threatening me. You should be fixing her quicker. You need to fix her now," I cry, hitting his chest with my palms. "You need to fix her," I cry.

"Cress—"

"NOW!" I interrupt and yell at him, "You need to fix her now because he's threatening to take my little girl from me. That's all on you." Pausing, I look at him, breathing heavily, "I want a new doctor on her case. I never want to see you again, Preston Knight. Get the fuck out of my daughter's hospital room. It's over. We are over."

"Cress, pl—"

"I said get the fuck out. Falling for you has caused all of this. This is all your fault, I hate you."

Turning away from him, I walk back to Lexi's bed and climb in next to her. I pull her close to me and cry.

I cry for Lexi.

I cry for losing Preston.

I cry because I hate Creed more than I ever thought possible.

And I cry for the shitshow my life has become.

Tears pour down my cheeks as I run my fingers through Lexi's hair. I've never been so scared in my entire life. I'm going to lose my daughter, and it's either going to be to the bacteria that's currently ravaging her little body, or to her dickwad of a father, and this is all Preston's fault. Quietly I murmur to myself, "Falling for Dr. Knight was the worst thing I have ever done."

29 PRESTON

"I WANT A NEW DOCTOR ON HER CASE. I NEVER WANT TO SEE YOU AGAIN, Preston Knight. Get the fuck out of my daughter's hospital room."

Those words play on a loop over and over in my mind. And each time, it's more crushing than the last. Sliding down the wall next to Lexi's room, I run my fingers through my hair. Pulling the strands in frustration, the follicles tear, but it gives little reprieve to my mood.

"What are you doing on the floor?" Andi asks as she slides down to sit next to me.

"Cress kicked me out and I think we broke up. No, we did break up, she said it's over."

"She didn't mean it. That woman loves you unconditionally." She squeezes my arm in the reassuring way she always does, but this time there's no reassurance at all. "It's a trying time for all, Preston. Give her space and just be you, she'll be back in your arms in no time."

"When did you get so wise?"

"I've always been this wise. You are just noticing it now."

I smile at her. "Thanks, Andi."

"Anytime, but can I make a suggestion?"

"Sure."

"Go home and shower, you stink like a sewer rat."

"There's the Andi I know but I'm not leaving, my girls need me." And I mean that, I think of Lexi as my own.

"Preston," she snaps. "Go home and shower. You have been here for four days straight, you need a break and a shower. Then come back refreshed and ready to fight, both the sepsis and for your girls. You've just administered the antibiotics that are gonna kick this thing's ass, now IS the time to freshen up besides, Lexi doesn't need a stinky broody doctor around while she's recovering."

"I'm not broody."

"But you are admitting you stink? I promise to page if there's ANY change."

"Promise?"

"Yes, now go before I vomit. You reek and no one needs that."

A laugh escapes me and I stand up, looking into Lexi's room, I see Cress lying in bed with her. Her cheeks are wet from crying, turning around I come face-to-face with Creed. "Told you to stay away but looks like the bitch woke up and dumped your sorry ass."

"Fuck off, Creed."

"Don't worry, Doc, I'll take good care of her. I'll show her how a real man fucks."

I shake my head. "How you can be thinking about that right now when your daughter is in there fighting for her life is beyond me, but it also shows you know nothing about Cress. Dick, and especially yours, is the last thing on her mind right now. Now, if you excuse me, I need to get back to work."

Stepping around him, I walk away, ignoring the taunts he's yelling at my back. Passing Steve from security, I nod at him and give him the 'I'll leave him to you' look. Stopping, I turn and watch as Steve escorts a yelling and cursing Creed from the ICU.

Once he's removed from the ward, I head down to my car and race home. As soon as I walk inside, I stop when I see one of Lexi's *My Little Pony* figurines sitting on the entry table. I pick up the purple pony and whisper, "I'm sorry for letting you down, Lexi, I'm going to make you better…I hope."

Stepping into the shower, I close my eyes and let the hot water wash over me. Lifting my head, I smile when I see all of Cress's products in the nook. Flicking open the cap of her shower gel, I breathe it in. The lime and coconut smell reminds me so much of Cress and happier times. Turning around, I slide down the tiles and sit on the floor. Leaning my arms on the seat, I stare at the bottle in my hands. The ringing of my phone grabs my attention. I turn off the water, wrap a towel around my waist. Stepping in my bedroom, I pick my phone up off the bed. I see that it's my brother, Keeton, calling. I'm not in the mood to talk so I let it go to voicemail. Throwing it back on the bed, I walk back into the bathroom and dry off. Walking naked into the closet, I change back into black slacks and a white button-down.

My phone beeps with a text, I know it will be Keeton, he's a persistent son of a bitch, so I sit on the end of the bed and reply to him without reading his message.

PRESTON: *Super busy. Catch up soon*
KEETON: *Looking forward to it…it's been forever. Call when you can*
PRESTON: *Will do.*

Throwing a few changes of clothes into a bag, I grab a few toiletries and head back to the hospital. Dropping off my things in my locker, I head straight to ICU.

Walking into Lexi's room, I find it empty and my heart stops beating in my chest. I spin around and before I can ask, Andi says, "They've taken her for another chest X-ray and I managed to convince Cress to take a walk. She's just as stubborn as you, no wonder you two are in love."

"She broke up with me, remember?"

"She's not thinking clearly. One problem at a time, and no offense to your ego, but that little girl should be our number one focus right now."

"Stop being rational."

"I can't help it that I'm the only one thinking clearly right now." She turns and walks away. She stops, turns and says, "Ohh, and by the way, that Creed douche, he's been removed from the hospital, he assaulted Steve."

"Really?"

"Really, really."

"That's good news, here's hoping the good news continues to filter in."

"Positive thinking and it will," Andi says, ever the optimist.

Walking over to the nurses' station, I sit down and look at Lexi's file. Her recent blood work looks better, but she's still not out of the woods, her latest X-ray is uploaded and when I look at it, I smile. Her lungs are improving and we are about to move her from ICU to the children's ward.

The air around me crackles and I know she's back. Looking up, I see Cress and even though she looks tired, she's still the sexiest woman I have ever seen. Her hair's up in a messy bun and she's wearing ass-hugging jeans and a simple black sweater. As usual, she makes a simple outfit look like catwalk couture.

Cress looks up and our gazes meet, she stops mid-step and stares back at me. I'm about to walk over to her, when Lexi is wheeled back in and our moment is over. I sit and watch as Cress races over to them. They wheel Lexi back into her room and what makes me smile, as she's wheeled past, I see her eyes are open and she's smiling. She sits up and tries to shout, "Prince Dr. Preston," her voice is quiet, but there's excitement in her eyes.

Standing up, I walk over to her room. "Princess Lexi, my favorite patient. How you feeling, Munchkin?"

"Better. Mommy says my medicine is working."

"It sure is. Sorry it took so long."

"It's okay. Can you stay?"

"Preston needs to get back to work, Munchkin, and you need to rest," Cress says without looking at or acknowledging me. It hurts but after my chat with Andi, I understand.

"Actually," Andi says from behind me as she enters the room, "now that you're better, we have a special ward for you. Do you want to see your new room, Lexi?"

"Yes, please." She looks to Cress. "And then we can watch Pony."

"Anything for you, Munchkin."

Stepping aside, I watch as Andi escorts Cress and Lexi to the children's ward with the help of an orderly. Looking up, I catch Cress staring at me. I smile but she quickly looks away. Standing in the now empty room, I spy another pony figurine on the rolling table and an idea forms. Racing out of the room, I head to the doctors' lounge to have some privacy and set my surprise up.

Walking into the lounge, Clay is lying on the bench and he's listening to music. "What song is that?" I ask him as I open my locker and grab out my laptop.

"It's "I Won't Give Up" by Jason Mraz."

Nodding my head, I smile. The words to this song sum up my feelings right now. I'm not giving up. I'm going to get Lexi better AND then I'm going to win Cress back. I'm not giving up, not ever when it comes to Cress and Lexi.

30   CRESS

Two days later, I wake up and like always, my eyes go straight to Lexi's bed and for the first time in almost a week I smile and it's a genuine smile. Her color is back to normal, she looks like Lexi again. The first thing I want to do is text Preston, but then I remember I can't. I was a total bitch to him and I broke us. Sighing, I realize I need to get used to not having him around anymore.

Lexi opens her eyes. "Mommy?"

"Yes, Munchkin?"

"I want toast."

Those three words mean everything to me. If she wants food, that means she's better. Preston did it, he fixed my little girl...and I pushed him away. "I'll see what I can do." Before I get a chance to get her some toast, the door to her room opens and a huge bouquet of balloons is delivered. It's filled with pink and purple love hearts, a Rainbow Dash 3D balloon and several round Pony gang ones. Then enters someone with a *My Little Pony* blanket that they place over the bed, a plush Rainbow Dash pony, and a basket of Pony figurines. Lexi grabs the plush pony and hugs it to her chest, it's just as big as her. The smile on her little face right now is priceless. Another person walks in behind with a lollipop bouquet, Lexi's eyes widen when she sees that. And lastly, someone hands me a venti-sized coffee from across the road.

"Holy duck," I say, as I take in the Pony explosion around us.

"Mommy, where did all of this come from?" Lexi asks me.

"I have no idea, Munchkin," I say, but I'm pretty sure I know where it all came from: Preston.

The hairs on the back of my neck stand on end, the air around me crackles and then I feel him behind me. My heart beats faster. My breathing becomes labored. It's been a few days since he's been this close to me and my body hasn't forgotten how he makes me feel.

"Morning," he says from behind me. The deep timbre of his voice warms me from the inside out.

"Prince Dr. Preston," Lexi beams. "Look what I got?" She holds up the pony and winces when she pulls on her IV.

Preston steps around me and over to her. "You okay, Munchkin?" His voice laced with concern; it pulls at my heartstrings. He really does care. Then I begin to wonder if I made a mistake. Did I overreact due to the situation with Lexi?

She nods. "I'm okay now," she says. "I haven't seened you much."

"I've been here. I've just been busy." He lifts his gaze to mine. He smiles but it doesn't reach his eyes. He looks tired. His face is covered in a light beard, and he looks fucking hot if I'm honest. "You like your surprise?" he asks Lexi.

"You did all this?" Lexi asks him.

He nods at her. "Yep, I wanted to cheer you up." He looks over to me. "And you too," he says.

"I don't know what to say," I admit, a lump forming in the back of my throat because he did all of this, even though I pushed him away. But then I remember Lexi asking about him and I realize that, yes, he has been absent the last few days. Maybe he doesn't care after all, but then if he didn't care, he wouldn't have done all of this. I'm so confused right now.

"You don't need to say anything, Cress."

"You shouldn't have, Preston. We are..." I stop because I don't know how to finish that sentence. What are we? I broke what we were because I was scared, will we ever get back from that?

Turning away from him, I stare out into the corridor. "Cress," he says, touching my shoulder. "I just wanted—"

"No," I say, turning to face him. "You shouldn't have, Preston." When he looks at me, I know without a doubt: I made a mistake pushing him away and breaking us was the wrong choice. "We...I...I need a minute."

Racing out of the room, my eyes well with tears. Everything becomes blurry with each step I take. Turning the corner I bump into someone, they grip my shoulders to steady me. "Cress, are you okay?" Andi says, her voice laced with concern.

"I...he...Preston...I broke up with him."

"What did he do now?"

"Everything. He's kind and spoiling us. It's too much. I need him to leave us alone. We are over. I broke us. I can't do this. I—"

"Cress, that man loves you and Lexi with everything he has. I have never seen him like this before. He'll probably kick my ass for telling you this, but he's been here twenty-four seven for the last week. Checking in on Lexi and making sure she was getting the best possible treatment every chance he got. He'd hover and wait for you to leave, or he'd hide out at the nurses' station and watch her remotely."

"What?" I say, completely shocked at her revelation.

"You didn't know?"

"No," I shake my head and hold my hand to my chest. My heart rapidly beating at this revelation. "I never saw him."

"He's been here in the shadows. Watching. Hovering. Doing what he does best." She purses her lips. "This probably isn't my place to say, but give him another chance, Cress. What happened with Lexi was no one's fault. These things happen and generally without warning, especially in kids."

"But—"

"No buts, Cress. He's gutted you broke up with him, and he's pissed at himself that he didn't see this coming. You are the one for him, Cress, and I think, deep down, you know it too."

"I...I need air, excuse me." Stepping around her, I head toward the fire exit and race up the stairs to the roof. I found this place the other day when I needed air after breaking up with Preston.

Pushing the door open, I step out onto the rooftop. Walking over to the edge, I place down my coffee and stare out into the distance. My mind is racing a million miles an hour. The questions coming at me at light speed. Lowering my head down, I begin to cry as it all catches up with me and then it hits me: I made the biggest mistake of my life pushing away Dr. Knight.

31 CREED

THIS IS TURNING OUT BETTER THAN I ANTICIPATED. CRESS BROKE UP WITH THE fucker and she's teetering on the edge. She'll be riding my cock, begging me for more very soon. It's a shame the kid pulled through, but if I play my cards right, I can make her hate Cressida. Or maybe Dr. Fuckhead will fuck up and miss something else, and then she'll die.

She races out of the room, tears pouring down her face. Dr. Fuckhead follows soon after, stopping at the nurses' station. When the coast is clear, I go into the squid's room. It looks like a fucking Pony explosion in here; balloons and toys are everywhere.

"What the fuck?" I snarl at the scene before me.

"Daddy Creed," she says. *Fuck, I hate it when she calls me that.*

"It's just fucking Creed, how many times do I have to tell you that?"

"Look what Prince Dr. Preston did for me," she excitedly says.

"Looks like he's trying to win you over for fucking up." She looks at me with a confused look. "You know you're in here because he fucked up and your mother is a whore."

"You are saying lots of naughty words."

"Joys of being an adult, kid. Where's Cressida?"

"She went for a walk, Prince Dr. Preston said she needed some air."

"Seems she doesn't care either."

"She does so. Mommy loves me."

"Really? That woman only knows how to love herself. She doesn't love you at all."

"Mommy loves me," she cries.

"If she did love you, she'd be here now. She clearly has more important things to do than sit here with you. Lexi, she doesn't love you."

"Mommy," Lexi cries, "does to love me."

"Shut the fuck up," I growl, reaching out, I pop a purple love heart balloon. The loud bang startling the squid and she begins to cry harder.

"For fuck's sake," I growl. "I'm your father, you need to listen to me and shut up. Stop with the tears." Anger courses through my veins. "Shut. The. Fuck. Up."

"I wish Prince Dr. Preston was my daddy, you're mean."

"And you whine too much. I'm your father, so you're stuck with me and if I have my way, you will be with me always."

"No," she cries, "I want Mommy."

"Tough shit. I want to see her and him suffer."

Deciding that my daughter is coming with me, I walk toward the bed. I wish I could see the look on the bitch's face when she realizes that her precious daughter is gone.

"Sir," someone says from the doorway, "I'm going to have to ask you to leave."

Turning around I see the doctor's side whore. "Fuck off, lady, she's my daughter. I have a right to be here."

"That maybe so, but I will not tolerate someone speaking to a child like that. The whole ward just heard how you spoke to her. You've upset her and she's still recovering."

"Yeah, recovering 'cause both that bitch and fucker fucked up. I can speak to her however the fuck I want." I pause and glare at the woman before me, but she's one tough bitch and just glares at me. "Get the fuck out. NOW."

The bitch turns on her heel and walks out of the room, leaving me with a crying kid. "For fuck's sake. Stop crying, tears are for the weak. When you are mine, I will beat you tough just like my daddy did to me. No kid of mine is going to be a pussy."

"Sir," a deep male voice says from behind, "I'm going to have to ask you to leave."

"Make me," I snarl, no one tells me what to do.

"Last chance, sir, you need to leave now."

Turning around, I stare at him, this fucker looks like he means business and if I'm going to fuck Cress over, I cannot lose my shit now. "Fine," I huff. "I'll go but I'll be back." Without looking at the squid, I walk out of the room, shoving the guard in the shoulder as I walk past.

Entering the elevator, a plan formulates in my mind. Cress is going down...but first, a little fun.

32 CRESS

PICKING UP MY COFFEE, I TAKE A SIP, IT'S STONE-COLD. "UGH," I WHISPER, "cold coffee, just another thing that's gone cold in my life."

Letting out a sigh, I continue to stare across the rooftops. I really wish I could call Ave right now, but she's still recovering and doesn't need this added to her worries. I know she'll kick my ass but she has enough on her plate at the moment.

The silence is broken when I hear my name, "Cress." Spinning around I come face-to-face with Preston. Worry etched on his gorgeous face.

"How did you find me here?"

"I will always find you, Cress, always." We silently stare at one another; again that déjà vu feeling washes over me. "When no one could find you, I just knew you'd be here because this where I come when I need to escape."

"It's beautiful up here."

"It sure is," he says, but his eyes are on me and I feel like he's referring to me and not the view.

We fall silent again and quietly stare at each other. The walls I previously put up begin to crumble and the regret at pushing him away festers within. My eyes well with tears when it hits me like a freight train; I want him. I need him. I love him. We need him in our life.

We.

Need.

Him.

But what if we've lost him? Because in haste, I pushed him away. That thought hurts like said freight train smashing into me, it utterly guts me that I pushed him away, I don't want that. I want Preston Knight in my and Lexi's life. "Preston—" I blubber.

He steps over to me and gently squeezes my upper arms. "Lexi is going to be fine...and so will we." *How did he know?* "Nothing will keep me from you. Not even an outburst when you thought your world was ending." He takes my cheeks in his palms and stares deep into my soul. "Cress, I'm never letting you go." He gently presses his mouth to mine and all the sadness, anger, fear, and unease I had evaporates as soon as his lips touch mine and I know, without a doubt, he's right.

I was falling for him from the moment I saw him and I want to fall even deeper in love with him. "I don't want you to let us go either, Preston. I'm going to jump in with both feet and give us my everything because you are my everything."

"Good, because me plus you and Lexi are my forever. My everything." He cups my cheek in his palm again. "I'm sorry I let you both down, but if you give me another chance, I'll never let that happen again. I was devastated at causing you this pain. When I lost you and Lexi, I thought my world was over. That little pony-loving princess has wormed her way deep into my heart, just like you have."

He wipes a tear from my cheek. "I love you, Preston," I whisper, leaning into his palm.

"I love you too, Cress. I never stopped and I never will."

Taking his cheeks in my hands, I press my lips to his. He slides his arms around my waist, pulling me into him. Wrapping my arms around his neck, I hold him tightly and pour everything into this kiss. He breaks the connection and rests his forehead against mine.

Everything is falling into place again. Lexi is getting better and I have Preston back in my life. Closing my eyes, I enjoy the moment.

Preston's pager goes off, he looks down and frowns "We need to head back down. Creed was just with Lexi and she's upset."

My eyes widen and my heart begins to race faster. "What?"

"He was just asked to leave."

My eyes widen, "We need to get back."

"Okay, let's go." He laces his fingers with mine and together, we head back inside and down to see Lexi.

When I step back into her room, my heart breaks. My little girl is sobbing and wrapped in Andi's arms. "Lexi, baby, what's wrong?"

"Daddy Creed is mean," she cries.

Fucking Creed, I think to myself as I race over to her bed. Andi stands up and I sit down and envelop Lexi into my arms. She cries and cries, it breaks my heart seeing her so upset.

Andi and Preston are quietly talking in the corner; from the look on Preston's face he's as angry as I am right now. Andi leaves and Preston walks over to us.

"Hey, Princess Lexi. You okay, Munchkin?"

She nods her head but the tears keep coming. "Wanna tell Mommy and I what happened?" he asks, as he pulls a chair to the side of her bed.

"He popped a balloon and said Mommy doesn't love me and he swore. Lots."

"Munchkin, Mommy loves you to the moon and back. You know this, right?" She nods her head. "Creed is just having a bad day," I tell her, hoping that this will make her feel better.

"He said he wants to take me from you."

My eyes pop open, rage simmers in my blood that he would say this to her. Shaking my head, I hold her tighter to me. "I won't let that happen, Lex. I love you too much to let you go." Kissing her head, I look to Preston. He looks like I feel—ready to explode.

"I'm going to speak to security, make sure he isn't allowed back in."

"Thank you," I say, reaching my hand out to his. He takes my hand and squeezes it before bringing it to his lips and kissing my knuckles. He leans over and kisses Lexi's head before he walks out to speak to security.

Lying on the bed with Lexi, I hug her to me. Her body relaxes and I know she's fallen asleep. My mind plays over everything that has happened. I find myself smiling when I realize things are looking up again. Lexi is better, and Preston and I are back together. I came so close to losing both him and Lexi, now that I have them back, I'm going to hold on with both hands. I'm never letting them go, never.

33 PRESTON

LEXI HAS BEEN HEALTHY FOR SIX MONTHS NOW. IF I'M NOT AT THE HOSPITAL, I'm with her and Cress. I'm watching her like a hawk, I will not miss her getting sick again. I'm in my office finalizing my proposal for the pediatric upgrade, the carrot offered to entice me to stay in Chicago. They weren't happy when I called them to decline their offer but by staying here, I get the job and the girls, making my life perfect.

I'm meeting with Dr. Jenkins tomorrow and if she agrees to my proposal, its going to be amazing to see my vision come to fruition.

My phone pings with a text, it's my brother. He and I have been playing phone tag for weeks now.

KEETON: *Hey, Doc. You free for dinner? I have news*
PRESTON: *Now's not a good time for dinner. What's the news?*
KEETON: *I'd rather tell you in person. Don't fret it's good news. Great news in fact.*
PRESTON: *Good news I can handle, maybe next week?*
KEETON: *Sounds good, let me know when and I'll set it up with Blair and Faith*
PRESTON: *Blair and Faith???*

What is my brother up to now? And why am I being invited to dinner with his business partner and some chick?

KEETON: *I'll explain over dinner. See you next week*

A few days later, Lexi, Cress, and I are in the blanket fort we made watching, you guessed it, *My Little Pony*. We are waiting for pizza to arrive when my phone rings and I smile when I see Keeton's name on the screen. "Hey, baby bro," I answer. I try and roll out of the fort but Lexi has a death grip on me so I lie back and get comfy.

"Are you alive? You didn't get back to me to arrange dinner," Keeton says.

"Duck, I totally forgot."

"Duck? Really?"

"Umm, yeah, I'm at my girlfriend's place and she has a kid.'

"Come again, girlfriend? With a kid?"

"Says the guy who wants me to have dinner with his business partner and meet some chick."

"Touché," he says, and I picture him nodding his head as he says this.

"So, are you going to tell me what's going on in your life?"

"Are you going to tell me about playing happy family?" he retorts back. I look to Lexi and Cress and realize I am, in fact, playing happy family but there's no playing. This is real life and I am one-hundred-percent committed to this family.

"You first," I counter.

"Of course, you'd say that. How about this weekend we all get together at your place? Enjoy the last of this good weather? Barbecue and swim?"

"Sounds great, let me just check with Cress."

"Pussy-whipped," he coughs down the line.

"Asshole," I whisper back.

"Prince Dr. Preston said a naughty word," Lexi says.

"He did, Mommy will punish him later." Cress winks at me and it goes straight to my cock.

"You guys free Sunday afternoon to meet my brother and his whatever they are?"

"Sounds good," Cress says, as Lexi asks, "Can we swim and have burgers?"

"Yes," Keeton shouts through the phone.

Cress and I laugh, "Of course, Munchkin."

Lifting the phone back to my ear. "So you heard that?"

"Yes, and tell Lexi she has great taste and Uncle K can't wait to meet her."

"You're a dick," I tell him.

"He said a naughty word again, Mommy."

"Double punishment is coming for him then."

"You're in trouble," Lexi singsongs.

"Thanks, bro, I'm in trouble 'cause of you."

"Happy to help. See you Sunday."

He hangs up and when I look over to Cress, her eyes are full of hunger and desire...I'm so looking forward to my punishment.

After pizza and more Pony episodes, I bathe and get Lexi into bed. Once she's asleep, I walk back into the kitchen, and notice Cress staring at her phone. "He text again?" I ask.

She lifts her gaze to mine, she smiles but it doesn't reach her eyes. "Yeah, but I did what you said, I deleted it straightaway." She walks over to me and wraps her arms around my waist and rests her head on my chest.

"Thank you," she murmurs.

"What are you thanking me for?"

"For being you. For loving me and Lexi like you do."

"I do love you both, with all my heart, Cress." She lifts her gaze to mine and smiles, this time it reaches her eyes. She presses her lips to mine and when she pulls back, her eyes are full of hunger and desire. Taking her hand, I lead her into her bedroom.

She pulls away. "I just need some water, give me a minute."

Nodding my head, I watch as she walks back into the kitchen, turning around I walk into her bedroom and remove my shirt and pants, leaving me in my boxers. I sit on the edge of the bed and fall back to the mattress, I'm shattered and cannot wait to crawl into bed with Cress. A throat clearing from the doorway causes my head to raise and when I look up my eyes bug out of my head.

Cress is leaning against the doorframe in the sexiest piece of lingerie I have ever seen. She's wearing silky black panties that match a sexy as fuck white satin bra adorned with black lace, that flows into a black mesh that stops just at her panty line. "Fuck me, Cress. You are the sexiest woman alive."

From behind her back, she has an open bottle of bubbly in one hand and a plate of chocolate-coated strawberries in the other. "We need to celebrate."

"What are we celebrating?"

"There's lots to celebrate, Dr. Knight."

"Come here," I growl.

Cress pushes off the doorframe and saunters over to me. Swishing her hips side to side as she goes. She places the plate of strawberries onto the bedside table and brings the bottle to her lips and drinks. She leans down and presses her lips to me, the bubbly going from her mouth to mine. Some spills down her chin and neck. Leaning forward, I lick down her throat and chest, lapping up the spilt bubbly.

Wrapping my arms around her waist, she straddles my thighs and stares at me. The air in the room is heated and thick with desire. Taking the bottle from her, I take a sip. Then I lift it up and pour some across her chest. Pulling her closer to me, I lick the cold liquid from her skin, goosebumps breaking out across her chest. Sucking her nipple through the material, it pebbles and hardens. Licking across her chest, I do the same to the other one. Her head drops back and I continue to lick and suck her chest. She circles her hips on my lap and cries out when she can't rub herself on me.

"Patience, my dear," I mumble against her skin.

"Fuck patience, I want your cock in me now," she mewls, grinding herself on my leg. She is soaked.

"Well, I want to savor this sexy as fuck outfit you have on," I taunt, squeezing her ass and pulling her back up so she can't rub herself on me anymore.

Gripping my cheeks, she stares intently at me. "Preston, I will wear this every day for a week, just fuck me now."

Staring back at her, I slam my lips to hers and fuck her mouth with my tongue. She moans into my mouth. My cock is rock-hard and I'm ready to fuck her, but I want to tease her a little longer. I increase my grip on her ass and gently slide her back and forth on my leg.

"Please, Preston," she begs.

Gripping the edge of her panties, I break our kiss. "I hope you aren't fond of these panties," I say before I tear them off her, the flimsy material disintegrating at the force. Before she can protest, I flip her on to her back, remove my briefs, and push inside her.

Her pussy welcomes my cock, hugging it tight. Pushing my hips, I thrust in and out of her. Sitting up, I lift her leg over my shoulder and continue to slide in and out of her. Her eyes are closed, her mouth open. She moans and groans in the sexiest way as I fuck her hard.

She reaches up, pulls down the cup of her teddy and plays with her breasts. "Cress, that is the sexiest thing I have ever seen."

Her eyes open and we stare at one another as I continue to pump in and out of her. She slides her hands between us and rubs her clit. Her walls tighten around me and together we explode. Our bodies shudder as we give ourselves over to the pleasure.

Lowering her leg. I pull out and stare down at her. She looks gorgeous with her flushed cheeks and chest glowing from her orgasm. Climbing onto the bed, she snuggles into my side, and we drift off to sleep wrapped in each other's arms.

The next day, I head to the hospital to see Dr. Jenkins. She agreed to everything in my proposal. I'm glad I turned down Boston, my life is here with Lexi and Cress. I've finished up another meeting and I'm heading to my car, looking forward to getting home to my girls. The elevator stops and Flynn hops in. "Hey," I say, noticing the bags under his eyes, "you finishing or starting?"

"Just finished. You?"

"Same." My phone rings as we enter the parking garage, I smile when I see it's Momma Cress. I slide to answer and before I say anything she cries, "Preston, we have a problem."

34 CRESS

MOM STOPPED BY AND ASKED TO TAKE LEXI FOR ICE CREAM, WANTING A FEW hours to myself I happily obliged. Taking the opportunity, I change from my pajamas into a black-and-white blouse and my black capris. Heading to the mall, I treat myself to a quiet coffee. My phone pings with a text and I freeze like I always do at the moment when I hear that sound. Creed is still text taunting me but I no longer read them, I delete them, but much to my delight, I see it's from Ave.

> **AVERY:** *Guess what?*
> **CRESS:** *What?*
> **AVERY:** *Bay is getting released next month.*

Rolling my eyes, I shake my head. Baylor Evans is the polar opposite of my best friend, even more so now that she has a criminal record. Ave assures me she's changed, but I personally think, *once a bitch, always a bitch.*

> **CRESS:** *That's great news. Wanna meet for coffee?*
> **AVERY:** *I'd love to, but Flynn and I are busy this afternoon*

I read that as code for 'we are going to fuck like rabbits.'

CRESS: *Fine, but we need to do drinks soon. Feels like it's been forever since I've seen you*
AVERY: *Sounds good...maybe you will finally spill the deets on you and a Channing Tatum look-alike doctor that you seem to be spending a lot of time with*

A laugh escapes at that. I'm not sure why I haven't come out and specifically told her about Preston and me. She's not dumb, or blind, but at the same time she hasn't asked, and we really haven't seen each other much in the last few months. Since Lexi got sick, she's been my main focus and since Ave moved in with Flynn, she's been in the honeymoon phase.

CRESS: *Tell me when and where for drinks, and I will bring ALL the gossip.*
AVERY: *It's a date...Jelember work for you?*
CRESS: *Hahaha, that sounds about right. When did we get so busy that we have to resort to text messages to communicate?*
AVERY: *When we got old*
CRESS: *Hey, I'm not old...you're old*
AVERY: *I'm ending this before you hurt my feelings. Catch up soon.*
AVERY: *Love your 'old' face **stick out tongue emoji***
CRESS: *Love your 'old' face too. See you soon, raccoon*

Clearly Preston is rubbing off on me when I read back that last message. Shaking my head, I finish my coffee and head back home. Stopping at the store, I grab a few things to start marinating the chicken for the barbecue tomorrow. I'm excited and nervous to be meeting Preston's brother and partners. Keeton, Preston's brother is in a throuple with Blair and Faith. I've never met anyone in a throuple, so I'm intrigued to hear and see how it works.

Realizing I left a bag in the car, I head back outside. I'm leaning into the back seat when I'm pulled by my hair from the car and spun around. "You fucking bitch," he snarls.

"Creed—" I don't get to finish that sentence because he slams my head into the side of the car. It hurts like a bitch. I see black-and-white stars and my hearing is now fuzzy, it sounds like I'm underwater. Creed is blurry. I blink rapidly and my sight returns. Creed is red in the face, I can see his lips moving but I still can't hear properly.

He grabs me by the throat and squeezes. Lifting my hands, I try to pry him off me but I'm not as strong as him. Fear bubbles inside of me, without thinking, I lift my leg and knee him in the balls. As soon as I do it, I realize it's a mistake because his face becomes even more enraged. "Ohh, you've done it now, bitch." He grips my hair, the follicles pulling from the force. He drags me up the front path and inside. I try to scream out but my voice is hoarse from him squeezing my neck.

He opens the screen door and throws me inside. Landing on my hands and knees, I flinch at the pain. He grabs me by my shoulders and flips me over. He straddles my waist, grabs my hands and pulls them above my head. He pins them down with one hand and rests the other next to my head. I stare up at him and I freeze, I have never seen Creed like this before.

My breathing is coming in short fast bursts. My heart is rapidly beating, it feels like it will burst through my chest. "Creed, please," I beg.

"I love it when you beg. Beg me to fuck you. Beg me, Babydoll. Beg me for my cock."

"Please, Creed," I cry. "Please don't hurt me."

"I'm not going to hurt you, Babydoll, I'm going to fuck you like you've never been fucked before, and then you are going to come with me and we will live together just like we used too."

"You are delusional. I'm not going anywhere with you."

"It's not like you have a choice in the matter. Now, do you want my cock in your ass? Mouth? Or cunt first?"

Shaking my head side to side, I try to wriggle free but it's no use. He's got me pinned down. He grips my chin tightly and forces me to look up at him. I close my eyes tight, ever so thankful that Lexi isn't here right now.

"Open your eyes, slut. I want to see the look in them when I sink myself inside of you."

Again I shake my head side to side. He slaps me hard across the cheek, my eyes fly open. My cheek stinging from the slap. My eyes well with tears. "Please, Creed." I beg him again. "Please don't do this."

He roughly grabs my breast, squeezing and pressing down on my chest. I gasp when he tears at my blouse and rips at the cup of my bra, then lowers his head and roughly bites me. I scream, pain tearing through my breast. He lifts his head and stares down at me. I've never seen a more sinister look on his face. He slides his hand down my stomach. I close my eyes waiting for him to slip under the waistband of my pants, but it doesn't come. Someone pulls Creed off me.

Opening my eyes, I see Flynn standing in the doorway. Preston is next to me, punching Creed in the face over and over. "Stop," I try to shout but my voice is hoarse. "Stop him!" I yell at Flynn.

Flynn steps to Preston and shouts. "Cress needs you, man." This causes Preston to pause mid-swing. He looks over to me and when our gazes connect, his eyes widen. He punches Creed once more and shuffles over to me. He takes me into his arms, I wrap mine around his waist, and I cry into his embrace.

Flynn has his foot pressing Creed's chest, holding him down. He has his phone to his ear, speaking to the authorities. Everything is muffled as I hold on to Preston and continue to cry.

Soon, my house is full with police officers and EMTs. The paramedic gives me the all clear and Preston agrees to watch over me, therefore saving me a trip to the hospital. Between Ave and Lexi in the last six months, I'm over hospitals.

Everyone has left and finally it's just Preston and me. We are sitting on the sofa when the front door opens, I look up and see Mom and Lexi walk in. "Hey, Munchkin, did you have fun with Nanna?"

"Yes. Not only did I get ice cream but I got to see a movie too."

"Wow, aren't you lucky."

It seems Mom was on her way back here when she saw the altercation with Creed, she kept driving and called Preston. Preston told her to keep Lexi away until she heard from him or me. I'm thankful Mom drove past when she did because who knows what would have happened otherwise.

Focusing on Lexi, I look around the room and smile. I have the three most important people in my life with me and after today, Creed will never be able to hurt or taunt us again. He was arrested for assault and will be behind bars for the foreseeable future. Apparently that agent who stopped by a few weeks back was building a case and this will add to that. Creed is going to be behind bars for a very long time to come. Lexi and I can now live life happy and carefree, with Preston.

35 | PRESTON

...six weeks later

I'M VISITING MY MENTOR, DR. TARA OLE, IN IDAHO. SHE LEFT THE BIG CITY when she retired and now consults at the local hospital here. I'm visiting, as I want to bounce some ideas off her before I present them to Dr. Jenkins. I officially start my new role next month, and we are going to transform our pediatric wing into the best in the country, sorry Boston. My team and I are going to make Western General THE top pediatric hospital in the country; again sorry not sorry, Boston. Dr. Jenkins has already approved stage one, but with Dr. Ole's help, I'm going to propose a stage two, really elevating the hospital.

It's been great seeing her again but I can't wait to get back to Chicago to see Cress and Lexi. I miss them both dearly, that little girl has wormed her way into my heart. Much like her mother has, if things go sour with Cress and me, I'll be devastated not seeing the Pony-obsessed little munchkin.

Today I'm assisting in the ER, as they are short-staffed. It's crazy busy. My next case is a little boy with a fractured arm; it will be an easy one to wrap up my time here. It has been great catching up with Dr. Ole. She has played a major part in my career. Without her, I wouldn't be half the doctor I am today.

Pulling the curtain back, I look up from the chart in my hand. "I'm Dr. Knight, seems our lil' slugger here has a fractured wrist." Clipping the X-ray up on to the light box, I step next to Dad and notice him staring at it too. He turns his head, and gazes at his partner. "It's a clean break, Autumn, he'll be fine," he says, confirming my suspicion that he too is a doctor.

"Your husband is correct," I agree, "Oliver's break is a clean one."

"He's not my dad," Oliver says from the bed.

"My mistake." My eyes dart between the three of them, there's clearly some tension between them, and I can't help but check out the woman before me. She is gorgeous: blue eyes, blonde hair, killer body but she has nothing on my Cress.

"Dr. Griffin Steel," he says, stretching out his hand to me.

"Dr. Preston Knight, visiting from Chicago." He shakes my hand, squeezing tightly, unofficially telling me to back the hell off.

His eyes widen, and then I realize he's heard of me before. Nodding my head, I smile. "Pleasure to meet a fellow colleague."

He ignores me and focuses on the woman again, "Autumn, seems Ollie here has the best pediatric specialist in the midwest on his case."

"How do you know he's the best?" she questions him.

"Preston Knight of Western General is the best in his field. Boston Children's Hospital wanted him to head their pediatric department, but he chose to stay at Western General and head up their new pediatric department instead. It caused quite the stir when he turned down the top job in Boston."

"What can I say, I don't like to conform to what's expected of me."

"So the rumors are true then?"

I shrug my shoulders and wink, seems the rumor about me turning down Boston is making the rounds, that's one of the reasons I came here to see Tara. I needed her to reassure me that I made the right decision. Wanting to change the topic, I look to Oliver. "So, Oliver, from here, we will get you cast up and then you can head home. I don't need to go through the instructions, as I'm sure Dr. Steel here will look after you."

"We don't need Griffin's help," Oliver's mom snaps. "Can you please tell me what I need to do?"

"Of course."

As I explain this to Autumn, I notice Griffin intently watching her. There's some major tension, sexual tension, between the two of them.

As soon as Ollie's cast has set, I drop off the discharge papers and watch them leave. From the outside, they look like a loving family but from the brief time I was with them, I know that's not the case. My phone buzzes in my pocket, removing it, I smile when I see it's from Cress. Sliding it open, I read.

CRESS: *Hey, Doc. When do you get back?*
PRESTON: *Hey, sexy lady. Will be back tomorrow*
CRESS: *Up for dinner and a sleepover? Mom and Lexi are having a sleepover so I want one too*
PRESTON: *Will this be a naked kind of sleepover?*
CRESS: *Is there any other kind?*
CRESS: *Your place or mine?*
PRESTON: *Can we do mine? I have to be at the hospital the day after for an early shift*
CRESS: *I will definitely be doing you and I don't care where we sleep… not that there will be much sleeping at this sleepover*
PRESTON: *Down, girl, I can't be sporting a boner right now, I'm in the middle of the ER*
CRESS: *I know the best medicine for that and I will happily administer it tomorrow **wink wink***
PRESTON: *Dammit, Cress. Your ass is mine when I get home*
CRESS: *Promise?*
PRESTON: *Fuuuuck, woman, I'm going now before I lose my medical license. I'll message you when I get home*
CRESS: *I can pick you up, if you like?*
PRESTON: *You'd do that?*
CRESS: *I'd do you **wink** and yes, I'd love to. Text me your flight details*
PRESTON: *Will do when I get back to the hotel. See you tomorrow, sexy lady*
CRESS: *Later, Doc. Love you **wink emoji***
PRESTON: *'Til then, penguin **kiss emoji***

The flight home is uneventful and we even land early. Walking out, I'm focused on my phone and I'm not watching where I'm walking and bump into someone's back. They spin around and it's Cress. "Cress, Love, I'm so sorry."

"It's fine. I shouldn't have stopped in the middle of the walkway. I was flustered 'cause your flight got in early and I wanted to be at the gate when you landed."

"Aww, did you miss me?"

"Maybe," she nonchalantly says. She stares at me and the hunger in her gaze has my cock twitching in my pants.

Wrapping my arms around her, I pull her to me and whisper into her ear, "Let's get you back to my place, I believe we have a naked sleepover to get to."

"Let's go." She slips her hand between us, squeezes my dick, winks, turns around, and walks away from me. Swinging her hips seductively with each step she takes toward the exit...I can't wait to get home.

36 CRESS

PRESTON AND I HAVE AN AMAZING SLEEPOVER, LIKE WE ALWAYS DO. THAT MAN knows how to bring my body alive, I don't think I've ever orgasmed as intensely as I do with him. Our bodies fit together perfectly, it's like we were destined to meet. He's the other half of me that was missing, when I'm with him, I'm whole and complete. Like that movie line, "He completes me."

Waking up in his arms is my most favorite way to start my day, I wish we could do it every day, but it's too soon to even think about moving in together. We haven't even been a couple for twelve months yet.

The morning flies by and before I know it, I'm off to school to get Lexi. When I pick her up, she's quiet and not her usual bubbly self. "What's wrong, Munchkin?"

"It's the daddy/daughter dance and I don't got a daddy now." My heart breaks at her words.

"I'm sure Preston would take you."

"But he's not my daddy."

"Ohh, Munchkin, come here." I drop down to my knees and I envelop her in my arms. "How about you ask him? I'm sure he'd love to go as your daddy."

"I wish he was my daddy," she sadly says.

"I do too, baby."

The car trip home is quiet today. I play Lexi's words over and over in my head, I too wish Preston was her daddy. When we get home, she heads straight to her bedroom. Making a chocolate milk, I grab some cookies and head down to her room. Knocking on her door, I step inside and find her on the floor playing with her ponies.

"Thought you might like a choccie milk and some cookies."

"Thanks, Mommy," she says.

"And we need to come up with a plan on how you are going to ask Preston to the dance."

"But he's not my daddy."

"Daddy is just a name. You may not call Preston Daddy, but I'm pretty sure he loves you like a daddy does."

"Really?"

"Yep. Now, let's come up with a plan."

Over cookies and milk, Lexi and I devise a plan.

The slamming of a car door outside startles me but at the same time, I smile, knowing what's about to happen. "Lexi, he's here," I shout from my spot on the sofa.

"I'm ready," she yells back.

Preston knocks. "Avon calling," he singsongs as he enters.

"You're a dork," I tell him.

"A dork who you love," he says, as he leans over the back of the sofa and kisses me. "Where's Lex?" he asks, looking around the room for her.

"She's in her room, she has something to ask you."

"Okay." He nods and walks down the hallway.

Leaning over the edge of the sofa, I try to peek down but I can't see or hear anything. The anticipation is killing me.

A few moments later, they both return. Lexi is in the outfit she picked, the princess dress Preston gave her a few months back, and she's holding his hand. The sight is adorable and has my ovaries doing summersaults.

"Mommy, Preston is going to be my daddy."

"That's great, baby."

"And you are going to be his queen."

Scrunching my face up in confusion, I look between the two of them. Lexi nudges Preston and he steps over to me, he drops down to one knee and takes my hand in his. "Cress, you and Lexi both mean the world to me. I already think of her as my daughter, I have from the first time I met her. You stole my heart the night we met and I'm pretty sure, I stole yours too." My eyes well with tears. "Lexi is right, I'm going to be her daddy because I want you to become my wife." From his pocket, he pulls out

Lexi's plastic ruby princess ring. "Cressida Rachel Bayliss, will you marry me?"

Nodding my head, I blubber, "Yes, yes I'll marry you."

Gripping my cheeks in his hands, he presses his lips to mine and kisses me, cementing our engagement. He pulls back and I stare into his green eyes, they are shining brightly right now. "I love you, Preston."

"I love you too, Cress."

"I love my mommy and daddy," Lexi says from beside us.

Looking over to her, I smile. "Did you know, Munchkin?"

She nods her head. "When I asked him to be my daddy, he asked me if I can be his daughter and you his queen."

Looking to Preston, I smile. My heart is so full right now. I have my daughter and I have my prince. Falling for Dr. Knight was the best decision I ever made, right after saying yes to becoming Mrs. Preston Knight.

EPILOGUE

...two years later

"Preston, get me drugs. Get me every fucking drug there is. It hurts so much."

"Cress, Love, I wish I could but you are too far along now," he says, wiping my forehead with a wet cloth.

I've been in labor for forty-two hours now, I'm ready for this baby to be out but mini Preston wants to stay inside. He's stubborn like his father. I don't actually know if it's a boy or not, but he's being an asshole right now...just like his father, who won't get me the good drugs. "What's the point in being married to a doctor if he won't give me the good stuff when I'm in labor?"

"It's nice to know you are only with me for my access to the good drugs."

"Ohh shit!" I scream as another contraction hits. It passes quickly, I'm panting heavily. "Preston," I cry, "I'm sorry I'm a bitch."

"It's fine, Love. You are doing great, we are so close to meeting our little princess."

"Prince," I say, as another contraction hits. "I need to push," I shout.

Dr. Jenkins looks up from between my thighs, and nods. "Yes, Cressida, it's time."

"It's fucking Cress," I growl at her, and I really shouldn't because she's doing me a favor delivering bub number two. The chief doesn't usually deliver babies but I managed to sweet talk her into doing this for Preston and I. The next contraction hits. I push and scream squeezing Preston's hand tightly in mine.

"I see the head. Cress, on the next one, I want you to push hard," she says, her eyes focused between my thighs.

Nodding my head, I close my eyes and push and scream with everything I have. The room goes quiet and then baby Knight lets out a cry. It's the most beautiful sound in the world.

"You did it, Cress," Preston says, kissing me on the lips. "We have a baby—"

"—girl."

"We have a Pepper," I cry.

"Do you want to do the honors, Dad?" Dr. Jenkins asks.

Preston looks to me and I nod. Looking down I watch as he cuts the cord and then Dr. Jenkins hands me our daughter. Taking her into my arms, my eyes well with tears. "Hi, Pepper. I'm your mommy and this is your daddy. Your big sister, Lexi, cannot wait to meet you, and neither can your cousins, Marvin and Marshall."

"And in nine months, she'll have another cousin to play with."

"Ave is pregnant?" I question.

Preston shakes his head. "No, Keet, Blair, and Faith are expecting."

"Oh My God, that's amazing. "Who's the daddy?"

He shrugs. "Both of them, I guess."

"That's amazing. Babies all round."

After I'm stitched back up, I'm wheeled back to my room. Mom and Lexi are waiting, Lexi's face lights up when she sees me. "Where's my sister?" she asks.

"How did you know it was a girl?"

"'Cause I asked Santa for a baby sister last year."

The door opens, and Preston enters, pushing the bassinet with Pepper in it. Lexi races over and stares down at her.

"Why's her head all squished?"

Mom, Preston, and I all laugh. "Lexi, your head was like that when you were born too," Preston says, pulling her into his side as they stare down at Pepper.

"Really?"

"Yep, it's true."

"Can I hold her?"

"Mom needs to feed her first, and then you can."

Preston reaches in, lifts Pepper up, and holds her to his chest. Seeing him with our little girl fills my heart with so much joy. He steps to the bed and hands Pepper to me. "Hey, Munchkin," I whisper, kissing her on the head before I start feeding her. It all comes back to me, as if it was just yesterday that I was doing this with Lexi for the first time.

Preston is standing with Lexi and Mom; he must feel me staring at him. He looks over his shoulder at me. Our eyes connect and that déjà vu moment hits me. I'm transported back to when Lexi was born. Dr. Jenkins came in for rounds and a doctor caught my eye. We had a moment, just like this one. It was intense. It was electric. It was perfect, his gaze penetrated deep into my soul; just like it does when Preston stares at me. And it hits me, Preston was that doctor. "It was you," I say.

"Who was who?" Mom asks.

"It was Preston."

"What was Preston?" Mom asks, as Preston says, "What did I do?"

"When I had Lexi, you were there. You were on rounds with Dr. Jenkins, we had a moment and then you left."

Preston stares at me and I see the moment he remembers too. "Oh My God."

He walks across the room and kisses me on the forehead. After all these years, I finally found my prince, and he happened to be the one I'd been dreaming about all these years. That explains why falling for Dr. Knight was so easy, our love story began before either of us knew it.

THE END!

PLAYLIST

Breakeven – The script
You Found Me – The Fray
Duck Tales – main theme – Geek Music
Let Her Go – Passenger
I Won't Give Up – Jason Mraz
Forever and Always – Parachute
She Will Be Loved – Maroon 5
Not Over You – Gavin DeGraw
Closer – Nine Inch Nails
SexyBack (feat. Timberland) – Justin Timberlake
Pony – Ginuwine
Torn – Natalie Imbruglia
Walking Away – Craig David
My Little Pony theme song – Twilight Sparkle
Bleeding Love – Leona Lewis
I'm Yours – Jason Mraz
Someone Like You – Adele
Girls Like You – Maroon 5
What About Us – P!nk
Heathens – Twenty One Pilots
Let You Down – NF
Letters from the Sky – Civil Twilight
I Will Wait – Mumford & Sons

Touch Me (I Want your body) – Samantha Fox
All of Me – John Legend
How to Save a Life – The Fray
You And Me – Lifehouse
Shake it Off – Taylor Swift
Hands to Myself – Selena Gomez
For the First Time – The Script
Secrets – OneRepublic
Lips of an Angel – Hinder
All The Right Moves – OneRepublic
Cheap Thrills – Sia
You're The One That I Want – Loving Caliber

This playlist can be found on Spotify.

falling for

AGENT COX

When love and
hate collide

A FALLING NOVEL

DL GALLIE

There's a fine line between love and hate.
A love fueled from hate, is the strongest of them all.

BAYLOR
My life hasn't gone as I planned, but it's all my doing.
I'm given a second chance.
But I didn't count on him—Agent Corey Cox.
He's on the straight and narrow, abiding by the rules.
He calms my inner beast and makes me want to be a better person.
When my past reappears, that wildness inside sparks to life again.
Is his love enough to stop me turning my back on everything I've worked so hard for?

COREY
I live my life by the book.
Being an agent is everything to me.
The lines are never blurred.
Until her—Baylor Evans.
She's wild, carefree, and marches to the beat of her own drum.
She brings out a side to me I never knew existed.
But it all implodes, when I'm faced with an impossible decision.
Either way I lose.

To Bec,
This dedication is because you told me to, you're welcome and its appropriate since you loved Baylor from the beginning. You coined #BaylorIsABitch so thank you for that.
...but seriously, thank you for your support and your stylish dress sense. I'll give you a non-hug next time we see each other

And Nicola, Agent Cox is yours

"The course of true love never did run smooth"
  ~ *William Shakespeare*

PROLOGUE

"Time's up, bitch," he snarls at me, "Time to choose who lives...and who dies." While delivering the ultimatum, his tone changes to sinister and downright frightening, especially on those last four words; how I was ever in love with this man—no, monster— is beyond me.

"No," I cry, my eyes flicking between them. The choice before me is impossible. The old me would've easily chosen in a heartbeat, consequences be damned, but the new me? Well, she cares. She has a heart now. She worries about things and people.

No matter what I choose right now, someone will die. Someone I care for will lose their life and there's nothing I can do to stop it.

My gaze darts between the two people who mean the most to me in this world. *How do I choose?* And then it hits me; I know what to do. "Me," I whisper.

"What?" he growls, spittle flying from his lips.

"Me," I quietly whisper. "I choose me," I say, louder this time, my voice clear and firm. The ramifications of my decision yet to sink in.

"No!" they both cry out.

"It's the only way," I reaffirm.

Looking back to *him*, I stare into his evil eyes. "I. Choose. Me," I confidently say, enunciating each word to prove my point. There's not a hint of hesitation in my voice; in reality, it's the complete opposite of how I really feel, but it's the only way to protect them. It's a sacrifice I'm willing to make. My death means they will live.

"Very well then." He raises his pistol and points it directly at me. My heart races as I stare down the barrel of his gun.

With death literally staring me in the eyes, a calmness washes over me as I wait. Closing my eyes, I breathe in deeply for the last time.

I'm ready.

His snicker pierces the silence and that sound grates through me. He clicks the safety and then all hell breaks loose.

Gunfire rings all around me. The sound is deafening as bullets fly around, and then it's silent.

Dead silent.

I'm frozen on the spot, waiting for death to take me. Waiting for the pain of being shot to register, but it doesn't come. Everything around me is moving in slow motion. Everything around me is fuzzy. I'm blinking rapidly to clear my vison but it doesn't clear. My heart rapidly races at the unknown.

In the distance, I vaguely hear voices and shouting but it's all muffled. In the blink of an eye, everything comes roaring back to life in high definition and surround sound.

I can hear the people around me shouting and running. The birds chirping in the trees nearby. The water lapping at the shore end, and then it hits me; I'm still standing.

I'm still alive.

Looking down, that's when I see it. My eyes widen at the scene before me. Tears begin to flow down my cheeks. My vision blurs as more liquid leaks from my eyes. I collapse to my knees and fall to the deck. I stare into lifeless eyes.

Someone is shouting my name but darkness is encroaching and engulfing me. It's pulling me under and I'm powerless to stop it.

My last thought before I drift into the dark abyss is they are dead...and it's all my fault.

1

COREY

STANDING IN THE ADJOINING ROOM, I STARE THROUGH THE TWO-WAY GLASS, flicking the mic switch on. I smirk when I hear her going off at the agent. With his back to me, I'm not sure who it is. I turn it off and shake my head; Baylor Evans has a smart and sassy mouth. From watching her just now, she intrigues me and I'm not sure if that's a good thing or not, especially with what I'm about to propose to her.

She's sitting at the table across from the agent, her clothes are torn, her hair is a mess, and her face is bruised and swollen. From what I can gather, she's been through a lot in the last four days. My eyes are locked on her. This woman has been at the forefront of my mind, ever since the boss handed me the file with her picture in it. I've stared at the photo more than I should have, and I've memorized every inch of her face and body: blonde hair, blue eyes, super fit, a killer rack—hey, I'm a boob man, shoot me. In three words, she's fucking hot, and just the person I need to wrap this case up.

Picking up the file, I go over it one more time, not that I need to because I know it word-for-word and back-to-front. I've been on the Vlahos case for eighteen months now, and this is the first positive lead I've had fall into my lap.

Looking back up, I watch her. She's angry right now, I need her to calm down before I approach her and offer her the deal of her life.

The door opens and in walks Agent Oats. "Oats," I say in greeting, shaking his hand.

"Cox," he replies, and knocks on the glass garnering the attention of his partner, Agent Hall. Yes, their names are Agent Hall & Oates—great, now I'm fucking humming "Maneater" by the famous duo.

Hall stands up and exits the interrogation room to join us. When he opens the door, we hear her. "You fucking dickwads, you can't keep me locked up. I was just kidnapped for fuck's sake. I have fucking rights. You ass—"

He pulls the door shut. "Fuck me," he mumbles, as he leans against the door he just closed.

"Well, she seems fun," I say, as I offer him my hand. He takes my outstretched hand and shakes it. "She's kind of a wild kitten with no filter, hey?"

"More like a foul-mouthed, fucking out of control tiger." The three of us laugh.

"You sure about this plan, Cox?" Oats asks me.

Nodding my head, I turn around and lean against the glass, crossing my legs at the ankle, while resting my palms on the window ledge. "Yep, Baylor Evans has the in that I need."

"But she's a live wire," Hall retorts.

"Exactly, she's perfect," silently I add, *in every-fucking-way,* "and that's why they won't suspect a thing."

"It's your career," he throws back at me. "But first, you need to convince psycho Barbie in there to cooperate with your crazy plan."

Turning around, I stare at her before turning my attention back to him. "Are you doubting my ability, Hall?"

"Fuck yes, I am. That woman is a time bomb waiting to explode, Cox. I hope you know what you're doing." With that, he and Oats walk out, leaving me alone.

Taking a deep breath, I pick up the file, a box, and open the door. I step into the danger zone, also known as the interrogation room.

"About fucking..." she snarls and stops when she sees it's me and not Hall. "Who the fuck are you?"

"Watch your mouth," I warn.

"Fuck you," she spits back at me.

I raise my eyebrows at her and she flips me the bird. Shaking my head, I walk farther into the room. "I'm Agent Corey Cox."

"Where's dumbass?"

"Not here," I say, taking a seat across from her. I slide the box over to her.

"What the fuck is this?"

"What have I said about your language, Ms. Evans?"

She rolls her eyes at me and we silently stare at each other across the table, assessing one another. The longer we stare, the thicker the air becomes in the room. *She really is more stunning in person. Focus, Cox, focus.*

"Well?" she sasses.

"Open it and see."

She eyes me suspiciously. I stare back at her, not giving anything away.

Finally she gives in and lifts the lid, her eyes widen in surprise. "How do you know that Grape Laffy Taffy is my favorite?" she asks, as she grabs a piece of candy and begins to unwrap it.

"It's my job to know everything about those I'll be working with."

She has the piece halfway to her lips, and asks, "What the fuck are you talking about?" She pops the taffy into her mouth and begins to chew... loudly...like a fucking horse.

"As I said before, Ms. Evans, watch the language, please."

"Oh, are you the swearing police now, Agent-whatever-you-said-your-name was?" She pauses, her eyes roam over me, trying to determine why I'm here. My thoughts are confirmed when she asks me, "What's this all about?"

"You and I are going to be working closely to bring down Kye Vlahos and his organization."

Her face drops at the mention of Kye, and it confirms to me she really has no idea he's still alive.

"Kye's dead," she whispers flatly.

"You sure about that?" Opening the file, I grab a surveillance photo taken three days ago and slide it across the metal table to her.

She picks it up and when she looks at it, her eyes bug wide open. "How? What? Why? This is a trick. You're fucking with me."

"No trick, Ms. Evans. And I'm not fucking with you either. Seems lover boy left you out of the loop and kept something pretty significant from you. Kye Vlahos is very much alive and well. His doppelgänger however, well, he's dead."

"What?" she says, her tone shocked at the doppelgänger revelation.

"Do you know who Kye Vlahos really is?"

"Obviously, I don't because I thought he was dead, but from that photo, clearly," she sasses, "he's not."

"Mr. Vlahos is THE king of the drug trade on the East Coast and head of the Vlahos dynasty. He faked his death to throw us, and his family off his trail, but we have eyes and ears everywhere, and well, you can guess the rest. We knew he was still alive, we just didn't know why or how or where he was hiding out. That was until he got cocky. He reappeared in person a few days ago. He's looking for someone." I pause for effect. "That someone...is you!" Her mouth drops open at this revelation, "He's been following you for weeks now, Ms. Evans. Well, his lackey, Creed Dawson, has been following you. Seems like Kye misses you."

"He's dead," she whispers, shaking her head. "I saw them kill him. I saw it with my own fucking eyes," she says, still staring at the photos of her not-so-dead ex-lover. She lifts her head to look at me. "Are you fucking with me?"

"Mouth. As I've already said, I'm not messing with you. You saw what they wanted you to see. And he wanted you, us, and everyone else to think he was dead."

She throws the photo on the table and starts shaking her head from side to side. "That fucking, dickwad, psycho asshole," she snaps, standing up, and slamming her palms on the table in anger. "I'm going to kill that fucker myself when I find him—"

"That's not the plan I have in mind," I tell her.

"Fuck you and fuck your plan. No one tells me what to do."

"Watch your mouth."

"Go fuck yourself, Cox."

"Do you want your sister to get hurt again?" I know it's a low blow using her sister like that, but I need Baylor if I'm going to crack this case.

Her heads snaps up toward me and if I thought she was angry before, she's furious now. "Leave my sister out of this," she growls between clenched teeth. "She has nothing to do with this."

"She became a part of this as soon as you did. You do realize she ended up in hospital because of *you*? They thought she was you. You don't want that to happen again, do you? Kye clearly wants you back and you are going to willingly go back to him because you are going to help me bring him and his organization down."

"And why would I do that?"

"Because it will shave time off your sentence and it will bring down the biggest drug racket since Pablo Escobar in the nineties."

"Why me?"

"Because you're our—well my—only hope." I tell her honestly.

She sits back down and picks up the surveillance photo. She stares at it and then quietly asks, "Can you promise me my sister will be safe?" She lifts her gaze to mine. Her face is etched with worry, but I think it's for her sister and not for herself. This woman is hard to read, which is why she's perfect for this undercover assignment. "I won't do this if she's at risk. I can't and won't let her get hurt again."

"I will do everything in my power to protect her but I can only do that if you agree to help me."

She stares at me and I have no fucking clue if she's going to help me or not. She grabs another candy and slowly opens it. She pops it into her mouth and chews. The silence, well apart from her chewing, is deafening.

Finally, she breaks the silence, shocking me when she agrees. "I'll do it, but if even a hair on my sister's head is touched or out of place, I will fucking chop your balls off and feed them to you, drenched in hot sauce."

"My, my, you're a feisty little kitten."

"Fuck you, Buster," she snarls, the tone of her voice and her sass turning me on, but at the same time, I'm convinced that given the chance, she absolutely would chop my balls off in a heartbeat.

"Meow," I sass before turning around and walking out of the room. Slamming the door behind me, I lean against the wood and let out a deep breath. A grin appears on my face and I shake my head, this case sure just got interesting.

2

BAYLOR

STARING AT THE DOOR AGENT COX JUST WALKED OUT OF, I SHAKE MY HEAD IN disbelief. My mind is racing. The last week has been crazy, like something from a movie. First, I pretended to be my sister when shit hit the fan. Then, I was kidnapped, and now I'm sitting in a police interrogation room being offered a chance to redeem myself by the hottest fucking agent, and rather than deciding what to do, I'm stuffing my face with Laffy Taffy and thinking inappropriate thoughts about Agent Cox and his chiseled jaw. His muscular arms. Gorgeous hazel eyes. Kissable lips. Tight perfect ass. I shake my head and scoff, I'm fucked when it comes to Agent Corey Cox but if I'm going to turn my life around, I need him.

Popping another candy into my mouth, I lean back in the uncomfortable metal chair, and mull over everything he offered. Instead of coming to a decision, I become angry when I think about how he spoke to me. To be honest, I'm fucking fuming right now. How dare he threaten me? Threaten the safety of Ave, fucking asshole.

Staring at the two-way mirror, I wonder if he's watching me. In case he is, I flip the bird toward the glass and stick my tongue out.

Standing up, I start pacing the room. My breathing becomes labored and my heart is racing, but it's not because of the decision before me, it's because of *him*, Agent Corey-fucking-Cox, and that I was beaten up recently.

Flopping back into the chair, I sigh as a slight throbbing begins between my thighs. I'm currently turned on by this sexy-as-fuck agent, what's up with that? How can I find him attractive when he holds my life in the palm of his hand? All I can think about is him bending me over this metal table and fucking the life out of me. *Seriously, Bay, focus.*

With a frustrated sigh, I lower my head to the table and wince at the contact. My face is a mess right now. I'm pretty sure I also have a cracked rib and I stink. The fucking assholes who took me messed with the wrong person, if they weren't already dead, I'd kill them myself.

The door opens again and my head lifts up to see a paramedic standing there. "Agent Cox sent me in to reassess you."

"I was assessed at the scene," I tell the lady.

"Won't hurt to get a second opinion," she says, walking into the room and placing her bag on the table.

"Fine," I huff, crossing my arms over my chest and wincing when my wrists rub against my shirt and I'm taken back to that room.

The rope cutting into my wrists.

The tight grip around my neck.

The sting in my cheek when they hit me.

She touches my shoulder and I flinch. "You don't seem fine," she sasses with a grin, reminding me of, well me.

"Fine," I concede, wiping at the corner of my eye, "I'm not fine. I hurt all over and I stink."

She steps over to me and stares at my face. "Looks like you went a few rounds with Mike Tyson."

"I feel like I went a few rounds with him AND Muhammad Ali."

"And you're still standing to tell the tale," she says. Taking my chin in her hand, she turns my head side to side, looking at my face. She scrunches up her nose. "You in any pain?"

"A little, but I'm a tough gal." She eyes me in that 'don't bullshit me' kind of way. "Fine, I'm exhausted and ready to collapse."

"Well, let's get you fixed up. You can chat with Agent Cox and then you can go on your merry way."

"Yeah, that's not gonna happen anytime soon."

She nods but doesn't say anything. She pulls out some medical supplies and gets to cleaning me up. Clearly, the first paramedic did a crappy job because the pile of used swabs is huge.

"I'll get you something to drink, and let Agent Cox know you are all cleaned up."

"Thanks," I tell her, and watch as she packs everything up and exits the room. Once again leaving me alone again with my dirty thoughts of Agent Cox.

The sound of the door opening startles me, seems I drifted off to sleep. The original officer enters again, and I deflate when I realize it's him. I'd much rather it had been Agent Cox, but I'm sure I will be seeing him again soon. Movement behind him catches my eye and I smile when I see it's Ave.

"Avie," I cry, pushing the chair back and standing up.

"BayBay," she blubbers, her eyes roaming over me.

Racing over to her, I wrap my arms around her and she returns the gesture. She squeezes me tightly, and it hurts like a bitch, but emotion overcomes me and together, we hug and cry. "I was so worried," she sniffles. "I've been going out of my mind with worry the last four days." Pulling back, she gently grips my cheeks in her palms. "Are you okay?"

"Yeah, I'm fine," I whisper, my voice is anything but and it totally gives me away.

Ave stares at me. "Wanna try again?"

"You know me too well."

Her face deflates. "I used to know you too well. Now, not so much," she says, pulling me over to the chairs. She sits down but I don't. She stares up at me, her face etched with fear and anger. "You need to start talking, Bay!"

"Always the responsible one," I grumble, getting pissed she's playing mother hen right now. Once again, perfect Avery to the rescue.

"Bay," she pleads. "What happened?"

"Long story." I nonchalantly reply.

"Bay," she warns. The tone in her voice affects me in a way I haven't felt since we were little.

"Fine, I'll tell you, but first, I need you to listen to everything I have to say."

Her face pales and I hate I'm putting her through this. "I'm not going to like this, am I?" she asks.

Shaking my head, I confirm, "Probably not..." I take a deep breath, wincing at the tightness in my ribs. "...but, Avery, I need to do this. I need to make amends for my actions. I need to do this for Kye."

"Who is Kye, Bay?"

My eyes well up again, they're a mixture of angry, sad, and confused tears. "I thought he was 'the one' and because of my actions, I thought he died. It should have been me, but he protected me. Like I told you at the hospital, I tried to walk away after that, but I was in too deep. Way too deep." I bite my lip and stare at her. "But it was all a farce, he tricked me and lied. Avie, this is my chance to put things right. This is my chance to make up for his death, well, for the death of, I don't even know his name." As I say this, I start to doubt if he was 'the one' and I have so many questions: who was I with? Kye or his doppelgänger? Why did he do this to me? How could I fall for his lies? "For once, I want to do the right thing."

"I'm so proud of you, BayBay." Her words shock me. "And that's the honest truth. Last week, I was broken up and hurt over your actions, and now, I could not be prouder of you." She squeezes my hand. "This the Bay I know and love. You are taking charge of your life. You are owning your mistakes and you are trying to put things right." I see nothing but happiness and pride in her face and it confirms I'm making the right decision. "Okay, now, tell me the plan that I'm not going to like."

Taking a seat next to her, I stare at my sister. "Well, when the agents found me, River and Smallie were being dickheads, as usual. They were waiting for orders from Kye—"

"You said Kye was dead."

"Spoiler alert, he's not. Cox just informed me he's alive and well. Apparently, the person I saw die wasn't him."

"This is like something from a movie."

"Tell me about it. Anyway, when you were attacked, they were coming to get me to take me to him, but when that went to shit, the plan changed. Once they got me, it went to shit again because I was rescued before the supposedly dead Kye turned up. In the process, River and Smallie were killed, which are all good things because for one, they were fuckers, and two, it led me to here and the redeeming of me."

"Okay, so what's the part I'm not going to like?"

"Cox—"

"Who's Cox?" she asks.

"Some agent," *a sexy as hell agent* "who needs my help to bring down Kye and his drug ring."

"Bay," she pleads, "I don't like this."

"Can't say I'm a fan either, but I need to do this, Avie. This is my chance to make amends for my actions and redeem myself. Also, my time served will be reduced, and I ain't gonna let that asshole get away with what he did to me. He needs to pay for that."

"Can't you just do jail like a normal person?"

"Nope, not my style," I nonchalantly say with a shrug.

"Why any jail time at all, if you're helping them?"

"The great gnome arrest from when I was twenty."

"Fucking gnomes," she scoffs and I laugh.

"Fucking gnomes," I agree. "Anyway, helping will reduce my time to twelve months rather than two years."

"Isn't there another way?"

Shaking my head, I reply, "No, Ave, there isn't."

"Is it wrong that right now I want Bitchy Baylor to appear, and for you to tell everyone to go fuck themselves or to fuck off?"

"Ohh, she did," Agent Cox says as he reenters the room. "Multiple times."

3

COREY

BOTH OF THEM TURN TO FACE ME.

"Fuck, you again," Baylor says, while at the same time her sister asks, "Who the hell are you?"

"Wow, for twin sisters you're different, yet the same," I say, walking over to Avery, I stretch out my hand, "Agent Corey Cox, it's a pleasure to meet you, Ms. Evans."

She shakes my hand but eyes me suspiciously.

"So you're the one with this plan for my sister." She air quotes plan and stares intently at me, her glare isn't as intimidating as her sister's, but it's still frightening. "What will you do to guarantee her safety?"

"I can't one-hundred-percent—"

"Then no, my sister will not be doing this."

"Ave," Baylor intrudes, "I have to do this. It's either this or jail. I really don't have a choice."

"Why?" her sister pleads.

"Because I need answers. I need to know why Kye did what he did, but more importantly, I want to bring the asshole down. No one fucks me over like that."

A laugh escapes my lips, causing Baylor to turn her head toward me, scowling, and raising her eyebrows defiantly. "What the fuck is so funny, asshole?"

"Watch your mouth, Baylor," she huffs and crosses her arms and winces a little but my eyes are locked on her pushed-up tits. She clears her throat and I lift my gaze to hers. "You constantly surprise me and that's exactly why you are the perfect person for this assignment. Even if you are a pain in my ass."

"Am not," she sasses back.

Shaking my head, I take a seat across them and look toward her sister. "Avery, I will do everything I can to ensure Baylor gets through this safely."

"But—" she protests, but Baylor interrupts her.

"Avie, I'll be fine," Baylor confidently says, reaching out to squeeze her sister's hand, "I can hold my ground with the best of them, besides I'm Bitchy Baylor, I've got this."

"No, you're my BayBay and I worry. I know you're strong but you're my sister, my twinsie. I don't want to lose you. I know you are a tough b-i-t-c-h, but—"

"Did you just spell bitch?" Baylor questions her sister.

Avery nonchalantly shrugs. "Yeah, and?"

"You are something else, Avie. Like seriously, how are we twins? We are—"

"Baylor, focus," Avery snaps. "Please don't do this. Choose time in jail. It's safer. I'll hire you a great lawyer, I'll do everything I can to help you. I just can't lose you, Bay."

"Avie, I choose Cox," she looks to me, and her words affect me in a way they shouldn't, "and his plan. I want do this." She looks me dead in the eye, "I'm one-hundred-percent in."

"Are you sure about this, Bay?" her sister questions again, clearly uneasy with her sister's decision. She's worried about her sister's safety and I get it, but I need Baylor to do this.

"Yeah, I'm sure." She looks back at her sister and smiles, but it's forced. Underneath her tough girl front, she's scared and she should be, this will not be a walk in the park. If I'm honest, there's a huge chance this will go tits up and Baylor's life could be in jeopardy, but it's a risk that needs to be taken, and I will do my darnedest to keep her safe and get my man. "I'll be fine, Avie. Promise." They hug each other and the moment between them reminds me of my brother, Hunter, and me, well before his death that is.

Avery's eyes widen and she pulls away from Baylor, "Ohh, candy," she says, reaching over to grab one from the box I left for Baylor, but before she can grab one, Baylor slaps her hand away.

"Mine," she growls at her sister, but what surprises me is she's staring at me as she says this and not at her sister.

"Wow, living up to your name of Bitchy Baylor right now." She shakes her head. "I forgot how possessive you get of your grape Laffy Taffy."

"See, you do know me...and you just swore," Bay sasses at her sister. Avery sticks her tongue out in that affectionate, sisterly way. "And yes, you may have one. Only cause you said bitchy." She emphasizes the word one. Avery leans over and grabs two candies, garnering a growl from the Laffy Taffy warden.

Baylor grabs one herself and pops the treat into her mouth, "So what's the plan, Stan?"

"Don't ever call me that again," I snap.

Baylor leans into her sister. "This one has a stick up his ass," she not-so-quietly whispers.

"I heard that."

"You were meant to. You really need to take a chill pill or get laid... maybe even both."

"Baylor," her sister warns, "Be nice. You just agreed to help Agent Cox."

"He needs me more than I need him," she snaps at her sister.

"Baylor, if you like, I can call Hall and Oats," Avery giggles at this, "and have you transferred over to the holding cell. My offer will be off the table and you can serve out your full sentence. It's no skin off my nose." I really hope she doesn't call my bluff because she really is my last hope. "The decision is yours, but believe me, my offer is better than what you are currently facing." I flick open the file and pretend to read but I know this file front to back. "You are facing charges for felony distribution, possession, and I'm sure I can find a few traffic infringements to add to the list too."

"Get fucked, asshole."

"Watch it. The way I see it, Baylor, you help me, or get used to the color orange for the next few years. What will it be?"

"I like you," Avery says, staring directly at me. She turns her attention back to her sister. "Baylor, I you need to listen to him. Tame your inner beast for once in your life."

"Harsh much?" Baylor snaps at her sister.

I hold back a laugh; I like this one too. For twins, Baylor and Avery Evans are total opposites but there are also many similarities, including their looks. If you didn't know better, it would be easy to mistake one for the other. I can see why River and Smallie thought Avery was Baylor.

"Baylor, seriously," Avery lashes out at her sister, no longer is she calm, cool, and collected. Her fears over her sister are surfacing and she's laying it all out in the table for Baylor. "Pull your head out of your ass. For once in your life, play nice and listen. You are literally being handed the best lifeline anyone could ask for, and you're going to piss it all away if you keep this up. Just stop being Bitchy Baylor and be Benevolent Baylor. Please, Bay," she begs, "do the right thing, if not, you will end up in prison for a long time, or worse...dead."

Baylor stares in disbelief at her sister, I don't think Avery has ever spoken to her like this before. Baylor is taken aback by the forceful nature of her sister just now, but I'm confident that Baylor can do this. Sure, she plays tough, but from my observations, underneath her bitchy exterior is a person with a heart who wants to do the right thing. She puts on a front, I know because her actions and personality remind me so much of Hunter. He, too, was in a similar predicament, but unfortunately for him, he didn't have someone watching his back and he lost his life. He's the reason I became an agent. He's the reason I want to help Baylor, because the similarities of their situation mirror one another, and I will not lose someone in that manner again.

Her shoulders lower and she reaches over to take her sister's hand again. "Ave, I'm going to do this. I already agreed. I know I need to do it. I don't have any other choice, plus as I said before, I'll get answers. But most of all, I need, no, I want to redeem myself." *BINGO, I knew there was a soft side to this woman*, I think to myself, but she shocks me when she quietly adds, "I don't like the person I've become, Avie. I want to be more like you. I want people to want to be around me. I want someone to love me like Flynn loves you. I want a friend who will drop anything to be there for me like Cress does for you. I want to start living life rather than just coasting through."

"Ohh, Bay," Avery cries. "I'm so proud of you right now."

The moment between the sisters is heartwarming but time is of the essence right now. "Sorry to break up this Hallmark moment, ladies, but we need to get this in motion. Baylor needs to get out of here so we can bring this all crashing down."

Baylor looks to me and confidently says, "Let's do this."

4 BAYLOR

AVE LEFT AND I SPENT THE NEXT FEW HOURS FORMULATING THE PLAN WITH Agent Cox and his superior. There was so much paperwork. I lost count of how many times I was threatened if I took off or betrayed him. Like I could go anywhere, he took my passport and I have no clue how to go underground as they say.

He's so anal with everything—the complete opposite of me—ensuring all the I's are dotted and the T's are crossed. I've never met someone as straitlaced as him… and Anal Avery is my sister. He sees everything as black and white, there's no gray or in between. And rules, fuck me side-ways. Him and his rules are going to drive me fucking nuts. If he keeps pushing me, I'll show him my claws like the kitten he keeps referring to me as. Little does he know, I'm not a kitten, I'm a fucking lion. I'm the queen of the jungle and I'm going to bring him, Kye, and this case, to their knees.

Thankfully I can still live at the apartment with Ave, but I will be suggesting she stay with Flynn more often than not. I don't want her to get hurt again. I keep playing the image of stepping out of the elevator and seeing River and Smallie standing above her limp, lifeless body and the events that unfolded after…

…I've had this feeling of being watched the last few days, but it's clearly my mind playing tricks on me because no one is there. Hell, I swore I saw Kye the

*other day when I was doing a drop-off for Creed. Stepping into the elevator, I press
the button for my floor; this is the slowest elevator in the history of elevators. The
doors open and when I step out, I see River and Smallie and wonder what they're
doing here. Then, I see Ave on the ground and a sinking feeling develops in the pit
of my stomach. Smallie lifts his leg back and kicks Ave like she's a football. My
eyes widen and I'm frozen, but then, instinct kicks in and I shake my head and
race out of the elevator.*

"Avie!" I scream, and this causes their heads to snap up.

*They look at me stunned, and then, one of them growls, "Fuck." Smallie kicks
her again and from the force, her head connects with the doorframe and I watch as
she loses consciousness.*

"What the fuck, guys?"

"We thought she was you," River says, looking agitated and guilty.

"Why are you here?"

"The boss wants what's his."

"And what's that?"

*But before he can answer, our nosey next-door neighbor exits his apartment.
"What's going on?" he asks, looking between the three of us, he hasn't noticed Ave
yet. Needing to cause a distraction and get the guys out of here, I shout, "Call
911," and race over to Ave.*

*"Fucking bitch," one of them yells, as they make a beeline for the emergency
stairwell.*

"Ohh, Baylor," I cry, keeping up the ruse that it's me who has been assaulted.

*"Emergency services are on their way," the neighbor says, but I stare at Ave
and hope that she'll be okay as I quietly whisper, "Shit, shit, shit. This is all my
fault."*

"Avery," the neighbor says, pulling me out of my thoughts.

"Yes," I answer, reaffirming that I'm Avery.

"Can I get you anything?"

*Shaking my head, I stare down at Ave and take her hand in mind. "Please be
okay," I whisper.*

*The elevator doors open and the paramedics walk over to us. They shuffle me
out of the way and get to work on Ave/me. She's loaded onto the stretcher and they
hand me her bag. I follow after them and climb in with her. We pull up at Western
General, where she's whisked away and I'm escorted to the waiting area in the ER.*

*Taking a seat, I stare at the two bags on my lap. My purple Prada and Ave's
simple black tote; even our bags are different. Her phone rings but I don't answer,
I just stare at the purses on my lap. Her phone pings that a voicemail has been left.
Without thinking, I reach in and grab her phone. I see she has a missed call from
Flynn.*

"Ms. Evans?" a nurse asks.

Lifting my head, I look up at her. "Yes,"

"Your sister is being taken to X-ray. We will know more soon."

Nodding my head, I watch her walk away. That should be me in there. Her phone pings again, so I look down at the screen and it's a text from Cressida. Ignoring that, I click on Flynn's name, he needs to be here for Ave. He picks up immediately, "Ave, babe—"

He thinks I'm her and before I can stop myself, I cry, "Flynn...it's Bay."

"What's wrong? Where are you?" His voice is etched with worry and jealousy courses though me. No one would worry or care for me like that.

"I'm at Western General," I tell him.

"I'm on my way."

"Hurry."

Hanging up from Flynn, I go back to staring the bags on my lap. Movement in the corner of my eye causes me to lift my head, and I see the nurse from before walking over to me with two officers. "Ms. Evans, I'm Officer Cooper and this here is my partner, Officer Devon."

I nod my head, "Hi," I mumble, gripping the strap of my bag tighter.

"Can you tell us what happened tonight?"

"It's all jumbled but I got home and two guys were standing over her. They were shocked to see me."

"Do you think they were after you and not your sister?" The officer's question shocks me but at the same time, I was also expecting it. Everyone knows Avery Evans is a saint and I'm not, so it's unsurprising they would ask that. I know this is the time to admit that it's Ave in there, but the lies continue to fall from my mouth.

"I...I don't know," I lie, because they were one-hundred-percent after me. Avery is innocent in all of this. Avery is always innocent and it's always me in trouble. I will myself to tell the truth. To say, "There's been a mistake, I'm Baylor, it's Avery in there. They were after me. I'm the bitch here." But before I can confess, Flynn enters the ER. My heart stops because I know I'm about to be caught. He's her boyfriend, he will know I'm not Ave but I don't correct them.

Taking a deep breath, I close my eyes, but when I open them, my gaze lands on him; I just can't do it. I live up to my 'Bitchy Baylor' name and continue the ruse that I'm Avery Evans. "Flynn," I cry, wrapping my arms around his waist and snuggling into him. I breakdown and weep into his chest. He wraps his arms around me, hugging me tight. I feel safe in his arms. It's nice to be held and wanted and loved, even if the person doing all of that thinks I'm someone else.

I know what I'm doing is wrong, but I can't stop myself...and I don't care a bit it's all a farce.

Tears fall down my cheeks. I don't know if I'm crying because I'll never have a love like this, or if I'm crying because my sister, my number one cheerleader, is in there because of me and my actions.

His embrace tightens and he soothingly whispers, 'Shhhh' over and over, reminding me so much of Ave.

Guilt sets in but when Flynn says, "Avery here is my girlfriend." It snaps my attention back to the present. This is when I need to come clean, but I like being someone's girlfriend again. I haven't had that since Kye and even if just for tonight, I can be happy and loved, then I'm going to take it.

The officers look at me, waiting for confirmation that Flynn is my boyfriend, so I nod in agreement. Flynn is Avery's boyfriend so that's not a lie. The only lie is I'm Baylor and not Avery.

The officer addresses Flynn, "Baylor was attacked by two unknown assailants, at the apartment she shares with her sister earlier this evening. Avery, here, inter-rupted them and probably saved her sister."

"I was so scared, baby," I say, snuggling into Flynn's side. Surprising myself how easy it is right now to pretend to be Ave.

Flynn places a kiss on my head. "Babe, I'm so glad you weren't home when it happened. Do you know who they were?"

I shake my head, and another lie slips through my lips. "No, I've never seen them before."

"Are they the guys from the other day?" he asks me. I have no idea what he's going on about. He eyes me suspiciously and then adds, "You mentioned two guys the other night?

"I...I don't know. Everything's all so fuzzy." Pulling away from him, I sit down and cover my face with my hands. This is getting out of control, I need to confess but when Flynn says, "What shit has your sister gotten into?" my blood boils. Of course he thinks this is all my fault. I look at him and snarl, "Who says it's her fault?"

"I didn't say that, I—" Before he can defend himself, a doctor walks over to us, Flynn stands up to greet him. I sit and watch them, after giving permission for Dr. Clay to speak freely, he gives us an update on me slash Ave.

"Avery, Baylor has a concussion and a laceration to her left cheek that needed five stitches, but luckily, no broken facial bones. She has three cracked ribs and a nasty bump on the back of her head. Her face and torso are bruised, likely from being kicked. She was also shocked with a Taser. There's two red barb welts on the side of her abdomen. All things considered, she's in okay shape." Dr. Clay adds, "She's still unconscious and we will continue to monitor her until she wakes up."

Rapidly blinking I process his words, but everything is all jumbled. Hearing the extent of her injuries concerns me. "Will...will she be okay?"

"Until she regains consciousness, we won't know about her mental state but physically, yes, she'll recover from the injuries sustained."

"Can I see her?"

Dr. Clay nods his head. "Of course. Come with me. Flynn, technically, you cannot see her."

"No, I understand," he says before turning to me. "You go see your sister and I'll see about getting her transferred to a room upstairs."

Wrapping my arms around him, I kiss him. I know I shouldn't, but I close my eyes and press my lips to his. He's stiff, it's like he knows I'm not her but he's too nice to say anything.

Pulling away, I follow Dr. Clay, leaving Flynn behind.

Taking a seat beside Ave, I stare down at her. My eyes well with tears. Taking her hand in mine, I squeeze. "Please wake up. I'm so sorry, twinsie. Please wake up for me."

Seeing her lying there changed something inside of me. Yes, it still took me some time to come clean, well, for Cressida to out me, but I feel remorseful for what I had caused, and after chatting with Ave once she woke up, I knew it was time to make a few changes in my life. I want to be someone she's proud of again. I wanted to be her BayBay.

Another deciding factor in turning my life around was when River and Smallie took me from the hospital. After being tortured for a few days, I was more than determined to change; this wasn't the life I wanted anymore and I definitely don't want to be tortured again. I never expected my chance to reform come in the form of a straitlaced sexy agent with an offer right out of the movies, but here we are. I'm about to go undercover to help him bring down a major drug ring that is run by my presumably dead boyfriend. *Tarantino couldn't write this shit*, I think to myself, as I walk toward the warehouse.

My second chance starts now, and I'm not going to let them down. With my hand on the doorknob, I push it open and enter.

It's go time.

It's showtime!

5
BAYLOR

STEPPING INSIDE THE WAREHOUSE, I THOUGHT I WAS PREPARED TO SEE HIM. I'D seen the surveillance photo of Kye, but there was still a part of me that thought Cox was fucking with me. But he wasn't because standing before me, alive and breathing, is Kye Vlahos.

My breath hitches. "You...you're...you're dead," I stammer, blinking rapidly. My eyes lock on the alive and breathing Kye Vlahos. Cox told me I needed to act surprised when I saw Kye for the first time, but I guarantee you, I'm not acting right now.

"Surprise, Sugar. Daddy's home," he says, stretching out his arms, smiling at me.

"H...how? W...what? How?" I stutter.

"I think we need to talk, Sugar," he says, walking over to me. My rapidly blinking eyes are locked on him. He cups my cheek with his palm, and my breath hitches again when his hand connects with my skin. Lifting my hand, I cover his with mine, leaning into it. Squeezing. Breathing him in.

"You're really here?" I whisper.

"In the flesh, Sugar." His voice is deeper than I remember but he looks exactly the same, except his hair is a little longer. "What did they do to you?" he whispers, gently running his thumb across my bruised cheekbone.

"Who?"

"Smallie and River."

"It doesn't matter what they did. How are you alive?"

"Yes, it fucking matters," he snarls. "No one touches what's mine." The vehemence in his voice is frightening. I don't remember him ever speaking like this before. "If they weren't already dead, I'd kill them myself."

Staring at him, I process his words and actions. He's being so nice to me. It's as if he does love me, but if he did, why did he let me think he was dead? Looking directly into his eyes, I glare at him. "If I meant so much to you," I snap, "you wouldn't have let me think you were dead these last few months." I pull his hand off my face and throw it to the side. I step back and spin around, shaking my head.

Turning back to face him, my eyes well with tears when the emotion I felt at losing him hits me with the force of a Category 5 hurricane, "Why, Kye? Why?" I cry, "Why did you make me think you were dead? I loved you. I thought you loved me too."

"It's complicated," he nonchalantly replies, slipping his hands into his jean pockets, rocking on his feet, as if he doesn't have a care in the world. As if he didn't just reappear from the dead.

"Don't give me that shit!" I yell, anger building at how calm and cool he's acting right now. "How dare you treat me like that!"

"Sugar," he interrupts.

"Don't fucking Sugar me. I want answers, Kye, and I want them now."

"Calm your tits, woman. I'm trying to explain but you're going all psycho bitch on me right now."

"Did you just, A. Tell me to calm my fucking tits, and B. Call me psycho fucking bitch? YOU," I point at him, "are the fucking asshole, dickwad cunt. You made me think you were dead." My eyes well up with tears. "I cried for you. My heart broke for you and all along, you were fucking alive."

"I know. I'm sorry I did that but if you let me explain..."

"You died, Kye. I saw it," I cry, tears are pouring down my face now. I thought I was going to be okay with his deceit, but seeing him alive and breathing, it cuts me that he didn't confide in me. "Why?"

"Sugar," he says, cupping my cheeks in his palms, "I had to get the feds off my ass and take care of a few family matters. I didn't want you to get caught up in this until it was safe."

"Why do they care about us? We are nothing. Nobodies."

"Baylor, Sugar. I'm Kye-fucking-Vlahos, head of the Vlahos family.

Since the recent demise of my father, mother, sister, and uncles, the family empire is mine." He pauses. "Mine."

My eyes widen, seems Cox left out a major detail, but then it hits me, he didn't know this. "What?"

"It was all planned, Sugar. I took out Father and his brothers, and no one suspected a fucking thing. Mother and sister were collateral, their deaths earlier today were unfortunate, but now, now I'm back where I belong."

"And where's that? Hell?"

He laughs at me, "No, in the seat at the head of the Vlahos family, where I rightfully belong. And Bay, Sugar, I want you by my side every step of the way from now on. What do you say, Sugar? Will you reign as my queen?"

6
COREY

Watching Baylor walk out of the room just now was harder than I anticipated. I've sent many people undercover, but this woman, she's affected me in a way like never before.

A knock at the door garners my attention, and I look up to see Hall standing in the doorway. "Saw Baylor leave, wanted to check that your balls are still attached."

"My balls are safe, thanks for your concern."

"Why the long face then?"

"I'm concerned," I tell him, rapping my fingers repeatedly on the file before me.

"Concerned about what?" he asks, walking into the room and taking the seat Baylor just vacated.

"This case."

"Having second thoughts about using such a wild card?"

"I'm not concerned about sending her in, I'm worried about what could happen to her. Kye Vlahos and his associates are crazy motherfuckers. I can normally see an endgame, but not this time."

"Lay it all out for me then, maybe you need an outsider's view."

"Okay, Kye fakes his death, and while he's 'dead', his family members all die in non-suspicious ways, which makes them suspicious. Then he reappears from the dead and takes the seat at the head of the family. What is he up to? A source tells me he's been following Baylor and then two of his men take her and rough her up. Why did they do that? There are too many crazy pieces, and I can't make them all fit together."

"Can't believe I'm saying this but by sending Baylor in, you're on the right track. Crazy plus crazy equals answers." We both laugh. "Look, give her time, she's been gone for ten fucking minutes."

"Yeah, I guess so."

"I still think she's a wild card and you are a crazy fucker for using her, but with the elements you just laid out, seems like she's exactly what you need to crack this case wide open... as long as she sticks to the plan and the rules." He stands up and slaps the folder before me. "Go home, get some sleep. Tomorrow's a new day." With that, he walks out, leaving me alone.

Leaning back in my chair, I link my fingers behind my head, and think back to earlier this evening when I laid out the rules to Baylor...

..."*Are you listening, Ms. Evans?*"

"*No, I'm just sitting here staring at your lips moving, thinking about cocktails and eating nachos while being on a beach in Mexico. Of course, I'm listening.*"

"*Well, what did I just say?*"

"*Ummm...*"

"*Exactly my point. You need to pay attention. Your life is on the line here, do you want to end up dead?*"

"*No one would care if I did die.*"

"*Your sister would.*"

"*Leave Ave out of this,*" she snarls, the glint in her eye darkening at the mention of her sister.

"*Well, focus, and I won't bring her up again but, Ms. Evans, this is serious. If it goes wrong, I can't guarantee your safety...and I really don't want to have to tell your sister you didn't make it. For a small thing, she's feisty.*"

"*She gets that from me.*"

"*No shit,*" I say, "*Now, can we get back to this?*"

"*Fine,*" she huffs, crossing her arms across her chest. She winces slightly. "*Can you start again, please?*"

"*Fine,*" I throw her words back at her. "*Once you leave here, you'll be on your own in the field, but we will be listening in via this,*" I lift up a phone, "*hidden in the case is a microphone that will transmit to us twenty-four seven. Once a week, I'll stop by the apartment at an agreed time, and we can discuss the plan forward. I'll be posing as a contractor you and Avery are using for upgrades on the apartment.*"

"*Like you've done a day of fucking hard labor in your life.*"

"You know nothing about me, Kitten." She growls but I ignore her. "As I was saying, we will meet up once a week, unless you make contact to meet earlier. You can reach me using this," I hand her a burner phone, "keep it at home at all times. Kye and his men cannot see or get access to this."

"Gotcha. What specifically do you need?"

"Anything and everything." I laugh, running my finger through my hair. "Names, dates, times, schedules, anything you think will be beneficial in bringing him down."

She nods her head. "Can I ask a question?"

"Of course."

"Do you really think I can do this?"

"I do. I think you can do anything you put your mind to. I think you hide behind this snarky bitchy front because you're scared."

"I'm not scared," she snaps, "I'm..."

"You're what?" I ask, my voice laced with concern. This is the first time Baylor has shown any emotion, other than sassiness. If she's one bit hesitant, I can't in good conscience allow her to do this.

"I...I don't know who I am or what I want in life. Ave knew she wanted to be a teacher since forever, she knows who she is. I've never found who I am and it feels like everyone compares me to her." She pauses and smiles. "She really is the best. Ave doesn't have a mean bone in her body and then there's me. Crazy wild me, marching to the beat of my own drum and not caring about consequences. You know, the first time in my life that I felt anything was when I started working with, well I guess, for Kye. They treated me with respect, they didn't compare me to Saint Avery but I guarantee you, if they met her, they would. Everyone loves her."

"Stop! I interrupt her, and the use of her first name startles her. Standing up, I walk around the table and lean against the edge next to her. She lifts her gaze to me. "I see you, Baylor, and I see a strong confident woman who just needs someone to believe in her. And guess what?"

"What?" she timidly asks, her eyes locked on mine.

They are filled with vulnerability but also fire, my little firecracker is still in there. She's scared of what lies ahead and she should be, but I won't let anything happen to her. Poking myself in the chest, "Me," I honestly tell her, "I believe in you."

Her eyes widen at my response, her mouth opens and closes a few times and then my sassy little kitten is back. "You're just saying that because you need me."

Shaking my head, I laugh. "Yes, I need you but, Ms. Evans, do you really think if I didn't believe in you, I'd send you in there?" Standing up, I walk around the desk and lean against the timber. "You are my winning piece."

"So I'm just a pawn in your game?" She pauses. *"It's me who's risking every-thing here."*

"Is my kitten afraid of a challenge?"

"I didn't say that," she sassily snaps back at me.

"But you didn't deny it either, Ms. Evans."

"You are infuriating, you know that?" I shrug at her. *"I was merely pointing out that I'm the pawn in this."*

"Ms. Evans, a lot of people may have underestimated you in the past but believe me when I say this, if anyone can bring down Kye Vlahos, it will be you."

We silently stare at one another, processing the words just spoken. Something passes between us. We've turned a corner in our relationship and for the first time since I formulated this plan, I think that we can actually do this. This blonde-haired, blue-eyed woman is going to bring down the Vlahos family and they won't see her coming.

"Thank you," she whispers, *"for believing in me. I won't let you down."* Taking a deep breath, she stands . *"I guess it's time to get this show on the road."*

"Yep," I say, letting the P pop.

She walks toward the door but before she opens it, she turns to face me. "Thank you, Corey. For the pep talk, even if I think you're full of fucking shit."

Before I can reply, she turns the handle and walks out of my office...

...My phone pings with a text. Picking it up, I read the message. It says two words *She's in.*

After she left here, I had her followed to make sure she didn't try and take off. I was positive she wouldn't run, but there was also a part of me that thought she might.

Picking up the photo of her we have in the file, I stare at it. At her. "It's all up to you now, Baylor," I whisper to the photo.

Placing the image back into the file, I pack up my things and head home.

I'm in my kitchen pacing, before I wear a hole in the tiles, I change into some sweats, pull on my sneakers, and go for a run. I bring up Spotify and Rammstein begins playing as I exit my building. I head toward the Lake-front Path and run along Lake Michigan. A quick ten-mile run is just what I need to clear my head, because right now, Baylor Evans is on my mind and I need to focus, especially if I'm going to get her through this alive.

7

BAYLOR

It's been seven days since I made my deal with Cox, and I'm no closer to getting anything from Kye. He's keeping me at an arm's length but at the same time, he tells me he wants me by his side as his queen. It feels like he's testing me, I don't know why he's doubting me, I've never betrayed him, or given him any reason not to trust me…unlike him.

I'm at the warehouse, waiting for Kye and Creed to return. That Creed guy is seriously unhinged. He keeps talking about Cressida and her new beau and how he hates him, blah, blah, blah. I tune out when he talks, but the last few times he's said some really sinister things about Cressida. Look, I'm not her number one fan but seriously, the way he talks about his baby momma, it's disgusting.

What's even more shocking, he brought Lexi here yesterday. Who does that? Who brings their kid to a place like this? She's cute for being Cressida's kid, not that I'd ever admit it out loud. It's a shame her dad is a dick and her mom is such a bitch. Her mom, Cressida Bayliss, is Avie's best friend so she's always at the apartment but lately, not so much, which is fine by me.

Gaga comes on and I start humming along to "Born this Way" when there's a commotion outside. The door swings open, and Creed and Kye enter. Kye is holding his side and leaning on Creed for support. "Kye," I shout. Jumping up, I race over to them. "What happened?"

"Fuckers got one up on me."

"Are you hurt?" I ask, placing my hand over his.

"Just a small stab wound," he says through clenched teeth, as Creed lowers him to the sofa.

"You need to go to the hospital," I say, crouching down next to him. He's sweating and looks pale. I'm no doctor but he looks like he's dying.

"Nah," he shakes his head, "the doc is on her way."

I stare at him, about to say something, when the door opens and I hear heels clicking across the cement floor. Looking over my shoulder, I see a brunette with fake tits and a dress that's painted on walking toward us. Her eyes roam over Kye and a ragey, stabby feeling begin to fester and flow through my veins.

"Kye, darling," she singsongs, her voice grating on my nerves. "What happened?"

"I got stabbed," he replies.

She leans down and kisses him, he turns his head—at the last minute— and her lips land at the corner of his mouth. A growl forms in the back of my throat seeing this.

Both of them turn their heads to look at me. "What?" I snarl.

"You jealous, Sugar?" Kye says, placing his hand on the bitch's ass, squeezing, licking his lips like a fucking pig.

Slapping his hand off her ass, I stand up and stalk away. He laughs at my retreating form and it pisses me off.

Storming down the hallway, I enter Kye's bedroom and slam the door behind me. Flopping back onto the bed, I sigh. Then I quickly stand up and tear the sheets off. He probably fucked her on these sheets. I don't know why I'm acting like this. I don't love him anymore, but the thought of him with someone else enrages me.

Grabbing the sheets, I open the door and throw them into the hallway before slamming the door shut again. Walking back into the room, I sit on the end of the bed and kick off my purple heels. Breathing rapidly, I fall back onto the mattress and stare up at the ceiling.

My outburst just now is confusing to me. I don't care for him in that way, but when I saw him with *her*, I became jealous. I'm not a jealous person. Resting my arm over my eyes, I sigh. I don't think I can do this. My emotions are all over the place and if I'm not careful, I'm gonna end up dead.

Why is doing the right thing so hard?

Closing my eyes, I drift off to sleep, only to be woken when there's a banging on the door. "Baylor, Bossman wants you!" Creed shouts through the door.

"Tell him to fuck off!" I shout back.

"Your funeral," he says.

"Whatever," I mumble, lifting my arm, I rest it on my forehead and exhale deeply. That fear of not being able to do this rears its ugly head again. "I can't do this," I whisper, my eyes welling with tears.

The door opens and Kye walks in.

Lifting my head, I wipe my eyes and see a shirtless Kye standing there, a bandage around his waist, color back in his cheeks. We stare at one another, neither one of us speaking.

"Did you fuck her?" I snarl, breaking the silence.

Sitting up, I pull my feet onto the edge of the mattress and wrap my arms around my legs, resting my chin on my knees. I look down at my toes, wriggling them. The purple polish sparkles in the dim bedroom light.

"Not today," he replies, walking farther into the room.

"So, you have before?" I snap, lifting my gaze to his. Staring at him, I notice his eyes are locked on me.

"Yeah," he says, reaching out, he goes to cup my cheek but I slap his hand away.

"Well, go and fuck her now. She can be your fucking queen, since I mean so little to you." I'm shocked at the anger coming from me right now. I don't want him in that way. I don't want him in any way. I just want to bring him and his lying, deceiving, non-dead ass down.

"Bay, Sugar," he coos, squatting in front of me, he places his hands on my knees, "She's nothing to me." When I continue to stare at my toes, he lifts his hand and places it under my chin, lifting my gaze to his. "You're my queen, Sugar. It's you I want by my side, not her."

I believe him, I don't want to but I do. I nod my head in agreement. Kye smiles at me, and for a brief moment, the love I used to have for him simmers below the surface. He leans forward, threads his fingers into my hair, and presses his lips to mine. We fall back to the mattress and kiss, just like we used to. I close my eyes and give myself over to Kye and the kiss, hooking my leg around his back. What surprises me is that behind my closed eyes, I see Corey-fucking-Cox. I groan in shock, which Kye takes it as I'm enjoying this. He lifts his hand and cups my breast, pinching my nipple through my shirt and bra. I moan again but this time, it's a pleasurable one. I'm still picturing Corey as I give myself over to the pleasure coursing through me.

Wrapping my arms around his neck, I deepen the kiss and pull him into me. He hisses in pain, which pulls me out of my lust induced state. I suddenly start remembering why he got stabbed earlier and more importantly, I'm kissing Kye; not Corey. *What the fuck is wrong with me?*

Gently, I push him off me. "Kye, babe, you're hurt."

"I'm fine. Doc stitched me up."

At the mention of *her,* my anger returns, and this time when I push, he rolls off me. I stand up, turn around, and stare down at him. "We need a new doctor," I spit at him before spinning on my heel and walking into the bathroom, slamming the door behind me. Leaning my hands on the vanity edge, I stare at my reflection and shake my head. *What have I gotten myself into?*

The door opens. I look up and in the reflection of the mirror, I see Kye staring at me. He doesn't say anything; it's unnerving. "What?" I snap.

"Wanna talk about your jealousy?" He crosses his arms and leans against the doorframe. I silently watch him in the mirror and let out a frustrated sigh.

Turning to face him, I lean against the vanity, crossing my legs and arms, mimicking his stance.

"I presumed that you fucked others when you were 'dead' but seeing it, it..."

"It what?"

"It didn't piss me off and that pissed me off."

"So you're pissed off that you're not pissed?"

"Pretty much. It makes no sense." I look to my feet, wriggling my toes in the fluffy floor mat for something to focus on that isn't Kye.

"Do you care if I fuck Monica now?"

Lifting my head, I stare at him and shake my head from side to side. "No, I don't." I pause, "How can I be your queen if I don't care that you fuck her or anyone else?"

He steps over to me and rests his hands on my hips, "I chose you to be my queen because you are one badass bitch. You hold your ground. You don't cower to anyone. You command respect from my men but most all, you have my back. Do I want you in my bed? Fuck yes, I remember how good it was with you, but am I going to turn you away because you don't want that? Hell fucking no. Pussy is pussy—"

"Charming," I interrupt and smack his shoulder.

"Dick is dick too."

"Touché," I reply.

"Baylor, what do you want?"

Staring at him, I bite my bottom lip and think about what I want. "I want to be by your side as your queen, but right now, I can't be in your bed. I'm still hurt over you letting me think you were dead. And I'm still really pissed off at you sending Smallie and River to get me."

"They went off the grid, I still don't know what happened there."

"Creed happened. He tried to fuck you over. I guarantee it. That guy is a loose cannon, but getting back to us, fuck who you want, but I don't want to see or hear it. If and when I'm ready to be with you, I'll let you know."

"And that there is why you are my queen. Soon, you and I will be the new age Bonnie and Clyde. The world ain't seen nothing yet, Sugar." I smile and nod in agreement because yes, he ain't seen nothing yet.

8
COREY

Sitting here listening to what sounds like Baylor and Kye making out pisses me off. I have no right to feel like this, but I'm jealous. I'm infuriated and fucking jealous that the bastard gets to kiss her, and all I can do is sit here and listen. Ripping off my headphones, I throw them onto the table and stand up. Gripping the back of my neck, I stare down at the file before me and shake my head. There's shit everywhere right now.

My eyes land on a photo of Baylor and Creed Dawson. This Creed guy is Kye's go-to man. Picking up the photo, I stare at it, well, I stare at her. She's sitting in a car with him, and doesn't have a care in the world. I wish I could be as carefree as she is.

Dropping the photo, I continue to stare at her. Then I look to Creed and I decide to focus on him. Sifting through the mess, I find his file and begin to read. Seems that Baylor is connected to him through her sister's best friend, Cressida Bayliss. No one has spoken to Ms. Bayliss so I decide to take a little trip and visit her.

Grabbing my things, I head down to my car and drive over to her place. Pulling up, I turn the car off and climb out. I walk up the stairs and knock on the door. An attractive woman opens the door and stares at me through the screen. "Can I help you?" she cautiously asks.

"I hope so. I'm looking for Cressida Bayliss," I state.

"That's me. I'm Cress," she says, her face etched with hesitation.

"I'm Agent Corey Cox, I'd like to ask you a few questions about Creed Dawson."

"Is he okay?" she asks, her voice raising an octave.

"As far as I'm aware, yes. Can you tell me about your relationship with him?"

She opens the screen door and steps out onto the porch. "Creed and I dated for a few years about five years ago. He's the father of my daughter, Lexi." She pauses. "Is he in trouble?"

"I'm not at liberty to discuss that, but he is someone we are looking into."

"Fucking asshole," she whispers, "I knew something was up."

That statement piques my interest. "How so?" I ask.

"He's changed recently." Those three words concern me and I'm not liking where this conversation is heading. "He's become verbally abusive toward me. He's telling Lex horrible things about me and when she comes home, she's upset. Lately she hasn't been enjoying herself when she's with him."

"How old is your daughter?"

"She's five."

"When was the last time you saw Mr. Dawson?"

"Probably a week ago when he dropped Lexi off, but he's texted me a few times. Do I need to be worried about him with my daughter?"

"You know him better than I do, Ms. Bayliss, but trust your judgment. You seem like a smart woman." She nods at me, but I notice that all the color has drained from her face. "Can I ask what your relationship with him is now?"

"Civil, I guess." She shrugs.

"No, I mean, personally?"

"We aren't in a physical relationship, if that's what you mean. He's the father, if you can call him that, of my daughter and that's it. I spend as little time with him as possible."

"Why is that?"

"He's a dick," she honestly tells me. "If it wasn't for Lexi, he wouldn't be in my life at all. I tolerate him for Lexi and for her only."

I'm processing her words when a deep voice says, "Cress, is everything okay?"

She looks over my shoulder at the man and nods, then she looks back at me, "As I said, Agent Cox, apart from handover with my daughter, I don't know what Creed gets up to. Hell, I don't even know where he lives."

Well, this was a bust, I think to myself. "Okay, well thank you for your time, Ms. Bayliss." Pulling a card out, I hand it to her. "If you think of anything else, please don't hesitate to contact me."

Nodding at her and the guy, I turn around and head back to my car. Once I'm behind the wheel, I open the file and stare at the surveillance photo of Creed Dawson. This guy is a smarmy son of a bitch, he's a loose cannon, and I don't like the feeling that's developing in my stomach when it comes to him. He's almost as crazy as Kye, but whereas Kye is calm, cool, and collected, this guy is a crazy psychopath.

My phone's alarm goes off reminding me to head over to Baylor's for our first catch-up in an hour. When I think of her, I think about what I heard before I came here and I grind my teeth. Why does the fact she was making out with Vlahos irk me so much?

Putting my car into drive, I head back to the headquarters so I can change and pick up my 'work' van.

Forty-five minutes later, I pull up to Baylor and Avery's apartment. These overalls are uncomfortable as fuck. With everything I need in hand, I head into the building. Taking the stairs rather than the elevator, I step onto their floor and walk toward their apartment.

Raising my hand, I knock. I can sense her shuffling on the other side, and when the door swings open, I'm taken aback at the vision before me. Baylor is wearing a white halter dress that hugs her curves and highlights her tits perfectly. On her feet are purple heels that elongate her legs, and I imagine her legs wrapped about my waist. The heels digging into my ass as I kiss the life out of her. Her voice snaps my attention back to the present. "Are you going to come in? Or are you just going to stand there and eye-fuck me?"

"Watch your mouth, Kitten."

"Stop fucking calling me Kitten."

"Meow," I say, as I step around her and inside. As I walk past her, I'm assaulted with her scent. It's sweet, like candy, the total opposite of her personality, which is dark and musty. I walk over to the sofa and sit, pulling out my files and stare up at her.

"Make yourself at home, why don't you?" she sasses.

"Thanks, I will. So got anything for me?"

"Nope," she states, as she sits next to me.

"Maybe if you stop making out with him, you'd have something for me," I vehemently snap at her, my words shocking me. I'm being extremely unprofessional right now, but Baylor brings out this side of me. I stand, needing to get away from her right now; I walk around the coffee table and stare over at her.

"I've kissed him once and that was after he was shot and stitched up."

"So you kiss anyone if they've been shot?"

"I'd like to fucking shoot you," she sassily snaps at me.

"Feeling's mutual, Kitten."

She stands and storms over to me and pokes me in the chest. "Stop. Fucking. Calling. Me. Kitten."

"Stop making out with the suspect and do your job."

We stand toe to toe, staring at one another. Something passes between us. The air thickens, much like my dick. Reaching over, I grip her cheeks in my palms and slam my lips to hers. She covers my hands and deepens the kiss. My tongue slides in and out of her mouth, while she wraps her leg around me, pulling us closer. Our kiss is frenzied and carnal. The sound of keys sliding into the front door lock grabs my attention. I push Baylor away from me, just as the front door opens and Avery walks in.

"Sorry, I'm late," she says. "Traffic was terrible." She looks over to us. Both of us are disheveled and breathing heavily. "What's going on?"

I'm at a loss for words right now; I have never acted so unprofessionally in all of my career. This woman causes my brain to stop functioning.

"I was telling Agent Cox here how I kissed Kye this morning, getting him to trust me the only way I know possible."

"Whoring yourself?" I say, and as soon as I say those two words, I instantly regret them.

"I'm just doing as you told me," she says, turning to face me. "You told me to do whatever it takes to bring Kye to his knees and trust me, I did exactly that." She winks and turns her attention back to Ave. "How was your day, sis?"

Her nonchalant actions piss me off but at the same time, I'm more turned on than I ever have been before. This woman is going to be the death of me...and possibly my career.

9
BAYLOR

HOLY FUCK, COX IS KISSING ME, AND HOLY FUCK, CAN THIS MAN KISS. COREY-fucking-Cox sure knows how to kiss a woman. I'm ready to rip my dress over my head, turn around, and let him fuck me senseless over the arm of the sofa, but Ave arrives and prevents that from happening. Thankfully…I think. When he calls me a whore, I see red and any feelings of wanting to fuck disappear as quickly as they came.

The next words out of my mouth are complete bullshit but fuck him. "…You told me to do whatever it takes to bring Kye to his knees and trust me, I did exactly that." I throw him a wink and poke my tongue into my cheek, insinuating I gave Kye a blow job.

Turning to face Ave, I smile sweetly. "How was your day, sis?"

"Good," she drawls the word out. She can sense she's walked in on something but she's too nice to state the obvious.

"That's great," I tell her, she stares at me. Imploring with her eyes for me to say something, but I'm at a loss to explain it right now. One minute we're bickering and the next, he's tongue fucking me. And can I say, it was the best tongue fucking of my life…I can only imagine what he'd be like between the sheets.

Shaking my head, those dirty disappear and I come back to the present to hear Ave and Cox talking about Creed. "…he's a dick. Plain and simple."

"That's putting it lightly," I add, "He's a crazy motherfucking dickwad." He eyes me intently. My body and clit is aware of his intense stare. It's getting annoying so, being the mature woman I am, I stick my tongue out at him and smirk.

"As I was saying, he's psycho crazy." I look over to Ave, "What did Cressida ever see in him?"

She shrugs. "Beats me. If it wasn't for Lexi, she wouldn't have anything to do with Dickwad Dawson."

"That's the best nickname for him. Lexi is a cute kid. She's sassy like her mom." Ave looks at me in confusion. "Dickwad stopped by with her the other day."

Her eyes widen. "Don't worry, Kye put a stop to that. He lost his shit when he saw her there with him."

"Who brings their kid to a place like that?" Cox asks.

In unison, Ave and I both say, "A dickwad." Then we laugh. In the last few weeks, our twin thing is returning.

"I'll give it to Kye," I add, "he refuses to hurt woman and children."

"Tell that to his sister and mother," Cox says.

My eyes snap to his. "They were killed by accident. He didn't want to hurt them." My defense of Kye is confusing right now.

"Accident or not, Kye's actions killed his mother and sister. Don't underestimate this man, Ms. Evans. Given the chance, he will end you too. I've seen men like him change in the blink of an eye. As they garner more power, it goes to their head and clouds their judgement. Kye Vlahos is a classic sociopath, please bear that in mind." The room falls silent and we process his words. "And with that, we'll wrap up today's meet. I'll see you again in three days' time. Unless you uncover something before then."

"Thank you, Agent Cox," Ave says, ever the polite one. "So far, you are holding up your end and keeping Bay safe."

"Please, I'm keeping myself safe. See you soon, Cox," I say, waving at him with a sweet smile on my face.

With that, he turns and walks toward the door. Ave says goodbye and closes the door behind him. She turns to face me, and I smile at her, "Thank you," I say.

"What for?"

"For always having my back. For always being by my side."

She walks over to me, throws her arm around my shoulder, and pulls me in for a side hug. "I'll stand by you, Bay. Always. I won't let anybody hurt you. You're my twinsie." She grabs my hand and leads me into the kitchen.

"And I won't let anyone hurt you either," I tell her, and I mean it. After what Smallie and River did to her, thinking she was me; I knew I had to make up for it, and my past actions too. "And I'll stop hurting you too. You're my twinsie, Avie, and I'm sorry. So so sorry for all that I've done and how I've treated you recently. You've always been on Team Baylor and I've let you down, but this is my chance to make you proud."

"And I am, Bay. I'm so proud of you right now for owning your mistakes, I just wish it was in a safe 'non-bring-down-a-mafia-drug-ring' way."

We stare at one another and a calmness washes over me. I know Avie and I will be fine. We will get back to our BayBay and Avie selves and be happier than we've ever been.

"Hey, Bay," she says, breaking the silence.

"Yeah, what's up, Avie?"

"Are you subconsciously singing that *I'll stand by you* song right now?"

"Yes." We both laugh. She grabs her phone, pulls up Spotify and clicks play. I open a bottle of red and pour us two glasses of wine. With our drinks in hand, we head into the living room and sit on the sofa. We listen as Chrissie Hynde from the Pretenders sings "I'll Stand By You." We join in singing the chorus, but Ave and I aren't half as good as Chrissie.

The song finishes and as is the emotional roller coaster that is Spotify random, we are now listening to "Butterfly" by Crazy Town.

Ave turns the volume down and looks over at me. I can tell from the look in the eye, she's about to interrogate me regarding what she walked in on. I was secretly hoping she'd forget, but Ave doesn't forget anything. "Okay, so..." She drags out the word so, waiting for me to talk.

"So what?" I ask, playing coy, but I know exactly what Ave's referring to...the kiss. The fucking out-of-this-world kiss that rocked me to my core.

"What did I walk in on earlier?" She raises her hand to silence me when I go to deny it. She gives me the 'don't mess with me' teacher look. "I have eyes, Bay, and I could feel the tension between you and Corey."

Not sure how to answer, I pick up my wine glass and chug back the contents. Since my glass is now empty, I stand up and walk back into the kitchen. Topping up my glass, I grab a new bottle and the open one, and walk back into the living room.

"Wow, a second bottle, this must be good," Ave teases.

"Not sure I'd describe it as good."

"Well, how would you describe it then?"

"Confusing in an already precarious situation."

"Okay, well start at the beginning and tell me."

"Cox and I kissed just before you arrived. One minute we were arguing about me kissing Kye and the next, he was tongue fucking me. If you hadn't walked in, I would have begged for him to bend me over the sofa and fuck me."

"You kissed Kye?" she questions.

"That's what you're focusing on now?"

"Well, yeah, I'll get to the Cox kissing but first, why did you kiss Kye? And how does Cox know?"

"There's a listening thingy-ma-giggy in my phone. Kye got stabbed—"

"What? How?"

"With a knife," I cheekily say, as Ave eyes me. "He was out with Creed and returned stabbed. Monica, his bimbo bitch doctor came and stitched him up, they've fucked before and I saw red. Don't know why I got angry, but I did. He found me and then we kissed, but while I was kissing him, I was picturing Cox. I stopped it before it went further. Anyway, Cox brought it up before you arrived, and then he kissed me and I kissed him back. Then you came home, and well, you know the rest."

"That's a lot of kissing," she says.

"Yep," I say letting the P pop. "And it will never happen again…with either of them."

"Bay, I don't believe you."

I look at her, purse my lips, and shake my head. "Yeah, I don't believe myself either."

We both fall silent and sip on our wine then Ave breaks the silence. "Can I ask you a question?" I nod my head, "Who's the better kisser?"

Without thinking, I blurt out, "Cox."

"That doesn't surprise me. That man is fine. I wonder what he's packing."

"Avery Evans," I playfully scold, "what has gotten into you?"

"Flynn," she replies with a wink. I shake my head.

"You dirty, dirty girl. What has happened to my sweet and innocent sister?"

"She met a sexy-as-sin Irish doctor, who makes her do things she would never ever do."

"Like what?" I ask. Ave and I really haven't had a chance to chat about her new relationship.

"Well, the night we met, not only did I have my first one-night stand but I also let him finger fuck me in the restroom alcove at The Tavern."

"Is it wrong that I'm kind of proud of you regarding this?"

"Cress said something similar." She takes a sip then adds, "I think Corey might be your Flynn."

"Nah, I need this to be over so I can forget about Corey-fucking-Cox."

"You really think you can forget about him after this?"

"I have to. We are too different. It would never work between us."

"Flynn and I are total opposites," she says. "We work." I ponder her words and wonder, could Cox and I be more than whatever the hell we are right now?

"You two are a classic opposites attract, I'm glad that my stupidity didn't ruin that for you because I have never seen you happier."

"Flynn makes me happy, he brings me out of my shell. I miss not seeing him when he's on nights." I realize that I too become sad when I don't see Cox. He has wormed his way into my cold, dead heart, but we can be nothing more than informant and handler. Maybe if we'd met under other circumstances, I could see us working out, but I'm a criminal and he's the law. He hates me and I, I don't know how I feel about him.

For the rest of the evening, Ave and I listen to music, drink wine, and hang out, just like we used to. It's the perfect way to end a stressful and confusing day.

Later that night, as I lie in bed, I think over everything that has happened and how my life has changed. Things concerning Agent Corey Cox are blurring and I don't know what to do. And that scares the living shit out of me.

10
COREY

I<small>T'S BEEN TWO WEEKS SINCE</small> I <small>KISSED</small> B<small>AYLOR AND EVER SINCE THEN IT'S ALL</small> I've thought about. Hell, I've even jerked off in the shower with visions of her on her knees. Her pouty lips wrapped around my shaft as it slides in and out of her mouth. Fuck, my dick is hard once again.

Thankfully I'm alone right now. I readjust myself and look across the road, still no movement. I'm staking out the doctor who has been working with the Vlahos family for the last few years. Flipping open the file, I reread the details regarding Dr. Monica Quinn. She's thirty-four years old. Graduated top of her class from Johns Hopkins and now runs a practice in the burbs. How does a successfully doctor like her end up working for the mafia? The door opens and out walks the lady of the hour. When I see her in person, I can see why she's their doctor. She has dark brown hair, killer legs, and massive fake tits. Why women do that to themselves amazes me.

She climbs into her black Mercedes and pulls out of the practice parking lot. Starting my car, I follow her keeping my distance and changing lanes to make sure she doesn't know I'm following her. She pulls up to a restaurant and stops at the valet. She flirts with the pimply faced teenager and walks into the restaurant. A few moments later, Kye and Creed arrive.

Her face lights up when she sees Kye and what shocks me most is the kiss that occurs between Monica and Kye. I thought he only had eyes for Baylor. This development doesn't sit well with me. I make a note to discuss it with her later. And speak of the devil, her ride drops her off at the front doors and she walks into the restaurant. Her head held high, showing just how strong she is.

From my spot on the street, I see that Baylor is unimpressed as she joins them. Grabbing my laptop off the passenger seat, I log into the surveillance system and hope that I can hear what's going on. Baylor must have her phone on the table because I can hear everything clearly.

"Baylor, Sugar. Calm down," Kye says.

"Do not fucking tell me to calm down. This bitch had her hands all over you."

"That's not all I had on him," Monica says to Baylor, taunting her. Oh, how I wish I was inside to witness this scene unfold live. Right now, I'm imagining Baylor's face turning purple, her fists will be clenched, and she'll be biting her bottom lip in frustration.

"You are fucking dead," Baylor seethes, "Either she goes, or I go."

"There's the door," Monica throws at Baylor.

"Enough," Kye growls. "Ladies, play nice. Baylor, we need Monica."

"There are a million doctors in the world, I say we get another," Baylor huffs.

"I quite like this one," Creed adds, the tone of his voice chilling.

"Of course, you would," Baylor snarks, "you like all the hoity-toity bitches."

"What can I say, I have a type."

"Thank fuck, I'm not your type," Baylor says, and right now I'm imagining her crossing her arms defiantly.

"Well, now that's out of the way. We have business to discuss."

"I need a drink, if she's going to be here," Baylor snarls.

"Day drinking, really?" Monica says. "Why is she even here, Kye? Why do you need her?"

"She's my queen. She'll be by my side always. You can be replaced, Monica; Baylor cannot. There is only one queen and Baylor is it."

"You say such nice things," Baylor answers. "So what's the plan, Stan?"

"Don't ever call me that again," Kye snaps, reminding me of when Baylor said that to me. "The plan is in motion, specifics are still being nutted out, but I need to know that the three of you are all on board?"

All three of them nod and say yes.

"Excellent." Kye explains, "The world won't know what hit it when this all comes to fruition."

"Wanna fill us in on the specifics?" Baylor asks.

"All in due time, my queen. All in due time."

They fall into general chitchat. I need to see Baylor so I take the opportunity. I exit my car and cross the street and head inside. Baylor sees me and her eyes widen, I nod toward the restroom as I take my seat at a table nearby, placing my back to them.

A few moments later, she walks by toward the restrooms. I order a drink from the waiter and after he leaves, I stand and follow Baylor. She's waiting in the alcove just near the restrooms.

"What the fuck are you doing here?" she snarls at me.

"Getting lunch," I nonchalantly say, "and—"

"I know, I know," she sasses, "language."

"Having fun antagonizing the good doctor?" She growls at me. "Are you jealous of her?"

"Pffft, please. There's no comparison between her and me." *I agree,* I silently think as my gaze roams over her. She's wearing a deep purple dress and what I have come to realize, her favorite purple strappy heels. "Now, what do you want?"

"Yes," a deep voice says from behind us. "What do you want with my queen?"

Turning around, I come face-to-face with Kye Vlahos. "I'm her contractor, Corey." I stretch out my hand. Kye looks down at it, then to Baylor and finally, he shakes. Squeezing harder than necessary to exert his power. I don't cower. I look him directly in the eye and do not waver. "I'm here meeting a potential new client and when I saw Ms. Evans, I thought I'd give her an update on the tiles. They were damaged in transit and there's now going to be a delay. We will need to extend the completion date by a few weeks."

"Ave will be upset," Baylor replies, "but these things take time. I'm sure it will all work out in the end." I get the double meaning to her words and nod.

"All the planning and waiting will be worth it in the end. You just need to keep your eye on the prize."

"I've already got my prize," Kye says, pulling Baylor into his side and kissing her temple. She smiles up at him but it doesn't reach her eyes. I start to wonder if maybe this is too much for her. Did I make a mistake sending her in?

I realize they are both staring at me. "Well, I must run," I tell them. "I'll be in touch, Ms. Evans, when I know more."

"Mmmhmpf," she nonchalantly replies. "See ya."

She takes Kye's hand and pulls him away. They walk back over to their table, say their goodbyes, and I watch them leave. They really are a stunning couple and she's playing the doting queen role well, but a feeling of unease is building. My gut has never let me down before, I hope this isn't the first time it does.

11
BAYLOR

The following day, I'm lazing at home with a slight hangover. Okay, a massive hangover. After running into Cox with Kye, I was antsy and not feeling myself. After the meeting, I returned to the apartment and was happy to see Ave was home. Just like we did the other week, we spent the evening together. We shared two bottles of red wine, watched *Ten Things I Hate About You*—hello Heath Ledger—and threw together an antipasto platter for dinner. I think I was Greek in a past life because I could live off wine, cheese, olives, and cured meats.

The serenity of my morning is broken when I get a frantic call from Kye. He needs me to meet him at a restaurant downtown immediately. He tells me to dress provocatively in a skimpy slutty dress. *Fuck him,* I think to myself as I walk into my room and grab out a pair of skintight leather pants, a black halter top with a deep V and, you guessed it, my purple strappy heels. "Perfect," I whisper to my reflection, before I add some nude lipstick and blow wave my blonde locks.

Not skanky-sexy like he requested, but I'm still fucking hot and that's all that matters.

Grabbing my clutch, I throw in my lip gloss, gum, some cash, and I'm ready to go. On my way out the door, I order an Uber. I'm waiting on the curb when Kye calls. I answer on the second ring, "Hey!"

"Where the fuck are you? When I tell you to come, you come."

"Calm your tits, asshole. I'm waiting for an Uber."

"Why are you Ubering?"

"I don't have a car," I tell him. "I always Uber it."

"Well, fucking get one," he snaps, seems this will be a fun afternoon. "No queen of mine Ubers it."

"Sure, I'll just whip thirty-seven grand outta my ass and go buy myself a Mini Cooper convertible." We both go silent just as my Uber pulls up. "My ride's here, see you soon." I hang up and mumble, "Fuck you," to my phone as I climb into the car.

Staring out the window, I sigh. Cox was right, Kye is a sociopath, but I'll raise the bar and add controlling dick-faced asshole. His actions are becoming unhinged, and to be honest, he scares the absolute crap out of me. He's definitely not the man I knew and loved, but I don't have a choice. I need to do this if I want to redeem myself, but at times like today, I question if it's all worth in the end.

The car pulls up at the restaurant and I thank the driver. I look up and see Kye staring at me from inside the restaurant. I smile but he doesn't smile back and a sinking feeling develops in the pit of my stomach. Putting one foot in front of the other, I head inside. I repeat to myself over and over. "I'm tough, I'll get through this." And I hope to high heaven that I do get through this.

To say the afternoon with Kye was fun would be a lie. It was a shit-show from the moment I stepped into the restaurant, but I showed him that no one fucks with me. I think I finally proved to him that I'm with him one-hundred-percent, no thanks to Cox anyway.

Walking over to see Kye, I see Creed and two other men sitting at the table. "Gentlemen," I say, as I take the empty seat next to Kye. His eyes roam over me and I see anger reflecting back at me.

"I said wear a dress," he barks at me.

"No one tells me what to wear," I tell him.

Reaching over to grab his drink, he grabs my wrist and squeezes. "Are you defying me?" he growls, increasing pressure around my wrist.

"This isn't nineteen twenty, asshole. I will dress however the fuck I want. If you don't like it, I'm quite happy to leave."

The grip Kye has on my wrist tightens, it's becoming painful but I refuse to show him that. Thankfully, one of the men sitting across from us breaks our Mexican standoff. "She's a live one."

Turning my gaze from Kye to the man, I raise my eyebrows at him in a 'what the fuck' way and at the same time, I pull my wrist free from Kye.

"And you are?" I ask, just as the waitress places a lychee martini in front of me. Looking to Kye, I smile my thanks and pick me drink. I take a sip and the liquor instantly calms me.

Licking my lips, I smile at the men as Kye introduces us. "Bay, my queen, this is Max and Bob." Those names ring a bell, but they also cause me to laugh because they are dog names. "We are discussing a new business partnership. I was hoping you can help sway their decision to join forces with us."

Placing my drink on the table, I turn to face Kye. "Are you whoring me out to Max and Bob?" My voice is cool and calm, but on the inside, Bitchy Baylor is raging. I'm no whore and he needs to remember that. He shrugs at me and that pisses me off.

Leaning into him, I breathe heavily on his neck as I slide my hand up his thigh. Palming his cock through his slacks, I increase the pressure. Licking up his neck, I whisper, "I'm no one's whore." I bite his earlobe and squeeze his dick hard in my fist. He clenches his teeth and hisses from the pain. "If you want me to be your queen, you need to remember that."

Letting go of his cock, I turn my attention to the men across from us. "Now, gentlemen," I purr, picking up my drink and staring across the table, "let's see if we can come to some other agreement that doesn't involve me and my virtue." Taking another sip, I watch the men.

"I like her," Max says to Kye, throwing a wink at me before he looks at Bob. The two of them have a silent conversation oblivious to myself, Kye, and Creed sitting here. I've nearly finished my drink when they turn their attention back to us. "You have yourself a deal, Vlahos," Bob confirms.

While Max adds, "On one condition." His eyes are locked on me as he says this and surprisingly, I don't cower under his gaze.

"Anything," Kye replies whereas I say, "Depends."

Both men laugh. "We want her," he points to me, "on the first drop. No Queen B., no deal."

"As long as it doesn't interrupt my schedule, or involve me on my back, I'm sure I can oblige." I have no clue what I'm agreeing to but this could give me the intel that Cox needs, and it will also reaffirm to Kye that I'm on his side. He's still keeping me at an arm's length. I need to do something that doesn't involve me sleeping with him. I won't go there again, my legs are closed to Kye Vlahos. Even if he wasn't a scary mafia king, that boat has sailed.

"Now, hold up a minute," Kye interjects, slamming his fist on the table, the cutlery rattling from the force. "I'm the boss here. I have the final say in things."

Turning my gaze to him, I sweetly smile. "And here I thought we were in this together, babe."

"Uh-oh, trouble in paradise," Creed teases.

Kye growls and turns his attention back to me. "You may be my queen but I am the motherfucking king. I have the final say."

"Whatever," I nonchalantly reply. Leaning back in my chair, I cross my arms, unintentionally pushing up my breasts. Four sets of eyes drop to my chest. *Men,* I think to myself as I lean forward, showing off the girls even more. If I lean forward any more, my nipples will be showing. I'm not prepared to whore myself but I will be a dick tease.

After a few more seconds, I reach out, pick up my martini, lean back, and sip. *The titty show is over, boys.* The four of them watch my movements intently. Looking at Kye, I see anger and lust reflecting back at me. Max and Bob are still staring at my tits; I see hunger in their eyes but also fear. They don't want to cross Kye, but at the same time, they are men, thinking with their dicks when the hint of boob is placed before them. When I look over to Creed, I shudder. His eyes are glued to my chest and the creepy fucker is licking his lips. Whereas Bob and Max's glare is playful, Creed's is deranged and dirty—I really hate that fucker.

Biting my lip, I hold back my smirk when Kye smiles. Finally, I am the fucking queen Kye wants me to be and I have four hapless pawns trapped in the valley of my breasts.

The word pawn takes me back to a conversation with Cox and for the first time, I think that he's right. I can do this, I can bring down Kye, and I will do whatever it takes to do so.

The next few weeks are much of the same: lunches with associates, new and old. Kye parading me around like a shiny new toy, showing off his queen to his minions.

In public, we are the ultimate power couple but behind closed doors, we live separate lives. There has been no further kissing Kye, or Cox, and I'm pretty sure he's still fucking that doctor bitch, but I don't care. At the end of the day, I'm his queen and that's all I need to be to get this done.

Besides, I'm lusting after the one person I should not be lusting over, Corey Cox.

Each night, as I drift off to sleep, I have inappropriate steamy dreams starring my sexy but annoying agent. I wake up and pleasure myself, whispering his name as my fingers bring me to climax. My digits are getting a good work out at the moment; maybe I'll need to invest in a B.O.B to give them a rest. Nah, it's the real deal or nothing for me.

After our meeting this week, Cox seems impressed with the intel I'm gathering, but it's still not enough to bring everything crumbling down around Kye. I've fully gained his trust now, but some days I feel like one of his lap dogs. Being at his beck and call. Dropping everything when he calls and running straight to him, well, driving to him in my new navy blue Mini Cooper convertible. A perk of being his queen, as well as a stylish new wardrobe.

After the Max and Bob wardrobe argument, he sent me on a shopping spree with a predetermined list of clothes. Thankfully, he wasn't with me so I could get the requested items but in the style I like. I've never had such an amazing wardrobe before, totally makes up for Creed being around.

As Cox promised, I'm safe and we have been able to keep up the ruse of him being my and Ave's contractor. Not sure how much longer we can use that cover but fingers crossed, I won't have to do this much longer because Kye is starting to scare me with his behavior. Cox was right, the power and control is going to his head. I need to end this and I need to end it soon. The sooner, the better,

12
COREY

It's been almost three months and I'm no closer to bringing down Kye Vlahos. The list of associate names I'm gathering from Baylor is great, but I need that smoking gun. I need that one piece of evidence that will close this close, bring it to an end, and put Kye behind bars for a very long time. The only downfall to that is my time with my Kitten will come to an end. As much as she is a pain in the ass, she's also intriguing and has piqued my interest.

We'd never work out as a couple. She's wild. I'm not. She's a criminal. I'm a law enforcement officer. We are two opposites, and there's the little fact she hates me. There's a fine line between love and hate, and we are teetering precariously on that line.

Throwing the file onto my desk, I rub the back of my neck in frustration. I'm starting to lose hope that this is going to work. I begin to wonder if sending Baylor in was the right thing to do when I'm given the Hail-fucking-Mary of all Hail Marys.

A knock on the door grabs my attention and I look up to see Oats standing there with a goofy grin on his face. "Hey, what's up?"

"Creed Dawson was arrested for assault."

"Come again?" I say, totally shocked at what I just heard.

"He attacked his ex-partner, Cressida Bayliss, earlier this evening."

"Shit, is she okay?"

"She's extremely lucky. Her mom happened to be driving past when he attacked. Mom called the current boyfriend and he managed to get there in time. Dawson was about to rape her."

"Fucking hell. I knew he was a psychopath, but that's just nuts."

"Thought you might want to talk to him, see if you can get anything from him regarding Vlahos and his plans."

"Yeah, thanks. I'll be right there."

Leaning back in my chair, I grin. Creed Dawson's arrest could work in my favor. If he's as delusional as Baylor says he is, I'm willing to bet my left nut he will sing like a fucking canary to reduce his time.

With a pep in my step, I walk into the interrogation room, his eyes widen when he sees me. "You," he snarls, "you're Baylor's contractor."

"One of my many jobs," I tell him, as I take a seat across from him. "So, Creed, I have a proposition for you."

"Thanks for the offer, asshole, but I don't suck cock."

"My cock isn't on the table but your ass can be. I'm sure Tiny in cell block 'C' would just love you and your ass."

His eyes widen. "What the fuck, man? What have I ever done to you?"

"Me? Nothing, but you attacked the mother of your child and you were about to rape her. Tiny doesn't much care for assholes who beat on women."

"Bitch fucking deserved it," he snarls, glaring at me.

"And you will deserve everything Tiny will give you, but..." I leave it hanging, waiting to see what he will do.

"But what?" he asks, all malice in his voice gone and I know I have him.

"You help me and I'll help you."

"How can I help you? I'm no one."

"You're not no one to Kye Vlahos."

His eyes widen at the mention of Kye. "What the fuck does he have to do with this?"

"I've been building a case against him, I need your help to wrap it up nice and neatly, so I can get my person safely out of there."

"You don't have an agent in there. Kye would sniff a fed out in a heartbeat."

"Never said it was a fed."

"Who, then?"

"I can't play all my cards in the first hand, can I? Now, Mr. Dawson, are you going to help me? Or should I give Tiny a call?"

"What do you want to know?"

BINGO! This is too fucking easy. I knew he'd turn. I didn't expect him to roll over so easily. I don't trust this asshole, so I'll be cautious with what he does tell me. Deciding to push my luck, I lean forward. "Everything. I want to know every single thing about Kye Vlahos and his organization."

"And you'll keep me out of jail? Away from Tiny? Safe from him?"

"Depending on the intel you give me, I'll do what I can."

"All right then. Kye Vlahos is a crazy motherfucker. You name it, he's into it."

"Be more specific or I'll tell Tiny you like it rough. The rougher, the better."

"Guns. Drugs. Human trafficking."

"Elaborate on the human trafficking."

"He needs men for labor."

"So no women and children?"

"Not women and children. He has a conscience."

A laugh escapes me, the fact he won't traffic women and children doesn't mean shit. Trafficking is trafficking and with all of this, he's going down for a very long time. "So when he hears that you beat the mother of his child, he'll let you go scot-free?" Creed's face pales as he registers what I just said. "I need specifics if you want my help and protection."

"Kye and that bitch." The mention of Baylor piques my interest. It feels like she's hiding her involvement in all of this and Creed here will either confirm my suspicion or prove me wrong. I don't have any proof she's deceiving me, but the doubt is there. But then again, Kye is keeping her at a distance because I don't think he trusts her either. *Which team are you on Baylor: Team Kye? Or Team Cox?*

"Which bitch are we referring to?"

"Baylor Evans. She's a smart one. Always there, plotting and planning. I don't trust her."

"And why's that?"

"That whore took my place as his number one. She opened her legs and he fell for it."

"So you're jealous because Kye is getting some from her?"

"I'm not jealous, I'm pissed off. She waltzes in after two of my men are mysteriously killed while retrieving her. I call bullshit. A little slut like her couldn't take down two men like that." His eyes widen when realization hits. "She's your insider. You were the ones to kill Smallie and River."

Shaking my head, I deny everything. "I'm not telling you who I have on the inside. And I'm not discussing some woman you're jealous of. I want Vlahos, I don't care about his bitch."

"It's her, it has to be. No one else would be stupid enough to cross him. That fucking whore is a dead bitch when Kye finds out."

"And you'll be a dead man if Kye finds out you ratted." His eyes widen once again. "I can't protect you, Mr. Dawson, unless you give me something to pin on him. So far, everything you've told me is in line with what I already know. I need something concrete from you for me to hold up the end of my bargain."

"There's a meet later this week, Kye is getting all the big players in to take them out. He wants more control. He wants to own the world."

"Now, that wasn't so hard, was it?" I tell him, sliding a notepad and pencil across to him. "I want names, a date, and a location for this meet."

Picking up the pencil, he starts writing. I'm not sure I trust this guy, I need to meet with Baylor and confirm everything Creed tells me, but can I trust what she's saying? If Dawson knew about this meet, why didn't she tell me? Or is this Kye keeping her in the dark again? I need to meet with her and see if she's withholding information from me and confirm, once and for all, what side she's on.

With the info from Creed in hand, I exit the room and call Baylor. Calling is risky but time is of the essence. "Hello?" a deep male voice I recognize as Kye Vlahos answers after the second ring.

"I'm looking for Baylor."

"And you are?"

"Her contractor. And you are?"

"Her king." Hearing him call himself that really pisses me off and makes the urge to take him down even stronger.

"Is she there? I need to speak with her urgently."

"She's tied up right now," I don't like his tone of voice, but before he can say anything, I hear her yelling in the background. "What the fuck are you doing with my phone?"

Their voices are muffled, but I can hear her yell, 'Fuck you, asshole!" A door slams, and I finally hear her through the line, "Hey, this is Baylor."

"It's Cox," I sternly say, my tone harsher than I intended.

"What can I do for you?" she sweetly says, and just hearing her voice calms the rage building within me.

"We need to meet as soon as possible."

"Sure, I can meet you at the apartment. Is there another issue with the project?"

Her comment stumps me and then I remember I'm her 'contractor.' "Kinda."

"Okay, well, I'll see you in an hour or so."

"Great, see you then." I hang up and smile. She really is in this for the right reasons. Creed is just getting in my head and trying to throw me off my game. With the end in sight, I need to focus on my endgame: bringing Kye Vlahos to justice. Grabbing my things, I head to my car and make my way to Baylor's place.

I'm parked out front but I don't see Baylor's car so I sit, wait, and watch. When Baylor finally arrives, I watch as she exits her new car and heads inside. I wait a few moments and then climb out of my work truck and head to her apartment.

She answers the door straightaway after I knock. "Hey," she says, but the smile she gives me doesn't reach her eyes. She looks tired and uneasy.

"You okay?" I ask as I step inside.

"Fine," she drawls, but from the tone of her voice, she is anything but fine.

"Kitten," I plead.

"I'm in a mood 'cause Kye's in a mood 'cause Creed was arrested and—"

"I know Creed was," I say, my confession shocking her.

"How do you know?"

"I know everything regarding Kye Vlahos and his crew. Seems you've been holding out on me."

"I've told you everything I know," she snaps at me, flopping down on the sofa and crossing her arms like a petulant child.

"Really? Everything?"

"Yes," she says, but her eyes dart around the apartment anxiously. The fact she won't look at me confirms she's hiding something.

"Look at me," I say and she lifts her gaze to me. "Thursday. 2:00 p.m."

"Is that supposed to mean something?"

"You tell me."

"What fucking game are you playing, Cox?"

We stare at one another. "Kitten, a source of mine tells me an important meeting is happening on Thursday with quite a few big players."

She scoffs and shrugs her shoulders. "This is news to me." From the look on her face, I believe her.

"I believe you," I confirm. "We're going to make our move on Thursday. I don't want you at that meeting."

"What do I do if Kye wants me there?"

"Lie. Cheat. Whatever. Just do not be at that meeting, Baylor. Please?"

"Okay," she says. She bites her bottom lip. "This is it, isn't it?"

I nod. "I think so."

She stands up and walks over to me. We stare at one another, "Cox, I, ummm—"

Her phone rings, breaking the spell that enveloped the two of us just now. She pulls out her phone. "Shit," she mumbles. "It's Kye."

"Answer it."

"Hey," she casually says. She listens to Kye and nods her head, saying, "Mmmhmpf," quite a few times. "Sure, I'll be there as soon as I finish with the contractor," she tells him. "Okay, see you soon." She hangs up and looks to me. "I, umm, ahh, have to go. Kye needs to see me."

"Okay, but remember what I said. Stay away from that meeting on Thursday."

We say our goodbyes and I walk out, leaving her alone in her apartment. This is what we've been working toward, but now that the end is in sight, I'm not ready for it to be over. I'm not ready to say goodbye to Baylor Evans, and that scares me.

13
BAYLOR

ON THE DRIVE BACK TO THE WAREHOUSE, I PLAY THE MEETING JUST NOW WITH Cox over and over in my mind. He's worried about me and it's not in the handler/informant way, it was in a caring I-don't-want-you-to-get-hurt kind of way. Before Kye called, I thought we might kiss again. I hoped to kiss him again and I think he wanted to kiss me too. I wanted to feel his lips pressed against mine. To have them all over my body. I wanted to strip him out of his suit and then lick him from head to toe, paying special attention to the appendage between his thighs.

I want him…but I can't have him. We are from two different worlds. Hell, we'd probably kill one another if we were under the same roof for longer than an hour.

As I pull up at the warehouse, it hits me; I'm falling for Agent Cox.

Shaking my head, I laugh, of course I fall for the one person I can never have; such is my life. Nothing can become of it because I'm me and he's him. I need to finish this job and then forget I ever met the sexy-as-fuck agent.

Sitting in my car, I stare at the steering wheel, feeling sad. I know I need to go inside but I can't. I want to drive away from here and never see Kye Vlahos ever again. A knock on the window startles me and I jump in fright. Looking up, I see Monica-fucking-Quinn staring at me. Seeing her here pisses me off. Any sadness I felt evaporates and is replaced with anger and brings Bitchy Baylor to the surface.

Pushing my door open, I step out. "What are you doing here?" My voice full of disdain, gives away how I feel about her being here.

"Kye called."

"So you come running whenever he calls you? Pathetic much?"

"Whatever," she sasses. "When he tires of you, he'll come back to me."

"Keep telling yourself that. I'm his queen; you are nothing but an employee of his. He only calls you when he needs you. I'm always here."

"I'm more than that," she mumbles quietly, but I hear it. Hearing those words piss me off and Bitchy Baylor makes an appearance.

"Say that to my face."

She steps to me, our noses millimeters apart. "I'm more than that. You might be his queen, but I'm the one he fucks."

"You're his fucking whore. Nothing more. Nothing less."

"You—" she snarls but Kye steps outside and interrupts, "Ladies, are you fighting over me?"

Arrogant dick, I think to myself, as I smile and look over to him. "You wish, dear," I tell him. "I was just telling the lovely doctor here that's she's nothing but your whore. You can fuck who you want as long as I stay your queen."

"And that is what you are, my queen." He cups my cheek and smiles at me. I shudder at his touch but thankfully there's a chill in the air. I can play it off as I'm cold, running my hands up and down my arms, trying to warm myself up. Leaning over, I place a kiss on his cheek. My gaze is locked on Monica. She's fuming right now. I think she thought she was more to him, but my words and his actions prove my point. The look on her face is priceless as realization sets in that she's nothing more than the mafia doctor and his side piece, a warm place to shove his cock.

Pulling back from Kye, I blow her a kiss and walk away, swinging my hips from side to side with each step away from them. Opening the door, I enter the warehouse. The only sound is my heels echoing off the cement floors, and with each step I take, my shitty mood evaporates. Nothing beats a good bitch smackdown and I just took Monica down without lifting a finger.

Pouring myself a glass of white wine, I fall into what's become my seat and wait for Kye and the doctor bitch to join us. As I sip on my wine, I smile to myself. The old Baylor would have been pissed that he was cheating on me, but the new me? Well she' doesn't give a flying fuck because she has the title of Queen and doesn't have to fuck Kye.

Kye finally joins me and I notice he's alone. The look in his eye right now is predatory and alarming. He pours himself a scotch and takes a seat next to me. He stares at me as he takes a drink, swirling the liquid around in his glass. "So...I called you here because I need you."

"What's new?" I cheekily say, lifting my glass to my lips. I drink and watch him over the rim.

He smirks at my snark. "I have a meeting set for Thursday afternoon. I want you there by my side. Showing everyone that we are the King and Queen of Chicago."

"I'm busy," I tell him, looking at my nails as if I'm bored, but in reality, I'm shitting bricks right now. This is what Cox warned me to stay away from not one hour ago. I need to get out of this but if I refuse, he'll know something is up. I'm so screwed and not in the fun, sweaty, naked way.

"Yeah, you're busy...with me." His tone is harsh and unnerving. "I need my queen with me at this meet, and if you want to keep being my queen, you'll be there."

The look in his eyes is scary. I've never seen him like this before. "Fine," I relent. "I'll be there." *Shit. Shit. Shit.*

"Like you had a choice." He places his hand on my thigh and squeezes tightly. I can feel his sinister gaze on me. "Are you hiding something from me, Sugar?"

Swallowing the sip I just took, I turn my head and stare into his eyes and smile sweetly. Leaning into him, I whisper, "Wouldn't you like to know?" Placing my glass on the coffee table, I stand and shuffle past him to head toward the bathroom.

My heart is pounding so loud that I don't hear Kye sneak up behind me. He roughly grabs the back of my shoulder and spins me to face him. His face is red with anger, "You may be my queen, but I am the fucking king. I can take you out whenever I want." He pulls me closer to him, one hand on my hip and the other now gripping my throat. His fingers dig into my skin and I can feel his breath on my face. He licks from my jawbone and up my cheek. "Maybe I need to fuck some sense into you, huh, Sugar, would you like that?"

"Please," I beg, fear coursing through my veins and for the first time since starting this undercover gig, I fear for my life.

He smirks, taking my plea as I want him, not that I want him to let me go. "You want my cock sliding into your cunt? Or maybe your mouth? Or if I remember correctly, you love a good ass fucking." He slides his hand from my hip to my ass, rubbing his finger along my ass crack, squeezing my asscheek roughly. The grip on my throat tightens. It's becoming hard to breathe, spots begin to dot my vision. "Is that what you want, Sugar? You want my cock in your ass while I finger your cunt?"

My eyes well with tears and fear bubbles throughout my body. I'm on the verge of passing out when he loosens his grip, but he's still choking me. "Please, Kye," I beg again. "I'm with you one-hundred-percent." I swallow deeply and fasten my gaze on him. I stare into his dead, evil black eyes. "I warned you about Creed. I warned you that he was unstable, and look, three days before the biggest meeting since you took over, your right-hand man gets arrested." He lets my throat go, and on instinct I lift my hand and rub. "I'm with you, Kye, one hundred and ten percent. I always have been and always will be. The fact you don't realize that, hurts. Maybe I'm not your queen after all."

Straightening my dress, I turn around, and with my head held high, I walk toward the exit. Once outside, I run over to my car. Unlocking the door, I climb in and grab my phone. I unlock it and send a message to the one person I need right now.

14
COREY

My phone pings with a text. I drop my pen, pick it up, and unlock the
screen. Opening my messages, I read.

> **BAYLOR -** *I need to see you.*
> **BAYLOR -** *NOW!*

I stare at her texts and that rumbling in my gut feeling from the other
day returns with a vengeance. My fingers slide over the screen and I
immediately text her back.

> **COREY -** *When and where?*
> **BAYOR -** *The apartment. Now.*
> **COREY -** *See you there.*

Closing my laptop, I grab my things and race to the parking lot to drive
over to Baylor and Avery's. She pulls up at the same time as I do, and I
don't like the look on her face.

Climbing out, I yell, "Baylor!" She looks up at me and smiles, but it
isn't her usual bright smile. Walking toward her, I stop in front of her but
before I can speak, she says.

"I'm scared, Cox. I don't think I can do this. I…"

"Kitten," I cup her cheek, "I won't let anything happen to you." I pause "Do you trust me?" She nods her head. "Good, then trust me. Let's go upstairs and we can talk."

She nods again. Like a robot on autopilot, we head inside the building and up to the apartment. We enter and Baylor heads straight to the kitchen, she grabs a bottle of tequila, pulls off the cap, and chugs. She bites her lip and stares at nothing.

"Kitten, you're scaring me. What happened?" She looks at me, but doesn't say anything; her silence is unnerving. "Baylor!" I shout and that garners her attention.

"You called me Baylor."

"That's your name."

"You either call me Kitten or Ms. Evans." She pauses and bites her lip. "I really like the way you say my name. The way your tongue wraps around the 'lor' is refreshing."

"That's great but what's got you so freaked? We met not three hours ago."

"Kye, he, umm, he choked me." Her hand instinctively goes to her neck and she rubs it. "He…he threatened me."

"I'm pulling you out now. This is over."

"No!" she shouts, shaking her head. "I can do this. I just had to get out of there. I…I need…can…can you hold me?"

Without missing a beat, I step over to her and wrap my arms around her shoulders. She slides hers around my waist and holds on for dear life. Her body is shaking but all I can think about is how great she feels in my arms right now. She sniffles. "Are you crying?"

She shakes her head. "No, I think I'm allergic to you." She lifts her head and pushes away from me. Immediately, I feel the loss of her and I don't like it. We stare at one another. The air around us heating and sizzling, but the next words out of her mouth freeze me to my core. "I'll be at the meeting this Thursday by his side. As his queen."

"I said no." My voice is loud and takes on an authoritative tone.

"Well, he said I needed to be there and after being choked an hour ago, I'll be there." She lifts her hand to her neck and runs her fingers back and forth across her skin. She looks me dead in the eye and my Kitten's spark is back. "Deal with it, Cox." She continues to stare at me, her gaze egging me to snap and say something, but I refuse to give in to her. "What? Got nothing to say?" she taunts. "The Almighty Agent Cox is speechless. First time for everything." Just like that, sassy Baylor is back and truth be told, I now want to strangle her, after I sink myself balls deep inside of her.

She's always defying me. Pushing me but I still want her. Lifting my gaze back to hers and even though she's being tough right now, I see vulnerability and fear reflecting in her eyes.

"Kitten, what happened after you left here?"

She swallows deeply. She licks her lips and stares into nothing. "When I got to the warehouse, Monica was there. I really cannot stand that skank. She got my hackles up, and then Kye and I got into it. He demanded I be there. At first I refused, your words were ringing in my head, but he wasn't taking no for an answer. I relented." She pauses. "Then he asked if I was hiding something. I don't think I hesitated but Kye is good at reading people. He didn't like my answer and that's when he choked me. I managed to convince him I was Team Kye, we kissed and made up." I growl at hearing she kissed him again. "Down, boy, it's a figure of speech. I managed to get him back onside but I had to get out of there. I wanted to see you." She quietly adds, "I needed you."

"Are you okay?" This is a side of Baylor I've never seen before, she's normally ball-busting, taking shit from no one, but right now, she's the complete opposite of that.

She turns her gaze to me. "I'm ready for this to be over."

"After Thursday, it will be. Thankfully, we have time to work on you and your safety into the plan. Nothing will happen to you, I promise. We want Vlahos only. We will need to arrest you to keep up appearances, but I'll be the one to cuff you."

"Kinky," she teases, "I never picked you as a deviant but then again, it's always the ones you least expect." And just like that, my Kitten is back. She jumps up on the countertop and winks at me. My cock twitches when she does this. *What is this woman doing to me?* "Should I bring my own cuffs, or will you supply them?"

Suddenly, I get a vision of Baylor cuffed to my bed. She's wearing a sexy virginal white lace bra and panty set. She looks like an angel, but in reality, she's the devil in disguise. "Yo, Cox. Earth to Cox."

Her voice snaps me away from my dirty thoughts. "Sorry, what?" I reply like a loser.

"Where did you go just now?"

"Trying to work out the best way to keep you safe," I tell her, impressed with myself for coming up with the ruse so quickly.

"I will be safe, won't I?" She looks down at the floor, swinging her legs back and forth to keep herself grounded.

Placing my finger under her chin, I lift her gaze to mine. "I will do everything in my power to keep you safe, Kitten."

"I know you will," she quietly murmurs, giving me a small smile. Her voice is soft, something you don't often hear from the firecracker that is Baylor Evans.

We stare intently at one another. A force takes over my body and I step closer to her. Nudging her legs apart, I step between them and reach up to cup her cheek in my hand. She leans into my palm and nuzzles into it. Turning her head, she places a kiss on my skin. Her lips are warm and silky soft. She reaches up and cups my cheek like I did to her. I too turn my head and kiss her palm.

With our hands cupping each other's cheek, we continue to stare at one another, the temperature in the kitchen rising with each passing second. Our breathing becomes labored and my cock is already at half-mast and we haven't even done anything yet. Her tongue darts out and she licks her bottom lip then bites it. "Fuck it," I whisper.

Gripping both her cheeks in my palms, I press my lips to hers. She drapes her arms over my shoulders and pulls me into her, deepening our kiss and connection. She wraps her leg around my waist. I can feel the heat of her pussy. She moans into my mouth and my cock is now standing at full attention.

Sliding my hand down her body, her nipples pebble from my touch but I keep moving south. Pushing up the material of her dress, I slip my hand between her thighs and cup her mound. Her panties are soaked with her arousal. I rub her through the material as I continue to kiss her. Our tongues sliding in and out of each other's mouth's.

Pulling her panties to the side, I slide my finger between her lips and my eyes widen when I feel the metal ring on her clit. *I can't wait to play with that*, I think to myself as I push two fingers deep inside her.

"Cox," she mewls against my lips, as I continue to thrust my fingers in and out of her.

Pulling my lips away from hers, I watch as she falls apart. Her walls clench around my fingers and when I press my thumb against her clit, she cries out as she climaxes. She falls back against the countertop and rides out the rest of her release.

Removing my fingers, I bring them to my lips and lick her juices off them. "You have the sweetest tasting pussy, Kitten. A man could become addicted."

She sits up and stares at me. Without saying a word, she slides off the counter and drops to her knees. She lifts her hands and I watch as she undoes my belt, flicks open the button, and lowers the zipper of my slacks. She slips beneath the waistband and grips my cock in her tiny hand, squeezing and tugging as she pulls it out. The head is angry, purple, and dripping with precum. She licks her lips and with her eyes locked on mine, she opens her mouth and sucks me like a lollipop. Her tongue swirls around the tip before she swallows me whole. She opens her throat and takes me deep into her mouth.

"Your mouth is like heaven," I groan, threading my fingers into her hair. I guide her head back and forth. The image of her sucking my dick is so much better in reality. Much sooner than I would like, my balls begin to tingle. "I'm about to come," I incoherently mumble, this is the best BJ in history of BJs. Her head bobs faster, my legs stiffen, and I come down her throat. She grips my asscheeks and sucks every last drop from me.

My cock pops out of her mouth, and she wipes at the corner, seductively sucking her finger. "Mmmmm," she moans.

Standing up, she stares into my eyes. I know I should feel bad about what just happened since I'm her handler but I don't. What does surprise me is her reaction. "I think you should go. I need to focus," she says. "I need you to go."

Cutting her off, I put my finger to her lips and nod. "I'll go. Baylor—"

"You called me Baylor, again," she says.

"That is your name."

She shakes her head, "You said that earlier too—" The moment is interrupted when the front door opens, "Bay, I'm home!" Avery yells out.

"Shit," I curse. I jump back and quickly put my cock away and rezip my pants.

Baylor laughs and sings out, "In here." My eyes widen at her response. Just as I've fixed my pants, Avery steps into the kitchen.

"Ohh, hi, Agent Cox."

"Corey is just fine and hello to you too, Ms. Evans."

"Well, if I can call you Corey, you can call me Avery."

"Hi, Avery," I say to her before turning to face Baylor. She's sitting back up on the counter, swinging her legs back and forth without a care in the world. She's grinning like the cat who caught the canary, me being the canary. She raises her eyebrows at me in that smart-ass way I'm coming to love. "Kitten, I'll be in touch once I have a plan formulated. Stay safe."

Reaching out, I squeeze her knee. We stare at each other for a few heartbeats and then I turn around to leave. Smiling at Avery on my way past, I exit the apartment and let out a deep breath.

Climbing into my car, I lean my head back and close my eyes. What the fuck have I just done?

15
BAYLOR

"Sooo, how was your day?" Ave teases, jumping up onto the counter next to me. She rests her head on my shoulder and I lean into her. I think about her question and internally laugh. Today has been crazy and chaotic, just another day in the life of Bailey Martine Evans.

"Long. Interesting. Frightening." *Erotic*, I silently add. "Take your pick."

She lifts her head and turns to look at me, her face etched with worry. I know these past few months have been tough on her but I'm happy she has Flynn. I'm glad that my actions didn't ruin that for her. Apart from the worry, I haven't see her happy like this in a very long time. "Why was it frightening?" She reaches over and squeezes my hand in that concerned sisterly way. Looking down at our joined hands, I take a deep breath and I tell her everything that transpired today.

"You gave him a blow job in our kitchen?"

"That's what you are focusing on with regard to everything that I just said?"

"I'll circle back to the rest. I want to know how you go from formulating a plan to bring down a drug kingpin to both of you going down on one another?"

"This is me, why are you surprised?"

"Touché." She nods, "So how did it happen?"

"Well, my mouth sucked his dick like it was a lollipop and he ate my vagina like a starved man."

"Crass much, Bay?"

"What can I say, Cress is rubbing off on me."

"More like you were rubbing one off on him."

"Avery Evans, I have never heard you speak so crassly before, I'm impressed."

"What can I say, Cress is rubbing off on me." We both laugh. "But seriously, Bay, how did that happen? I thought you hated him?"

"I do, he's a straitlaced dick with a stick up his ass. Always doing the right thing. Always riding my ass but..."

"But what?"

"But I can't stop thinking about him. He's fucking hot in that suit and his dick, fuck, Ave, it's the most beautiful one I've ever seen."

"Dicks are ugly."

"Not this one," I say, a goofy grin on my face as I think back to his dick in my hand and mouth.

"Okay, so he's hot with a beautiful dick and he pisses you off. Sounds like the start of a beautiful love story to me."

"Pffft, I never said I was in love with him."

"No, but you are falling for him."

I've already fallen, I silently say. "Doesn't matter, we can never be. We are too different."

"Flynn and I are different."

"We are different in that I'm a lawbreaker and he's a lawmaker. Can't get more different than that."

"You're not a criminal."

"Tell that to my record," I snap at Ave, my voice harsher than I intended but regardless, Corey and I can never be. "I just need to finish this thing and then forget I ever met Corey Cox."

"If that's what you want but for what it's worth, I don't think that is what you want."

A laugh escapes me, "Ave, I don't know what I want."

"There's plenty of time to figure it out." We both fall silent and I think about what she said. However, time is not my friend, if this all goes to plan, by the end of the week this case will be wrapped up, and Corey will move onto the next case, and I'll be off to jail.

Ave jumps off the counter and breaks the silence, "It's Wine Wednesday, let's see if we can come up with a plan over a bottle of red."

"Ave, I don't think wine will fix this but I'm happy to give it a shot."

"No, we don't shoot wine, we sip it and savor it."

"I'm not posh, Ave. Hell, give me a wine box, a straw, and I'm good to go."

She snort-laughs as she reaches into the wine fridge, grabbing a bottle of red, while I jump down and grab two glasses. She opens the bottle and pours two generous glasses. Handing me mine, her face shines brightly. "Cheese, we need cheese."

"Yes, nothing beats wine and cheese."

Like a well-oiled machine, Ave and I put together a kick-ass cheese platter. With our wine and platter in hand, we head into the living room. We both sit down and in sync, we tuck our legs under ourselves and snuggle back. I look over at Ave and realize she and I are in a good place. "I'm glad we're back on track," I tell her.

"Me too," she says. "I thought I'd lost you there for a while, but who knew that a mafia drug dude would bring us back together?"

"At least Kye is good for something." Taking a sip, I sigh.

"It's a good vintage, hey?" Ave says, mistaking my dejected sigh as a sigh of appreciation for the cab merlot.

"It is, but that's not what the sigh was for."

"Wanna talk about it?"

"What's there to talk about?"

"Whatever's bothering you."

"I...I feel..."

Ave leans forward and places her glass on the coffee table, then she scoots closer to me, and takes my hand in hers. She squeezes it reassuringly. "Bay, let it all out. Just spew the words; maybe you don't need advice. Maybe you just need to get it all out."

"Spew the words, so eloquent." She eyes me in that mom/teacher way and I think, *Fuck it.* Taking a huge gulp of wine I purge it all out. "I'm scared that once this is all over, I'm going to get into trouble again. I'm annoyed Kye isn't who I thought he was, and I'm sad that come Thursday, I'll never see Corey again. You're right, I *have* fallen for the straitlaced sexy agent but because I'm me, we can never be. And I'm concerned that when I do my time, I'm going to fall into the wrong crowd and be led astray again. I don't want to turn into Bitchy Baylor again. I want to be Badass Brilliant Baylor."

"Do you want advice? Or were you just venting?"

"Will I like the advice you give me?"

She shrugs at me and makes a face. "Just then you remind me of Porky from *The Little Rascals* when he shrugs."

"I made Flynn watch that recently, he'd never seen it before."

"What? How can he not have seen that movie?"

"I know, right? I rectified that...with red wine and sexy naked times."

"Avery Evans, you dirty, dirty girl...I'm so proud of you, joining the dirty side."

"You sound like Cress. She called me skank-hopper the weekend I met Flynn."

"Skank-hopper, I love that." I look to Ave, "Okay, yes, I do want advice. What do you have for me?"

"Step one. Drink more wine." She leans forward, tops up our glasses, and hands me mine. After she settles back into the sofa, she looks at me. "It's one thing at a time. First, bring down Kye and get rid of him. Put him in the 'later mater, nice knowing you' pile. Then you do your time. Twelve months isn't all that long. When you get out, look up Agent Cox and see what fate has to say."

"So I basically leave it up to fate then?"

"Pretty much. If it's meant to be with Cox, it will be."

"Well, that's not an easy fix."

"Life isn't easy, Bay, and the sooner you realize that, the sooner you'll find your own happiness."

"When did you get so wise?"

"I've always been wise."

"No one likes a gloater."

She sticks out her tongue at me and I can't help but laugh. Taking a sip of my wine, I think about what she said. This path to redemption is long and arduous, there's no quick fix. I wonder if I will ever get my happily ever after? Or if I'm destined to be alone for life since I'm such a screw up. Whether it be with Cox or someone I haven't met yet, I hope it's not too late for me.

16
COREY

TODAY IS THE DAY I BRING DOWN KYE VLAHOS AND RATHER THAN EXCITEMENT for this, I'm upset that today will be the last time I see Baylor. That woman has wormed her way into my heart. Her frustrating, snarky, foul mouth has grown on me. A knock on my door snaps my head up and I smile. "Charli Davis, what the hell are you doing here?" I say as I walk over to her and wrap my arms around her.

"Dean and I are here finalizing the details for the Underdown trial."

"Bet you'll be glad to see the backend of that case. It was a never-ending shitshow."

"Tell me about it. Thankfully, the ducks were finally in a row and the case closed itself. Now we can hand Underdown over to the prosecution and we can move on to the next case."

"Any idea on what that is?"

"Nah, not yet but I'm sure the next person needing protection will be just as lovely as him."

Charli and I went through the academy together. If ever I were to work with a partner, it would be her. She's a ball-buster but she gets the job done. She's the best WitSec handler there is. She's never lost a witness under her watch.

"Got time for a coffee?" I ask her.

"Sure, Dean is catching up with a detective buddy of his, so I've got a few."

"Sweet." We walk toward to break room and I fill her in on the Vlahos case, leaving out my feelings, or whatever they are, for Baylor Evans. Just as we've sat down, her partner, Dean Chikatilo, walks up to us. "Let's roll," he rudely says, ignoring me. I'm not a fan of his and the feeling is mutual. Dean is a cowboy, how Charli puts up with him is beyond me but they seem to work well together.

She looks up. "Sure, give me a sec," she says to him. Looking back to me, she smiles. It's a megawatt Charli smile. "Good luck with the Vlahos takedown today. Seems your risky plan using Evans was a good move."

"I'm hurt you ever doubted me." I fake offense and she laughs.

"Everyone doubted you, Cox," Dean snarls, his gaze locked on me. "Using a junkie as your way in was stupid and fucked up, if you ask me."

"Not me," Charli interrupts, breaking the tension. "I was rooting for you and knew you could do it."

"Of course you were," Dean says, rolling his eyes. "Let's go." He turns and walks out without a goodbye.

"Bye, Dean," I quietly quip at his retreating form.

Charli laughs, "Thanks for the coffee. We should do drinks soon."

"A proper catch-up sounds good," I tell her.

"Awesome, let me know when and where. Later, Corey." She stands and walks out but pops her head back in. "For what it's worth, I would have done the same thing as you. You've got this, but good luck."

Before I can reply, she's gone again. Sitting here, I stare into my mug and shake my head. The end is here and rather than focusing on the game plan for today, I keep thinking about her. If I lose focus, everything I've worked toward is going to come crashing down and it will all be for nothing. I need to put Baylor Evans out of my mind and focus. My goal is to bring down Kye Vlahos and see him behind the bars for the rest of his life, not get the girl...but is there a way to do both?

BAYLOR

My mind is all over the place today. I'm so nervous I want to vomit. Kye keeps staring at me and it's making my skin crawl. I wish I could hug Ave one last time because I have a feeling that after today, I'm never going to see her again. We said our goodbyes this morning after our wine and movie night. Not only did we watch *The Little Rascals*, we also watched *Ten Things I Hate About You* and *Empire Records*. We stayed up later than called for mid-week, but it was what Ave and I, especially me, needed. When she left for work this morning, we hugged each other tighter than usual. I was glad when she said she'd be with Flynn for the next few days. With everything that's about to go down, I don't want her anywhere near the apartment…or me.

Kye growling my name snaps me back to the present. I shake my head, trying to clear the fog. "Sorry, what?"

"Where's your head at? You've been aloof for the last few days."

"Just tired," I offer with a smile that's one-million-percent fake than fake smile. "Didn't sleep much last night."

"You worried, Sugar?"

Nodding my head, I decide to go with honesty. "Yes, I am. I don't want to be there today—" he goes to interrupt but I stand up, walk over to him, and press my finger to his lips, "but I promised I would and as your queen, I'll be there. Not sure what my presence will accomplish but a promise is a promise."

"And that's why you're my queen." The anger from the other day is gone and replaced is the arrogant egotistical Kye Vlahos that we all know and hate. "You know, you can have a more active role if you wish. I'd give you anything, Baylor." He cups my cheek in a loving way. "One day, I hope we can get back to where we were before I set all of this in motion. Sugar, I know my death affected you and I'm sorry I did that but at the same time, I'm not because now...now I can give you the world. After today, the city will be ours. I want to share and bask in this glory with you."

Staring at him, my heart begins to race; this feels like a do-or-die moment. You know that moment in the movie when it's all about to change, that's what this feels like, but in reality, the decision is not so easy to make. With what's being offered, the old me would have jumped at the chance to be Queen Bitch: ruler of the city with minions at my beck and call. Without blinking, I would have shoved anyone in my way to the side and stomped on them. The new me, however, she's hesitant but Kye is literally offering me the world and that's kind of hard to resist.

He grips my chin and lifts my gaze to his. He stares intently at me and something passes between us. My hatred toward him begins to thaw. Those feelings from before surface and slam into me like a tidal wave. My heart begins to beat faster. My skin heating at his touch. "Will you rule by my side? Be the queen you were born to be?"

Without any hesitation, I whisper, "Yes, I'll be your queen and together we will rule this city." As those words pass my mouth, a sinister smile appears on my face. With this decision made, I feel freer than I have in weeks. Bring. It. On.

When my words register, Kye, too, smiles. It sends shivers down my spine. He cups my cheek, "The city will be ours, My Queen." But like everything that is in my life, it all comes crashing down.

18
COREY

To say today was a clusterfuck is the understatement of the fucking century. I should have trusted my gut but no, I went with my heart and it nearly cost me everything.

Leaning back in my chair, I replay everything that happened in the last five hours…

…It's go time. My team and I are doing the final preparations before we leave to take down Kye Vlahos. Baylor has been silent for the last few days, and I have a sneaking suspicion that she's going to screw me over…and it's all because of me and my actions. After our last meeting, when things happened that should never have happened, it blurred the lines between us. I think it pushed things too far. There's a feeling deep in the pit of my stomach, yelling to me that something is amiss. And then there's my head, thinking about Baylor and her gorgeous fucking lips wrapped around my dick. And finally, we have my heart. It's beating with little love hearts for the blonde bombshell, who can never be anything more than my informant…and someone who gave me the best blow job of my life.

Shaking my head, I slip on my vest and look to my team. Charli and Dean are joining us since they are between cases. I'm happy to have them along with us because we need all the manpower we can.

Everyone's eyes are on me. "Let's do this," I declare to the team. "Our main objective is to bring Kye Vlahos to justice. If we can nab his cronies or those whom he's meeting with too, then great, but Vlahos is our main target. Baylor Evans needs to be kept safe if possible, she's been a great help in gathering this intel and I'd hate to see her hurt or killed."

"You sure we can trust the bitch?" Dean asks.

My hackles rise when he refers to her as a bitch. "Yes, we can. She hasn't indicated otherwise."

"That's not what Creed Dawson says."

"Why were you talking with him?"

"It doesn't concern you." His response doesn't sit well with me but I don't have time to dwell on him, or Dawson.

"Let's get in and out and hope that it's smooth."

"You just jinxed that," Charli adds, shaking her head as she fastens her vest.

"Wanna bet on it?"

"You bet. Less than five casualties, it's my shout. Anything above five, and it's your shout."

"You're on, Davis," I tell her, outstretching my hand to shake on it.

"You're going down, Cox."

After we seal our bet—with the others making bets of their own—we all file out and climb into the van. Looking around, I trust eight of the nine agents and officers in here. My eyes are locked on Dean, I hate that fucker but he's Charli's partner. She wouldn't work with someone she doesn't trust, and I trust her with my life so I have to trust he has our backs too.

We pull up across the road from the meeting, it's being held at a restaurant in Little Italy just off Sheridan Park. We watch as multiple crime bosses along the East Coast enter the restaurant one by one. If we can take them all down, it will be a great win for us, and a huge hit to the drug and trafficking trade on the East Coast.

A car with tinted windows pulls up and I know she's here. The door opens and a long slender leg appears and then she climbs out. She's a fucking knockout at the best of times but today, fuck me sideways, she looks like a queen. She's wearing sky-high black heels and a figure-hugging purple dress that accentuates each and every delectable curve. The neckline plunges and showcases her tits spectacularly. She walks around the back of the sedan and joins Vlahos on the sidewalk. He says something to her and she smiles at him. The look she gives him lights up her face and it hits me straight in the balls. A groan emits in the back of my throat. Charli looks at me questioningly and Dean, the fucking dick, smirks and not so subtly readjusts his cock.

Vlahos slips his arm around her waist and the two of them walk inside, along with his henchmen.

Grabbing my laptop, I log into the app for the recorder installed on Baylor's phone, and wait for it to connect. It's staticky at first and then I hear his voice and what he says has me clenching my fist and grinding my molars, that is until Baylor replies. "Kye, we are here to discuss business not how fucking fabulous I look. Everyone in this room knows I'm hot and in a few moments, they will feel my wrath if they don't stop eye fucking me, you included. Now, everyone take their fucking seats and let's get started."

"She's a firecracker," Charli says, and I find myself nodding.

"You have no clue, Davis."

Chuckles erupt from my team, most of them were there the day Baylor was brought in and I floated this plan with the captain. They all thought I was crazy, hell, most of them still think I'm crazy, but if this all goes down how I hope today, my crazy plan will have paid off.

"When are we going in, boss?" Coombs asks.

"Let's wait and see what this meeting is all about. Plus, backup is still not here."

"Cox will know when," Charli says. "His instinct is always on point."

Looking to Charli, I nod. I'm glad she's here today; she will ground me and keep me in line. Her faith in me restores my confidence this will work out. Heat sensors show they are all congregated in the back of the restaurant in the large private dining room, making our entrance that much easier and more of a surprise.

Kye introduces everyone to his queen, and now that the introductions have been made, they start discussing business. Kye really is a piece of shit, someone in that room might take him out before we get in there.

All eyes are on me, awaiting the go signal. Backup still isn't here but I don't want to miss my chance. I have a good team, minus Dean, so I make the decision to move. "Remember, Vlahos is the main target. Anyone else we detain is a bonus and don't forget, Baylor Evans is technically one of ours."

Everyone nods in agreement and with that, it's time for me and my team to make our presence known. "Let's move."

The ten of us file out of the van. Two head left, two head right. The restaurant has no back access so that makes things easier for us. The remaining five and I head toward the front entrance. Dean is the first to shoot when two men exit the restaurant. He pops them both off, one after the other. He looks at me in that smarmy 'you're welcome' way.

"That's two," Charli says with a wink, as she and Dean fall into sync and enter the restaurant before me. Following each other's lead, I notice they work well together. Stepping over the bodies Dean dropped, I enter the behind them.

We fan out and approach the rooms at the back. My heart is racing. I've been involved in many sting operations but this one is the first time where I'm nervous and on edge. Our plan is rock-solid; the only variable is Baylor-fucking-Evans.

456   DL GALLIE

The teams outside radio in and tell us they are in place, they are our backup in case Vlahos escapes. There are two entrances into the room, which is perfect for us. Looking at everyone, I raise my hand and indicate on three. I flick up one finger and when all three are up, I indicate it's go time.

Raising my leg, I kick open the door and step into the room.

"What the fuck?" Vlahos snarls, just as the back door to the room is also kicked in. The six of us have our guns pointed toward him. There are eight men sitting down, plus Baylor. Kye is standing at the head of the table; his face is laced with shock right now. He draws his weapon as he steps over to Baylor and places his hand on her shoulder. He squeezes it, she looks up at him lovingly, and that one look guts me. He leans down and presses a kiss to her temple. It seems the prick really does care about her, or it's a ploy and he'll use her to protect himself. But from the look she's giving him in return, it seems like she cares for him too. I'm really hoping that it's all an act. That she's a really good actress and playing the doting girlfriend role.

Snapping my attention back to him, I clear my throat. "Kye Vlahos, you are under arrest for drug trafficking, human trafficking, and murder."

"Like you have shit on me, pig," he spits at me. "I suggest you turn around and walk out of here. That way we can pretend you didn't just interrupt this reunion, and everyone can go on their merry way."

All eyes in the room are flicking between the two of us. My gaze keeps dropping to Baylor but I try and maintain eye contact with Vlahos. "Yeah, that's not going to happen. Now we can do this the easy way, or the hard way. Choice is yours."

"I'm going to have so much fun," Kye says, his voice a sinister tone and I know that this is all about to turn to shit, and shit is an understatement. Kye pulls the trigger and that sets off a chain reaction of gunfire. Even through all the gunfire, I hear Baylor's screams.

Without thinking, I rush forward but I'm stopped when Vlahos raises his arm and presses the barrel of his gun to my head. On instinct, I raise my arm and point my pistol at him. Each of us staring the other down. The room falls silent; all eyes are on us. Baylor crawls out from under the table. She stands up and when she turns around, she gasps in shock. Her eyes dart back and forth between us.

A lone gunshot cracks through the air. My eyes widen and the next moments are played out in an ultraslow motion. Baylor screams as Vlahos falls to the floor, clutching his shoulder. Baylor drops to her knees and presses her hand to his shoulder. "Kye, no-no-no," she cries, tears cascading down her cheeks. She isn't faking her concern for him. She looks over the table and stares at someone. Turning my head, I see Dean standing there, arms still outstretched. He has a smirk on his face and then he pulls the trigger again. I feel the bullet fly past my head with millimeters to spare and a grunt emanates from behind me.

Turning my head, I see one of Vlahos' henchmen fall to the ground at my feet. A knife slipping out of his hand as his lifeless eyes stare up at me. A bullet hole in the center of his forehead.

"You shot him," *Baylor cries over and over. Her hands are covered in blood when they come back up, an agent pulls her away kicking and screaming. They cuff her and that's when she really lets loose.* "Get the fuck off me," *she screams,* "you fucking dicks."

I growl as I walk over to her, she's using excessive language right now but I guess it plays into her cover.

"Fuck you," *she spits at me* "Fuck you all."

Kye groans and her eyes snap to his. "Help him, you fuckers. He's been shot."

Her concern for him pisses me off. "Get her out of here," *I tell the officer who cuffed her. He nods at me and without a word, escorts a still screaming Baylor out of here.*

Walking over to Kye, I drop to my knees. "Seems your day didn't quite go as planned."

"You are a fucking dead man. You hear me? You're fucking dead."

"We'll see about that." *A paramedic arrives and Kye is placed on the stretcher and cuffed to the bed rail. He's escorted out of here with two officers. I look around at the carnage. We lost two agents today. With the two outside and the one in here, a total of five people lost their lives, but we arrested Vlahos and all eight of his guests.*

Kye is wheeled past and I taunt him, "Don't drop the soap."

He flips me the bird and is escorted out of the restaurant.

"Great job," *Charli says to me as she leans against the table.* "You got him."

Nodding my head in agreement, I remind, "We got him."

"Then why do you look like your kitten just died?"

My head snaps up at her choice of words because it does feel like my kitten died. She was absolutely distraught over Kye and that cuts me to the core, more than I would like to admit. Not wanting to discuss this, I go with the obvious answer. "Paperwork."

"Ugh, paperwork," *she says, nodding her head.* "So it seems after all the paperwork," *she whispers the word paperwork,* "you owe me a night out."

"It seems I do but you totally cheated."

"How so?"

"Your partner killed three of them, you had inside help."

"Yes, because Dean and I colluded together for me to win a night out at your expense."

"See, I knew it." We both laugh. *"How about I finish this paperwork back at the office and tonight we head out."*

"Sounds good to me."

We both exit the restaurant and head back to the precinct.

…and that brings me to now.

The paperwork is completed. All my I's dotted and all my T's are crossed. Kye Vlahos is behind bars and will be for a very long time. I should be over the moon that this is over, but all I feel is sadness at never seeing Baylor again. By the time I got back to the precinct, she'd already been processed and was on her way to The Metropolitan Correctional Center.

I will never see Baylor Evans again, and that upsets me more than it should.

19
BAYLOR

CLIMBING OUT OF THE CAR, I CAN FEEL EYES ON ME—COX IS HERE. IT'S comforting knowing he is but at the same time, I'm shit fucking scared for what's about to transpire. Stepping onto the sidewalk, I look up and see Kye eye fucking me. My body heats from the intensity of his gaze. I smile seductively at him. He steps to me and slides his hand around my waist. "Fuck, you are a vision. My cock is throbbing at the sight of you in this dress."

"Well, let's get this over with and then..." I don't finish that sentence because there will be no after if all goes according to the plan. Kye licks his lips and we make our way inside. I look over my shoulder and up at the sky. It's clear blue, not a cloud in sight. Taking a deep breath, I hope I will see daylight again.

We enter the dark and dimly lit restaurant and a feeling of dread develops in the pit of my stomach, but I push it aside and follow Kye into a banquet room in the back. As soon as we enter, all conversation stops. Every head turns to face us. All eyes roam over me as if I'm a piece of meat. I remember the time Kye called, demanding I dress like a whore, and I smile at how far we've come. I look to him and I see the power emitting from him. He was born to lead. He's thriving as the head of the Vlahos family and if today goes according to plan, he will be THE head honcho of the East Coast. Watch out world, Kye-fucking-Vlahos is coming.

But then I wonder, can I stand by him and watch what he does? The drugs I can handle, but it's the human trafficking and the murder I can't deal with.

He slides his hand around my waist and I'm snapped back to the present. He squeezes my hip in a possessive way and it reminds me of Cox the other night when he pushed me back to the counter and went down on me. I shudder at the memory and clench my thighs to ease the throb.

Fuck, how can I be thinking of that, and him, right now?

Looking over to Kye, I focus on him. "Gentleman, I give you Baylor Evans. My. Queen. Isn't she gorgeous?"

A murmur of agreements and head nods come from the men before us. *Pussies,* I think to myself as I raise my hand to silence them. "Kye, we are here to discuss business, not how fucking fabulous I look. Everyone in this room knows I'm hot and in a few moments, they will feel my wrath if they don't stop eye fucking me," turning to face Kye, I add, "you included. Now, everyone take their fucking seats and let's get started."

Pulling away from him, I take my seat, lean back and look around the room. These eight men are the evilest of the evil and each one of them deserves everything that will be coming through that door any moment now. I sit and listen to Kye ramble on and I come to the realization that he is just as evil as them, if not more so. He killed his own family to get where he is, there's nothing more despicable than that. I wonder if he will do that to me too, if I piss him off?

"My queen has a point," Kye says, leaning on the table. "We are here because I have a proposition for you all. As you know, I have recently taken over as head of the Vlahos family—"

"Rumor has it," a man to my left interrupts, "you killed them, including your own mother, to get this position of power. I speak for myself when I say, I'm not comfortable with that."

"And what proof do you have for this rumor?" Kye asks him pointedly. He's met with silence. "Exactly. It's all hearsay."

"Then why did you fake your death?" another asks.

"Because I didn't want to end up dead like them."

The room falls silent as everyone processes his words or should I say lies. For crooks, I can't believe they cannot smell the bullshit coming from Kye's mouth right now. *Fucking idiots.*

Before any more can be said, the door to the room is kicked open. The cracking of the wood startles me and Kye growls, "What the fuck?" Just as the other door is also kicked in. His eyes widen as six agents storm into the room. All six of them ignore every other person in the room and have their guns pointed toward Kye.

A hand squeezes my shoulder and when I look up, I see Kye, too, has his gun drawn. A fake smile is still on my face, and he glances down at me and winks. He thinks this is all a joke. I'm scared shitless right now but I cannot remove the smile from my face. I'm frozen with fear.

At the sound of Cox's voice, I turn my head and stare at him. He's all decked out in his combat gear and holy fucking hotness, Batman. A man in uniform is hot, but a man in combat gear, fuck, it sets my insides ablaze. He's focused on Kye and from next to me, I can feel the anger and rage building within Kye. He's on the edge, one wrong move and this is going to end in a gunfight, I don't have a good feeling for Cox and his team.

Kye antagonizes Cox. "Like you have shit on me, pig. I suggest you turn around and walk out of here. That way we can pretend you didn't just interrupt this reunion, and everyone can go on their merry way."

The room is silent, except for the heavy breathing of every person. Everyone's eyes are darting between Kye and Cox. The barbs are tossed back and forth between the two of them and when Kye's tone turns sinister, I begin to inch toward the front of my seat. Ready to drop and hide. I didn't sign up for this and if I die today, I will be coming back to haunt Corey Cox for the rest of his days.

I'm not sure who fires first but after that first shot, a symphony of gunfire follows. Grunts and bodies collapse all around me. I'm not sure if they are dropping from being shot or from hiding.

Dropping to the floor, I cover my head and crawl under the table. Curling into a ball, I make myself as small as possible. Someone is screaming and then I realize, it's me. Fear courses through my veins. My is heart racing, beating loud and fast in my ears.

Opening my eyes, I see legs moving but they stop suddenly and the room falls silent. A few seconds ago, it was chaos, and now, nothing. Taking a few deep breaths, I crawl out from under the table and when my eyes land on the standoff between Kye and Cox, I gasp in shock. I don't want either one of them to get hurt, but I know that one of them will not be walking out of here alive.

It all happens so fast, yet at the same time, so slow. Kye drops to the ground, clutching his shoulder. His eyes wide open with shock. Dropping to my knees, I crawl over to him. "Kye, no-no-no," I cry, as I press my hand to the bullet wound. Deep red blood stains his shirt. I've never seen blood up close before, it's definitely not like it is in the movies.

Lifting my head, I glance over the table and I see an agent with his arms raised. My eyes widen as realization hits that he's going to kill Cox. My heart begins to race at the thought of Cox getting shot. He pulls the trigger, and I wait for Cox to collapse to the ground but to my surprise, one of Kye's men grunts and drops to the ground before me.

His eyes are vacant, staring into nothing. A trickle of blood drips down his nose from the single bullet hole in the center of his forehead.

Kye groans and my attention snaps back to him. Gently I lift his head and cradle it in my lap. Over and over I repeat, "You shot him." My cries becoming louder and louder. Someone grips my arms and lifts me into a standing position. Kye's head drops to the blood-stained carpet and he grunts again. My arms are twisted behind my back and I'm cuffed.

"Get the fuck off me," I scream and wriggle, "you fucking dicks."

I try to pull free of the officer but he's got me cuffed and in his grasp. I look at Cox; I want nothing more than to hug him, but as Ave reminded me, I need to pretend I don't know him. So I spit at him and growl, "Fuck you. Fuck you all."

Kye moans and my eyes drop to him. He deserves everything that's coming but no one deserves to be in pain, I'm guessing getting shot hurts like a bitch. "Help him, you fuckers. He's been shot," I cry again. "Please," I beg. "Help him."

Tears pour down my face as the adrenaline pumping around my body begins to fade. Lifting my gaze, my eyes meet Corey's but I don't see the man who cares about me. I don't see the man who made me come on his face the other day. All I see is a straitlaced professional agent.

The final knife to my heart is when I hear him say. "Get her out of here." Those five words hurt like a sledgehammer.

He won't meet my gaze and it seems he really did only want me for my help to get Kye. He doesn't care about me at all. I stupidly thought after the other night that when this was all over, we could try something but I guess, I was wrong.

The officer escorts me out of the restaurant and into an awaiting cruiser. I'm taken to the station and placed into a holding room. I hated being in this room a few months ago and I hate it even now. It's so cold and sterile. The door opens and a female officer walks in. "Baylor Evans?" she asks. It's on the tip of my tongue to say no and be a snarky bitch but I just nod at her. "You're being transferred in ten."

"Where's Cox?" I ask her.

"Not here. I will be processing your transfer to MCC."

"What the fuck is MCC?"

"The Metropolitan Correctional Center. It will be home for the next," she looks at the file in her hand, "twelve months for you, Ms. Evans."

"Can I see my sister before we go?"

She shakes her head, "I'm afraid not. Details will be passed on to your family regarding visitation in the coming weeks."

"Weeks?" I shout, my eyes well with tears at the thought of not seeing or speaking to Ave for a few weeks. "I need my sister," I blubber.

"I'm sorry."

"Well, can I see Cox then?"

"As I said, he's not here. If I see him, I'll let him know but he's currently out in the field."

"I fucking know that," I snap. "I was with him when this all went down. Don't you know who I am? What I did for you people?" I know I'm being a bitch right now, but this is all happening too fast. I knew it was going to happen but knowing and reality are two different things.

"Curb the language and your attitude, Ms. Evans. I'll be back to collect you soon."

The door closes and I mumble, "Fucking bitch." Her words remind me of Cox and I smile to myself. *Fucking Cox.*

Resting my head on the table, I sigh in defeat and begin to cry again. I did all of this for my freedom. Forgetting that before I get my freedom, I'll be locked away. Tears cascade down my cheeks as the reality of it all sets in. I'm upset I can't say goodbye to Ave. That I can't tell her my plan to cozy up to Kye and be his queen worked. I'm sad I won't get to see Corey again. That I can't see the joy on his face at getting the bad guy. That I won't get to kiss him again or sleep with him. I know we are different but we could work, if we tried.

Sitting up, I lean back in my chair and whisper, "Falling for Agent Cox was fucking stupid. I will never fall for a man again, it hurts too much when it turns to shit."

20
COREY

…twelve months later

A KNOCK AT MY DOOR HAS ME LIFTING MY HEAD AND GRINDING MY TEETH AT the interruption. That anger is put aside when I see the captain at my door. "Captain," I say in greeting. "What can I do for you?"

He walks in and takes a seat. From the look on his face, I know it's not going to be good. "I have some news," he tells me.

"Okay." His demeanor is scaring me. I begin to think that something has happened to Mom and Dad but if it were in regard to them, Aunt Bec would have called me.

"It's Vlahos," he says, his tone unnerving.

"What about the asshole?" His lawyer has been a douchebag this last twelve months. He's tried to have the charges dismissed multiple times but I have an ironclad case, and each time the DA and I get their motion for dismissal denied.

"He escaped."

"What the fuck," I shout. "How the fuck did that happen?"

"He was taken to hospital with suspected appendicitis and with the help of his associates on the outside, he escaped. He killed two officers and severely injured a nurse."

"Fuck me." Rubbing my forehead in frustration, I glance up and from the look on his face I can tell there's more. "Just spit the rest out."

"Creed Dawson was found dead in his cell a few moments ago."

"Fuck me," I groan, "and let me guess, it looks like a suicide but you and I both know it's not."

"Not this time, Cox. He was definitely murdered." He's still shuffling and I just know there's more. I wish he'd just spit to out.

"Why do I feel like there's more?"

"Because there is," he confirms.

"Shit comes in threes," I tell him, "What's the third shitastic news you have for me?"

"A note was found near Dawson's body. It was addressed to you and let's just say, it's very concerning."

"What did it say?"

"It said, 'Rats like to squeal. You and that bitch are going down.'"

"What bitch?" But as soon as I voice it, I know exactly who Vlahos is referring to, Baylor Evans.

"I'm guessing he's discovered Ms. Evans was helping you."

"Baylor-fucking-Evans, I thought I was rid of her," I tell him, but it's a lie, a big fucking lie. She's been on my mind every single day for the last twelve months. Hell, I even dream about her and have woken up on several occasions with a rock-hard dick. I'd either have to take a cold shower or whack one out just so I could get back to sleep. "Where is she right now?"

"Funny you should ask, she was released from prison today. The timing is quite the coincidence, if you ask me."

"Is she aware of the threat made?"

"Not as yet. I came to see you to get your opinion on what we do from here."

"Me? Why do I care what happens?"

"Because she was your informant. I thought—"

"No, no, I get it. I'll reach out to her and tell her to be careful."

"Maybe you should put someone on her. Just to be safe."

"I'm sure it'll all be fine. Let's just find this fucker and put him back where he belongs."

"Corey, you need to be careful, too. Don't go all cowboy on this."

"You first named me, you really are concerned."

"When a threat is made against one of my agents, you bet your fucking ass I'm concerned. Now, I want you to arrange surveillance for Ms. Evans and you need to go see her and give her a heads-up."

"Fine," I relent. "I'll get on it after I finish this report."

"Now, Cox. The timing of all of this is too much of a coincidence. My gut is telling me this is going to turn to shit and as I said, I refuse to lose an agent or informant."

The look on his face doesn't give me any room to negotiate, so I nod my head and begin to pack up, looks like I'll be seeing Ms. Evans once again.

BAYLOR

Today is the start of my new life...or so they say.

Today I'm being released from jail for my part in the drug sting. I'm not the same person I was when I first went in. Hell, I'm not the person I was before I went undercover. I'd heard stories that prison changes a person. I thought they were full of shit but once again, I was mistaken.

Don't get me wrong; I'm still a bitch. But now, I'm a lovable one. I still love all things purple and bagels with cream cheese are still THE best food items ever created in the history of foods...and grape taffy is life. But now, I have a future. I actually care about my future and have dreams. I want to work in a bar and I want to become a mixologist. I'm also looking forward to spending some time with Ave and her soon-to-be fiancé—that is if she says yes tonight.

Flynn came to visit me the other week. I was shocked when I walked into the visitors' room and saw him alone. At first I thought Ave was in the bathroom but when it became clear she wasn't, my thoughts turned to the worst. She was dead, or sick, or she was abducted by aliens. Thankfully, she was fine—no alien anal probing for her—and he was here to ask, well, tell me, he was going to propose. I squealed in delight, garnering odd looks from the guards, inmates, and their visitors.

Flynn really is the perfect person for my sister, sure they are polar opposites but as the saying goes 'opposites attract.' I nearly ruined that for them when I was in over my head, but I'm glad my meddling last year didn't wreck this for them.

That day still haunts me and I can never take it back, but I will spend the rest of my days making it up to my sister. I have a recurring dream of when Smallie and River kidnapped me from outside the hospital while Ave was recovering. The shrill sound of her screams as they drove off with me in the back of that van still haunt me, even when I'm awake…as does the last time I laid my eyes on Corey Cox.

He's the one who got away. Not that I stood a chance with him but now that I'm out, it's time to focus on me. Love will come when I least expect it.

Flynn and Ave walk back inside and the smile on my sister's face is the biggest I've ever seen, she's beaming. I don't think I've ever seen her so happy. Cress races over and hugs Ave and then grabs her hand to get a look at the rock on her finger. Flynn and Preston do the man hug thing and they both then join us. Preston embraces Ave, after a nudging from Cress

"So how long have you two been banging?" I ask Cress, just as she takes a sip of the celebratory champagne. She spits it everywhere and her eyes widen in surprise but before she can answer, Lexi comes racing over.

"Mommy, I need to go poo poo," she says, crossing her legs and rocking on the spot.

Quicker than I have ever seen someone move in regard to shit, Cress jumps up, grabs Lexi's hand, and escorts her down the hallway to the bathroom.

"Saved by the poop," I say to Preston, who I notice hasn't said a word. He neither confirmed nor denied my question and in my experience, when people are silent, they are trying to come up with a rebuttal.

"Bay," Ave says, "leave her alone. It's been a rough time for them—"

"Lexi is doing much better now," Preston interrupts. "Cress and I are watching her like a hawk. I won't miss anything like that again."

"Miss what?" I ask. I'm genuinely concerned 'cause Lexi is a kick-ass kid.

Ave looks to me. "I'll fill you in later." She turns back to Preston, who kinda looks like Channing Tatum. "Glad all is well."

Cress returns with Lexi, who now has a lollipop and my mouth waters. I haven't had candy in so long. My mind drifts to Laffy Taffy and as if she's a mind reader, Ave walks over to me with a rectangular box and a smile breaks out on my face. "Is that what I think it is?"

"It might be."

"You are the best sister, ever," I tell her, grabbing the box and ripping it open. Two-point-five seconds later, I'm popping a purple chewy candy into my mouth. I close my eyes and savor the flavor, as a moan breaks free.

"Would you like us to leave you and your candy alone?" Ave says.

Opening my eyes, I look up and see everyone is staring at me. "It's sooo good."

"That purple shit is nasty," Flynn says, "I much prefer the green ones."

"Nah uh, buddy. Purple all the way."

We all head outside to enjoy the rest of the evening. We drink champagne and eat our weight in hors d'oeuvres; the food is amazing. It sure beats prison food, I'm going to end up so fat from eating all the things I missed out on while being locked up.

Looking around, I smile. Flynn outdid himself. The patio has been transformed into a romantic oasis. There's no way Ave would say no. It's such a romantic scene, and my mind drifts to Corey Cox. I wonder what the straitlaced sexy asshole is up to right now. I'm brought back to the present when Cress, Preston, and Lexi announce they are leaving. They say their goodbyes and soon after, it's just Flynn, Ave, and me.

Tonight could not have been more perfect, even Cress wasn't as annoying as I used to find her to be. Seems getting laid has mellowed the bitch. My sister is still beaming, Flynn went all out with the proposal but Ave deserves that and so much more. It's funny, the old me would have been majorly pissed off that my release from the slammer was overshadowed by the proposal, but seeing the happiness on my twinsie's face warms my little dead black heart.

Deciding I need some air, I excuse myself and head downstairs. Exiting the elevator, I pause mid-step when I see *him* standing in the lobby. My heart stops beating, I'm shocked at seeing him here. After that day, I never thought I'd see him again. Over the last twelve months he has gotten sexier, if that's possible.

He stops in front of me and we stare at one another. The air around us simmers and raises the temperature in the lobby. He speaks first and the sound of his voice vibrates through my body. Every nerve ending sparks to life and my clit jumps and pulses like it's at a rave. Twelve months of no contact and two words almost bring me to my knees.

I'm so screwed.

22
COREY

"I'M NOT YOUR FUCKING KITTEN," SHE SPITS AT ME. MY EYES RAKE OVER HER body and she's just as sexy as I remember.

"For a woman, you have such a potty mouth." My gaze drops to her lips and I remember the feel of them pressed against mine. Wrapped around my cock. Even though that occurred over twelve months ago, my body remembers as if it happened just moments ago.

"Fuck you, asshole. I'm not your Kitten. Never was and never will be."

"Kit—"

"You better watch your back, Cox. I have claws and I won't hesitate to use them on you. Now, what the fuck are you doing here? I've done my time. I'm a good girl now."

"I have no doubt you would scratch and mark me, but, Kitten," stepping into her personal space, I lean closer and whisper, "I promise you when it happens, you will be purring. All. Night. Long." Stepping back, I notice her swallowing deeply. *Score one for me* I think to myself. "I need to talk to you."

"What do you think we're doing now?"

"Don't sass me, Kitten." I see she's still sassy…and sexy as ever. "Can we go upstairs and talk? I have something important to discuss with you."

She shakes her head. "No, you can tell me here."

Looking around the lobby, it's empty except for the concierge and us.

Stepping closer to her, I lower my voice. "Kye Vlahos escaped from custody today and a threat was made against me...and you."

She wobbles on her feet as my words sink in, "Wwww...what?" she says, her voice wavering. Any and all sass gone. "How?"

"He faked illness and managed to escape while in hospital."

"Why would he threaten me? He doesn't know I was a part of it, does he?"

"It looks like he knows. I think Creed Dawson told him."

"Fucking asshole, I'll kill him if I ever see him."

"That might be hard, he was murdered earlier today."

"What?"

I tell her about Creed's untimely death earlier today and mention the note threatening us. "I...I...we, I nee—"

"Kitten, listen to me." She lifts her gaze to mine and fear is etched all over her face. "I won't let anything happen to you. I have a man stationed out front and you will be protected." Stepping closer to her, I cup her cheek. "I promise." I run my thumb over her bottom lip. Her eyes droop closed. When she opens them, they are cloudy with desire. My head begins to lower to hers, but the moment is interrupted when I hear a soft voice from behind me. "Agent Cox, what are you doing here?"

Pulling away from Baylor, I turn to face her sister but before I can say anything, her eyes lock on Baylor and she immediately knows something is wrong. "BayBay, what's wrong?"

Baylor looks to her sister and hearing her voice unravels her. The floodgates open and she begins to cry. "Avie," she blubbers, falling to her knees. Covering her face with her hands, she cries as her sister embraces her in a sisterly hug.

The elevator doors open and my head snaps up, I see a gentleman step out, he looks familiar but I can't place him. His eyes lock with mine, then they drop to the sisters embracing and he races over to them. Squatting down, he rests his hand lovingly on Avery's back. "Ave, baby, what's wrong?"

She lifts her head to look at him. Concern is plastered all over her face. "I don't know," she tells him. "I came down to find Bay with Agent Cox and when she saw me, she fell apart."

"He's going to kill me," Bay murmurs.

"Who's going to kill you?" Ave asks her sister.

"Kye," she whispers.

"Who's Kye?" the man questions them.

"The guy Bay helped Agent Cox bring down. But he's in jail. I don't know what's going on." Avery stands up and turns to face me. "Care to explain, Agent Cox?" The tone of her voice reminds me so much of Baylor when she's pissed off.

"How about we take this upstairs?" Flynn says, looking over his shoulder toward the front desk. "We can discuss this in private."

"Good idea, Flynn." She looks to her sister. "Come on, Bay, let's get you upstairs."

Bay nods, but when she stands up, she wobbles on her feet and stumbles. Stepping forward, I wrap my arms around her. "I've got you, Kitten," I tell her, as I lift her up bridal style.

She wraps her arms around my neck and snuggles into my chest. As we walk toward the elevators, she whispers, "He's going to kill me," over and over again.

Following behind Avery and Flynn, I whisper, 'Shhhh' over and over, but she's lost in her mind right now. This isn't how I expected her to react. I was expecting my feisty kitten to tell me he can try, but no one will bring her down. I certainly didn't expect her to break down like this. I guess prison has mellowed her. My inner voice says, 'If you'd kept an eye on her, you'd know her better.' So many times over the last twelve months, I wanted to reach out. Make sure she was okay but the agent in me knew that was crossing a line.

The elevator doors open and we step into a gorgeous foyer. Flynn and Avery live in the penthouse, the four of us enter and my eyes dart around the place. Must be nice to have cash to spend on a flashy home like this. It's open plan with light walls, a large dark sofa with bright throw pillows, and doors leading to an amazing outdoor area. The kitchen is gorgeous. With dark chocolate-brown granite with wooden cabinetry, it's the ultimate dream kitchen.

Everyone walks to the living room and takes a seat on the sofa. Bending down, I go to place Baylor next to her sister, but she's gripping me tightly and not letting go. Turning around, I sit next to Avery with Baylor still attached to me like a monkey.

"What's going on, Agent Cox?" Avery asks.

"I got word today that Kye escaped. I came to warn Baylor to be on the lookout."

"Why do I feel there's more?" she questions.

This woman misses nothing. "As well as Kye escaping, Creed Dawson was murdered this morning in his cell."

"Ohh my God," she gasps, covering her mouth. "Does Cress know?"

"I'm not sure, but when Mr. Dawson was discovered, there was a note left."

"What did it say?"

"'Rats like to squeal. You and that bitch are going down.'"

"Oh My God," she says again, covering her mouth as the enormity of this sinks in.

"Will Bay be safe?"

"I will not let anything happen to her."

"What about you?" Flynn asks.

"I'll be fine. My concern is Baylor. I never imagined this would happen, if I had thought it would, I never would have used her to bring him down."

Baylor's head snaps up. "You used me," she growls, pulling away from me, she stands, and glares down at me. "You used me to get him and once you got your man, you tossed me aside like a piece of trash. Hell, you didn't even say goodbye after it all went down. I did exactly as discussed, I cozied up to the fucker. I pretended to want him. To be his queen. To be by his side. I did everything. Then once you got him, I became a footnote in your report. You forgot all about me." She turns and stalks toward the windows. She stops and takes a deep breath then spins to face me again. She points at me angrily. "You used me," she says softly, "and now my life is in danger because I tried to do the right thing." Tears streak down her cheek. "This always happens to me. I try do right and it all blows up in my face." She wipes away her tears and locks her eyes on me. "If I die, Cox, I will fucking haunt you for the rest of your days."

She turns and storms down the hallway. Slamming a door in anger, the force causes the doors out here to rattle. "Well, that went well," I say to break the silence.

Turning to face me, Avery stares at me. "She's right, you know."

"How so?"

"She did all this for you and then you ghosted her. After the moments you shared, she thought you cared, but in reality, you just did what was needed to get what you wanted."

Shaking my head, I protest, "That's not true at all. I...it's...it's complicated."

"You need to tell her that. She feels used and betrayed, and I don't blame her." The room falls silent again. "I think you should leave, Agent Cox." Avery stands. "You better keep Bay safe because if even a hair on her head is harmed, well, let's just say, you don't want to see what I'm capable of. If you think Baylor can be bitchy, wait until you meet 'Angry

Avery', she has nothing on Bay. Agent Cox, my sister means the world to me. Sure, she's done some unsavory things, but she's owned her mistakes and has made up for them. You need to keep her safe so she can have her second chance."

Standing, I face Avery. "I will keep her safe." Walking to the door, I look over my shoulder with my hand on the door handle. "And for what it's worth. I do care about her...more than I should."

Opening the door, I step into the foyer and walk over to the elevator. Pressing the call button, I wait and think about what just went down. I realize how badly I fucked up when it came to Baylor and me. This is my chance to show her I don't just think of her as an informant. Maybe I will get my chance with Baylor Evans after all.

BAYLOR

CURLING INTO A BALL ON MY BED, I HUG MY KNEES AND LET IT ALL OUT. I CRY like I do when Thomas J dies in *My Girl.* I should have known something like this would happen. I never get a free pass, no matter what I do. Shit always hits the fan. This was meant to be my redeeming moment but now, now my life is on the line because I tried to do the right thing.

A knock on my door startles me, but I don't want to talk to anyone right now so I ignore it. Through the door, I hear Ave. "I'm here when you want to talk, BayBay. I love you."

"I love you too," I quietly whisper.

Rolling to my back, I let out a deep sigh and stare at the ceiling. Hours pass by and the events of the evening continue to play over and over in my head. One minute I'm over the moon to be released. Then I'm on another high celebrating my twinsie's engagement. And then it all comes crashing down around me when Cox tells me Kye escaped and that my life has been threatened.

Fuck. My. Life.

Closing my eyes, the image of Cox when I stepped out of the elevator pops into mind in high definition, full color vision. He really is a sexy-as-sin man. As soon as my eyes landed on him, my breath hitched. My heart started racing like I'd run a marathon and I'm no runner, so it was freakin' fast. My skin is still tingling from being in his arms. If only it wasn't due to my life being on the line. If only he was here to sweep me off my feet and ravage me.

At the thought of him ravaging me, my clit begins to tingle and throb. Sliding my hand down my body, my nipples pebble as I brush past them. Flicking open the button on my jeans, I slip my hand in and under the material of my panties. My clit sparks to life as I slide the pad of my finger over the ring and down between my folds. I'm wet already. Cox has that effect on me. My finger easily slides inside and I quietly moan. Biting my lip to keep myself quiet, I continue to thrust my fingers in and out, grazing my clit as my hand slides by. Gripping my breast through my shirt, I explode around my fingers. Moaning his name as I ride out the pleasure coursing through me.

Removing my fingers, I stand, grab my things, and skip across the hall to the bathroom and have a shower. I change into my pj's and once back in my room, I slip back into bed. The orgasm doing nothing to ease the worries swirling around my mind.

The next morning, I walk into the living area to find Ave at the kitchen counter with a coffee cup in hand. "Morning," I say, as I climb onto the stool across from her.

"Morning," she replies, as she fills a mug for me and hands it over to me. "Sleep okay?"

"Ish," I reply. Wrapping my hands around the mug, my palms warm from the heat of the hot black yummy nectar inside. Bringing the mug to my lips, I take a sip. Closing my eyes, I savor the flavor, my taste buds dancing and zinging to life. The coffee in prison was horseshit so to finally drink something good—no amazing—I can't help but moan.

"Would you like me to leave you and your coffee alone?" Ave teases, as she takes a seat on the stool net to me.

"Ave, you have no idea how shit the coffee was in there. This right here is everything."

"What's everything?" Flynn asks.

"Coffee," Ave and I say in unison.

Flynn leans down and kisses Ave on the top of her head. She leans back into him and closes her eyes. The love radiating between them is enough to heat an entire city block. Grabbing my mug, I slink back to my room, leaving the two lovebirds alone.

Snuggling down in the armchair in my room, I grab my Kindle and devour *Benched* by *Rebecca Barber*. I'm not normally a fan of the man bun but the way Rebecca describes Hunter-Caveman-Mitchell, I have been swayed.

A knock on the door pulls me away from my book and I smile when I see Ave. Her cheeks are flushed, indicating she and Flynn just got down and dirty. "Hey, what's up?"

"Just checking to see how you are? You disappeared earlier."

"I'm getting there. Yesterday was a lot, but I think I'm okay."

"You know you can talk to me."

Nodding, I place my Kindle down. "I know. I just don't want to rain on your parade. You should be celebrating your engagement. Not worrying if my mafia kingpin ex-boyfriend is going to make good on his promise."

"Well, I wasn't really worried about it until you put it like that. I was more checking on how you feel after being out? From all that I've read, it can be an adjustment for those being released."

A laugh escapes me. "Why am I not surprised that you looked all of this up?"

"What can I say, I like to know what to expect."

"Ave, I'm fine." I stand and walk over to her. "I promise."

"Just promise me you'll talk to me if things get too much?"

"Yes, Mom, I'll do that. Now, I'm going to walk to the store, get myself some wine and cheese, and then I'm going to binge watch movies all afternoon."

"Want some company?"

"I'd love some."

Ave and I do exactly that, Flynn even joins us. He just shakes his head when we watch *The Little Rascals* and recite every line word-for-word. The credits roll and I hop up to stretch, I've been sitting for too long. I look over to see Flynn and Ave making goo-goo eyes at one another. "Remember the first time we watched this together?" she asks him.

"How could I forget? You were naked and we ended up making sweet, sweet love 'til the wee hours of the morning," he not so quietly whispers.

"Lalalalalalalala," I singsong as I pop my fingers in my ears. "I don't need to hear this shit. That's one of those 'you know it happens but we don't talk about it' things."

They both laugh.

We tidy up the mess we made and we all head to bed. Just as I'm about to step into my room, Ave grabs my arm. "I'm taking you to brunch tomorrow." I try to interrupt her, but she commands, "Uh, don't argue. We're doing it."

"Yes, Mom," I tease again. "Night, guys."

In unison, they say, "Nite-nite," and head into their room.

Climbing into bed, I fall asleep immediately. The emotional toll of the last few days has finally caught up with me.

"This has been nice," I tell Ave, as I lift my mimosa and take a sip. The tang of the orange juice mixing with the tartness of the bubbles is the perfect combination...and it allows me to drink before midday, but then again, it's always 5:00 o'clock somewhere in the world.

"Yeah, it has. I can't remember the last time you and I brunched together," she says, as she shovels in a mouthful of her omelet.

"Probably before I went off the rails," I reply sadly, looking to the table. Ave reaches over the table and squeezes my hand. "Bay, look at me." Lifting my gaze, I look at her. "That's in the past and it needs to stay there. Focus on the future and what's ahead."

"I'm trying but it's hard. With Kye on the loose, I'm pretty fucking scared, Avie," I honestly tell her. For the last two days, that's all I've thought about. I know that if he gets his hands on me, I'm dead. Literally.

"Cox won't let anything happen to you," she confidently says, but I'm not so sure. Kye is a crazy motherfucker, what I ever saw in him confuses me now. He's nothing like *him* but no one is like him. He's like the ultimate alpha that got away. And that there is another fucking problem in my life.

When I saw him two days ago, I was feeling all the emotions; angry at him for not saying goodbye or reaching out. He knew where I was, it's not like I disappeared, and then there's that attraction, which isn't just one-sided. I know he feels it too. The air definitely crackles when we are together. I haven't been with anyone since him. I think of that afternoon constantly and we never even had sex.

"He was that good, huh?" Ave asks me, as she takes a sip of her drink.

Nodding my head, my mind drifts to the feel of his tongue licking me. His fingers gripping my hips. Oh fuck, I need to get laid. "I need to use the bathroom."

Excusing myself, I stand up and walk toward the restrooms when I hear my name being screeched like a banshee. Turning around, I see Dr. Bitch aka Monica, Kye's side-piece standing next to Ave. Before I can say anything, she raises her hand and slaps Ave, hard across the face.

"You fucking bitch," she snarls, "I told Kye you couldn't be trusted and it looks like I was right."

"Oi, Monica, get your fucking hands off my sister."

Her head snaps to me and I storm toward them. "You okay, Ave?"

"I'm fine but I'm bloody sick of getting slapped in the face when it comes to Kye." My face scrunches in confusion. "I'll tell you later," she says, cupping her cheek.

Looking back to Monica, I stare at her. "What the fuck do you want?"

"I want to fucking kill you for what you did, you bitch. Kye doesn't deserve what you did to him."

"What I did?" I growl, "What I did? You do realize he is the worst of the fucking worst, right? You standing by his side shows you are just as bad as him. I'm not perfect, I know that better than anyone, but you two are the fucking scum between my toes." Ave giggles at my *The Little Rascals* reference. "I suggest you turn around and leave before I really show you how bitchy I can be."

"Watch your back, bitch," she snarls and then turns on her heel and storms out of the restaurant.

"You okay?" Ave asks me, resting her hand on my back in the reassuring way she does.

"Yes. No. I don't know," I tell her, the joy I felt not five minutes ago has vanished.

"Let's go home," she suggests.

Shaking my head at her, "No, let's enjoy our brunch. I'm not letting my salmon bagel or my mimosa go to waste."

Without a word, Ave sits down and lifts her drink. "A toast."

Lifting mine, I ask, "What are we toasting to?"

"To us, the Evans twins. Back together and better than ever."

"I'll drink to that."

Bringing my drink to my lips, the hairs on the back of my neck prickle. Looking over my shoulder, my mouth drops open and my breath hitches in my throat when I meet the evil stare of Kye Vlahos. But as quickly as I saw him, he's gone again. Clearly my mind is playing tricks on me again. I guess this situation is messing with my mind. Turning back to Ave, I focus on her. She's staring at the bling adorning her ring finger.

"I haven't seen you smile like that in a long time," I tell her.

She looks up at me, and she's beaming, her smile brighter than ever. "I'm happier than I've ever been, Bay. I have my sister back and I'm engaged to the most amazing man. Life is brilliant right now."

"I'm so so happy for you, Avie." Reaching across the table, I squeeze her hand.

We finish our brunch with no more interruptions or bitch-slaps. We decide to leave the car with the valet and head into the mall for a girls' day. We get manis and pedis. I spoil myself with a new pair of kick-ass purple heels and some lingerie. Lots and lots of purple lacy sexy lingerie. After wearing tighty whities for the last twelve months, I deserve a splurge.

We stop at Olive Garden and grab takeout for dinner. We have enough to feed an army but leftovers are always good. With our food in hand, we wait for the valet to bring Ave's car around. Staring up at the sky, I smile, it's a gorgeous sunset this evening. I missed views like this while being locked up.

"Gorgeous sunset, tonight," Ave says as I pop a taffy into my mouth. Before I can reply, all hell breaks loose.

24
COREY

I<small>T'S BEEN A FEW DAYS SINCE THE PROVERBIAL SHIT HIT THE FAN AND EVERY</small> waking moment has me thinking about *her,* Baylor Evans. She has been at the forefront of my mind when I'm both awake and asleep. I think of her first thing in the morning. She's my last thought at night. I even dream about her. I've whacked off to visions of her, more in the last few days than I've whacked off in the last twelve months. I feel like I'm a horny teenage boy again,

Letting out a frustrated sigh, I lean back in my chair and close my eyes. Once again, the blonde-haired angel appears before me. A knock at my door has me sitting up in my seat and my happy thoughts disappear when I see Dean Chikatilo standing there.

"Hey, what's up?"

"Charli and I are heading to Bin 501, wanna join us?"

"Didn't pick you as a wine dude."

"I lost a bet so it was her choice."

"That's my girl," I tease, and the look he gives me is murderous. I really hate this asshole. "Sure, I'll meet you guys there in an hour."

"I'll let Charli know. See you soon," he says with a smile but it's sinister.

How Charli can work so closely with him amazes me, but then again,

Charli is a tough badass who can deal with the best and worst of people. Hence, why she's great as a WitSec handler. The people she deals with are always colorful, with different backgrounds and varying levels of danger. She and Bay would definitely get along; thankfully those two won't ever be in the same room together.

Deciding to call it a day, I shut down my computer, grab my things, and head to my car to drive over to the bar to meet Charli and Dean. Traffic is light and I make it to there in record time. Looking to the sky, it's a vivid red and orange sunset this evening—it's absolutely gorgeous.

Opening the door, I step inside and immediately spot Charli and Dean. They look cozy together and a prickly feeling develops as I watch the two of them. Charli and I are friends, platonic friends, but seeing her with Dean right now doesn't sit right with me.

Making my way over to them, Dean looks up and a shocked expression appears on his face but he quickly schools it. "You made it," he says, his voice laced with shock.

"Yep, decided to cut out early."

"You sick, Cox?" Charli teases, "You never leave early."

"Trying something new." I shrug my shoulders and tell her, "You guys need a drink?"

They both raise their glasses. Nodding, I turn and head to the bar. There's an attractive brunette behind the bar. Her blue eyes are amazing, "What can I get ya?" she asks as I walk up to her.

"A glass of merlot, please."

"Coming right up." She spins on her heel and gets to preparing my drink. A guy walks up to her and places his hand on her lower back, he leans in, and whispers something to her. "Branson," she scoffs and hits him in the chest, "down, boy."

Clearly the two of them are together, the love radiating between the two of them is off the charts.

She replaces the cork in the bottle and walks back over to me. Placing the glass on the bar top. "Sorry, it's fuller than usual, but I got distracted." Her cheeks darken and the pink tinge is adorable on her face. Reminds me of a sassy blonde I know who rocks that shade when she's aroused. Dammit, I'm thinking of her again.

"No complaints here," I tell her, as I grab my wallet from my back jeans pocket but before I can pay, there's an explosion from outside, shaking the bottles and glasses behind the bar from its force.

Turning on my heel, I race toward the entrance and meet Charli and

Dean. We step outside and my mouth drops open at the scene. "Fuck me," I growl, linking my fingers and resting my hands on the back of my head.

Shaking my head, I assess the scene before me and then I notice that the center of the blast came from where I parked. "My car."

"You were the target?" Charli asks, just as a hail of bullets start flying.

"Get down," I shout, as I throw myself at Charli, shielding her with my body.

A piercing pain shoots through my shoulder as Charli and I fall to the pavement. The wind is knocked out me, as the shock of being shot causes me to land not so gracefully.

Rolling off Charli, I stare at the gorgeous sky above. It's the last thing I see before darkness engulfs me in the blood red of the sunset sky.

An incessant beeping from beside me grates through my head. My eyes open and droop closed again. My eyelids feel like lead weights. Blinking repeatedly, I finally manage to keep them open. The room comes into focus and I realize I'm in a hospital bed. Then the events of the evening come crashing back to me.

Sitting up, I wince at the pull in my shoulder. Looking down, I see I'm shirtless and there's a bandage covering the bullet wound. I try to look behind me and see if it went through, but when I twist, a burning pain shoots through me.

"It was through and through," Charli says from next to me, I hadn't even realized she was here.

"Are you okay?" I ask, my eyes scanning her for injuries but she seems okay.

"Apart from a few bruises from having your lard ass crash-tackle me, I'm good." She pauses. "Thank you, Cox."

"Why are you thanking me?"

"I would have taken that bullet if you hadn't thrown yourself at me. So, thank you. I owe you one."

"You can repay me by getting me the fuck out of here. I hate hospitals."

"That I can do, but I don't think you'll like what I have to say next."

Before she can tell me the next batch of bad news, the door to my room opens and in walks Flynn Kelly, Baylor's sister's fiancé. "Corey, nice to see you awake."

"Nice to be awake." He steps into the room and I notice Charli slip out before the door closes. "So when can I get out of here, Doc?"

"You were just shot."

"But I didn't die."

He ignores me and continues, "The bullet went through so you didn't require surgery. It missed everything major, X-rays show no further damage but you will be sore for a few weeks. Try to rest up and keep the wound dry."

"So, sponge baths for the foreseeable future?" I raise my eyebrows at him.

"Sorry, I'm taken and bat for the other team," he teases, "but I will see what I can arrange on your behalf."

"Thanks, Doc, appreciate it." He nods and exits the room. A few moments later, Charli walks back in.

"All good?"

"As well as a gunshot can be, I guess." She still has that sheepish look on her face. "Out with it, woman. Whatever you have to tell me can't be any worse than my car getting blown up or being shot." She purses and lips and that's when I realize what she needs to tell me is worse than that. "Just tell me, Davis."

"An attempt was made on Baylor Evans' life at the same time as you were to be blown up. It's looking like it was a coordinated attack."

"Is she okay?" I ask, trying to sit up, but the pain in my shoulder is making the task difficult. Charli assists me into a sitting position.

"She's fine but the valet that she and Avery Evans were with, while they waited for their car, wasn't so lucky."

"Fuck me." I say, lifting my good arm to run over my face. "Where is she now?"

"Awaiting transfer to a safe house."

"That's good." I nod and look over at her and again, I can tell she's still hiding something. "What else is there?"

"You're going to the safe house with her," she says this really fast because she knows there's no way in hell I'm going into WitSec.

"Like fuck I am. I need to get out of here and bring down this motherfucker."

"Not happening, cowboy. Dean and I have been assigned to watch over the two of you up at Silver Springs Lake until he is back in custody."

"Like fuck you are," I scoff at her.

"Yes, fuck we are. You and Baylor Evans are officially in WitSec until Kye Vlahos is apprehended."

Flopping back to the bed, I shake my head in defeat and wince at the pain in my shoulder. I wanted to see her again; I didn't want to be living with her. Then I laugh, Baylor will *not* be happy with this. The next few weeks and/or months are going to be fun, seems I have three new room-mates and one of them is my feisty little Kitten.

25
BAYLOR

I T'S AMAZING HOW ONE MINUTE YOU'RE STARING UP AT THE GORGEOUS SUNSET and the next, you're ducking for cover as bullets fly everywhere. Once again, Ave was in danger...because of me. We were both taken to the hospital to be checked out. Apart from a few scratches and bruises, we are fine. We were lucky, very lucky but the valet dude, not so much.

Flynn meets us in the ER and the scene between him and Avie was right out of one of the DL Gallie's romance novels I've been reading. It was perfect and romantic in every way, if you remove the ER, the attempt on our lives, and the disheveled state of both of us.

Flynn being Flynn, commands responsibility of our care. We are escorted into a treatment room and assessed immediately. We are waiting in the room when a lady walks in, reminding me of Lara Croft from *Tomb Raider*, which means she's kick-ass. I already like her and she hasn't even spoken a word.

"Baylor and Avery." She looks between us, unsure as to who is who.

"I'm Baylor," I tell her. "That's Ave," I add, flicking my thumb to Ave.

"Nice to meet you both. I'm Agent Charli Davis from WitSec. I've been assigned to watch over you, Baylor." She walks farther into the room and I take her in. Slim but muscular, with long dark chocolate-brown hair. Along with the Lara Croft vibe, she also reminds me of that chick from *One Tree*

Hill, Sophia someone. She's badass and hot, basically she's the brunette version of me.

"Watch over me, how?" As soon as I say those words, I know that whatever comes next is going to suck major donkey balls.

"Due to the attempt made on your life today, you will be entering witness protection under my watch until Kye Vlahos is apprehended."

"Like fuck I am," I snap at her, she doesn't deserve my rage but it seems, once again, Kye is fucking with my life.

"I'm sorry, ma'am, you don't have a choice."

"Don't fucking call me ma'am."

"Baylor, language," Ave scolds me. "Look, I only just got you back but I agree with the agent. You need to go with her. I want you safe until this man is caught. I can't lose you, BayBay." She begins to cry and seeing her upset, upsets me, and my eyes well with tears too. "I won't lose you."

Wrapping my arms around her shoulders, I pull her in for a hug. "What about you?"

She pulls back and stares at me. "I have Flynn, he won't let anything happen to me. I'll be safe."

"And we will have someone watching her since you look so alike," the agent adds. "Avery, you need to remain vigilant in the coming weeks."

"I will, I promise. Just keep my BayBay safe."

"Is there any other way?" I plead. "Can I speak with Corey Cox? He was my original handler person."

"He, umm, ahh, is unavailable right now." Her response is confusing to me.

Taking a deep breath, I purse my lips. I really want to flip her off and run away but the new me relents, "Then I guess, I'm going with you." It's hard, and no fun, being good.

"Glad you are coming willingly, Baylor. I'll give you a few moments to say goodbye to your sister, and I'll arrange for my partner to escort you there. I'll join you later once I've finalized a few things here in the city." Again I get the feeling she's hiding something from me but before I can press her, she exits the room leaving Ave and I alone.

Looking back to my sister, I see tears in her eyes. "Don't cry, Avie, I'll be fine."

"But I just got you back."

"And I'll be back again soon…ish."

"But what if—"

"Nope, no what-ifs. I will be back. Promise."

She wraps her arms around me, tighter this time. I do the same. We hug each other, squeezing each other for dear life. A knock on the door pulls us apart, we look over and in steps Flynn with a guy I recognize from the day the bust went down. He gives me the heebie-jeebies.

"I'm Dean Chikatilo, I'll be your escort today."

"I'm Baylor. This is my twinsie, Ave, and her fiancé, Flynn."

"Nice to meet you all. Ms. Evans, we must get moving. Say your good-byes and leave your phone and purse with your sister."

"I can't take anything with me?"

"I'm afraid not. Everything you need will be provided."

"Ohh, okay then." Standing, I look at Ave. "I guess this is goodbye, again."

She shakes her head. "No! It's not goodbye, it's I'll see you later."

"See you later, I like that." We hug each other one last time and surprisingly, Flynn wraps his arms around the two of us. Ave and I are both blub-bering when I pull away.

"I love you, BayBay," she tearfully says.

"Love you too, Avie."

Turning away from my sister, I follow Agent Chikatilo out of the room. The sound of Ave crying stays with me as we walk away.

He escorts me to an awaiting van, opens the door, and I climb in. He follows and takes the seat next to me. Looking to the front seat, I see Agents Hall and Oats. "What's up, guys?" I say.

"Ms. Evans," they both say in their stick up their ass, hoity-toity agent way. Turning back to face the front, they pull away from the hospital curb. Settling in, my eyes become heavy and I drift off to sleep.

I'm shaken awake. "We're here," Agent Chikatilo says, before he opens his door and hops out. He comes around to my side, opens my door, and offers me his hand. I take it and he helps me out. My body is stiff from the uncomfortable position I was in, we drove through the night and the sun is just starting to rise.

Behind the gorgeous cabin is a lake. "Where are we, Agent Chikatilo?"

"Silver Springs Lake," he tells me, as we begin walking toward my new home. "And call me Dean. We'll be together for the foreseeable future and my full name is a mouthful and a half. So Dean is fine."

Nodding my head, a creepy feeling runs over me. I don't like this guy but since we will be roomies for who knows how long, I smile at him before turning my attention to the cabin before me, it's gorgeous. This won't be such a bad place to live for the foreseeable future. It has a rustic charm to it with a wraparound porch, shutters, and planter boxes. Climbing up the few stairs, we walk around the side and my mouth drops open at the view before me. The cabin sits right on the lake and has its own private jetty. Looking around, there doesn't seem to be any other dwellings nearby, hence why we are here, dear Baylor.

Dean unlocks the door and steps to the side to let me pass. Stepping inside, I find I'm in the kitchen. This place is nothing like I pictured. I imagined a dingy room in the bumfuck of nowhere. I got the bumfuck part right but the living quarters, I was way off base. Looking around, I smile at the room before me. It's a dreamy country-inspired kitchen; I'd love to bake up a storm with Avie in here. The farm-style sink sits under a picturesque window that overlooks the outdoor patio area and lake. An island counter with a marble top sits in the middle. The rich wooden cupboards complement the hardwood floors. Past the kitchen is the dining room and off that a large living room with stone fireplace. Off the living room is a hallway leading to the bedrooms, bathroom, and stairs up to the master suite.

"Dibs on master suite." I shout, as I make my way over to the stairs.

"No, can do," Dean retorts, stopping me in my track as I step onto the first step. "You need to be on the ground floor so we can easily protect you."

"Fuck that," I snark, as I make my way up the stairs and much to my dismay, there are already things in that room. Turning around, I stomp back downstairs.

"Who's up there?"

"Charli," he says, as he walks past me and heads down the hallway. "This is yours," he says, stopping in front on the first door. "Mine is down the hall across from the laundry and next to the bathroom."

Nodding, I walk into my room and sit on the bed. *At least the mattress is comfy*, I think as I flop back.

"Get some sleep," he tells me, "Charli will be here in a few hours and then we can go over everything."

Nodding, I stay where I am and I drift off to sleep straightaway.

I'm woken a few hours later from an amazing dream. As I wake up, I must still be in my dreamland because I hear *his* voice, as if he's here with me. Shaking my head, I wipe the sleep from my eyes. Swinging my legs over the edge, I sit there for a few moments and when I hear his voice again, I realize it wasn't a dream. He IS here.

Standing up, I walk down the hallway but before I make myself present, I stop and listen to them talking…about me.

"She's a wild one," Dean says.

"That's the understatement of the century but she's...she's, I have no words for Baylor Evans."

Hearing that pisses me off, so I make my presence known. Dean and Corey both turn their heads to look at me. Corey is sitting on the sofa and Dean is in the armchair. "And I have no words for you too, asshole," I snap. "I'm in this mess because you guys didn't do your job."

"Baylor—"

It's the first time he's used my real name in forever and hearing that hurts, he's always called me Kitten. Clearly, I mean nothing to him. My anger and hurt explode and I scream at him, "I fucking hate you!"

"I fucking hate you, too!" he spits back at me. "You're a stuck-up, pain in my ass who won't take responsibility for anything. It's always someone else's fault."

"For once, asshole, this isn't my fault. Creed fucking Dawson ratted on me and now I'm stuck here in the bumfuck of nowhere with you, Lara Croft, and Agent Wankstain." He has to hide the laugh right now. "What the fuck are you laughing at?"

"Watch your mouth, Kitten."

"You're not the boss of me."

"No, I am," Lara Croft aka Agent Davis says, as she steps into the living room from the kitchen. "I suggest the two of you learn to live together because for the foreseeable future, we will all be living in close quarters." She emphasizes the word all.

"As long as HE stays out of my way, I have no problem."

"As long as SHE stays out of my way, I have no problem."

Corey and I stare intently at one another, these next few months are going to be fun...or not.

26
COREY

Baylor and I continue to glare at one another. It's a Mexican standoff and neither one of us is willing to make the first move and concede defeat. This woman is frustratingly stubborn but guess what, Kitten? So am I.

Dean stands up and breaks the silence, "I'm doing a perimeter check." He heads toward the front door and exits the cabin.

"Great," Charli says, "I'll get started on lunch." She turns around and walks back the way she came.

Now it's just Baylor and me in the living room. We continue to stare at one another. Surprising me, she walks over and sits down next to me. That's when she notices my shirt undone and the bandage covering me.

"What happened?" she questions, and I hear genuine sincerity in her tone.

"Got shot," I tell her.

"Kye?" she questions.

"Courtesy of him, yes."

"Are you okay?"

"Yeah," I reply nodding my head. "Takes more than a car bomb and a few bullets to bring me down."

Her eyes widen at my confession. I see concern in her eyes and I hate that she's hurting for me. I hate that this is all because I brought her in. I never should have floated this idea because now, she's in WitSec and that asshole is roaming free.

"Baylor," I say, while at the same time she says, "Corey."

We both laugh. "You first," she says.

"I'm sorry," I tell her.

She scrunches her face in confusion and it's adorable to see. "Why are you sorry?"

"You're in this mess because of me."

She shakes her head from side to side. "No, I'm in this mess because of me and a fucking psycho, narcissistic, dickwad asshole named Kye Vlahos."

"Watch your mouth, Kitten." She smiles when I say this. "Why are you smiling?"

"You called me Kitten again."

"I always call you Kitten."

She shakes her head, "Not since arriving here. You've called me Baylor and while I like the way you wrap your tongue around my name, I prefer when you call me Kitten." She purses her lips. "It's almost as if you care." She lifts her head and stares at me.

"Kit—" but before I can answer her, Charli pops her head in.

"Lunch is ready."

Baylor smiles at me and hops up, offering me her hand when she notices I'm struggling to stand on my own. Placing my palm in hers, an electrical current zaps between us. From the look on her face, she felt it too. She pulls me into a standing position and we stare at one another. Her blue eyes are so radiant in the light; it feels like she's staring deep into my soul. "

"Thank you," I tell her, that's when she realizes she's still holding my hand. She quickly drops it and steps around me toward the dining room. She looks over her shoulder and states, "I'm glad he didn't kill you." Then she turns around and continues on.

Shaking my head, I follow, and when I enter, my eyes widen at the spread before me. "Holy shit, Charli, when did you become a MasterChef? This all looks amazing."

"It's nothing," she nonchalantly says as she takes a seat next to Baylor.

Taking my seat across from Baylor, my eyes take in all the food before us. There's two different salads, chicken strips, chicken skewers, dinner rolls, corn on the cob, and behind her on the counter are her famous brownies. "Can I just skip to dessert?"

"Not until you eat your salad," she tells me.

"Yes, Mom," I tease.

She flips me the bird. "Just sit down, asshole."

"How come you don't get mad at her for swearing?" Baylor asks me as she fills up her plate.

"She owns a gun and knows how to use it," I tell her, placing a chicken skewer on my plate.

Baylor looks to Charli. "Think you can teach me to shoot?"

Charli nods. "Sure."

As I growl, "No fucking way."

"Watch your mouth," the two of them sass me in unison.

"Jinx!" Baylor yells at Charli.

"Double jinx!" Charli shouts back.

"Triple jinx." Baylor's throws back at her with a laugh.

"Quadruple jinx," Charli sasses in return, leaving Baylor speechless. And then the two of them cackle like hyenas. Putting these two together is going to be trouble; I can just see it now.

"Oh My God, it's like dealing with children," I say, biting into a chicken skewer.

"Your just jealous you didn't get to play," Charli says, taking a sip of her soda.

"Yeah, so jealous," I sarcastically reply.

"Why you jealous?" Dean asks, the kitchen door slamming shut behind him. He sits next to me, fills a plate, and digs in.

"Wash your hands, you grub," Baylor says, her face scrunched up.

"Fine," he huffs, standing up he walks into the kitchen and washes his hands.

"So how do you two know each other?" Baylor asks Charli.

"Corey and I went through the academy together and over the years we've stayed in touch. Met here and there on cases. This is a first though."

"How so?"

"He's the first colleague I've had under my protection. It's a little daunting, to be honest."

"Pffft," I tell her, "there's nothing daunting about me."

"I agree," Dean says, rejoining us. "Just like you, Baylor, he's just another witness we're babysitting. He's nothing special." He looks to me. "No offense."

"None taken," I tell him, but from the tone of his voice, I know he's full of shit. This guy really grates on my nerves, it was easy to mask it when I'd only see him here and there but living with him, well this is going to be fun.

Looking across the table, I see Charli and Bay chatting away. Those two clicked immediately. It's nice to see Bay finally relaxing. When I first saw her earlier and we began to fight, that wasn't how I wanted this to go. What I really want to do with her is not appropriate but ever since I saw her almost a week ago now, I've wanted nothing more than to fuck the life out of her.

Dean nudges me and asks, "You gonna tap that?"

"What?" I ask him, unsure if I heard him correctly.

"You gonna tap that?" he says, enunciating each word and royally pissing me off.

"Charli and I are friends. Nothing more," I tell him, but I know he's referring to Baylor. I know that what I want and what I should do are two different things and I really don't want to voice it aloud.

"Not referring to her."

Looking to him, I stare at him, unsure what to say.

"Your silence tells me everything." He stands up, leans down, and quietly whispers, "I'd tap it the first chance I got."

Grinding my molars, I glare at him and breathe deeply. It's taking every ounce of my strength to not deck this motherfucker right now. If I hated him before, now I despise him.

He laughs as he grabs his empty plate and walks into the kitchen.

Watching him walk away, I feel her eyes on me. Turning my head, my gaze catches her and we stare at one another. She brushes a tendril of blonde hair behind her ear and smiles. It punches me right in the heart and it hits me. Ohh fuck, I'm falling for Baylor Evans.

BAYLOR

…two weeks later

ONCE AGAIN, THE SUN IS SHINING BRIGHTLY BUT AS SOON AS THE SUN STARTS to dip, there's a chill in the air. I'm sitting out on the end of the jetty with a coffee in hand and a bag of taffy. Someone, I'm guessing Corey, arranged for them to appear in the groceries each week.

Sitting out here, it's my happy place. It's so peaceful. When I sit out here, it's as if everything is right with the world. I pretend I'm not in WitSec. I pretend that Corey is my husband watching me from the deck of the house and not an agent also under protection. Charli is my best friend and not our handler. The best friend part is the only true statement. She and I bonded immediately, I feel as if I've known her longer than two weeks. The only thorn in my side is Dean. There's something about him that grinds me the wrong way, but I can't put my finger on it.

If it wasn't for Charli, I don't know that I'd be able to survive this. Charli really is a kick-ass chick and my original assessment of her being a cross between Lara Croft and that chick from *Chicago PD* is one-hundred-percent true. Her mannerisms remind me so much of Ave, she calms me in the way Ave does. Thinking of Ave, it hits me right in the chest how much I miss her. I miss her like crazy. At least when I was in prison we could talk on the phone, but while I'm here, it's radio silence. I'm not sure how much longer I can take the isolation. Being here is different from my time on the inside. In prison, I had jobs to keep me busy. But here, there's not much to do at all. Living with three people is hard, especially when one of those three is a douchecanoe, wankstain asshole.

The jetty jiggles and I know my serenity will be broken any minute, but I don't mind because I know it's *him* coming to join me. Whenever he's near, the air around me crackles and zings to life. I've never felt this before, but it can never be more than a fantasy. If our circumstances were different, I'd make a move but I know that once this is all over, he'll go back to being the sexy-assed agent he is, and me, well I have no clue what I'm going to do. I do know that Bitchy Baylor has left the building; I just wish I knew what I wanted to do with my life.

"It's beautiful out here," he says, taking a seat next to me.

"It sure is. Sitting here at the end of jetty is my most favorite spot to be."

"I guessed that."

"How so?" I ask.

"You're down here each and every day." I laugh. "You know, it's probably not the safest spot to hang out."

"There's no one around for miles. We are literally in the bumfuck of nowhere."

"You underestimate Kye. He will find us."

"You trying to scare me?"

"No," he says shaking his head. "Just being realistic. And I..." He drifts off.

Turning to face him, I rest my hand on his knee. "And I what?" I ask. I really want him to finish that sentence.

"I don't want to see you get hurt."

"Awww, does the big bad agent care about me?"

"Yes, I do," he honestly tells me. His eyes are locked intently on me. In this light, I can see flecks of gold around his irises. He really has the most mesmerizing eyes. "Kitten, I don't want anything to happen to you. You're here because I didn't protect you."

"Cox, no," I say, shaking my head. "I'm in this mess because Kye Vlahos is a fucking psychotic asshole, who thinks the world owes him. Now, before you berate me for my language, there are no other words to describe him so I'm given a pass when it comes to him."

He smirks and I find myself grinning back at him.

"You really are something," he tells me.

"Something good or something bad?"

"Something that could get me into a lot of trouble," he lifts his hand and brushes a strand of hair behind my ear, "but it would totally be worth it."

We both fall silent, processing the words he just uttered. My eyes drop to his lips and I want him to kiss me. It would be the most perfect moment, and we start to lean forward. We are millimeters away from kissing when the sound of an engine has Cox pulling away. Seconds later, Charli comes racing down.

"Inside, now!" She demands.

"Kitten, go," Cox says.

"You too, Cox."

He stands up and offers me his hand. He pulls me up and we flee toward the house. My heart is racing when we step inside the kitchen. Corey locks the door behind us and we walk to the windows and watch as Charli stands on the end of the jetty and talks to driver of the boat.

As I watch, my heart beats faster and faster. Fear rumbles through me. My breathing is labored and my vision begins to dot. I wobble on my feet but Cox catches me. "Breathe, Kitten."

Blinking rapidly, I feel like I'm going to pass out. Corey grips my cheeks and lifts my gaze up to him. "Focus on my voice, Kitten. Deep breaths. Slowly," he soothes. Gently, he runs his fingers along my cheekbone. "Breathe in. Breathe out." He mimics the breathing motion and somehow, my body follows his lead.

My breathing and vision return.

My heart rate begins to slow down.

My body and senses relax.

My skin prickles and comes back to life at his soothing touch.

Lifting my hands, I cover his on my cheeks. Looking into his eyes, I feel secure in his embrace and I know, he'd do anything to keep me safe.

Without thinking, I lift to my tippy-toes and press my lips to his. He doesn't kiss me back and I feel like I've made a mistake, but then it happens. His tongue pushes through my lips and into my mouth. He's kissing me back. It starts out slow but it quickly turns heated and carnal.

It's the best fucking kiss of my life.

Wrapping my arms around his neck, I pull him farther into me, deepening the kiss and our connection. You can't tell where he starts and I end. We become one as our tongues continue to slip and slide in and out of each other's mouths.

He spins us around and with our lips fused, he walks me backward through the living room, down the hall, and into my bedroom. Once across the threshold, he kicks the door closed and guides us toward the bed. The back of my knees hit the mattress, instead of pushing me down, he lifts me up, spins around, and sits on the edge of the bed with me straddling him.

His cock presses into me, I can feel every ridge because I'm only wearing black leggings sans panties. He grips the hem of my purple slouchy sweater and pulls it over my head. Our lips separate for a few moments but as soon as the material passes, our mouths are once again joined.

He slides his hand around my ribs and unclasps my bra. Slipping the straps down my arms, my skin comes alive at the brief touch of his fingers. Dropping it to the carpet, he kisses down my neck toward my breasts. My head drops back, pushing my chest toward him. He cups my boobs and sucks the taut peak into his mouth. "Fuuuuuuuuck," I moan at the sensation.

Lifting his gaze to mine, I stare into his heated eyes. I know he wants to berate me for swearing so, I taunt him, "Maybe you should spank me?" But the joke's on me, before I can process what's happening, I'm flying through the air and I land on my stomach on the bed. He grabs the top of my leggings and pulls them down, exposing my ass. He runs his hand gently over the cheek and my skin breaks out in goosebumps at his touch. They quickly disappear and they're replaced with a stinging sensation. The asshole slapped my ass.

"Did you just fucking slap my ass?"

"Yes," he growls, as he lands another two slaps in quick succession.

"Fuck," I cry out.

"Watch your mouth or I'll fill it with something to shut you up."

He slaps my ass again and again. My insides quiver and I moan in delight. "You like me slapping your sexy ass, Kitten?" he whispers into my ear, as he slaps me repeatedly. My desire building each time his hand connects with my flesh.

"Please," I beg, rubbing myself against the comforter but I can't quite reach where I need to be rubbed.

"What are you begging me for, Kitten?"

Looking at him over my shoulder, I tell him honestly, "Everything."

28
COREY

THE ONE WORD IS MUSIC TO MY EARS.

My cock was already hard but hearing her say that has it painfully pressing against the zipper of my cargos. Flicking open the button, I'm about to lower my fly when there's a knock at the door. "Living room, now," Dean yells out.

Baylor is staring at me, breathing heavily. "To be continued," I reassure her, bending down and pressing my lips to hers. She rolls onto her back and wraps her arms around my neck, pulling me down so I'm cocooning her. I give myself over to her and the kiss.

Nothing else matters right now except for Bay's breasts pressing into my chest and my tongue plunging in and out of her mouth. Another banging interrupts. "Now!" Dean roars. Clearly we lost ourselves in each other and lost track of time once again.

Staring down at her, I brush her hair off her forehead and cup her cheek. "Kitten, we WILL continue this later."

She nods her head and reluctantly, I climb off her. Standing up, I readjust my cock and redo the button. Outstretching my hand, I offer it to Baylor. She places her tiny hand in mine and I pull her into a sitting position. My eyes drop to her tits.

"My eyes are up here, buddy."

"I know," I tell her with a wink, "but have you seen your tits? I have no words."

"I see them every day. There's nothing special about them," she says, as she climbs off the bed and pulls her leggings back into place. She reaches down for her bra and unfortunately for me, she slips it back on. Bending down, I grab her sweater and hand it to her. "Thanks," she whispers, putting it back on. She's only wearing leggings and a sweater but fuck me sideways, she is a vision.

Another pounding on the door startles Bay and she jumps at the sound. "Coming," I shout, as I walk to the door and swing it open.

"Already?" Dean teases, "Thought you had more stamina than that, Cox."

"Fuck you, asshole," I spit at him. Pushing past him, I make my way down the hall.

"I don't know what you see in him when you could have me," I hear Dean say to Baylor, spinning around, I'm ready to let loose on him when Baylor steps into the hallway. She backs him up to the wall opposite her room, and she places her hand on his chest. "I don't know why you'd even think I'd want to be with you, but I'll spell it out for you. He has none of your characteristics. The possibilities with him are endless. He thinks of me as a person and just not a possession. Those are just a few of the things that make him, and not you, appealing to me." Tapping his cheek, she smiles and walks away. Just as she reaches Charli and me, she looks over her shoulder and adds, "And have you seen his ass?" She squeezes my ass for effect and continues down the hall.

Charli and I both laugh at her reply and follow her into the living room. She curls her legs under herself on the sofa and waits for us. Charli sits next to Bay, while I lean on the sofa arm next to her. She presses her head onto my thigh and I smile at the contact.

Dean finally joins us, and he looks pissed off but Charli doesn't give him a chance to whine like the little bitch he is. "Dean, take a seat, we need to talk," Charli says, breaking the silence.

Dean drops into the armchair. "What's up, boss lady?"

"That was a close call earlier. Baylor, I don't want you going down to the jetty anymore. That boat could have been Kye and his men. We can't take that risk."

"But—" she tries to interrupt.

"No buts. Your safety is my number one priority."

"Can I still go outside? Or am I trapped in here like an animal at the zoo?"

"Accompanied? Yes. Alone? No."

"I feel like I'm in prison again," she says.

"I'm sorry, Baylor, but I can't risk it." She looks to Dean. "I want you to recheck the perimeter."

"I did it this morning," he snaps back at her.

"I want you to do it again."

"Fine," he grunts. He stands and exits through the front door, slamming it behind him.

"What's his problem?" Baylor asks us.

"You just rejected him. He doesn't take too kindly to women doing that."

"Well, he shouldn't be such a douchehole."

I laugh at Baylor's assessment of Dean. "How do you put up with him as a partner?" I ask Charli.

"He never used to be like this but he's changed in the last few weeks. He's being secretive and his mind isn't on the job."

"Should I be worried?" Bay asks.

"No," Charli and I say together.

"Bay, I'm not going to let anything happen to you." I tell her, "You need to listen to Charli's orders. If you do that, you'll be safe."

"What about you guys?"

"We'll be fine. We're trained for this," Charli reassures her. "I need to call HQ and update them on our visitors today. Can I trust you to behave?"

We both nod our head. It appeases Charli because she heads upstairs to make her call.

I take a seat on the coffee table in front of Bay. "You okay?" She nods but I don't believe her. "I call bullshit."

"How can you be so calm about this?"

"It's my job to be calm. You just need to trust us and relax."

She stares at me and she bites her lip. "I think I know how we can relax." She shuffles to the edge of the sofa and stands up. She stretches out her hand to me. With a smile, I place mine in hers. Lacing our fingers together, she pulls me back down the hallway and into her room. She closes the door behind her and turns to face me.

"You, Agent Cox, have far too many clothes on."

"As do you, Ms. Evans."

"Call me Kitten," she seductively says, lifting her sweater over her head then dropping it to the floor.

"Okay, Kitten, you still have too many clothes on."

She grips the top of her leggings and ever so slowly peels them down her legs. She pulls them off and stands up. With her eyes locked on me, she reaches behind her back and removes her bra. She is gloriously naked before me.

Licking my lips, I step to her. I need to touch her. She grabs my hand and shakes her head. "Uhh ah, Agent Cox. You cannot touch me until you remove your clothes, too."

Quicker than I have ever stripped off before, I remove my shirt, cargos, and briefs. The discarded items join Baylor's clothes on the floor. "Much better," she purrs, as the little minx slides her finger down the valley between her breasts.

Mimicking her words from before, I reach out and grab her hand. "Uhh ah, Kitten. Your body is mine."

She lifts her gaze to mine. "Have at it then, Agent Cox."

29

BAYLOR

Standing naked before him, my heart beats faster than it ever has before. How I can be turned on right now, when not five minutes go, my safety was once again in jeopardy, is beyond me. But when it comes to Agent Corey Cox, my rational thinking takes a vacation.

He steps toward me like I'm his prey, sliding one hand around my waist and the other into my hair. He tugs me into him and slams his lips against mine in a heated all-consuming kiss. *I fucking love kissing him.* I feel his kiss all over my body. My skin is heated and thrumming with desire for the man before me.

"Please," I murmur against his lips.

He breaks the kiss. "What do you want me to do, Kitten?"

"Everything," I tell him, and it's true. I want him in every way possible. He may piss me off to no end but at the same time, he turns me on. He brings my body to life in a way I've never felt before.

"Everything it shall be, then." He smirks at me. Gripping my waist, he throws me over his shoulder and walks us over to the bed. Resting a knee on the mattress, he drops me down and I bounce a few times. A giggle breaks free.

"I love when you laugh like that," he tells me, his eyes eating me up.

"I love having you make me laugh like this." I stare up at him and take a moment to appreciate the fine specimen before me. Abs on abs. The elusive V pointing to his cock, his impressive cock. There isn't an ounce of fat on the man. He is muscular in the most delicious way. There are no tan lines on the man; he is hot AF.

"Like what you see?" he cockily says.

My eyes snap up to his. "Fuck yes, I do. I want to lick every crevice on your body. I want to suck your dick until you see stars. I want to kiss you forever, but most of all, I want—no I need—you to fuck me into next week, right this fucking second."

"Normally I'd tell you to watch your mouth, but fuck, Kitten, I want all of that too. You are a vision and we will not be leaving this room until I have explored every inch of your delectable body. Now get ready, 'cause, Kitten, I'm about to fuck you. All. Night. Long." He enunciates the last three words and my body, which was already buzzing with desire, quivers with what's about to happen.

"Have at it, Agent Cox." I lie back into the pillows and spread my legs wide. Sliding my hand down my body, I flick my clit ring before slipping my finger between my folds but before I can insert a finger, he grips my wrist.

"Uh ah, Kitten. That pussy is mine." Before I can protest, he lowers his head and licks me from taint to clit. He sucks on my piercing as he thrusts his fingers inside of me, and immediately I see stars. "Fuuuuck," I moan in delight, as he continues to assault me with his tongue and fingers. He hooks his finger around inside of me and I explode. I scream his name as the most intense orgasm of my life slams into me like a wave to the shore in the middle of a Category 5 hurricane.

My body is mush when he removes his fingers and face from between my thighs and stares down at me. "I love that shade on you."

"What shade?" I breathlessly ask him.

"Just fucked pink."

"Don't think I've seen that color at Sephora."

"You won't ever see it there because it's a limited edition color that's solely for me."

I don't know how to reply to him, so I lift my hand and beckon him to me with my finger. Like a panther stalking his prey, he crawls up my body. He doesn't touch me but his nearness is enough to have my body coming to life again. He hovers above me, staring deeply into my eyes. I see nothing but lust and desire reflecting back at me.

Reaching up, I cup his cheek. "Where have you been all my life?"

"Catching bad guys and waiting for you and your sassy mouth to be in interrogation three."

His words cause the smile on my face to drop, he's right. We met because I'm a criminal and he's an agent, but before I can dwell any further, he covers my hand with his. "Don't go there. Stay here with me. Think of the here, the now, and what's next."

"And what IS next?"

"Me fucking you."

"About fucking time."

"Kitten."

He growls my name in warning to my excessive swearing, but I love taunting him. I stare at him and smirk. "Fuck. Me. Now."

"You're asking for another spanking."

"I'm down with that but first—" I don't get to finish my taunt because he thrusts himself deep inside of me. I thought I saw stars when he used his fingers and tongue but fuck me sideways, I'm seeing the whole fucking universe right now.

He lowers his head and kisses me aggressively. His tongue thrusts in sync with his cock with perfect timing. Wrapping my arms around his neck, I hold on tightly as he fucks the life out of me.

"Cooooooorey," I moan, as his cock continues to fill me up. He slides in and out, hitting that magical spot with each thrust.

"Come for me, Kitten," he demands against my lips. I want to tell him to go fuck himself, but it's like he knows my body because I'm right on the cusp. He slips his hand between us and when he presses on my piercing, it's just what I need. I scream his name as another intense orgasm unleashes.

My walls clench his cock and my juices soak the mattress below. His body tenses and he, too, comes, his seed spilling deep inside of me. My eyes widen when I realize we didn't use protection. Looking up at him, I see the recognition on his face too.

"Fuck," he spits.

"We just did," I say with a laugh, wanting to lighten the mood. Loosening my grip around his neck, I smile at him. "Don't worry. I'm clean and on the pill."

"I'm clean too. I've never been careless like that before but with you, all rational thoughts left my body. All I could focus on was sliding into you and fucking you."

My grin widens at his words. He climbs off the bed and walks to the door, he looks out, then darts across the hall to the bathroom. He returns with a washcloth. He kicks the door closed and proceeds to wipe me clean. I was worried that after we did the deed, it would be awkward but it's not.

I'm happy and content. At that thought, my smile drops because lately, whenever I'm happy, shit soon hits the proverbial fan.

"What's wrong?" he asks me as he climbs back onto the bed, pulling me into his side. I snuggle in, throwing a leg over him, and running my fingertips over his chest.

"It's nothing."

"Don't lie to me, Kitten, what's got you frowning?"

"I'm happy," I honestly tell him.

"That's a good thing."

A laugh escapes me. "I know that but my with my track record, whenever I'm happy, it all turns to shit."

"That was then. This is now." He tells me and places a gentle, reassuring kiss on my temple. It instantly calms me—and it hits me—he calms my inner beast. He brings out the goodness I have buried deep down.

"How do you do that?" I ask him. Lifting my head off his chest, I rest my cheek in my palm and I look up at him.

"Do what?" His face is laced with confusion.

Sitting up, I spin around and cross my legs. I stare down at him and smile. "Put me at ease with your words. You calm me, Corey. Ave was the only one to ever do that but since I met you, you've brought me to life and make me look at things in a different light. You've dug deep inside of me and you're pulling out the best version of me."

"Kitten, I haven't done anything. That's all you. If I remember correctly, you told me to go fuck myself when I first offered you that deal. Sitting here now, I wish I had listened to you," my face drops at his words, "no, not like that." He sits up and faces me. We are both naked having a pretty deep conversation right now. "If you hadn't of agreed to go undercover, you'd be back in the city living a good life. Instead, you're trapped here because you helped me."

"And I'd do it again because it was the right thing to do."

"Your big heart is one of the many things I love about you." My eyes widen at the mention of love. Sure I have feelings for him, and he does for me, but love, no. No one will ever love me. "If anything, you've brought me to life. I now see life in color rather than just black and white."

"You really are something else, Corey Cox."

"As are you, Baylor Evans. Now come here, I need to fuck you again."

And that's what we do for the rest of the night. I lose count as to how many orgasms he pulls from me but I do know one thing, after last night, I have completely fallen for Agent Cox.

30
COREY

WAKING THE NEXT MORNING, I SMILE WHEN I REALIZE IT WASN'T A DREAM. Baylor and I finally fucked and I can unequivocally say, it was the best night of my life. But what surprises me the most is my feelings for her have grown dramatically in the last twelve hours. She constantly surprises me. Sure, she puts up a bitchy front, but underneath all that is a woman with a beautiful soul who just got lost.

Looking down at her sleeping form, I watch her sleep. She looks so peaceful and content right now.

"Stop staring at me, you creeper," she huskily says, her voice laced with sleep.

"How did you know I was? Your eyes are closed."

"I could feel your gaze on me."

"Can you feel this too?" I ask, rolling to my side, I thrust my morning wood into her thigh but it backfires on me when with her eyes closed, she grips my cock in her hand and begins to stroke. "Fuck me," I moan and she squeezes me tighter and tighter with each flick of her wrist. "Kitten, if you keep that up, I'm going to come and I would much rather do that inside of you."

"Mouth or pussy?" she taunts me.

"I don't care. I just need to be inside you…now."

Quicker than I've ever seen her move, she rolls on top of me and slides down my shaft, impaling herself. She purrs in that sexy way she does when she's aroused. "Fuck, hurry up, Kitten. I'm ready to burst."

She rocks her hips back and forth. With one hand, she tugs on her nipple, and with the other, she circles her clit before gently tugging on her piercing. When she does this, I feel her walls tighten around me. "Now," I grunt and together, the two of us tumble over the orgasmic cliff.

She opens her eyes and stares down at me, "Good morning, Agent Cox."

I fucking love hearing her call me that. Reaching up, I cup her boob and gently massage the plump mound. "Morning, Ms. Evans," I say, as I sit up and wrap my arms around her.

"Kitten, my name is Kitten to you."

"Duly noted." Leaning forward, I take her nipple into my mouth and suck. She moans and circles her hips, my dick coming back to life even though I just came moments ago. Letting the taut peak pop out of my mouth, I gaze into her vibrant blue eyes. "Should I fuck you again? Or feed you?"

"Fuck, then feed." Her breathing is heavy. Her hips rocking back and forth, her pace increasing the longer we stare at one another. Her movements are slow and sensual. Our gazes fused to one another as we both rock backward and forward.

"I need more," she pleads. Leaning forward, I take her nipple into my mouth and suck. Gently biting the tip before sucking again. "Yes," she mewls, as our movements increase.

She grips my cheeks and slams her lips to mine. Her tongue plunges into my mouth as she rides my cock. Sex just gets better and better with her. She bites my lip and it sets me off, out of nowhere, I erupt inside of her. We haven't once used a condom but I don't give a flying fuck. I'd happily have a million kids with Baylor Evans.

"Coooooorey," she roars as she, too, climaxes.

We stop moving and with my forehead against hers, we both get our breathing under control.

A knock on the bedroom door startles us, "Corey, I need to speak with you," Charli says.

"Give me a sec!" I shout back.

"Okay, meet me in the kitchen," she says, and then we hear her footsteps as she walks away.

Baylor and I stare at one another and for the first time in twelve hours, she looks frightened. "What's wrong, Kitten?"

"It's nothing," she denies, but I can tell from the look on her face, it's something.

"Don't deny it, missy, it's written all over your face. What's wrong?"

"Hearing Charli, it brought me back to reality. I'm in WitSec 'cause my crazy ex is trying to kill us. After this is over, who knows what will happen."

"What do you want to happen after all this is over?"

She stares blankly at me. Her mouth opens and closes a few times. "Don't answer me now. Think about what you want and when you know, let me know." I cup her cheek in my palm, she snuggles into it and stares at me. "But I will confirm, I want this. I want you. Any way you'll have me."

"Naked and on a beach?"

"Sure. After this, I'll take you to a tropical oasis and we can do exactly that."

"I'd like that." She climbs off me. "I'm going to take a shower. You go chat to Charli." She stands up and grabs her robe. Pulling it on, she looks at me over her shoulder. "And, Corey," I look up at her, "I want you any way you'll have me, too."

Before I can reply, she opens the door and steps into the bathroom across the hall.

Climbing out of bed, I re-dress and head to the kitchen to meet Charli and Dean. Dean looks pissed off. I wonder what's crawled up his ass but before I can say anything, he pushes his chair back, "I'm doing a perimeter check." He storms out of the kitchen, slamming the door behind him.

"Was it something I said?" I say to Charli, as I pour myself a coffee.

"Beats me. He needs to pull his head out of his ass and start pulling his weight."

"What do you mean? He's doing the perimeter checks, what more should he be doing?"

"Actually checking it for starters, I watched him last night from my room upstairs. He walked down the drive and that's all he did. He was on his phone, not doing his job. I called him out on it, and now he's got his panties in a twist."

"Is that normal for him?" I question, as I take a seat at the dining table across from her.

"Lately, yes. It's like his mind is elsewhere. Anyway, I wanted to discuss further what we talked about yesterday."

"What about it?"

"Are you okay with the changes made?"

"I'm fine with it and I think, Bay is too."

"Bay hey? What happened to Ms. Evans?"

"Ohh, piss off. You know perfectly well that our relationship has changed. It's..."

"Complicated?" she offers.

"Well, yes that, but I was more thinking along the lines of the start of something."

"No shit," she scoffs, "I never thought I'd see the day that Corey Cox finds 'the one' and focuses on something other than work." She air quotes 'the one' and I find myself grinning when I realize she might be right. From the moment I saw Baylor, I knew she was special. "It's nice to see you relaxing while us mere mortals are slaving away keeping you safe."

"Ohh piss off, Davis. This is just as much of a holiday for you as it is for me. It's not often you get stationed in the woods by a gorgeous lake like this. How did you pull that off?"

"I didn't. Dean did. He's the one who planned and signed off on the location and logistics. It was nice to see him step up for a change. Just wish he'd step up now that we're here."

"You need to chillax, Charli. Grab a book and sit out on the deck and enjoy the day."

"Where's Corey Cox and what have you done with him? The Corey I know is a workaholic, I fully expected you to demand a shift and to be involved in the day-to-day operations while being here."

I shrug at her. "What can I say, I'm a changed man."

"I think it has something to do with a certain blonde-haired, blue-eyed chick who is also living here." She pauses. "It's nice to see you smiling and relaxed for once."

"I smile," I retort.

She laughs at me. "Dude, before, you looked like Arnie in the Terminator movies when he'd smile or like you were constipated. Now, you actually smile, like a normal person."

"There's lots to smile about, now."

She shakes her head, "Whatever the reason, I'm happy. And I'm going to take your advice. I'm going to fill my coffee mug and go sit outside in the sun and read."

"Sounds like a plan."

Following her into the kitchen, I grab a mug and fill it up for Baylor. Charli heads outside. Grabbing the tub of taffy and her coffee, I head down to the hallway toward her room.

Stepping inside her room, my heart sinks when I see the window open and no sign of Baylor.

31
BAYLOR

With a pep in my step, I skip over to the bathroom. Pulling open the shower door, I reach into the cubicle and turn the faucets on, letting the water heat and steam up the room.

Looking at my reflection in the mirror, I smile. I look well fucked and rested, and it couldn't be more true. Last night was everything I dreamed it would be and more. Grabbing my toothbrush, I squeeze on some toothpaste and begin brushing. My mind drifts to last night and this morning, and my body comes alive at the memory.

Spitting out, I rinse my mouth and grab some mouthwash. Swishing it around, I climb into the shower where scalding water feels amazing on my body. I haven't had a workout like that in a very long time. Cox has some stamina, that's for sure.

Grabbing my bodywash, I lather up. Looking out, I see a silhouette through the frosted glass door. He doesn't realize I know he's here so I decide to play with him…and myself. I bend down, like they taught me at the pole dancing class I once took. My ass points in the air. When I straighten back up, I run my hands up my body. He will be able to see what I'm doing, and I hope it's turning him on as much as it's turning me on.

Turning to face him, I press myself against the frosted glass, squishing my breasts. The cool glass pebbles my nipples, and I gently tug and an illicit moan slips through my lips. Stepping back, I slide my hands down my body, flicking my clit ring and letting out another groan. I can't wait any longer, pushing on the door, I poke my head out and my eyes widen, "What the fuck?" I snarl, when I realize that I just did a sexy shower show for Dean.

"He said you were a kinky slut," he says, gripping his dick.

"Who did?"

"You know who." I stare at him blankly, I have no fucking clue who he's referring to but before I can question him further, he turns and leaves me staring at his retreating form. He quietly closes the door behind him. I stare at the wood for a few moments and shake my head in confusion.

Stepping under the spray, I rinse off and step out. Grabbing the fluffy purple towel, I dry off. Realizing I didn't bring any clothes in with me, I wrap the towel back around me, and step into my bedroom. I quickly pull on my jeans and a purple tank top. Sitting on the edge of the bed, I slip on my, you guessed it, purple Chucks.

After tying the laces, I fall back onto the mattress and sigh. Why was Dean in the bathroom just now? And who was he referring to? Surely Corey wouldn't have told him about last night, those two hate each other. And their hate is why I will be keeping this little peep show a secret. No good will come from Corey knowing what happened.

The room feels stuffy so I walk over to the window and open it. Looking out, I smile at the gorgeous sunny day before me. I'd love to go sit at the end of the jetty but Charli has forbidden that. Then I remember seeing a swing on the front porch. I grab my Kindle and climb out of the window. I don't want to run into Dean right now, I'm embarrassed at what he witnessed.

Taking a seat on the swing, I push off and relax back into the cushions. I'm up to the part in *Benched* where shits gonna hit the fan but before I get to the good part, I hear Corey screaming. He's yelling that I've been taken.

Standing up, I walk to the front door but it's locked. I can hear them inside so I walk around the side of the cabin and enter through the kitchen.

"He's taken her!" I hear Corey shout at Charli. "How the fuck did he find us here?"

Charli sees me and relaxes but Cox is still unaware I'm behind him and okay.

"Corey," Charli says, but he's in his own head mumbling to himself.

"She's a fighter. She's gonna be okay. We'll find her." He runs his hands through his hair. Even with his back to me, I can feel the concern radiating off him.

Falling for Agent Cox

"Cox!" Charli shouts. She steps over to him, grips his chin, and turns his head toward me. His eyes land on mine and they instantly fill with relief.

"Kitten," he breathlessly says, as he stalks over to me, wrapping me tightly in his arms, and hugging to his chest. "Where were you? I was so scared." He pulls back and grips my cheeks but before I can answer him, he presses his lips to mine. He breaks the kiss and rests his forehead against mine.

"Calm your tits," I tell him, "I—"

"Do not tell me to calm my tits." He steps back from me and runs his fingers through his hair. I've noticed he does this when he's frustrated. "When I walked into your room and saw the window opened and you nowhere in sight, I panicked."

"Overreact much?"

"Not when there's a fucking psychopath on the loose trying to kill us both I'm not."

I can't help it and I roll my eyes. He shakes his head. "I knew you were trouble when you walked in, but you know what?"

"What?" I quietly whisper, unsure of what he's about to say.

"The first time I looked into your eyes, I knew underneath your bitchy, snarky exterior was a girl wanting to be loved and be accepted for who she is, warts and all." He pauses. "No one is perfect, Kitten. I know I'm certainly not, but it's how we act that decides if we are worthy and you, Baylor Evans, are worthy."

"You are so full of shit, Cox. You're perfect, me? Not so much."

He shakes his head. "If only you could see what I see."

"What do you see?"

Stepping over to me, he cups my cheek and whispers, "You."

That one word is laced with so much, no one has spoken to me like this before—ever. No one has said that about ME before. My eyes well with tears. This can't be my life. This doesn't happen to people like me. I feel like I'm in a movie, or a dream, right now because this clearly is not real. Never has anyone professed their like for me as Corey just did. Ave? Yes. Me? Nope, no way in hell.

A tear breaks free. He swipes it away with the pad of his thumb. "Why are you crying, Kitten?"

"I...I, no one has ever said that to me before. I've never, I..." I'm really confused right now, hence my gibberish. "Are you sure?"

"Sure about what?"

"That you like me? I think you have blood loss, or you hit your head while we were fucking last night and you have a brain injury."

He laughs and I find myself laughing with him. "You really are something, Baylor Evans, but I promise you, every word I just spoke is true."

"Really?"

"Really, really. Now come here and kiss me."

"You come here and kiss me," I tease back. Raising my eyebrows at him.

"With pleasure." He closes the distance between us, grips my cheeks, and presses his lips to mine.

A sniffle from behind us garners our attention. We pull apart and look over at Charli who's wiping at her eyes. "You all right, Davis?" Corey asks her.

"Yeah, got a bug in my eye. I'm going to get back to my book outside. Leave you two lovebirds alone." She walks past us, grinning. The door closes behind her and it's just Corey and me.

"Sooo," I offer. "What now?"

"Promise me you won't scare me again like that?"

"Promise. I didn't mean to scare you, Core." His smile widens suddenly. "Why are you grinning like the cat who caught the canary?"

"You called me Core."

"And?" I ask him, genuinely confused right now.

"I usually hate when people call me Core, but when you say it, I kinda like it."

"Look at us, evolving. I like it when you call me Kitten and you like me calling you Core. Kitten and Core, a match made in WitSec."

"Leave the WitSec part out and it's perfect."

"My life hasn't been perfect in a very long time."

"Well, Kitten, this is only just the beginning."

32
BAYLOR

…five weeks later

TIME IS SOMEHOW FLYING BY BUT AT THE SAME TIME, IT'S DRAGGING ON. COREY and my relationship is moving along in leaps and bounds. I've never been in a relationship like this before. He's so attentive but more than that, he can read me like a book. He knows when I'm down and he knows exactly how to turn my frown upside down.

"Morning, Kitten," he says, as he enters the kitchen. He's shirtless and sweat covers him. Even all sweaty and gross, he's the sexiest man I've ever laid eyes on.

"Morning, Core," I say, as I hand him a cool glass of water. Our fingers brush and like every time we touch, an electrical current flies through my body. "I don't know why I can't go for a run with you."

"You know why," he tells me, as he finishes his water. We have this argument each time he goes for a run.

"You're in just as much danger as I am."

"Don't argue with me, Kitten."

"But—"

"No buts, don't make me handcuff you, Kitten."

"Maybe I want to be handcuffed," she throws back at me.

"It can be arranged but unlike the spankings you so enjoy, you won't enjoy this."

"Wanna make a bet?" I sass, resting my hand on my hip and cocking it to the side. The material on my sundress pulls down, revealing the top of my breasts. His eyes drop to my chest and darken with lust. He lifts his heated gaze back to mine.

"Don't tempt me, Kitten."

I wink at him and sashay out of the room. Looking over my shoulder, I notice his eyes are on my ass, so I add an extra swing as I walk away. I step into the bathroom and from the other room, I hear Corey murmur, "Fuck me." I bet he's sitting there, running his hands over his face in frustration.

An idea forms in my head and with a grin on my face, I duck into my bedroom. With everything I need in hand, I head back out. He's still on the sofa and he's resting his elbows on his knees with his head down. He's so lost in thought he doesn't hear me return, which is perfect for what I have in mind.

Silently, I snap one side of the handcuffs around my wrist and then the other to his wrist. His gaze lifts to mine in shock. "Oops," I cheekily say, "did I do that?" That's when he notices I'm only wearing a sheer purple teddy. *Thank you Ave for including this in my care package.*

"What happened to your dress?"

"I took it off," I nonchalantly say, as I push him back onto the sofa and straddle his thighs. "Now, since we are cuffed, and alone, I think we should have some fun."

"I'm listening," he tells me, his gaze locked on mine.

"Well, since you are attached to me, literally and figuratively, I thought…" I stop talking and trail my fingertip over his chest, letting my fingers to the talking.

"You thought what?"

With my eyes on his, I keep moving my finger over his chest. Sliding lower and lower. Tracing my finger along the top of his cargos, I lean closer. My breasts pressing into his chest, I take his earlobe into my mouth and nibble. "I thought we could explore each other's bodies with our hands and tongue and teeth."

"I'm down with that but I have one amendment."

"I don't think you are in a position to bargain but I'm open to suggestions," I breathe heavily into his ear, garnering a groan from him.

"Do you trust me?" he pants.

Pulling back to stare at him, I reply honestly, "With my life."

"Good," he says and before I know it, he lifts me into his arms bridal style and walks us into the bedroom. He lays me down on the bed and cocoons me, pressing his lips to mine and kissing the life out of me. I'm so lost in the kiss I don't realize what he's doing. He laced our fingers together and unbeknownst to me, he slipped the cuff off his wrist and now I'm attached to the bed via the cuffs, with my arms stretched above me.

"What the?"

"You should know better than that, Kitten. I will always win." He stares down at me and my body heats just from his gaze. "Now, what shall I do with you?"

"I have a few ideas," I tell him.

"Uh uh, I'm in charge now."

He climbs off the bed and ever so slowly he removes his pants, followed by his boxer briefs. Once he's naked, he stands beside the bed and stares down at me, languidly stroking his cock.

"If you uncuff me, I can do that for you."

"You can also help me while cuffed, you have a perfectly good mouth."

"Well then, come here." I lick my lips and open wide, waiting for his cock.

"Ohh, Kitten," he says, resting a knee on the edge of the mattress. He continues to stroke his cock, while my clit pulsates with need.

"Shut the fuck up, Core, and shove your cock in my mouth."

"Yes, ma'am."

"Don't fucking call me ma'am."

"Watch your mouth, Kitten."

"Fill my mouth with your cock and you can watch it for me."

He straddles me and taps his cock against my chin, smearing precum on my skin. I'm about to protest again when he thrusts his hips forward and his cock passes between my lips. It hits the back of my throat causing me to gag a little. As he moves his hips back and forth, I pucker my cheeks and suck as best as I can. "Fuck, Kitten, your mouth feels like heaven."

When he stares down at me, I have never felt more wanted or desired in my life. His cock twitches and I know he's close to coming. Gently, I graze my teeth on his shaft. He hisses and then I feel the first hot spurt hit the back of my throat and I suck every last drop from him. He removes his cock from my mouth and leans forward and shoves his tongue into my mouth, kissing me deeply.

His hand slides down my side. My skin prickles at his light touch. Slipping his hand between my thighs, he cups me. "Kitten, you're soaked," he murmurs against my lips. "What should we do about that?"

"Fuck me," I tell him, my body is on the edge right now. He doesn't move, but I'm ready to combust. "Fu—" But I don't get to finish my curse because he thrusts two fingers inside me. My heads drops back and I give myself and my pleasure over to him. He kisses and nips down my neck toward my breasts. Massaging them, he continues to finger fuck me. My orgasm is just about there but as soon as I feel like I'm about to explode, the asshole stops moving his fingers.

"Corey," I beg when he starts to move them again. "I need to come."

"Not until I say so," he tells me.

He uses his knuckle and nudges my piercing with each outward stroke. My body is buzzing with the need to come. My walls clench around his fingers and just before I explode, he slides down my body and sucks my piercing into his mouth. That suction sets me off and I come harder than I ever have before. He continues to shove his fingers in and out and suck on my clit as I come and come and come. Finally, my body relaxes and I recline into the mattress.

"Holy shit," I pant.

Corey lifts his head from between my thighs, his chin glistening with my arousal. Beckoning himself forward, he crawls up my body and hovers over me. "Kiss me," I demand.

"Yes, ma'am." And before I can protest at him calling me ma'am, he presses his lips to mine and slides his tongue into my mouth. We kiss like teenagers at the drive-in on a Saturday night, but unlike teenagers, we make it through all the bases and he hits a home run. Corey slides into me and fucks me slowly. His cock moving in sync with his tongue in my mouth.

Corey and I languidly make love to one another. This is definitely making love because it's slow and sensual. It's perfect in every way possible. Together we come, moaning into each other's mouths. We continue to kiss and eventually, we fall asleep. Corey on my chest and me still cuffed to the bed.

Startling awake after a nightmare, I realize I'm alone. Corey must have uncuffed me while I was sleeping. Looking at the clock on the side table, I realize it's late afternoon. Slipping my dress and underwear back on, I cross the hall to the bathroom and freshen up.

Looking at my reflection in the mirror, I don't recognize the woman staring back at me. There's life in my eyes and for the first time in a long time, I realize I'm happy and I'm falling in love. Splashing water on my face, I wipe it dry and head into the kitchen for a drink.

With my drink in hand, I head out the front door and sit on the porch swing. Tucking my legs underneath me, I rub at my wrist. It's a little chaffed from our sexcapades earlier. I think if, no, when, we do that again, we'll need to get a fuzzy pair of cuffs to prevent chaffing.

"What's got you grinning?" Charli asks me as she walks up the front stairs.

"Nothing," I say.

She sits down and turns to face me. "I call bullshit and from the red marks and moaning I heard earlier, I'd say you're on a sex high."

"Maybe," I nonchalantly shrug at her. She eyes me. "Okay, yes, I'm on a sex high."

"Again," she teases. "I'm so happy and not jealous at all."

"I'm sorry."

"No, you're not."

"Yeah, you're right, I'm not really that sorry. You could always hook up with Dean."

She scrunches her face and shakes her head, "Hard pass there. He's my partner in a work sense and that's all it will ever be. Plus, he's not really my type."

"What IS you type?" I ask her.

"Not him," she laughs. "I don't know. I've been married to my job for so long now, I haven't really had time for a relationship or love."

"I get that but you really need to look out for yourself, too. You're a hot chick; don't you want that giddy feeling when they're near? Or the happiness that comes from being with someone?"

"Can't say I've ever had that. Not sure I'm cut out for love."

"I bet you will meet someone one of these days and when you do, it will be love at first sight and you will fall hard and fast."

"Yeah, I wouldn't bet on that."

"Never say never," I tell her.

We both fall silent and I can see our chat racing through her mind. Standing, I look down at her. "It's Tuesday, you know what that means?"

Together we singsong, "It's Taco Tuesday."

Linking arms, we head inside and begin prepping dinner.

After a delicious taco dinner, sans margaritas—damn WitSec and no alcohol—Corey and I spend the rest of the evening in my room, devouring each other's bodies like we do most nights and I fall asleep in his arms, blissfully happy.

Waking the next morning, I stretch out my muscles from head to toe. My body aches in the most delicious way. A noise startles me and I quickly sit up. My Spidey senses are on high alert. "Corey?" I yell but I'm met with silence. That feeling of unease increases.

Staring up, I pull on my robe when the door to my room swings open. My heart stops beating when I see who's standing there; they were the last people I expected to see.

33
KYE

Soon everything I've worked so hard for will be in place. Sure, my base of operations has been taken to another country but I'm Kye fucking Vlahos, no one can bring me down. *She* and the feds tried, but I'm like a cat with nine lives.

The door opens and Monica slides into the seat next to me. Just as the door closes, my driver pulls away from the curb. She turns her head and stares at me. "It's all arranged."

"Excellent," I tell her.

There's hunger in her eyes and I know she'll do anything I ask of her. Right now, I need her more than she needs me, but she's so clueless she doesn't realize I'm using her to get what I want, Baylor Evans. She is my one true queen and even though she betrayed me, she will rule by my side. I will make sure of it…and I know exactly how to make her comply.

Grabbing my phone, I scroll through my contacts list and when I get to the one I'm after, I click their name. "What?" he growls on the second ring.

"It's time."

"I told you, I don't have it yet."

"I have a new repayment in mind. Give me what I need now and we'll call it even."

"I'm listening," he tells me. I can hear the desperation in his voice but when you have nothing to live for, you look after number one. Consequences be damned.

"I need an address."

"An address?" he repeats with confusion and as soon as the penny drops, he mumbles, "Ohh."

"Ohh, indeed."

"I'll tell you what you need but you need to promise me something."

"You aren't really in a position to be bargaining with me."

"If you want that address you need to guarantee me that she won't be harmed."

"Which 'she' are we referring to?"

"You know who I'm referring to. Guarantee me her safety and not only will I get you an address, but I'll help you secure the package."

This is a change of events I didn't see coming and it can work to my advantage if I let him think he's in control. "You have a deal. Two days and it's all going down."

"Why wait?"

His eagerness to get this over with shows his desperation. Looking to Monica, she nods her head that she can move up her timeframe. "Tomorrow, lunchtime," I confirm and then I hang up. "You sure you can get it done sooner?"

"Do you not trust me?"

"No, I don't. I don't trust anyone, Monica. And I especially don't trust anyone without a penis between their thighs."

"Sexist much?" she scoffs, crossing her arms and pushing her tits up. She's not wearing a bra under her dress; she's such a fucking slut.

Leaning over, I trace my fingertip across the hem of her dress, sliding my hand under the material and cupping her tit. Squeezing her nipple painfully between my thumb and forefinger, I pull the flimsy material down and suck the tip into my mouth. She reaches across, grabs my cock, and begins to stroke. Gripping the back of her neck, I throw her to the floor and like the good little slut she is, she pulls out my cock and begins to suck. This woman sucks like a Hoover and before long, I'm coming down her throat. Like always, I imagine it's Baylor sucking me off and her name passes through my lips as I empty my load down Monica's throat.

"Did you just moan that bitch's name while you came?" she asks, wiping at her lips.

"Yep," I honestly tell her. "Just like I imagine it's her every time."

"You're a fucking asshole. That whore betrayed you and you still want her. What makes her so special?"

"She isn't you and the fact you can't see it says it all." I tell her, "Now, I suggest you pull your panties out of your cunt and concentrate on the plan." I stare intently down at her. "Don't fuck this up for me, otherwise you will meet a nasty demise. Am I clear?"

"Crystal," she huffs, sliding back into the seat next to me. I think about what she said, she's right, Baylor did betray me and that betrayal is why I want her by my side. She will be miserable for the rest of her days and that's the best form of punishment.

"Good," I tell her, looking out of the window, I watch the city fly by. Tomorrow everything will change. My queen will be back by my side and the future will be mine, but first, I need to tidy up a few loose ends.

Dropping Monica off at her practice, I head to the warehouse and swap cars. I sit in my car and watch. I've been following her, biding my time and finally, that time is here. I didn't get to where I am from making rash decisions. No, I got here because I'm meticulous and plan everything methodically. Sure, I didn't plan on *her* betraying me, that blindsided me, but I will not let that happen again.

Like clockwork, they step onto the street. She kisses him goodbye and walks down the street. He heads back inside and in three minutes, he will pull out of the underground parking lot. Like clockwork, his car pulls onto the street and he drives off, leaving me acess to his most prized possession.

Driving down the street, I pull into the side alley. Climbing out of my car, I wait. I hear her steps getting closer. Stepping onto the sidewalk, I stop in front of her. She stops and looks up at me. She stares at me and the moment it clicks as to who I am, she scoffs and turns to run, but I was waiting for that.

Grabbing her, I pull her into me and start walking toward my car. "Hello, Avery," I whisper into her ear. Opening the back door, I grab the syringe filled with Propofol, and inject it into her neck.

Shoving her inside, I look down at her. Her eyes are getting heavy and before she passes out, I tell her, "Let's go see your bitch of a sister."

34

COREY

Waking up next to Baylor is fast becoming a habit and the best way to wake up. I can count on one hand the number of times in the last five weeks I've slept in my room. Quietly climbing out of bed, I pull on my sweats and shirt and head into the kitchen.

Looking up, I'm surprised when I see Dean standing at the back door, looking out into the yard. He hasn't heard me enter the kitchen, some WitSec agent he is. "Morning," I say, startling him, the reaction is odd but then again, it's Dean. He is odd.

"Hey," he says, and then turns his attention back outside. "Doing my morning check, back soon." He opens to door and heads outside, leaving me alone.

The smell of coffee hits my nose and I smile. *At least the asshole made coffee,* I think to myself as I grab a mug and pour a cup. Taking a sip, I moan as the caffeine hits my bloodstream. With my mug in hand, I step out the kitchen door and walk toward the stairs down to the backyard when out of my peripheral vision, I see two men near the tree line. Turning my head, my eyes widen when I see it's Kye Vlahos and Dean. The two of them are standing there having a conversation like two old chums catching up.

A creak on the decking boards turns my attention away from them. Turning around, I see a woman standing there. When she sees me, she lunges at me and injects something into my neck. Dropping my mug, I take a few steps backward and begin to tumble down the stairs. Landing on my back with a thud, a shadow appears above me but the drug injected combined with my fall blurs my vision. Darkness engulfs me and I pass out.

—◦◦◦—

When I come too, I realize my hands are tied behind my back. Next to me, someone sniffles. Turning my head, I'm relieved to see Baylor. "Kitten," I say, my voice croaky. "Are you okay?"

"I'm Ave," she says and my heart drops. "I'm okay, but where is she? Where's Bay?"

"You'll see her soon enough…" Kye says, and then adds, "maybe."

"Let Avery go. She has nothing to do with this."

"No, she doesn't, but it's so much fun messing with people. That bitch fucked with me so I'm going to fuck with her, but mark my words, Agent Cox, after today, Baylor will be mine and not yours."

"Over my dead fucking body," I snarl, trying to break free from the ropes currently binding my wrists behind my back.

"That's the plan," he growls. Raising his fist, he punches me in the face. My head snaps back, colliding with the railing.

From beside me, Avery begins to sob. "Shhhh, it's okay, Avery."

"How? And where's Bay?"

"My queen is still sleeping," Kye tells us, "She'll need her sleep for what I have planned for her."

"What are you going to do to her? To us?" Avery asks him.

"I can't tell you everything. There needs to be some mystery in this. We just need to find Agent Davis and then the games can begin."

Shit, Charli. She hadn't even entered my mind. Late last night she was summoned to the city so she left after dinner. When she gets back here, she'll be walking into an ambush. I need to get loose and get Avery and Baylor out of here. Their safety is my one and only priority.

"Don't even think about it, Cox. You are at my mercy. Don't try and play hero, otherwise you'll end up dead sooner. Actually, go for it. I can't wait to end you."

Dean jumps up from his spot near the stairs, knocking over the trash can. In the quiet of the morning, it echoes loudly. Piercing the serenity.

"You all right there, heffalump?"

"There was a bug," he whines like the little bitch he is and I can't help but laugh. This pisses him off. He storms over to me and in quick succession punches me in the face. "You're a fucking dead man," he snarls.

"Enough!" Kye bellows, when from inside we hear Baylor yell my name. A sinister smile appears on his face, "It's showtime."

He roughly grabs Avery and drags her inside. Tears are pouring down her face, and she keeps tripping over her feet as the fear in her increases. I'm helpless to do anything. The kitchen door closes behind them and I'm left with a psychotic Dean and the woman who injected me earlier.

From the corner of my eye, I see Charli through the veranda railing. She stares at me and the scene before her. She mouths something to me but I miss what she says because the kitchen door swings open. She ducks down out of sight. Kye steps onto the deck, pushing Avery and Baylor in front of him. He's using them as a shield in case he's been caught.

A laugh escapes me. "What the fuck are you laughing at, asshole?" Dean growls.

"Big bad Kye Vlahos is using two women as a shield. He's a fucking pansy."

He shoves Baylor and Avery to the side and storms over to me and pulls out a pistol, pressing it to my temple. A feminine scream pierces the quiet of the morning. We all look over to Baylor who is currently walking toward him. "If you love me at all, Kye, you will not pull that trigger."

"What makes you think I still love you?"

She stops in front of him and cups his cheek; that contact makes my blood boil. She stares at him, just like she did the day of the takedown all those months ago, and I suddenly feel like she's been playing me this whole time. That she was just biding her time for *him* to come and rescue her.

She looks to me and smirks. "I'm Baylor fucking Evans, everyone fucking loves me."

Eight words is all it takes for my world to coming crashing down around me and confirm my fear. She used me.

35
BAYLOR

WHEN I SAY THOSE WORDS, MY WORLD AROUND ME COMES CRASHING DOWN. Corey actually believes I've turned and that hurts me to my core. Before I can try and clue him in that it's all a ruse, Kye slides his arm around my waist and slams his lips to mine. I'm shocked and when my mouth opens, he shoves his tongue inside. My eyes close and a tear falls free.

"Fuck, I've missed those lips," Kye tells me.

I smile at him; it's all I can manage right now. From next to me, Ave cries and that sound snaps me back to the present. Looking around, I need to figure a way out, and I'm positive the only way to do so is to continue this charade with Kye.

Lacing my fingers with his, I squeeze his hand. "Let's get out of here," I tell him and I try to drag him away.

"Bay, what are you doing?" Ave pleads.

Looking to her, I see it in her eyes, disappointment. I wish I could tell her I love her. That I'm doing this to save them but I can't right now. As much as it pains me, I need them to think I've turned. Their safety hinges on this.

"Not so fast. Before we go, you have a choice to make."

"And what choice might that be?"

"Her or him?"

"Excuse me?" I question him, but I think I already know.

"In order for us to leave, someone needs to die. You, as my queen get to choose."

Dean grabs Ave and marches her over to Corey. He pushes her to her knees and roughly squeezes her shoulder. My eyes well with tears as my gaze flicks between the two most important people in my life. No matter what I do right now, someone I love will die.

From behind me, a woman laughs. Looking over my shoulder, I see Monica fucking Quinn. I'm not surprised at all that she's here, helping him. She's a fucking scum, I was no better before I started all this but now, I've changed. I'm not the selfish bitch I used to be and that's why this choice is impossible.

"She can't choose, Kye, because she loves him. It's written all over her face." Monica sneers, "She never loved you, not like I do. I'm your true queen, Kye. Give me that gun and I'll prove how much I'm yours. I'll kill—"

A gunshot rings out and I look over to see Monica collapse to the deck. Looking back at Kye in shock, I'm sick to my stomach when I see the sinister look on his face.

"No one threatens my queen or tells me what to do." He looks to me and cups my cheek. "Now, who do you choose?"

"I...I..." I can't answer him. I don't want either of them to die. I can't live without either one of them. I just can't.

"Time's up, bitch," he snarls at me. "Time to choose who lives...and who dies."

Looking back to Kye, I stare into his evil eyes and that's when my decision hits me. "Me," I whisper.

"Sorry, I didn't hear that."

Taking a step closer to him, I stare at him. "I. Choose. Me," I confidently say, enunciating each word to prove my point. My voice is strong and confident; the complete opposite of how I really feel, but it's the only way to protect them both. It's a sacrifice I'm willing to make because I realize in this moment; I love him. This will be my ultimate act of love.

"I love you," I murmur. Turning my head, I stare at Corey and smile. "I love you." Turning my gaze to Ave, I swallow back a sob. "I love you too, Ave."

"You love him?" Kye snarls, grabbing my shoulder roughly, spinning me to face him.

"Yes!" I shout at him. "I love him with every fiber of my being, therefore to save them, I chose me. I'd rather be dead than spend a day breathing at your side without one of them here. Kye, you don't get to dictate my life anymore. I make my own decisions and I choose me!" I shout, "You were the worst decision I've ever made. I give my life for theirs, it's the ultimate sacrifice I can make."

"And it's one more shitty decision you've made, Baylor." He raises his pistol and points it directly at me. My heart is racing but as I stare down the barrel of the gun in Kye's hand, I know I'm doing the right thing. The click of the safety causes me to jump. Taking a deep breath, I close my eyes. I'm ready for death but as with everything in my life, it doesn't go according to plan.

Kye sneers and it hits me, he's not going to just kill me; he's going to kill them too. I've just fucked this up for everyone, but before I can come up with a plan, gunshots pierce through the silence. The sound of the gunfire is deafening. My ears are ringing; everything is muffled. Everything happens in slow motion.

I'm frozen on the spot, staring into the distance when it comes roaring back to life. People are yelling. Feet are pounding on the deck. Someone is crying nearby and as I stand here, it suddenly hits me. I'm still alive.

Shaking my head, I look around at the chaos before me. I look down and my eyes widen. I gasp and cover my mouth. My eyes well with tears and everything, once again, becomes blurry.

The first tear drops and it causes an avalanche to flow behind them. I fall to my knees and stare into lifeless eyes.

Kye is dead.

Looking next to him, my heart stops when I see it's Corey lying next to him. His eyes are closed and there's a growing red spot on his chest. Vaguely, I hear Ave yelling my name, but I continue to stare at Corey. He's not moving. He's not breathing. There's so much blood and it continues to seep out of his chest.

Black spots hinder my vision.

Blinking becomes difficult.

Breathing hurts.

Everything becomes muffled.

My last thought before I drift into the dark abyss is that he's dead and I'm not, how will I live with that?

36
COREY

Opening my eyes, I blink a few times. My shoulder is throbbing, my head is fuzzy, and there's an incessant beeping coming from the machine next to me. Looking to the side, I see someone in the chair by the window. My vision is quite blurry so I can't make them out clearly, but I can tell it's a woman.

Clearing my throat, I garner their attention. They sit up immediately and when they see me, they stand and walk over. I watch her as she walks over to me. My vision is still shit and I can't see her properly, but her eyes are a vivid blue. Her lips are moving but I can't hear what she's saying, it's muffled. Her form becomes blurrier. My eyelids become heavy. Blinking is difficult. I close my eyes and drift off into darkness again.

The next time I wake, my shoulder still hurts, my head is less heavy, the beeping is still loud, but this time my eyes stay open. The room comes into focus and I look to the chair but this time, there's a brunette sitting there. When she notices me staring at her, she stands. "About time you woke up, Sleeping Beauty."

"Very funny, Davis. What happened?"

"What do you remember?" she throws back at me.

"It's all hazy right now." I swallow but my mouth is drier than the Sahara desert right now. "Water," I croak out.

She grabs the pitcher from the rolling table and fills it up. She brings it to my lips and I drink. I gulp down the whole cup in a few seconds. "More."

She shakes her head, "Not too much, otherwise you'll be sick. You've been out for forty-eight hours now. Surgery went well."

"Surgery?" I question, but then I remember my shoulder, lifting my right hand I rub over it and missing pieces come back to me. A cabin by a lake. A man with a gun. Two women who look the same. Gunfire. Then nothing. "What happened?" I ask again.

"You were shot—"

"No shit," I fire back at her. "Who shot me?"

"Kye Vlahos," she says and then stares at me, not elaborating further.

That name is familiar but I can't quite place it. "Why do I know that name?"

"Because…" Again she doesn't say anything.

My mind is all jumbled right now. Closing my eyes, I lie back, and like a strike of lightning, I remember facing off with Kye. We were in a banquet room, but it was him who was shot in the shoulder. The woman from earlier was with him and that confuses me even more.

My head begins to throb, blood whooshing in my ears. The machine I'm attached to begins to erratically beep, much like the thudding of my heart right now.

The door to my room swings open and it's pandemonium. My body feels heavy and the darkness once again envelops me and I drift off.

This time, I dream of the blue-eyed woman. We are standing on the end of a jetty, a cabin behind us. I'm in black board shorts and she's wearing a purple string bikini and she looks fucking amazing. Taking her hand in mine, I pull her and we jump into the water. She wriggles free from me and swims away. She turns around and we stare intently at one another when a gunshot rings through the silence.

Turning my head, standing on the end of the dock, I see Kye Vlahos. His arm is outstretched and in his hand is a smoking gun. He's grinning and moves his gaze from mine and then he lets out a sinister laugh. Looking over, I see the woman floating in a pool of red bloody water. Another gunshot rings out but I wake with a start.

My heart is racing as I inhale deeply. "Fuck me," I moan, as the wound in my shoulder pulls from the deep breath I just took.

Lifting my right hand, I rub my fingers over my forehead. That dream felt so real but what I want to know is, why am I dreaming of this blue-eyed woman? And why was she here earlier? Maybe I dreamt that too.

The door to my room opens and in walks, Charli. She smiles when she sees me awake and walks over to take a seat next to my bed.

"Don't you ever do that again!"

"Do what?" I ask, genuinely confused. I'm in a hospital bed, what could I possibly have done?

"Flatline like you did. You scared the absolute shit out of me, Cox."

"My apologies. I'm sorry I got shot and my body decided to do whatever the hell it just did."

"Apology accepted. Now, how do you feel?"

"Like I got shot."

"Hardy fucking har."

"Watch your mouth, Davis." As soon as I say this, a warm and fuzzy feeling envelops me. I'm so confused right now. Nothing is making sense. "Can you fill me in, please?"

She takes a deep breath. "It seems that Dean was working with Vlahos and gave up our location, hence how he found us."

"I never trusted that fucker," I snarl.

"I did and it pisses me the fuck off that I didn't realize he'd turned. I knew something was up with him but I never thought he'd do this."

"Don't beat yourself up. I didn't even click, I just presumed he was being a dick 'cause he is one."

"Well, I'm the bigger dick because I didn't realize my partner was dirty. That was actually why I was called away that night."

"Thank fuck you were called away because had you not, the outcome would have been very different."

"The outcome was still shit. You got shot. Vlahos died. Dean got away. At least Baylor and Avery are now safe."

"Who're they?" I ask her, I don't know anyone by those names.

She looks at me, concern on her face. "You're messing with me, right? You know who they are."

I shake my head. "I have no clue who you're talking about."

We both fall silent and then the door to my room opens and in walks the blue-eyed woman from my dream. When she sees me awake, her face breaks out in the most beautiful smile. She races over to me and hugs me. "Core, I'm so glad you're awake. I was so worried." She pulls back and cups my cheek and stares at me.

"Who are you?" I ask and my question removes the smile from her face.

"Hardy har, Mr. Comedian," she says, reaching up to cup my cheek.

Shaking my head, I push her hand away and look to Charli. "Charli, who is she?"

"Core, it's me. Baylor. Your Kitten."

"I don't know you. I don't have a kitten. I hate cats." I stare at her, trying to remember her, but the first memory I have of her is when I woke earlier and then again when she appeared in my dream.

Quietly, I whisper, "I don't know you."

37
BAYLOR

"I DON'T KNOW YOU. I DON'T HAVE A KITTEN." THOSE WORDS PLAY ON REPEAT as I turn away from him and exit his room. The tears fall as I walk down the corridor. Exiting the hospital, I lean against the building and slide down. The brick wall scratches and digs into my back as I fall to the ground and cry.

Resting my head on my knees, I sob my broken heart out.

He doesn't remember me.

I don't know how long I sit out here but when I have no more tears to cry, I stand up and decide to go home. I've taken two steps when the hairs on my neck prickle. Looking up, I see Corey and Charli standing in the doorway of the hospital. My first thought is why is he out of bed? He only woke up a few minutes ago but when I look around, I realize it's dark. Clearly I've been sitting here crying for much longer than I thought.

Our gaze connects and we silently stare at one another. I plead internally for him to recognize me, but he continues to stare through me. My heart breaks all over again at his blank stare. My chest tightens and I realize I've been holding my breath. I try to breathe but I can't. I'm literally breathless right now. The more I try to inhale, the more it hurts. The panic building within me increases which halts my breathing further. My vision begins to dot; I stumble and fall. My head connects with the cement and then nothing. I let the darkness engulf me because I have nothing to live for anymore. Without him, I am nothing.

When I stir, I realize I'm in a hospital bed. Even though I'm awake, I keep my eyes closed because when I open them, it will all be real. Corey won't remember me and I'll be all alone. At least if I stay asleep, I can pretend he didn't just destroy my heart and soul.

Two people are talking; it's Ave and Flynn. I can hear from the pain in her voice that she's worried about me. I don't want her to worry but I also don't want to wake up and not have him in my life anymore.

"Why did this happen?" Ave cries.

"It seems the shock from the last week became too much and it caused her to lose consciousness. Her vitals are good, Ave. Now we just wait for her body to reset and then she'll wake up."

"She's been out for twelve hours now. Why won't she wake up, Flynn?"

"She's been through a lot, babe, and with the Corey thing, it's all caught up with her, but her body is doing what it should. Trust me, I know what she needs right now."

"Well, I need her to wake up," she snaps at him. "Flynn, I can't lose her." Ave murmurs, "I can't lose my BayBay."

"You won't," I croak out. Hearing the sadness in her voice hurts too much, I can't pretend to still be asleep anymore. "I'm sorry," I tell her, as she sits on my bed and takes my hand in hers.

"Why are you apologizing?" Ave asks me, as she brushes my hair off my forehead.

"'Cause I made you worry, again," I quietly tell her.

"Bay, I will always worry," she confirms to me, and I can tell by the tone of her voice she means it.

Lifting my gaze to hers, my eyes well with tears. "He doesn't remember me," I tell her. A tear breaks free and then an avalanche follows behind. Ave pulls me into her embrace and I cry into her shoulder. The clicking of my door causes me to lift my head and I see that Ave and I are alone. "Ave, why doesn't he remember me?"

"Flynn said it's some sort of short-term memory amnesia, he remembers stuff from years ago but not recently." I sadly nod as I listen but all I hear is, he doesn't remember me. "But if it makes you feel better, while you were out, he came to visit."

"Not really but it's something. I guess."

"He seems upset, Bay. He was asking about your relationship, but

Flynn said to not say too much otherwise it will confuse his mind and may block it permanently."

"I should have known that something like this would happen. I'm not destined for a happily ever after."

"Yes, you are," she says, squeezing my hand. "The past is in the past. You need to look to the future. Your future with Corey." She pauses and then adds, "And as a kick-ass aunty."

My mouth drops open and my eyes widen. "I'm going to be an aunty?"

She nods. "Yes, we found out yesterday. I have my first scan in a few weeks."

"Ohh, Ave," I cry, "I'm so happy for you." Pulling back, I look down at her belly, which looks a little pudgy up close. "Twins?"

She shrugs. "I don't know."

"I'm betting it's twin boys," I tell her as I lie back in my bed, smiling for the first time today. "You think you can grab me some—"

"Taffy and a coffee?"

"You know me so well."

"I sure do." She stands up and walks to the door, before she opens it, she looks over her shoulder, "It will all work out, Bay, I promise."

She exits my room and I stare at the closed door. I hope she's right because I really do love him. I hope I get my chance at happiness but as with everything in my life, the door to my room opens and once again, shit hits the fan.

38
COREY

When I saw that Baylor woman collapse, my heart hurt for her. I don't remember her but it seems we know each other. No one is telling me shit and it's pissing me off. There's a knock on my door and it opens, that woman's twin, Avery, pops her head in. They are very similar but I can tell she's not her. She smiles that sad 'I'm sorry' smile. "Can I come in?" Nodding my head, she steps inside but stays by the door. "Just letting you know Bay is awake and everything is okay."

Relief at hearing she's okay floods my body. "That's great," I pause, "how...how is she?"

She steps farther into my room. "Confused. Sad. Upset. Feels she deserves this."

"Why would she deserve me not remembering her?"

She bites her bottom lip and an image of Baylor doing that flashes in my mind and I smile. "What did you just remember?" Avery asks me.

"Does she do that?" I question.

"Do what?"

"Bite her lip like that. It sparked a memory of her sitting on a kitchen counter doing that."

She smiles at me. "Yeah, she does. Would you like to see her again?"

"Yes. No. I don't know," I tell her, as I rub the back of my neck in frustration. "I don't want to upset her again. She ended up in here because of me."

"No." She shakes her head. "She ended up in here because she's been through hell."

"Because of me."

"No!" she shouts. "Because of Kye and Dean. It's not your fault, Corey. Please for me. For Bay, go and see her. If me biting my lip sparked something, maybe spending some time with her will spark more memories." She bites her lip again and a vision of Baylor with a lake behind her flashes before my eyes. "Look, I don't know you very well, but I know you are good for her and I know that deep down, you feel something for her. Please don't give up on her."

Before I can reply, she exits my room. Leaving me alone with my thoughts and visions of Baylor biting her lip. As I keep thinking about that, my heart beats faster. It's as if it knows who she is. "Fuck it," I mumble to the room.

Hopping out of bed, I slip my feet into my slippers and I go to see her, hoping Avery is right and something she says or does will reboot my memory.

Stopping outside her door, I take a deep breath but I hear a commotion on the other side. Stepping into the room, Dean is standing beside her bed. He has his back to me and hasn't noticed me yet. He's focused on Baylor, her eyes are locked to his and that's when I notice he has a knife in his hand.

I can't see his face but his shoulders are hunched tightly and his breathing is deep and erratic. He's on edge and completely unhinged, Baylor is in trouble.

"Get the fuck away from me, asshole," Baylor growls at him, and those seven words cause everything to come crashing back to me. I remember.

Watching her in the interrogation room.

Her sassy tongue the first time we spoke.

Kissing her in her kitchen.

Arresting her the day we took down Kye.

Seeing her for the first time in the lobby after her release.

Waking up next to her at the cabin.

Handcuffing her to the bed.

Sliding my cock into her.

Her lips around my cock.

The look on her face when she pops a piece of taffy into her mouth.

Her smile.

Her laugh.

I remember…everything.

"Watch your mouth, Kitten," I say, causing both of them to turn their heads toward me. They both have shocked looks on their faces. His filled with malice at my arrival, and hers in shock that I'm here and I called her Kitten.

"You remember?" she whispers.

Nodding my head, I smile. "Everything. I remember everything, Kitten."

Tears well in her eyes, I want nothing more than to take her into my arms and kiss those sassy pouty lips, but Dean turns to face me.

"Well, isn't this nice?" he sneers. "The happy lovebirds are reunited just before they die." He looks back to Baylor. "Kye was right, you are a fucking cunt." He turns his attention to me. "And you, Corey-fucking-Cox, are nothing but a waste of space." He steps toward me and I realize, I have no weapon and I'm recovering from being shot.

He takes another step closer; I back up and hit the wall. I'm trapped and have nowhere else to go. *This is not good*, I think to myself but at least he's focused on me and not my kitten.

His eyes widen and then he falls to the ground. Behind him, Baylor stands there with her dinner tray in her hands. "Take that, you stupid fucker," she says to his crumpled body.

Normally I'd want to scold her for swearing but she's right, the fucker deserved that and more. We stare at one another. She smiles at me and bites her bottom lip. A smile appears on my face at seeing that because I remember everything about the woman before me. All the feelings I have for her bubble to the surface and I need her in my arms.

At the same time, we lunge for one another. She jumps over his body and I step forward. She wraps her arms around my waist and I throw my good arm around her shoulders, pulling her into me. I breathe her in. "I remember," I whisper into her hair. "I remember everything."

"I thought I'd lost you," she blubbers into my chest.

"I will always find you, Kitten."

She lifts her gaze to mine, and I cup her cheek and bend down to kiss her. As soon as our lips touch, everything is right in the world once again. A groan from Dean pulls us apart, just as the door opens and Ave walks in. Her eyes widen when she sees Baylor in my arms and then she smiles. Her gaze drops and her eyes widen farther when she sees Dean on the ground. Without saying a word, she turns back around and exits the room, leaving Bay and me alone, with a moaning Dean.

A few moments later, the door opens again and Charli is there with a uniformed officer.

She looks to Dean, "Dean Chikatilo," she says, her voice wavering, "you are under arrest for the attempted murder o..." She reads him his rights, but all my attention is on the blue-eyed woman in my arms.

"Kitten, I'm so sorry I didn't remember you," I honestly tell her, cupping her cheek in my palm. She leans into it and rubs her cheek on my hand.

"You have nothing to be sorry for."

"Yes, I do. You're the best thing to have come into my life. There's no way in hell I could forget someone like you. I also need to apologize for not saying it sooner."

"Saying what?" she asks, her face scrunched in confusion.

"I love you, Baylor Evans."

Her mouth drops open in shock and then she smiles. I've never seen anything more stunning in my life.

"I love you too, Corey Cox."

She reaches up, grips my cheeks, and presses her lips to mine. Everything around me fades away. It's just my Kitten and me. We may have hated each other when we first met, but there's a fine line between love and hate, and a love fueled from hate like ours is the strongest of them all. And my kitten is the strongest person I know.

39
BAYLOR

...three months later

COREY WENT BACK TO WORK THIS WEEK AFTER BEING SHOT, HIS SURGERY, AND rehabilitation. He's a shitty patient but after purchasing a pair of fuzzy handcuffs and a slutty nurse's outfit, he became a pliant and willing patient. I'm sure the sexy outfit and a prescription of BJ's, spankings, and handcuffing had something to do with it.

And me? Well, yesterday I enrolled in community college to do a degree in mixology. I start next semester and I'm excited for the adventure ahead. In the meantime, I will keep trying to pull Charli out of her funk. She and I are meeting up for drinks tomorrow night. She's devastated that her partner betrayed her, but what upsets her the most is that she didn't see it coming. She knew Dean was acting strange but she put it down to his hate for Corey. Never in her wildest dreams did she think he was working for Kye. We still don't know why he was helping him; the asshole is refusing to give anything away.

We spent the evening at Avery and Flynn's. Today they had another scan and as I guessed when she first told me, she's pregnant with twin boys. The four of us had a lovely dinner, we've decided to try and do this weekly, but sometimes Flynn will be absent due to his shifts. I'm so glad

Avie and I are back to being twinsies and that Flynn and Corey get along so well.

Ave and I join the boys at the door. "Yeah, my Kitten got me good!" Corey says to Flynn with a smile on his face. Stepping beside him, he pulls me into his side and kisses my temple. "She's a wild one, but she's my wild one," Corey says to Flynn and Avery. His words make me smile but it's true, he got me good and I wouldn't have it any other way.

Corey and I are walking down the street toward his car after saying our goodbyes. Our fingers are laced and I've never been happier. Looking over to him, I grin.

"What?" he asks.

"I love you," I honestly tell him and it hits me, I want to be with him forever. Pulling on his hand, I stop us. "Core, marry me?"

"Come again?"

"Marry me? I love you. You love me. I want to be with you forever. Life is too short but I know without a doubt, I want to grow old and gray with you."

"Isn't the guy supposed to ask the girl?"

"Probably, but I don't give a flying fuck, and before you tell me to watch my mouth, I know, language. So what do you say, Agent Cox, will you marry me?"

He stares at me. He's silent and I begin to wonder if he doesn't want what I want when he finally breaks the silence. "Fuck yes, I'll marry you."

I can't resist. "Watch your mouth, Core."

"Great, it's started already. You bossing me around."

"Get fucked, fiancé," I sass at him, "Now take me home and ravage me. We have some celebrating to do."

The trip back to our place is quick, I'm pretty sure Core broke a few road rules to get us back here but I don't care. I need him and I need him now.

We race inside and head straight to our bedroom. I make quick work of my clothes; my body ablaze with want and need for him. Core stares at me and with his eyes locked on me, he pulls his shirt over his head in that sexy one-handed way that guys do. My gaze unashamedly roams his chest that was carved by the gods. He removes his jeans and briefs together. He's gloriously naked and my eyes once again roam over his body, I will never get enough of this man. His cock is hard and erect with the tip already glistening with precum. It makes my mouth water; I want to devour him. "Core, get your sexy as fuck ass over here now."

He growls at my swearing and that noise vibrates through my body.

Who knew a sound like that could cause my body to react like this, but Corey-fucking-Cox does things to me. "I'd much rather watch your cock slide into my mouth but potato patatho."

He stares at me. The temperature in the bedroom rises the longer we eye fuck one another. "Get on your knees, Kitten."

"Why?" I ask, my heart rate increasing as he stalks naked toward me.

"Because I'm going to do exactly as you asked." He stops halfway to me. "I'm going to fuck your sassy mouth, and then I'm going to make love to my fiancé until the wee hours of the morning."

"You had me at fuck your mouth."

"Kitten," he growls.

With a wink, I drop to my knees and crawl toward him. Stopping at his feet, I gaze up at the man whom I love unconditionally. Licking my bottom lip, I bite it as I beckon him closer to me. His cock is right in front of me, the head weeping with his arousal. My tongue darts out and I swipe it across the tip. Core hisses and it turns into a groan when I suck his shaft into my mouth.

"Fuck, I love your mouth," he pants, as he guides my head back and forth. My eyes flick to the freestanding mirror and I watch our reflection as Core does exactly as he threatened: he fucks my mouth. And fuck me sideways, it's the hottest thing I've ever seen. I was wet before but watching ourselves in the mirror has me dripping with need. Sliding my hand down between my legs, I flick my piercing before slipping two fingers inside myself. I moan around his dick. I'm so turned on right now. I look back up at him and I look toward the mirror. He follows my gaze and I watch his cock slide in and out of my mouth. His gaze is a little lower and he watches my fingers glide in and out of my folds.

"You are fucking everything, Baylor Evans. You are mine. Now and forever," he groans, increasing his thrusts, causing me to choke on his dick. He pulls back and drops to his knees in front of me. He grips my cheeks. "You okay, Kitten?"

Nodding my head, I cover his hands with mine. "Better than ever. I fucking love you so much."

"Kitten," he growls, in that delicious way I've come to love.

"Fuck you," I sass at him. Falling to the carpet, I lie back and spread my legs open. My clit is swollen and throbbing, my fingers won't cut it anymore. "I need you, Core."

"You have me, Kitten," he says, as he slides his cock into me. My walls clench and hug him tight. "Fuuuuck," he groans. He drops forward and rests on his forearms. He fucks me like the stallion he is. He literally takes my breath away.

"Now!" he shouts and the two of us come together. Screaming each other's name as we tumble into that glorious orgasmic abyss.

Opening my eyes, I stare up at him. I love this man with all my heart and soul. Who knew getting arrested, going undercover, doing jail time, and a stint in WitSec would lead to all of this?

Falling for Agent Cox was the best decision I ever made.

EPILOGUE

WHEN BAYLOR SURPRISED ME AND PROPOSED, SHE TOTALLY RUINED WHAT I had planned for the following week, so I had to quickly rearrange my plans but either way, we were engaged. And now, my Kitten and I are married and on our honeymoon. Avery and Flynn gifted us a trip to Oasis in Castaway Grove and it's fucking gorgeous, its literally an oasis. Not as gorgeous as my wife, but nothing is as gorgeous as her.

Lying in bed, I watch her sleep. My wife, I love saying that, is perfect in every way possible. She rolls over in her sleep, pulling the sheet down and baring her amazing tits to me. Sparkling in the morning sunlight is her engagement ring. The one I gave her after her surprise proposal, almost ruining mine...

...Leaving her sleeping, I quietly sneak out to the kitchen, I need to make a few adjustments and bring forward my proposal plans. I've just finished rearranging them and making coffee, when she slides her hands around my waist and kisses my shoulder blades. "Morning, fiancé."

"Morning, fiancée," I say back, spinning around to face her. I rest my hands on her lower back and stare into her gorgeous blue eyes. "Sleep well?"

"Like a baby. You?"

"Like a king."

"A king, hey, does that make me your queen?" As soon as she says this, her

face drops. *That was what Kye used to always say to her, not wanting her to be upset,* I shake my head.

"You are my Kitten and my fiancée."

"Well, you are mine and my fiancé." She grins at me. "Is it just me, or is it fucking awesome to say fiancé?"

"Watch your mouth, Kitten."

"I know how you can shut me up."

"You are insatiable," I tell her, as I slide my hands down her purple satin nightie and cup her ass. "I always want you but I need you to get dressed. I have a surprise."

"I like surprises. What is it?"

"If I tell you, it won't be a surprise."

She pouts, "You can spank me."

"I can do that anytime I want, now if you behave, I will spank and cuff you later."

"Promises, promises," she says, as she pulls away from me, turns, and walks out of the kitchen. She stops at the entrance and clears her throat. Lifting my gaze, the minx is standing there naked, her nightie hanging from her index finger.

I'd love nothing more than to ravage her, but my surprise will be here in ten minutes and for what I have in mind, I need more than ten minutes.

"You are going to be the death of me, woman. Go and get dressed and I promise, later."

"You better, fiancé, otherwise I'm taking back my proposal."

"No take backsies!" I shout as she stomps, yes, stomps away.

Picking up my mug, I bring it to my lips and shake my head.

When she returns she's dressed in jeans that look like they were painted on and a purple halter top thingy. My eyes roam over her and when I get to her face, she's smirking. "Like what you see?"

Nodding, I hand her a coffee. "Fuck yes, I do."

"Watch you—" She doesn't get to finish because the doorbell rings. "You expecting someone?" she asks, as she walks to the door. She swings it open and the doorway is filled with a balloon bouquet of at least twenty balloons in different shades of purple. It's attached to a box, filled with grape taffy.

"Core," she coos, "you shouldn't have."

When she turns around, I'm down on bended knee with a ring box in my hand. "Baylor, you may have beaten me to the punch with the proposal, but mine has all the romance and taffy you could desire. I think I fell for you the moment I heard you sassing at Agent Hall, I've fallen more and more in love with you each and every day since then, and I will do so until my last breath. Baylor Martine Evans, Kitten, will you marry me?"

A tear cascades down her cheek and she drops to her knees in front of me. She grips my cheeks and slams her lips to mine. She kisses me deeply, knocking us back to the floor with her on top of me. "Is that a yes?" I ask against her lips.

"Yes, a thousand times, yes."

Rolling her to her back, I remove the ring from the box and slip it onto her finger. "I love you, Kitten."

"I love you too, Core."

…What are you grinning at?" she asks, bringing me back to the present.

"Remembering the day I asked you to marry me."

"That was the second best day of my life."

"The best being when you officially became Baylor Cox?"

"Nope," she says, shaking her head, "The best was the day I was arrested because it led me on the path to you."

"Who knew an arrest could lead to all this?" I ask her.

"Certainly not me. What shall we do today?"

"Weeeeelll," I draw the word out. "We are on our honeymoon and your ass is looking mighty fine. I was thinking a spanking."

"How about we work on my ass's tan and then tonight, you can turn it pink after I suck your cock."

"I fucking love your dirty mouth," I tell her, pulling her into me and kissing her deeply.

"And I fucking love you."

The spanking comes sooner than anticipated due to my wife's sassy mouth, and with her ass nice and pink, we change into our swimwear and head downstairs to work on her ass tan and have a few cocktails.

We are walking toward our cabana when an old friend and I run into each other. "Burton fucking Hayes, what are you doing here?" I say, as we do the one-armed bro backslap hug.

"I live here now, man. I bought Castaway Coffee."

"No shit."

"Yes, shit."

My eyes dart around, "Did Trina come too?"

He shakes his head. "Nah, we split. That's one of the reasons I came here."

"You finally woke up and saw the light, eh?" Trina was a crazy bitch, always out for herself. I always got the feeling she was hiding something but I never said anything 'cause Burton seemed happy.

"You could say that." His demeanor changes slightly but just as quickly, his face lights up when a gorgeous brunette walks toward us.

"Hey, baby," she says, snuggling into his side. She looks to me and stretches out her hand, "Hey, I'm Nix"

"Corey," I say, placing my hand in hers and shaking. For a small thing, she has a good grip.

She turns her head to look up at Burton, love radiating between the two of them. "Kain is here, he and Talia just had another argument."

"Again?" Burton questions

"Yeah, those two just need to fuck already. Like seriously, penis in vagina, pump and repeat. Once they fuck away the tension, peace will return to the grove. Blind fucking Freddy can see they want each other, but they are too stubborn to see it."

"Love blinds some people, they don't see it until it smacks them up the side of the head when they least expect it."

"Are we speaking from experience?" Nix asks me.

Nodding, I grin. "Yeah. My Kitten came into my life when I least expected it."

"No shit," Burton says, "Agent Corey Cox has finally met 'the one.'"

"After he arrested me," my gorgeous wife says, sliding her arm around my waist joining us.

"You and I are going to get along smashingly," Nix says.

Burton rolls his eyes and whispers, "Ohh shit." He looks to Bay. "If she offers you a cocktail, run the other way."

"What can I say, I make killer cocktails." Nix nonchalantly shrugs but the look she is giving Burton right now is carnal and heated, it's similar to how Baylor looks at me when she wants to get down and dirty...or kill me.

There's a fine line between love and hate and Baylor and I walk along that precarious knife's edge each and every day. Baylor is my complete opposite but at the same time, she's my missing piece. Our love and hate collided spectacularly but I wouldn't change a thing. Well, maybe the getting shot part but the recovery blow jobs were amazing, so yeah, I'll keep the getting shot part.

"Killer, more like downright dangerous," Burton mumbles, but loud enough for all of us to hear.

"You love them...and me." Nix winks at him and then links arms with Bay, dragging her toward the Grove Bar. Like the lovesick puppies that Burton and I are, we follow them.

After way too many of Nix's killer cocktails, Baylor and I stumble toward the beach. We collapse into a cabana and snuggle into one another. We stare up at the night sky. There are a million tiny little stars twinkling in the night sky. "Core, you think that somewhere up there is a couple like us, snuggling and in love?"

"I've never really thought about it," I tell her, "But I do know that I'm happy to be snuggling here with you." Rolling to face her, I rest my head on my hand. Brushing a tendril of hair off her face, I lean in and kiss her nose. "I love you, Baylor Cox."

"I love hearing that," she tells me.

"I love you," I repeat.

She shakes her head, "No, not that. I love that I'm officially Baylor Cox. If you had told me the first day we met that I'd be married to you, I would have told you to drop the crack pipe. Never in my wildest dreams did I think this would happen but seriously, getting arrested was the best thing to ever happen to me, because it led me to you."

"Arresting you was the best arrest of my life."

"Technically Hall and Oats arrested me. You just needed me to bring down the bad guy."

"Potato patahto. But you know what?"

"What?"

"I wouldn't change a thing either. Falling for you was the best thing I ever did."

"Aww, you say such sweet things. Now, take me back to our room and fuck me."

"Watch your mouth, Kitten."

She leans over and kisses me, "You wouldn't have me any other way. Now, let's go."

It's true, I love her just the way she is.

THE END!!!!!

PLAYLIST

Anywhere - Rita Ora
Purple Rain - Prince
Unstoppable - Sia
The Last Time - The Script
Bitch - Meredith Brooks
Born this Way - Lady Gaga
You're The one I Want - Loving Calibre
Sober - Demi Lovato
Stronger - Kelly Clarkson
Love the Way You Lie - Eminem feat. Rhianna
When Love and Hate Collide - Def Leppard
What About Now - Daughtry
ICH TU DIR WEH - Rammstein
Set Fire to the Rain - Adele
I Knew Your Were Trouble - Taylor Swift
Butterfly - Crazytown
Story of my Life - One Direction
True Colours - Cyndi Lauper
Apologise - Timberland
Dusk Till Dawn - ZAYNE feat. Sia
Not in Love - Olin and the Moon
The Reason - Hoobastank
Animals - Maroon 5

Girl on Fire - Alicia Keys
Sweet but Psycho - Ava Max
The Diary of Jane - Breaking Benjamin
Broken - Seether feat. Amy Lee
I'll Stand by You - The Pretenders
FourFiveSeconds - Astrid S
Maneaster - Hall & Oats
Nothing Like Them - Loving Calibre
Better Than Me - Hinder
Without You - Hinder
You and Me - Lifehouse
Bring me to Life - Evanesence
Hey Hey, My My - Battleme
Way Down We Go - KALEO
Bad Reputation - Joan Jett and the Blackhearts
Cruel to be Kind - Letters to Cleo
Can't Take my Eyes off You - Frankie Valli
Even Angels Fall - Jessica Riddle
The Weakness in Me - Joan Armstrong
My Happiness - Powderfinger
Iria - The Goo Goo Dolls

This playlist can be found Spotify.

falling for
AGENT CRUZ

Nothing is as
it seems

A FALLING NOVEL

DL GALLIE

There's no rhyme or reason when it comes to happily ever afters. Falling in love happens when you least expect it.

CHARLI

I was betrayed, now I don't trust easily.

One night I let loose and do something crazy.

When my new partner is assigned, I'm shocked to find we've already met.

From the moment my eyes land on him, again, I know I'm screwed.

Dominic Cruz crashes through my fortress and I start to trust again.

Until I don't.

Things happen that will once again change me, and everything I thought I knew.

DOMINIC

This new assignment fell into my lap.

I was reluctant but then I met my new partner—Charli Davis.

The one who rocked my world and left in the morning.

Our connection was instant and it's still as intense.

My future is finally looking bright.

Then the past reappears.

Now everything is uncertain, but nothing is as it seems.

To my Henchwench, Tara
Thank you for being my wench XoXoX

There is never a time or place for true love. It happens accidentally, in a heartbeat, in a single flashing, throbbing moment.

~ *Sarah Dessen*

PROLOGUE

BETRAYAL.

Verb.

To fail or desert especially in time of need…and for the second time in as many months, I've been betrayed. Once again, someone close has let me down. This time it hurts so much more because the person who betrayed me is also the man who stole my heart.

I knew he was too good to be true and rather than listening to my head, I listened to my traitorous vagina and heart. *Assholes.* Now, my life is in the toilet—like my head currently—but this time, I have more than myself to think about. All I want to do is crawl into a ball, drink myself into oblivion, and eat my weight in Doritos, but I can't. I have to be strong because people are relying on me, but just once, I'd love for someone to look after me.

Sitting up, I rest my back against the tub and stare into nothing. "Stronger" by Britney Spears starts playing from the living room and as I listen to the words, they hit me hard.

Standing up, I stare at my reflection in the guest room's mirror and decide that yes, I am strong. I can do this, alone. No more wallowing. I will not let a penis ruin my life. I'm Charli fucking Davis, kick-ass agent…and soon-to-be mom.

CHARLI 1

…ten weeks earlier

"…HE'S DIRTY, CHARLI," AMANDA, THE BOSS, TELLS ME.

"Come again?" I question, but I'm already processing what she just told me and deep down I know everything she said is in fact one-hundred-percent correct.

"Dean is working for Vlahos. He was responsible for the explosion that took out Corey's car. Bomb making pieces, similar to what forensics retrieved, were found in his apartment."

"That's pretty dumb of him."

"I'd guess that when he failed to take Corey out, he was rocked and skittish. From memory, you guys moved to the cabin straight after the attempt. He clearly didn't have time to clean up his mess."

Shaking my head in disbelief, I rub my forehead. "So what do we do now?"

"A team will return with you now and try to catch him in the act."

"He'll be suspicious if I return with backup."

"Which is why we will have a cover story stating that another threat has been made against Cox and since he's a fellow agent, everything is being done to keep him safe."

"That will work. Will they return with me? Or come up later?"

"Both. Agent Barber will return with you now to have an extra set of eyes and ears inside. Agents Isaac, Jenkins, Drake, and Thorpe will be on stakeout, they are all set to go once we've formulated everything. Charli, it's imperative that Dean doesn't know about this."

"I won't be letting anything on. I want to take him down as much as you do. I'm just pissed I didn't put two and two together. I knew something was amiss with him, but I just thought it was his hatred toward Cox affecting him."

"Don't beat yourself up over this."

"Easier said than done," I tell her. Some agent I am, I didn't even realize that my partner is dirty.

"Davis," Amanda snaps, "I need your head in the game."

"I'll be fine, Boss."

"Good," she says and she leaves my office.

Leaning back in my chair, I stare at the ceiling, frustrated with myself. I'm an agent, a federal fucking agent, and I missed all the signs pointing to my partner being a corrupt asshole. I should've known something was up with Dean, but he played me like a fool. However, I will have the last laugh. I will do everything in my power to bring him and Vlahos to justice.

Grabbing the file Amanda left, I go over all that she has and I add my suggestions and notes for how to proceed from here. By the time I have the plan amended, it's early in the morning. I should be sleeping but I'm running on adrenalin, caffeine—a lot of caffeine—and anger right now.

A knock on my door, startles me. I was so lost in my head, I didn't hear my name being called. "Davis, we are ready to finalize the plan," Agent Barber tells me.

"Thanks, Bec," I respond.

Standing up, I follow her down to the conference room. Everyone falls silent when we walk in. I pause at the entrance to the room and they all stare at me. I hate the look of pity reflecting in their eyes. "Okay, yep, this sucks. I don't want to hear 'sorry' or anything along those lines. All I want to do is bring him to justice and put Vlahos back where he belongs. If you have a problem with that, there's the door." I point behind me. No one moves or utters a word. You could hear a pin drop in here. "I'll take the silence as we are good."

Stepping into the room, I close the door behind me and take a seat. "Okay, here's the plan."

Exactly thirty minutes later, Bec and I are in my car and on our way back to the cabin. The others will follow and get to their tasks while we get to ours.

"I know you said to not say anything, but since I'll be living with you for the foreseeable future, I feel I have like a roommate privilege." I laugh at this. "How are you doing with all this?"

"I feel like a fool. I'm a federal fucking agent and I didn't see what was happening right under my nose."

"He had everyone fooled, Charli."

"Yeah, but I'm his partner. I've been living with him for the last few weeks and I didn't suspect a thing. He was doing all of this right under my nose. He and Vlahos must be laughing at me and my ignorance."

"And that will play perfectly into this. His cocky ass won't see us coming."

"I hope you're right, Bec."

The sun has been up for about an hour when we reach the cabin. As we approach, I notice a car in the driveway and my senses tell me something is up. Immediately, I'm on high alert and pull to the side of the road. Without saying a word, Bec grabs her phone and calls the office for a plate check. It comes back registered to a Dr. Monica Quinn.

"Fuck," I scoff. "He's here." Looking to Bec, I order her, "Call the other team and tell them to get here ASAP, I'm going to go in."

"Alone?" she questions.

"Yep, I'm meant to be there so they won't suspect anything if I'm caught walking in. They won't expect me to have backup so we have an element of surprise, even if I'm discovered."

"Be careful," she reminds me.

Nodding my head, I reach over to the glove compartment and grab my gun. Climbing out of the car, I slip the weapon into the waistband of my jeans. Once it's secured, I make my way over to the cabin.

Ducking by Monica's car, I hear voices coming from around the back. Sneaking onto the property, I press myself to the side of the cabin and slink around the side. Ducking below the deck, I move farther into the yard. Peeking under the railing, my eyes widen at the scene before me.

Corey and Avery Evans are bound and on opposite sides of the deck. Monica Quinn, Dean, and Vlahos are standing around. Dean startles and trips on his deceptive fat feet and knocks over the trash can on the deck. The loud noise echoes in the quiet of the morning, "You alright there, heffalump?" Vlahos spits at Dean.

"There was a bug," he whines, this causes Corey to laugh and it pisses Dean off. He storms and punches Corey a few times, pushing him to the deck. "You're a dead man, Cox," he snarls at a beaten and bloody Corey.

"Enough," Vlahos bellows. Then from inside we hear Baylor yell for Cox. A sinister smile appears on Vlahos's face, "It's go time."

"Shit," I mumble, I was hoping backup would be here before this happened. Kye grabs and roughly manhandles a quivering, and visibly shaken, Avery inside. Cox spots me and I mouth, 'Backup is on the way' but before he can acknowledge me, the kitchen door swings open again.

Dropping down out of sight, I sneak another look and see Kye step back out onto the deck, pushing Avery and Baylor in front of him. I shake my head when I realize that he's using them as a shield. He really is a piece of work.

Cox laughs and everyone turns their heads to face him. "What the fuck are you laughing at, asshole?" Dean growls.

"Big bad Kye Vlahos is using two women as a shield. He's a fucking pansy." *You dickhead*, I think to myself, typical macho man trying to show off in front of his woman. From the corner of my eye, I see Bec and backup on the street about to enter the property. I nod at her and raise my hand in a stop position. She and the team stop and duck down out of sight since we don't know if Kye has any men inside and watching the house. I'm presuming not since I made it here undetected.

Looking back to the deck, my eyes widen. In the few moments I was watching the street, Kye has pulled out his gun and the barrel is currently pressed into Corey's temple. "Fuck, fuck, fuck," I whisper, just as Baylor begins walking over to them.

"If you love me at all, Kye, you will not pull that trigger." Her voice is strong but I can tell from the shaking of her body, she's shit scared right now.

"What makes you think I still love you?" Kye sneers at her.

Baylor, reaches up and cups his cheek. "I'm Baylor fucking Evans, everyone fucking loves me."

A grin appears on my face, only Baylor could, and would, say that. Kye slides his arm around her and slams his lips to hers. I see the moment Cox's heart breaks. He's fallen hard for her but right now, he feels betrayed by her. Her acting is on point but then again, fear causes people to do crazy things. I hope he knows she's acting. Well, I hope she is, otherwise this situation has just taken another turn I never saw coming.

"Fuck I've missed those lips," Kye croons, and I see Corey's face once again shatter at Baylor's betrayal, but I'm positive she's playing Kye's game. I've lived with the two of them these past few weeks and their connection is strong.

She takes his hand in hers. "Let's get out of here," she tells him, trying to pull him away from Corey and Avery, that slight movement shows me this is all a ruse to save Corey and her sister, who is a blubbering mess.

I miss exactly what Baylor says next but it's enough for Avery to plead with her. "Bay, what are you doing?"

Bay ignores her and tugs on Vlahos's hand again, but he pulls and stops her in her tracks. "Not so fast, Sugar. Before we go, you have a choice to make."

"And what choice might that be?" she sasses.

"Her or him?"

"Excuse me?" she huffs. I don't think she was prepared for this. Seems she has underestimated Kye Vlahos once again.

"In order for us to leave, someone needs to die. You, as my queen, get to choose who lives and who dies."

Dean grabs Ave and marches her over to Corey. He pushes her to her knees and roughly squeezes her shoulder.

Nearby a woman laughs; it's Monica. She walks, well saunters, toward Kye and Baylor. "She can't choose, Kye, because she loves him." She points to Cox. "It's written all over her face. She's never loved you, not like I do. I'm your true queen, Kye. Give me that gun and I will prove how much I'm yours. I'll kill—"

A gunshot rings out and Monica's body falls to the deck in a heap. Everyone is open mouthed and in shock. "No one threatens my queen or tells me what to do." He looks back to Baylor and cups her cheek again. Ignoring the fact he just killed a woman. Sure, she was a bitch but no one deserves to die like that. "Now, who do you choose?"

"I...I..." Baylor is in shock and is mumbling.

"Time's up, bitch," he snarls. "Time to choose who lives...and who dies."

Shocking us all, Baylor whispers, "Me!"

Dropping his hand from her face, he growls. "Sorry, I didn't hear that."

"I. Choose. Me," she confidently says, stepping toward him. Each word uttered with force and emotion. Turning her head, she tells Corey she loves him before repeating the same endearment to her sister.

"You love him?" Kye snarls, grabbing her shoulder roughly and spinning her to face him. His face is etched with anger and betrayal. *Ohh shit, this is going to end badly*, I internally whisper to myself.

Baylor doesn't help the precarious situation when she shouts, "Yes, I love him with every fiber of my being, therefore, to save them, I choose me! I'd rather be dead than spend a day breathing at your side without one of them here. Kye, you don't get to dictate my life anymore. I make my own decisions and I choose me. You were the worst decision I ever made. I give my life for theirs, it's the ultimate sacrifice I can make." I'm so proud of her for stepping up, but at the same time I'm yelling internally at her because she has just pissed off a madman. And that madman has been known to make rash decisions, for example, Monica. Case in point.

"And that is one more shitty decision you've made, Baylor." He raises his pistol and points it directly at her. That's when I signal for Bec and the team to come forward. Pulling my pistol from my jeans, I quietly click off the safety and make my way to the stairs.

Sneaking up them, I raise my weapon just as Kye flicks off the safety on his. Without hesitating, I pull the trigger and hit him right between the eyes. He too got off a shot and Cox falls to the deck. Looking around, I can't see Dean, seems the asshole got away in the commotion, but mark my words, I will get him. His betrayal will not go unpunished if it's the last thing I do.

Looking over, I see Baylor is frozen on the spot, staring at the scene before her. "Baylor," I yell, but she's so lost in her head she doesn't hear me as I begin to untie her sister's hands. As soon as Avery is free, she races over to her sister, but before she can reach her, Baylor collapses and loses consciousness.

The paramedics arrive. Corey and Baylor are rushed to the local airfield to be transported back to Western General. I leave Bec to handle things here and I escort Avery back to the city and her sister.

If we thought this was bad, it only gets worse in the coming days.

CHARLI 2

…five days later

LIFE IS SLOWLY RETURNING TO NORMAL, WELL FOR EVERYONE ELSE IT IS, BUT for me, I'm stuck in a rut. I keep focusing on the betrayal of my partner and it's really pissing me off that I'm pissed off. I'm still flabbergasted my partner turned and betrayed me. He was working for the enemy and I never saw it coming. After we apprehended the asshole at the hospital, he remained tight-lipped as to why he did what he did, but one of these days he will give me the answers I deserve. It's the least he can do for betraying me like he did.

The funny thing about the whole situation, I'm not pissed that he turned, what I'm most annoyed about is I didn't see it happening. We were living under the same roof and he was doing it right under my nose. What kind of shitty agent does that make me?

Internal Affairs is taking their sweet-ass time with their investigation. However, I'm not worried because I know I've done nothing wrong and clearly my boss, Amanda, agrees, because a new partner has been assigned. I hate that everyone in the office now looks at me differently. I'm the sucker who missed her partner joining the dark side. Well, fuck them. Fuck them all. When my new partner arrives next week, I'll be watching them like a hawk, I will not be made a fool of again. Fool me once, shame on you. Fool me twice, shame on me.

Deciding to torture myself a little more, I paid Dean another visit, hoping to get finally answers. But like the dickwad asshole he is, he's refusing to give me anything. *Asshole.* I almost wish we never apprehended him at the hospital, because seeing him and not getting closure is more frustrating than if we'd never arrested him—out of sight, out of mind kind of thing.

After my third visit with him, I'm still no closer to finding out why he did what he did and I won't be able to put it aside until I do. Why did he turn? What made him turn his back on the oath he swore to uphold? Was he forced? Was I just blind to what was in front of me? So many unanswered questions.

"Fucking asshole," I mumble to myself, as I lean back in my chair and think over the meeting just now with him...

...*"Just tell me why?" I plead with him.*

"Why?" He nonchalantly replies, shrugging his shoulders.

"You owe me."

"I don't owe you shit, Davis. I did it, I turned. The end."

"But why, Dean? This isn't the Dean I know."

"Clearly, you didn't know me like you thought you did." He looks down and quietly adds, "I had no choice."

"Everyone has a choice, Dean."

His head snaps up, obviously I wasn't meant to hear that. "That's your problem, Davis. You think everything is black-and-white. Life isn't all unicorns and rainbows, the sooner you realize that the sooner you can move on."

"I will never let this go, Dean. I cannot move on until I get answers."

"Well, you will die an information-less old lady."

Standing up, I shake my head at him and turn toward the door. With my hand on the handle, I look over my shoulder at him. "Dean, I'm not going anywhere. I will be back here each and every week, until I get my answers."

"Don't hold your breath because I will never tell."

Stepping out of the room, I close the door and lean against it. Dean is a stubborn asshole but I'm even more stubborn. I will get my answers, I refuse to give up...

· · ·

A knock on my door has me lifting my head and I see Bec standing there. "You went to see him again, didn't you?"

"Maaaaaybe," I say, drawing out the word.

"You are a glutton for punishment, Charli. He's never going to tell you anything."

"But I need to know why. I need to know how I missed what was happening right under my nose."

"It wasn't just you he fooled, he fooled us all."

"But—"

"Not buts, Charlotte."

"Ohh, you mean business, you real named me. Next thing you'll be middle naming me too."

"If I knew your middle name, I would."

"Thankfully for all involved no one knows my middle name."

"One day I will find out, and then it's on."

"Whatever, Rebecca."

She flips me the bird and walks out of my office and my phone pings with a text from Bay.

BAYLOR: *You + me + wine + cheese*
CHARLI: *Do we have to go out?*
BAYLOR: *Yes, we are going out for girls' night*
BAYLOR: *No arguments*
BAYLOR: *Meet you at Bin 501 at 6 p.m. sharp*
CHARLI: *If you promise to be on time, I can agree to this*
BAYLOR: *...or close to 6*
BAYLOR: *......this is me after all*
CHARLI: *FINE...you, but you are buying the wine and cheese*
BAYLOR: *deal...see you later*
CHARLI: *Bye, you bully*
BAYLOR: *You love me*
CHARLI: *No, I love wine and cheese*
BAYLOR: *with a side of Baylor*
CHARLI: *6pm, don't be late*

Looks like I now have plans this evening. After seeing Dean, I'm not really in the mood but have you ever tried to say no to Baylor Evans? Yeah, no one has. That woman has you agreeing before you have even processed what's happening. She seriously could sell ice to Eskimos...but I wouldn't have her any other way. Life is definitely more fun with Baylor in it and I can say, without her by my side through Dean's betrayal, I'd be a quivering mess in the corner, drinking wine and eating cheese alone. She's become my person since the shit hit the fan, and I'm thankful every day she fell into my life.

With my new plans set, I head home to get ready for a night that will once again change everything.

DOMINIC 3

Getting transferred to the Chicago office came at the perfect time. Things with Bianca ended badly and the relocation was just what my soul needed, plus a good friend of mine recently opened a wine bar here and well, wine. Once I'd signed the transfer papers, I packed up all my shit and shipped it off. Then I jumped on my Ducati and started my cross-country road trip to the Windy City. I was on a time crunch so I couldn't take my time and really enjoy the ride, but being on the road was just what I needed to clear my head and be ready for the new adventure ahead. One day, I'd like to do it again and take my time so I can enjoy in the sights along the way.

I've unpacked the last box and I flop onto my black sofa. I lean back and let the cushions envelop me. This was the reason I bought it, the comfort is next level and recently, it was where I slept most nights. Lifting my feet and resting them on the coffee table, I close my eyes and let out a sigh. I'd love nothing more than to drift off to sleep but I've arranged to meet up with my old school friend, Branson Holmes, at his wine bar tonight. He and his brother, Kody, started it together. He runs it by himself now after his brother was tragically killed. Kody's death was a shock to all and adding to the shock, Branson is now with Kody's ex, Kasey, which isn't surprising really, as those two always had a close bond and most people always presumed he was with her. Guess fate has a funny way of working sometimes.

Jumping up, I head into my bedroom and strip off as I walk through. By time I reach the en suite, I'm stark naked. Stepping into the shower that's large enough to fit a football team in, I turn the hot faucet on and wait for the water to heat up. Once it's steaming hot, I step under the spray. The hot water feels amazing on my muscles, which are aching from all the heavy lifting I did today. You'd think I'd have been stiff after my long ride but nope, lifting a few boxes is what got me.

Once I'm all clean, I hop out, dry off, and change into my black jeans and a black Henley—in case you hadn't guessed already, black is my favorite color. Running my finger through my hair, I style it in that 'I didn't style it, it's naturally like this' way, pull on my boots, and I'm ready to go. Grabbing my wallet and phone, I slide them into my pockets. Then I slip on my black leather jacket, grab my helmet, and head into to the garage. Pressing the buttons, the garage door opens and I smile when I see my bike all shiny and black.

Straddling my baby, I turn her on, and rev the engine. There's no better sound than the roar of a bike in an enclosed space. Once I've had my fun, I drop it into gear and make my way to Bin 501.

Pulling into the parking lot, I kick the stand down, remove my helmet, and rest it on the seat. Stretching out my sore muscles, I groan at how good the stretch feels and decide that tomorrow I'll hit the gym to get back in shape. I kinda let myself go these last few months. When things started to go pear-shaped with Bianca, I stopped caring. Not wanting to dwell on the past, I grab my helmet and make my way inside.

The door hasn't even closed when I hear my name being yelled out, looking up, I smile when I see Branson walking toward me. "So good to see you," he tells me as he pulls me in for a hug, slapping me on the back.

"Good to see you too, this place is amazing," I say as I look around.

"Yeah, I'm pretty proud of this place too. Just wish Kody was..." He drifts off and doesn't finish that sentence.

I nod. "Sorry to hear about Kody, you guys were always so close."

"Thanks," he tells me, the grief of losing his brother etched on his face. He's clearly still heartbroken about the sudden death of his brother.

Wanting to change the subject, I broach a happier topic. "I hear congratulations are in order," I say, breaking the awkward silence. "You got married and had a kid."

"Yep, I'm a dad now, Kase gave birth to our son KJ and we're currently engaged," he replies with a huge grin. "getting married later this year."

"Well, congrats, man. Seems like all your dreams are coming true." As soon as I say that, I realize how insensitive it was since Kody is no longer here, but before I can apologize, a gorgeous brunette joins us.

"Branson, babe, can you help me in the back please?"

She smiles at me. "Sure, but first, I want you to meet someone." He pulls her into his side and the look on his face is pure love and adoration. "Dominic, this is Kasey."

"Nice to meet you," she says, offering me her hand.

"You too. And congrats by the way." She looks confused. "The baby and engagement." Her eyes brighten as my words register.

"Thank you. So, how do you two know each other?"

"Dominic, Kody, and I went to high school together." When I say this, a wave of sadness rushes over her when I say Kody's name.

"You and I will have to catch up one night and you can fill me in on all the mischief you guys used to get up to."

"Sorry, that goes against bro code," I tell her, "It's like fight club, what happened at school, stays at school."

We all laugh. "I can see why you guys were friends. I'll leave you to it." She looks to Branson. "I'll be in the office." She winks at him then turns and walks away.

"You did well, man."

"Yeah, I did. I love her with all my heart, but sometimes I feel like an ass because I only got my chance because Kody died."

"He'd want you both to be happy."

"That's true. Would you believe he left us each a letter, basically giving us his blessing? It's like he knew deep down."

"That sounds like him."

"Yeah." He nods and sadly smiles. "He really was the best brother anyone could ask for."

I'm at a loss as to what to say next when, thankfully, he's called away but we agree to catch up later.

Walking over to the bar, I take a seat and wait to be served. Looking around, a feeling of contentment washes over me and for the first time since arriving in Chicago, I feel at home and at peace. Moving here really was the best decision I could have made, both personally and professionally. I'm looking forward to starting in the Chicago office on Monday, and the usual nerves regarding who my new partner is begin to fester. Will we get along? Will we find our groove and be kick-ass at what we do? I really hope I get along with him, or her. There's nothing worse than having animosity between partners, especially in our line of work.

Finally I'm served and I order a glass of red. The server places my glass down and when I look up to thank him, from the corner of my eye I see someone take a seat at the other end of the bar. Looking over to them, my breath hitches in the back of my throat when my gaze lands on the most beautiful woman I have ever seen. Chocolate brown hair. A smoking hot body. Killer rack and even from here, the most mesmerizing hazel eyes. There's a sadness about her but when she smiles, fuck me sideways, she's stunning.

Our eyes keep briefly meeting but she always looks away. Finally they lock on one another and our staring contest continues, but the moment is broken when her friend arrives, snapping her attention away from me. *Game on, Angel*, I think to myself.

Picking up my wine, I watch her over my glass. Her friend takes her glass of wine and proceeds to drink it. They clearly are good friends. She signals the bartender to get his attention, but as he walks toward my Angel, I stop and tell him, "Hey, I'd like to buy the lady there her drink."

He nods at me and goes about serving her.

Once again she keeps looking at me but each and every time, she quickly looks away when our gaze connects. Her friend turns around and immediately spins back to face her. The two of them have an animated and heated conversation. I sit and watch as the bartender delivers my glass of wine to her.

She smiles and nods her head in thanks. Lifting my glass, I salute her and take a sip. With our eyes locked, she too takes a sip. I intently watch as she swallows and my mind turns to her swallowing my cock. I really need to get laid, maybe a night with her is just what I need. I haven't been with anyone since Bianca and after what she did, I don't want a relationship. I just want a night of no-holds-barred fucking and when I see her biting her lip, I know she's the one I want to take home tonight. Lip biting is my weakness and only cements to me, she will be coming home with me.

Bringing my glass to my lips, I watch her and wonder, how I can get her to lower her guard and let me take her home tonight?

CHARLI 4

I'm sitting in my car outside Bin 501 and no surprise, I'm waiting for Baylor. She's late, like I knew she would be. She's probably having wild monkey sex with Corey but if I was blissfully in love like those two are, I'd be getting down and dirty all the time too.

Looking around the parking lot, I realize that the last time I was here, Corey's car blew up after Dean planted a bomb. Then to top off an already shitty evening, Corey was shot protecting me. The thought of what Dean did to Corey, and in general, annoys the ever-loving fuck out of me but tonight is about letting my hair down and having a good night with Baylor…if she ever gets here.

The rumbling of a motorcycle engine garners my attention. Lifting my gaze I see a sleek black Ducati Monster pull into the parking lot. The rider pops the stand and climbs off. Holy fucking hotness, Batman, this guy is at least six foot five and full of muscle, and not in the eww way, in that, I want to lick every crevice and groove kind of sexy muscle way. He's wearing black jeans that accentuate his height and a leather jacket hugs his muscular frame. It's taut across his shoulders and hangs loosely around his ass, his ohh so fine jean-clad ass. He removes his helmet and I let out an audible groan, crap on a cracker this man is stunning.

Like a creeper, I sit in my car and ogle the fine specimen before me. He looks around the parking lot and for a brief moment our gaze connects. I duck down in my seat, not wanting to be caught being the peeping Tom that I am.

Lifting my head up, I sigh in relief when I see that parking lot is empty, except for creeper me.

Grabbing my phone, I check the time and shake my head. "Dammit, Baylor," I say to myself, frustrated that she is really, really late now.

My eyes keep gravitating toward the bike, if I had lady balls, I'd head into the bar and proposition that sexy as sin man, but that's not me. So I stay where I am and hide like the big-ass pansy I am.

After staring at the bike again, I decide to head inside. Maybe I'll see Biker Boy and his fine looks can keep me occupied while I wait. Climbing out of my car, I walk across the parking lot to the bar. Opening the door, I step inside and like a heat-seeking missile, my eyes lock on my sexy Biker Boy and I find him sitting at the bar, alone.

Walking toward the bar, I take a seat at the opposite end, with a clear view of him, and order myself a glass of red and pull out my phone to text Bay.

> **CHARLI:** *Once you've finished getting down and dirty, I'm seated at the bar waiting for girls' night to start.*

Placing my phone on the bar top, I pick up my glass of wine and take a sip. I close my eyes and enjoy the robust flavors currently dancing on my tongue. When I open my eyes, my gaze connects with him and I freeze. Everything around me fades away; it's just him and me. Our moment is interrupted when Baylor collapses into the seat next to me.

"Sorry, I'm late," she pants, "I was…"

"Giving Cox a kiss goodbye?" She stares at me blankly. "Don't try and deny it, Bay, your lipstick is smudged." She wipes at her mouth and I laugh, "Haha, gotcha."

"Huh?" she asks, grabbing my wine and taking a sip.

"Your lipstick is fine but my assumptions as to why you're late are correct."

"Hardy har har," she sasses back at me and drinks the last of my wine. "That's for being a bitch."

"You love me." I shrug, as I signal the bartender back over. Looking back at Bay, I smile at her but I'm really staring at the man behind her. I can't stop looking at him, he has a magnetic pull that is beyond my control to ignore.

"Lucky for you I do love you. Now, how are you?" she asks, but I'm too focused on him to answer her. She swivels around and I know the moment she sees him because she spins back to me, and her face lights up like a Christmas tree. "You HAVE to go home with him tonight."

"No," I confirm. "I cannot do that."

"Why not?" she questions. "That man is fucking hot. If I didn't have my own hottie, I'd be over there right now."

"Well, we are here for girls' night and he is not a girl."

"Charli," she says, her tone lowering. "Let loose for once in your life. Go and have a night of wild monkey sex with that fine as fuck man and come morning, become straightlaced Agent Charli Davis once again." She pauses and then laughs. "I can totally see why you and Core are friends. You are two straight and narrow peas in a pod."

I process her words and thankfully, the bartender arrives and places a glass of red in front of me. "Courtesy of the man over there." I follow his finger and realize he's pointing at my Biker Boy, well not MY Biker Boy but the Biker Boy I was ogling earlier. I smile and nod my head in thanks. He lifts his glass and salutes me.

"Just do it," Baylor says, and then turns her attention to the bartender. "Can I please get a bottle of that," she points to my glass, "and a charcuterie board for us to share?"

He nods and gets to opening the bottle of wine that Bay just ordered. My eyes keep drifting over to Biker Boy and each time, he's staring at me. Biting my lip, I contemplate what I should do, but my thoughts are interrupted when Bay says, "I'm going to the bathroom and then I'll get us a booth."

Nodding my head, I pick up my wine and take a sip. Just as my glass reaches my lips, a body bumps into me and I spill red wine all over my shirt, thankfully it's red wine red in color and it won't stain, but he spilled my wine and that there is sacrilege. It's the equivalent to a toddler spilling their milk, not good. "You all right?" I inquire.

The guy turns around and his eyes roam over me, I shudder at the lewdness in his gaze. It's nothing like Biker Boy's gaze. Finally his creepy once-over reaches my eyes. "Did it hurt?" he asks me.

"Did what hurt?" My face scrunching up at his weird and random question.

"Did it hurt when you fell from heaven?"

"Seriously? You are using that lame line on me after spilling my drink? The words coming from your mouth should be, 'I'm so sorry, I'll get you another' but no, you have to use the corniest pickup line in the history of pickup lines."

He stares at me and I don't like the intensity in his gaze. "My my, you are feisty. I bet you fuck like a wild animal."

"Excuse me," I shout, just as I feel a heat behind me.

"Yo, dickwad, apologize to the lady now."

"Get fucked, asshole, I was here first."

"Actually, bud, no, you are not number one. This lady here is mine." He places his hand protectively on my shoulder and my body comes alive at his touch. "Now I suggest you apologize and then scurry away before I lose it and my fist becomes acquainted with your face."

Normally I'd be pissed at hearing someone call me 'mine' but coming from him, I want to strip out of my wine-soaked blouse and fuck him like the wild animal Creeper McCreeperson says I am. That reaction shocks me because I don't do that. I don't fall under a man's spell so easily. I'm pushing thirty and I've never had a one-night stand.

"Sorry," Creeper McCreeperson mumbles, his voice wavering in fear at the presence of Biker Boy here. He throws a ten spot on the bar top and walks away but when I say walk, I mean he runs like a scared little boy. Mind you, Biker Boy is pretty intimidating. Whereas Creeper McCreeperson is scared, I'm enthralled with fake rescuing boyfriend.

"Pretty sure he just pissed his pants," I tell Biker Boy. Craning my neck, I look up at him and smile. "Thank you."

"You're welcome."

We stare at one another and just like earlier, everything around us disappears and it's just the two of us. Our moment is interrupted when Bay returns. "I got us a table." Her eyes widen when she realizes who I'm with. "I'll just take this," she grabs the bottle of wine and her glass, and whispers, "I'll be over there." She turns and walks away. Pausing, she spins around, grabs my hands, and says, "Charli, just do it." She throws a wink at me and then I watch as she walks over to the booth we will be in for the rest of the evening.

"Do what, Charli?" Biker Boy asks me; his voice is deep, gruff and has my body tingling. All that from only three words.

"With Baylor, she could be referring to anything."

He steps closer to me and leans down. I can feel his breath on my neck. Just from his breathing, my body buzzes with anticipation. He whispers, "I think she's referring to you doing me and I agree with your friend, Angel" He stands up and I instantly miss his closeness. "I'll be waiting. The ball's in your court." He winks and walks away from me, returning to his seat from earlier.

Sitting here, my breathing is labored and my clit is pulsating like never before. Grabbing my wine glass, I take a big gulp-like sip, and then stand up and head over to Bay. I feel his eyes on me with each step I take across the room.

My mind is racing with a million and one questions and thoughts right now. Can I do it? Can I have a one-night stand? What if he's a serial killer? Will the charcuterie board have smoked cheese? A random thought I know, but hello, cheese. Then my mind drifts to what it would feel like to have his lips on mine. His hands on my body. His breath on my neck was enough to turn me into a pile of goo and if his breath can do that, then I can only imagine what else he could do to me. Maybe I should just go for it.

Taking my seat across from Bay, I'm aroused at the thought of what might be but also hesitant to take that leap. Looking back over to Biker Boy, I wonder if, just for one night, I should just let go like Bay is suggesting.

Gah, I have no idea what to do.

DOMINIC 5

Seeing that guy hit on her makes me ragey mad. Before I know what I'm doing, I'm stalking over to my girl—yes she's mine, she just doesn't know it yet—and staking my claim. "Actually, bud, no, you are not number one. This lady here is mine. Now I suggest you apologize and then scurry away before I lose it and my fist becomes acquainted with your face."

The asshole scurries away after mumbling a quiet apology. Pulling out the chair next to her, I take a seat. We silently stare intently at one another but I don't notice anything but her. Her friend returns, whispers a few things that I can't quite hear but my ears perk up when she says, "Charli, just do it," before leaving us alone again. I'm pretty sure she's referring to 'doing me' but Charli—beautiful name for a beautiful woman—is hesitant. It's nice to know her friend is on my side, now to get Charli to come over to Team Cruz too. She seems shy so I need to play my cards carefully, but I want her to know how I feel without coming on too strong. I lean into her and breathe her in, she smells divine. Her skin prickles from my breath and I know she feels what I'm feeling too, so I decide to throw caution to the wind and go for it. "I think she's referring to you doing me and I agree with your friend, Angel." I stand up and stare down at her, "I'll be waiting. The ball's in your court."

Walking back to my seat, I have no idea if I have a chance in hell of her coming home with me tonight, but I do know I haven't felt a pull like this in a long time. I don't think I ever felt like this with Bianca.

I can feel her watching me but as I told her, the ball's in her court now.

A hand touches my shoulder and when I turn my head, I deflate when I see it's her friend. She's grinning at me. "Hi, I'm Baylor."

"Dominic," I offer, and really hope she doesn't try to hit on me.

"Charli is my girl and I want to see her happy. I need you to man up and swoop her off her feet, even if just for tonight," she pauses and steps closer to me, "BUT if you hurt her, I will hunt you down and hurt you a million times worse."

This woman is crazy, I should let her know she just threatened a federal agent, but I want what she wants for us so I nod. "Even without your pep talk," I tell her, "I was contemplating doing exactly that but how am I meant to woo her? She seems closed off."

"Leave that to me," she says matter-of-factly and then turns away and walks back to the booth they have snagged. Charli is nowhere to be seen and then I see her, returning from the bathrooms. Her cheeks are flushed, but I can't wait to see her flushed from arousal while she's riding my cock.

She rejoins her friend and I continue to sit here and watch the two of them, waiting in the wings, or wine bar in this case, for my moment to swoop in and woo her. Finally the moment is here, it's time to make my move. She's giggling and seems to be tipsy. I really hope she's drunk enough to let go, but not too drunk that she'll regret her decision in the light of day when she's sober.

Walking over to them, her eyes lock on me, and she watches as I get closer to her. Her eyes rake over me, and from the glint in her eye I know she wants me. She's ready to let loose and have a night of fun with me as I suggested earlier. "Ladies," I say as I reach them.

"Hey, Biker Boy," Charli says with a smile, her voice deep, husky, and ohh so sexy.

Her cheeks are a gorgeous flush of pink, and I hope it's from my presence and not the wine, then I click that she called me Biker Boy. "How did you know I ride a bike?"

Her eyes widen in shock. "Ummm, ahhhhh, your jacket. It's a bike jacket, not just a sexy leather jacket."

"Nice save," Baylor quietly says, lifting her glass with a cheeky smirk. She takes a sip. "Sooo, what's your intention with my friend?"

"Baylor," Charli scolds, "you can't say shit like that."

Baylor shrugs and focuses on me, raising her eyebrows in that 'tell me now' way.

"Well—"

"A hole in the ground with water in it," Charli says, and then she giggles at her own joke. The sound is music to my ears. It's the first time I've seen her so relaxed since I've been watching her—shit, that makes me sound like a stalker. I smile at her response while Baylor shakes her head and rolls her eyes. "You seriously are a dork, Davis."

"An adorable dork," I add, gazing at her and basking in her tipsy beauty.

"Did you just call me a dork?"

"No, I called you an adorable dork, there's a difference."

"Mmmhmpf." She stares back at me. The air around us thickens. Her breaths have become labored and the pink of her cheeks continues to darken as her eyes roam over me. Then she says five words that make my night, hell my whole year. "Take me home, Biker Boy."

From next to her Baylor squeals and from the megawatt grin on her face, I think she's happy with Charli's decision too, "I'll call Core to come get me." She hops up and walks away to call Core, whoever he is.

Reaching out, I cup her cheek in my palm. An electrical current jolts between us, her eyes widen, she felt it too. "You sure about this, Angel?"

She nods and nuzzles into my palm, "I've never been more sure of anything in my life."

CHARLI 6

I CAN'T BELIEVE I JUST AGREED TO GO HOME WITH HIM. THERE MUST HAVE BEEN something in the wine, the cheese, or I've entered an alternate universe because I don't do things like this, I don't tell men to 'take me home.' This is so out of character for me but as soon as those words left my mouth, I felt so confident. Now that he's actually 'taking me home' and my brain has kicked into gear, I'm having second thoughts.

His thumb gently runs along my jawbone and he continues to cup my cheek. Lifting my eyes, they lock on his and within seconds, any doubts I had evaporate. Hell, all thoughts leave my brain and I lose myself in his rich chocolate brown orbs. A calmness washes over me and I'm left with a buzzing body filled with desire, want, and need for the man standing before me.

He removes his hand from my cheek and I sigh at the loss.

Baylor rejoins us, grinning at me. "Core will be here in ten," she says. Picking her glass up, she chugs back the last of her wine before grabbing her things and walking toward the exit. Dominic offers me his hand and helps me out of my chair. Like when he cupped my cheek, a spark jolts through me when my fingers touch his palm.

Once standing, he escorts me outside and we wait with Bay for Corey. I feel bad for ditching her but from the megawatt grin on her face, she doesn't care.

The heat from his hand on my lower back causes my body to react in a way that I haven't felt in a very long time. He's barely even physically touching me and already I want more.

Corey pulls up to the curb, climbs out, and makes a beeline for Baylor. When he reaches her, he dips her back and kisses the life out of her, as if he hasn't seen her for months and not just hours. It's over the top for being in public, but it's them to a T. He brings her upright again and then looks to me and notices Dominic standing at my side.

"Who are you?" he asks, all big brother protective like.

"Dominic Cruz," he says, stepping forward, offering his hand to Corey.

"Corey Cox," he replies, shaking his hand. The alpha male testosterone pinging all around us.

"Settle down, Core. Nic here—"

"Dominic," he interrupts Baylor.

"Sorry, Dominic and Charli here are going to have a lovely night together. She doesn't need you going all caveman big brother on her. Now, take me home and ravage me." She links her fingers with his and pulls him toward the car, as she looks over her shoulder at me. "Don't do anything I wouldn't do," she singsongs as she opens the door and climbs in.

Corey closes it and looks back to us, specifically me. "Charli, call me if you need anything."

Nodding at him, he walks around the hood, climbs in, and we watch them drive away.

"So," he says breaking the silence, "shall we head back to my place?"

Looking over at him, I nod. "As I said before, take me home, Biker Boy."

He laces his fingers with mine and we walk toward the parking lot, his bike comes into view and I smile. Remembering sitting in my car and watching him earlier, I shake my head when I realize all those dirty thoughts I had are about to hopefully come true.

"What are you smiling about, Angel?"

"I saw you pull up earlier and I sat in my car over there." I point to my car. "I was totally checking you out."

"Well," he croons, grabbing my hips and pulling me to him, "As soon as I saw you, I was checking you out too. Seems this was inevitable."

"I don't believe in that bullshit."

"What do you believe in?" he asks me.

"What's right in front of me. What I can see, touch, and feel."

"And what can you see, touch, and feel?"

"You...and I can't wait to touch and feel you in private." My words shock me, I'm not normally so brazen like this. Clearly Bay is rubbing off on me.

"Have at it, baby," he says, stepping back and opening his arms wide.

He stares at me and my body comes alive at the intensity of his gaze. Brazenly, I step to him and I slide my hands under his shirt and up his stomach. My fingers brush over ab after ab, sliding my hands around to his back, I slip them down and squeeze his ass.

"Like what you touch?" he asks me. Biting my lip, I nod. "Well, I definitely like what I see and I'd very much like to see, touch, and lick what's underneath your clothes. Shall we get going so we may touch, see, and feel each other in privacy?" Again, I nod my head. "Good," he replies.

Leaning down, he kisses the tip of my nose. The tip tingling from the connection with him.

He turns around and from a secret compartment, he produces a helmet and hands it to me. "I can bring you here tomorrow to get your car."

"Okay," I say, as I pull the helmet on. I'm suddenly nervous. My hands are shaking and my heart is racing. He reaches out and squeezes my hand in his.

"Let me." Dropping my hands, he reaches up and within two seconds the helmet is fastened and secure on my head.

He throws his leg over the machine and climbs on, never have I seen anything so sexy and all he did was sit on his bike. "Your turn," he says, twisting to face me. He offers me his hand and I take it. Carefully, I hop on behind him. Slipping my arms around his waist, I hold on tight. He smells amazing, sandalwood with a hint of mint. I inhale deeply and sigh.

"Did you just sniff me?" he asks, looking over his shoulder at me.

"No," I defensively return.

"I call bullshit, Angel."

"Shut up and drive," I tell him.

"Hold on."

With pleasure, I think to myself. He starts the bike, the engine vibrating beneath me. Wrapping my arms tighter around him, I hold on tight. He pulls out of the parking lot and we zip through the streets. The cool wind flying past us but I don't feel it. All I can feel is my body pressed to his.

Even though we are zipping through the streets, I feel safe with him. I have never felt more content in my life.

All too soon, we pull into a driveway and the garage door automatically opens. He pulls the bike in and the door lowers behind us. My heart rate picks up but I don't move. I sit where I am, hugging him tightly.

"You can let go now, Angel."

"Maybe I don't want to."

"Well, if you don't let me go, how can I see, feel, or touch you?"

"Point taken but…" I pause, fear envelops me because I'm don't know how to voice what I want.

He turns his head to look at me and my breath hitches, his eyes are full of hunger but at the same time, they are so calming. "But what?"

"I…ummm, ahh…"

"You ummm, ahh what?"

Deciding to throw caution to the wind—seems to be the trend tonight —I tell him what I want. "I want you to bend me over your bike and fuck me." I've never had the desire to fuck on a bike before, but right now it's all I can think about. This is so not me. I kinda like sexy, brazen, and semi-relaxed Charli, Dominic seems to bring out my inner sexy minx.

"I've never actually done that before but I'd be honored if you'd pop my bike fucking cherry."

Holy shit, he's about to fuck me over his bike.

DOMINIC 7

SHE WANTS ME TO FUCK HER ON MY BIKE? I DID NOT SEE THAT COMING BUT I can unequivocally say, I'm down with that, so down with the bike fucking plan. This woman looks like an angel sent from heaven, but in reality, she's a seductress sent from hell to tempt men like me…and I cannot wait to sin with her. Not only is she smoking fucking hot but it seems she has a dirty, kinky wild side too. I'll have to thank Branson for inviting me out tonight, "Ohh shit," I mumble.

"What?" she asks, her voice laced with concern and it hits me she possibly thinks I don't want this anymore.

"It's nothing," I reassure her.

"I can go if you like," she offers, her voice quivering.

"That is the last fucking thing I want. You are not going anywhere, Angel, until you are well fucked. The ohh shit was in reference to not saying bye to the owner of Bin 501."

"You know the owner?"

"Yeah, he's why I was there tonight. Wine bars are not usually my thing—"

"Ohh," she quietly says, interrupting me. "That place is my favorite."

"Weeeelll, Angel, it just so happens, it's now a favorite of mine, but I think it's more to do with a sexy as fuck patron than the delicious wines on offer." She smiles at my words and it lights up her face in the dim garage light. "Rumor has it, you would like to be fucked on my bike." She shyly nods and bites her lip. "Since this is your fantasy, how shall we proceed?"

My eyes drop to her teeth digging into her plump bottom lip, my cock twitches at the motion. He's done that several times now when it comes to my Angel. "Fuck, I love when you do that."

"Do what?"

Lifting my hand, I run the pad of my thumb along her lip, "When you bite your lip, makes me want to bite it...and more."

She leans into me and whispers, "I'd like that very much. However, right now, I need you to climb off your bike and remove your clothes, BUT I want you to do it slowly so I can admire your body."

"And what will you do while I strip for you?"

Lifting her hand she waves her fingers in front of my face. I grab her wrist and gently squeeze, "Uhhhh uh, Angel, all your pleasure will come from me tonight...all of it."

"Well, you better get to it, Biker Boy...I'm waiting and I don't like to be kept waiting." She rakes her gaze over me. "I really want to see what's hidden under your clothes."

"You and me both, Angel, but in order for me to do that, I need to reluctantly let go of you. However, I absolutely promise, as soon as I'm as naked as the day I was born you can touch me, again. And again. Anywhere and everywhere, all night long. But first, let's make your bike fucking fantasy a reality."

She swallows deeply and nods. Letting go of her wrist, I climb off without bumping her. Spinning to face her, I grab my shirt at the neck and pull it over my head and drop it to the ground.

"I said slowly," she scolds me.

"My apologies but at the thought of you naked on my bike, I can't go slow."

She smirks at me and nods. "Fair enough." We stare intently at one another. "Well then, have at it, Biker Boy."

With my eyes locked on her, I flip open the button on my jeans and slowly lower the zipper. Gripping the top of my jeans, I pull them and my briefs down. My cock springs free, hitting my stomach. Her eyes bug wide open when she sees my dick. In a very non-sexy manner, I kick off my shoes and clothing, leaving me gloriously naked in front of the sexiest chick to ever sit on my bike.

"I think we have a problem," I tell her.

"What's that?" she huskily replies.

"You have far too many clothes on."

"That's an easy fix." She sits up straight and spins her leg over, now sitting sidesaddle on my bike. She slips her hand under the spaghetti strap of her navy top and slides it down her arm and repeats the process on the other side. Slipping her arms out, she grabs the material at her breasts and pulls it down, baring her tits to me. Her nipples are dusty pink and erect, begging for me to suck on them. She stands up and continues to slide her shirt down, once she reaches her hips, she keeps pushing down, revealing sexy black-and-white boy shorts. Wriggling her hips, the material floats to the floor, leaving her only in her panties.

I'm so confused right now.

"Jumpsuit," she says, but I have no fucking clue what that means, all I know is that she's now standing next to my bike in nothing but her panties and sexy-as-fuck heels.

Stepping to her, I cup her cheek, "Fuck me, you are a vision." Her cheeks darken at my compliment, leaning down, I press my lips to hers for our first kiss. That electrical current once again jolts us, she gasps in shock, and I take the opportunity to slip my tongue into her mouth. She slides her hands around my neck and deepens the kiss and our connection. As first kisses go, this one is pretty amazing.

Sliding my hands down her back, I cup her ass and lift her up, placing her back onto the seat. She spreads her legs and I step between them. Moving away from her lips. I kiss along her jaw, her head drops back, elongating her neck, and giving me unobstructed access to her neck. Kissing and nipping along her skin, I make my way down to her chest.

Cupping her breasts in my hands, I push them together before taking one of her nipples into my mouth, nipping the tip before sucking the nipple into my mouth. "Nic," she moans as I suck harder. Letting the tip pop from my mouth, I kiss across her to her other nipple. I squeeze it between my thumb and forefinger, garnering a hiss from her. My tongue darts out and I circle the nub before gently biting and sucking. Once again, she moans. Gripping my head, she pushes me farther into her.

Lifting my head, I gaze into her eyes. "Time to make your fantasy a reality."

CHARLI 8

HOLY HOTNESS, BATMAN, THIS MAN IS FINE. ALL HE'S DONE IS KISS ME AND play with my tits and my body is already buzzing with desire, want, need, lust, and everything in-between. I've never been more turned on than I am in this moment. The hunger in his eyes matches mine, when he says, "Time to make your fantasy a reality," I nearly climax on the spot. Biting my lip, I nod my head.

When he slides his hands down my sides, a giggle breaks free. "That tickles," I playfully laugh.

"Sorry," he responds, with a smirk that indicates he totally is not sorry. He grabs the waistband of my boy shorts and begins to pull them down. I lift up and he removes them, dropping them to the garage floor and the pile of already discarded garments. Leaving me naked, except for my shoes on his bike. "Fuuuuck, Angel, you are...I have no words."

"I could say the same about you," I pause and bite my lip, "now fuck me, Biker Boy." My brazen words shock me but at the same time, they don't. Clearly Baylor is rubbing off on me, and right now I really want Dominic to rub himself on me.

"With fucking pleasure," he growls.

He grips his cock and strokes it a few times, as he steps closer to me and rubs the tip up and down my lips. Leaning back, I use my core strength to hold myself up and grip on to his upper arms for added support. He taunts me a few more times and then he thrusts his hips and slams into me.

"Nic," I moan, as he continues to slide in and out of me.

We stare at one another as we fuck on his bike. My hips meeting him thrust for thrust. That tingling feeling begins to develop in my belly. "I'm close," I pant.

"Me too," he growls. His grip on my hips tightens, and he continues to slam into me over and over, faster and faster. My eyes close and I scream out his name as the most intense orgasm of my life detonates. My body stiffens. My skin tingles and the air around us zings with electricity as we each let our release take over us.

We are both panting heavily. Opening my eyes, we stare at one another as we control our breathing. Sweat glistens on our skin as we both come down from our euphoric high.

Without saying a word, he lifts me up. Instinctively, I wrap my arms around his neck and my legs around his waist. His cock is still hard and inside me as he turns and walks toward the door leading inside. How he's still hard after what we just did amazes me. He opens the interior door and walks down the hallway and enters his bedroom. He steps through the room and into the en suite. Reaching into the shower, he turns it on and steps in. The cold spray splashes us and we both hiss.

"Shit, that's cold," he says, but the water begins to heat. He lowers himself down and sits on the shower seat with me straddling him. His gaze is locked on mine. Leaning forward, I press my lips to his. My tongue presses along the seam of his lips and slips into his mouth. Our tongues caress one another and my hips begin to circle. His cock hardens further inside me and before long we are rocking back and forth for round number two.

We both come much quicker this time. Resting my forehead against his, we each calm our breathing. "You are everything I imagined, and more, Charli." His places a quick kiss on my lips. "Now, let's get washed, then we can sleep a little, and then we can go again."

"So cocky," I tease him.

"Not cocky, just stating the facts."

"Ohh really," I say, as I climb off him. My legs feel like jelly but the warmth from the hot water raining down on me is heaven on my muscles and I moan.

"You keep moaning like that, and I'll have to take you again."

"I'm down with that," I tease.

Winking at him, I step back under the spray. Closing my eyes, I drop my head backward and let the water wash over me. I open my eyes, when I feel him standing in front of me. Even with the water obscuring my vision, I can see every gorgeous inch of this man. Lifting my hand, I cup his cheek. "Thank you," I honestly tell him.

"Why are you thanking me?" he asks me.

"For tonight."

"It's only just getting started," he says.

Lowering his head down, he presses his lips to mine and before I can process what's happening, he lifts me up and presses my back into the tiles. My legs close around him and his cock slides into me again. Our bodies join as one, it's as if we were made from the same mold.

"Nic," I moan against his lips, as orgasm number three begins to build. Startling me, he pulls out of me and lowers me to my feet.

"Turn around," he demands, his tone rough, but it sparks me to life and I spin around. "Hands on the wall." Lifting my arms, I press them to the tiles. "Don't move or I'll stop and we will go to bed." Nodding my head, I spread my legs and push my ass toward him, circling my hips on his rock hard cock. "Didn't I tell you not to move?" he warns.

Turning my head, I look at him over my shoulder and shrug. He slaps my ass, the skin stinging from the connection but before I can scold him, he grabs my hips and slams himself back into me. Pistoning his hips back and forth. From this angle he hits that pleasure spot. "Niiiiiiiccc," I moan. As my orgasm tears through me, he follows as I'm riding out the pleasure wave.

He slides his hands around my front, cupping my boobs. Turning my head to face him, he presses his lips to mine for a kiss that takes my breath away. He breaks the connection and stares at me. Neither of us utter a word as I spin to face him. With my eyes on his, I grab his shower gel and squeeze some into my palm and I begin to wash him. My hands slide over his body, once he's all clean, I push him back under the spray and watch as the soapy bubbles slide down his torso. A torso that was carved by the gods.

Reaching out, I squeeze some more soap into my hands and I soap myself up. I notice his gaze intently follows my hands as I wash my breasts and stomach. Sliding my hands between my thighs, I shudder when I brush my clit. It's swollen and throbbing. He grips my wrist, "What did I say about your pleasure tonight?"

"I'm washing myself, it's not my fault that you have my body buzzing and when I brushed my clit, it decided to quiver."

He stares intently at me. "Fine, I'll allow it."

"Tough shit if you didn't, Biker Boy."

Pushing him out of the way, I step under the spray and wash the soap off, paying extra attention to my breasts just to taunt him, but it doesn't work. He shakes his head and steps out, and the asshole flicks the faucet to cold, causing me to squeal when the coldness hits my heated skin. Jumping out of the shower, I glower at him as he laughs.

He leans down, giving me a perfect view of his tight, taut ass and grabs out two fluffy towels. He hands one to me and we silently dry off. He throws his to the floor and takes mine, dropping it on top of his. He grabs my hand and pulls me into his room. He pulls back the comforter and climbs in, patting the sheet next to him. "You coming?"

"I just did…three times."

"If you keep staring at me like that, I'll be making it four very soon."

"As much as I'd love that, my vagina needs a rest. Maybe in the morning, if you don't hog the bed and snore, we can make it four."

"I don't snore."

"So you're a bed hog?" I tease, as I climb in next to him.

Pushing him to his back, I snuggle into his side. He wraps his arm around me and I throw my leg over him. I'm not normally a snuggler, but with Dominic I seem to be doing many things I don't normally do.

"Goodnight, Angel," he whispers, pressing a kiss to my temple.

"Night, Biker Boy," I reply, pressing a kiss to his pectoral.

Sleep comes quickly and I have the best night sleep I've had in a very long time. Probably because I'm exhausted after three amazeballs orgasms, but it could also be because I'm the most relaxed I've been in a very long time.

Dominic Cruz is the prescription I needed and I have a feeling life will be good from here on out…or not.

DOMINIC 9

I'm pleasantly woken the next morning with Charli's lips wrapped around my dick. Lifting my head, I look down and see my cock slide in and out of her perfect mouth. Her eyes are locked on me as she blows me. She winks and continues to suck my dick and fondle my balls. Sooner than a grown man should, I come down her throat. Grunting and gripping the sheets in my fists through my release, she sucks and licks every drop from me. My cock pops out of her mouth and she seductively crawls up my body. "Morning, Biker Boy," she murmurs before pressing her lips to mine. *Yep, definitely the best way to wake up.*

Threading my fingers into her hair, I hold her to me, deepening the kiss and our connection. Flipping her to her back, she squeals, and smiles up at me. Her smile hits me right in the chest. "Morning, Angel."

We stare at one another and something passes between us, but as quickly as it appears it's gone. She reaches up and cups my cheek. "Thank you for last night, I guess I better get going."

"Or..." I offer.

"Or what?" she asks, running her thumb along my jaw.

Leaning down, I nibble her neck and whisper, "Well, for starters, I need my breakfast. You've already had yours. After I've had my breakfast, we can have a nap because when we wake, it will be midmorning fuck time." I nip her earlobe. "Which will lead into our lunchtime fuck," I suck on her earlobe, "then I'll feed you...food as you'll need your energy for your afternoon fuck." I kiss that sensitive spot behind her ear. "Only then, will you 'get going' as you put it."

"I think I like that plan," she breathlessly pants, as I continue to kiss down her neck toward her gorgeous tits, taking her nipple into my mouth, and gently sucking.

"Fantastic, now let me have my breakfast."

She likes this plan because she pushes on my head, guiding me down her body. I can smell her arousal and I've barely touched her. She spreads her legs, opening herself up. I breathe her in and moan before I slide my tongue between her folds.

"Biker Boy," she moans, pressing my head into her farther. "Fuuuuuu-uuck," she wails, as I bring her closer to the brink. She explodes on my face when I slip the tip of my pinky into her ass. Sliding back up her body, I stare down at her. Her cheeks are flushed, I have never seen a more gorgeous sight. "We will totally be exploring your ass later."

She bites her lip and nods her head.

"Fuck me, you are perfect in every way," I tell her before I slam my lips against hers. The force of my kiss shocks her, her mouth opens, and I slip my tongue inside. My cock thickening with each sweep of her tongue against mine.

"Fuck me, Biker Boy," she breathlessly whispers against my lips.

Without waiting a beat, I rub the tip of my cock up and down her slit. She tilts her hips and the head edges in slightly. Staring down at her, I thrust forward and push the rest of the way in. Pausing, I hold myself still and let her warmth envelop me and then I begin to rock back and forth. Her forehead rests against mine as I continue the thrust in and out of her. This is more than fucking, it feels like we're making love. That thought should scare me but it doesn't. That thought lingers in the back of my mind as Charli and I continue to thrust back and forth.

She rakes her nails down my back and grips my ass, pulling me into her farther. Our bodies are one as we both rock our hips. The connection between us is palpable. The air pinging with desire and lust. It's filled with moans, groans, and grunts.

My eyes are closed and I give everything I have to her. Her body stills beneath me and she lets out a guttural wail that sets me off. Together we come and I come hard. Harder than I ever have before. Opening my eyes, I stare down at her. She's breathing hard.

Reaching up she cups my cheeks. "Fuck me, Biker Boy, that was—"

"Amazing. Out of this world. The best fuck you've ever had."

"Wasn't what I was going to say, but I totally agree."

Rolling off her, I lie on my back, and she cuddles into my side, just like she did last night, and I have to say, I love having her close to me like this. Normally after a hookup it's uncomfortable but with Charli there's no awkwardness.

Her fingertips gently run across my pecs, my skin coming to life under her touch. I internally laugh, this woman is turning me into a mushy ball but I don't care. After the clusterfuck that was Bianca, it's liberating to be at ease with a partner.

Seems moving to Chicago was not only great for my career but personally too. Charli and I click on all levels. I wasn't expecting to meet anyone last night but I'm glad I met Charli. She is the complete package. Killer body. Wicked sense of humor. Amazing mouth, but most of all, she's honest and real. I know I don't know her well, but she's everything I imagine when I think of who I want Mrs. Cruz to be. Again, that thought doesn't scare me. I don't think it does because she is who I have been waiting for all my life.

Charli's breathing evens out, she's drifted back to sleep. I stare down at her and smile. *I fucking love Chicago,* I think to myself. Gently I place a kiss on her head and close my eyes. My last thought before I drift off to the land of Nod is that this is the beginning of something amazing.

CHARLI 10

I'M LYING IN BED WITH MY EYES CLOSED. MY BLADDER IS SINGING OUT FOR ME to get up and relieve myself, but my bed feels amazing and I don't want to get out. A rustling next to me causes my eyes to open wide and that's when I remember, I'm not at my place…and I'm not alone.

Looking to the side, I'm met with a muscular back. My eyes trace the red finger marks I left on his skin last night. They start at his shoulders and go all the way to his ass. His ass has bruises from my fingers. Between my thighs begins to tingle as memories of last night, and earlier, flash before my eyes. Then I remember I need to pee.

Climbing out of bed, I pad over to the en suite bathroom. Sitting on the toilet, I relieve myself. As the tightness in my bladder decreases, my chest and lungs begin to tighten. My breathing begins to speed up and the urge to flee is strong. "I need to get out of here," I whisper to myself. I wipe and stand up, glancing at myself in the mirror. The girl reflecting back looks like me, but she's relaxed and well fucked. And well fucked, I am. Both figuratively and literally.

Last night was amazing, the best night of my life, but I need to get out of here.

Taking a deep breath, I peek back into the bedroom and see that Dominic has rolled to his back. His chest is on display and I get the sudden urge to lick each and every crevice on his delectable body. His cock rests against his stomach and I remember what it felt like in my mouth earlier. If I was brave, I'd crawl back onto the bed and ride him like the stallion he is, but I'm not that ~~brave~~ brazen woman anymore. I'm back to being a big-ass chickenshit who's about to sneak out.

Ever so quietly, I tiptoe across his room and into the living area. I look around for my clothes and then I remember they're in the garage. I open the garage door and like each time you try to be quiet, it sounds like a herd of elephants heffalumping about. I look over my shoulder but I don't hear or see Dominic. I slip into the garage and quickly redress. Once I'm clothed, I grab my phone and I order myself an Uber. Thank fuck for location tracking, as I have no clue as to where I am. Luck is on my side and a car is only a few minutes away.

With my ride on the way, I quietly head back inside. Tiptoeing to the front door, I'm almost free when his voice startles me. "Leaving without saying goodbye?"

Spinning on my heel, I stare at him, and holy crap on a cracker, this man is fine. His hair is messy in that sexy I-just-crawled-out-bed way. A pair of gray—yes gray—sweatpants hang low on his hips, accentuating every rugged ridge on his body. "I...umm, ahh—"

"Sneaking out so there's no awkward goodbye?"

Nodding my head, I smile. "Yeah, pretty much. Look, Nic, I've never done this before. I don't know the etiquette for the morning after."

"Sneaking out without saying goodbye is not the best way to end what I can unequivocally say was the best night of my life."

Again I find myself grinning. "Yeah, it was pretty amazing."

"So why are you sneaking away then? We could have this all the time. Maybe?"

"Just because we had a great time between the sheets doesn't mean we will connect emotionally too."

"I'd be surprised if we didn't because, Charli, I have never, N-E-V-E-R felt a connection like I do with you."

I did too is what I want to say, but instead I go with, "Nic, please just let me go."

"Give me one good reason why."

He walks toward me. "Because..."

"Because? That's all you've got?"

Looking to the floor, I close my eyes and take a deep breath, lifting my head, I stare at him. "Nic, I'm not looking for anything right now. If fate has other ideas and we meet again, then we know that it was meant to be, but for now I'm gonna go." Stepping to him, I press my lips to his for a quick goodbye kiss, but as with us, it quickly turns heated. He slides his hand around my waist, pulling me to him. His tongue pushes through my lips and into my mouth. Wrapping my arms around his shoulders, we melt together into one perfect goodbye kiss.

Pulling back, I whisper, "I'm sorry." My phone pings, indicating my ride is here. "Goodbye, Nic." Turning toward the exit, I bite my bottom lip, and breathe deeply. He reaches around me and opens the door for me.

"I'll walk you out," he tells me, leaving no room for argument.

We step out onto the porch and I see the sedan idling out front. We silently walk down the pathway, his hand resting on my lower back. My body thrums with desire from his brief touch. A part of me wants to stay but there's also a part that needs to get out of here. As if the moment isn't mortifying enough, a car pulls up behind my Uber. A male and female climb out, followed by two young boys from the back, they are bickering between themselves and oblivious to what's going on around them.

"Boys," the father says, garnering their attention. The six of us awkwardly stare at one another.

"Hi," I shyly say.

"Hello," the father, well I presume he's the father since the three boys all look similar. "Are you the agent here to show us the house?"

"Huh?" I question like a goof. "No, I'm just leaving…"

"Ohh," he says, and then recognition hits that I'm doing the morning-after walk of shame, and his eyes flick between Dominic and me. With a knowing smirk, he turns and walks toward his wife and kids, leaving Nic and I alone.

Nic reaches out and opens the car door for me. "Thank you," I say as I climb in. He closes the door and I look up to see him staring down at me. There's hurt in his eyes and I feel like a bitch that I'm the reason he's hurting. I knew having a one-night stand was a mistake. This is an awful feeling and it's not one I will be repeating. Ever. One-night stands are not for me.

"Fuck," I quietly mumble to myself.

As the car pulls away, our eyes are locked on one another. I stare at him and his house as we drive down the street and turn the corner. Guilt has taken up residence within and I'm close to telling the driver to turn back around when my phone rings from my clutch. The noise startles me and I jump at the sound. Digging in my bag, I retrieve my phone, and smile when I see Bay's name flashing on the screen.

"Morning," I say in greeting.

"More like afternoon, and where the fuck are you?" In the background I hear Corey tell her to watch her mouth.

I laugh at Corey berating her before I answer, "I'm in an Uber on my way to my car."

"Your dirty fucking skank. I'm going to get wine and then I'll meet you at yours."

"Make it tequila."

"This is gonna be good. See you soon, skank." She hangs up before I can reply.

Shaking my head, I drop my phone back into my clutch and lean my head against the window, and I watch the city go by and think about Bay's words. She's right, I am a skank. A gutless skank who walked away from the most perfect man I have ever met and after the best fucking night of my life. Dominic and I clicked on every level. Our bodies melded together as one. He's ruined me when it comes to sex, never will I experience anything like that ever again.

The car stops outside Bin 501. I thank the driver and climb out. Walking over to my car, I unlock it and climb in. My eyes drift over to where Nic parked last night and my heart aches at the thought of never seeing him again. "Stupid stupid, Charli," I berate myself as I start my car and head home.

When I pull up at my place, I see Baylor is already here. "Hey hey, skanky lady." She sings this in tune to "Foxy Lady" by Jimi Hendrix as I walk up to her. I give her 'the look' and her eyes widen. "What's wrong, puddin?" Now she's channeling her inner Harley Quinn. My mouth opens and closes a few times. I don't know where to begin, the first tear falls and without saying a word, she pulls me in for a hug.

Wrapping my arms around her, I begin to sob. "I had the best night of my life with Biker Boy," I sniffle, "and then I left, saying if it's meant to be it's meant to be, but I think I made a mistake. I should have stayed. I should have gotten his details. I shouldn't have been a skank. I should have been a mature adult."

"Why did you do all of that if it was the best night your life?"

"'Cause I'm a dickwad."

She pulls away and cups my cheek in a motherly way. "Don't cry, Charli. Let's go upstairs and you can spend the afternoon with me and Jose. We can make you forget all about Biker Boy." She lifts the bag with her and jiggles it about. I can hear bottles clinking together. I nod and for the first time since I got home, I smile through my tears.

Bay and I link arms and we head inside and up to my apartment. She and Jose certainly do make me forget all about the sexy bike-riding Adonis…that is until Monday morning when I come face-to-face with him in the most unlikely of locations.

DOMINIC 11

Watching Charli drive away in her Uber just now gutted me. *Man, I'm turning into a chick with all these 'feelings,'* I think to myself, as I watch the car turn the corner at the end of the street. I'm left standing here with my crumpled heart, alone, but movement beside me catches my attention. When I look up, the man, his wife, and sons are still standing here, staring at me.

I smile at them, the man has a knowing looking on his face. His wife has a scowl on hers and the kids; they are none the wiser as to what just transpired. Nodding my head, I smile, and watch as they walk toward the house next door. It was recently sold, I'm guessing they're my new neighbors. *Perfect first meeting,* I think to myself as I head back inside.

Closing the door behind me, I walk toward the kitchen. "I need coffee," I mumble to myself, as I grab my mug and place it under my Keurig.

Leaning against the counter, I wait for the nectar that is coffee to brew. My mind flits over last night and this morning. I woke up to an empty bed, and my heart deflated when I realized I'd been fucked and chucked. I really thought we had a connection, but the conversation just now proves that, once again, when it comes to chicks, I know jack shit. My dick is rock fucking hard right now, it clearly didn't get the memo that I'm alone.

With my coffee in hand, I pad across the living room and step out onto the back deck. The deck was the reason I got this place. It takes up the majority of the backyard but it's perfect. To the left is a sunken hot tub and to the right is a gourmet outdoor kitchen. I treated myself and have ordered an outdoor table and matching lounger that my sister, Elena, helped me pick out. She's another reason coming to Chicago has been great. I never realized how much I missed her. She's currently a first-year med student at Western General. I'm so proud of her, if only Abigail, or Abi as she prefers, was as focused as Elena. Abi, is the baby of the family and in Mom and Dad's eyes, she can do no wrong. She's definitely the wild child of the three of us, but in saying that, I wouldn't change a thing about her.

As if she knew I was thinking about her, my phone pings with a text.

ABI - *What's up Boogerbutt?*

DOMINIC - *Having a coffee on my big deck*

ABI - *I don't want to know about your big deck*

DOMINIC - *Can't wait for you to sit on my big deck*

ABI - ***middle finger emoji***

DOMINIC - *You love me **kiss emoji***

ABI - *Only cause I have to*

ABI - *Can't wait to visit you*

ABI - *Mom says hey*

DOMINIC - *Tell her, her favorite son loves her*

ABI - *You're her only son*

DOMINIC - *Hence her favorite, der.*

DOMINIC - *How are you?*

ABI - *I'm texting you on a Sunday afternoon so clearly I'm bored.*

DOMINIC - *Feel the love. What's up?*

ABI - *You ever feel lost?*

That last message concerns me so I bring up FaceTime and call her.

"You didn't need to call," she says in greeting.

"I know I didn't but I think this conversation will be easier in person rather than via text."

"I'm fine," she confirms, but I can tell from the look on her face she is anything but.

"Abi," I warn, "don't bullshit me. Whenever you, or any woman, says they are fine; they are definitely not fine. What's got you down?" She goes quiet, and then her eyes well with tears. "You're scaring me, Sissy."

"Donovan broke up with me."

"Well, he's clearly a dick and not worthy of your tears."

"But I..." She drifts off and then it clicks.

"Slept with him."

She nods. "He humped and dumped me." She's full-on crying now.

"I know how you feel and—"

"You don't know shit," she sasses, wiping at her tear-stained cheeks.

"I know more than you think, Sis." My mind immediately drifts to Charli, *I know exactly how you feel, Abs, but the difference is, I'm not a seventeen-year-old girl.*

"I thought he loved me, Nic." I growl when she calls me Nic. My name is Dominic but as soon as I think that, I realize that most of the night, Charli called me Nic and I didn't correct her. In fact, I didn't mind her calling me that at all. I normally hate it when people call me Nic. *Another reason we were perfect,* then I hear Abi say, "...I was only a bet." My mind forgets about Charli and I focus on my sister.

"Say that again?" I growl, my big brotherliness kicking in.

"It was all a bet," she cries.

"He bet on you?"

"Yep, he and his friends have a bet on how many girls they can bang before Christmas break."

"What a bunch of dickwads."

"That's nicer than what I said when I found out. Any chance you can arrest the pindicked assholes?"

"As much as I'd love to help you with that, I can't."

"Maybe Elena can get me a severe shits inducing drug. I can give them all a case of the mega shits."

"Just go to pharmacy and do it yourself. No need to incriminate Elena like that, or ruin her career before it's even begun."

"You're so smart."

"You're just realizing this?" I tease. "But I promise, you'll get over it, and then when you least expect it, you'll meet Mr. Right and you'll forget all about the dickwad who broke your hymen and heart."

"Speaking from experience?"

"Well, since I haven't found Mrs. Right and don't have a hymen, I can't say for sure but look at Mom and Dad. They're blissfully happy and in love."

"It's so gross seeing old people being all lovely-dovey."

A laugh breaks free but I smile because Mom and Dad are VERY affectionate people. I think that's why I'm a sensitive soul at heart. "You'll change your tune one of these days."

"Yeah, but I won't be gross in front of my kids."

"Yeah, you will, you're a Cruz."

"Thanks, Dominic, you really are the best brother."

"I know," I cheekily say. "Now go to CVS and show that dickwad what happens when you mess with a Cruz."

We say our goodbyes and then I head back inside. Placing my mug in the sink, I decide to tackle the rest of the boxes sitting in my office. Connecting my phone to the stereo system, I get to it. A few hours later, my office and spare rooms are all set up. My stomach rumbles and I realize I haven't eaten all day. Not in the mood to cook, I order a pizza.

Grabbing myself a beer, I lean on the kitchen island, take a sip, and think about tomorrow. I'm excited for this new job. I wonder what my new partner will be like. I've been lucky, since becoming an agent, I've mostly worked alone. This will be the first time I'm with someone for a long-term assignment.

There's a knock at the door, I walk down the hallway and swing it open to find my pizza waiting for me. Taking my pepperoni on thin from him, I head back to the kitchen. I grab another beer, jump up onto the counter, and eat my pizza.

When I've eaten more pizza than I should have, I clean up my mess and head to bed. Deciding to get an early night before my first day tomorrow. As soon as I step into my room, my senses are assaulted with her scent mixed with sex. At the thought of her and last night, my cock stirs. Much like it has all day whenever my mind drifted to her. Maybe I need to visit Bin 501 again this weekend and hope I come face-to-face with my Angel again. Little do I know, I'll be coming face-to-face with her much sooner than that.

CHARLI 12

"UGH, I'M NEVER DRINKING AGAIN," I MUMBLE TO MYSELF AS I CLIMB OUT OF bed when my alarm blares at stupid o'clock to get ready for work. The sun is not yet up but I always start my day with a run, even when I'm hungover. I didn't get one in yesterday but I think I got my exercise in another way, so I give myself a pass. I'm still sore, but that's no surprise, because Nic fucked me into the middle of next week, no, year. Baylor thinks I'm a 'fucking moron'—her exact words—for running out on him, and not that I'd ever admit it to her, I think I agree. Sneaking out like I did was one of the biggest mistakes I've ever made, but there's no point in dwelling on the past.

With that thought in mind, I change into my running gear and head out. Jogging first thing in the morning reinvigorates the soul and I always have a great day when I start like this. I'm meeting my new partner today, can't say I'm looking forward to that. After the betrayal from Dean, I'm not keen to have a new one.

After hitting five miles, I make my way home to shower and change. I decide to head in early, to get on top of some paperwork. Since it's early, I stop at the coffee shop downstairs and grab myself a salted caramel latte, my new favorite coffee, and a ham and cheese croissant.

When I arrive at the office, I'm the only one here. No surprise since it's not yet 7:00 a.m. The silence is peaceful and it allows me to get in and tackle the mountain of paperwork on my desk.

A knock at my door startles me and when I look up, I see the captain. "Morning, Boss," I tell her.

"Morning. Your new partner is here. Can you meet us in the conference room in five?"

"Can do."

She nods and exits my office. I quickly finish the file I was working on and then I make my way into the conference room. Amanda is facing the door and a man is sitting with his back to me, "Charli, I'd like you to meet your new partner, Dominic Cruz."

My world freezes when my new partner turns around. My mouth drops in shock and my eyes bug wide open. My new partner is *him*. "Hi," I manage to squeak out. Walking into the room, I offer him my hand and he takes it. Just like on the weekend, an electrical current passes between us.

"Nice to meet you, Charli," he says, his tone void of any feelings whatsoever. It's not like the deep, gruff sexy-as-sin voice from Saturday night/Sunday morning.

"You too," I say, playing along with the charade that we don't know each other.

"I was just telling Nic here—"

"It's Dominic," he interrupts.

"Sorry, Dominic, I was updating him about our upcoming cases and your current predicament with IA. I have reassured him that you're innocent and he has nothing to worry about."

"I'm sorry you're going through this," he says, his voice showing some compassion, not that I think I deserve any compassion from him after running away like a coward yesterday.

"Thanks, I'm sure it will all be over soon. As Amanda would have told you, I have nothing to hide."

"Well, I'll leave you two to get aquatinted." Amanda stands up and walks toward the door. "It's good to have you aboard, Dominic."

We silently stare at one another. I fall into the chair across from him and shake my head.

"Looks like fate had other ideas for us," Dominic says, breaking our silent stare off.

"I think we, umm, ahh, should talk about what happened," I nervously say.

"I think we should too, but not here. Maybe we can get drinks later?"

Nodding, I smile. "I'd like that."

With the awkwardness put aside, we get to it. For the rest of the morning, I show Dominic around the office. Introducing him to those we will be working with, there's not much to catch up on file wise, as I'm in between cases right now, and well, the whole IA/Dean thing. I show him to his office and tell him, I'll be in mine if he needs me.

I head back to my office and close the door behind me. I rest my head back against the wood and close my eyes. Of course my one-night stand is my new partner, that's just my freakin' luck. Walking over to my desk, I grab my phone and text and Bay.

CHARLI - *So, I just met my new partner...*
BAYLOR - *And???*
CHARLI - *You've met him*
BAYLOR - *????*
CHARLI - *Dominic from Saturday night is my new partner*

My phone rings immediately and it's Bay. "No fucking way," she squeals. "Is he just as fucktasticly gorgeous when you're sober?"

Yes. "Umm."

"And when will it be happening again? This is like fate."

"That's what he said too, but I think it's more like karma for being a ho."

"How many times do I need to say it, you are not a ho for having a night and morning of fan-fucking-tabolous sex."

"Well, considering he acted like he didn't know me when Amanda introduced us, I don't think we will be having fan-fucking-tabolous sex again." I pause, "He did agree to have drinks and discuss things."

"Well, that's a good sign, if he didn't care he'd just play dumb and forget it happened. Me thinks you'll be having fan-fucking-tabolous sex again with him."

"You need to get your loved-up head out of the clouds."

"Pffft, whatevs. Make sure you call me after drinks and fan-fucking-tabolous sex."

"There will be no sex with him, but I promise to call after we discuss things."

"I bet my left nut you fuck him again."

"You don't have nuts," I remind her.

"Fine, I bet Core's left nut that you fuck him again."

"I don't want to be thinking of your man's nuts." I pause and think about her words and then I shake my head. "Corey's nuts aside, there will be no more fucking between us."

"You keep telling yourself that, you'll be banging his brains out later this evening. Trust me because the chemistry between you two is too hard to ignore."

"You know nothing, Baylor Evans," I tell her.

"Don't be going all *Game of Thrones* on me, I'm more like the oracle from *Matrix*, I see it all and I see fan-fucking-tabolous sex between you and your sexy agent." Before I can reply, in typical Baylor fashion, she hangs up on me.

Shaking my head, I throw my phone onto my desk and wonder if she's right. Will I be having fan-fucking-tabolous sex with him again? Movement in my doorway garners my attention and when I look up, my eyes widen when I see who's standing in the doorway to my office. "Darren, what are you doing here?" I ask him, staring over at him.

"I'm here to get what's owed," he says, stepping into my office, closing the door behind him.

"Excuse me?" I question, having no clue as to what he's referring to.

"My brother said you didn't know, but after the mess Dean's now in I don't believe a word out of his fucking mouth." He shakes his head. "I should have known he'd fuck it all up."

"What are you taking about?" My confusion is increasing by the second.

"Just give it up and I won't need to take this further."

I stare at him dumbfounded, I have no idea what he's wanting me to give up. "Darren, I really have no idea what you're talking about."

"Looks like we're doing this the hard way then."

Before I can reply, he opens the door and walks out. Slamming it behind him. "What the hell was that?" I whisper to myself.

It opens again a few seconds later, but it's Bec standing there now. "Was that Darren Chikatilo?"

I nod. "Yep. He's freakin' deluded like his brother."

"What did he want?"

Shaking my head, I recap what just happened and then add, "I have a feeling I'll find out soon."

And soon is sooner that I thought. With what is revealed, I'm screwed...and not in the sexy naked on a motorcycle kind of way. I'm screwed in the 'better get used to the color orange' kind of way.

DOMINIC 13

Of all the people in Chicago, my new partner had to be her. Guess fate wants us to be together after all. Alternatively, fate is just a cruel bitch who is messing with me. You'd think after the shit with Bianca I was due some good luck, but no, that's not the case...or maybe it is? Maybe I shouldn't judge things until after Charli and I chat tonight.

Walking to the break room for more coffee, I think about the morning with Charli. She was the epitome of professional once the shock of me being her new partner wore off. And after spending the morning with her, I think we will make a smashing team. Now I just need to convince her that we can work outside of the office too.

With a coffee in hand, I head back to my office and I go over the office rules with a fine-tooth comb. There's nothing in here forbidding us from having a relationship so tonight when Charli and I meet up, I'm going to broach the subject of an us. I know I haven't known her, well actually, I don't really know her at all, but I know that we could be something. You don't have a connection like we have for just one night, a connection like that is meant forever. I just need to get her on board with the idea of a future with me.

My phone rings and when I glance at the screen, I sigh when I see Bianca's name. Clicking the red decline button, I send the call to voicemail. Two seconds later, it rings again and again; I decline the call. This happens three more times before I angrily answer. "What?" I snarl down the line, my tone leaving no confusion as to my mood.

"Dominic?" she questions.

"You know it's me, you've been calling nonstop for the last five minutes."

"I need to talk to you."

"Well, I don't want to talk to you."

"Please," she begs, "I've already apologized."

"You think two words are going to ease the pain of what you've put me through? Bianca, we are over. Done. Dusted. Kaput."

"But—"

"No buts, lose my number. Don't call me again."

I don't give her a chance to reply, I hang up. Throwing my phone onto my desk, I lean back in my chair and stare up at the ceiling. Memories of that day come crashing back to me like a heart-crushing tsunami…

…The case wrapped up early and I cannot wait to get home. B isn't due home for a few hours, so I can cook us dinner and then we can have a quiet night in. Stopping in at Jewel-Osco, I grab everything needed to cook pastitsio. I use a family recipe that has been handed down to mamá from her mamá and so on. But no one makes pastitsio like γιαγιά. With everything in hand, I grab a lovely bottle of red to accompany our dinner and head home.

Parking my car, I grab my bag, the groceries, and head up the stairs toward the front door. I can hear a muffled noise from inside and I deflate when I realize that B is home and it will ruin my surprise. Pushing open the front door, it's me who is surprised. In the middle of our living room is my girlfriend, bent over the coffee table and plowing into her from behind is our neighbor, Lawrence. He has her ponytail wrapped around his fist, and the other grips her hip as he pistons his hips back and forth. The two of them are so lost in their desire, they don't notice me. He roars as he comes inside of her and she moans through her release.

Clearing my throat, they both snap their heads toward me. Bianca's eyes widen when she sees me, in a fluster, she lifts herself up and her head connects with Lawrence's nose. A crack sounds through the living room. He jolts back and because his pants are around his ankles, he stumbles backward and trips over the armchair. His ass and balls in the air for all to see.

"Honey, I'm home," I sarcastically say before I turn on my heel and walk out, slamming the door behind me. I stomp down the stairs and head back to my car.

"Dominic," Bianca shouts. Closing my eyes, I take a deep breath and turn around to face her. Tears are streaking down her cheeks. "I'm sorry," she cries.

"Sorry you cheated? Or sorry you got caught?" My question stumps her, she just stares at me. Her mouth opening and closing. "Exactly like I thought."

"I'm sorry," she cries again.

"Sorry doesn't mean shit, Bianca, when his jizz is currently running down your leg." She looks down and presses her thighs together. "How long?" I snarl between clenched teeth.

Her silence pisses me off, shaking my head, I turn to my car and open the door. Before I climb in, I look over the door at her. "I'll be by to get my things later."

Climbing into my car, I start the engine and back out of the driveway. I head over to my parents' house. Mamá will cook me my pastitsio and Dad and I will drink copious amounts of red wine until I forget that I ever met Bianca Rowe...

...shaking away that thought, I focus on the positives in my life. My new job. My new house. Charli and our dinner tonight and as I think of her, it hits me. Had it not been for Bianca cheating on me with Lawrence, I never would have moved here and then I never would have met Charli. "Thanks, Bianca," I quietly whisper, seems her cheating on me WAS a good thing after all.

Sitting up, I grab my pen and start filling out the paperwork I need to file with HR. Once it's completed, I drop it off at HR and as I'm returning to my office, there's a commotion down the hall. Looking up, I see a group of agents I don't recognize following Charli into the conference room.

"What's up with that?" I ask Rebecca.

"Higgins and Laelyn from LOTUS are here, they finally have a lead to take down The Flower."

"I thought that was all myth?"

She shakes her head, "Nope, it's one-hundred-percent true."

"All of it?"

"All of it," she matter-of-factly says.

"No shit."

The Flower is a secret organization that LOTUS—Locate and Oust Traitors of the US—has been trying to take down for years, but The Flower is really good at what they do and no one has been able to infiltrate them. This will be a massive win for them if they can do this.

Heading back to my office, I start to familiarize myself with upcoming cases, I feel like I'm being watched and I look up. I smile when I see Charli standing in the doorway to my office. "Hey," I offer in greeting.

"Hey, I, umm, ahh, need to postpone our drinks. I'm going to assist LOTUS with The Flower takedown."

"Need any extra help?"

She shakes her head. "Nah, we've got this. Can we catch up later in the week?"

"Yeah, that's fine."

From down the hallway someone yells, "Let's go, Davis."

"Catch ya later," she says with a wave, turns, and walks away. She quickly spins back. "Nic, I'm really glad you're my new partner." Before I can say anything she walks away, and once again I realize that I don't mind being called Nic. My cock agrees too because he's harder than steel right now, and it's really inappropriate since I'm in the office. Thankfully I'm sitting down at my desk, a rock-hard dick on your first day isn't a good way to say hello to my new colleagues.

Within the five minutes we were chatting, she managed to reset my pissed-off mood after my call with Bianca, and even though our chat has been postponed, I'm happy we will still get to talk, plus it gives me time to formulate my game plan to win Charli over. Leaning back in my chair, I grin. This is definitely fate at work and I cannot wait to see what the bitch has in store for Charli and me.

CHARLI 14

Iᴛ's ꜰɪɴᴀʟʟʏ ᴛʜᴇ ᴡᴇᴇᴋᴇɴᴅ ᴀɴᴅ ᴀs I sɪᴛ ᴏɴ ᴍʏ ᴠᴇʀᴀɴᴅᴀ ᴡɪᴛʜ ᴀ ɢʟᴀss ᴏꜰ wine and a cheese platter, I think over the past week. It sure has been one crazy ride. First my one-night stand turned out to be my new partner. To say I was shocked when I walked into the conference room and saw him would be the understatement of the century, no, millennium. After walking away from him and regretting it, I never thought I'd see him again but fate obviously had other ideas.

It was a few days before he and I actually worked together, as I was helping Tannen, Higgins, and Laelyn with The Flower takedown. That was a major win for LOTUS and the US in general.

It's only been a few days but Nic and I seem to work well together. And I have to admit, in the sober light of day, he's just as fucking gorgeous and our connection, it's still there and just as intense. It's going to be hard —pun intended—working with him day in, and day out.

Next on the crazy week list was the visit from Darren, Dean's brother. His cryptic visit was confusing but then again, he is related to Dean. Speaking of Dean, he refused to see me when I tried to visit him yesterday. I just want answers, it feels like the dickwad is going to take the truth to his grave. I know that's irrational since we are only in our thirties, but I don't think I will ever get the truth or answers I desire when it comes to Dean Chikatilo and his betrayal.

And kicker number three, happened this morning. I was late after getting stuck in the elevator—that's isn't the kicker—when I finally made it to my office, I was met with Amanda and two new assholes from IA. They are still convinced I'm in cahoots with Dean and they interrogated me for over three hours. Three-fucking-hours answering the same questions over and over. My answers have not changed since I was first interviewed, but they are like a dog with a bone and won't let it go. Without Dean confessing, I have no clue how to prove my innocence.

Taking a sip of wine, I let the robustness of the red infuse my soul and all my worries begin to dissipate, that is until my phone pings with a text.

NIC: *Looking forward to tomorrow night*

After the shitshow that was this week, I kept changing the subject and putting him off regarding us discussing last weekend, but today I relented and agreed to head to his house tomorrow afternoon to discuss us. Well not us-us, but what happened last weekend and how we proceed from here.

Baylor thinks I need to just go for it, her exact words were, "You only live once and amazingly good sex is hard to come by." She's right on that last part, amazing sex is hard to come by and sex with Dominic is out of this world amazing. My nether regions tingle each and every time I think about last weekend, that has NEVER happened before. Maybe Bay is right, maybe I need to go for it with him. Just to be sure, I went through the HR rules and regulations and there's nothing in there preventing us from being a couple, it's all up to me, and him, I guess.

With a sigh, I chug back the last of my wine and head inside. Placing the dishes into the dishwasher, I turn it on and head into my bedroom to get ready for bed. Changing into my satin nightie, I climb under the covers, turn off the light, and close my eyes, but sleep doesn't come. Every time I close my eyes, I'm taken back to last weekend when Dominic and I fucked on his bike.

Flicking the light back on, I reach into my top drawer and grab my vibrator. Flicking it on, it buzzes and then stops. I flick the button—not that button—and nothing happens. The batteries are dead. "For fuck's sake," I moan. Throwing the useless appendage to the side, I lay back and slide my hand inside my panties. I'm already soaked, it's embarrassing how wet I am at the memory of last week, but thankfully, no one is here to judge me. Running my finger up and down my folds, I focus on the task at hand. Separating my lips, I rub my clit and moan. That little bundle of joy zings with desire and thrums to its own beat. Sliding my hand farther down, I slip a finger inside, curling it around to hit that magic spot.

My finger is no dick but right now, it's getting the job done.

When I grip my breast and tweak my nipple through my nightie, that's the ignition source I need and I explode around my fingers. My toes clench. My back arches off the bed. My body spasms and I moan in delight as pleasure ricochets throughout me from head to toe.

With a contented sigh, I collapse and relax into my mattress and blissfully drift off to sleep.

Stretching the next morning, my muscles are taut from my self-induced orgasm, my mind drifts to this afternoon and I wonder what will happen. Will Dominic and I see eye to eye on this? But more so, what do I want to happen?

Sure he's hotter than hot. He seems like a nice guy and we get along both inside and outside of the bedroom. Am I open to a relationship with him? I haven't been in a relationship in such a long time. I've been married to my job but maybe it's time I look out for Charli and not Agent Davis. Work is going great guns so it seems like the perfect time to focus on me.

Deciding to leave it up to fate, I crawl out of bed and head into the kitchen. I smile when my eyes land on the full coffeepot—thank you automatic timer. Grabbing my 'Fucking Amazing FBI Agent' mug, I pour myself a cup. Bringing my mug to my lips, I take a sip.

Picking up my phone, I realize I didn't reply to Dominic last night. Shit, I think to myself, I must have mentally replied. I quickly type out a message.

CHARLI: *Sorry, I mentally replied last night. Looking forward to today too. Do you need me to bring anything?*

Immediately I get a reply.

NIC: *Just yourself will be fine*

Smiling at his reply, I finish my coffee and head into my en suite to prep for this afternoon. I shave, everywhere, not that I'm expecting to get laid, but hey, a girl's gotta be prepared. I wash and blow wave my hair. Deciding to go for casual, I slip into my denim jeans that make my ass and legs look amazing and I pair them with a figure-hugging, plain white tank. And finally, my black ballet flats.

Looking up, I realize that time's gotten away from me and if traffic is shit, I'm going to be late. Grabbing my purse and keys, I head down to my car. Climbing into my mini, I drive over to Dominic's place.

Parking on the street, I look up at his house and I take it in. The other morning I didn't have a chance to appreciate the beauty of the architecture before me. It's a classic Chicago bungalow, with a dormered second floor, a large pine tree takes up most of the front yard, and the stairs are adorned with flowerpots. It screams Dominic.

Looking to the house next-door, I see the man from the other morning in the front yard weeding. I smile politely and head up the stairs. Taking a deep inhale, I ring the doorbell. When the door opens, all breath leaves my body as I stare at the man before me. My eyes rake over his body and before any words are said, I realize I could quite easily fall for Agent Cruz.

DOMINIC 15

SWINGING OPEN THE DOOR, MY MOUTH DROPS AND MY EYES SHAMELESSLY RAKE over Charli from head to toe. This woman is the epitome of a sexy siren and she's dressed casually in a simple—sexy as hell—white tank and jeans that look like they're painted on. "You really are an angel."

Her cheeks darken at my compliment and a smile graces her face. "Thank you." Her eyes roam over me and her smile widens. "You're not too bad to look at yourself, Biker Boy." I'm wearing dark denim jeans, a black Henley, and I'm barefoot since I'm home.

"Please, come in," I say, sweeping my arm out and stepping aside so she can pass.

"Thanks." She steps in and as she walks past me, all I can smell is her. My cock likes it and twitches in my pants. Subtly I adjust myself and close the door. I follow her inside and my eyes drop to her ass, and fuck me sideways, it's delectable. The denim molds to her body, accentuating her gorgeous curves. Swallowing deeply, I think about naked grandmas, I didn't invite her here to fuck, I invited her here to talk, BUT if that did happen to occur, I wouldn't be too upset. I am a man after all.

Stopping at the kitchen island, I grab the stereo remote and turn it down, Mumford and Sons are singing about fucking it up and I really hope that I don't fuck this up. Seeing Charli here again is something I never thought would happen, but it seems fate had other ideas.

"Can I get you a drink? Wine? Beer? Water?"

"Wine would be great," she says, looking back over her shoulder and with the sunlight beaming through the back windows, she's glowing. Like the angel I keep referring to her as.

"Take a seat at the island and I'll get it. Red or white?"

"White, please."

Nodding my head, I grab a bottle from the fridge. I go to twist off the cap and groan when I realize it has a cork. Digging in the drawer, I find the corkscrew and open the bottle. Placing it on the counter, I turn and grab the glasses from the overhead cabinet. When I turn back, I notice Charli checking me out. Internally I fist pump because that means she still feels what I feel.

Pouring two glasses, I hand her hers and when our fingers brush a spark zaps through me, and from the look on her face, she felt it too. Walking around the island, I take a seat next to her. Lifting my glass, I look over to her. "A toast."

"What are we toasting to?" she asks and lifts her glass.

"To us and whatever the future holds."

With a smile that lights up her face, she nods. "I like that. To us and whatever the future holds!" She taps her glass gently against mine and brings the glass to her lips. I watch as her lips wrap around the thin edge. She takes a sip, closing her eyes, she quietly moans and savors the crisp flavor before swallowing.

When she opens her eyes, she catches me staring at her. We silently stare at one another. Her tongue darts out and I follow the movement before she bites her bottom lip. "This is awkward but not," she says with a laugh.

"I know, right? I don't want it to be awkward between us," I honestly tell her.

She shakes her head. "Me neither. I…"

"You what, Angel?"

She places her glass down and stands up. She walks into the living room before turning on her heel and walking back toward me. "I've never been more confused in my life." I go to reply but she continues, "I thought leaving was what I wanted, but then when I left I realized it wasn't what I wanted, but I had no way to reach you so I left it to fate. Fate seemed to have a plan because lo and behold, you're my new partner. And this connection between us doesn't seem to be a one-time, fleeting thing." She's still pacing as she gets this all out. She animatedly uses her hands and it's cute to watch. "The connection between us is there. It's strong, really strong, and I've never felt anything like this before. I feel you before I see you. I can predict what you're about to say. I miss you as soon as you leave and when you return, I feel free. Content. Happy. When I'm around you, it's like there's nothing wrong in the world, everything is rainbows and flowers and unicorns. For the first time in forever, I feel alive and that I'm seen. I don't feel invisible with you by my side." She stops and turns to face me.

"You're cute when you ramble," I tell her.

"I don't ramble."

Nodding, I scrunch my face and playfully add, "Yeah you do, but you want to know something?" She nods. "I agree with your rambling. Every single word of it. And for the record, you could never be invisible, Charli Davis. You are the brightest star shining in the sky, outshining every other one." Standing up, I walk over to her and take her hands in mine, lacing our fingers together. "Charli, I want to see what's between us. I don't for one minute think we were meant to be a one-time thing, and I think fate agrees too."

"Fate's a bitch," she says.

"A bitch who led us to each other so she can't be that much of a bitch."

"Touché." She pauses and we continue to stare at one another. "So, where do we go from here?" I seductively raise my eyebrows at her and she laughs. "As much as I'd love that, Nic. I want to get to know you in here," she pulls her hand from mine and rests it over my heart, "before we get to that again, but believe me when I tell you, I want that so much." She bites her lip. "Last weekend was the best night of my life."

"Mine too and since I've already had a taste, I know the wait will be worth it."

"The Way You Look Tonight" by Frank Sinatra begins to play and I offer her my hand. She smiles and places hers in mine. I spin her around and pull her back into me. She slides one arm around my waist and the other over my shoulder. Resting her head on my chest, we sway to the music. She begins humming along to the music. The songs changes to "You Are So Beautiful" by Joe Cocker, and we continue to sway to the music.

Quietly I whisper, "You really are beautiful, Charli."

She lifts her head from my chest and gazes into my eyes. Lifting her hands, she grips my cheeks in her palms, leans forward, and presses her lips to mine. "Thank you for a wonderful afternoon."

She rests her head back on my chest and we continue to sway to Joe. I press a kiss to her head and close my eyes, photographing this moment. Cataloguing the feelings coursing through me for future reference because I always want to feel like this. It's in this moment I realize I'm falling for Charli Davis.

CHARLI 16

...five weeks later

It's the weekend and I'm in my kitchen cleaning up the breakfast dishes. Dominic is in the shower, he told me to leave the dishes but my OCD refuses to let them sit. Those filthy little bastards are sitting on the counter waving their dirty jazz hands at me singing, 'I'm dirty and you know it.' I've closed the door on the dishwasher when "Sexy and I Know It" by LMFAO comes on, I laugh as it's super close to what my dirty dishes were singing at me. I turn up the volume and begin to shake my booty around the kitchen. I dance and sing my heart out.

Spinning around, I jump in fright when I see Dominic in the doorway, leaning against the frame. He's staring at me with a grin on his face. "Don't stop dancing around on my account."

Feeling brazen, I spin back around and shake my booty at him. Gripping my sundress, I slide it up and down my thighs as I dance around. Glancing over my shoulder, I notice his eyes are locked on my ass. I take the opportunity to stare at him. He's barefoot. His jeans are torn and only half of the buttons on his shirt are done up, exposing his muscular tanned chest.

Turning around to face him, I shimmy over and wink, before I spin back around and rub my ass against his crotch. Running my hands up his neck and around the back of his head, he rests his hands on my hips and grinds himself into me.

Stepping backward, I shake my ass once again before spinning to face him. My hips still swaying side to side, I step closer and press a kiss to his chest. Kissing down his torso, I reach his buttons. Using my teeth, I begin to pop them open, one by one.

"Most people would use their hands to undo buttons on a shirt," he says, his voice so deep it vibrates through my body.

"I'm no ordinary woman," I reply with a wink.

"You most certainly are not ordinary, Charli. You are fucking extraordinary."

His words hit me right in the chest. Standing up, I grip his cheeks in my palms and slam my lips to his. Wrapping his arms around my waist, he pulls me into him. My breasts push against his bare chest. The kiss is frenzied and frantic. It's downright perfect, leaving me light-headed and wanting more. Breaking the connection, I drop to my knees and tear at the remaining shirt buttons. They fly about the kitchen, pinging on the floor. His shirt falls open and I take the moment to appreciate his gorgeous physique. Abs upon abs that lead down to that delicious 'V' that causes woman to go cray cray.

Licking my lips, I lift my gaze to his. With our eyes locked on one another, I pop open the button and lower his fly. Sliding my hands in, I push his jeans and briefs down. His cock springs free, and a smile graces my face when I see how hard he is. Lifting my hand, I grip the base and begin to slowly stroke him. Leaning forward I lick the tip, my tongue swirls around his slit as I pump my hand up and down. His precum coating my tongue. I moan as I suck his shaft into my mouth.

With my eyes locked on his, I relax my throat and take him deep into my mouth. "Fuck, Charli," he groans, as I continue to slide his dick farther down with each thrust. Holding on to his thigh for balance, I suck his cock as if it's a melting Popsicle on a hot summer's day. His hips gyrate in sync with me.

His cock twitches.

His body stills.

He groans as the first spurt of hot salty cum sprays into my mouth. I lick and suck every last drop from him. His dick pops out of my mouth and I wipe at the corner of my lip. Seductively slipping my finger into my mouth, I suck.

Dominic drops to his knees, removes my finger from my mouth, grips my cheeks, and kisses me. Much like the one earlier, it's frenzied and heated. With our lips locked, he shuffles us around so I'm straddling him. He pushes my dress up, pulls my panties to the side, and slides his finger up and down my slit. "So wet," he murmurs against my lips. Pressing a finger inside me, I moan into our kiss.

My hips begin to move against his hand, the pressure inside me building. "Please," I whimper against his lips.

He removes his finger, grips his dick which is once again hard. Lifting me to my knees, he lines himself up at my opening and I slide down his shaft. Moaning as his dick enters me. When I'm fully seated on him, I rest my hands on his shoulders and begin to ride him. I slide up and down his shaft, my thrusts becoming faster and faster. He lowers his head and sucks my nipple through my dress. My head drops back and I let the pleasure building envelop me. He bites my nipple and I scream as a powerful orgasm detonates. I ride him like a cowgirl as I come and come and come. I'm still riding my high when I feel him release inside of me.

Resting my forehead against his, I close my eyes and savor the moment. Both of us breathing heavily. Pulling back, I grin. "Well, that took a turn I wasn't expecting."

"You and me both. I was going to suggest a picnic but I think BJs and kitchen sex was a much better idea."

"We can start each and every Sunday this way from now on."

"I like the sound of that."

Dominic's phone rings but neither one of us moves. It stops, only to start ringing again. "You better get that."

"I should but I'm quite content just being here with you."

"I'm content too, but my knees are starting to hurt and there's a perfectly comfy sofa in the living room. How about, you get that," I nod toward his once again ringing phone, "I'll freshen up and we can have a lazy day."

"Can we have tacos for dinner?"

"Deal." Placing a kiss on his nose, I stand up and offer him my hand. He places his in mine and I help him up. We stare at one another, I know it's only been a few weeks but those three words are on the tip of my tongue, I'm just about to say them when his phone rings again.

He steps around me and picks it up. "Hey, Abs," he says when he answers, and I can hear Abi berating him from where I'm standing and I laugh. Walking past, I head into my bathroom and freshen up. By time I return, he's on the sofa and has a strange look on his face.

"You okay?" I ask, as I sit next to him.

He nods. "Yeah, I'm fine." Much like when a woman says they are fine, I don't believe him.

"You sure?"

"Yeah, I'm sure. How about we order in our Mexican fiesta?"

"That sounds great. I'll see if Bay and Corey want to join us."

"Perfect," he says, but I can tell his mind is elsewhere.

Bay and Corey are busy so it's just us. We order enough food to feed the entire country. After eating my weight in Mexican, Dominic and I head to bed. I fall asleep after a mind-blowing orgasmcap, my new favorite bedtime nightcap.

Just as the sun is rising, I wake up and feel queasy. I think I overdid it on the Coronas last night and as soon as I stand up, my stomach rolls. I race into the bathroom and throw up. Once I start vomiting, I can't stop.

Dominic is a saint and looks after me. He runs the shower for me and I climb in once the water is hot. When I get out, I feel much better. Stepping into my room, I smile when I see my navy blue pantsuit on the bed waiting for me. With a smile on my face, I get dressed and when I step into the kitchen, Dominic hands me a cup of peppermint tea. "Thanks," I say as I wrap my hand around the mug.

Dominic and I head into the office but a few hours later, I start to feel sick again so I head home. I climb into bed and fall asleep straight away. I wake when there's a knocking at my front door. Shuffling through my apartment, I open the door and see Bay.

"Well, you look like shit."

"Hello to you too," I snarkily reply.

"Ohh, I'm sorry. Hello, Charli, you look like shit."

Flipping her the bird, I turn around and collapse onto my sofa. Bay comes in and sits next to me. "You okay?"

"No," I shake my head, "I feel like shit and I can't stop throwing up. I think the Mexican we had yesterday is not agreeing with me."

"Or you're preggers," she teases.

"Hardy har har, Evans."

She shrugs. "Can I get you anything?"

I shake my head. "No, I just need to get this bug to pass and then I'll be fine."

"Okay, well, I'm going to go 'cause I don't want to catch anything. Call Corey if you need anything."

"Why not you?"

"I don't want to catch what you got."

"Feel the love," I tell her.

She stands up and places a kiss on my head. "You know I love you but I don't do vomiting or poop."

"You'll make a great mom one day."

"I know I will."

"You do know that babies poop and vomit...quite a lot from the little that I know."

"And that's where Core comes in."

"You are something, Baylor."

"Something awesome," she confirms. "Laters, lady."

And as quick as she was here, she's gone again.

Picking up my phone, I see a text from Nic.

NIC: *Hope you are feeling better, let me know if you need anything*

I grin as I read his message, he really is a sweetheart.

CHARLI: *Feeling better. Hoping a good night's sleep will help. See you tomorrow*

Placing my phone on my bedside table, I close my eyes and begin to drift off to sleep when her words cause my eyes to open and I sit upright. "Shit," I grumble.

Slipping on my running shoes, I grab my bag and keys and jump into my car. I drive to Walmart and I race to the pharmacy. With a test box in hand, I head home and make a beeline into my bathroom. I open the first box and read the instructions. Pee. Wait two minutes and then I'll know. It all seems pretty simple but trying to pee on a little white stick is much harder than it looks. Finally, I hit the stick and place it on the counter, before I have finished washing my hands, two pinks lines stare back up at me. Ever the optimist, I think maybe it's a false positive, so I open the second test and repeat. As before two pink lines stare back at me.

Not trusting the first two, I race back to Walmart and grab two more boxes, different brands this time. I pee on the extra four and like the first two, they all come up positive.

Sliding to the floor, I lay all six tests on the bathroom mat. I stare down at the six white sticks, all with two pink lines waving their pee-pink jazz hands in my face. "Shit, I'm pregnant," I whisper to myself.

Lifting my knees up, I rest my elbows on my knees, and cover my face with my hands. I've felt off this past week but I thought it was due to stress, or food poisoning, but no, it's because I'm pregnant. My periods have never been regular due to having polycystic ovarian syndrome, or PCOS, so my lack of period since meeting Dominic didn't really register. When I think of him I smile, he will make a great dad. Sure, this is sudden, but we are in a good place, it will all be fine...but ohh am I wrong. The next day at work, the shocks just keep rolling and life will never be the same again.

CHARLI 17

LAST NIGHT I TOSSED AND TURNED ALL NIGHT LONG. BY TIME THE SUN RISES, I'm dressed and ready for work. So I head in early. I still feel queasy but not as bad as yesterday. With a peppermint tea in hand, I head into my office and start looking over the upcoming case files. At 9:00 a.m. I call my doctor and I manage to get an appointment in forty-five minutes. Calling the boss, I tell her I have an appointment and head to the doctor. Like I knew, she officially confirms I'm pregnant. She does a scan and tells me that I'm roughly nine weeks pregnant. Seems Dominic knocked me up on our first night together.

"How can I be nine weeks along and not know it?"

"All women's pregnancies are different. There are no set rules when it comes to babies."

Nodding my head, Dr. Clark continues to do her baby doctor thing. She assures me everything looks good and hands me a printout. "My baby's first picture," I say with eyes full of tears as I stare at the picture in my hands. The baby just looks like a blob, but it's our baby and I cannot wait to tell and show Dominic.

With a billion pamphlets and some prenatal vitamins in hand, I head back to the office with a stop at McDonald's for something to eat. I tell myself that it's almost lunchtime so it's okay, but in reality, I've been thinking about cheeseburgers all morning. I notice a woman enter the elevator behind me and she's pregnant, my eyes drop to her belly and I smile. *That'll be me in a few months' time*, I think to myself.

We both get off on floor seven. I go left and she goes right, when I look up I see Patrick Fitzpatrick—yep, he's a double Patrick—from IA with the Boss Lady. "Good morning, Patrick. Amanda," I say with a smile, nodding at them both, but the animosity radiating from Patrick does nothing to ease my already churning stomach.

"Charli, can you meet with us in interrogation three, please?" He's all official and stick up his ass like, I don't envy the people in IA at all. They get a bad rap but they are only doing their job.

"Sure, I just need to drop off my bag and grab some water." Not waiting for a reply, I head to my office. Patrick follows me and I notice that he's watching my every move. An eerie feeling runs up my spine. With my water in hand, I follow him into interrogation and just as I take my seat, a wave a nausea hits me. Covering my mouth, I take a few deep breaths and manage to keep the vomit at bay.

"You okay, Charli?" Amanda asks when she walks in.

Nodding my head, I smile. "Yeah, the sickness from yesterday is still lingering," I tell her and silently I add, *"And it will for the foreseeable future."*

She nods and takes a seat. I look up and from the look on her face, I know it's not good news. "What's going on?"

"Charli—" she says but Patrick interrupts her, "Agent Davis, you are officially on suspension. We have reason to believe that you were, and still are, working in cahoots with your previous partner, Dean Chikatilo."

"That's bullshit!" I shout and stand up. "You don't honestly believe I would be involved with this?" I stare down at him. "I—"

"It doesn't matter what I believe and I will ask that you contain yourself, Agent Davis."

Turning to Amanda, I plead with my eyes but she shakes her head. "I'm sorry, Charli, my hands are tied with regard to this, this is all IA."

Dejectedly I sigh and fall back into my chair. Patrick continues to talk and tell me what's going to happen from here on, but I don't register a word he's saying. Once I hand over my badge and gun, I exit interrogation and walk in a daze back to my office. In a matter of twelve hours my life has been turned upside down and inside out, and the hits haven't finished coming.

A wave of sickness hits and I race into the restroom. I just make it into a cubicle before I empty my stomach. Ever so thankful that I grabbed a cheeseburger from McDonald's on my way back, otherwise I'd be throwing up nothing. Grabbing some toilet paper, I wipe my mouth and flush. Washing my hands, I look at my reflection and sadly smile at myself. "Nic," I mumble, "I need Nic."

Exiting the bathroom, I take the long way round to his office and as I get closer, I hear raised voices coming from inside his office. The door is slightly ajar and I peek through the gap. My eyes land on him and I notice that he's angry. A woman is sitting with her back to me. "I don't give a flying fuck that you're pregnant, Bianca. I will not be a part of this kid's life. It's all yours. Not my responsibility."

Those words shatter me. Here I am, outside his office door to tell him that I'm pregnant with his baby, and he's telling who I presume is his ex that he doesn't want to be father to her baby. If he doesn't want to be a father to hers, he sure as hell won't want to be a father to mine.

Walking backward slowly, I turn on my heel and race to my office. I need to get out of here so I grab my things. The air is stifling and the need to get out of here intensifies. I need fresh air and I need it now. Amanda is calling my name but I keep walking, ignoring her. Reaching out I punch the elevator button and thankfully it opens immediately. I can't deal with any of this right now, I dive into the metal car and quickly press the close door button.

A voice yells, "Hold the elevator," but I don't want to be near anyone so I repeatedly punch the close button. "Please, please, please," I mumble. The doors finally begin to close and I sigh. "I'm free," I whisper as the car begins its descent to the ground.

Stepping backward, I close my eyes and my stomach lurches. I'm not sure if it's from morning sickness, betrayal of what I just heard, or at the prospect of losing my career. The elevator doors open into the lobby and I race over to a trash can. Resting my palms on the edge, I empty my stomach. I'm heaving when I hear the ding of an elevator. I freeze, hoping it isn't the boss, or *him*, and I'm relieved when I don't see either of them. It's a woman but that relief turns to dread when I see she's pregnant and I immediately know it's her: she's Dominic's other baby momma.

Turning back to the can, I vomit again.

Thankfully she doesn't stop and from the corner of my eye, I watch her waddle through the lobby and outside. Wiping my mouth on the back of my hand, I follow the path she took and step outside. The cool air hits my face and the tears I've been holding back begin to fall. Pulling out my phone, I dial the one person who I know won't judge me. Before they say anything, I blubber, "Bay, I need you."

DOMINIC 18

A KNOCK ON MY DOOR STARTLES ME. DROPPING MY PEN, I LOOK UP AND SEE the last person I expected standing there. "Bianca, what are you doing here?"

"Hi, Dominic," she says. My eyes are locked on her as she walks into my office and sits down across from me. Why the hell is she here?

"What do you want?" My tone is harsh, but I said all I needed before I left.

"I…umm, ahh, I wanted to see you."

"Why?" I question again.

"Lawrence and I are no longer seeing each other."

"And?"

"I'm pregnant," she quietly whispers.

"Congrats," I tell her.

"It's, ummm—"

Shit, fuck no, is my immediate thought. "Is it mine?" I ask, not sure I really want to hear the answer.

She shakes her head. "No, I'm twelve weeks. The last time you and I had sex was way before that. Lawrence is the father."

Phew, I think to myself. "So why are you here?"

"I want you back, Dominic. I made a mistake with Lawrence, I see that now. I want you, me, and this baby to be a family."

"You expect me to play daddy to his child?"

"It would be our child."

"No, it's his child. And not my problem, Bianca. You have some fucking nerve coming to my workplace and dropping this on me."

"I'm alone and pregnant," she cries.

"I don't give a flying fuck that you're pregnant, Bianca. I will not be a part of this kid's life. It's all yours. Not my responsibility. Go back to where you came from and work this shit out with Lawrence."

"He...he doesn't want me or the baby." She's crying now, a part of me feels bad for her but there's also a part that doesn't give a shit. She did this to herself.

"Look, Bianca. I really am sorry you're in this mess but it's not my problem. You broke us and any future we had when you cheated on me. Now, please leave."

"I thought you were better than this," she snaps.

"Well, I never thought you'd cheat on me with the neighbor. So there's that." We stare at one another across my desk. Leaning back in my chair, I dismiss her, "Good bye and good luck."

Without a word, she nods, stands up, and exits my office. "Fuck," I mumble and rub my forehead as I watch Bianca leave my office. The nerve of that woman to come here and grovel for me to take her back because she's knocked up...and not even with my baby. Lifting my hands, I link my fingers and rest my hands behind my head.

Sighing I shake my head, I need to see Charli.

Looking up, I see it's nearly 1:00 p.m., maybe I can take her out for a late lunch. Pushing back from my desk, I stand up and smile as I walk out of my office only to be met with Amanda, my new boss, calling my name. Turning around, I face her. "Can I speak with you in private, Dominic?"

Nodding my head, I smile. "Yeah, sure." But inside I'm pissed 'cause I need to see Charli. I need a hug from my Angel. A cuddle from her will make this, and me, feel better. Following Amanda, I enter her office and take a seat across from her. "What's up, Boss Lady?"

"You know I hate being called Boss Lady."

"Sorry," I say with a shrug, but she knows I don't mean it. Calling her Boss Lady is a running joke in the office.

"Dominic, all your upcoming cases are being transferred until I can find you a new partner."

I scrunch my eyes in confusion, "Shouldn't Charli be here for this?"

She shakes her head, "Charli is officially suspended, under suspicion of working with her old partner, Dean."

"That's bullshit!" I shout, "Charli is—"

"I know as well as you do that she's innocent but IA sees it differently."

"Where's Charli now?"

"She left."

"What?" I question. "Why didn't she come and see me?"

"She was pretty upset when she left. I know you two are close so I'm happy for you to head out early and make sure she's okay. She's an integral part of this office and I will do everything in my power to get this wrapped up quickly and have her officially back on the team."

"Thanks, and I will do what I can too." I shake my head. "How is this happening? And why? Why Charli?"

"Your guess is as good as mine, but we need to work together as a team to clear her name."

"I'll do anything to help. But first, I need to see if she's okay."

Without waiting for a reply, I stand up and exit the boss's office. I swing via mine and grab my things and head over to her place.

On the drive over, I try calling her but it goes to voicemail. "Angel, it's me. I'm on my way to your place. I just heard the news, I'm so sorry this has happened to you. I'll be there soon." Disconnecting the call, I focus on the road. An accident on the freeway delays me and it takes me nearly two hours to get from the office to her place.

Knocking on her door, I'm met with silence and nothing. "Charli? Angel? It's me. Open up."

Resting my forehead on the wood, I close my eyes and sigh. "Where are you, Angel?" I whisper. Pulling my phone out, I call her and again it goes to voicemail. I dial again and press my ear to her door to see if she's inside but I don't hear anything. Again voicemail picks up. Not giving up, I dial again and this time the call connects. "Angel, where are you?"

"Don't call again," a voice that isn't Charli's growls down the line before hanging up on me.

Confusion mars my face at what just happened. Dialing her again, it goes straight to voicemail without ringing, her phone has been switched off. "What the hell?" I murmur to myself, as I make my way back to my car.

Just as I climb in my phone rings, my heart deflates when I see it's my sister, Elena, calling and not my girl, Charli. "Hey, Sis," I dejectedly say on a sigh.

"Hey, Boogerbutt. Why do you sound like your cat died?"

"Rough day," I tell her.

"Wanna tell Dr. Cruz all about it?"

"I thought you were going into pediatrics and not psych?"

"Potato. Vodka," she nonchalantly replies. "But seriously, what's up?"

"Bianca for one."

That name causes her to groan. "What's your witch of an ex want now?"

"She's pregnant—"

"Did you not wrap it with her? Seriously, Dominic, how could you be so stupid? Especially with an evil hobag skank like her."

"Thanks for the vote of confidence, Sis. And for the record, it's not mine. It Lawrence's but when she told him, he dumped her."

"Karma is awesome in this instance. So why, and how do you know?"

"She wants me back."

"Of course she does. I hope you told her to stick it where the sun don't shine."

"Not in as many words but yes, I told her it's not my problem."

"Okay, well that's shit, but I know that isn't what's got you down. My sister senses are on high alert, wanna meet for an early dinner? I don't have to be at the hospital 'til tomorrow morning."

"Sure," I tell her. Even though I want to see Charli, hanging with my sister will be fun. Charli clearly needs time to process this IA thing. Since someone hung up earlier, I know she's not alone, but I have to say, it hurts she didn't come to me. I'm her boyfriend, surely she'd want comfort from me. I know if I were in her shoes I'd want her by my side, but she is in shock and hurt right now so she's probably not thinking clearly. I'll spend tonight with Elena and then tomorrow, I'll find my Angel and together, we can come up with a plan to fix this mess. "Meet you at my place?" I offer.

"It's a plan, taco-man."

Then together we say, "Mexican."

"You do the beer. I'll do the food. And, Boogerbutt, don't let that mole get you down."

"Thanks, Sis. See you soon."

Hanging up from Elena, I smile. A night with her is just what I need, but I'd much prefer to be with Charli. I'll give her tonight but tomorrow, she will be talking to me. Before I leave her place, I send her a quick text.

NIC: *Just letting you know I'm thinking of you.*
NIC: *See you tomorrow*
NIC: *Love you*

Placing my phone in the center console, I drive to the liquor store and grab a six pack of Corona since Elena and I are having Mexican. With beer in hand, I head home and when I arrive, Elena is already waiting for me.

"Did you speed?" I ask her, as she walks into my garage to meet me.

"No, did you go to Mexico to get the beer? My tacos better not be soggy now."

"Suck it up, Buttercup," I tell her.

She sticks her tongue out at me and heads inside. We make our way into the kitchen. Our brother-sister bond sparks and in sync we serve up our dinner. I place the beers in the fridge and grab the plates and cutlery while she unpacks the food and plates it up.

"That smells amazing," I tell her, as I uncap two beers and slide one over to her.

"Only the best for my Boogerbutt." She raises her bottle toward me, we clink, and I take a sip.

Elena and I spend the night together and it was great to chill and catch up. After she leaves, I grab a shower and climb into bed. I try Charli again but it goes straight to voicemail. I don't like this silence. Tomorrow is another day and this time, I won't back down 'til I see my girl.

CHARLI 19

STANDING ON THE SIDEWALK, TEARS STEAK DOWN MY FACE WHILE I WAIT FOR Bay. She pulls up to the curb and I climb in. Without saying a word, she leans over and hugs me, which causes more tears to flow.

She breaks away and sadly smiles at me. She reaches up and cups my cheek in that loving way; it eases my hurt ever so slightly. "We'll talk when we get home." Nodding, she puts the car into gear and pulls back into traffic, taking me to her and Corey's place.

We walk inside and I head straight to her sofa. She joins me a few minutes later with a bottle of wine and two glasses. She pours me one and hands it to me. I take it and I'm about to take a sip when I remember I'm pregnant. "Can I just have water, please?"

"Are you sick? You never turn down wine."

"I'm, ummm, ahh—"

"Holy shit, you're preggers?"

Nodding my head, I begin to cry. "Ohh, babe," she says, taking a seat next to me she pulls me into a sideways hug. "What did Daddy Dom say?"

At the mention of Nic, I cry harder. "He doesn't want a baby."

"What?" Baylor screeches.

"I went to tell him and I heard him telling a woman that he doesn't care she's pregnant and he doesn't want to have to do anything."

"That fucking dick monkey. I'm going to kick his ass. Did he tell you this too when you told him?"

I shake my head. "I didn't tell him. I just got out of there." We silently sit here and I process my words. "That's not the only shitty thing to happen."

"What more shit could there possibly be?"

"IA suspended me today. They have evidence against me relating to Dean."

"They need an ass kicking too. Fucking dickheads."

"Watch your mouth, Kitten," Corey says, walking into the room. He places his messenger bag by the side table and walks over to kiss Bay on the head. Seeing them so lovey together hurts. He looks to me and sadly smiles.

"How you doing?"

"I've had better days," I tell him.

"IA will come to their senses and see that you're innocent."

"That's the least of my worries," I tell him, and he looks quizzically at me. "I'm pregnant."

My eyes widen when I realize something. "Oh My God, Bay, I ate gooey cheese. I drank wine. I went for a run, I'm bad mom and the baby isn't even here yet. Bay," I cry. "I had sex on a motorcycle." A tear breaks free and I wail, "I'm a shitty whore mom." She wraps her arms around me and the tears continue to flow as I let all my grief out.

"You are not a whore, nor are you going to be a shitty mom. This baby is lucky to have you as their mom and they are even luckier because Aunty Bay and Uncle Corey are going to spoil them rotten."

My eyes well with tears at her words, damn pregnancy hormones. I never cry, but for the last few days it feels like that's all I've done. According to the books, this will be the new norm until my lil' munchkin arrives.

The three of us eat dinner that Corey cooked and I have thirds, it's was yummy, and I wash it all down with two bowls of ice cream. The ice cream is not because of the pregnancy; it's my go-to food when I'm upset. And with the upsetting events from today, I deserve ALL the ice cream.

Saying good night to Bay and Corey, I head toward the spare room. Changing into a nightshirt that Bay gave me, I crawl into bed and take a deep breath as I turn my phone back on. It goes ballistic in my hand. I have a gazillion missed calls, voicemails, and texts. I click on Dominic's texts and read over them.

The last one, I keep reading over and over.

NIC: *Love you*

He loves me but he won't love you, I think to myself, rubbing my still flat belly. I alternate between reading his texts and staring at the ceiling. This time when I read his text, anger builds within me. I'm just about to place my phone down when it pings in my hand and I see his name on the screen.

NIC: *Good night, Angel. Please let me know you're okay? We will get through this IA thing. I promise.*

A laugh escapes me, I completely forgot about that. I've been so focused on being pregnant and alone that I forgot my job is in jeopardy right now. Seems my life is just one big shitshow right now. And then he follows up with another text.

NIC: *Just remember, I love you*

"You love me but you won't love our baby," I whisper to myself, as another avalanche of tears break free. Stupid pregnancy hormones. I choke on a sob and let out a guttural cry.

The door to my room opens and Bay walks over to the bed, climbs in, and pulls me into her arms. She hugs me tightly and whispers, "Shhhh," over and over as I continue to cry.

"What am I going to do?" I blubber into her shoulder.

"Be the super awesome kick-ass person that you are. We'll clear your name and then you can focus on being the best mom to BJ."

"BJ?" I question.

"Baylor Junior."

For the first time all day, I laugh. It turns into a full-on belly laugh as I think about the name she suggested. "I am NOT calling my baby BJ. I'll save that name for your and Core's baby."

"Ohh, yes, good call. BJ is mine."

"Do I want to know why you two are discussing BJs right now?" Corey asks, leaning against the doorframe.

"See?" I tell Bay, "People immediately go to a blow job and not Baylor Junior."

"You're going to call the baby Baylor Junior?" Corey asks.

"No," I say while Bay says, "We are."

"We're pregnant?" he asks her.

"Not yet, but when we are we will call our lil' girl BJ and if it's a boy, CJ."

"I like that," he says.

Hearing him so excited for their nonexistent children hurts and I begin to cry again. "Why can't Nic be like Core is over your fictional babies?" I hiccup on a sob. "I'm going to be alone, fat, and pregnant in jail."

"You won't be in jail," Bay tells me. "I'm going to prove your innocence."

"How?"

"I haven't figured that out yet, but I promise you, your lil' Jelly Bean will NOT be born in jail and you will not be alone. Babe, I'll be by your side every step of the way."

"What did I do to deserve you?"

"Swore to protect me when my life spiraled out of control 'cause of the dumb decisions I made when I was a whorebag." She pauses. "You know, that right there is why you will be the best mom in the entire universe. Charli, you have a heart of gold. You're kick-ass. You're strong and resilient AAAAAND you're going to be the hottest pregnant woman ever...well, until I get pregnant that is."

A smile graces my face. "Thank you. You always know how to cheer me up."

"I know," she cheekily says. On anyone else it would sound cocky but coming from Baylor, it's not. That's just her. "Now, get some sleep, tomorrow we figure out how to get you out of the shit mess you are in."

"You don't have to do that."

"Yeah, I do, 'cause if it wasn't for me, Dean wouldn't have gotten involved with Kye and you wouldn't be in this mess."

"This isn't your fault."

"Not directly it isn't, but because of me and my shitty decisions, you are now in this mess. I refuse to let you wear orange 'cause it really doesn't go with your complexion."

"You really are something else, Baylor Evans soon-to-be Cox."

And with that, she and Corey leave me alone with my thoughts. My mind drifts to Nic. "Why couldn't you be happy for this?" I whisper to the room, sadly adding, "Guess I didn't know you as well as I thought."

DOMINIC 20

It's lunchtime and I still haven't seen or heard from Charli. It's not like her to go off the grid like this. Then again, I've never been suspended from the job that I love, and Charli loves her job with all her heart and soul. Heading to the break room, I see Corey is making a coffee. "Hey," I say as I grab my mug.

He head nods and quickly exits the break room. *That was weird,* I think to myself as I make my own coffee. With my mug in hand, I head toward his office. I knock on the door, he looks up and there's a murderous look on his face. "Cruz," he says, his tone anything but friendly.

"Got a minute."

"Nope." His curt one word answer confuses me even more.

"When you have time, I'd love to bounce ideas off you."

"Mmmhmpf," he nonchalantly replies. The air is stifling. Animosity is radiating off him in droves. He looks up at me and shakes his head. "You have some nerve coming in here acting like nothing is wrong."

"Huh?"

"Stop playing dumb and get out of my sight."

His dismissal is confusing but not wanting to enrage him further, I leave him alone. Guess he won't be helping me to come up with a plan to clear Charli's name. Heading back to my office, I grab my phone and dial her number, again. This time it rings and my heart beats faster at the thought of hearing her voice. And I do, via her voicemail, again. "Charli, Angel, it's me, again. Please call me. I'm worried about you."

Throwing my phone on my desk, I lean back in my chair and sigh. "Where are you, Charli?" I mumble when there's a knock at my door. "Hey, Bec, what's up?"

"How are we going to clear our girl's name?"

A smile graces my face and I laugh. "I just stopped by Cox's office to ask the same thing, but he's in a mood."

"You would be too if you were engaged to Baylor."

"What's wrong with Baylor? She's Charli's BFF, right?"

"Bay has the nickname of 'Bitchy Baylor' and she lives up to that name one million percent."

"Surely she isn't that bad?"

She shrugs. "Enough about Bitchy Baylor, how are we going to clear Charli?"

"I have no clue. Have you spoken to her?"

"She texted to say she was fine but we all know when a woman says fine, they are anything but."

"She isn't talking to me."

"Ohh no, trouble in paradise?" I shrug my shoulders. "Well, I can only imagine what she's going through right now and because of her issue, you have been taken off all your cases. She probably feels bad that you too are caught up in this."

"I never thought of that but it makes sense…even if it is far from how I feel."

"Just be there for her. That's all you can do."

Nodding, I agree but there's also a niggling in my stomach that it's more. But to show her that I do care, I'm going to clear her name, and as Bec and I agreed, we need to go to the source of all this shit, Dean Chikatilo.

An hour later, Bec and I are in an interview room waiting for Dean. "What this guy like?" I ask Bec.

"An asshole through and through. Most of his partners would last one case, if that. Charli was the only one who could work with him. They'd been partners for almost a year before the Vlahos case."

"So that's why IA are riding her."

"Yeah, but I know Charli, she wouldn't do what they're accusing. Even his brother, Darren, thinks she's involved."

"How so?" I question.

"He paid her a visit a while back—" Before she can finish, the door opens and in walks Dean. The guard uncuffs him and he takes a seat across from us. He eyes us with disdain.

"Barber," he says, "this is a pleasant surprise." He looks to me, "And you are?"

"Dominic Cruz."

He nods his head. "The new partner...and more, from what I've heard."

"Cut the shit, Dean," Bec interrupts him. "Why won't you tell IA that Charli isn't working with you?"

"Who says she isn't?" I grind my molars at the audacity of this asshole.

"You and I both know that Charli would never do what she's accused of. Are you seriously going to let your ego bring down one of the best agents we have? She was your friend, for fuck's sake." He shrugs. "I hope you drop the soap and become someone's bitch. You're a disgrace." She pushes back from the table and storms out of the room, slamming the door behind her.

"I think I pissed her off," he jokes.

Slamming my palms on the table, I lean forward. "I will prove Charli's innocence with or without your help." Standing up, I walk to the door. With my hand on the handle, I look over my shoulder. "And tell your brother to stay away from Charli."

"Darren visited Charli?" He seems genuinely shocked by this.

"Don't play dumb, you know he visited her. How about you give him what he wants and clear Charli's name at the same time."

"You don't know what you're talking about. Tell that bitch to watch her back." That line pisses me off, I turn around and without thinking, I walk over to him and slam my fist into his face. His nose crunches under the force, with a satisfied smirk on my face, I walk out of the room and join Bec.

"Get anything out of him?"

"Nope, but I think I broke his nose."

She grins. "Well, that's a start."

"He threatened Charli."

"We need to get this sorted and fast," she says. "I don't have a good feeling about any of this."

"You and me both, Bec."

Bec and I head back and as soon as we step into the office, Amanda is waiting for us with a look on her face that tells me I'm in trouble. "Care to explain, Cruz, why Dean Chikatilo is in the infirmary with a broken nose?"

"He fell into my fist." She eyes me. "He threatened Charli, I couldn't let him get away with that."

"As much as I admire you standing up for your partner, you can't go around assaulting people." She pauses. "Next time, get him in the ribs, that's easier to blame on a table."

"Yes, Boss."

"Good. Now, did you get anything from him?"

"Nope," I say, shaking my head. "He seemed shocked that Darren paid Charli a visit. This whole thing doesn't make sense. Both Dean and Charli's financials are clean. What was Dean doing for Vlahos? And what does Darren think Charli has? There are too many pieces and none of them fit together."

"Hope you like puzzles," she tells me.

"Not so much, but I will give this puzzle my all. If only to clear Charli's name."

"Speaking of, how is she?"

"I don't know. She won't talk to me."

"She's fine." Cox says, and I swear I hear him silently add, "not that you deserve to know." He walks toward the elevator with his messenger bag on his shoulder, not offering any further information.

"Give her time, this must me hard on her," Amanda tells me, as she squeezes my shoulder and makes her way back to her office. Grabbing my phone, I dial Charli again. And again, it rings out. It doesn't even go to voicemail this time. I'm starting to get worried but what can I do?

CHARLI 21

It's been three days since shit hit the fan. I'm still hiding out at Bay and Corey's place. Dominic is relentless with trying to reach me, but I keep playing what I heard over and over in my mind.

"I don't give a flying fuck that you're pregnant. I will not be a part of this kid's life. It's all yours. Not my responsibility."

How could I have been so wrong about him? I never thought he would be so heartless. I guess it's good that I knew before I told him, if he'd said that to my face I would have been more gutted than I am right now. Sitting on the floor in Bay's guest bathroom, I lean back against the tub after vomiting, again. Closing my eyes, I take deep a breath and find the sickness disappearing…probably 'cause there's nothing left in my body to throw up.

"Stronger" by Britney Spears starts playing from the living room and as I sit here and listen to the words, they hit me hard. I am strong and I will be fine. I don't need *him* by my side to raise munchkin because I'm kick-ass and strong, just like lil' munchkin who's growing in my stomach.

Standing up, I rinse my mouth and then stare at my reflection. I may look like shit right night—thanks, morning sickness—but I'm tough. I will get through this. I'll put my big girl panties on and tell Nic that he's going to be a father. I would never hide something like that from him but before I tell him, I need to look after me. A few more days won't hurt, I'm just not there mentally yet, but I will get there because I'm Charli fucking Davis, kick-ass agent...and soon-to-be mom. I need to be strong for this baby since I will be all he or she has. At least I have Momma and Daddy on my team. That conversation went much better than I thought it would have...

...My head is in the toilet again, whoever dubbed it morning sickness is a lying asshole. It hits at any time of the day and can last for a few minutes or a few hours. I was worried with how much I was throwing up, but Dr. Clark assures me that it's normal to which I replied, "Well, normal sucks."

My phone rings and I reach up to grab it off the counter. I smile when I see it's Mom. "Hey, Momma," I say as I answer.

"How's my baby girl?" Hearing her cheery voice sets me off and I begin to cry.

"It's all turned to poo, Momma."

"Frank, get in here," she yells, "Charli Bear needs us."

"I'm fine, Momma."

"We all know what fine means."

This causes me to laugh. "Daddy is here, we are switching to FaceTime." It rings and I answer the call.

"Ohh, baby, what's wrong?"

"Everything," I cry. Momma and Daddy let me cry, they offer sweet nothings but I don't hear them because I'm too busy crying like a baby.

"Charli Bear," Daddy says, "what's going on?"

"I'm suspended and...and...I'm pregnant."

"We're gonna be grandparents?" Momma asks.

"Yes, but he doesn't want me, or the baby."

"Say that again, Charli Bear? Because I'm sure I heard that he has abandoned you."

"I overheard Nic telling a woman who's also pregnant that it's not his problem."

"Who was this woman? How many women has he knocked up? I'm not sure I want him to be a part of yours or this baby's life."

"I don't know, I ran away."

"Charli," Mom says in the mom tone, "does he know?" I shake my head. "Charli, you need to tell him. Maybe it will be different with you."

"But what if he doesn't want me? I don't think I can do this on my own."

"You won't be alone. Daddy and I will be there for you, you know that."

"I know but my life is in the toilet right now, much like my head."

"Is the morning sickness bad?"

"Bad is an understatement."

"When Mom was pregnant with you, she too had horrible sickness at any time of the day. She also ate Brussels sprouts by the ton."

"No wonder I hate those green slimly suckers."

We all laugh.

"Now, what's this suspension all about?" Daddy asks.

"It's to do with the Dean fiasco from our last case."

"Maybe I need to pay this Dean guy a visit. No one messes with my Charli Bear and while I'm there, I can kick baby daddy's ass too."

"Or you could just come and visit me and hug me."

"Or we can do that." He looks to Momma. "What do you say, June, we go to the big city and visit our baby girl?"

"Big city? You guys live outside of Houston, that's a big city too."

"We live outside the city, therefore not IN the city," Daddy says.

"Potato. Vodka," I tell them.

"Ohh, I just read that book," Momma says. "That Alley girl really knows how to write dirty and I cannot wait to read the Dirty one, I really hope Maddey ends up with the brother but then again, the SEAL man is pretty swoony too."

"You've always had a thing for a man in uniform," Daddy says.

"Ahh, hello, your daughter is still on the line."

"Down, Frank," Momma says.

"Uggh, shoot me now," I groan but I also tear up. I thought Nic and I had a love like Momma and Daddy, but clearly I was wrong.

"Frank, book the tickets, our baby needs us."

"Thanks, Momma," I blubber.

"You never need to thank me. I will always be there for you, baby. Always."

...Momma and Daddy will be here next week and I'm excited for their visit. I could really do with a Momma hug right now. Don't get me wrong, Bay hugs are good but they're nothing like a Momma hug. If I'm half the momma that my momma is, then this baby is going to be fine.

Walking out of my room, I find Bay in the living room. Stuffing her face with purple taffy. "Morning, sexy momma."

"Morning," I say, taking a seat next to her. I reach over and grab a taffy. She slaps my hand.

"Mine," she growls, Bay is very protective of her taffy.

"Did you just beat up a pregnant lady?"

"Yep, and I'll do it again if she tries to steal my taffy."

"I'm hungry," I tell her, as I pop the candy I just stole into my mouth.

"Let's go out for brunch then. You've wallowed enough. It's time to get back into the real world."

"Can I borrow some clothes?"

"Nope, you are going to go home to get your own, and I also think it's time for you to get back on the horse, as they say."

Looking over at her, I scrunch my face up but I know she's right. I can't hide out here forever. "Fine," I relent.

"Like you had a choice. Let me go change and then we can go."

Twenty minutes later, she's in a black maxi dress and purple sandals. We climb into her mini and head over to my place. Bay takes a seat in my living room and I head into my bedroom to change. Ten minutes later I emerge in a navy shift dress and my ballet flats.

Bay looks up and smiles. "That's a nice dress."

"Thanks, it has pockets." I tell her, as slip my hands into said pockets, stretching my fingers to indicate them.

"I've always wanted a dress with pockets."

"Maybe we can go shopping and find you a pocket dress and me some maternity clothes after brunch?"

"You had me at shopping, let's go," she says, as we link arms and exit my apartment.

We head back down to her car and as we pull away, I see Dominic pull up on his bike. My breath hitches when I see him. He looks so freakin' hot on that bike, but then I remember the words I overheard and any hotness evaporates.

Baylor scores a parking spot right out front of our favorite café, Sassafras. This place has the most amazing French toast, which is fantabulous because I'm starving. Food is all I seem to think about these days but food is a good comfort right now. It can't hurt me, well unless I get diabetes it could, but life surely couldn't be that cruel to kick a woman when she's already down.

With our bellies full, Baylor and I walk down the street and enter Nordstrom's. We head to the women's department and begin looking. Bay finds a stunning purple—no surprises there—dress that has no pockets but it looks amazing on her, so she grabs it.

I have a pile of clothes and I'm happy with my haul. I've just pulled my dress back on when a stabbing pain rips through my abdomen, I double over and grunt in pain. "You okay, Charli?" Baylor sings out.

Opening the cubicle door, I look up at her and shake my head. "Bay, something's wrong."

DOMINIC 22

It's still radio silence from Charli and I'm starting to get worried. It's not like her to ignore me and not return my calls or texts. No one in the office has heard from her, and Corey is being a right royal cocksucker to me at the moment.

The mail guy knocks on my door and hands me an envelope. I stare at the orange rectangle in my hands. My name is scrawled on the front; no other postmarks or details give me any clue as to whom it's from. Sliding my finger under the flap, I open it and pull out a single card, it falls from my fingers to my desk. Picking it, confusion once again mars my face and I scrunch it up as I read the card.

MANHATTAN VAULTS

VAULTS 154, 155 & 176

"If the wind changes, your face will stay like that," Elena says from the doorway.

"Har har, very funny," I say. "What are you doing here?"

"Thought I'd stop by before my ER shift and see how you're doing. It's been a few days and I thought you would have called me with an update."

"I have no news, I haven't spoken to Charli."

"Why not?" she sasses, as she takes the seat across from me.

"She's not answering my calls."

"Have you been to her place?" I nod. "Have you made a grand gesture so she knows you're thinking of her?"

"I punched the dick that's making her life hell right now and broke his nose."

"And they say chivalry is dead. But seriously, Big Bro, I think you need to up your game in the romance department. FYI, punches aren't really all that sexy to a woman."

"I think I have a lead to clear her name...but it means I have to go to New York."

"Then you better book flight to The Big Apple. I wanna meet the lucky lady who has your balls in a twist."

"Please never refer to my balls, or them being in a twist ever again."

"But it's ohh so fun teasing you, Brother."

"Lucky I love you."

"You have no choice."

"That's debatable."

"Got time for a coffee?"

"Always for my pain in the ass little sister."

Placing the card back in the envelope, I slip it into my drawer and grab my wallet. Slinging my arm around her shoulder, we exit my office. We run into Corey on the way to the elevators and the look he gives me is murderous.

"Corey, this is—"

"Don't care," he snarls, "How many do you have on the go?" Then he quietly mumbles, "She's fuckin' better off without you."

Before I can ask him for clarification, he storms away. Leaving me even more confused.

"He seems nice," Elena says, as we enter the metal car.

"He normally is but his fiancée is a bit of a loose cannon from what I've heard around the office."

"That's no reason to be a dick monkey."

"Dick monkey? You been speaking with Abi?"

"Yeah, I think she's lonely now that we're both no longer in town."

"Maybe she can visit over spring break."

"I think she'd like that. You think Mom and Dad will let her?"

"So they can have alone time? Hell yes."

She laughs as we reach the ground floor. We walk through the foyer and across the street to the coffee shop. She grabs a table and I go order. While waiting I grab my phone and try Charli but like usual, she sends me to voicemail. "Hey, Angel. It's me. Again. Please let me know you're okay. Love you."

I'm starting to get worried. I really need to get this accusation quashed so Charli can come back to work and I can see her again. I miss her like crazy.

My name is called, snapping me back to the present. I grab our coffees and join Elena at the table she snagged.

After our catch-up, I head back to the office and grab the envelope. Pulling out the card, I read it again. Waking my computer, I pull up Google and search Manhattan Vaults. Dialing the number it rings a few times, "Manhattan Vaults, this is Lana, how may I help you?"

"I'm chasing information on box 154?" I'll start with the first number and go from there.

"Certainly, let me look that up." I can hear keys tapping in the background. "Okay, Mr. Davis, how can I assist you today?"

"I'm sorry, did you just say Davis?"

"Are you not Dean Davis?" she questions, her voice pitches high but not in that 'I just fucked up way.' I can't put my finger on it but she seems almost happy that she was discovered. Disconnecting the call, I grab the card, stand up, and exit my office. I make my way to the boss's office and knock. "You got a minute, Boss Lady?" I ask her.

She glares at me and points to the seat across from her. "Of course."

Entering, I take a seat and hand the card to her. "This was delivered to me earlier today. It's to do with Charli's predicament."

"That's a big leap."

"Well, when I called them, the lady who answered called me Mr. Davis when I gave the first box number, and when I questioned my name she called me Dean Davis."

Her eyes widen. "So much for security but that is quite the coincidence, no wonder IA think she's involved."

"I know, right? Is this enough to get a warrant to get access to the vault and their records?"

"No, but I would like you to head to New York and see what you can garner in person. This could be what we need to clear Charli and nail Dean further to the wall."

Nodding, I stand up. "I'll be on the next flight."

"Keep me posted and, Dominic," I look back to her, "don't tell anyone about this."

"You got it."

Exiting her office, I head back to mine and I book an American Airlines flight leaving O'Hare at four thirty this afternoon. Shutting down, I grab my laptop and things and head home to pack for my flight.

After checking in, I make my way to the departure lounge. A loved-up couple sits across from me and my mind drifts to Charli. I wish she was coming with me. This time of year is always magical in New York, maybe once all this shit is over, she and I can go on a trip somewhere together. But in order for that to happen, I need to clear her name, and I'll stop at nothing to do that.

Charli is worth going to hell and back for. I've fallen hard for her and I'm not letting her go.

CHARLI 23

BAY RACES ME TO WESTERN GENERAL, I'M PRETTY SURE SHE BROKE SEVERAL laws on the way here, but I'm fine with that because I'm really worried right now. She parks her car in the emergency lot and when we enter the ER, she goes all Bitchy Baylor and makes a scene. She's yell that she's Dr. Flynn Kelly's sister-in-law and that I need to be seen straightaway because it's life or death. I wouldn't go that far but as soon as she says I'm pregnant, they sure change their tune.

I'm escorted back to a cubicle where they take my vitals. A doctor pulls back the curtain, she looks to me and smiles. Her eyes look familiar but I haven't seen her before. "I'm Elena, what seems to be the issue?"

"I—"

But Bay interrupts me, "We were shopping and Charli made a sound like a pig dying and when I opened the door she was huddled over and looked like shit." She looks to me. "Sorry, but you did." She turns back to the doctor. "I hauled ass here. Now please tell me that this lil' bubba is okay, my girl here doesn't need any more shit to happen. I know they say things come in threes, but we don't need a third shit thing to happen."

"Would you mind getting a lemonade?" the doctor asks Bay.

"Yep, sure, no worries." She turns to me. "Be right back."

She exits the room leaving me with the doctor. "She's kinda full-on," she says to me.

"She's Baylor. She marches to the beat of her own drum."

She laughs and nods. "Well, now that it's just us. You want to tell me what happened?"

"She pretty much said it all. We had brunch. Then went shopping. I was changing back into my dress when a stabbing pain ripped through me. I've never felt anything like it before."

"And how far along are you?"

"Almost ten weeks."

She nods. "Let me grab the Doppler and I'll check the baby's heartbeat and then we can get you a scan. If you can, change into the gown and then hop up on the bed. I'll be back in a sec."

Nodding my head, I take a deep breath and take the gown from her. I change into the gown and climb onto the bed. Lying back, I stare up at the ceiling and close my eyes. They pop wide open when I hear someone say, "Dr. Cruz, where did you want the ultrasound machine?"

Dr. Cruz, shit, she's Nic's sister. The curtain pulls back and it's Bay. "I need to get out of here," I tell her.

"Did the doctor give you the all clear?"

Shaking my head, *no*, I whisper-shout, "She's Nic's sister."

"No fucking way?" she screeches in surprise. "There's your third thing." She looks to me wide eyed. "You don't think she knows who you are?"

"I don't think so. He's mentioned me but there's a million Charli's out there, I could be anyone."

"How do you know she's his sister?"

"Someone called her Dr. Cruz."

"Maybe there's a million Dr. Cruzes out there?"

"No, this is karma biting me in my fat pregnant ass for lying and keeping this from him."

"You haven't lied. You just haven't been honest." I raise my eyebrows at her, "Okay, well, yeah, it's kinda sorta a lie."

"I'm so screwed," I cry.

The curtain to my cubicle is pulled back and a male doctor is standing there. He steps into the area. "Hey, Flynn," Baylor says to him, wrapping her arms around him for a hug.

"Baylor, I hear you caused a scene on arrival."

"Charli needed a doctor and you're the best I know. Actually, Preston would be better. He deals with kids, can you get Preston?"

"He deals with children, last I checked Charli is an adult."

"But her baby isn't."

"You're pregnant?" he asks me.

"Almost ten weeks along," I say, nodding and shuffling into a sitting position.

"Very well—"

"Can you treat me? I'm sure Dr. Cruz is good, but I'd prefer if you saw me."

"Can I ask why?"

Biting my lip, I stare at him. My mouth opens and closes a few times, I don't know how to voice this, but thankfully, Baylor does it for me. "The baby daddy is Dr. Cruz's brother. He doesn't know yet and to be honest, he doesn't deserve to know because he's a jerkface cockwank."

"And why is he a jerkface cockwank, as you put it?"

"He told another chick to deal with her pregnancy herself, he don't want to play daddy."

"Ouch," Flynn says. "Leave it with me and I'll take over."

"Thank you," I quietly say.

He exits again and leaves me with Bay. "Thank you," I tell her, "I appreciate you getting Flynn to take over my case."

"Anytime, but what's the point in knowing people in high places if you can't call on them in a time of need?"

"You really are a bitch," I tell her.

"Once a bitch, always a bitch," she says with a shrug and drops onto the end of my bed, and to be honest, I wouldn't have her any other way. Baylor is Baylor and I'm so glad to have her on my team right now. I think I'll be needing her more than ever in the coming months.

Three hours later, Baylor is fluffing my pillows at home, my home. I got the all clear from Flynn, everything is okay with the baby, but my blood pressure is a little elevated. He recommends I take it easy and thinks I need to tell Dominic about the baby. I know he's right but I don't think I'm emotionally ready to hear him tell me what he told that woman. I don't think I'll ever be ready to hear those words, but Flynn's right, he needs to know. Taking a deep breath, I dial his number.

My heart races as it rings. "Charli," he says when he answers, "I don't have time to talk. I'll call you soon." And he hangs up, without letting me get a word in.

His actions crush me and only cement to me that I, no we, are better off alone and without him. Rolling to my side, I curl into a ball and begin to cry. Through my tears, I wail, "Falling for Agent Cruz was the dumbest thing I ever did."

DOMINIC 24

Of course Charli calls me just as I've boarded my connecting flight. Yes, in my rush, I booked a flight via Charlotte with a one-hour layover, and due to bad weather, that layover time has doubled. I quickly tell her I can't talk and hang up. After the death stare of all death stares from the stewardess, I pocket my phone with the intention of calling her first thing tomorrow morning, because it will be close to midnight before I get to my hotel.

The landing in LaGuardia is bumpy and after what feels like a million hours, I finally make it to my hotel. Collapsing onto the bed, I fall asleep immediately.

The blaring of my alarm wakes me. It feels like I only just went to sleep a few moments ago, but I've been asleep for nearly six hours. It's just before seven, still too early to call Charli so I decide to go for a run. With my headphones in, I head toward Central Park. It's absolutely gorgeous here this time of year, actually, I love New York any time of the year. It's a great place to visit but I could never see myself living here. It's too peopley.

Heading back to the hotel, I grab a shower and decide to head straight to Manhattan Vaults. The sooner I can get the proof I need, the sooner I can clear Charli's name and life can get back to normal. Well, a new normal because I plan on living life to the fullest, with Charli by my side. I want to grow old and wrinkly with this woman. I want to see her stomach swell as our future babies grow inside her. I want to travel the world with her by my side, I want it all with her. She's it for me.

Pushing open the brass door, I step into the opulent reception area of Manhattan Vaults. It's such a pompous place but I will admit, the security is top-notch. I walk toward the front desk and I'm greeted by a woman with pink hair. I see her name tag says 'Lana.' She's the lady I spoke to yesterday.

"Welcome to Manhattan Vaults, how can I help you?"

"Hi, I'm hoping you can help me, Lana. I'm Agent Dominic Cruz from Chicago. I'm looking into a case and Manhattan Vaults came up. I was hoping I can get details on three of your vaults."

"We take security and privacy here very seriously, Agent Cruz. Unless you have a warrant, we will be unable to assist you." She's acting more professional than she did yesterday. I can't gauge if this is all a ruse or if she really is following protocol and yesterday was just a slip of the tongue."

"Is there a manager I can speak to? This is of grave importance and time is of the essence."

"I will see if Mr. Anders is available to see you, but I assure you, he will tell you exactly the same."

Leaning on the counter, I stare down at her. I'm about to play hardball and Lana here won't know what hit her. "I'm sure Mr. Anders would be interested to know that you, Lana, confirmed the name on an account to me over the phone without verifying whom I was." Her eyes widen. "In case you're confused, I'm not the account holder. I think Mr. Anders would be very interested to hear about that security breach."

Her eyes dart around. "Please, I'm sure I can assist you without really breaking any privacy rules." She glances around again, and then whispers, "I can't get you access to the vaults, but I'm more than happy to give you names and entry records."

"That would be wonderful, Lana."

"What are the vault numbers?"

"I'm interested in vaults 154, 155, and 176."

"Give me a few moments to bring it all up."

"Thank you, Lana. I appreciate your help."

Ten minutes later, I'm on my way back to my hotel with a folder of paperwork to go through. Stopping at a coffee shop, I grab a coffee and sandwich. With food in hand, I head to the hotel and up to my room.

Sitting on the bed, I begin to read everything that Lana gave me. My eyes widen as I read, this isn't enough to clear Charli but it's enough to cause doubt. I need to get back to Chicago and pay Dean a visit.

"You again," he smartly says as he's escorted into the room. The guard removes his cuffs and he sits across from me. This guy really is an asshole.

"Thought I'd pay you a visit, Dean Davis." His eyes widen when I use that name.

"I think you have the wrong person, my name is Dean Chikatilo."

"Not according to paperwork at Manhattan Vaults."

"How the fuck do you know about that?"

"I'll be asking the questions here, asshole. Does Charli know you were using her as a cover for your laundering?"

"How the fuck did you figure this all out?"

"I didn't, but you just confirmed my suspicions." His eyes widen again. "When I discovered you were using the name Dean Davis, it expanded my searches. You'd be surprised at what I found…but then again, I don't think you would be since you and your brother are the masterminds behind this. The only thing that confuses me is, why did you to get involved with Kye Vlahos?"

"I ain't telling you shit. If you had anything solid, it wouldn't be you here interrogating me."

"Ohh believe me, they will be. I just wanted to confirm for myself before I hand all this over, but I do have one question, I—"

"I ain't telling you shit."

"I want to know why you bought Charli into this."

"It's always about her. That bitch can never do anything wrong. She's like Mary-fucking-Poppins, always cheery. She can do no wrong. Everyone loves her but she never…"

"Never what?"

"It doesn't matter because when I go down, she goes down. Collateral damage as such."

Shaking my head, I stare at him. "This isn't over, Chikatilo, mark my words, you and your brother are going down."

"And Charli will come with us."

"Not if I can help it."

Standing up, I exit the room. Closing the door behind me, I lean back, close my eyes, and exhale deeply.

"What are you doing here?" a voice says from my left.

Turning my head, I look over and see Corey Cox. "Fuck," I mumble, "trying to clear Charli's name."

"Like you care about her."

"What's that supposed to mean?"

"Don't play dumb, Cruz. Just leave her alone. She's better off without you."

"Why do I get the feeling you know something that I don't?"

"Wow, very astute of you. Just leave her alone."

He shoves me in the shoulder as he storms off. Shaking my head, I stare at his retreating form and I play his words over and over. I feel like I'm missing something, but what?

Climbing into my car, I drive straight to the office. Making my way upstairs, I head to Amanda's office. She makes time for me and I fill her in on everything I've discovered. "Visiting Dean was stupid, Dominic. We've now lost the element of surprise."

"But it proves Charli is innocent," I tell her.

"It won't be enough for IA. We need solid evidence that Charli had nothing to do with any of this." She pauses. "Do you think you can get the sign in/out paperwork for the vaults? If we can prove that Charli isn't associated with the vault and it was Darren and Dean who set it up, that should be enough."

"Not without a warrant. Had Lana not messed up when I called, she wouldn't have given me what I got."

"Leave it with me. I'll reach out to a colleague and see what we can come up with. Good work, Dominic. Make sure to tell Charli all of this. Won't be long and her smiling face will be back in the halls here."

"Will do."

Leaving Amanda's office, I decide to head over to Charli's place. I've missed seeing her and I really want to give her this news in person. I'm stuck in traffic when my phone rings. "Branson, what's up?"

"Just checking to see where you are? Kasey and I are waiting for you."

"Shit," I remark, "I totally forgot, give me twenty and I'll be there."

"Sure, no worries. See you soon."

Changing my destination, I head to Bin 501 for dinner with Branson and Kasey. It's been great reconnecting with him since moving here, and Kasey, she's just a gem. I still can't believe they are together but if I'm honest, I always saw a spark between them but Kody swooped in first and won the girl. I still can't believe he's gone but as the saying goes 'the good die young' and Kody definitely falls into that category. However, in saying that, had he not passed Kasey and Branson never would have gotten together, he'd never do that to his brother.

Traffic is much lighter heading this way and I arrive at Branson's wine bar quite quickly. Walking inside, I smile when I see Branson, but I'm stopped in my tracks when a blonde bombshell slaps me across the cheek. "You're a fucking dick," she snarls at me.

Rubbing my cheek, I take a good look at her and then I register that it's Baylor, Charli's best friend and Corey's fiancée.

"Nice to see you again too. Mind telling me why you slapped me?"

"Mind telling me why you're a fucking dickwad?"

"Watch your mouth, Kitten," Corey says, running his palm down her upper arm.

"He deserves every curse word I'm spewing for what he's done."

"What have I done?" I ask, genuinely confused.

"You really are a piece of work. Charli doesn't need you in her life."

"Is Charli okay?"

"Like you care. Where have you been?"

"New York. I'm following a lead to clear her name."

This stops her in her tracks. "Ohh, well that's good, but what about your baby? You going to step up to the plate and be a father?"

"What baby?"

"Your baby, you told your baby momma to fuck off."

"I did," I confirm. "But—"

"But nothing, you need to be there for your baby, dickwad."

"It's. Not. My. Baby," I say through gritted teeth.

"Of course you'd say that. Men always say that." She looks to Corey. "But not you, you're amazing. You'd never do that." She looks back to me. "Unlike this dickwad."

"The baby isn't mine...hang on, how do you know about this?"

"Charli heard you telling her you want nothing to do with your baby."

"I said that because it isn't mine. My ex got pregnant by the guy she cheated on me with. He dumped her and she came crawling back to me."

"Ohh," she says, her eyes widen. "Ohhhhhhh, shit. You really need to tell Charli this."

"I plan on seeing her later, if I can find her. She's been on my mind all week and it's killing me not seeing her. Since she was suspended she's been ghosting me. I miss her. I love her. I only went to New York for her."

Baylor looks to Corey and mumbles, "This is a big pile of shit."

"Why do I get the feeling there's more to this big pile of shit, as you so put it?"

"Because there is more, but you need turn around and go find Charli, and you need to go find her now and sort all this out."

"Is she okay?"

A smile graces her face. "She will be now."

"Everything all right?" Branson asks, as he walks over to us.

"I have no clue," I tell him.

"It will be, once he gets to his girl." She's now calm, her demeanor just now reminds me of Jekyll and Hyde. "You need to leave, now."

Looking to Branson, I ask, "Can we get a rain check? I need to get to my girl. I don't know why but I just know I need to see her."

"Of course. Call me later and fill me in."

Nodding my head, I exit the restaurant and head back to my car. I climb in, start the engine, and gun it. I need to get to Charli and I need to get to her now.

CHARLI 25

BAY AND COREY JUST LEFT, THEY INVITED ME TO GO WITH THEM TO BIN 501 but A. I don't feel like going out, and B. That's where I met *him* and I'm trying to forget about *him* right now. I finally reach out and he shuts me down, promising to call, and days later it's radio silence from him. This is what I get for reaching out, well screw him. This baby and I don't need a dickwad like him around.

Turning on the TV, I bring up Netflix and start watching *Prison Break* because hello, Wentworth Miller and Dominic Purcell. After three episodes my eyes become heavy so I turn everything off and head to bed. I've just crawled under the covers when I hear a knock at my apartment door. I'm pretty sure I know who it is but I don't have the energy right now to deal with *him,* so I lay here. Ignoring the banging and pleading from Nic.

Knocking.

Silence.

"Please, Charli, open up."

Silence.

"I love you and miss you."

Silence.

"Please open up, Angel. I need to see you."

Silence.

"Please."

Silence.

More knocking.

"I know you can hear me, I'm going to go now but just know I love you, and I'll be back tomorrow."

Silence.

"Angel, I will be back morning, noon, and night until you open up and talk to me because," pause, "I love you, Charli Davis."

Silence.

Closing my eyes, I take a deep breath and decide it's time to face him. I shuffle though my apartment but when I open the door, he's not there. I step into the hallway and look both ways but it's empty. "Dammit," I mumble to myself, as I close the door and head back to bed. Just as I snuggle in, my phone pings with a text. Opening the message, I read it.

NIC: *Please just let me know you're okay. I miss you and love you, Charli Davis. That will never change. NEVER. I'll be back tomorrow and every day until you see me. You are it for me, Angel. I love you to the moon and back.*

My eyes well with tears as I read his message. "But will you still love me when I tell you I'm pregnant?" I tearfully mumble to the room.

Rolling to my side, I cry myself to sleep.

Waking the next morning, I feel like shit and for once, it's not from my pregnancy. I feel like shit because I miss Nic more than anything in the world. I'm a hormonal emotional mess right now. A run will help clear my mind so I hop up, change into my running gear, and set off to reinvigorate my soul and clear my mind.

Unfortunately for me, neither of those things occur. If anything, my run only made things worse. It gave me time to think, and thinking isn't good right now because my mind runs wild, really wild, and it's also playing tricks on me. I feel like I'm being watched.

Taking a seat on a nearby bench, I bend down to fake retie my laces and I covertly look around. Nothing seems out of place, clearly my mind is playing tricks on me. Sitting back up, I realize that I'm hungry, and then I start thinking of a cheeseburger. I eat at least one a day right now.

Standing up, I take one last glance around and when I don't see anything suspicious, I jog to the closest McDonald's and order a cheese-burger meal. Sitting down, I devour my meal and then I order two more. Hey, sue me, I'm pregnant.

With my belly full, I make my way home and that feeling of being watched hits me again, but this time when I look around, I see a van that heightens my unease. The driver and I make eye contact, this causes their eyes to widen and they quickly drive off. "That was weird," I tell myself, and I continue to make my way home.

When I step inside my apartment, I get the feeling that someone has been here. Nothing appears to be out of place but the air has a smell to it that wasn't here before I left. Walking into my room, I strip off my clothes and climb into the shower. The hot water feels amazing on my muscles. Soaping up my hands, I wash myself. My breasts are very sensitive at the moment and when I brush over them, I moan. My whole body comes alive in a way that only Nic has ever pulled from me.

Closing my eyes, I run my hands over my stomach and I slide down farther, between my thighs. Spreading my legs, I slip my finger between my folds and shudder when I touch my clit. Circling my finger around the sensitive bundle, I massage my breast with my other hand. Pleasure builds down low, my breathing picks up as I continue to twist and rub myself. Sliding my finger down, I press my digit inside of me. Hitting the bundle of joy within. Inserting another finger, I pump my fingers in and out. Twisting my finger, hitting that magic spot each time, I moan Nic's name as I come. My body trembling at the intensity of my climax.

Pulling my fingers out, I turn around and slide down the wall. Tears stream down my face. "I miss you, Nic," I blubber. Resting my head on my knees I cry, wishing he was by my side and kicking myself for not answering the door last night.

Deciding I need to speak to him, I hop out and dry off. I pull on a cute sundress and apply a little makeup. Grabbing my purse, I head down to my car and drive over to Nic's place. Taking a deep breath, I walk up his front stairs and knock.

But I'm met with silence.

Turning around, I walk back to my car, hop in, and dejectedly I drive back home. Stripping off my dress, I pull on my sweatpants and FBI hoodie. Grabbing a pint of Ben and Jerry's, I collapse onto the sofa and watch more *Prison Break*.

My phone rings and I look down to see it's Baylor. "Hey, Bay," I quietly say.

"Hey hey, sexy lady," she cheerfully says. "What you doing?"

"Eating ice cream and watching *Prison Break*."

"Ohh, Wentworth Miller. Totally sucks that he's gay."

"Yep," I reply, letting the 'P' pop.

"Well, since you aren't doing anything. Come on over for dinner. Corey cooked waaaaay too much and if I eat all of this, I'll end up fat."

"Bay, I really don't feel like going out again."

"Well, that's too bad. You need to stop moping and get on with life. Get your ass over here now or I will…"

"Will what?"

"I don't know but I will do something that gets you over here."

"You aren't going to give up until I agree, are you?"

"You know me too well," she cheekily says, "See you within the hour."

"I hate you," I tell her.

"Love/hate, same-same. See you soon."

Huffing I stand up. I look at what I'm wearing and consider changing back into my dress from earlier, but Bay is making me go against my wishes so I don't care that I look like a homeless slob. At least my hair and makeup is still on point.

Once again, I grab my purse and head down to my car and head over to Bay's place.

Knocking on the door, I wait for Bay to answer. I grab my phone and see that I have no new texts from Nic. The door swings open and Bay looks me up and down. "Glad to see you dressed up for the occasion."

"Bite me" I tell her, and the bitch does exactly that. "Did you just bite me?"

"You told me to," she says with a shrug.

"It's a figure of speech, you bitch."

"Whatevs, come on, the food is getting cold."

We walk inside and when I step into the kitchen my eyes widen when I see who's standing next to Corey. "Nic, what are you doing here?"

DOMINIC 26

Leaving Charli's place just now killed me. Knowing she was inside but not answering really hurt me. Something is going on, I can feel it in my bones. I need her to know that I'm here so I send her a text. I lay it all out for her, telling her she's it for me via text isn't the most romantic way to do it, but I need her to know how deeply I care for her. I know it's only been a few months but when you know you know. It was the same for Mom and Dad, and it seems, well I hope, it's also the case for Charli and me.

Pulling away from her place, I notice a van across the street. Seems a bit late for a delivery but then again, I'm not a delivery worker, I don't know what hours they keep.

Making my way home, I head inside and collapse onto my sofa. I stare up at the ceiling and think about the last time that Charli and I were here…

…We have just cleaned up the dinner dishes. Charli cooked me an amazing risotto dish and we washed it down with a lovely red. With our wine glasses in hand, we are now snuggling on the sofa watching a movie. It feels very domesticated and I laugh.

"What's got you giggling?" she asks, looking up at me.

"This feels all domesticated." I pause. "It's perfect."

"It sure is perfect and you know why?"

"Why?"

She sits up, takes my wine from me and places our drinks on the coffee table. She straddles my lap and stares into my eyes. "It's because you are perfect, Dominic Cruz."

"I think you have that the wrong way around, YOU are perfect, Charli Davis. You are perfect in every way."

Gripping her cheeks in my palms I press my lips to hers. She places her hands over mine and kisses me back. Our tongues languidly slide in and out of each other's mouths. My cock hardens between us, there's no way she can't feel how hard I am. She breaks our kiss and shimmies back along my thighs and drops to the floor. She makes quick work of my button and before I can process what's happening, her lips wrap around my cock and she sucks.

"Fuuuuck," I moan, and she continues to blow me. "Your mouth feels sooo good but you know what's better?"

"What?" she huskily asks.

"Your pussy."

Lifting her back onto my lap, I'm glad she's wearing a dress because I can't wait. I shove the material up, pull her panties to the side and thrust my hips upward.

"Nnnnniic," she moans.

She holds on to my shoulders and rides me. Our eyes are steadfastly locked on one another as she goes to town on my cock. She meets me thrust for thrust and together we reach our peak. Grunting and growling through our release.

She rests for forehead against mine. Our breathing hurried. "I love you, Nic."

"I love you too, Angel."

...as that memory fades, I realize my cock is just as hard now as it was then. As much as I want to pleasure myself right now, I want to save my release for Charli. She owns them, just like she owns my heart.

Standing up, I walk into my bedroom and strip off, heading into my bathroom for a cold shower to ease my cock. It doesn't work though because memories of Charli and I assault me while I'm in here, and I can't help myself. I grip my cock and pump vigorously. Sooner than a grown man should, I spray my cum all over the shower wall.

After my self-love, I wash myself and climb out. Drying off, I slip into bed naked, and drift off to sleep where I dream inappropriate sexy things about Charli and me.

When I wake the next morning, I decide to head into the office to see if

I can find out anything more about Darren and Dean Chikatilo. Grabbing my helmet, I ride my bike, hoping the freedom of the ride will clear my head, plus it will soon be too icy and dangerous to ride so I'll take the opportunity while I can.

Parking my bike, I make my way to the elevator, pushing the call button, I wait. The doors open and Baylor and Corey exit.

"Hey," I offer in greeting.

"Morning," Corey says.

"Hey," Baylor enthusiastically says. "How did it go last night?"

"It didn't."

"What do you mean it didn't?" she snaps at me, her voice laced with anger. If looks could kill, I'd be six feet under right now.

"Calm down, Kitten," Corey placates her.

"I went to her place but she wasn't there, or she was ignoring me. I really don't think she wants to see me."

"She does," Bay assures me, "she just needs to pull her head out of her ass." She pauses. "Do you trust me?"

I eye her, I don't know this woman from a bar of soap, but for some reason I do trust her when it comes to Charli. "Can't believe I'm saying this, but yes, I do trust you."

"Then be at our place tonight and leave the rest to me."

"What are you planning?" Corey asks her.

"I'm planning on getting my best friend and this dude back together again."

"We didn't break up," I tell her.

"Semantics. Just be at our place tonight and I will make sure she's there so you guys can clear the air and get back on the same page 'cause right now, you are in two different chapters and I need you guys to get your HEA."

"What's a HEA?"

"Duh, it's a Happily Ever After. If anyone deserves it, it's my girl Charli and she just so happens to deserve her HEA with you. Now, our place tonight." She smiles at me and walks off, leaving Corey and me alone.

"Should I be worried?" I ask him.

"When it comes to her," he nods his head toward her, "definitely."

"Thanks, I think."

He slaps me on the shoulder and walks over to Baylor. He scoops her over his shoulder and she squeals. She slaps him on the ass and he returns the favor. I smile watching them. I want that for Charli and me...and maybe after tonight I will get it.

After reaching several dead ends, I look up and realize it's 4:00 p.m. already. Shutting down my computer, I make my way over to Baylor and Corey's place. She smiles when she sees me. "You need to hide you bike."

"Does Charli not know I'm coming?"

"Ummm."

"Please tell me she knows."

"Ummm, she knows." I go to tell her I'm leaving when she grabs my arm, digging her nails in. "Please stay. I know deep down she wants to see you but she's, well, she needs to see you, and this is the only way I can think to get her here. Now that you're here, I can get her here without it looking suspicious."

"Fine," I relent. "But if she's pissed, I'm leaving after I tell her this was all your idea. I don't want to cause her any anguish."

"Trust me, you won't. Now move the bike and I'll message Charli."

"Are you sure this is going to be okay, Baylor? I really don't think she wants to see me," I question Baylor again, still not comfortable about being here.

"She needs to see you." She keeps saying that, but why?

"Can't you just tell me why she needs to see me?"

"Nope, not my place, just trust me."

Again, she keeps saying that but before I can wonder any more, there's a knock at the front door. She's here. Nerves rack through my body as I wait for Baylor to answer the door and let my Angel in.

CHARLI 27

I'M GOING TO KILL MY EX-BEST FRIEND, I THINK TO MYSELF AS I STARE AT NIC standing before me. Why is she meddling? Why is he here? And why is he so fucking sexy? If we weren't currently standing in Corey and Bay's living room, I'd totally mount him like the stallion that he is. *Damn pregnancy hormones.*

"Hi, Angel," he says, even his voice is divine.

"Hi," I hesitantly say, "what are you doing here?"

"I've missed seeing your beautiful face."

"You have?"

"Yes."

That one word shoots straight to my heart. My eyes water and then Baylor says a sentence that causes my eyes to pop wide open.

"Wow, those pregnancy hormones have turned you soft, you're crying again."

"Pregnancy hormones?" Nic questions.

"Oops," Bay says, and for the first time since knowing her, she seems shocked at what just came out of her mouth.

"You're pregnant?" he asks, and my head nods on its own. I wait for him to tell me to go to hell and it's not his blah blah blah, but he doesn't. "You're pregnant? With my baby?" Words once again elude me and I nod.

He's silent, his eyes keep darting from my belly to my face and then the biggest smile graces his face. "We're having a baby." It's not a question, it's a statement and I realize he's happy.

"You're okay with this?" I question.

"Absolutely. We're having a baby," he says again. He steps to me and takes my hands in his. "Why didn't you tell me?"

"I heard you with Bianca the other day and—"

He cups my cheek in his palm and shakes his head, "Her baby isn't mine."

"It isn't?"

"Nope. It's Lawrence's." My eyes widen.

"Ohh shit, I've made such a mess of things."

"How so?"

"I thought you didn't want to have anything to do with her baby, and I freaked out thinking you'd react the same way when I told you. So I pushed you away because I couldn't deal with heartache like that."

"You weren't going to tell me about the baby?"

"I was, eventually. I was just trying to deal with the prospect of doing this solo." I stare up into his chocolate brown orbs. "I should have known there was more to it. I know you. I know you wouldn't turn your back on your baby. Please forgive me for doubting you."

"There's nothing to forgive. Given what you heard, I understand why you thought what you did. Does it hurt that you thought that? Yes, but I've heard pregnancy hormones are crazy so no apology is necessary. Just know, Charli Davis, I will be by your side every step of the way." He places emphasis on the last five words.

"Really?" I question again.

"Really, really." Not giving me a chance to question or protest, he presses his lips to mine, reaffirming his love for me…and our baby.

"Fuck me," Baylor says from beside us, "I think I just got pregnant from that kiss."

"Watch your mouth, Kitten," Corey says, "Let's give these two some privacy."

"Piss off, I want to watch the Charli and Nic show."

"Dominic," Nic growls at Bay.

"How come she gets to call you Nic?"

"Because she's the mother of my child."

"That's pregnancy prejudice and one-hundred-percent not fair."

Corey shakes his head, takes Bay's hand in his, and drags her protesting from the room.

"Are you sure?" I ask him again, still amazed he wants me and the baby.

He nods his head at me. "You are everything I need and more, Angel."

"You have that the wrong way around, Nic. I need you. We need you. This baby needs you."

"And you have me. I'm sorry that you misunderstood what I said to Bianca. I would never turn my back on my child. Momma would have my ass if I did."

A laugh escapes me. "Your momma sounds amazing."

"She is and she's going to be stoked to become a γιαγιά."

"Yeay whata?"

"Γιαγιά. It's Greek for grandma."

"Γιαγιά, I like it. What's grandad?"

"Pappoús but my dad will go by Papa, just like his and so on."

"I love that."

"What will your parents want to be called?"

"Granny and Grumpy." He laughs and it's a deep belly laugh.

"Grumpy, really?"

"It's totally an affectionate term."

"Well, I love that too. Sounds like this little one will be spoiled by his or her grandparents."

"And her aunty," Baylor says, handing me a gift bag.

"What's this?" I ask.

"Open it and find out."

Pulling out the tissue paper I find three items. I pull them out and lay them on the back of the sofa since it's the closest surface. There are three shirts with Daddy Agent, Mommy Agent, and Baby Agent printed on them.

"Turn them over," Bay says.

On the back is #TeamCruz with the number three.

"Bay," I cry, "this is amazing." Throwing my arms around her, I hug her to me and whisper, "Thank you."

"You are welcome. Just remember that Baylor is a great girl's name." I laugh. "I'm serious. At least gimme the middle name since I sorted this all out for you."

We all laugh at Baylor but from the look on her face, she's deadly serious. "How about Nic and I have a name chat first."

"Fine," she huffs. "Let's pop some bubbly to celebrate."

"Mean much?" I tease her.

"Name her Baylor and we will all have grape juice with you."

Again, we all laugh and head into the kitchen to get drinks. The guys have beer, Bay has bubbly, and I have grape juice. "To baby Cruz," Corey says.

"To baby Cruz," we all echo. The guys head outside to start the grill, while Bay and I stay inside to finish prepping the meat and salad.

"Grill's ready," Corey yells.

Since I'm closest to the meat tray, I grab it and head outside when I overhear Corey. "I owe you an apology, Cruz."

This causes me to pause. "Why?"

"I've been a dick to you all week, thinking you'd turned your back on Charli. I guess we all judged before having the whole story."

"If the shoe was on the other foot, I would have jumped to the same conclusion. But I meant what I said before, I will be there any way that she'll have me."

"She wants you by her side," I say, stepping outside.

Handing the meat to Corey, I walk over to Nic, and slide my arm around his waist. "I mean it, Nic. We need and want you by our side."

"And I want to be there. Every step of the way."

Lifting to my tippy-toes, I press my lips to his. My pregnancy hormones decide to wave and shake their jazz hands on my clit, and I unabashedly moan into the kiss, rubbing myself on his leg to ease the friction currently pinging between my thighs.

"You getting a clit boner?" Bay asks, as she places the salads on the table.

"A what?" I ask, pulling away from Nic and blushing at my brazenness.

"A clit boner?" I scrunch my eyes in confusion. "You know, when your clit tingles and grows, a clit boner."

Shaking my head, I laugh. "I'm not answering that."

"That's totally a yes," she says. "You guys alright for drinks?"

They both nod their heads indicating they are good. She heads back inside and returns a few moments later with a wine bucket and her drink. In the bucket is her bubbly and my grape juice.

The four of us have a chillaxed and quiet evening. It's the most content I've felt since I discovered I was pregnant. We laughed. We—well they—got drunk but most of all, Nic was by my side.

Later that evening, I fold a drunk Nic into my car and drive back to my place. He and I make it upstairs and we fall into bed. Lying in Nic's arm, I have a smile on my face. This is the first time in days that I feel happy and content. No longer do I think falling for Agent Cruz is bad, falling for Daddy Cruz is the best thing I've ever done.

DOMINIC 28

When I wake up, I realize it wasn't a dream. I'm in bed with Charli and she's snuggled into my side. I have the hangover from hell—remind me never to go shot for shot with Baylor again. Now I know why Corey said no.

"Ugh," I groan.

"Feeling a little under the weather?" Charli asks me, lifting her head to stare up at me. Her chin resting on my pec.

"Why didn't you warn me about Baylor?"

"'Cause everyone needs to at least once go shot for shot with her. You are officially a team member now."

"I like being a part of Team Davis."

"And I like being on Team Cruz." I pause and smile. "I can't believe Baylor got us #TeamCruz shirts."

"She really is something else."

"She's Baylor. You either love her or loathe her."

"Well, I know I love you, Charli Davis, and I'm never letting you go."

"Is that so?" she says, as she straddles me, rubbing herself on my growing cock. It's then I realize we're naked and I wonder if we had sex last night. "No, we didn't," she says, garnering my attention.

"How did you know I was thinking that?"

Reaching up, I cup her breasts with my hands and massage them. She moans. "Because I know all your tells."

"I think I know yours too."

"And what do I want?" she breathlessly asks, as she continues to circle her hips on my cock.

"Right now, you want me to fuck you."

"Mmmhmpf," she says. Her eyes still closed as she continues to ride me.

"Then what are you waiting for?"

She opens her eyes and stares down at me. "Nothing." She lifts her hips and slides down my cock. Her walls hugging me tightly. With her eyes locked on mine, she rides me as if she's a cowgirl. Bucking, fucking, holding on like her life depends on it. And unlike a rodeo, I last for longer than eight seconds.

Together, we reach our crescendo and we shout each other's names as we bathe in orgasmic pleasure. She collapses onto my chest, "I've missed that," she mumbles into my neck.

"So you only missed me this past week for my cock?"

"Not just your cock." She lifts her head. "I've been miserable without you, Nic. I'm sorry that I didn't give you a chance to explain what I over-heard. I'm sorry I eavesdropped. I'm sorry I pushed you away, but most of all, I'm sorry I didn't tell you I was pregnant sooner."

"You have nothing to apologize for. We're together now and that's all that matters, and I promise you I'll be here every step of the way, Charli. Can I come to your next appointment?"

She lifts her head. "You can come to them all." She leans forward and presses her lips to mine. What starts out as a slow and sensual kiss, quickly turns heated and carnal. Flipping Charli to her back, I line my once again hard dick up at her entrance and slide in.

Her pussy was made for my cock.

With our eyes fused to each other, we make love.

Slow and sweet love.

Charli Davis is it for me, now and forever.

After a lazy morning in bed together, we order an Uber and head back to Baylor and Corey's place to collect my bike. When Charli heard I rode over, she was excited to go for a ride. We showered separately, because if we'd showered together, I would have taken her again and I don't think my cock, or her pussy, needs another work out.

Baylor and Corey aren't home so Charli texts her to let her know we've collected my bike. Charli hops on behind me, having her pressed against me is the best feeling in the world. Not wanting to go straight home, I ask her if she's up for an adventure. She nods so I jump on to the I-94 E and head toward Michigan City.

Parking my bike, we head to a hole-in-the-wall fish and chip shop and then head to the water's edge for a midafternoon picnic.

"It's so beautiful here."

"It sure is," I tell her, my eyes locked on her and not the view.

"I meant the view."

"I know, the view from where I'm sitting is the most gorgeous view I have ever seen. Angel, you are glowing."

She looks to me and smiles. "Would you believe today is the first day that I haven't been sick since I found out?"

"Really?" I question.

"Yep, and I think it's because of you. Since seeing you yesterday afternoon and clearing the air, I've felt this weight lift. I'm not as anxious or stressed."

"Well, that's good, because anxiety and stress are not good for babies."

"And when did you become Mr. Baby-Know-It-All?"

"This morning when you were asleep after you sexually attacked me."

"I sexually attacked you?" she questions.

"Yep, I was just lying there when you straddled me and took advantage of lil' old me."

"I didn't hear you complaining."

"Not complaining, just stating that you started it."

"Keep that up and you won't get attacked ever again."

"Like you can stay away from this?" I jump up and strike a pose. Charli laughs and it's like music to my ears. Offering her my hand, I pull her up and into my arms. Sliding one around her waist, I stare into her eyes. "For what it's worth, you can sexually attack me like that anytime you want."

"Anytime, eh?"

"Yep, anytime."

"How quick can you get us back to your place?"

Throwing her over my shoulder, she squeals and laughs as I hoof it back to my bike. Slapping her ass for good measure. She moans and it goes straight to my cock.

"Did my slapping your ass just turn you on?"

"Yes, everything about you turns me on and since I've become pregnant, my sexual appetite has increased. I hope you're ready for this."

"If it means I get to fuck you twenty-four seven, then bring it on."

"Then take me home, Biker Boy, and—"

Cutting her off, I place a chaste kiss on her lips. We climb on my bike and I speed back to my place, breaking quite a few road rules, but the fines will be worth it. My girl wants to fuck and what my girl wants, my girl gets.

DARREN CHIKATILO 29

SHOULD HAVE KNOWN THAT DEAR OLD BROTHER WOULD FUCK ALL OF THIS UP. I told him not to get involved with Vlahos. I told him we had enough and would be fine, but no, he didn't listen and now he's in jail and our money is in limbo. And to top it off, that bitch is playing dumb. I was hoping getting her suspended would get her to falter and give me the location of the money, but she's locked up tighter than a nun's cunt. Seems she's loyal to Dean and only him, she should know that I'm the one in charge.

I'm sitting on an uncomfortable chair in the visitation area at the prison, waiting for my brother. I've had enough of this shit, I want my money and I want it now. My patience has run out and it's time for them to give me the answers I need.

Looking at my watch, I shake my head when I realize I've been waiting here for twenty minutes, he's still not here and the anger I was already harboring is getting stronger by the minute. The buzzer sounds and I look up to see Dean walking toward me, he has a black eye and a busted nose.

"The fuck happened to you?"

"Dominic Cruz."

"The partner?"

He nods. "The fucker sucker punched me when I wouldn't give him information to clear Charli's name."

"Speaking of the cunt, what are we going to do about her? She's still not complying."

"It's hard to comply when you don't know shit," he tells me, but I know that she knows something. You don't work closely with someone like those two did and not know about every aspect of each other's life—legal and illegal. Besides, he wouldn't be protecting her otherwise. I'm starting to suspect that she and my brother are conspiring against me. He better still be on my side, I don't give a rat's ass that he's family, if he's betrayed me, I will have no qualms in taking him out.

"You cannot tell me that she knows nothing. Why are you protecting her? Just get her to give up the goods and this can all be over."

"I've told you, I hadn't implemented the incrimination of her before I was incarcerated."

"So you say, I need to get this finalized. I can't hold them off any longer."

"Once I'm out of here, it will all work out."

"I can't wait that fucking long. This is all because you got involved in something I told you not to. If you'd just stuck to the original plan, I'd be free of my mess and we'd be on a beach living it up in Fiji."

"We needed him for protection, you know that."

"And look at what you ended up getting instead?"

"You need to get past this, Darren. I will be out soon and then we can proceed with the final steps." Reaching over, he taps my cheek. "Patience, dear brother. Patience."

"My patience has run out," I growl, slamming my fist on the table. "I fucking told you not to get involved with Vlahos. I knew something would happen and what do you know, I was correct. He's dead. You're locked up, and the money is in limbo because you fucked up."

"Fuck you, asshole," he snarls. "As I've repeatedly told you, we needed the protection he could offer us."

"And I told you I had it sorted, you've ruined this for me...I mean...us."

He shakes his head and glares at me. "I will get you what you want as soon as I'm out of here. That was always the deal."

"I'll just pay the little bitch a visit, she'll give it up and then I'll work on getting you out."

"You can try but I assure you, she doesn't know what you want to know. I keep telling you that, but you aren't listening."

"Don't protect her. I will kill her and you if it have to."

"Right now, brother dearest, you need me more than I need you. Look around," he waves his hand around, "three meals a day. Roof over my head. I'm safe in here, you can't touch me. You, on the other hand, you're out there without the one thing you want. I have the power to bring you down if I so choose, but I gave you my word and I still stand by that. Now. Get me the fuck out of here and we can finish what we started."

I growl at my brother, "Don't mess with me. One call and I can end you in there." I point behind him.

"And then you'll be up shit creek without a paddle." He leans forward. "Get me the fuck out of here and then I will help you. Until that happens, my lips are sealed." He mimes zipping his lips. Rising up, Dean rests his palms on the edge of the metal table and he stares down at me. "Get me the fuck out of here, Darren." He turns on his heel, and stalks away from me, just before he steps out of sight; he looks over his shoulder. "Clocks ticking, asshole."

Slamming my fist on the table, I growl, "Fuck." Standing up, I stride out of the room, my head held high, not letting on that I'm pissed the fuck off. My blood is boiling. Signing out of the prison, I walk to my car, climb into the driver's seat, and head back to my place.

Walking inside, I flop down on the ratty sofa. I'm running out of patience. I want my money and I want it now. I need to up my game if I'm going to get this sorted quickly. It's time to up the stakes. Charli Davis is about to pay up. She needs to realize, I always get what's owed and my brother can fuck right off if he thinks I'm waiting. I wait for no one. Game on, bitch!

CHARLI 30

WAKING IN NIC'S ARMS IS FAST BECOMING MY FAVORITE WAY TO WAKE UP. BUT it comes a close second to his head between my thighs. The pregnancy sex hormones are running rampant through me at the moment. Lately, each and every time I look at Nic, my panties dampen and I have to jump him. My sexual need has gotten so out of control that he bought me a rabbit to give his cock a break. And I have to say, using 'Ronnie the Rabbit' while he's watching me is such a turn-on that usually after I've given myself a self-induced orgasm, he gives me a Nic-induced one too. Hashtag winning.

"Morning, Angel," he says, in his deep and gruff voice. It sends shivers through me and I shudder in his arms. "Did you just come from me saying good morning?"

"No," I smack his chest and giggle, lifting my head up, I gaze into his baby blues, "but my panties are now soaked."

"You're not wearing any," he whispers as he rolls on top of me, cocooning me under him.

"Are you complaining?" Raising my eyebrows suggestively at him, I spread my legs and lift my hips, rubbing myself on his morning wood. His cock hardens further between us. Grabbing my arms, he raises them up, pressing them into the mattress as he begins to slide the tip of his dick up and down my slit. His eyes are locked on mine when he presses his length inside of me.

"Nic," I moan, as my body adjusts to his girth. He thrusts in and out of me, ever so slowly. "Faster," I mewl, scratching my nails down his back. He presses his lips to mine and kisses me deeply. Our tongues slide back and forth in sync with his dick down below.

Breaking the kiss, he stares down at me and lifts my leg over his shoulder. Hitting that magical spot with each thrust of his hips. "Niiiiiiic," I scream as my orgasm explodes. My body coming alive from head to toe as pleasure courses through me.

Nic's body tenses and he grunts through his release, "Fuck, I love you."

"I love you too," I pant, as he lowers my leg and collapses to the mattress next to me.

Rolling to my side, I snuggle into him. "What do you think of the name Carter if it's a girl."

"Carter Davis, I like it."

"No, Cruz. She, or he, will have your last name."

"Are you sure?"

"Yep, because hopefully one day, I'll have that last name too."

"Charli Cruz, I like that just as much as Carter Cruz."

"And if it's a boy DJ, Dominic Junior."

"I don't hate that either."

"Then it's sorted, Carter for a girl and DJ for a boy."

With a smile on my face, I lie here and enjoy the moment, not knowing that in the coming weeks, my bliss bubble will be popped when everything unravels.

CHARLI 31

...ten weeks later

I'm sitting out on Nic's deck, enjoying a cheeseburger and biding time 'til my doctor's appointment later this afternoon. The joys of being on suspension for something that you didn't do, time, lots of time on my hands. Nic is going to meet me there and we will get to see our baby and maybe find out the sex. I think I want a surprise, there are very few surprises in life but Nic, along with Bay, want to find out.

My phone rings, halting my decision/thoughts on finding out the sex. Looking down, I scrunch face up when I see it's Patrick from IA calling me. I know he's just doing his job but he doesn't help the stigma given to Internal Affairs agents, he really is a power hungry asshole.

"This is Charli," I say as I answer.

"I need you to come into the office," he says, no greeting or pleasantries.

"I'm sorry, who is this?" If he wants to be a dick I can be one too.

"It's Patrick from IA," he snaps.

"Hi, Patrick," I say, stalling, and wanting to piss him off. "How are you today? I'm great, thanks for asking."

"I need you to come into the office, now."

"I'm sorry, Patrick, I have a doctor's appointment, I can come in after that."

"I said now," he shouts down the line.

"And I said, I'll be there after my doctor's appointment. See you later."

Not giving him a chance to reply, I hang up and throw my phone down next to me. "Asshole," I growl, as I take a big bite of my cheeseburger.

Nic and I walk back into the office hand in hand, he's still gripping tightly to the sonogram picture of our little girl, showing anyone and everyone the picture of our lil' munchkin. I decided yes, in a spur of the moment decision when the doctor asked if we wanted to know the sex, I wanted to know.

Our elation soon dissipates when we step into the office and are met with a scowling Patrick from IA. "Follow me, Agent Davis," he growls, turning on his heel and walking toward the conference room.

"Do you want me to come with you?" Nic asks me.

Shaking my head, I smile, "Nah," watching him walk away, I add, "I have nothing to hide, I'll be fine." I follow him to the conference room and wonder how can someone be so unpeopley? I used to feel sorry for Patrick and the IA guys but after this, nope, not at all. They are power hungry dicks, plain and simple.

Before I've sat down, Patrick cuts to it. "Charli Davis, you are officially terminated from the FBI."

"Come again?" I ask him. "Did you just say I've been terminated?" Clearly, I heard wrong just now.

"Yes, I did." He growls at having to repeat himself. "You no longer are an employee here. We have found the smoking gun I need to bring your deceptive lying ass down. Did you think I would not discover that you've been laundering money?"

"What evidence?" I ask.

"You've been laundering money that links back to Vlahos, Ciccone, and several other illegal operations that we have been investigating."

"Whatever you have is fake," I tell him again. "I'm innocent," I protest but from the stern look on his face, he doesn't believe me.

"That's what they all say." He pompously stands up and glares down at me. "I suggest you find yourself a good lawyer because with what I have on you, you'll be joining Dean behind bars very soon, and if I have it my way, the two of you will be going away for a very long time."

"But—"

"No buts, Davis, you're out." He picks up his file and smugly adds, "Better get used to the color orange."

He walks out of the conference room leaving me stunned, alone, and jobless. A hand touches my shoulder, startling me. Lifting my head up, I see Nic staring down at me. Concern etched on his gorgeous face. "What happened?" he asks, his voice laced with apprehension and worry.

"I...I've been terminated."

"What?" he growls, "This is horseshit."

Nodding my head, I begin to cry. "Nic," I wail, "Our baby is going to be born in jail. I'm a shit mom before she's even taken a breath."

"No!" He drops to his knees in front of me and grips my hands in his. "Our baby will not be born in prison. I will figure this out...somehow. I won't let that happen."

"How?" I cry. "He seems pretty confident that what he has will stick and I'll be sharing a cell with Dean."

"I don't know how yet but, Angel, I promise. I will not let you down."

Resting my head on his shoulder, I continue to cry and think how I'm going to get out of this, but before I can think, Patrick the IA jackass—his new name—returns.

"You need to leave the premises, Davis, you are no longer an employee of the FBI."

"I'm her partner, she's here visiting me."

"She's a known criminal, Agent Cruz, and is no longer allowed, or welcome, in the building."

"You—" Nic goes to berate Patrick, the IA jackass, when I interrupt, "It's fine, I was just leaving."

Turning to Nic, I cup his cheek. "I'll see you at your place later." Lifting to my toes, I place a kiss on his lips. Picking up my bag, I exit the conference room and when I step out, I feel everyone watching me as walk toward the elevator.

"Charli," Bec says just as the door opens, "I will fix this."

"You sound like Nic," I tell her and sadly smile.

"Well, then listen to us, he and I will fix this."

Nodding, the doors close and the metal car takes me down to the parking lot. Walking over to my car, I climb in and before I head home, I make a stop to visit Dean.

Going through the check-in procedure, I wait in the visiting room. He walks toward me, looking confused to see me.

"What are you doing here?" he asks me.

"Like you don't know," I snarkily say.

"Has something happened?"

"You could say that. I've been fired because apparently you and I have been laundering money together." His eyes widen when I say this. "Is that why you were working with Vlahos? To launder money?" He stares blankly at me. "Why are you doing this to me, Dean? I was nothing but a good partner and friend to you, and this is how you repay me." My eyes well with tears, "Why, Dean? Why?" My hand drops to my belly, I lift my gaze and plead. "I'm pregnant, Dean." His breath hitches and his eyes widen at this revelation. "The stress of this isn't good for me, or the baby." I pause, wiping away a stray tear. I take a deep breath, "Be the man I know you are, Dean. Deep down you're a good guy, you've just lost your way. Don't let what you and your brother have gotten yourselves into affect me anymore. Own your mistakes and do the right thing, please. It's not just my life at stake anymore."

Standing up, I turn and walk away. Before I exit, I look over my shoulder. "Do the right thing, Dean," I tell him before I push the door open and walk away from him. I have no idea if my plea will make a difference or if it all just fell on deaf ears. I hope with everything I have that I got through to him.

Looking back through the glass, I see him still sitting there, staring into space. He's processing my words and I have a feeling he's going to do the right thing, well I hope he is.

Stepping outside, I walk down the stairs and turn toward the parking lot and take a deep breath. I hate the smell of the prison. I need to go home and have a shower and wash off all the icky prison stench. Then I'm going to laze on the sofa, order McDonald's delivery—again—and eat all the cheeseburgers. Once my tummy is full, I'm going to crawl into bed, sleep like Sleeping Beauty and then tomorrow, I'll come up with a plan to end all this.

That feeling of being watched has the hairs on the back of my neck standing on end. Looking around the open parking lot, I see that I'm the only one here. Shaking off the feeling, I climb into my car and head toward home but a few miles down the road, I see a McDonald's and decide to stop in for a cheeseburger...or four. At this rate, our little girl is going to come out looking like the Hamburglar.

Pulling in, the lineup for drive-through is massive and I'm in no mood to wait so I park my car and head inside. Ordering four cheeseburgers and a Sprite, garnering a Judgey McJudgerson look from the cashier, I pay for my order that could easily feed two, and technically I am two, so screw her and her Judgey McJudgerson face. With my receipt in hand, I smile politely and step aside to wait for my food.

Living up to its 'fast food' name, my order is called quickly.

Smiling at the cashier, who is still judging me, I grab my food and drink and head back to my car. Reaching into the bag, I pull out one of the delicious burgers and take a bite. Closing my eyes, I moan in delight as the greasy burger fires up my taste buds. Resting my drink on the roof my car, I dig in my bag for my keys. I'm so engrossed in looking for my keys, that I don't hear someone sneak up behind me. Before I register what's happening, everything goes dark for me and munchkin.

DEAN CHIKATILO 32

WITH CHARLI BEING PREGNANT, THIS CHANGES EVERYTHING. I WAS WILLING TO bring her down to save my ass, but now that it's more than her at stake, I don't think I can do that to her. I knew using her as my scapegoat was going to bite me in the ass, but desperate times call for desperate measures. As the days go by, Darren is becoming unhinged and if he unravels any further, this will all turn to shit, well, a bigger pile of shit than it already is. Maybe it's time I fess up to everything, but I haven't come this far to lose now. I need a new plan that clears Charli but still keeps my hands clean…ish.

"Phone call, Chikatilo," the guard growls at me from outside my cell.

Nodding at him, I rise to my feet and walk over to the wall of phones. Picking up the receiver, I answer, "Hello,"

"It's happening," Darren bellows down the line. The tone and shake of his voice unnerves me. He's teetering on the edge right now and I need to be careful how I proceed from here.

"No!" I growl, "I say when it happens. You need to back off of Charli. Things have changed, she's—"

"—pregnant, I know. We need to wrap this up before she goes into labor. I want what you promised me. I've got this, Baby Brother. You will soon be free. We will have the cash. Just trust me, everything is in motion."

"What do you mean everything is in motion?"

"I'm doing what I should have done as soon as you were arrested, I'm taking control of this operation."

"But—"

"But nothing, this is happening, Dean, and there's nothing you can say or do to stop it."

He hangs up and I mumble, "Shit. Fuck. Shit." I stare at the wall, Charli is in danger and it's all my fault. This is turning into a raging inferno. I need to act now if I'm going to protect what's mine, as well as Charli and her unborn baby.

Picking up the receiver again, I dial the one person who I know will help me.

"Dean?" a shy timid voice says after accepting the call.

"Yeah, baby, it's me."

"What's wrong?" she questions.

"Darren is going to do something and I need to try to stop it because things have changed."

"What's changed?" she asks.

"Charli is pregnant."

"Wow, that certainly wasn't expected."

"I know, kinda throws a wrench in the works, and with Darren becoming more and more unhinged, I need you to stop him from doing something stupid."

"I'll do what I can, baby." The line goes quiet, and then Lana quietly says, "I think I did something wrong that may have added to Darren's mood."

My gut churns. "Lana, baby, what did you do?"

"A while ago, I sent a message to that agent you mentioned, Cruz. Hoping to throw the focus on to Darren because I know deep down you don't want to hurt Charli. The Cruz guy, well he came here. I ummm, ahh, I gave him hints without incriminating us or anything. And Darren, umm, knows he was here. I'm sorry, I didn't mean to lie to you but I just want you home. I miss you. I thought if I cleared your name, you'd be out."

"Yes, it was stupid, but I've been feeling the same." Closing my eyes, I rub my forehead and sigh, "Baby, it'll be fine. I'm...I'm thinking of coming clean. Darren is losing it and I don't know how much longer I can keep up this charade. Now with Charli—"

"Darren was ranting and raving about her while he was here. Saying she knows but is being a c-word about it all, and it's time for him to make her pay. Does he mean what I think he means?"

"If you think he means taking her and getting the info he wants then yes, you are thinking like him." I pause. "Baby, I need you to do me a favor."

"Anything," she says, and I know she means it. She may play the dumb bimbo but underneath that facade is a kick-ass woman who I'm crazy about.

"I need you to get in touch with Cruz again and this time, I need you to tell him everything."

"Everything?" she repeats, her voice laced with concern, but the time to confess all is now.

"No, don't tell him everything, everything, but enough to get him intrigued and then you need to convince him to come and see me."

"Are you sure about this?"

"No, but this has gone on long enough and it needs to end."

"Will you be safe?"

"I'll be fine, baby." *I'm not one-hundred percent sure.* "But it's Charli I have concerns for now. She doesn't deserve Darren's wrath for my lies and deceit."

"Will Darren kill us?" she fearfully asks.

"Us? No. Charli? Possibly, but this is a risk we have to take. I can't let an innocent woman and her unborn baby take the fall for my mess. I never should have involved her, but desperate times—"

"—called for desperate measures. I know, baby. I don't like this but I will do everything you've asked." She pauses. "I love you and I'm so proud of you. Sure, this hasn't quite gone to plan but together, you and I can conquer anything thrown our way."

"I love you too, baby, but whatever you do, do not—I repeat—do not, let on to Darren that we're going to flip on him. He will kill you in the blink of an eye and I can't lose you."

"I promise, Dean. My lips are sealed when it comes to your crazy brother."

We say our goodbyes and hang up.

Walking back to my cell, I hope with everything I have that Lana can get in touch with Dominic and keep Charli safe, but I know my brother, he will stop at nothing to get his money. He'd even kill a pregnant woman who, like Jon Snow, knows nothing.

DOMINIC 33

WATCHING CHARLI LEAVE RIGHT NOW WAS HARD. I WANTED TO SMASH Patrick from IA in the face but I know that won't help Charli, or me. Turning on my heel, I walk into Amanda's office, slamming the door behind me. She looks up and purses her lips at me. "This is horseshit," I snarl, dropping into the seat before her.

"I agree," she says, leaning forward she rests her elbows on her desk and her chin in her fingertips. "What are you suggesting we do?"

"Clear Charli's name."

She nods. "And how do you propose we do that?"

"I was hoping you'd have an idea because I have nothing right now. What's this so called evidence they have?"

"They haven't disclosed that to me."

"This is horseshit," I scoff, again. Staring at the floor, I lean forward and rest my elbows on my knees and cradle my head. I let out a frustrated sigh.

"So you've said. Twice now." Lifting my head, I stare across the desk at her.

"Well, it is," I say like a petulant child.

"Cruz, I want you to go home and be with Charli this afternoon. She will need you, even though she'll be stubborn and pretend like she doesn't." I nod and grin at this because that's exactly what my Angel is like. "We can meet again tomorrow morning with a fresh and horseshit-free head. Then we'll come up with a game plan to fix this mess."

Nodding in agreement, I agree, "I like this new plan. I'll see you bright and early in the morning."

Tapping her desk, I stand up and exit her office. I head back to mine to grab my things and just as I enter my desk phone rings. I contemplate ignoring it but something compels me to answer. "Cruz," I say in greeting.

"This is Lana."

"Lana," I repeat, the name sounds familiar but I can't quite place it right now.

"From Manhattan Vaults."

"Yes, Lana, how can I help you today?"

"I...umm...ahh, Dean—"

"What about the asshole?"

"He's not an asshole. He asked me to call you and warn you."

"Warn me about what?"

"Darren."

"What about Darren?"

"He's going to do something stupid if you don't get to him first."

"What's he going to do?" But as I ask the question, I think I already know what she's going to say.

"He's sick of waiting and he's going to go after Charli. He...he's going to plant evidence—"

"You're a bit late with the warning, that's already happened."

"Ohh," she says, "I'm booked on a flight later tonight, can I meet with you?"

"Why do you want to meet with me?"

The line is silent for a moment and then she says, "I'll tell you everything when I get there."

"Why are you helping me now? Why the change of heart? When I came to see you, you were locked up as tight as your vaults."

"Dean doesn't want anything to happen to Charli, now that he knows she's pregnant."

"How does he know she's pregnant?" I ask.

"He didn't say but now that she is, it changes things. Can I meet with you tomorrow?"

"What times does your flight get in?"

"Around six, as long as Delta is on time."

"Come straight to my office, I can't wait 'til tomorrow to see you."

"Okay, I'll see you later, Agent Cruz."

Hanging up from her, I grab my phone to call Charli and give her the good news. It goes to voicemail. "Hey, baby, it's me. I'll be home later than I hoped but I think I have something that will clear your name. Love you."

Standing up, I walk back to Amanda's office and fill her in on the call with Lana just now. "That's great news," she says. "I'd like to be here when you meet with Lana too."

"Of course," I tell her.

Heading back to my office, I sit down at my computer and try and concentrate but my mind can't focus. I keep looking at the clock, I swear time is actually ticking slower. My phone pings with a text and I see it's from Abi.

ABI: *Check this out, I'm getting it for baby Cruz **link attached***

It's a website that makes baby clothing and Abi's getting a onesie that says, "A U N T I E, I'll be there for you." In a *Friends* layout. I laugh and shake my head.

NIC: *Love it. So will our little girl*

No sooner do I hit send, my phone rings in my hand. Swiping, I answer but before I can say anything, she screams, "It's a girl!"

"Yep," I confirm, grinning that I will have a little girl in a few months' time. "We found out this morning."

"And why am I only finding out now?"

"Because I have work and the world does not revolve around you, Abs."

"A text would have sufficed." Then she adds, "Mom is gonna flip her shit when she finds out she's getting a granddaughter."

"Umm, how about Dad? He's more gaga for this baby than Mom is."

"This is true," she agrees. "This lil' princess is going to be spoiled rotten but she will love her Aunty Abs the most."

"Don't let Elena hear you say that."

"Pffft, like she stands a chance against me." Shaking my head, I just laugh. "Anyway, Aunty Abs has to go. Give Charli's belly a kiss for me and punch yourself in the face."

Before I can reply, she hangs up. Throwing my phone onto my desk, I bring up the website Abi sent me on my desktop. I start looking at the site and when I see a pink onesie with "Daddy's Little FBI Agent" on it, I order one straightaway.

After completing the transaction, I call Charli again, but again it goes to voicemail. Worry seeps in but if I know her, she will be curled up on the couch with a cheeseburger, or three, and will be engrossed in reruns of *One Tree Hill*.

A knock at my door garners my attention, and when I look up I see Amanda and Lana standing there. "Hey," I say to them both, as I stand up and round my desk. "Should we talk in here or in the conference room?"

"Conference room," Amanda says, she turns, and walks away. Silently Lana and I follow her. Closing the door behind me, I walk to the other side of the table and take a seat across from Lana and Amanda.

"Okay, Lana," Amanda says, "Dominic tells me you have information that may help Charli."

She nods her head, "Earlier today, I got a call from Dean—"

"What's your relationship with him?" Amanda asks her.

"He and I have been seeing each other for just over twelve months now. We met when he and his brother came into Manhattan Vaults."

"And why did they need your services?" Amanda asks her. This is the first time I've seen Boss Lady in agent action and she's a no-holds-barred agent. She's totally badass and I can see why she's the boss around here.

"At the beginning, I had no idea of what they were up to, but as Dean and I got closer, my role changed. I started to accept the deliveries. Darren wasn't too impressed that I was assisting them. Darren likes to think he's the boss but he's dumb as dogshit."

"Okay, how does Charli and Vlahos fit into this?"

"Dean wanted protection and he thought Vlahos was the answer. During the setup with Vlahos taking over the security, he was arrested and all assets that Dean had fronted were seized. As fate would have it, Dean was assigned to watch the witness girlfriend chick and the agent. Vlahos went off track and wanted revenge, he wasn't impressed with being screwed over by his supposed queen. Dean managed to locate the frozen assets and retrieved them from evidence, using Charli as his scapegoat. All evidence against her is fabricated by Darren, Dean, and me. The IA guy investigating Charli is in Dean's pocket too."

"That fucking asshole," I growl, slamming my fist on the table. "I knew Patrick was a cocksucker."

"Cruz," Amanda warns me. She turns her attention back to Lana. "You're telling me that Patrick Fitzpatrick is working with Dean?"

She nods her head. "You'd be surprised how money can sway people."

"So why are you telling us this now?"

"Dean is worried that Darren is losing control and now that Charli is pregnant, he doesn't want her to stress over this and cause harm to the baby."

"So if she wasn't pregnant, he'd still be letting her take the fall?" I question her.

She shrugs at me. "How do we know that this isn't just another ploy? For all we know, you could be throwing Patrick under the bus too?"

"Why would I incriminate myself with more lies?" She has a point but I'm still not convinced.

"Will you be willing to testify to this?" Amanda asks her.

She nods. "Yes, I'm willing but I would like to make a deal for myself and Dean."

"For you, that's possible. For him? Not a chance in hell."

Excusing myself, I step out of the room and dial Charli's number but this time it goes straight to voicemail. I can't wait to tell her the good news, but I will be here with Amanda for the next few hours getting this all documented. It's too late to visit Dean tonight to get him to corroborate Lana's story, but my gut is telling me it's the truth.

Walking back into the interrogation room, I feel lighter. I can't believe that this time tomorrow it will all be over. Charli is going to be so relieved to be free of these accusations.

CHARLI 34

Opening my eyes, everything around me is fuzzy. The last thing I remember is eating a cheeseburger on the way to my car and then nothing. Blinking a few times, the room comes into focus and my heart rate increases as I glance around. I'm in a basement, the walls are cement and covered in grime. In the center of the room is a set of rickety-looking stairs that head upstairs. From the dim light coming from a single bulb above me, I continue to look around and apart from the chair I'm tied to, the room is pretty bare. There's a busted water heater in a corner and a few boxes scattered throughout. There's a musty smell in the air from there being no windows and it's a little on the chilly side down here.

I've never seen this place before and I have no idea where I am. Panic begins to fester but I know for the sake of munchkin, and me, I need to remain calm. Closing my eyes, I take a few deep breaths but it has the opposite effect on me and I vomit. Turning my head to the side, I empty my stomach on myself and the floor—now the rooms smells musty and vomity.

The door at the top of the stairs slams open and I hear feet stomp down the stairs, looking up my mouth drops open when I see Darren Chikatilo walking toward me.

"You're finally awake," he teases, but the playful look on his face drops when he sees the vomit on the floor and all over me. "Ugh, you dirty fucking bitch," he snarls, the playful look is gone and it's replaced with disgust. "Why'd you vomit?" He stands there staring at me, waiting for me to answer him. "I asked you a fucking question, why did you fucking vomit?"

"The smell down here didn't agree with me."

"Tough fucking shit. Do not vomit again."

We stare at one another, the air thickening with disdain for one another. My stomach rumbles, breaking the silence and then I remember I was at McDonald's when he took me, "Where are my cheeseburgers?"

"What?" he snaps

"My cheeseburgers and Sprite, where are they?" From the look on his face, my burgers and drink are not here and he doesn't give a rat's ass about them. "Think you can get me some more?" I ask, hoping that if I keep him occupied, I can find a way out of here, but unless I become Houdini, I'll be stuck to this chair for the foreseeable future.

"Fuck you and fuck your cheeseburgers. Gimme what's mine and then you can have all the fucking cheeseburgers you like."

"I can't think on an empty stomach," I sass back. His face morphs from nothing to anger in the blink of an eye. This guy is seriously unhinged and I need to stop taunting him. My burgers will have to wait but as soon as I get out of here, I will be eating my weight in the cheesy greasy burgers.

He storms over to me and rests his palms on my thighs, digging his fingers in painfully. For a scrawny guy, he sure has some strength. I wince in pain as his nails dig farther in, thankful to be wearing linen pants to prevent him from breaking the skin but I will surely be bruised. "Give me my fucking money!" he yells in my face, spittle and his foul heated breath hits my skin, causing my stomach to roll again. I can feel the lump building in the back of my throat, I'm going to vomit any second. If he was pissed before at me hurling, he'll really be pissed if I vomit on him.

Lady Luck is on my side because he pushes himself back, letting me breathe. The dank basement smell isn't much better but at least the need to vomit has disappeared, ish.

"This will be home until I get what's mine." He stares at me. "Give me what I'm owed and then you can breathe some fresh fucking air."

"I really don't know what it is you want, Darren."

"Don't fucking lie to me. You, Dean, and his lil' bitch are conspiring to cut me out. I just know it."

"Cut you out of what?"

"Shut up," he growls, stepping toward me he slaps my cheek. My head snaps to the side from the force. Copper fills my mouth. The taste of the blood causes the need to vomit to reappear and before I can stop myself, I vomit all over myself. It comes up so quickly that I don't have time to turn my head and I vomit down the front of me.

"Ugh, really?" He turns his back on me and storms back upstairs, slamming the door shut behind him.

My eyes well with tears. Closing my eyes, I take a few deep breaths, the feeling to vomit is still there and increasing with each breath. The smell down here really isn't agreeing with me. Taking a few more deep breaths, I calm my racing heart but it doesn't do much to ease the ill feeling building in my stomach. Opening my eyes, I stare at a spot on the wall and try to calm myself down, I cannot let fear take over right now. I need to remain strong, for me and munchkin. That determination is the only thing keeping me going right now, I will not let this asshole win.

The door above flies open, slamming into the wall again. Turning my head, I watch as dust and dirt particles flutter in the air. Darren marches back down the stairs with my handbag, my phone is in his hand. He walks over and stops in front of me. "Passcode" he growls. Waving my phone in my face, I stare at him blankly. "Passcode," he snarls through clenched teeth. "Your phone is going off so we need to text lover boy so he doesn't come looking for you."

"Where is here?" I ask, hoping he'll give me something to work with, but I don't think he's that dumb.

He ignores my question. "Passcode!"

"465702," I tell him, he punches the code in, and smirks. "Seems lover boy misses you, there's a few voicemails and texts."

He begins to type a message and reads as he types.

CHARLI: *Need space. Today has been hell. I'll be in touch when I'm ready.*

"That should keep the asshole at bay." He presses send and stares at my phone in his hand, his eyes widen. Nic must be typing back. "Ohh look, a reply." He reads it to me.

NIC: *Please don't push me away, Angel. We will fix this, I have something that may clear you. Just remember I love you. I'll see you tomorrow XoXoX*

"Aww, he thinks he can clear you and that he'll see you tomorrow. How sweet...and naïve." He looks at me with a sinister grin. "He might be able to clear your name but see you tomorrow, well that's entirely up to you." Without saying another word, he walks back upstairs and turns the lone light off, leaving me in darkness.

The basement is eerie and scarier in the dark.

I can hear him stomping around upstairs and then it's silent. As the saying goes, 'silence is deafening.' I can't handle the silence anymore so I start to sing to myself. First I start with my mantra song, "Stronger" by Britney, which morphs into "Fighter' by Christina Aguilera. I'm belting out "Sweet Home Alabama" by Lynyrd Skynyrd when the door above flies opens.

"Shut the fuck up!" Darren shouts down the stairs, slamming the door shut once again.

Not wanting to anger him further, I close my eyes, hoping to get some sleep. Exhaustion takes over and I drift off to sleep, but I'm rudely woken the next morning when Darren throws freezing cold water on me. "Shit," I mutter as the cool water trickles down my arms and front.

"You going to tell me what I want to know?" he asks, leaning against the wall, he crosses his arms over his chest and he stares at me.

I shrug. "I don't know what you want."

"You know what I want," he growls.

Shaking my head side to side, I stare up at him. "I don't, Darren. I really have no clue what it is you think I have. I wish I knew because I would give it to you in a heartbeat if I did."

Clearly my answer isn't what he wants because he storms toward me, pulls his hand back, and slaps me hard across the face, repeatedly. My head flopping side to side from the slaps. His motion become wilder and faster. The chair begins to rock from the force, I feel like I'm going to topple over but at the last minute, he viciously grips me by shoulders and steadies me. Digging his fingers roughly into my arms.

"You will tell me," he snarls before walking away. He spins on his heel, lifts his hands, and laces his fingers, bringing them to the back of his head. Flexing his arms, he glares at me. "Where's my fucking money?"

"I don't know," I tell him, again.

"Don't lie to me!" he shouts, the tone in his voice unnerving. He's starting to lose control, I need to placate him, who knows what he'll do next. "Dean said you didn't know but I know the two of you are conspiring to cut me out. He's a cunt. You're a cunt. You're all cunts who think they can pull the wool over my eyes. I refuse to be cut—"

"Cut you out of what?" I interrupt, "Darren, listen to me, I really," I place emphasis on the word really, "don't know what you're talking about."

"Bullshit," he scoffs, gripping my upper arms again, he stares into my eyes. His pupils are dilated. His face is full of anger and rage. I know no matter what I say, it will fall on deaf ears. "I will get what's mine and I don't care if I have to kill you, him, and anyone who gets in my way." He shoves me away from him and the chair topples backward. I land with a thud. My head bouncing on the cement. Both of my arms are pinned under the chair, I scream out in pain at being trapped. He stares down at me manically laughing, it reminds of a witch's cackle. He shakes his head and walks away from me, leaving me trapped.

Wriggling around, I eventually manage to get my left arm free but my right is pinned and from the angle I'm currently lying in, I'm pretty sure my shoulder is dislocated. With everything I have I roll, wriggle, and rock. Trying to free my pinned arm but nothing works. I'm halted in my efforts when a searing pain tears through my shoulder, yep, it's dislocated. I try again but I can't free myself and each time I move the pain increases.

Not giving up, I try one last time but this time, a pain worse than what I just experienced with my shoulder begins low in my stomach. Breathing through clenched teeth, my eyes widen when a piercing stabbing pain rips through my abdomen from front to back, followed by a warm wetness between my thighs. My eyes widen and I freeze, when I look down, I see my linen pants are stained with blood, the patch getting bigger before my eyes. "Noooo," I cry. I try and wriggle free but each time I move that pain in my shoulder and belly intensifies. Through my tears, I whimper, "I'm losing my baby."

DOMINIC 35

Leaving the precinct, I head to my place but when I arrive home, I find it's empty. I try calling Charli but once again, it rings out, sending me to voicemail. Jumping onto my bike since it's faster, I head over to her place but when I let myself in, I find it empty too.

Dropping to her sofa, I lean back and sigh. My phone pings with a text, I smile when I see it's from her.

CHARLI: *Need space. Today has been hell. I'll be in touch when I'm ready.*

Her words hurt, I get wanting to be alone but I want to be there for her. Even if it's just to hold her while she cries, plus I have news that will surely cheer her up. Guessing that she's at Bay's, I decide I'll give her tonight but tomorrow, tomorrow she will talk to me and I will tell her no more blocking me out. We are in this together and I want to be there to help her when times are tough, not just when they're good. I've never felt like this about anyone before and now that I have her, I'm not letting her go. She can push me away but I will always push back, always.

I send her a text reconfirming all of this.

NIC: *Please don't push me away, Angel. We will fix this, I have some-*

*thing that may clear you. Just remember I love you. I'll see you
tomorrow XoXoX*

Standing up from her couch, I lock up and head back to my place. Falling into bed, sleep doesn't come easy because I'm worried about Charli. Eventually I drift off but I wake with a start just as the sun is rising, a feeling of unease washes over me.

I know it's early but my need to see Charli is strong, so I grab my things and head into the garage. Normally I'd take my bike but it's raining so it looks like I'll be driving and not riding today. I stop at McDonald's and grab four coffees and four cheeseburgers. Knowing that these will be what my girl wants/needs.

With the coffees and food on the passenger seat, I drive over to Baylor and Corey's place. My face scrunches when I don't see her car out front. "Maybe she's on the side street," I whisper, as I grab the drinks and burgers. Ringing the doorbell I wait, nerves flutter in my stomach the longer I wait. Pressing the doorbell again, the door finally swings open and I'm met with a sleepy scowling Baylor. "Is there any reason you're on my doorstep at stupid o'clock, Cruz?"

"I need to see Charli."

"So why are you here?"

"She's not here?" I question.

"No, why would she be here?" Bay asks. "Did you do something stupid again?" She notices the coffees and helps herself to one.

"What's going on, Bay?" Corey asks, a towel around his hips. His eyes widen when he sees me in the doorway. "Cruz, what are you doing here?"

"He's looking for Charli 'cause he obviously did something stupid again," she says, taking a sip of the coffee she stole and from her sass and snark just now, I hope she burns her tongue, or chokes, or both. "He's going all out with coffee and I presume cheeseburgers, since we have coffee from McDonald's."

"I haven't done anything but after yesterday, she said she needed space so I presumed she was here with you."

"What happened yesterday?" Baylor and Corey ask in unison.

"She was fired. Dean and Darren planted fake evidence."

"That dude seriously needs to be dick punched," Baylor says, "But she's not here. Did you try her place?"

I nod and the sinking feeling that woke me earlier comes back with a vengeance. "Well, if she's not here, where is she?" I ask them, but they both shrug.

Without saying anything, I turn around and stalk to my car and head into the office, that's the only other place I think she'd be. Since it's early, traffic is light and I arrive quickly. Looking around the parking garage, I don't see her car. Picking up the coffee and burgers, I head up to our floor. It's empty when I step out of the elevator; this place is eerie when no one's here. I walk over to Charli's office but when I push the door open, a brown packing box sits on her desk. My heart hurts when I see that, but it doesn't last long because I know today we will have the evidence in hand to prove Charli is innocent and then she can get back to work.

Dejectedly, I walk to my office. Grabbing my phone, I pull up Charli's number and I hit dial. Once again it rings out. Throwing my phone onto my desk with more force than I intended, it slides across the top and bounces onto the floor. "What did that phone ever do to you?" Bec asks as she bends down, picks it up, and hands it back to me.

"Charli is missing."

"What?"

"She left here yesterday and now I can't find her."

"You don't think Dean and Darren did something? I know the girl-friend confessed to all last night, but can we really trust what she's saying?" I shrug. "I think you need to go pay Dean a visit."

Nodding, I grab my keys and head toward the elevator. The car arrives and I step in, Bec and Amanda follow. "We're coming too," Amanda says. "I heard what you told Bec. It's not like Charli to disappear like this and Bec is right, until Dean confirms what Lana said, we have to presume it was all ruse to throw us off track."

Silently we exit the elevator. We walk over to my car and climb in. Twelve minutes later, we arrive at the prison. I may have broken a few road rules to get here, but Charli is totally worth the fines. It's still early and the guards are less than impressed with our surprise morning visit, but fuck them, my girl is missing.

After what feels like an eternity, Dean is escorted into the interrogation room. "Good morning," he cheerily says, his demeanor of nonchalance pissing me off.

I snap. "Where is she?" I snarl. Grabbing him by the collar, I throw him up again the wall and press my forearm across his chest. I stare into his eyes waiting for him to answer.

"Where's who?" he asks.

"Charli, where the fuck is she?"

He shrugs. "Beats me, you should keep better track of your baby momma."

Pulling my fist back, I slam it into his face. A loud crunch echoes through the room and blood sprays all over me. "Fuck, my nose," he cries.

"Cruz," Amanda warns, "step back from the asshole. If you beat him to a pulp we won't be able to find Charli." She turns her attention to Dean. "Take a seat, Chikatilo, you and I need to have a chat and you will not lie or deceive me. Understood?"

"Yes, Boss Lady," he says, as he shoves past me and takes a seat across from Amanda.

"Call me that again and I will let him," she flicks a finger toward me, "have at you again. Now, your little girlfriend paid us a visit last night. Is everything she said true?"

He nods. "Yes, it's all true."

"Why should we believe you? You've had months to confess."

"Desperate times. Desperate measures."

"You were so desperate that you threw your partner of four years under the bus and then blackmailed the IA agent investigating your mess?"

"Desper—"

"No," Amanda emphasizes, "that's a cop-out and you know it. Charli is one of the best agents we've ever had, as were you. She was your friend and of all people you know, she doesn't deserve this. Now, where is she?"

"I don't know where she is, honestly," he tells Amanda, and from the tone and sincerity in his voice, I think he's telling the truth. "But I'll go out on a limb here and say that Darren has her. He called me yesterday and threatened he was going after her. I told him to hold off, hoping that Lana would confess all to you then she and Charli would be safe, but seems my dear old brother decided to go against my wishes."

"Where would he take her?" Bec asks. I completely forgot that she came with us.

Dean shrugs. "I don't know. You could try his place but I don't think he'd be stupid enough to go there."

"Fuck," I growl, raking my hands though my hair when it hits me. "Her phone."

"What about it?" Amanda asks.

"Charli texted me which means it's still on and it rang out to voicemail earlier this morning, we can get IT to trace it."

Before anyone can argue or agree, I turn on my heel and race out of the room, heading back to my car. Pulling my phone out while I wait for the elevator down, I dial Kat, our tech guru. "What up, Cruz?" she answers on the first ring.

"I need you to trace a cell ASAP."

"I love when you go all super secure agent suave on me, what's the number?"

"It's Charli," I say.

"Baby momma Charli?"

"Yep," I reply, letting the 'P' pop.

"Okay, leave it with me and I'll send you the coordinates of the last location as soon as I have them," she tells me.

"You're a rock star," I tell her.

"I know, find our baby momma and let me know if I can do anything else to help."

"Roger that," I tell her and disconnect the call. I climb into the driver's seat and I look over to see Amanda and Bec racing toward my car. Amanda opens the passenger door, just as my phone pings with a text from Kat. "I've got her location."

"Give it to me and I'll call for backup," Amanda says, as she takes her seat and the phone from me, she gets to arranging backup. Glancing in the rearview mirror as I back out of my spot, I see that Bec has her phone to her ear, no doubt arranging medical for my girl.

Pressing my foot down, I haul ass out of the parking lot and head to the location that Kat sent me a few moments ago. Pulling into the morning gridlock, I slam the steering wheel in frustration. "Fucking traffic," I growl. Gripping the wheel tightly in my hands, I whisper, "I'm coming, Angel. Just hang on a little longer."

CHARLI 36

TEARS POUR DOWN MY FACE AS I LIE HERE TRAPPED. THE PAIN IN MY ABDOMEN isn't as bad as it was earlier but it's still there. Every time I look down, I see all the blood that I've lost and more tears fall. There's so much blood. I'm sure there's no way that munchkin could have survived. She's a fighter but I don't think she will survive this, because I don't think I will. I'm going to die here trapped. Alone. And pinned under a chair.

As I lie here, a vision of Nic appears before me and I realize that he's my everything. I hope he lives a full and happy life without me and munchkin. Nic will never know how much I've truly fallen for him. I fell so hard for that man, he came into my life when I didn't even know I needed him. "I love you, Nic," I whisper, as a guttural sob breaks free at the thought of never seeing him again. I cup my belly with my free arm and I cry.

My self-pity moment is interrupted when I hear a commotion upstairs, followed by a lone gunshot.

My eyes widen.

Fear builds within.

I hold my breath waiting.

I'm frozen and then I hear, "Charli, Angel, where are you?"

"Nic," I whisper. "Nic," I shout a little louder but I'm so choked up with emotion that I can hardly speak. "Down here," I yell, but I don't think anyone can hear me. With all my might, I scream like I've never screamed before. "Niiiiiiiiiiic!"

"I'm coming, Angel," he yells, and then the door above slams opens. Footsteps pound down the stairs; I can't see who it is but I know it's him, "Charli," he yells, "I'm here." He flies down the stairs and his eyes widen when he sees the blood and me trapped.

Sobs wrack through my body when my brain registers that he is here. He's really here. "You're here," I whisper, as he drops to his knees and stares down at me.

"Nic, help me. I'm...I...I think I lost the baby," I cry.

"Shhhh," he coos, as he brushes a tendril of hair off my face, "I'm here, Angel." He cups my face and looks lovingly at me. "I'm here," he repeats, his voice instantly soothing me.

"I'm gonna get you out of here," he says, "I've got you."

Leaning over me, he reaches behind me and unties my trapped arm. I collapse to the floor, wincing in pain when my shoulder connects with the cold cement. It was only a few inches but after being pinned in this position for a few hours, it felt like I fell off a cliff edge.

Rolling to my back, I take a deep breath at finally being free, but it doesn't ease any of the pain coursing through me right now. The room above me starts to spin. My vision blurs and everything around me becomes muffled. Nic is hovering above me, I can see his lips moving but I can't hear anything he's saying. All I can hear is a loud whooshing noise echoing in my head.

The last thing I see is Nic's gorgeous brown eyes staring at me before the darkness engulfs me.

—ᅟᄿᄿᄿᄿᄼᄼ-O˚O-ᄿᄿᄿᄿᄿᄿᄿᄿᄼ-

When I open my eyes again, a bright light shining above causes me to close them quickly and groan.

From my side, Nic says, "Angel," and he squeezes my hand.

Turning my head toward the voice, I carefully open my eyes. "It's so bright," I whisper. He stands up and reaches over me. The sounds of a switch flicking vibrates through my head but the overhead lights turn off, leaving only a yellow glow from the wall behind me.

He sits back down and grips my hand and with the other, he runs his fingertips up and down my cheek. "Hi, Angel."

"Hi," I croak out. "Where am I?" I ask, everything is fuzzy and I can't remember why I'm here.

"You're in the hospital," he says. "Darren had you."

When he mentions Darren's name, my eyes widen and it all come crashing back to me. I pull my hand free from his and drop it to my stomach. I still have a slight pooch, "Munchkin?" I ask.

He stares at me, not saying a word, his silence is unnerving and then he smiles. "She's fine."

"Really?" My eyes widen at his words. He nods at me, "Really, really? Carter is okay?"

"Ohh, I love that name," a voice says from behind me. Turning my head, I see a group of people standing huddled together. My gaze flits over the group and then I realize my mom and dad are here. And so are Mr. and Mrs. Cruz, Abi, and Elena. I recognize them from photos Nic has around his place and Elena from my visit here when I was shopping with Bay.

"You're here?" I say, my eyes locked on Mom's.

"Of course," she says, pushing past Dad and walking over to me. "As soon as we got the call from Dominic, Dad and I jumped in the car and drove straight here." My eyes well with tears, Mom and Dad are here. Munchkin is fine and I'm safe.

I go to move my hand toward her to squeeze it but I wince in pain. Looking down I see my arm is in a sling and then I remember I was pinned. Turning my head back to Nic, I ask him the one question I'm not sure I want the answer to, "Where's Darren?"

"He's dead. Amanda shot him when we found you. He pulled a gun on us, she didn't hesitate and pulled the trigger."

"And Dean?" He doesn't get a chance to answer because the door to my room opens and Dr. Flynn Kelly walks in.

"Charli, you're awake," he says, as he walks to the end of my bed. He picks up my chart and looks over it. Lifting his gaze back to mine, he smiles. He really is good-looking, add in that sexy as hell accent and I can see why Avery fell for the dashing doctor.

He looks over to my family. "Can I ask you all to step out for a moment?"

They all nod and a chorus of "Glad you're okay," "We'll be back," and "I need coffee," can be heard as they all shuffle out. Nic stands too, bends down and kisses my forehead. "I'll be just outside."

Squeezing his hand, I shake my head. "Please stay."

He looks to Flynn and he nods. "That's fine by me."

The door closes behind our family and Flynn steps around to where Mom was standing. "How are you feeling, Charli?"

"Wiped," I tell him.

"That's to be expected. You have a dislocated shoulder and you suffered a placental abruption."

"What's that?" I ask, he's speaking English, I think, but I have no clue as to what a pla-thingy abruption is.

"A placental abruption is when the placenta partly or completely separates from the inner wall of the uterus. It occurs in one percent of pregnancies. It can occur at any time after twenty weeks. It's most common in the third trimester but I'd say the trauma of the last few days is the contributing factor to this happening to you now at just shy of twenty weeks."

"What does that mean for munchkin?"

"We will keep you in for the next few days so we can monitor you, since you are still bleeding quite heavily. You've already had one transfusion but at this stage, everything with the baby seems fine. Her heartbeat is strong and she's still wriggling around in there."

"What happens if I don't stop bleeding?"

"You'll need to discuss those plans with your OB, but from what I remember from my stint in maternity, we would get you past the thirty-four-week mark and then you'd have an emergency C-section to deliver the baby. You'd be administered medication needed to help your baby's lungs mature and to protect the baby's brain due to the early delivery. I've spoken with your OB and updated her of what recently transpired. I'll inform her that you're awake and she'll stop by to discuss the rest of your pregnancy."

"But right now, the baby is fine?" I question him, my hand hasn't left my stomach since he started talking.

"Baby is strong. She's a fighter, like her mom." He points to my shoulder. "We've popped your shoulder back in and you'll need the sling for a few days, but you will make a full recovery from that injury."

"Thanks, Dr. Kelly," I tell him, relieved that munchkin and I are okay.

"Please call me, Flynn."

Before we can discuss anything else, the door to my room swings open and Baylor barges in, Corey is close behind her. "Don't do that again, lady. I've been worried sick about you and BJ," she says, hugging me tightly. I wince from the pain in my shoulders but I can't really do much so I one-arm hug her back.

"Who's BJ?" Nic ask.

Bay turns to face him. She points at my stomach. "Baylor Junior," she says in a 'duh' tone of voice.

"We are not calling our baby BJ," Nic tells her.

"Well, what are you calling her then?" Baylor huffs, clearly annoyed we won't name our baby after her.

"Carter," Nic and I say in unison.

"I don't hate that," Bay tells us, "therefore I will allow it."

"Don't think you really have a choice, Kitten," Corey says, pulling Baylor into his chest. He whispers something into her ear and from the pink tinge that fills her cheeks and neck; I'm guessing it was something dirty.

"Glad you're okay," Bay says. Grabbing Corey's hand, she pulls him to the door, yes, he whispered something dirty to her. "I'll be back tomorrow with a billion cheeseburgers."

Before I can say anything, she and Corey are gone. If this was a cartoon, there'd be a Baylor and Corey shaped hole in the door to my hospital room.

"She really is something," Nic says to me.

Nodding my head I laugh. "You have no idea but she's my someone." Looking at him, I pat the mattress beside me. "But you're my number one so come snuggle with me."

"You sure? I don't want to hurt you."

"I'm sure." I shuffle over and try hide the discomfort on my face but I don't do a very good job. "I'll be fine, Nic. I need you to hold me."

"Well, when you put it like that, how can I resist?" He looks to Dr. Kelly. "Can I?"

"That's fine. I'll leave you for now but page me if you anything changes or if you have any questions."

Dr. Kelly turns and leaves my room and Nic climbs onto the bed. Carefully we maneuver ourselves so I'm snuggled into his side without injuring my shoulder, or Carter.

"You really sure we want to call her Carter?" I ask him.

"Yep, Carter Davis is a badass name."

"You mean, Carter Cruz is a badass name," I tell him. I press a kiss to his chest. "One day we will all be Cruzes," I say. My eyes become heavy and I drift off to sleep in Nic's arms. Our baby is safe and everything is right in the world again.

DOMINIC 37

After her ordeal with Darren, Charli spent two weeks in hospital. The bleeding from the placental abruption stopped after ten days and our doctor agreed that if Charli promised to stay off her feet, she'd be allowed to go home for the rest of the pregnancy, as long as no other complications arise. And by home, I mean my place. I managed to convince Charli to move in with me…

…We're lying together in Charli's tiny hospital bed, My Angel is asleep and wrapped around me like a monkey. Even though I'm uncomfortable, I wouldn't be anywhere else in this world. It's been ten sleepless nights but knowing that Charli and Carter are safe, I don't care that I'll need to see a chiropractor for the rest of my life. Their safety and happiness is all that matters to me.

Dr. Clark told us that Charli can go home in a few days, if she promises to take it easy and stay off her feet—ha, I can't see that happening—you've met Charli Davis, she doesn't know the meaning of taking it easy. I'm one-million-percent sure that my Angel would have agreed to anything to be able to go home, and I'm not ashamed to admit that I totally took advantage of this scenario. When this situation arose, operation 'Get Charli to Move In' commenced.

Knowing that I'd need reinforcements for this, I called in June and Frank, Charli's parents, to help me convince her that this was the best option, for her, the baby, and me. Surprising to me, they agreed that this was the best plan, even going so far as offering to help move her in.

If I thought asking them to help with convincing their daughter to move in was hard, I can only imagine what it will be like when I ask for their permission to marry her, because that's totally in the cards...and soon. Charli Davis is it for me. My heart and soul belong to her, I think they have from the moment my eyes landed on her in the bar just a few short months ago.

So with their approval, I am waiting for the right moment to ask. "I can hear your brain thinking from here, what's on your mind, Biker Boy?"

A chuckle breaks free. "You haven't called me Biker Boy in a while."

"I was dreaming about your bike, I can't wait to jump on again."

"Not 'til after Carter is born. You heard Dr. Clark, you need to take it easy."

"Sitting on a bike IS taking it easy."

"You and I both know that it's never just sitting on that bike. It leads to fucking on said bike, and as much as it pains me to say, there will be no bike fucking, or fucking in general, until our little munchkin safely arrives."

"No fucking, that's a bit much, don't you think?"

"Nope, I've read up on placental abruptions and we are so lucky that you didn't go into labor. I'm not risking Carter for the sake of a fuck. We will have the rest of our lives to fuck, I think we can manage for a few months without."

She groans, "Ugh, you are so mean to me."

"Fucking is not in the cards, Agent Davis, but I never said anything about my tongue."

She lifts her head to stare at me. "I like that plan...think I can get a tongue preview?"

This is the perfect opening to drop my request, "I might be able to oblige but I need you to agree on one thing first."

"And what is your one request? You know I'll pretty much agree to anything to get your tongue between my thighs."

"I'm counting on that."

She lifts herself up farther. "I'm intrigued now so, Biker Boy, what is your condition?"

"Move in with me?"

Her eyes widen. "Come again?"

"I want you to move in with me. I want you, me, and Carter to be one big happy family under one roof."

"It's too soon."

"Angel, we are about to have a baby together, I think the soon boat has sailed."

"Are you sure?"

Nodding my head, I take her hands in mine. "I've never been more sure of anything. Charli Davis," dropping her hands, I cup her cheek, "I'm truly, madly, deeply in love with you, and you agreeing to move in will make me the happiest man in the world."

She nods her head. "Nic Cruz, you are my everything and I would love to move in with you. I love you to infinity and beyond. Now take me home and give me your tongue."

"We have to wait for the doctor's clearance but I promise, as soon as we are given the all clear, my tongue is yours."

Charli clearly really wants my tongue because later that day, she manages to sweet talk Dr. Clark into letting her out. I swear this woman could sell ice to Eskimos. It's really hard to say no to her but I don't mind at all because she's coming home...with me!

...and now here we are, but rather than following doctor's orders, Charli is gallivanting around the city. When I found Charli's note telling me she'd gotten an Uber to go and see Dean, I was furious. I had never felt anger like this before. She was just released from hospital and is meant to be on bed rest but no, my fierce baby momma is still playing super agent.

Leaning against my car, I fold my arms and wait for her to exit. I feel her before I see her. Looking up, I smile when I see her step outside and like she does after each prison visit, she looks to the sky and takes a calming deep breath. Prisons give her the heebie-jeebies, which is funny since in our line of work we visit them quite often.

She looks over and when she sees me, she's smiles but that smile drops when she sees the angry scowl on my face. Walking toward me, she's smiling, trying to placate me, but my anger must be showing on my face because her eyes show hesitation.

"Hey, what are you doing here?" she says, leaning into me to give me a kiss, but I turn my head and she kisses my cheek.

"More to the point, what are YOU doing here? You're supposed to be home. On bed rest."

"I needed to see Dean. I needed him to look me in the eye and confess everything."

"And you couldn't do that via FaceTime? Skype? Zoom? There's this thing called technology."

"Don't you dare sass me, Dominic Cruz." Shit, she called me Dominic, she's just as pissed as I am. "I'm pregnant, Nic. I'm not a damsel in distress who's made of glass. I needed to see him. I needed to hear everything from him. I needed closure so I can move forward and focus on munchkin. And you."

"And do you have your closure now?"

"Yes," she nods. "It's all closed and locked away, never to be actioned again." She reaches up and cups my cheek, just from her touch, the anger begins to dissipate. "I appreciate the concern but I'm fine. Really. Now take me home and get me five cheeseburgers along the way."

I want to be mad but she has a way of charming me, it's one of the many things I love about this woman. "You are lucky I love you, Charli Davis."

"You bet your fine ass I'm lucky and I promise from this moment on, I will stay home in bed...naked."

"Don't taunt me like that, woman, you know I can't ravage you like I want until after this baby is born."

"Weeell, we—"

"Nope, no hanky-panky 'til munchkin is born. I need you both healthy and safe." Raising my hand, I wiggle my fingers. "I'll be fine with Mrs. Palmer for the next few months."

"What about me?" Shrugging my shoulders, she pouts and it's totally adorable. "You are just mean, mister, taunting a bedridden pregnant woman like that."

Leaning into her, I whisper, "If you play your cards right and behave... in bed...with clothes on, I'll sweet talk the doctor at our next check up and get permission to ravage you, if AND when she deems it safe for you both."

"You better, Biker Boy. Now, since we can't get down and dirty, get me my cheeseburgers, that's the next best thing right now."

Placing a chaste kiss on her lips, I open the car door and drive her to the nearest McDonald's, where she eats an insane number of cheeseburgers before I take her home and we snuggle—fully clothed—in bed with my hand resting on her tummy.

We've just hit the thirty-six week mark and Charli is glowing. Dr. Clark is amazed that we, well Charli, has made it this far, but my girls are fighters, there's no stopping them.

Lifting my head, I rest it in my palms and watch her sleep—hey, it's not creepy when I do it. She really is the most beautiful woman in the world, add in her pregnant glow and I'm speechless.

"Are you watching me sleep again?"

"Maybe," I tell her.

"No maybe, baby, I can feel your gaze on me."

"Is that so?" I say, running the tip of my finger down her cheek. Her eyes open and land on mine. She smiles and like always, it hits me in the chest and brings me alive like never before.

"Mmmhmpf, but I'd much rather feel something else."

"And what might that be?" I ask, trailing my finger down her neck.

"Your tongue..."

"What about my tongue?" I tease back, sliding my finger between her breasts that since becoming pregnant have increased in size, and I'm not complaining one bit.

"I need it..." she pants, when I lean forward and suck on her nipple through her silky nightgown.

"Need it where?" Rolling her to her back, I climb between her legs and kiss down her stomach. Dr Clark gave the all clear two weeks ago for us to get down and dirty, but there has been no bike or crazy wild monkey sex. There has been lots of tongues and fingers, I will not do anything to hurt Charli or the baby.

"A little farther," she mewls, pushing my head down.

Situating myself between her thighs, I push her nightgown up and I blow on her. "Niiiiiiic," she moans, "please."

"Patience, my Angel,"

She lifts her head and due to her stomach, I only see her eyes but they are firing daggers at me right now. Before she gets any angrier, I lean down and nuzzle my nose along her panty-covered slit, giving her want she wants.

"Yes," she pants, gripping my hair in her fingers, pulling on the strands. "More," she demands and from the breathiness of her words, I can tell she's on edge. Pushing the material of her panties to the side, I lick her from taint to clit, giving her what she wants. "Yeeeeesssss," she hisses, as I assault her slit with my tongue.

Nibbling on her clit, I slip a finger inside. Her walls clench around my digit, twisting around, I hit that magical spot deep within. Charli moans loudly when I suck hard on her clit and wriggle my fingers inside her. She saturates my face with her release. "Nic," she says and from the tone of her voice, the pleasure zone she was in only moments ago has disappeared, "my water just broke."

CHARLI 38

"I FUCKING HATE YOU," I SCREAM AT NIC. "YOU AND YOUR DICK ARE NEVER coming near my vagina again."

I've been in labor for five hours now, Dr. Clark agreed that I can try but right now, I wish I'd taken the C-section option. I have never felt pain like this before and I'm going all crazy psycho lady and taking it out on Nic. The contraction passes and then I begin to cry. "I'm sorry, Nic. Please don't hate me."

"Shhhh, Angel, it's fine."

"It's not fine," I snap, "I'm being a Baylor."

"Angel, you are about to push a watermelon out of your vagina, you can Baylor away."

"Charli," Dr. Clark interrupts us, "you are only two centimeters dilated, you need to start thinking about going for a C-section. With your abruption and the slow labor, I have concerns." My eyes widen when she says the word concerns.

"Concerns how? Is Carter okay? What's wrong?"

"Everything is fine, for now," she reassures me, "but I would really like you to consider a C-section. If we can prepare it will be less rushed and much easier for both you and the baby, BUT if you want to keep trying, we can. I'll have the team on standby for an emergency one, but I would like to avoid that if we can."

"Do it," I say without thinking.

"Are you sure?" Nic asks.

Looking to him, I nod my head, and sadly smile. "Yes, I'm sure. I'm tired and it hurts. I don't think I can do this."

"You can do this," Nic encourages.

"I can't...I just want to hold our little girl." Looking to Dr. Clark, I reaffirm, "Let's do it."

No sooner do I say those three words and it's all go-go-go. I'm wheeled into the operating room. Nic is whisked off to scrub up—FYI, he looks hot in scrubs. A needle is shoved into my spine, numbing me from the waist down—and let me tell you—it's the weirdest sensation ever. You can't feel what they are doing but you can sense what's happening.

Before we know it, the most magical cry rings through the room and Carter Cruz takes her first breath, well, screech. Holy crap on a cracker, can that little girl screech. I watch as Nic cuts the cord and then our lil' munchkin is whisked away to be checked over. Nic hovers next to the nurses doing their job and when one hands him our little girl, I burst into tears. The sight of him holding her will forever be etched into my mind.

He looks over at me and smiles. "Let me introduce you to your mommy," he says as he walks over to us. "She's the most beautiful woman in the world and, kid, you and I are lucky to have her on Team Cruz." He stops next to me. "Wanna hold your daughter?"

Nodding my head, he places her in my arms and as soon as I hold her, I'm instantly in love. I've heard other moms say that but I thought they were full of shit, but nope, it's one-billion-percent true. What I feel for Carter is unconditional ever-lasting love, much like my love for her daddy. As if he knows I'm thinking about him, Nic places a kiss on my temple. Looking up at him, he's grinning. "We did good, Daddy Cruz."

"Sure did, Momma Cruz."

Our Hallmark family moment is interrupted when Dr. Clark informs me that I'm being transferred to recovery. Nic and Carter can come too and I'm thankful for that, I don't want to ever be away from her. It's only been a few moments but I'm addicted to her. Everything about her is perfect. Her button nose. Her chubby cheeks—probably from eating too many cheeseburgers. Her full head of dark hair and her eyes. Her eyes are a mirror image of mine, just in mini form.

After spending a few hours in recovery I'm finally transferred to my room. I spent a long time there as I had some bleeding in relation to the placenta rupture. With medication, oxytocin, and some abdominal massaging, we got my uterus to contract and the bleeding stopped, saving me from having to have a D&C, dilation and curettage, surgery.

There's a knock at my door and Elena pokes her head in. "Hey," she says with a smile. Her eyes drop to the bundle of joy in my arms. "How's my niece doing?"

"She's perfect," Nic proudly says. He's been sporting the biggest smile since Carter was placed into his arms. He pouted, yes pouted, when he had to give her to me so I could feed her. As soon as Carter finished feeding, he swooped in and took hold of her again.

"You're going to have to put her down sometime soon," I tell him. I look to Elena. "He's had her in his arms since she was born."

"Aww, is my big brother a softie? Does wee lil' Carter have you wrapped around her teeny tiny little finger already?"

"Yep, and I don't care. Carter Cruz is the most beautiful baby in the world," he proudly declares, as he looks over to me and adds, "Just like her mommy is the most beautiful angel in the entire universe."

"Ohh my God," Elena whines, "shoot me now. When did you grow a vagina?"

"Don't say that word around her," Nic says, cupping Carter's ear.

Elena and I both laugh at him but if I'm honest, it's sexy as fuck seeing Nic in dad mode.

—◦○◦—

We are finally home from hospital after a five-night stay. Nic and I are watching Carter sleep. Who knew a sleeping baby could be so entertaining? Sliding my arm around Nic's waist, I snuggle in. He presses a kiss to my head and whispers, "Marry me?"

My head snaps up and I stare into his eyes, from what I see reflecting back at me, he means it and without missing a beat, I whisper back, "Yes."

"Really?" he says, spinning me around to face him. He cups my cheeks in his palms. "You really will marry me?"

Nodding my head, I smile. "Yes. A thousand times yes."

He lowers his hands to my waist and lifts me up hugging and kissing me. It's romantic but at the same time, so painful. I wince and groan in pain. "Ohh crap," he says, lowering me to my feet. "I'm so sorry, Angel."

"It's fine, we got caught up in the moment. Now, where's my ring?"

He grabs my hand and drags me out of Carter's nursery and into our room. He pulls open his underwear drawer and digs into the back. He pulls out a Tiffany blue box and turns to face me. With a smirk on his face, he drops to one knee and takes my left hand. "Charli Davis, will you do me the honor of becoming my wife?"

Nodding my head, my eyes well with tears and I blubber, "Yes. Yes I'll marry you."

He pulls out the ring I've been admiring online, it has a diamond platinum band with a square mixed-cut diamond and slips it onto my left hand. Lifting my hand, I inspect the ring. It's everything I wanted and more. Looking down to my fiancé, I cup his cheek in my palm, the diamond on my finger sparkling in the afternoon light. Leaning down, I press my lips to his. Resting my forehead on his, I whisper, "I'm yours forever, Nic, and I cannot wait to officially start our life together."

DOMINIC 39

In a few short days, Charli will officially become Mrs. Cruz and I cannot wait for us to officially become a family, well, in the eyes of the law official. We were a family as soon as those two pink lines appeared on all six tests Charli took.

The last few months, since Carter arrived, have been one crazy roller coaster but I would not change one single thing. Who knew someone so cute and cuddly could A. Scream as loud as she does, B. Poop so much, and C. Projectile vomit. If projectile vomiting was a sport, she'd win hands down. Actually, I'd change the vomiting. Poop and pee, easy-peasy, but vomit, yeah nah, I'd rather have a root canal.

Tonight I have arranged a special date for my Angel. It will be our first night time away from Carter but I plan to keep Charli in such an orgasmi-cally blissed state that she won't notice. Aunty Bay and Uncle Corey are having Carter for the night. Charli is packing her overnight bag and I'm changing her. "Now, my lil' munchkin," I say to her, "please poop lots for Aunty Bay and if you can have a number three explode over her while you are in her arms again, that'd be great." A chuckle breaks free when I remember the first time Carter did a number three and Bay happened to be the recipient, and so far, the only recipient of one.

"Did you just ask our daughter to shit on Bay?" Charli questions from the doorway. Looking up, I see my Angel standing in the entrance to

Carter's room staring at me. She's wearing a navy sundress that hugs her curves and showcases her gorgeous tits. Charli always had nice tits but her tits since having Carter are even more plump and delectable.

"Yep," I say, letting the 'P' pop. "If anyone deserves to be shit upon, it's your best friend. Don't get me wrong, she's great but..." I shrug, leaving that sentence open-ended. Looking back down at our giggling munchkin, I grin when I see a twinkle in her eye that I take as her confirming that she'll shit on Bay for me. "That's my girl," I tell her, bopping her on the tip of her nose.

Charli shakes her head at me. "You are terrible, Agent Cruz."

"I'll show you just how terrible I am as soon as we're alone." Picking up our daughter, I wink at my Angel and notice her cheeks darken. She's biting her lip in that 'fuck me now way' and she's clenching her thighs together, from that action I know, tonight is going to be fucking—literally —amazing.

We've just said goodbye to Carter, Charli seems a little sad but I'm sure a soon as we get home, I can get her mind off our daughter. Reaching over, I rest my hand on her knee and squeeze. She covers my hand, I can feel her gaze on me. "What's on your mind, Angel?"

"Is it silly that I miss her already?"

"Not at all." I glance at her and smile, turning my attention back to the road. "I miss her too, but I promise that I'll do my best to keep you and your mind occupied."

"And what do you have in mind?"

"I cannot reveal all my secrets to you...but I will say, I'm ever so glad you're wearing a dress."

"And why is that?"

"For starters, I can do this." Sliding my hand up her thigh, I slip it between the gap. She widens her legs for me and I run the tip of my finger up her panty-covered slit. She shudders and I can't help but grin, but I'm also cursing myself. We are still ten minutes from home and just from running my finger over her panties, they're soaked and my cock is now rock-hard.

"And then what?" she breathlessly says. Pressing on my hand and pushing my palm against her heated mound.

"And then nothing." Her eyes widen and she shoots daggers at me. "Nothing because if I keep going, I will either crash or pull over and fuck you on the side of the road, and for what I have planned, I don't want any interruptions."

"Well, hurry up and get home, because I need you now, Nic."

She doesn't need to tell me twice, so I increase my speed and make the remaining ten-minute trip in seven. We pull into the garage and I turn the car off. Turning to face Charli, I find her staring intently at me. We both lean forward at the same time and our lips slam together in a heated and carnal kiss. I thread my fingers into her hair and deepen our connection. Her tongue licks along my lips before slipping into my mouth. The temperature in the car rising with each lash of our tongues together.

"More," she moans against my lips.

Breaking the connection, I pull back and stare. Charli is gorgeous at the best of times but when she's glowing with arousal, fuck me sideways, she's stunning. Her cheeks are flushed, her chest rapidly rising and falling with each breath. "Don't move," I growl at her. Pressing a kiss to the tip of her nose, I pull back, unbuckle my belt, and climb out. I round the hood of the car and open her door. Staring down at her, I offer my hand. She places her palm in mine and an electrical current zaps through me, every nerve ending in my body buzzing with desire.

Pulling her up, I slide my hand around her waist and pull her in. Grazing my nose up her neck, I nibble her earlobe and whisper, "I'm going to fuck you on my bike and then we are going to take a ride. When we arrive home, I'll fuck you on the bike again and then I'm going to feed you. Then I'll carry you to our bed and I'm going to make love to my fiancée all night long." Lifting my head, I stare at my Angel. "Nod if you agree with this plan."

Her tongue darts out and she licks her lip. She nods her head, steps around me, and walks over to my bike. Along the way, she lifts her dress over her head, leaving her in her panties and bra. She looks at me over her shoulder and drops her dress to the cement. She spins to face me, and walks backward to my back. She lifts herself up onto the seat and spreads her legs. She leans back on her hands and stares at me intently. Raising her eyebrows she seductively says, "What are you waiting for, Biker Boy?"

"Abso-fucking-lutely nothing." Stalking toward her, I grip the collar of my shirt and pull it over my head, stopping between her spread legs.

"Man, it's hot when you do that."

"Do what?" I ask, as I unbutton my jeans.

"Remove your shirt with one hand like that."

"Duly noted." I kick off my jeans and briefs. My cock springs free, the tip glistening with arousal at the sight of a lingerie-clad Charli on my bike.

"I stand corrected," she says, her eyes roaming over my naked body, "you fully naked is the hottest sight ever."

"You in lingerie on my bike is the hottest thing ever."

We stare at one another and like in the car moments ago, the temperature in the garage increases with each passing moment. Charli lifts her hand and drags the tip of her finger down her chest and under her panties. "I stand corrected, you on my bike in lingerie with your hand in your panties is the hottest sight ever."

With my eyes locked on Charli, I take the final step toward her and I slide my hand into her panties with hers. Together we slide our fingers in and out of her slit. The material of her panties is in the way; pulling my hand out, I grip the side and tear them off her body. Dropping to my knees, I nudge her hand out of the way with my nose, and inhale before licking her from taint to clit. "Niiiiic," she moans. Gripping my head in her hands, she presses my face into her mound as I begin to lick up and down her slit. Pushing my tongue inside, she moans, thrusting herself against my tongue. I slip a finger inside, pulling out, I thrust back in and it sets her off, she orgasms—loudly—and coats my face with her arousal.

When her body tremors cease, I kiss up her body. Her skin breaking out in goosebumps. Kissing up her neck, I lift her leg, and wrap it around my waist. Lifting my head, I gaze into her hazel orbs as I press my length inside her, her head drops back as I slide myself in to the hilt. "Watch," I growl, she lifts her head and together we watch my dick slide in and out. Thrusting my hips back and forth, in and out. We rock ourselves into oblivion, both of us crashing over the edge at the same time. Murmuring each other's name as pleasure courses through our veins.

Resting my forehead against hers, I vow, "I love you, Charli Davis."

"I love you too."

It's the middle of the night and Charli and I are naked in bed, she's cuddled into my side and is sound asleep. We did exactly as I planned and now we are both exhausted, well fucked, but exhausted. I lost count as to how many orgasms I gave my Angel, but the image of her fingering herself on my bike will be engrained in my memory forever.

Brushing a tendril of hair behind her ear, I stare down at her. She really is beautiful, and lives up to her name of Angel. She's pure on the inside and out. I'm still amazed that she's mine. Sure, our journey here hasn't been easy but anything worth fighting for is worth it, and I would go to hell and back for her, and Carter. Those two own my heart and soul.

"Are you staring at me again?" she asks, lifting her head to look up at me.

"Yep, I can't help it."

"You are too sweet but if you don't get some shut-eye now, tomorrow with our lil' munchkin is going to be tough."

"It will be worth it. You are worth every sleepless moment."

"You are such a sweet talker and I love it, but we need sleep."

"Fine," I huff, "but in the morning…"

"…we can do it on your bike again before we go get Carter."

"I was going to suggest waffles but I'm okay with another bike fucking."

"Waffles on the bike," she suggests.

"Charli on the bike…waffles off Charli in the kitchen."

"I like that plan." She presses a quick kiss to my lips. "Now sleep."

She snuggles into my side and like she always does, she drifts off to sleep in my arms. This is the best way to fall asleep, and I'm lucky because I get to do this every day for the rest of my life. I'm one lucky son of a bitch.

CHARLI 40

TODAY IS MY WEDDING DAY AND I'LL OFFICIALLY BECOME MRS. BIKER BOY. I cannot wait to start my life with Nic and Carter officially as a Cruz.

Staring at my reflection in the mirror, I think back to when I first met Nic and my heart flutters, just like it did that night when I saw him pull up on his bike at Bin 501. I was never into the biker boy thing, but that night I did many things I'd never done before, and I'm glad I took the chance because it led me here.

A knock on the door startles me. "Come in," I yell.

"I can't," a deep gruff sexy voice says through the wood, "it's bad luck to see the bride but I needed to see you."

Walking over to the door, I rest my palm flat against the surface. "Well how can you see me, if there's a door in the way?"

"I can feel your presence whenever you're around." *Swoon.*

"You've already sealed the deal, Biker Boy, no need to go all out with the swoon."

"I will swoon you like you've never been swooned before, Angel. Now, in the front pocket of your overnight bag is a little something for you."

Walking over to my bag, I unzip the pocket and inside is a long black box. "What did you do?" I ask.

"Open it and see."

Lifting the lid, I gasp. Inside the box is a Pandora bracelet with three charms: baby booties with a pink stone, a motorcycle, and last but not least, a rose gold infinity heart dangle charm.

"Nic," I cry, "it's beautiful."

"Just like you. Carter and I cannot wait to see you, now dry those tears and come marry me."

Nodding, I stand here and stare at the bracelet when I hear Baylor yelling, "Dominic Cruz, what are you doing here? You better not have seen her."

"Calm your tits, woman, I stayed in the hallway this whole time."

"You better not be lying to me. I don't care that it's your wedding day, I will kick you in the nuts if you ruin this for my girl in there."

Swinging the door open, Baylor lifts her hand and covers Nic's eyes, even though his back is to me. "He can't see you," she growls at me over his shoulder.

Pushing Baylor's hands out of the way, I cover his eyes with my hands and step in front of him. I press my lips to his. "I love the bracelet." KISS "I love you." KISS "And I cannot wait to marry you." KISS

"I love you too, Angel, and I cannot wait for you to officially be mine."

"Seriously," Baylor growls. "You," she pulls on my arm and covers Nic's eyes, "inside, and you, get to the altar so you can make her yours."

"Yes, ma'am."

"Don't fucking call me ma'am," she growls at Nic, and I can't help but laugh.

"Watch your mouth, Kitten," Corey snarls from behind her and I laugh again. I notice Bay's eyes glaze over when she hears Corey's voice. "Sorry to break up this Hallmark moment, but it's go time, people."

"See you soon, fiancé," I whisper into Nic's ear. "I'll be the one in a white dress."

"And I'll be in the one in a tux with his eyes glued to you."

Corey drags Nic away from me and Baylor pushes me back into the dressing room. "Seriously, I leave you alone for five minutes and you do this."

"Well, you shouldn't have snuck off to fuck you husband in the room next door."

"How did you know?" she asks, as she attaches my veil.

"I have ears and you're not all that quiet when you come. I see nothing has changed since the WitSec cabin with you two."

"You're just jealous that I got some just now and you have to wait until after the ceremony."

"Touché," I tell her, but really I'm fine because last night before Nic took off, he and I had one last romp on his bike. Doing it on his bike is one of my favorite extracurricular activities to partake in. Taking a deep breath, I run my hand down my dress and stare at myself again.

Looking over to my best friend I proudly say, "Let's go get me married."

I am now officially Charli Cruz; we are the Cruzes. I love saying that just as much as I love my husband and our daughter. Carter is in Nic's arms and we are walking back down the aisle as a family. I'm grinning from ear to ear, I have never been happier than I am in this moment.

Looking up at my husband—love saying that already—and daughter, my grin widens. Happiness, love, and everything in between courses through my veins. Falling for Agent Cruz was the best decision I ever made.

EPILOGUE

Charli

...three years later

WATCHING NIC IN A PINK TUTU WITH CARTER IN HER ORANGE ONE HAS MY ovaries bursting at the seams, if I wasn't already pregnant, I'm sure I would be. Nic is the best dad and he treats our little princess like a queen. I can't wait to see what he's like with our little princes, Davis and DJ—Dominic Jr.—when they arrive in a few short weeks.

A few weeks ago we moved into our forever home. With twins on the way, the old place wasn't big enough for a family of five but this place, it's big enough for a football team but after DJ and Davis, no more kids for us. Carter is already a handful, so I can only imagine what my two new Cruzes are going to be like when the three of them are together.

Nic and Carter are still in the living room dancing around together. If I wasn't the size of our new house, I'd be up with them, but instead I'm sitting on our new blue sofa eating, you guessed it, cheeseburgers. The burger craving from having twins is out of control, thank the heavens for twenty-four seven McDelivery.

"No eating on the sofa, Mommy," Carter says.

"I think Mommy gets a free pass," Nic says, scooping her up into his arms and flying her around the room. "Growing babies is hard work, so we need to make things as easy as possible for Mommy until the boys arrive."

"Okay, Daddy," she says. "Can we go for a swim?"

"If you have a nap, sure."

"Put me down," she says to Nic, she races over to me and grips my cheeks. "Daddy said if I nap, I can go swimming so I'm going to nap."

"Okay, munchkin. Do you want me to tuck you in?"

"No, I'm a big girl now, I do it." She rests her hands on my big belly and gets close, then she whispers, "I'm going to nap, baby boys, and then swim." She kisses my stomach and my eyes well with tears at the scene before me. Damn pregnancy hormones making me emotional at the drop of a hat.

Sitting here, I watch Carter skip to her room. "We did good, didn't we?" Nic says, taking a seat next to me and pulling me into his side.

Nodding my head, I wipe away a stray tear. "We sure did." Leaning my head back, I stare up at him and I'm overcome with emotion. "I really am a lucky woman and I'm so glad I climbed on the back of your bike that night."

"Me too, Angel, me too." He kisses my temple and drapes his arm over my belly. Snuggling into him, I pull his arm tighter around me and sigh. #TeamCruz really is the best team to be on, and I can't wait for our trio to become a quintuple.

THE END!

BONUS
EPILOGUE

Charli
…nineteen years later

"I CAN'T BELIEVE OUR LITTLE GIRL IS GRADUATING COLLEGE TODAY," I SAY TO Nic, as he steps out of the bathroom. A towel around his waist with his abs on display, rendering me speechless when my gaze drops to the illusive 'V.' Nic is just as good-looking today as he was twenty-two years ago when we first met.

The doorbell rings, snapping my attention away from the dirty thoughts that were playing through my mind at the sight of my husband semi-naked. "I'll get it, you," I twirl my finger at him, "put some clothes on."

"You don't tell me to do that often," he teases with a wink.

"Down, boy. We cannot be late for our daughter's college graduation."

"Spoilsport," he whines, dropping his towel and giving me an unobstructed view of his sexy as sin body.

"I was going to say maybe when we get home we can go for a ride, if you know what I mean, but if you're going to be like that…"

He grabs my arm and pulls me into his chest. "We are definitely going for a ride later, Mrs. Cruz."

"I'll hold you to that, Biker Boy."

He presses his lips to mine and what starts out as a sensual kiss, quickly turns heated. The doorbell rings again, pulling us apart.

"Coming," I yell, as I walk away from Nic to answer the door.

"You will be later," he teases as I close the door behind me. Walking down the hallway, I open the door to see Mason, Avery and Flynn's son and Carter's boyfriend, standing in the doorway.

"Hey, Mase," I greet him. "I thought you'd be with Carter?"

"I...I...I wanted to talk to you and Mr. Cruz before the ceremony."

"Okay, come on in. Nic is just getting ready."

"Can I get you a drink?" He shakes his head. "You look nervous, is everything okay?" He nods his head, sweat beading at this temple.

"Mason, what are you doing here?" Nic says, walking into the living area doing up the cuff on his dress shirt.

"I wanted to speak with you and Mrs. Cruz."

"How many times have we told you, it's Dominic and Charli."

"Okay, Dominic and Charli, I wanted to speak to you both."

"Is everything okay?" I ask him, he looks like he's going to throw up.

"Yeah, I'm just nervous."

"Why are you nervous, son?" Nic asks him. I have a sneaking suspicion I know why he's here but my loving husband is clueless.

"I wanted to ask you both something."

"Okay, what did you want to ask?" I offer, hoping my tone will ease the poor boy's nerves.

"As you know, your daughter and I have been seeing each other for a few years now." Carter and Mason have been seeing each other since we went to Bora Bora for Avery and Flynn to renew their wedding vows three years ago. Seems our kids got caught up with the love associated with the trip, and when we returned, they were glued at the hip and have been together ever since. "Well, I love your daughter very much and I want your blessing to ask her to marry me."

Bringing my hands to my lips, my eyes well with tears at the sweetness coming from him. I look to Nic and I notice he's clenching his teeth. As I watch him, I have no idea if he'll be okay with this. Carter is his baby girl, her getting engaged means her daddy is no longer her number one, but what he doesn't know is, a girl's daddy is always her number one. I know mine is.

"You want to marry my daughter?" he asks, I internally giggle at his use of my and not our.

"Yes, sir. I love her more than anything and I want to spend the rest of my life with her."

"She's my baby, I can't just give her to the first person who comes asking."

"Nic," I chide and scowl at him.

"I understand, sir, but there is no one out there who will love her like I do. I will treat her like the princess she is and I'll give her anything and everything I can."

Nic stares at Mason. The poor boy is shaking in his boots. "You ever hurt her, and I will end you. I don't care that your father is one of my best friends. I will end you if my daughter ever sheds one tear because of you."

"No sir, only happy tears, unless we're watching *The Notebook*, those tears I have no control over."

Nic out stretches his hand. "Welcome to the family, son."

"I need her to say yes first."

"She will," Nic reassures him. "She loves you like I love her mother but remember my warning."

He nods. "I'll remember but I will never hurt her. My dad would be in line after you to kick my ass to Ireland and back."

"Looks like it will be a double celebration today," I excitedly say. "I better organize more champagne for the celebration afterward."

The doorbell rings again and I walk over, answering it, I smile when I see Avery and Flynn standing there. Grinning. Seems these two were privy to what Mason was here to ask us. "Looks like we will officially be family."

"Looks like it," Avery says, pulling me in for a hug. When she pulls back she has a look in her eye.

"Why do I get the feeling you know something I don't know?"

"Boy do I have the gossip of all gossip for you," she excitedly says. Linking arms with Avery, I pull her inside, Flynn follows. "Lily and Clay eloped and are pregnant."

Pausing midstep, my eyes open wide as I process her words. "Come again? Did you just say Lily Cox and Clay Knight are married?"

"Yep," Avery confirms. "Bay and Cress are now officially family."

Baylor and Cress are what you'd call frenemies. Those two love to pick at each other. It's quite entertaining to watch. "Holy shit," I say, "I better order extra tequila for later."

"Yep," she says, letting the 'P' pop. "Lots and lots of tequila will be needed."

"How did this happen?" I ask Avery.

"Seems those two have been sneaking around for a few months and when she discovered she was pregnant, they decided to fly to Vegas and get married."

"Lily really is a mini Bay. And I bet right now Bay is fuming."

"Actually, she took the news much better than I thought. Corey and Preston, on the other hand, not so much. They are both livid right now."

"I'd hate to be those kids at this moment," I say.

"I know, right?"

Holy shit, this day just got interesting and we haven't even left the house yet. I thought our daughter graduating was going to be the highlight but no, her boyfriend wants to propose, and my best friend is about to become a grandma and gained a son-in-law. Life with kids sure is interesting. I'm just glad that my three are the sane ones within our group.

"Angel, we need to get going, if we are late, Carter will kill us," Nic says, interrupting my thoughts.

"Okay, let me grab my purse and jacket."

Standing up, I grab my things. We stop at Elena's to pick up Elena, Davis, and DJ—they had a sleepover at their aunt's place last night—and then the five of us, make our way to Carter's graduation.

They day is perfect, surprise baby and wedding included.

Our little girl looked amazing up there on stage and now, she's a newly engaged woman. My heart is full right now. Watching my daughter fall in love and get her happily ever after is just as amazing as when I got mine all those years ago.

There is no better feeling than falling in love and getting to live your very own happily ever after with the one you love. I've got mine and so has my daughter. I just need my sons to get theirs and then my life will be perfect in every way possible.

I thank Dominic Cruz every single day for falling for me.

Nic walks over to me, he has a glint in his eye. "Mrs. Cruz," he croons, pulling me into his arms, pressing a kiss to my temple.

Looking up at my husband, I smile. "Take me home, Biker Boy."

"With pleasure."

Linking hands with my husband, we leave our friends and family to celebrate, while we celebrate in our own way at home, just the two of us.

Want more?
Keep your eye out in 2022

Falling

THE NEXT GEN

ALSO BY DL GALLIE

STAND ALONES

Out of Nowhere

Antecedent

Doc Steel

Oops

Fractured:A driven world novel

Deck…the Balls - coming 30 November 2021

Seven Nights

Seven Kisses - coming 28 December 2021

In the Dark of Night anthology**

Secrets anthology**

***only available in paperback direct from me*

FALLING NOVELS

Falling for Dr. Kelly

Falling for Dr. Knight

Falling for Agent Cox

Falling for Agent Cruz

THE UNEXPECTED SERIES

When it comes to love, expect the unexpected

The Unexpected Gift

The Unexpected Letter

The Unexpected Package

The Unexpected Connection

The Unexpected series:The Complete Collection

THE CASTAWAY GROVE COLLECTION

Love has arrived in the Grove

Oasis

Unequivocal Love

Five Words

Broken Rules

...and a few more to come.

The Castaway Grove Collection, Vol 1

THE LIQUOR CABINET SERIES

Liquor has never been so disturbingly saucy

Malt Me (Book 1)

Tequila Healing (Book 2)

Wine Not (Book 3)

The Final Shot (Book 4)

The Liquor Cabinet: Series boxset

FACEBOOK ~ INSTAGRAM ~ BOOKBUB

GOODREADS ~ WEBSITE

dlgallieauthor@outlook.com

Sign up to my newsletter

ABOUT THE AUTHOR

DL Gallie is from Queensland, Australia, but she's lived in many different places all over the world, including the UK and Canada. She currently resides in Central Queensland with her husband and two munchkins. She and her husband have been together since she was sixteen, and although they drive each other crazy at times, she couldn't imagine her life without him.

Shortly after her son was born, DL began reading again. With encouragement from her husband, she picked up the pen and started writing, and now the voices in her head won't shut up.

DL enjoys listening to music, drinking white wine in the summer, red wine in the winter, and beer all year round. She's also never been known to turn down a cocktail, especially a margarita.

Made in the USA
Middletown, DE
29 January 2022